The
MAL'LAM
VOYAGERS

Jim Leslie

Published by Crusader eBooks, Perth, Western Australia

Typesetting, Layout and Cover Design by Site211 Media

Illustrated by the author

This edition printed and bound by CreateSpace, *https://www.createspace.com/*

National Library of Australia Cataloguing-in-Publication entry:

Author: Leslie, Jim, 1939 -

Title: The Mal'lam voyagers / Jim Leslie.

ISBN: 9780987553744 (paperback)

Dewey Number: A823.4

Acknowledgements

Books with a long gestation period, like this one, require more than a handful of thank yous. The initial inspiration for this novel was the work of Hawai'ian artist and visionary, Herb Kawainui Kane, an official *State Treasure*, now deceased. Herbs' words of encouragement to me, as well as his superb renditions of prehistoric life in the Pacific, still inspire me.

The life's work and controversial opinions of one Thor Heyerdahl continue to annoy and stimulate the world of archaeology. His ideas find life in my work also. Thank you Thor.

More personally, and more importantly, is the patient faith and encouragement of friends and family: My brother and sister-in-law, George and Marian Wilkins and my hopeful nephews and nieces. Sister-in-law Juane Lindner and her family. My daughter Lisa Grant. Dear old friends: Kim Morris, Ed Sherman, John and Colleen Beach, Jan Lofthouse, Carey Murray, Margaret and Norm Thursby, Tom and Jan Bain as well as others who couldn't wait any longer.

The generous assistance and encouragement of my publisher, Gil Hardwick of *eBooks West* over there in Perth, Western Australia, has rescued my writing career. Thank you Gil.

And now to the lady whose love and graciousness has flown with me on this journey: my wife Brenda. For forty years my best friend. The voyage isn't over yet honey!

This book is dedicated to the Alo'ha Spirit . . .

and other miracles.

CHAPTERS

PROLOGUE

In that great, archipelago-cast expanse of sea called the Western Pacific, some three thousand five hundred years ago, numerous tribes and cultures were on the move. Drought, greedy neighbors and population pressures were the spurs, plus not a little sense of adventure. These peoples were, in the main, of East Asian stock; somewhat Mongoloid in facial caste but possessing a more robust physique. Dark-honey in skin color with black, slightly wavy hair, they were obviously not of the same stock which would succeed them and become the people we know as Southeast Asians.

They were uniquely different in their societal makeup as well. Forced to rely more and more upon the sea for their livelihood due to the aggressive pressure of those who had already commandeered their inland territories, these people's lives were increasingly focused upon the sailing vessel. Not a warlike society by any means, they were unable to resist the growing numbers of tribes from the northwest bearing down upon them. First they clung to the shoreline, sailing but a few miles from their villages as they harvested the inshore fisheries.

Dugout canoes soon augmented their vessels which were at first just rafts of lashed-together bamboo culms, stable but limited in carrying capacity and seaworthiness. These canoes gradually became larger and more sophisticated as these seashore-people became more adept at selecting and shaping ever-larger tree trunks into sea-going vessels. The Gods and Spirits which they, as hunter-gatherers and slash-and-burn horticulturists, had invented to assist them in coping with their inland lives now needed reinforcements.

The *Great Earth Mother* remained their primary deity. This God of creation and renewal was deeply revered. Considered omniscient and omnipresent and possessed of a totally benign nature, no negative attributes were ever assigned to *Her*. As well, no images were made to represent *Her*, while lesser Gods required some visual representation to make them more believable. There were woodcarvings depicting *Daw*, the God of Storms and *Shat'lal*, the God of Fire and Earthquake. Some people gave heed to these supposed deities, the supplication of whom might bring about intervention and prevention of disaster. But most of these peaceful people preferred to accept the vagaries of wind, rain, fire, earthquake, even illness and occasional madness, as the incomprehensible but unavoidable nature of their world. *Great Earth Mother*, as she breathed in and out, brought about the cycles of life, joyous or sad. Laughter and joy, tears and sorrow were accepted as equals in living in *Her* world.

Few such societies exist in our present world. Small and isolated and constantly under threat of dispersal and dissolution by the 'Modern World', they are a living echo of those ancient people whom I shall call, the Mal'lam. Why the Mal'lam? Because that's what Kinau Ho'opai Kaiser called them. And she should know. She knew them as her ancestors. And one listened carefully when Tutu Kinau spoke of the *world before*!

~ ~ * ~ ~

I had come to the University of Hawai'i in Honolulu as a summer graduate research assistant. After a previous summer holiday in these magical islands, I had determined that I would become an Hawai'ian and live happily-ever-after in Paradise. Oh yeah? Little did I know then that it took more than a surfboard and a smattering of *pidgin* to make it as a local. Professor Yukihara, my boss on this research project, an Hawai'ian native himself and a very no-nonsense person who had little patience with mainland *haoles*, soon set me straight on a number of things:

Number one: "Forget everything you think you know about Hawai'i and Polynesians. You don't know anything!"

Number two: "Don't wear a Bikini … wear shorts and a T-shirt and try to present yourself as innocent and willing to work and learn. And be very polite to everyone; you're the outsider here … don't forget that!" By this time I was getting more than a little nervous. I, Valedictorian of my high school class, daughter of a successful surgeon father and a psychologist mother, holder of the Girl's Surfing Cup … never mind.

Number three: "Go to Hanalei on Kaua'i and see 'Tutu' Kinau. Tell her I sent you. Here … take this letter and introduce yourself. And be respectful!" With that, the grumpy, middle-aged Japanese man dismissed me and left the interview room as if he'd encountered a bad smell. This was not how my dream assignment should begin, by any means, I thought. But, there it was. Nuts to you, Professor! I'll show you!

Two days later, knapsack and briefcase in tow, I found myself hitchhiking from the airport at Lihue, up the coast toward Hanalei. A Hippie couple picked me up and gave me a ride as far as Kilauea. I resisted the offer of a joint of marijuana but questioned them intensively about Tutu Kinau, up at Hanalei. They were too stoned to give me coherent answers so I just sat back and enjoyed the view until they dropped me off to hitch another ride. I didn't have to wait long. A car full of local people, mostly kids in shorts and T-shirts and all sucking on popsicles, pulled up and without a word of invitation, opened the back door and the kids squeezed over to make room for me and off we went. The driver was an elderly woman, obviously mostly Hawai'ian, who sat far back in the drivers' seat, wheel at arm's length and she began speaking to me over her shoulder, glancing back at me in the rear-view mirror.

The kids were making a lot of noise and I had to lean forward to hear her. One loud exclamation from her … "Shoosh, you kids!"… was all it took to bring a welcome silence. None of the kids looked at all abashed. They just shut up and sucked on their popsicles. "Where you headed, honey?" she asked, and our eyes met in the rear-view mirror. Her eyes held a playful gleam, rather than a question. "I'm going to Hanalei," I said. "I'm looking for someone who lives there. Her name's Tutu Kinau. Would you know her?"

At that moment the little girl who sat crushed warmly against me in the back seat nudged me and with her popsicle, pointed toward the woman driving. She looked up at me and smiled with a twerpy expression. From her orange-stained mouth came one word. "Tutu!" Again I looked up to the mirror and saw that smiling face which was to so alter my life. "O.K!" she said over her shoulder. "You're the one!" Then the kids began chattering again, none of them paying the slightest attention to me. The lady driving never said another word until we arrived 'home'.

I found myself relaxing and just enjoying the trip, careless of what was going to happen next. And that was very much *not* my usual style. I'm known as a control freak, always in charge of a situation. But at that moment I was happy to just cruise along with the kids and the breeze through the window and the occasional glance up at the rear-view mirror. She seemed always to be smiling back at me when I did. When we finally arrived at the old, run-down wooden shack at the end of the potholed road up Hanalei Valley, I was astounded by the peaceful silence and beauty of the place. And then the kids piled out behind me in a noisy jumble of rascality, faces now painted in the pastel colors of various-flavored popsicles.

A menagerie of chickens, geese, ducks and silly, woofing dogs greeted us. Off in the distance the high mountains were collecting shards of afternoon clouds, preparing to amalgamate a shower for later on. Just at my left foot there was a puppy, intent on catching my attention. It was all chocolate brown with a white blaze on its forehead, slightly off-center. I was compelled to reach down and pick it up and immediately it bathed me in licks and kisses.

Tutu Kinau, for that was who I now assumed she was, gestured over her shoulder for me to follow her into the ramshackle house at the end of the long, wide yard. The air was rich with the smell of over-ripe guavas. Huge clumps of banana plants bordered the yard and tall coconut palms, heavily laden with nuts, waved gracefully in the onshore breeze. I felt transported. I was suddenly in an environment of peaceful otherness.

This was Hawai'i as I had never yet experienced it. I reluctantly set the puppy down on the ground. I'd forgotten to get my backpack and briefcase from the car. The puppy looked up at me with a momentary condemnation, and then waddled away to join its littermates as mom lay down in the shade and invited her puppies to relieve the pressure on her huge mammaries. This was certainly not her first litter. Two male dogs, flea-bitten and lazy and quietly lying down again, deigned to raise their heads and cast a glance my way. Then, back to snoozing.

For some reason, the covered carport with its pronounced lean to the right was at least forty feet short of the house. Since this area is a heavy rainfall zone, I never have been able to make sense of this bit of local tradition. Many of the properties I visited in the valley were similarly laid-out. The pathway to the house was a muddy track this day because last night had seen some heavy showers. Aha! Near the bottom step to the porch was a graveled area, boxed in by 2x4's and attended by a water faucet and short length of hose. Everyone in this household was disciplined in the procedure of rinsing their feet and slippers or shoes before ascending the steps, regardless of pouring rain. Tutu Kinau told me, "No one has ever melted away in the rain yet!"

I copied the routine which the children followed: take off shoes/slippers; rinse feet and footgear; hurry up the steps (if it's raining) and lay your shoes/slippers neatly in a row to the right of the front door. Since my previous visit to Hawai'i had introduced me to the local custom of removing footwear before entering a house, it was now second nature. One of the kids though watched carefully to see that this *haole* knew what was required. All of seven years old, he gave me a grave nod of approval, then turned and ran into the house to join the cacophony his playmates had begun. At least the kids thought I was *akumai;* Hawai'ian for, pretty smart.

By now I was in dire need of a pee. Tutu, with a not unreasonable suspicion of my need, pointed to a doorway to the left rear of the large main room of the house. The interior of the house was somehow larger than the outside would imply. I found the toilet with no problem and was pleased to also find it clean and neat. With all these kids, I was quite impressed. The toilet paper had Donald Duck printed on it. Cute.

Almost before I'd finished, someone was knocking urgently on the door. When I opened the door, there stood a little girl I'd not seen before, certainly not one of the kids in the car with me. Without ado she pulled up her short skirt, dropped her panties and plopped down on the seat. I was still washing my hands. She looked at me with not a hint of embarrassment as she sat there, tinkling sounds coming from beneath her, and said, "I'm Tina! What's you're name?" And so I was introduced to one of the most fascinating children ... no, *persons* ... I've been blessed to know. She and her Grandmother would take me on a most fantastic voyage into the past. And this is the story they told me. Make of it what you will.

Chapter One - Kaua'i Dreaming

I begin this story with love. Love for the many people who allowed me to enter into the secret places of their souls. I pledge my oath of honesty and integrity in recounting what they have shared with me. I am a person who has received great blessings from their presence in my life and the trusting revelation of that which is sacred to them.

My first week with Tutu Kinau and her family was one of overwhelming acceptance. They knew me only as Katherine, the *haole* lady who spoke funny and didn't know how to shuck a coconut but could play the piano. I had asked Tutu Kinau how she knew that, "I was the one!" I'd expected an answer having to do with some spiritual power, which made her especially sensitive to one's aura, or something like that. No. "Professor Yukihara called me the day before I met you and said to look out for a *haole* girl with big brown eyes and a briefcase who'll be looking for me. That's about all you'll ever get from Jiro. He's a man of few words. But he's really a darlin' man. You'll see, in time." The main puzzle here was that Tutu Kinau's house didn't have a phone. Oh well, she must have been contacted at someone else's house. I never did sort that one out.

That first week it rained a lot. Not uncommon for Hanalei. But it was summer and the rain was warm and the Trade Winds were moderate. Tutu's old upright piano caught a workout that week because there wasn't much else to do, confined inside as we all were. Well, most of us. The little kids were irrepressible in their energy and adventurousness. They even conned me into going with them one stormy afternoon to go mud sliding. Oh Boy!

A nearby hillside, used for many years for this purpose, became a shallow stream in the heavy rain. Water sluiced down over the red dirt and with a bit of juvenile engineering, became a slippery-slide of rather awesome capacity. Covered from head to foot in red mud, they all called out, "Katherine, come on. It's just perfect now!" Slipping and sliding and grasping at clumps of grass as I struggled up the slope, I thought to myself that if I was going to brag about being a top surfer-lady, I'd better be as keen as the kids or they'd think I was a wuss. Not smart, Katherine! My first slide down the slope was a joy of splashing mud and squeals. In an ordered line, we re-ascended the slope and one-by-one, took our turns for another go. I was last, of course, and mud-covered faces with white teeth in wide grins egged me on. Only this time, as I reached maximum velocity, my butt ran over a hidden rock protruding up through the mud. Oh, God, but that hurt! I limped for the next two days, actually relieved to not have to prove myself to the kids any more.

'Tutu' tut-tutted my recklessness, with her usual sly grin, and she and her cousin Helen, an equally sturdy lady with hands like grappling hooks, gave me an Hawai'ian massage to ease the pain and speed healing for my bruised *okole*. Shit! I thought they were going to tear my butt off. But, surprisingly, the next day as I stretched my neck to look over my shoulder in the bathroom mirror, I saw only a small, dark bruise on my left buttock. It still ached but got better really quickly. Thankfully, the clouds parted that day and no further mud-sliding was possible. The little girls, Tina amongst them, all wanted to see the bruise on my bottom. Cheeky kids! The cheekiest was little Roland, all of six, who wanted to see too. Tina soon gave him the bum's rush and slammed the door on him. Kids!

Wednesday of the second week the kids all scrambled aboard a broken-down old bus and headed off for a field trip sponsored by the local church. Tutu Kinau had been keeping me busy helping her with weeding the vegetable garden since the rain had stopped. I was quite enjoying this but on that morning, as we waved the kids off to their adventure, she turned to me and stated, "Today I want to show you some things of importance!" Without ado, she set out across the garden and headed toward the mountains. I scrambled back to the porch, hurriedly pulled-on my hiking shoes, sans socks, and ran after her. There were few preliminaries with this woman.

We climbed up the increasingly steep slopes toward the cloud-wreathed mountains at the head of the valley, her heavy stride pushing me to keep up. Through scrub and Lantana, then into the deeper forest above, we continued on for at least forty minutes. When finally she called a halt, I was gasping. She was too, but she had the advantage of knowing where she was going. The jungle, for that's what it must be called, was deeply shadowed and the humidity very high. It was dripping with moisture in fact. Mosquitoes hummed around us and both of us began a routine of slapping and rubbing ourselves."Let's keep going, Katherine. Too much mosquito here for stopping."

As I had become accustomed, her speech was a lilt of *pidgin-English,* with a sometimes-surprising use of precise and very erudite phrasing. On this day I was to learn that Kinau Ho'opai Kaiser was a graduate of the University of Hawai'i and a high school teacher for more than thirty years. Whether with pidgin or proper, educated English, Tutu Kinau had no difficulty in expressing herself. The combination of the two speech patterns was delightful. And this day would reveal many delights to me. Another half-an-hour saw us above the thick forest and onto a mostly grassy slope. The view back down the valley was marvelous. Green! So very green and sculpted. *Taro* patches with water a foot deep glistened in the morning sun and fruit trees and big swathes of banana plants framed them. Beyond was the sea. It was glorious!

We sat down on some smooth rocks which protruded darkly here and there through the grass. "Notice anything about these rocks?" Tutu asked. I looked around, stood up again to have a better look but could not see anything specific, no special feature yet. "Look hard." She said. I did look hard and then I began to see a pattern emerging. The stones, boulders some of them, were aligned in a series of rows spreading left and right of where we sat. The rows were parallel to the sea beyond us. I told her I thought it must have been a man-made structure of some kind.

"You're standing on one of the oldest *heiaus* in all of Hawai'i. You know what a *heiau* is?" Before I could answer that, yes, I thought they were sacred sites, she continued: "This *heiau* is more than a thousand years old. Jiro and some of his scientific staff dated it about ten years ago. Few people know it's here though. And that's how we want it kept; unknown to the outside world."

Tutu Kinau excused herself for a couple of minutes to pee, then came back and stood gazing across the hillside, from side to side. I could tell this place was very special to her. I felt the need to remain silent and still. I actually felt a sense of specialness too. Not only this place, but also the fact that she had brought me here was special. Then Tutu did something which made goose bumps all over me; 'chicken skin', they call it here. Standing with her broad back slightly arched, her arms spread wide, she began chanting; her face uplifted, eyes closed, she had a beatific expression like a black woman singing in a church choir. It sounded like ...'*Ah eh ohhhh. Alohaaa nooo!*'

I was immediately mesmerized by the rich, powerful sound and must have been open mouthed, looking up at her. She repeated the opening phrase, but I lost the words from then on. She chanted for not more than a minute. When she stopped she stood like she was listening for something. Long moments. Then she smiled, reached into a pocket in her long dress and took out a handful of ripe Strawberry guavas. She bent and laid the fruits like an offering on a low, flat stone just in front of her. I knew then that she had done this many times before. I had just witnessed my first Hawai'ian ceremony. First, that is, not part of a commercial production for tourists. This was the real thing and I was still 'chicken skin'.

"Come now," she said, smiling down at me, "The sun's getting hot. We go up there and sit under that *kukui* tree." It was not only pleasantly cool beneath this big tree but there was a small trickling stream just below it and we were both thirsty. After long drinks from cupped hands we both found comfortable seats and I waited for her to do something, say something. She looked intently into my eyes for a few moments, smiled and looked away down toward the *heiau* again. And then Tutu Kinau began to speak to me directly and her words were measured and precise. And there was no lilt of pidgin; rather her speech was soft and held only a faint accent which I could not place. It was beautifully spoken English. She mesmerized me with her voice and quite astounded me with her meaning.

"Katherine, what I have to tell you now comes from my heart. It also comes from the hearts of my people who have gone away from us, oh, so many years ago. My people, the souls who speak to me, are not Hawaiian. They are people who called themselves the *Mal'lam.* You know of them only in the corrupted, meaningless tradition of the 'Menehune'. There never were little, magical people who built fishponds overnight, or cast spells on others. That is all rubbish which began with the Hawai'ians themselves and other Polynesian peoples when they overwhelmed and subjugated people already indigenous to various island groups.

Humans often tend to try to diminish and make *Other*, those whom they abuse and destroy. Some of this, I know, is already a developing theory among those of you studying ancient cultures. But it is knowledge held and passed down by my ancestors, my *Mal'lam* ancestors, and here on Kaua'i. You see, I have both Hawaiian blood and European blood in my veins. But it is my *Mal'lam* heritage which has always dominated my soul. You have been sent to me to learn what I know to be the truth of the first people who sailed to these islands of Hawai'i. That was more than forty generations before the Polynesians, of what is called Tahiti, even knew these islands were here."

Kinau paused briefly and shifted her large body to a more comfortable position. I, meanwhile, could not move a muscle. Yes, I was aware of a current school of thought in anthropology which coincided with what she was saying. But I knew there was much more to come which was going to amaze me. There was just something so compelling in her manner and voice. And that altered form of speech continued.

"When I was a child, no more than ten or eleven, I began to hear voices speaking to me from the forest behind our house. Yes, the house I live in now. Quite strangely, I was not frightened. You may know that many Hawai'ian people are very superstitious and so was most of my family. But tales of Gods and ghosts and evil spirits never, even as a child, interested me much. Of course had I told anyone, even my mother, of these voices, she would have been in panic and have raced me off to a *kahuna* or a minister.

Nowadays, I would be taken to a child psychologist and probably be diagnosed as schizophrenic! Well, I didn't tell anyone, at least not for many years. And the voices continued. I heard them often, day and night. And when we visited family on the other side of the island, up a valley which I will take you to soon, the voices were even more numerous and stronger. And what did these voices say to me? Ah, so many tales they had to tell! They told me of the sweet land they lived in, of the peaceful life they led among the forested hills and along the seashore. They told me of how their own ancestors had come here from the other islands to the east and how, after many generations, they had forsaken sailing between the islands and ventured only far out enough upon the sea to fish. Everything they needed was here on Kaua'i. And then they told of the coming of the fierce people from the southern seas that stole their lands and drove them into the mountains and away from the sea.

Fear came into their lives with the arrival of the foreigners. And fear became a disease which slowly killed the *Mal'lam*! And yet there is no fear or sorrow in the voices which have spoken to me for most of my life. In fact, they taught me to laugh. And rejoice. For you see, I was an unhappy child and laughter was seldom heard in our house when I was young. But that is not part of my story which I tell you now. That time is long-gone. I am so very happy to be with you and to tell you of my life with the souls of my ancestors. I know that we shall share much laughter, for already they have welcomed you as my sister. My dear, little, *haole* sister!"

I sat there with tears streaming down my face, choking back sobs and trying to be objective and, very *haole*! But when Tutu Kinau leaned forward and took me in her big, strong arms and kissed me on the forehead, I wept like a baby. And then, through tears and around sobs I began to laugh, nearly choking myself which made me laugh even harder. In moments we were holding each other, both of us shrieking with laughter and rocking back and forth. I think I peed myself, I was so out of control. This madness, such sweet madness, slowly abated and we leaned back away from each other, our emotions temporarily exhausted. We continued to giggle and snort and wipe our eyes and faces for minutes as around us a sudden shower of rain, so common on summer days here, splashed and rushed down in buckets. The *kukui* tree was our big, green umbrella, even if it leaked a bit.

When the rain stopped, as suddenly as it had begun, Tutu Kinau slapped her thighs with her big hands and said, "Well, we gotta go home now, seestah! Lots of work to do! Big luau this weekend." She saw the puzzled look on my face, grinned and asked, "Eh? Nobody tol' you? Waagh! The whole family comin'. You'll have a good time. Let's go." The shift in her voice to the *pidgin* was somehow a relief after the drama of her soliloquy of minutes before. This abrupt change in her presentation would take getting used to. And with a couple of grunts and a groan, she hefted her big body off the moss-covered rock and set off downhill. In spite of her size and age, boy, could Tutu Kinau walk, especially downhill!

My mind was filled with a thousand questions but lack of breath and the need to pay attention to the rain-slick trail prevented me from asking. Kinau was an indomitable force descending the long hill. We plunged down through the still-dripping forest and the stones and logs covered in treacherous lichens and mosses almost as if we had a deadline to meet. We came out far to the left of where we had entered the forest on the way uphill, skirted around the uppermost *taro* patch and down smooth grass to the house. I was sweaty and smelling embarrassingly of peed-pants. No one else seemed at home so I went to the water faucet designed for washing feet and soaked myself down from head to foot with the short length of hose. I'd just squeejeed myself down as best I could when a dry towel flew through the air and landed exactly into my waiting hands. Ah, Kinau, you're a lifesaver. My *seestah* to the rescue!

The rest of that day was pretty well taken up with harvesting and cleaning the foods which this lovely property provided: sweet potatoes and taro from the gardens up the hill; tomatoes and peppers, garlic and onions from the near-by vegetable gardens. Then there were fallen coconuts to gather and green nuts to cut from the Dwarf Philippine coconuts.

Around three that afternoon the kids returned home, the old bus honking a greeting as it splashed through the many mud-puddles up the driveway. Out piled the kids, all loud voices and empty bellies! Tina was last off. I had noticed before that she carried herself with an un-childlike grace. Not aloof, but somehow self-possessed. An inner calmness seemed her prevailing mien while still looking the cute, pubescent twelve year-old she was. While the wild horde of younger children assaulted the kitchen and whatever edibles they could lay their hands on, Tina walked over to Kinau and the two strolled slowly toward the house, each with an arm around the other, chatting quietly.

I helped with bathing the younger ones that evening before dinner, Tina assisting me with getting them dressed. While we sat on the edge of the bathtub together, pulling T-shirts over protesting heads, she smiled up at me and asked, "You and Tutu had a good day up at the *heiau*?" I answered that I found it fascinating, and a bit spooky. I was not surprised that Tutu Kinau would have told her of our journey up the mountain. Her next statement did surprise me.

"Did Tutu tell you that I have my Spirit voices too?" No, she hadn't and now things were getting really interesting. Just then young Roland, who often liked intruding on people's conversations - what an ego he had for a six year old - charged into the bathroom full speed and shouted, "Unca' Teddy is here! He got a big pig fo' the *luau*!" And then he was gone again in a flash, his loud voice trailing off outside and into the yard. Tina only chuckled and finished dressing little Lani. "We better go see." she said, and we both went out into the front yard to see Unca' Teddy's pig. Boy, what a pig! And it was alive. I'd expected a carcass; a depersonalized hunk of meat which would hardly resemble a living thing, especially when cooked to perfection in the earth oven. No way! This one had a chain attached to a ring in its nose and was led squealing as only a pig can, fully suspecting that something unfortunate was going to happen to it.

Uncle Teddy Ho'opai was a small, wiry man of Filipino appearance, belying his Hawai'ian name. All smiles and friendly waves and comments to the children around him, he was nevertheless struggling mightily with this huge porker. The fat sow was determined to go in exactly the opposite direction in which Teddy was trying to guide it - and that was into a decrepit, ramshackle old pen near the back of the house. One boy, Samuel, about eight and big for his age, grabbed the chain and tried to help Unca' Teddy. The two of them still struggled and the pig's shrieks were growing louder. Deafening!

"Katherine! Give the boys a hand with that stubborn old sow." Tutu's voice held a touch of humor. I looked up to where she stood, leaning against the porch railing. No, she wasn't kidding. She wanted me, a certified urban lady who'd never even touched a pig before, to somehow assist in herding a reluctant porker to its doom. Then Tina came to the rescue. 'Why hasn't anyone thought of this before?' I asked through clenched teeth, trying to grab hold of the rusty, taut chain. Tina jogged down the steps with a handful of taro leaves and stood in front of the pig. The pig stopped. Sniffing, its beady little eyes seeming to struggle to focus on this new human assailant, it ceased squealing and took a few steps toward the proffered greens. Tina backed away, holding the taro leaves out before her. The pig was now intent on at least a last meal. Soon Tina's intervention had the pig in the pen, noisily slurping up the greens. Teddy took the chain off the sow and everyone quickly left the pen, the rickety gate then secured with the rusty links. Everyone smiled broadly now, satisfied with a job well done. Even I got into the moment and grinned as if I'd really accomplished something. Gee, we're a silly bunch sometimes!

Tutu Kinau managed to organize the kids into a working bee, gathering firewood from the big pile of Ironwood behind the house. Teddy, ever-smiling and now with a bottle of beer in his hand, directed the two older boys in digging the sand pit for the *imu*. The kids obviously loved this man. It turned out that he was Kinau's cousin, Aunty Helen's son. Although this large family claimed many surnames, I was to learn how closely knit they all were, apparently with few exceptions. I didn't know one could have so many cousins.

The next two days were busy, busy! Relatives and friends coming by all day, more kids running around, getting under foot. I quickly lost track of peoples' names but no one seemed to mind. The kitchen was filled with ladies and girls. I mean, these big family *luaus* are really important. This gathering was in celebration of a child's first birthday, a most significant ritual in Hawai'i. I helped out wherever I could and was finding this experience delightful. All the women, even the young girls, seemed to accept a strange *haole* in their midst without question. I had not felt as at home and part of something really important since I was a young girl. Christmases at my Grandmother's were a bit like this; all warm friendship and family closeness. But this was *biiig!*

Friday night was when most of the men arrived. Cases of beer were opened and the heavy, and messy, work began. Teddy and three other men brought out the big pig, this time with less effort as Teddy used Tina's trick with taro leaves. Poor pig! I retreated into the house but most of the kids gathered around to watch the slaughter. A short burst of squealing was followed by a painful silence. Even the chattering boys were stilled by the drama of the death of a large animal. I busied myself with the other women in the kitchen. That entire evening people continued to arrive; individuals, couples, but mostly families and more kids. Some were neighbors, some just friends from as far away as the other side of the island. Then, late in the evening when I was drooping from fatigue, wondering how all these women kept going all day like they did, I turned in response to a familiar voice. It was Jiro Yukihara, *Professor* Yukihara, my project director from the University! He was the last person I expected to see here. He walked through the door to the kitchen, a beer in hand, and gave me a big, warm smile. I almost fell over.

Tutu Kinau, her hands stuck into a big bowl of *poi*, leaned sideways to receive a kiss on the cheek from him. She smiled over to me and said, "Katherine. You go rest now. Get some *kau kau* and a plate for Jiro and go out and relax, Eh?" I didn't need a second invitation. I was bushed. And starving! Even though I'd been around food most of the day, the killing of the pig had put me off my feed. There was a long table set up on trestles in the living room, loaded with food. I took two plates and some cutlery and a couple of napkins and walked over to Professor Yukihara. Was this really the rude, gruff, cranky old bastard who had so curtly dismissed me? His face now glowed with warmth and geniality.

He took the plate and we worked our way together around the table, piling our plates to overflowing. Jiro struggled to keep hold of his beer bottle in the process. We walked together onto the *lanai*, Jiro giving two cheeky kids *stink-eye* until they gave up their seats on the broken-down, overstuffed old chairs. I thanked the kids as they grumbled away. One of them, a boy about twelve, threw a friendly grin over his shoulder at me. Obviously, everyone knew Jiro Yukihara and when he turned his *stink-eye* on you, you moved. But there was also no rancor involved. Jiro was a well-liked man in this huge, extended family. My gratitude only increased as he graciously signaled that I should take the less dilapidated of the two chairs.

A young man came up onto the porch - sorry - *lanai*, about as we sat down and asked if we would like a beer. Jiro quickly upended his bottle and held it out to the fellow. "Yep, and one for Katherine too!" The handsome young man grinned and threw me a wink. He was back in a very short while with four bottles. Jiro Yukihara and I sat eating and drinking our two beers in relative silence. Around us, the noise level was growing. Out in the yard the *imu* was being laid, the pig butchered and prepared for cooking in the earth oven and many bottles of beer being consumed. There were at least twenty-five children of ages one year to fifteen adding to the general cacophony.

The *imu*, or earth oven, was a large hole in the ground which had been filled with beach sand. It was now emptied of sand and the hard, hot-burning Ironwood logs cleverly stacked into a conical shape. A large log had been placed upright in the center and kindling placed around it, larger logs laid upon that. Wadded-up newspaper was placed among the bundles of kindling. No artificial fuel like gasoline or diesel was used because of the flavor it might impart to the food. This method of cooking was thousands of years old. Jiro and I sat, sated now, our bellies more than full, watching the *imu* being readied for a four A.M. firing. So early? Yes. The pig alone weighed in at over three hundred pounds and there would be that much weight in other food added to the cooking. It would take at least six hours of cooking to do the job.

The part I found so fascinating was the placement of the volcanic rock. Specially shaped stones had been selected, all gleaned from riverbeds so that they were smooth and rounded. Some were elongated so that they would fit inside the pig's carcass near the joints. None were larger than a loaf of bread. When the wood was all properly stacked in the fire pit, the rocks were carefully laid over the woodpile. The center log was then removed and a torch of rolled-up newspaper was dropped down the hole the log had left. When the fire, and it would be very big and very hot, had burned down to coals, the rocks would lay over them in a concave cone against the walls of the fire pit, most of them red hot. The specially selected stones laid near the top of the initial fire structure would be extracted with long, bent bamboo tongs, soaked overnight in water for flexibility and heat resistance. The specially shaped stones would be inserted into the pig's carcass and the pig then wrapped in chicken wire.

The trunks of banana plants, smashed flat, would be laid over the hot coals and rocks and the pig laid first into the *imu*. Then another layer of banana trunks and leaves. Then the other food items, wrapped in *ti* leaves, would be laid on top of the covered pig's carcass; whole chickens, fish, sweet potatoes, corn, a dish called *lau lau* which was fish or corned beef and taro leaves, quite like spinach, wrapped in *ti* leaves along with breadfruit and anything else which offered itself for cooking. All that food was then covered with more banana leaves laid thickly and in opposing layers. Then the whole thing was covered with cut-open gunnysacks soaked in water, and old-fashioned fabric tarps. The sand then was shoveled over it all, up to two feet in depth. During the cooking process the men in attendance would throw more sand over any area which was allowing steam to escape. Years of experience allowed the 'cooks' to gauge when the food would be ready. Then everyone would gather around and watch the opening of the *imu*. It is quite a ritual and with a delicious outcome!

By this time the night was deepening into a quiet hum of low conversation with a background of chirruping crickets. Little kids were giving out and falling to sleep in parents' laps. Soon they would be carried off into beds in the back of pickup trucks or into the back seats of cars. Not a few adults, mostly men with too many beers aboard, also crashed out. There was a whiff of marijuana in the air. Some of the younger people had gone off into the shadows beyond the range of the floodlights and lit up. From somewhere near the garage came the sound of ukuleles and guitars. From the kitchen came the constant clatter of dishes being washed and happy female chatter.

This was a beautiful evening. Until now, Jiro, as he had asked me to call him, had said little. Neither had I. We were simply enjoying the sights, sounds and ambience of this quite wonderful night. I no longer held any animosity toward 'Professor Yukihara'. All that gruffness and incomprehensible rudeness three weeks ago had evaporated. No discussion had been necessary to bring about this peaceful reconciliation. It just occurred spontaneously. We accepted another beer each, proffered by the same handsome young man, who by this time was beginning to look mighty good to me.

"I'm so glad things have worked out well for you here, Katherine." he finally said. "Have you had time to make many notes so far?"Surely he was joking! I'd been so busy with just the day-to-day ritual of life in Tutu's world that I'd not even opened my notebook. Wow! Until this moment I hadn't even been aware of this terrible transgression on the part of a student archaeologist. What's happened to me? I must be losing it! and then I became aware of the mischievous little smile which the dim ambient light betrayed. You rascal, Jiro!

"Katherine, you'll forgive me I hope, for giving you a hard time that day at the University." I peered hard in the dimness to see the meaning in his eyes but there was inscrutability there and it wasn't just his Oriental squint. Crafty old codger! "I've been keeping an eye on you these past weeks, through Kinau of course. She thinks you're very *akamai*. Also, you have a special quality which is very important to her. To me too, for that matter. You listen. And believe me, not too many *haoles* listen like you do."

I didn't know whether to be embarrassed, proud or what. But I did believe he was being honest. Just then young Tina, whom I hadn't seen since early in the evening and now carrying a toddler on her hip, came up to us and climbed onto Jiro's lap. Jiro put his arms around her and gently cuddled her. Looking over at me he said, "Tina is my Goddaughter. Did you know?" At that moment fatigue and that last beer got to me. I didn't think I could handle any more surprises that night. All I could do was smile and shake my head. I stood up, and nearly fell back into the chair but regained my composure enough to steady myself and stand. "I really need to go to bed now, Jiro."

I leaned forward and patted them both on an arm and said, "Thank you Jiro. I'll see you in the morning. Thank you. Goodnight Tina." I left them both smiling warmly at me and made my way, rather unsteadily, through the big main room, waving a goodnight to Kinau and the other ladies in the kitchen and went through the doorway into the small bedroom down the hall. Wouldn't you know? There on my bed were two tiny, sleeping figures. Oh well. I took a folded blanket from off the chair near the bed, gently pulled a pillow from beneath one of the little sleeping heads and lay down on the floor. I don't even remember saying my prayers.

Chapter Two - The Luau

I awoke to the smell of smoke and kitchen clatterings. Struggling up on one elbow I saw that the two little ones were still asleep on my bed. Gee, but they were cute! Then I was aware of an urgent need to go to the bathroom. Oh oh! There was a short lineup in the hallway; three other ladies all looking groggy and in the same situation as me. We all managed to save our honor though we were all grimacing and crossing our legs and doing those things which forestall accidents. The men, it turned out, were obliged to use the outdoor toilet, leaving the proper bathroom to the ladies and kids. Boy, that room got a workout that day.

After doing my business, brushing teeth and hair and a quick wash-up, I joined the ladies in the kitchen. There was Tutu Kinau looking fresh and cheerful, organizing the other ladies into work teams. She gave me a hug and then asked me to help with setting up the big serving tables. With me on this task were four other younger women whom I'd met only briefly the night before. Everyone seemed so cheerful and full of energy. I was dying for a cup of coffee and was definitely a bit hung-over. And what time was it? Good Lord! It was only six thirty!

The smoke of course, was coming from the *imu*, the fire having receded now into a glowing bowl of coals. Teddy and another man were prodding the stones among the coals with long sticks, each with a fresh beer in hand. Both looked a bit under the weather. Hair-of-the-dog, I think. Two other fellows were unwrapping the pigs' carcass from under a large tarp. Banana leaves had been wrapped around the pig first. From many feet away, the heat from that fire was awesome. Teddy and his friend didn't seem to mind, though they did back off from time to time. Didn't want their beers to get warm I guess.

Someone must have been reading my mind because in a few minutes, as the girls and I were laying out the tablecloths, Aunty Helen came down from the house carrying two mugs of steaming coffee. I thought she was going to join me in an eye-opener but just then Jiro came around the corner from the direction of the outhouse. He looked disgustingly bright and wide-awake. Helen passed him a mug and whispered a short message to him. We exchanged greetings and then, with a toss of his head, indicated I should follow him. I asked the girls if they would excuse me. My request was met with bright, tolerant smiles from two of them. The third, Joy her name was, didn't respond.

I was later to learn that she didn't much like *haoles,* even if they were a friend of Tutu Kinau. I followed him to a couple of rather hazardous looking old wooden chairs beneath the big mango tree, about fifty feet from the house. We sat down in relative seclusion from the increasing bustle around the house. We both blew and sipped on the hot coffee for a few quiet minutes. Then he sat back and began speaking, looking not at me but somewhere off into the distance. "No one will mind if you sit here with me for a while Katherine. There'll be plenty of work to do later. Now, I suppose I owe you some explanation . . ., again, . . . not an apology mind you!" and he turned his head slightly toward me and winked. "I gave you a hard time that day at the University for a reason. I must be slipping in my technique, or maybe I was already convinced about you. I was testing you. Needless to say, you passed the test!" A bit emboldened now by his recent friendliness, I asked him what was being tested. What did he expect me to do in the face of rudeness?

"If you'll recall the moment," he continued, "I was looking you straight in the eye. I saw, first, a bit of shock. Quite natural. But it was the gleam of indignation and determination which answered my basic question about you. I felt sure that you were the kind of person who would dedicate yourself to something and follow through with it." He set his empty mug down on the grass, crossed his legs and began explaining some things which had been puzzling me for days.

"Kinau and I were in contact the day after you arrived here. You see, she and I go back a long way. Way back. We grew up together, brother and sister. Her parents took me in when I was just a tadpole. Three years old I was. My parents had died of T.B., both very young. Adopting stray kids is still pretty common in Hawai'i. No lawyers or judges or legal papers then. People just took some little squirt like me and said, 'you're with us now!' The Hawai'ians call this, *hanai*. I felt a chill of 'chicken skin' when he said this. I had heard stories of this wonderful tradition before, but coming into first- hand contact, well, it was just so sweet. "As you have already discovered, there's something very special about our Kinau. She was always, since a little kid, staring off into space as if she was listening to something far away. She was indeed, as she's no doubt told you?"

He looked over and I nodded in confirmation. "Well, Katherine, what I'd like you to do is just continue what you've been doing. And don't worry too much about taking notes. There'll be no exam for you to pass. I want you to totally immerse yourself in this family, become a part of the scene here. Don't worry about fitting in. Kinau already loves you, as does Tina. Oh yeah. About Tina!" And here Jiro swiveled around on his chair and faced me. "Tina, even more intensely than Kinau, is in contact with the 'Old People'. Do you know what I mean?" No, I didn't. This was the first time I'd heard of the 'Old People'. I thought Kinau was in touch with the, 'Old People'.

"No. Tina's *contacts*, if you will, are not the people who lived in Hawai'i for a long time before the *Hawa'ians* came, as we know of them now. Tina is in contact with the Spirits of the people who were to become known as the *Menehune* long before the Hawai'ians had ever discovered Hawai'i!" This was going to take some working through! Katherine, what have you gotten yourself into? Here's a highly respected scientist, a university professor of world reputation who's telling me to continue a study of a twelve year old child's communication, on the psycho-whatever-level, of a people who may never have existed!?

Just then a commanding voice called to me from the tables where I'd been earlier assigned. "Eh! Haole girl! You come help now. Come Katherine. Time to make the flowers!" Then Jiro threw another stunner at me; "Katherine, I've just signed your request for an extension of your grant. You've got an income for another year!" I stood up in total confusion: did I turn and give Jiro a big kiss? Did I run back to the growing crowd of workers, preparing a great tribute to a little child on its first birthday? I did both. I threw Jiro a kiss and ran with exultation toward the life I was to lead for the next twelve-plus months on this magical island of Kaua'i! Oh, Katherine! What have you done?!

That morning saw a short, light shower which seemed to worry no one. It quickly passed and a warm sun played hide-and-seek with fluffy, rainless clouds for the rest of the day. I loved 'making the flowers'. Each of the six long tables set up on trestles and covered with spotless white sheets as tablecloths, were to be decorated with floral displays every three feet. The three other girls and I were kept busy for over an hour, learning how to arrange the flowers. Coconuts, cut in half, the husks still on them, were pierced with thin strips of bamboo and laid on the table. Plumeria blossoms were then threaded onto the skewers and the result was a visual shower of blossoms, accented by the wonderful fragrance of the flowers themselves. The Plumeria were of many colors and the colors alternated down the long tables. There were bowls of Tuberose and a few scant remnants of the season's Stephanotis, heady with their perfume, glorious in their pristine whiteness. For color were Hibiscus, Gingers and Ixoras. Fern leaves accented the arrangements, making them even more full and magnificent. I'd never attempted flower arranging before. It has, since that day, become a passion of mine.

Men now surrounded the *imu.* It was time to put the food parcels, the huge pig first, into the rapidly cooling earth oven. Timing was critical. All these men had grown up with this task; this ritual, actually! In went the first layers of crushed banana trunks; then the pig in its huge, wire-wrapped parcel; then came the smaller parcels wrapped in leaf, many bound with commercial string, some still using vine and twisted banana fiber. Whole Breadfruits were placed among the more articulated food parcels. These big, kind of prickly fruits had been cored and butter and brown sugar pushed into the hollow centers and the cutaway tops replaced, stem still sticking up proudly.

When at last all the food to be cooked was in place, the whole oven was covered in its layers and sealed with sand. The opening of the *imu* was scheduled for about three-thirty in the afternoon. Phewww! There was now an hiatus of about four hours in which most of those dozens assembled could relax and enjoy other pursuits: like, bathing the kids, feeding the kids their breakfasts, bathing ourselves, but not in the bathroom! The nearby stream, which fed into the main river, had lovely bathing beaches with coarse sand. I joined many other women in washing away the sweat and grime of the morning's labors. I heard that most of the men not needed for the *imu* watch had gone down to the beach to surf or fish. Here I was, a former surfing champ, not even interested, on this day, in the former passion of my youth! Extraordinary!

We women were having a ball splashing and playing in the stream, little kids among us, gossip flowing along with the waters. Then that little ratty kid, Roland, was discovered perving on the ladies. His mother, Rachael, who lived on Oahu and really spent little time with him, chased him off into the brush. We heard squeals of horrible torture as she caught up with him. Of course, the torture was simply in being caught and humiliated. A few whacks on the bottom elicited similar wails of agony but soon all was quiet and his mother shortly emerged from the creek-side greenery, without the naughty boy, and with a smile of triumph. "I've been trying to catch that little buggah spyin' on women for months! Got 'im this time!" A round of laughter and soon the conversations spread out upon many separate topics, little groups of women and girls moving through the water to join a topic of especial interest. Not surprisingly, most topics had to do with men, or what they did or even what hung off them. Tsk tsk!

By midday it was time to return to the *luau*. Then the real party would begin! When Kinau and Aunty Helen and I walked together up the slope and back toward the house, I was amazed to see twice as many cars and pickups and dozens more people than had been there earlier. There were more than a hundred people gathering. It was so colorful! Most of the older women outshone the younger ladies; voluminous *mu'u mu'u's* in every color, flowery patterns prevailing. Some of the younger girls, late teens and early twenties, wore shorts and rather revealing tops. Some even sported hippie-like long dresses and smelled of incense. This is, after all, the early '70's and mainland culture is making strong inroads into local culture. A few bearded young *haoles* accompanied the local girls. Most of those seemed slightly ill at ease.

To their credit, the local boys made a generous attempt to be hospitable and soon the beer was flowing and ukuleles and guitars began what was to be a daylong serenade. Impromptu hula dances started. Old Tutus, little kids, women and girls of all ages joined in. A couple of *mahus*, young men of the female persuasion, also joined the rows and circles of dancers and laughter and applause rose and fell beneath the *swaying coconut palms* (sorry, I had to say that!) Then it was time to open the *imu*. One older man, I forget his name now, blew on a conch shell, in the old tradition, and everyone began to gather near the earth oven, crowding together to better see the ritual of the opening.

Teddy was again the master of the *imu*. Small and slight though he was, he wielded a mighty shovel and hot sand began to fly as the six or seven men with him sweated to remove the covering from the buried food. Steam began to rise and delicious smells rose with it. *Ti* plant leaves and banana stalks impart a very particular, unforgettably delicious fragrance to cooked food. Even before the canvass covering, then the gunnysacks and layers of crushed banana stalks were removed, ohhs! and ahhhs! dominated the soundtrack of this marvelous drama. Little kids shoved against grownup legs and pushed aside skirts to get a view of what was happening too. Really little kids were hoisted onto Dad's or uncle's shoulders.

A *luau* is a huge confection of sounds and smells and color; the easygoing friendliness and joy were the icing on the cake. I couldn't remember ever being happier. Aunty Helen had brought me a beautiful, flowery *mu'u mu'u*, the long flowing dress patterned after the 'Mother Hubbards' which the missionaries had enforced upon the women of Hawai'i. Even in this often-hot environment, naked breasts and legs were abhorrent to those 19th century God-botherers. But the present day garment is more open and of a light, airy fabric. I felt quite like a queen in my borrowed dress. Tutu Kinau insisted that I wear a cluster of Plumeria flowers in my hair, on the right side. Right side meant you were 'available', left side meant your heart was already taken. I thought it all wonderfully romantic!

The parcels of food were laid out on a long table covered in old- fashioned and very practical oilcloth. Large stainless steel trays, borrowed from someone's' cousin's restaurant, were soon filled with the contents of the larger food packets The huge cooked pig was carried last from the *imu* by four men and laid upon a large platter of fresh banana leaves on the ground. There was joking and laughter among the food servers: one of the men taking the pig from the earth oven had burned his feet on hot rocks and sand. He'd forgotten to wear his *zoris*, or slippers. Even he was giggling. He'd been drinking beer since about 9A.M., so was feeling no pain. Tomorrow would be a different story, I'm sure.

Pork cooked at an Hawai'ian luau is really well cooked; some would say over-cooked. Never-the-less it was delicious. There is a flavor which can never be duplicated with any other manner of cooking. The offal, including the eyes, was consumed with ostentatious delight by some of the older men. That seemed to be their prerogative, although the younger men crowded around the rapidly disintegrating carcass to claim their bits. Macho rascals! People lined up in orderly fashion to fill their plates and find a place to sit down and enjoy this feast. I found a place among a group of young women, most of whom had flowers in their hair, on the right side of their heads. The girl-gossip began almost immediately, between bites and chews and swallowing. I was fascinated really, learning how the local girls thought and carried on about other people. Boys and young men walking by underwent scrutiny and comment, much like where I come from in California. I just listened, smiled on cue, occasionally laughed at a particularly witty observation, but mostly ate in silence - and in gratitude.

The young lady sitting on my right - Lovey was her name, a not uncommon first name here - and I quickly formed a rapport. Her flowers were on the left side of her head. A large cluster of pink and apricot Plumeria blossoms they were and she shyly confided that she was engaged to a boy from Oahu, a distant cousin on her mother's side. Unfortunately, he could not get away from work for the celebration. He worked for Aloha Airlines as a flight attendant and did shift work. Her lovely face displayed both sadness and pride. She really was in love. All day long these open, friendly and generous associations arose with the most delightful spontaneity. I was truly at home here! Accepted, even loved, and filled with Alo'ha! And by nightfall, full of beer and looking for somewhere quiet to lay my head. Of course, I wasn't alone in this. Surprisingly, I discovered my own bed empty of kids. I brushed my teeth, had a quick wash-up and lay down on a pillow which wanted to be silly and go around in circles. But before long I was vaguely aware of drifting pleasantly off to sleep.

Chapter Three - Above Kala'lau

In spite of the huge amount of food I'd eaten and the way-too-much beer I'd drunk, I awoke refreshed and happy. And I had another little kid sleeping beside me whose arrival the night before I'd not consciously noted. She was sleeping quietly so I eased myself out of bed, put on my shorts and T-shirt and tiptoed out to the bathroom. No one was waiting; no one yet occupied the amenities. I had a quick shower, cold water only, and boy, did that wake me up. I amazed myself by realizing that I was hungry! And a hungry riser couldn't hope for a better spread of breakfast: along the tables, which had been moved inside overnight (and I felt a twinge of guilt at not being there to help with that) I found two other early risers, one of them Jiro, loading up plates while trying to be quiet about it.

We all exchanged grins and whispered good mornings and left the kitchen as a small band of raiders and went outside to sit under the big mango tree. A few other people were up and about, mostly kids but being especially quiet - for kids. The smell of yesterdays' cooking hung sweetly in the still air. A young *haole* fellow was sitting up in his bedroll, lighting a cigarette; I'm not quite sure what kind, but he drew on the smoke with utter seriousness. I'd forgotten my watch. I asked Jiro what time it was. Around a mouthful of food he muttered, "Don't ask!" I reached over and turned his wrist gently so that I could read his watch. My God! It's only six o'clock! The young man sharing our breakfast grinned widely around his mouthful and nodded affirmatively. Well, on a beautiful morning like this you might as well be up and at'em.

When we'd finished eating, Jiro and I sat together in the shade and chatted. I asked him about this custom of a big party for a child's first birthday. I commented that it seemed that this child had gotten wealthy overnight. There were lots of envelopes and most of them bulging with money. The party guests, after eating, had come over to where the young mother sat with the little one and laid the envelopes and other gifts on her lap. The proud father sat behind them, beaming. They were both but in their late teens. "Yes, I suppose it might seem that the baby is suddenly rich. Keep in mind though, the rolls of bills are often only one-dollar bills, the most that one family could afford to give. Putting twenty ones in an envelope instead of one twenty-dollar bill of course makes the gift look better. That's not a problem. The true value is in the giving itself and the recognition that the baby is a new addition to the larger family. Also, Katherine, these youngsters have survived a year together since the birth of their child, and the child is almost always a surprise. So what the community at large is saying is, 'You've done well so far, and now your baby is well and growing. We'll help you all we can to make a home for yourselves and your child. God bless you three. We love you!"

How could I possibly contest the logic, more importantly, the humanity of this argument in support of this old and enduring tradition? But being a serious student of anthropology, I had to ask my mentor this: "How is it though, that the local community is unable, in so many cases, to continue this kind of support for its own people? A lot of young Hawai'ians, and mixed-race youngsters, seem to be floating away into legal and criminal trouble?"

Jiro didn't hesitate in his reply. And his words still echo so positively in my heart: "Katherine, your short time here with Kinau and the family has introduced you to many wonderful, humane people and a wonderful society of love and generosity. However, you will, in time, discover that we too have our misfits and, excuse the language, assholes! Like any society we are hierarchical; that means some group of people enforces a rule of prejudice. The American *haoles* rule here, and have done for over five generations. But if it weren't them then it would have been someone else. The ruling *Alii* of the Hawai'ians themselves were the most brutal and prejudiced people you could imagine. Only power over others mattered to them. Frankly, I'd rather be alive now under the *haoles* than under those bloody *Alii!*" His vehemence rather startled me actually, and we both fell silent for a time. A reassuring smile from him though, brought me back to our conversation.

"I could carry-on for hours with this diatribe of course. I won't. What I hope you will find in your stay here is, a tale of another society of people, centuries removed from ours, who found a way to overcome the worst aspects of human nature and establish a culture which survived in relative peace for many generations. Perhaps, and this is my fervent wish, you will discover some element of sanity within that society which we might apply to our world today!" Then Jiro leaned toward me and took my hand in his and said, "And if you don't, I'll flunk you in your course!"

My sinking heart was gently raised back up by his wonderful smile. I could have kissed him but just then we were interrupted. "Hey Katherine! You like help now? Plenty of clean-up to do!" It was Aunty Helen and her voice held a smile. Two hours later we had cleaned up the mess in the kitchen and the leftover food was equitably distributed among the departing guests. About two o'clock a group of young people asked me if I'd like to go surfing. Would I!? We all crowded into the back of a beat-up old Chevy van, loaded with the scrappiest bunch of surfboards I'd ever seen and headed down toward Lihue to 'Donkey Beach'. The surf was not big but regular and inviting. I surfed until I was nearly exhausted. Finally coming ashore when the shadows were long and the sea darkening, my surfing mates expressed an ungrudging admiration for my ability. Tired as I was I reveled in their acceptance. The drive home was a casual, low speed cruise. I refused as graciously as I could the proffered joints without hurting feelings. What a marvelous, challenging and mysterious weekend this had been. The following week would knock my socks off!

~ ~ * ~ ~

Monday morning everyone was up early. Jiro had a plane to catch at the Lihue airport, seven o'clock. Aunty Helen was up by five thirty, helping get the kids dressed and ready for a day down at the beach near Hanalei. Jiro was still sleeping and had to be awakened. He and some of the older men had stayed up late, dutifully finishing off leftover cans of beer. He was a bit seedy and grumpy that morning but a hot coffee and two fried eggs and rice had him going again. I helped Tutu Kinau pack some things for our trip around to the dry side of the island and up Waimea Canyon. I was as excited as a little kid myself. Tina, Kinau and I were the only ones going today, after dropping Jiro off for his flight. Kinau had family living up the mountain and we would be staying for at least two days. I loved the casualness of the Hawai'ian lifestyle: 'we going stay with Aunty Bev. Maybe be back Wednesday, maybe Friday. We'll see"

We packed clothes. Mine had arrived the week before from the mainland. Now I didn't have to wash clothes every day. Blankets too, went into the trunk of the car. It can get cold at night up there, even in summer. Food, we would pick up along the way. With no sense of rushing or fear of lateness, we four managed to be in the car and off at a quarter past six. Jiro and I sat in the back and chatted casually but I had one ear cocked toward the conversation between Kinau and Tina in the front seat.

I finally had to whisper to Jiro, "What language are they speaking? It's not Hawai'ian." Jiro guffawed and slapped me on the knee. "What you're hearing is a conversation in *Mal'lam* - between the only two people I know who speak it!" He was still chuckling when we drove into Lihue airport. Jiro really did think this was the funniest thing. Maybe it had been the expression of my face when he told me. Kinau and Tina and I got out of the car in the car park and accompanied Jiro to the departure lounge. The plane was leaving in five minutes. Pretty close timing for such a casual approach to schedules! Such things used to bother me greatly, being late that is. But all of that uptight, self-imposed stress seemed to be, daily, sloughing away from me. I was becoming Hawai'ianized!

Big hugs from Jiro for all three of us. As he hugged me he whispered, "Just pay close attention. Don't ask too many questions. Important things will be explained before you can even ask. Have a wonderful week up the mountain." And then he was gone and we turned and went back to the car. Tina, to my pleasant surprise, took my hand as we walked back. Kinau invited me to sit up front with her so that she could point out some of the places of interest. "Just like a tourist!" she said. In fact, I had never been to this part of the island before and was so looking forward to the trip, especially to see Waimea Canyon.

Tutu Kinau was a very careful and very slow driver. If I'd been in a hurry, she'd have driven me nuts. The car, a big old Chrysler, rode like a limousine and the engine, a big eight cylinder, just purred along. Teddy Ho'opai, a mechanic by profession who worked for the sugar company, kept most of the family's vehicles running well. He was, I would discover, a very exceptional fellow. So we purred along through the cane fields past Lihue, Lawa'i, and Kalaheo and stopped at Hanapepe to do some shopping.

There was a small grocery store there, run by family friends who had a wonderful fruit and vegetable selection, all home-grown produce. I bought us all a Coke and some potato chips while Kinau bought the *good* food. Tina tittered away at my purchase, saying she knew I wouldn't be able to resist *haole* food forever. But she ate her share of the chips and didn't hesitate to pop open her Coke. We were developing an easy and open relationship. Actually, Tina most often acted like a twelve-year-old-going-on-twenty-two. She laughed easily and had a clever wit. And she was forever giving me little digs; gently reminding me that I was still a *haole* in many of my attitudes, but usually following these jokes at my expense with a devilish grin. I liked her very much.

Shopping bags stowed away in the trunk, we continued on toward Waimea. The countryside began to look drier and more barren, mostly scrub and thirsty-looking *kiawe* trees, coconut palms still lining the shoreline along with the conifer-like Ironwood trees. As we approached the Waimea River Bridge, off to the right somewhere in the dusty old town itself rose the most magnificent tree I'd ever seen. It was taller than the coconut palms, broad and absolutely the most gorgeous golden yellow. I mean, it was covered in blossoms and was like a neon sign in broad daylight. "What is that?" I asked Kinau, pointing. "That's a Golden Trumpet tree." she answered, I think happy that I'd commented on it. "That tree maybe eighty years old, 'was there when I was a little girl. Pretty, eh? When that tree in full bloom, like now, it's time to gather *limu*. You know, seaweed." She also told me that that one tree could be seen for miles offshore, guiding fishing boats into port for the two weeks it bloomed. How important just one single plant can be!

We drove through the decidedly run-down little town of Waimea. Everything looked dusty and tired. This was a sugar cane workers town, old and staring the end of Hawaiian sugar production in the not-kindly face of international competition. The buildings, many of them, had the false, two-storey fronts one sees in American Western movies. The difference was the names: Yukimura's Hardware! Chin's Dry Goods! Texeira's Automotive Repairs! The *Wild Hawaiian West*! But I wouldn't have wanted to live there. Too dry. I like rain and Waimea gets precious little, except in flooding downpours!

Then the signs, large and hard to miss:

WAIMEA CANYON TOURIST DRIVE

GRAND CANYON OF THE PACIFIC!

Could that be a bit of Chamber of Commerce hyperbole? I'd have to wait only a few minutes to test that theory. Up we went, the gradient increasing markedly and the road getting more winding. Then the growth alongside the road got denser as we got higher. Now there were glimpses of the lower end of the canyon and I began to crane my neck to see more. Deeper and steeper the scenery became, more sharp the curves in the road. Kinau seemed very familiar with the road because she actually increased her speed and seemed also to enjoy taking the corners. Finally, when the tantalizing glimpses of an increasingly dramatic view became breathtaking, she pulled off the road into a parking area on the right. We got out and walked to the wooden railing near the drop-off.

Wow! Truly magnificent! Layers of soil revealed colors from bronze to red to tan. Most of the canyon walls were so shear that only a goat could climb them. "Look at the goats!" Tina said, obviously as enthralled as I, in spite of having been here many times herself. Below us, maybe two hundred feet down, was a family of goats with little kids running about the adults. I held my breath for one of them as it first butted an adult playfully, then leapt up and turned around in mid-air and charged off to what looked like a certain death-plunge over the cliff. Nope! It turned at the last second and pranced back to the previously abused adult with amazing insouciance. Awwww! They were so cute!

We watched the goats and the amazing scenery for about five minutes. This truly was a 'Grand' canyon. Then Kinau said, "Time we go now. Aunty Bev will be waiting." With some reluctance I retreated from this wonderful vista, vowing to return again with a camera, and more time. Back in the car Kinau said, "Aunty Bev's place is a ways further on. We have to drive on dirt road for a while first. You not gettin' carsick or anything, Katherine?" I looked to see if she was joking. No, she was serious. Well, maybe other folks got carsick on this road, but me, I was enjoying every second of this magic carpet ride! Carry on!

We drove on up the paved road for another five minutes, me still craning my neck to see another view. Then we turned left off the main road onto a gravel road, still quite wide and well engineered, and headed into thick rainforest. I commented on the tiny, bright red birds which had flown across the road ahead of us. "They're *apa'pane*," Tina told me, "They're native birds which live above three thousand feet. The old Hawa'ians used to capture them for their feathers for the fancy cloaks the chiefs wore." Gee, she could be articulate!

I had read some time ago that in the latter part of the nineteenth century, Americans had imported exotic birds from Asia as well as from North America.

I suppose, believing that the native bird life somehow fell short of what a tropical paradise was supposed to provide, they felt it necessary to enrich the avian population. What actually happened though was that some of the birds carried a form of Bird-Malaria. This, combined with the accidental infestation of the island with mosquitoes, of which Hawaii had been previously innocent, resulted in the native fauna being decimated by this introduced horror. Mosquitoes, the disease-carrying kind, don't thrive above three thousand feet altitude. Therefore, above that a few species of truly Hawai'ian birds still survive, some thriving. The displacement of one type of creature by another is an old, familiar tale in Hawai'i. And not only birds were to suffer this fate. I was on the trail of that tale, here beneath the huge mountain called, 'Wai'ale'ale'.

Aunty Bev and her husband, Warren Kapuna, lived about three miles off the main road. The road to there got a bit rougher the further along we went, but it was quite serviceable. The forest through which we were driving got thicker and taller, really large *Ohia lehua* and *Koa* trees becoming more common. Wild chickens scattered in front of us at one stage and moments later we scared up a wild pig which plunged recklessly off the road and into the thick brush. Suddenly the vista opened up and there was a large grassed area and a neat little house nestled among fruit trees. We were there!

As Kinau drove up the gravel driveway to the house, I noticed how neat and well maintained everything appeared. Even the trunks of the fruit trees were painted with whitewash. There were no coconut palms in evidence though. Up at this altitude they don't thrive. When we parked, Kinau honked the horn lightly and we got out. There, striding around the corner of the house was a tall, deeply tanned woman, wiping her hands on her apron. She appeared to be in her early fifties. Her smile of greeting warmed me to the core. She embraced, first, Kinau, then Tina, whom she grabbed and swung around her in great enthusiasm. Tina was obviously a favorite here. Then she came to me as Kinau introduced us and wrapped big, strong arms around me too, only I guess swinging me around was a bit daunting. "Alo'ha. Alo'ha. Welcome young lady! You are so welcome here!"

Aunty Bev spoke with a strange accent; not pidgin but with a soft melodious tone in her voice, evident even in those few words. She and Kinau began speaking Hawaiian, no mistaking that language now, while Tina and I began unloading the car. "Tina," I asked quietly, "where is Aunty Bev from? I can't pick her accent." Tina grinned, and hefting a pile of blankets onto her shoulder replied, "She's from Ni'ihau island. She spoke only Hawai'ian until she was in her teens." Off she went then, me following behind with the heavier bags of groceries

We entered a house that immediately embraced me with warmth and richness. It was immaculate and smelled faintly of bleach and pine oil and Plumeria blossoms, a heady bouquet. Other senses were stirred by the plethora of paintings, photographs, and maps and framed letters or documents. The walls were nearly fully covered. An American flag hung on one wall and the Hawai'ian State flag next to it. I followed the older ladies into the neat kitchen to unload the weighty bags of groceries. The smell of baking bread was the dominant perfume here and I suddenly realized that I was starving, again.

It must have been the fresh air and the altitude. I heard a toilet flush somewhere. Soon Tina appeared and pointed and said, "It's around the corner there, Katherine." So you're a mind reader already? Aunty Bev put the hot water on for tea and coffee, opened a brightly painted tin cookie container and loaded a plate with its rich-looking contents. She and Kinau never stopped talking all the while, their conversation full of laughs and giggles and a glance or two my way. Of course they were discussing me, in part. I'd never heard myself spoken of in Hawai'ian before, that I knew of anyway. Tina sat down without being bidden and started in on the cookies. I remained standing momentarily, but Aunty Bev, pausing in her conversation with Kinau, turned to me with a grin and said, "Go ahead girl. Sit down. Better have some cookies or that little guts'll eat 'em all. Tina looked quite unabashed and reached for another cookie. I did sit down but just looked around the room, then at the leafy view through the large kitchen windows. It' so homey here!

Soon the tea was steeping; loose tea, not tea bags in this house, and I chose the option of a cup of instant coffee. The Aunties seemed to have gotten off their chests the private conversation they needed to have and they sat down at the table with us 'kids'. The next forty minutes ran away with questions, laughter, more questions, some long explanations, more laughter, and the cookie plate became empty and so did my second cup of coffee.

"Tina," said Tutu Kinau, "Why not takes Katherine around the gardens, eh?" I was grateful for this because these recent hours of sitting were getting me down. I needed to get up and move around. Tina led the way out the back door from the kitchen, down a short flight of steps and onto a lovely, deep carpet of turf. A fog was moving in around us as we walked downhill toward the vegetable garden. "Won't last long!" Tina said. "Sometimes comes in this time of day, then burns off again." That was encouraging because I was thinking of going back inside for a sweater. Tina walked close beside me and put her arm through mine.

Jiro's admonition returned to remind me; don't ask too many questions! Tina pointed out the various plants in the vegetable garden and seemed quite conversant with the flowering plants too. The whole area was so neatly maintained that I of course had to ask … who took such good care of the gardens?" Aunty Bev and Uncle Warren both do. Uncle Warren hardly stops. He's always busy. You'll like him. He's a really nice man." Her definiteness was final. I would like Uncle Warren! So I was prepared to. "Sometimes, though, he doesn't like *haoles*." Oh great! But her tweak on my arm and the grin she threw up at me eased the surprise. "Naw!" she added, "He'll like you. Everybody likes you Katherine. You're *cool*!" My ego did a spin-out but I managed to control it and simply said, "Thanks, twerp!"

Tina suddenly let go of my arm and ran forward, down to the large *taro* patch below the vegetable garden. "Look at this!" she exclaimed, waving over her shoulder for me to catch up. In one corner of the *taro* patch, its water nearly a foot deep, rose the most beautiful leaves and huge pink flowers; certainly not taro plants. The leaves stood at least two feet above the water and the big flowers rose above them to three feet. The single blossoms were nearly a foot wide and the most gorgeous flowers I had ever seen.

"What are they?" I asked. "Don't know" she replied, "But they're pretty special, aren't they?" They certainly were. I later learned from Uncle Warren, who didn't seem to mind this *haole* too much, that they were Sacred Lotus which he had gotten from a botanical garden around the island near La'wai. Warren, a carpenter and cabinetmaker by trade, was a very keen gardener who, I think, almost resented having to waste his time making a living as head maintenance man at a Government project site. He loved this piece of land and it certainly showed.

Tina seemed in a garrulous mood, which I'd been hoping for, and she began to tell me about some of her family. 'Don't ask questions, just listen!' Jiro's words echoed.

"Tutu is my grandma, but she raised me from when I was a baby. Did you know that?" She looked up at me quickly and saw me shake my head. "Yeah, I never knew my real dad or my mom. My real dad, well, nobody seems to know who he was. And my mom … she's somewhere on the mainland. She's kinda lost, I guess. But Tutu and her husband raised me. Uncle Willem was his name. I called him Daddy. I loved him very much. I miss him." Tina was silent for some time as we walked together around the perimeter of the garden. She paused and pulled two long stems of succulent grass from a tussock and handed me one. We continued walking and chewing grass for a few more minutes. I thought I saw the gleam of tears in her eyes but refrained from asking anything. Then she began speaking again, her voice clear of tears but soft.

"That's where Tutu gets her last name. Daddy's name was Willem Kaiser. He was a merchant sailor who jumped ship in Honolulu. He and Tutu met in Honolulu, when she was going to teacher's college. They had two children; one was my real mom, one was my Uncle Kawika. He's nice too, like Daddy was. He lives in California." Tina skipped over to another tussock and refreshed our grass stems, then she continued.

"Daddy died about four years ago. That's when I began hearing the Spirit voices." Tina had said this so matter-of-factly that I nearly didn't take it in. Whoa! Now we're getting somewhere my girl! I suggested, trying to be off-handed, that we sit down on an inviting, green garden bench beneath a big loquat tree. Tina was agreeable and began her tale again even before we'd sat down."Tutu was so broken-up when he died. They were really very special together. He was so understanding of her and her association with the Mal'lam Spirits. He made little jokes about it, but only to the family. He believed in God; but he wouldn't go to church. 'A lot uff *hu'hu* !', he used to say." Her approximation of a Dutch accent in a deep voice was quite good. *Hu'hu*, of course is Hawai'ian for rubbish talk, or, … bullshit!

"I was at school when he had his heart attack, Tutu was at home with him. He hadn't been sick at all and no one ever suspected there was anything wrong. Aunty Helen picked me up at school and took me to the hospital in Lihue. Tutu was just so upset. I'd never seen her cry so hard, and I couldn't stop crying either. Aunty Helen and Tutu and me and a few other family and friends were all just wailing out loud." A little grin tweaked the corner of her mouth and she flashed me a glance. "Boy, we must have deafened people there in the emergency ward!" She pulled her legs under her and sat cross-legged on the bench, facing more acutely toward me now.

"Daddy had died shortly after they got him to hospital. Aunty Helen drove Tutu and me home. It was almost dark and as we got close to the turnoff to home, I began to hear Daddy's voice! It was distant, kinda like he was talking from the other end of a big, empty building. It scared me at first. But pretty soon I was just listening hard to hear what he was saying. Then his voice got clearer and closer. As we drove up the road to the house, I heard him say he would come back soon and talk with me. And for me to give lots of love to Tutu." I reached out my hand and patted Tina's knee when her voice broke and she looked down at her hands in her lap. I was sure she would cry.

But she looked up at me, dry-eyed and smiling again. "Katherine, I think I need to tell you these things. And lots of other things too. Daddy's voice still comes to me. It did the night I first met you. He said, 'This *haole* lady is your friend. She's your big sister!' Will you be my big sister?" It was my turn to cloud up and threaten tears now! I leaned forward and we had a good hug and cuddle. Actually, tough, uptight-*haole*-me was trying to hide dripping eyes. Dummy! She didn't care. She hugged me back for a few moments then returned to her story, while I sat sniffling.

"Tutu was alright a little while after Daddy's funeral, maybe three weeks or so. She took me up to the *heiau* with her and she told me then about her spirits and I told her about Daddy talking to me. She looked at me really funny at first, and then asked me to close my eyes and just open myself up to Daddy. Remember, I was only eight then and not as grown up as now, but I did that and Daddy did speak to me. He said one word, which isn't important to repeat now; it was a special word between Daddy and Tutu. Tutu started crying and laughing at the same time. She came to me and gave me a big hug and said that I was a 'blessed child!' She said that only she and Daddy knew that word. Actually Katherine, I can't remember it. Isn't that strange?" Tina's expression held all the wonderment and fascination of any pubescent child. But I knew that I was now 'big sister' to a person neither child nor totally adult. She was indeed a 'blessed child'!

"Tinaaa! Katherine!" It was Kinau calling us from the house. "Better go now." Tina said, "Uncle Warren must be home." And with that Tina sprang off the bench like a cat and jogged uphill toward the house, leaving me to unravel slightly stiff muscles and follow after. And speaking of cats, a big black and white kitty burst out of the shrubs ahead of me and raced after Tina. I hadn't seen any cats here earlier and as I ran after my 'little sister', I called, 'kitty, kitty,' after it. It totally ignored me. Just like a cat!

I mounted the short steps to the back porch and went in through the screen door. I could hear a male voice in the kitchen. Uncle Warren's back was to me as I entered. He turned to face me as Aunty Bev signaled my arrival with a nod of her head in my direction. By golly, but he was big! "This is Katherine." Tutu said, smiling. Warren faced me and gave me what I call a 'Polynesian scowl'; heavy brows knitted over fierce brown eyes, a mouth turned down in immediate disapproval. It remained but a moment and then melted into one of the broadest, warmest smiles I've ever been blessed with. Wheww!

"Alo'ha, Katherine!" rumbled from him and before I could brace myself, he'd wrapped his huge arms around me and nearly, but not quite, crushed me in a hug. He smelled of sweat, wood shavings and paint thinner. If that combination could be bottled, it'd be a best seller! He held me at arms length a moment, dark eyes scrutinizing me carefully, then released me and, over his shoulder said to Tutu Kinau, "She got good eyes, Kinau. You make good choice here. Reminds me of Willem!." I glanced at Tutu Kinau and she was smiling. Then Tina piped up with, "She's my big sister now, Uncle Warren!"

Warren Kapuna stepped back a couple of paces to where Aunty Bev stood. He put an affectionate arm around her ample waist momentarily and gave her a squeeze. "I got work to do in the taro, Bevvy. When *kau kau* ready?" His eyes were still on me, still assessing, but benign. "One hour." she replied. He turned and gave her a quick kiss on the cheek and walked off into the laundry room where the beer-fridge stood waiting. Warren made his own home-brew. He returned to the kitchen with two tall bottles in hand and asked me if I'd like a beer.

I would have said yes but assumed that Kinau and Aunty Bev were both tee-totalers. I'd never seen Tutu drink any alcohol. Later that evening though, I weakened and joined him in an after-dinner drink. Tina and I decided to go out with Warren to the garden. I was curious as to how he maintained his own *taro* patch. The big black and white cat followed Warren like a puppy, trotting along behind him, tail in the air like a flag. Warren strode quickly, sucking on a bottle of beer as he went. By the time we'd reached the *taro* patch, he was using his jackknife to open the second one.

Tina and I took off our slippers while he removed his work boots and socks and rolled his jeans up to his knees. In just half an hour I learned how backbreaking tending *taro* could be. Bending over constantly to pull weeds, twisting to throw the weeds onto the grass beside the water, bending to pull more weeds. Boy, good for the waist but rough on the back! We worked in total silence, my attempts to engage Warren in conversation meeting with grunts. Shut up and work, Katherine. Tina too, worked in silence, her supple body and quick hands keeping up with Uncle Warren's work output.

Suddenly he straightened with a small groan, rubbed his lower back and said, "You girls work too fast for old man like me. *Pau hana* now!" and with that declaration of 'finish-work-time', we waded out of the sticky mud and went uphill to a faucet near the garden to wash our hands and feet. A gentleman, he allowed us girls to clean ourselves up first. As we walked back up toward the house, Tina went up beside Warren and took his free hand in hers. I wondered if he might be fulfilling some surrogate role. He seemed very gentle and accepting of her. The mad cat came racing past us, tail up like a flag again, leapt up the back stairs and meowed at the screen door. Before we reached the porch, Aunty Bev opened the screen and Kahuna, that was the cat's name, whisked past her legs and inside.

Dinner that evening was delightful. Not just the delicious food with home-baked bread but the laughter and conversation. Warren told some funny stories about his workmates; especially funny was one about his mainland-*haole* boss. Warren didn't suffer fools kindly, it seemed. Aunty Bev related her run-in with a snoopy wild pig early that morning. I was rather surprised to discover that she was a real raconteur, and as funny as her husband. Dessert was apple pie. Tina and I pretended to squabble over who was going to eat the last piece, which garnered some laughter. The biggest laugh came though when Warren simply picked up the pie plate and ate the last piece himself, making exaggerated slurping sounds and grinning at Tina and me. Then he pushed back his chair and burped politely behind a big hand. Kahuna jumped into his lap then, apparently an after-dinner ritual, and lay across his legs, purring loudly as Warren stroked him.

The two ladies refused to let me help with washing-up, even the clearing away. Tina helped though, chattering and giggling happily. Well, I thought, I guess I'm supposed to keep Warren company. I walked around the living room, gazing at the family photos, framed awards and other mementos which hung there. Old photos, especially those sepia depictions of days long before I was born, have always fascinated me. I didn't know where Warren had gone but then I heard a cough from out on the lanai. I went to the doorway and could just see a pair of crossed feet off to the right. I went out the screen door and he smiled up at me from a big, well worn, overstuffed chair.

"You like a beer with me now, maybe?" I replied that that would be nice, if Aunty Bev wouldn't mind. "Hah! No botha yo' head 'bout dat. Bevvy don't mind a Sherry or two herself. 'Be right back." And he pushed himself up from his comfortable chair and went around me smiling, going through the doorway to the laundry porch. He was back shortly with a tall bottle of home-brew and a tumbler. I took a chair from the other end of the lanai and sat near him, a small table between us. I thanked him for the drink. He smiled and nodded and then as I sipped my beer, he sat up in his chair and I knew he was going to tell me something. So far, Jiro, your admonition has worked well.

"I'm happy that you and Tina-girl are good friends, Katherine. She's a lonely kid, sometimes. I love her like she was my own. Bevvy 'n me don't have children. Has to do with a fever I got in Korea. 'Made Bevvy sad for a long time tho'." He laughed his wonderful, deep chuckle and added, "Now we got cats!" and he laughed merrily as Kahuna entered the scene and claimed Warren's lap once more. "We got God's garden an' His birds an' those nuisance pigs in the woods. An' we got each other an' our families. Not too bad for poor folks!" Just then another kitty, this one a marmalade cat, crept out onto the lanai from somewhere. It meowed and walked hesitantly toward us, suspicious of me. "Kitty, kitty ... come." And Warren held out a long arm to entice the shy cat to him. Just then Tina, released from her kitchen chores, bustled onto the lanai with a message in her mouth. The marmalade cat disappeared off the edge of the lanai in one leap.

"That cat scared of everythin", Warren laughed and turned to face Tina as she approached us. She hadn't seen the cat herself but realized that she'd interrupted something. "Come sit down Tina-girl." Warren invited, "Katherine an' me talkin' story." "Talking story" was pidgin for a long chat, and Warren spoke a heavy pidgin, which only my experience of the past few weeks allowed for easy interpretation. Tina too, dragged a chair over from the other end of the lanai and set it down facing us. Then Kinau and Bev joined us, each with a small glass of amber liquid in hand!

Soon we were all happily ensconced in a rough circle around Uncle Warren, Kahuna still purring happily on his lap. The light was fading fast and a mist was falling around this cozy cottage. It was growing quite cool and there was a short interlude of women getting up and disappearing, returning with sweaters or shawls, me among them. I'm not quite a shawl person though, at least not yet. Only Tina and Uncle Warren seemed not to feel the cold creeping in with the fog. Warren was on his fifth beer so maybe he was better insulated.

"Warren," Kinau said, "Tina is going to take Katherine up to the 'Kahuna Baths' tomorrow morning. Can you drive them to the trail on your way to work?" Warren approximated a serious mien, rubbed his chin in concentration as if this was a real problem. Aunty Bev said, a slight tone of impatience in her voice, "Warren! Just say yes!" Warren burst into a wide grin and nodded to his wife, "Sorry Bevvy. Just kiddin'. Sure. No problem. But I leave early, girls. You got to be ready by six-thirty. Hardly time for breakfast!" I think Warren's beers were beginning to make him a bit silly, but we got the message. A short silence reigned and then Warren stifled a yawn and got up stiffly from his chair. Warren obviously had a bad back, not that he would admit it. "Time I was in bed, ladies. Too much good *kau kau* and good company always make me sleepy."

He lumbered over to his wife and gave her a kiss, turned and kissed Kinau on the cheek and walked away out of the lanai, giving Tina and me a blown kiss. This man had already had a hard day's work, starting at seven in the morning, some work in the garden and now it was nine o'clock. Of course, those beers didn't help keep him awake. Tina too, was looking droopy - about how I felt. It had been a long day for all of us. My 'little sister' and I lay our blankets out on the living room floor, on top of two inflatable sleeping mattresses. Even before we had claimed our beds, the kitty, Kahuna, decided that my bed was quite the one to use for his night's sleep too. I heard Bev chuckling as she said goodnight and went off to join her already snoring husband. Kinau said goodnight and retired to the guest room. My last recollection of that evening was of a loud, but pleasant, purring close to my head.

I awoke before anyone else and made a beeline for the bathroom. When I'd finished my ablutions, I crept as quietly as possible out to the lanai and sat on the steps, Kahuna coming up to join me. Rubbing himself against my arm, demanding attention, I began petting him. There was a heavy mist about, not uncommon for these parts. The gardens had a special, magical quality about them; I almost expected a fairy to emerge from the forest. No, but some wild chickens did. I sat watching them for quite a while until I heard someone stirring inside the house. I picked Kahuna up, still demanding pats, and walked into the kitchen where Bev was lighting the fire under the water kettle.

"Good mornin' Katherine." she whispered and gave me a pat on the arm as she went toward the bathroom. I stayed and kept guard over the kettle, Kahuna finally having enough of my half-hearted petting and jumping down to the floor. He left a couple of minor scratches in the process. Little twerp! It wasn't long before everyone was up; Warren was off to the outdoor toilet, magazine in hand. Kinau had next go at the bathroom while Tina pulled the blankets over her head for another few minutes snooze. I playfully disabused her of that intent and pulled the covers off her. Then Kahuna invaded her space and she gave up. Everybody up!

Warren left early, about six-thirty, we ladies not able to get organized in time to go with him. A large lunch pail and a thermos under one arm and his tool belt in the other hand, his gracious goodbyes warmed me in the cold, foggy damp which had descended. When I went back into the kitchen, Kinau was sipping a cup of coffee, Bev was cleaning up Warren's breakfast dishes and Tina was stuck into a bowl of 'Wheaties'. She pointed to a place set at the table for me, her mouth too full to speak. Bev said, "It's going to be a hot day!"… Could have fooled me! By seven-thirty, sure enough, the fog was burning off and Kinau said Tina and I should get ready for our hike. That we would be going up the mountain toward Koke'e had been mentioned last night but I thought we would all be going. No, just Tina and me, Kinau driving us up to a road which led to an outlook over Kalalau Valley. Not the Tourist Drive road, but rather another dirt road which the locals used.

We packed our backpacks with sandwiches which Bev made, sun-cream for this pale *haole* and a couple of candy bars. Fresh stream water would be readily available. I was really excited about this; just Tina and me alone for most of the day, an opportunity to learn something about her 'Spirits'. I was to find the experience quite stunning, and I even managed to scribble some notes later that evening. What follows is an expansion of my memory of that day, based on those few notes and the extraordinary impression her words made, and still make, on this researcher's mind.

Research Notes: Impressions and General Observations

Subject: Tina Pua'lani Kaiser, Kaua'i, Summer 1972

Tina and I had been driven to the end of a dirt road by Kinau (Tutu) Approx. 8AM. Getting warm already. 15 minutes down rough track through chest high Bracken Fern and *Ohia* lehua trees all around. Lots of tiny native birds. Getting glimpses of Kalalau Valley as we descend. Tina points out special plants of medicinal use as well as Shampoo Ginger in large clumps. Pig tracks on the trail but Tina says not to worry about them. Sure. Now onto a narrow ridge with the most spectacular views of the valley. Just below a large grove of *Ohia* trees is our goal. The most beautiful natural pool fed by a small creek! We are both sweaty so strip to our basics (Tina doesn't yet wear a bra) and ease into the cold pool. There's a natural ledge in the pool and we sat chest-deep and admired the unbroken view down into Kalalau Valley. Extraordinary! Still getting hotter but water beginning to chill us. Sit on grassy verge and Tina begins to tell me of her 'voices'. As we heat-up, we slide into pool again for few minutes. We do this many times while Tina continues her story.

This is the beginning of Tina's story of the Mal'lam, the proto-Polynesian people who were Hawai'i's first settlers:

"After Daddy died, and he began speaking to me from 'the other side', he started to tell me about some other people who wanted to talk to me too. I began to hear strange voices, speaking in a strange language, kind of faint but slowly they got louder. These voices, never frightening or anything like that, kept coming to me at strange times. Daddy came to me less and less then. I was sorry for that. But slowly these people's voices became familiar to me and I began to look forward to their 'appearing', you might say. But I never did really see the people telling me things; just impressions, like out of the corner of your eye. And the impression they were giving me was that they were people like Hawai'ians.

By that I mean they seemed to be Polynesian but they weren't speaking Hawaiian. Their language had r's and s's and t's and f's. And they had a shh' sound which was in a lot of their words. Hawai'ian doesn't really have these sounds. So, after getting used to the voices and the sounds of their language … and here's the strange part … I began to understand what they were saying! I can't really explain that. It's still a mystery to me. Anyway, after quite a few weeks I got so that I could ask some questions; you know, like, who they were, where they came from, where they were now?

Slowly I began to put together an idea of what they were all about, what they wanted from me. I began to wait really anxiously for them to come to me because I was so interested in what they had to say. And they were really happy people too! They began to make me laugh. Little jokes just between us or descriptions of people and things they did. Sometimes, though, I'd get caught having a conversation, maybe laughing out loud when other people were around. It could be embarrassing. If Tutu hadn't known what it was all about, I'd probably be in a nut house by now. She used to cover up for me if people commented. Some of the family know about this, my voices, but I guess with all the superstitions around the place, most don't worry about it. At least no one calls me crazy to my face.

Anyway, I've got a couple of cousins who are *really* crazy, and *they're* running around loose! One day last winter, I was home from school with a cold. Just Tutu and me were home. I'd been having lots of conversations with my 'voices', mostly at night when I could be by myself. That day though, lying back in bed, I kinda went into a trance. Tutu said I was sleeping for three hours and every time she'd check on me, I'd be muttering. She said she understood some of the words to be Mal'lam, as she knew it. See, her voices taught her to speak that language too.

Well, during that time, and I remember it all really clear, my voices told me about where their people had come from. Oh, it was so wonderful, the world they told me about! I had these visions of the open sea and the Mal'lam canoes sailing in a hard wind and how the sails billowed in the wind and the people aboard were gazing to the rising sun, expecting something! Then, and this is when I really began to understand about who the Mal'lam were, they began to tell me a story of how their people began the long, long journey to here, to Hawai'i! They haven't finished their story yet. Gee, I don't know how long it will go on, but I can't wait for them to tell me more. Who needs television?!"

This is what their story started with. I swear I haven't made anything up, Katherine. They told me it was like this.

Chapter Four ~ The Mal'lam Exodus

The pack was growing heavy on the old man's shoulders. But now as he strode from beneath the layer of mountain fog the dark blue of the sea greeted his tired eyes. The thin air of the snowfields brought a heavy fatigue to him on these journeys now. This would be the last of his 'gatherings' of the highland medicines. He was sure he would miss these journeys for they had been his greatest joy in his youth, when he had accompanied his own master. It was the annual harvest of the sacred lichens and herbs and ice-flowers, so important as catalysts for his people's complex pharmacopeias.

It would be both the first and the last such journey for his young apprentice too. The boy had whined and complained since they had left the tree line, three days before. Why had he allowed his better judgment to be diverted by the old woman's pleadings? The boy was useless. He obviously hated the mountains. "Even my brain is getting weak!" he muttered, turning his head to look over one shoulder at the boy behind him, his own grand-nephew. Head down, his steps clumsy and uncoordinated, the twelve-year-old lad struggled to keep up with the old man even though his load was only half as heavy. "Come on boy - keep up!"

Tal'ma Herb-Master growled and increased his stride on the grassy path, worn to a well-marked smoothness now by generations of journeys such as this. Ahead and below waved the roof of the giant-bamboo forest, the rattle of the heavy culms against each other in the freshening wind still distant and subtle. A flight of Snow Larks shrilled above them and swerved in unison like a school of fish and disappeared downhill. Clear now of the heavy clouds that had covered the mountain during the night, the man and the lagging boy felt the sun's heat on their bare legs with gratitude. Even in early spring, as it was now, ice could form in the gourd water jugs they carried. The nighttime cold could make sleeping a misery beneath the layered, woven-fiber blankets they carried.

"When will we have breakfast, uncle?" The boy's thin voice rasped the old man's nerves again and he replied, "When we reach the groves, boy. Save your breath now and just follow." Tal'ma immediately regretted the curtness of his reply. He was hungry too. Since he'd decided that the boy would never be suitable as an apprentice to a Herb-Master, there was no need to discipline him with gruffness. Besides, he really did like the boy. In fact he'd always thought of him as quite special.

"Not long now, my boy. Maybe ten minutes and we'll stop." This was by way of an apology, but the best he could manage. His head ached even though the air grew warmer and thicker by the minute. He found it a struggle to maintain the pace he normally set going downhill. Strange, he thought. Fifty years of self-discipline had ingrained that tendency to push on through fatigue, to rekindle the embers of his strength. Though his joints and muscles ached, his lungs drew in and expelled the scented air effortlessly and he began to softly sing the traveling song of his craft:

"Though far you be, and high and rare,

I come for you with a heart that's free.

Ascend, ascend, ascend I there,

To meadows 'neath the snowline.

And down now, down and down,

The bamboos greet my journey.

To the sea and home and people mine,

Their health and joy assured!

Tal'ma felt a twinge of love-born guilt as he heard the boy's voice trying to echo his song, breathlessly struggling. "Ah, boy! Why are you so weak, so afraid up here on this magical mountain?" he asked himself silently, wondering at his own tiredness. This apparent weakening of body and spirit among the younger generations of herbalists, all of whom made this great journey, had worried him for years. The same seemed to apply to those other crafts who's work brought them here to the highlands. Each generation, in his memory, had suffered more stillbirths, more strange maladies, than the one before. Too many women had died in childbirth; even so his beloved surrogate daughter, Marana, wife to his son, Faldo, oldest of his five boys.

When they had halted within the shelter of the towering bamboos, the boy surprised him by hurrying unbidden to help him remove his heavy pack. They sat on the smooth, moss-covered boulders near a stream and unpacked their last meal on the trail. As they ate, a flock of fowl appeared near them from out of the close-packed stems of the giant bamboo. Beneath the creak and clatter of the waving culms the birds' rustling and scratching among the leaf-litter was a pleasant, welcoming sound. Smaller than their domesticated cousins, which roamed at will among the huts of the villages below, these gaily-colored birds were one of the old man's favorite creatures. Alert but unafraid, their busyness and light-hearted bickering always brought a smile to his craggy face. They reminded him warmly of the women of his childhood and youth as they planted and harvested, wove and plaited in chattering, gossiping groups. "Do they really work and chatter and gossip as keenly as they did then?" He didn't think so. It seemed to him that everyone was more serious these days, more preoccupied with private worries which seldom found voice.

Though Tal'ma, like most of his older cronies, spent less time with the younger people, preferring to sit with old friends and reminisce and relax, they all never-the-less kept ears and eyes tuned to the mood of their people. Many others too, sensed an unsettling strangeness creeping into their community. "Something is wrong! Something is growing in the hearts of the people. I can almost smell a fear growing there! Why?"

The question walked with him down through the great bamboos and into the upper reaches of the rainforest. Here the air became still and heavy, the wind only a whisper among the tops of the towering hardwood giants. Small animals scurried unseen among the buttress roots of the huge trees. Small saplings strained in their desperate climb upward toward the sunlight. Tal'ma could hear the boy's breathing become easier as he walked behind his great-uncle. His footsteps were becoming more regular and assured as he hurried to follow. "Perhaps the boy is simply unsuited to the forests and the highlands." Tal'ma thought, "Perhaps he *is* best suited to the Seaman's life. He swims like a dolphin and bothers the seamen with his constant questions."

Part of Tal'ma's strength, his major talent, one could say, was in directing his people, in his subtle manner, toward their true callings. His expertise in his craft as a Herb-Master lent him unquestioned respect, an opportunity to act as an advisor in many realms. Tal'ma was revered as one of his people's most knowledgeable old Grey-heads. His own sons had benefited from his wisdom. Faldo Sea-Master, his oldest, was encouraged to take up that craft when he was only the age of this boy, A'lan. His twin sons, N'sho and N'sh'lam were both master Wood-workers, among his people's best; until they both had died that terrible day when the great waves had swamped the coastline.

Faldo too, was no longer among them, having one day sailed too far, or not far enough. He had disappeared along with his vessel and crew, twelve years ago. And dear Sh'kal the Musician! Tal'ma's youngest and his favorite, though he kept that preference secret even from his now-departed wife, was gentle and kind in all moments. He who listened only to the sweet harmonies of sky and earth and sea had died so young of some strange and sudden malady less than a year before. Oh, how he had warmed the hearts of all who knew him! And wasn't that about the time that this fear had become so evident? Still unarticulated, therefore mysterious. Yes! It had begun when the music died!

Tal'ma shook his head to clear these thoughts from himself, unable to withstand the sadness which pulled at his throat and threatened his eyes with tears. The forest had begun to thin now as they traveled at a fast walk down toward their home village. Behind the old man came A'lan's voice, singing softly of fishes and dolphins; strangely out-of-place it was, but soothing. Tal'ma smiled, his previous thoughts confirmed.

"Wait, boy!" Tal'ma barked and the boy nearly stumbled into the back of the old man. Ahead on the trail lay a large snake, black and gold markings gleaming on a new skin, head held above the ground, red and black tongue testing the air in their direction. Man and boy stood stock-still in the middle of the trail, the boy's eyes wide with fascination, and some fear. "Is it an omen, uncle?" A'lan asked in a whisper. He knew this snake only from the skins of others which were preserved and worn as belts on very special occasions. This big and dangerous snake was quite rare. "Perhaps, boy! Perhaps." The man pondered a moment and then said softly over his shoulder, "I've not seen one in over five years. And never this far up the mountain. Be still now, don't move."

The Talpa, as this reptile was called, was one of only two deadly snakes found in this small archipelago. Thankfully, they were seldom seen. So poisonous was its bite that no one was known to have survived its fangs, in spite of all the healing skills available. Still as a dead limb, the snake tested its surroundings, decided that no immediate threat existed and finally slid quickly away into the undergrowth beside the trail. Its disappearance had been so swift that A'lan asked himself if it had ever really been there. The spell was broken when the old man said, "Come now boy. Let's carry on. And stamp your feet as you go!" Their heavy treading, calculated to spur the snake on its way, soon evened into their previous easy gait. Tal'ma mused, "An omen? Perhaps. Perhaps indeed!"

The two descended for another hour along the well-used trail through more, quite expansive stands of bamboo. These massive timbers were destined for the huge rafts which carried trade between the islands. Many of these great culms were lashed to stakes in the ground by thick ropes, the resulting curves in their lengths determined for specific purposes in the construction of the great rafts. Along the trail were piles of such forcibly shaped lengths of bamboo, awaiting curing and transport down to the seashore for construction of a new vessel.

Soon Tal'ma and A'lan came out of the shady gloom and into the wide expanse of grassland which nearly encircled the island at this altitude. Below them they spied activity, figures moving about in the deep grass. Then dogs, small, curl-tailed mutts of a honey color spotted the newcomers and began barking and running uphill to investigate. Behind the dogs a man stopped his work and, shielding his eyes, peered up the slope to see who was coming. Finally recognizing the old man, the thatch-gatherer called out to the dogs to stop their barking and return to him. They did, albeit reluctantly, turning in their retreat to woof again at these intruders.

"Hello, Tal'ma Herb-Master! The man called out, climbing up toward where Tal'ma had signaled to his apprentice to halt. "Bless you for your journey!" A young girl, perhaps twelve years old, her brown legs a blur of movement, ran toward the old man and A'lan. She passed Tal'ma with a courteous smile but swept past to stand in front of A'lan, panting slightly from her uphill run. "A'lan," she said, "Papa says I can go to the sea for a time this year. Will you teach me to swim like you? Will you? Please?" All this without an intervening breathe and then she stood smiling whitely in front of the boy. Her hazel eyes were wide and expectant, beckoning to the boy's surprise, pleasing him but stunning his tongue with boyish embarrassment.

As Tal'ma watched what passed between the two children, he was mildly surprised at his mental tardiness. How had he not seen it more clearly before? Of course! The girl confirmed it. Already, in the vibrant, dynamic world of these youngsters, his brother's grandson was marked by uniqueness. Not just this one child's fawning attention but now the remembered events where this sturdy boy was the center of attention among his peers. Other adults had often commented upon it. And this little woman-to-be was plying her wiles already and A'lan was her target and she was eliciting all the proper responses. Tal'ma hid his smile behind a casual wipe of his face. Then he turned to the slight child who bubbled with barely controlled energy.

"I'm sure A'lan will teach you the ways of the water, girl." The boy glanced thankfully at his great-uncle, shifted the heavy pack and managed a smile. "Yes. Of course I will Tina." He blushed again and stood like a puppy on a leash, itching to be let loose - to flee.

"Tinaaah!" her father called from down the hill, rescuing the boy from further embarrassment. "Tina. Start the fire. It's time for a meal. Hurry now, and none of your mischief." The girl frowned and one had the impression of a mental foot being stomped. Then she smiled ingenuously at Tal'ma and turned and ran to her duties, calling over her boney shoulder, "You promised, A'lan! You promised." A'lan watched her disappear behind a small knoll, rolled his eyes heavenward as his body relaxed. He glanced sheepishly at Tal'ma and looked away, glad to be rid of the moment's discomfort.

"Are you well and dangerous, my friend?" Tal'ma asked the thatch collector as he made his way casually uphill. Such slightly licentious references were common among the men. "As dangerous as a man with a younger wife and three daughters can be, Tal'ma. They don't allow me the time for any mischief! "The men gripped hands in formal greeting and began to chat about weather conditions, the crop of thatching grass this year and other pastoral subjects.

A'lan, meanwhile, stood looking out at the dark sea beyond and to the dozens of rocks and reefs which seemed to have been scattered offshore by some giant hand. Then he focused on that cloud. The brownish-grey plume was growing out of the top of the perpetual cloud cover which hung over that great volcano, Roro Votu, over thirty sea-miles away. That monster mountain, whose last eruption had caused the terrible waves and taken so may lives here on this Set, or island, was bellowing forth its destructive fury once more. Sha'ham-Set was again in danger!

"Uncle, excuse me - but look!" Both men turned to the direction in which the boy pointed. The billowing cloud was even darker than when A'lan had first spied it. And now as the three watched, there came a dull rumbling 'Boom' from that direction, followed by dimmer sounds of those massive detonations at a distance which only the fastest canoe could travel in a day.

Tal'ma Herb-Master's distance vision was still keen and he quickly discerned the magnitude of the eruption. He laid his hand on the boy's shoulder and said, "We must get back to the village now, A'lan. As quickly as we can." A'lan hitched his pack again and tightened the straps and stood waiting for his great-uncle to lead. Tal'ma gripped hands with the harvester again. "My best to your good wife and your whole family, Lan'ta." Then he turned downhill and quickly strode onto the track. The harvester waved to the two departing backs, and then stood gazing in concern as the threatening cloud in the distance grew even darker and more ominous.

After minutes of watching, he turned away to look down-slope in another direction to where his two daughters were moving about at their camp near a spring which bubbled forth from an outcrop of basalt. As chief gatherer of the thatching grasses, he must remain here on the highlands until the other crews had returned with their bundles, much later in the day. It was unlikely that they would be aware of Roro Votu's eruption for they were working somewhere on the slopes to the west. It might take hours to find them. "Best we remain here and wait for them." Lan'ta murmured. "When they return I'll send Tina ahead to be with her mother."

As he bent to pick up the carrying pole which he also used to ease his sometimes aching back, he nearly lost his balance, catching his forward fall with one hand. The first tremor of an approaching catastrophe rolled under him. He stood quickly and regained his balance, then looked down toward where his daughters were. Both girls were looking toward him but were too far away for him to read their faces. Flocks of birds were wheeling about the sky overhead, having taken wing before the tremor struck, reading signs beyond a human's normal sensitivity.

There was another sharp jolt and a deep rumbling just within the threshold of human hearing. Then an eerie silence began as even the sky-born birds ceased their calls and the chattering bush fowl stopped their constant noise. A shiver ran up the harvester's spine as he jogged down the slope toward his daughters. The middle daughter, Lan'la, sixteen now, stood with both hands over her face but he could see her wide and fearful eyes. She was a nervous child; always, since infancy. Tina however, ran toward her father on strong, skinny legs, her face alive with excitement and enthusiasm for this startling phenomenon. The father thought how dissimilar all three girls were as she skidded to a halt in front of him. "She has the spirit which many fathers of boys would envy."

Just then the small dogs who always accompanied them up here for the grass harvesting began to howl. Then another tremor, sharper than that first one, rolled beneath the open grasslands. The rock structure which held the spring shuddered and split open, an increased flow of water spurting strongly into the pool beneath. The renewed flow splashed loudly in the silence, which had again returned to the hillside. The middle daughter cried out and ran to her father, throwing herself into his protecting arms. Tina turned to look at the sea and the smoke of the distant volcano. But something inside her mind focused her awareness not on the distant conflagration but internally: the words came clearly, as if spoken by another voice within her: "It is not *that* mountain which shakes you, girl. Take care! Take care Tina-an!"

As the grey-headed old Herb-Master and the boy ran down the grassy slopes, the boy outdistancing the old man, neither were able to feel the trembling beneath their flying feet. A'lan, however, noticed flashes of blue-green light running across the ground. Indistinct and ephemeral, the manifestation never-the-less existed in his vision. Long tradition of certain people with a special sensitivity to aural or visual phenomena had currency this day, all over this island. As a young child A'lan had become aware of these 'earth-lights' as he called them. On any given day or night, moonlit or dark, he would notice lines of various colors flitting about the landscape.

At times too, there were simply small flashes of color. Never frightened by this phenomenon, much as Tina was not frightened of the voices which sometimes invaded her awareness, A'lan could find no one to explain it to him. Most adults passed it off as boyish imaginings. Others simply told him to wait until he was older and he would understand. Not very helpful to a curious intelligence. Among those who truly understood the significance of his sensitivity, his 'sight', as it was referred to, was his mother, his grandmother, and the Sea-Master, Tel'an. All three of these people sensed a special dimension to the boy. Strangely, his great-uncle Tal'ma, while loving the boy for his brightness and quiet character, was not yet quite convinced of those same special qualities.

It was A'lan who first reached the gardens above the village, the men and women there gathered in small, excited knots of speculation and fear. The paddies of *taro* and the herbs and root vegetables were forgotten in the present disruption. Tools lay randomly where they were dropped when the first tremor struck. One man stepped from the group and waved the boy toward him. Then, seeing the Herb-Master just clearing the windbreak trees at his slower run, the man called out to him. "Tal'ma! Come!" and moved at a fast walk toward the old man, ignoring the boy for now.

But A'lan jogged beside the man. Face glistening with sweat and his breath racing too, he told him, "The volcano on Sht'o-Set. It's erupting!" Still the man preferred to ignore the boy's story and hear what the respected elder's account might be. A'lan gave up and sat down on the muddy garden-side soil, a small anger seething in his young mind.. It hurt him when others ignored his enthusiasms, and of course, this was *really* important! "Greetings, An'hola!" the old man called out as he approached the gardeners. He was breathing heavily and, An'hola thought, looking unwell. "The boy has told you? He asked, leaning on his staff for support.

"Yes, but did you not feel the earth moving as you came down the hill? There were two tremors, the second the stronger." Others of the gathering now approached the newcomers and soon ten gardeners were jostling for a position near the Herb-Master, all ignoring the young boy. "No," replied Tal'ma, "running as we were we felt nothing." He glanced over at his great-nephew for confirmation. That made A'lan feel better and he rose to his feet and replied, "No, great-uncle, but I did see strong lights all around us on the ground among the pine groves!" He immediately wished he'd not mentioned that for a woman in the group guffawed in derision. The head gardener however nodded at the possibility, but said nothing.

Ignoring the chatter around him, Tal'ma spoke in a loud, authoritative voice. "Now listen, all of you!" Many stepped back from him a pace or two out of deference to his rank. "We must all return to the village, now! There is danger in all this earthshaking and we must see to the rafts and canoes!" Without waiting for assenting comment, Tal'ma shouldered his way past the others and nodded meaningfully to A'lan. The boy shifted his pack again and followed Tal'ma, then passed him and set off at a dead run, the pack of plants and lichens on his back weightless now in his enthusiasm.

By the time the boy had reached the village, most of which was located on a rocky slope well above the grey sand beach, a confusion of hurrying people was moving generally toward the shore. Already men were hauling the bamboo rafts and double-hulled canoes up the steep slope toward safety ... they hoped ... and young boys carried nets and paddles and other lighter gear to the highest parts of the beach. Women called to children and to each other and voices reflected fear, but not yet panic. All cast glances at the sea, expecting to see at any moment the waters receding in dramatic fashion. This deceitful withdrawing of the waters, preceding the arrival of a large, quake-born wave, had cost the lives of many loved ones not three years ago. Never before in the experience of any living Mal'lam had this occurred.

Those elder citizens, men and women, Tal'ma among them, set about establishing some order to what threatened to become chaos. With measured calmness and authority they barked orders and directed the young people. As they did so, it was often with great effort because that last horrible encounter with a sea-gone-mad had cost many of the grey-headed Mal'lam loved ones. Only a few who possessed uncommon prescience suspected that today's emergency was but prelude to something truly awesome! One of those people stood beneath the covered porch of her small hut. Her name was Pha'an. She was grandmother to the boy A'lan and sister-in-law to Tal'ma. Pha'an was a highly psychic person, her gift being centered on the very earth itself; its massive moods and movements and the weather it engendered.

This day she was nearly overwhelmed with the messages the earth was sending her. She clutched her stomach in pain, so powerful was its message. The fear knotted there was a familiar one. Inspired by her 'sight', her sensitivity revealed to her the life within the land itself. Its movements this day called out in voices of urgency. She knew more than she revealed of her knowledge, more even than she really wished to know. At this moment she was listening to messages quite like those the young girl Tina was hearing, there high on the slopes of the great mountain."Take care - take care! Disaster comes your way!"

By sunset all valuable possessions and equipment had been stowed away high above the watermark of the last great immersion. Families moved even higher to an open area beneath the community gardens, an air of forced jollity building - proof against fear. Tightly wound bundles of fiber, soaked in fish oil, were mounted on poles stuck into the sand at the seashore, a few feet into the water. These would serve as torches at nightfall, their glow illuminating the sea's surface, allowing a visual warning should the sea begin to recede during the night. Watchers would attend throughout the dark hours, renewing the torches as needed. Meanwhile, large bonfires were lit and a communal meal was being prepared as the villagers determined to spend the night away from their homes as comfortably, albeit nervously, as possible.

Having been served their meal first, as was the custom at communal feasts, the elders of the community retired to the natural hot-spring baths for a long soak and an evening of discussion and gossip. The elder women took their places in the large, partially covered baths behind a screen of fruiting shrubs. The men retired to a similar in-ground pond, also partially covered, for their relaxing ritual. A wide, pebble-paved area surrounded the baths, an area for scrubbing and rinsing tired bodies before ensconcing themselves in the warm spring water. Each village on this Set was intentionally located to take advantage of these natural phenomena. There were three other, smaller, near-by villages on Sha'ham-Set, all performing a similar ritual this evening. The nearly constant temperature of these baths had made them a dependable venue for the social ritual for the Mal'lam of this lovely island. Only, tonight, much would change.

Chapter Five ~ The Desperate Days

Tal'ma Herb-Master lathered and scrubbed with the root of the shampoo ginger, creating respectable foam to help carry away the day's sweat and grime. He then rinsed himself with gourds of hot water from the baths. Around him other elders did likewise, some preceding him into the comforting heat to soak. Tonight would be a night of serious discussion. Rumors of foreboding, not directly pertaining to the eruption of the great volcano on Sh'to-Set, had been circulating all day. That cataclysm was quite visible from the baths; a dull, copper glow showed from across the thirty-mile passage of open sea and flashes of holocaust-spawned lightening glared repeatedly through cloud and smoke. As he rose from the low stool upon which he had sat to wash himself and rinse his tired body, Tal'ma felt the earth shudder beneath him. He and the other older men froze momentarily in whatever posture they found themselves, waiting! Nothing more happened. Old eyes looked to others, heads nodded and Tal'ma climbed into the natural tub of basaltic stone which nature had left, seemingly by generous design.

The cooling night air drew a misting of steam from the baths, casting a strange glow on the bathers in the light of the numerous torches burning around the bathing area. Tal'ma settled into the warm water with a long, drawn-out sigh, as did others. Such luxury! He sank himself up to his chin while some others submerged totally, surfacing shortly with much blowing and spluttering, wiping the water from their eyes. Soon all were present and had rinsed and relaxed back against the stone walls of this marvelous gift from the *Earth Mother* herself. Tal'ma was the first of the Elders to speak. His voice was tired and soft. "My sister-in-law is holding her stomach again." he said smiling, and some of the others laughed knowingly, acknowledging his meaning. The dim torchlight from outside the covering structure glistened on the rippled waters, lots of steam rising as the outside air cooled. Grey and some balding heads nodded slightly as they waited for Tal'ma to continue.

"My sister-in-law says nothing but looks with concern at the mountain ... our mountain! There is fear in her eyes which disturbs me." There was another period of silence until Tel'an Sea-Master, a dear friend of Tal'ma's, spoke in his high, stringy voice.

"The light-lines are confused!" he said gravely. He was referring to those emanations of energy beneath the sea, visible to only a few with a specific sensitivity to that energy level. That was part of the 'sight', which some few individuals possessed, whether it be vision, sound or some other psychic sense. "I've never seen them as they are now. Last night I was afloat, fishing with my eldest nephew, and below us they were flashing in strange sequences, running from shore out to sea but not in the manner I've known since my youth. Even my nephew, who doesn't claim the 'sight', commented that he'd seen them! That caused me concern. Something is amiss within Sh'ham-Set!"

Anho'la, the village's chief horticulturist, now added, "So too, are the plants confused! The new gourd flowers are distorted. The bees are very agitated and many cannot find their hives. They are found dying everywhere. And the taro shoots are withered this year. I too, am worried!" Another long silence until Tal'ma again spoke. "Today I saw a Talpa. The snake was at an altitude which I've never seen them at before. Have any of you seen them among the upper groves of bamboo or in the deep forest?" No one answered for a moment until the Bamboo-Master replied, "No, thank the Gods!" and chuckling followed.

Panto'al Feather-Master, master of bird knowledge, raised himself slightly on the stone seat, his shoulders smoking with steam. "The high-country birds are coming down the mountain very early this year. And yet, there's plenty of food above for them. They are in great numbers in the grasslands already, competing with the song-larks. I've never seen it thus before!" Interrupting the almost requisite pause in the stylized method of debate, Kol'sha Wood-Master rose from the water and said, "Phew! Is it my meal working upon me or is this water getting hotter?" Others stirred and the steam off their bodies rose as it would on a cold night, which this was not. Someone called out to a younger man who was in attendance upon his elders that evening. "Pa'paho. Come feel this water for us."

The man, tall and stoop-shouldered, ducked under the outer edge of the shelter roof and plunged his hand into the bath's steaming water. "Are you all trying to cook yourselves? I've never felt the water so hot!" By now the billows of steam were flowing out beyond the eaves of the shelter and into the soft evening breeze. Then the first spitting and gurgling began in the trough which fed the baths. A greater volume of water began surging forth spasmodically, splashing scalding water onto the tub's occupants. There was a mad dash of elders as they evacuated the ever-hotter water. Some, stiff and a bit awkward in their old age, tumbled painfully onto the pebble paving around the bath, one slipping and falling heavily. Two miles away, in another village, similar scenes were occurring, another bathhouse made untenable by this sudden incursion of extremely hot water. There, even closer to the actual seam of rock structure which fostered the formerly beneficent warm waters, men and women screamed as the hot water burst forth explosively, burning some rather painfully.

Tal'ma Herb-Master, standing naked outside the verandah of the bathhouse with the other old men and a gathering crowd, looked toward the women's baths and saw a similar exodus occurring, accompanied by high-pitched squeals and cries. He went with two other men to see that no one was injured. His sister-in-law, Pha'an, met him and took his elbow and led him aside, out of the hearing of the others."Tal'ma-luv," she said, using the term of intimacy allowed within families, "I have great fear. We must speak, now!" Still clutching his elbow with one hand, as much for support as to direct him, the other hand clutching her wrap around her, she led him to a secluded spot near the fowl yard. In the dim glow of bonfires and torches he looked into her seamed old features - attentive. In spite of their habit of mutual insult and denigrating banter which they had cultivated over the years, there existed a deep regard and respect. It was to this respect that she spoke and he regarded each word carefully.

"Tal'ma! oh, Tal'ma! The mountain speaks to me in such pain. Soon it will die, Tal'ma!" Her tears began to flow and he clutched her free hand with both of his in support against her distress. "Sh'ham-Set will die, Tal'ma! In only a few days. Do you hear me? We have only days!" So intense were her words that Tal'ma was forced to take a step back, still holding her hand, gaping at her, trying to think of some reason to disbelieve her. He surrendered to nearly sixty years of experience of this strange, psychic woman. He believed her! Tal'ma made his decision at that moment. He leaned forward to embrace his sister-in-law, kissed her wet face and then turned to rejoin the elders again. A Council was being convened and he must attend it. He now had a message which must be presented and acted upon! "Tal'ma-luv!" she called, causing him to pause and turn to face her again. "Keep the boy with you. Now more than ever. Promise me!"

Of their combined family of six boys and young men, they had both always referred to A'lan as, 'the boy', so special was he to the old woman, his grandmother. Tal'ma too, now shared a special regard for 'the boy'. Tal'ma placed his hand over his heart by way of a pledge and before he turned away to his other duties, he blew her a kiss for the first time in their relationship. Pha'an stood watching her old friend and sparring partner return to the gathering, heard his strong voice addressing them, exhorting them, spurring them to action. As she stood, she suddenly clutched her belly against the painful wails of her island as they assaulted her yet again. She too had decisions to make.

On the broad slopes of the open grasslands, some one-and-a-half miles above the village, Tina walked warily lest she stumble. It was full dark now and only starlight guided her footsteps. An hour ago her father had ordered her to go alone back to the village. Never before had he done such a thing. The other gatherers had not yet returned from their work area, far around the slopes. But what of that, she thought, they sometimes do stay overnight if they are really busy. Why did he seem so worried, so abrupt with both her and her sister? And why didn't Lan'an come too? Why does Daddy always think she's so fragile?

Tina was angry, hurt and just a little frightened. Lan'ta had sent one of the dogs with her and she held its leash tightly, gaining some comfort in its presence. Although there were no dangerous animals here, the dark and the tension of the past few hours made her jump at any strange sound as she threaded her way carefully over stones and clumps of grass, trying to stay to the trail. But, as was Tina's nature, she soon turned her thoughts to the task at hand and was increasing her speed, the trail familiar now, even in the dark. She let the dog off its leash then, confident in her own independence.

It quickly began to search for its own adventures, scooting off into the shadows, sniffing and snuffing as if on the trail of something interesting. She had to call him back to her repeatedly. It was like a small game they were playing and it distracted her from thinking of whys? And what's? Unknown to Tina was her father's deep disquiet. And it was this vague unease which had prompted him to send his dear, obstreperous, youngest daughter downhill to the distant village, back to her mother and oldest sister and safety. Safe from what? a part of him kept asking. He kept his middle daughter close to him when she and Tina accompanied him on these harvest trips, afraid for her own fear! This night they sat close together near the fire and watched their supper warming on the flat stone next to the hot coals. They chatted about simple things, both enjoying the quiet and the comfort of each other's company.

The glow of the uncommon bonfires above the village flickered between the trunks of the pine forest, a beacon to guide Tina, and a source of curiosity. She had never seen such bright illumination from the village before while up here on the lower slopes of the mountain. Just then the young, rambunctious dog returned and whimpered beside her. Strange, she thought. She bent down to pat the short-legged dog, and then thought it might be wise to put its leash on again. It remained at her side and tolerated her slipping the woven fiber rope around its neck without complaint. Again, strange behavior. She usually had to cajole it to stand still for this procedure. It then trotted beside her without straining on the rope as it usually did. It still uttered whimpers from time to time. Its behavior made Tina uncomfortable, a bit uneasy. Then to add to her unease came her *voices* again: "Take care!" they said, "Take care!" Tina's skin was all goose bumps, as sometimes occurred when her *voices* spoke to her unexpectedly.

But now, as she neared the gathering of her people around the huge bonfires, the smell of food replaced her previous nervousness with hunger. Oh, but she was hungry! Her mouth watered, her empty stomach growled in complaint and she began to run. Then she stubbed her toe on an unseen root. Instead of stopping to investigate the pain, she hopped for a time on one foot, releasing the dog to fend for itself, dragging its leash along behind it. And she swore! Hopping on one foot, growling words women were not to use, especially young girls, she made her way to the shelter of her community.

Entering the circle of light from the bonfires, she used their welcome glow to try to locate her mother and oldest sister, Sht'ana. Friends her own age called out to her to come and join them but she only smiled and waved and continued searching. She finally found Sht'ana sitting with some of her own friends, still eating. She was told that their mother was at the baths with the other elders and would be there for some time. Although in years their mother, Sha'lat, did not qualify as an elder, it was her standing as one of the supreme Herb-Mistresses of her people that required her to attend gatherings where important decisions affecting the whole community were being discussed - such as this night's concerns about giant waves and prognostications of doom and other disturbing phenomena.

Tina had gone to where the food for the village was being prepared and served that unusual night and returned to where her sister sat with her friends. She carried a half of a banana leaf, on which food was normally served, heaped with baked fish, fresh baked *taro* and breadfruit. She had only begun to eat when cries and shouts began rising from the direction of the baths. The real drama had begun for the Mal'lam in noise and confusion in the villages. But up on the hillsides it was manifesting itself insidiously, murderously, with quiet stealth.

For nearly three years faults within the structure of the great mountain which was the heart of this beautiful island of Sh'ham, had begun to separate. Responding to a greater geological pressure that was also acting upon the other islands of this archipelago, the great explosion across the sea, earlier this day, had been but a signal of greater activity to come. The invisible swelling of the northeast slope of this mountain had forced long, narrow apertures which in some cases reached to the surface.

One such vein of access had surfaced near the cold-water baths on the slopes above the village where women and girls gathered to bath and gossip, their day's work in the fields and paddies and work sheds complete. It was here also that Tal'ma's dear, youngest son, Shk'al the musician, would come and secrete himself among the boulders above the pool and play his flute and sing for the women below. He would lay back against the great boulders and gaze detachedly up at the scarf of clouds on the top of the mountain. Nearly every afternoon they were there, waving down to him, encouraging him to play ever more beautifully. Over many months, small quantities of a deadly mixture of gases seeped up through the stone faults and dissipated into the usually breezy high-country air. On still days though, these gases, invisible and scentless, would accumulate in injurious amounts. In their burrows and rock crevices would die thousands of tiny animals, the natural food of the dangerous snake, the Talpa. It would be hunger which would drive those snakes that survived to seek food at higher altitudes.

That same gas bubbled into the spring which fed the cold-water baths, dissolving in the water and entering the bodies of the most susceptible women in minute amounts. In some it would accumulate, causing damage to internal organs. The placentas of the mothers protected their babies from the direct effects of the poisons, but the mother's deteriorating health often led to miscarriages and stillbirths. Too many children did not survive their first year of life. Among a vigorously healthy people, this all brought great concern. The Herbalists and Healers were at a loss to explain it. And the Mal'lam was not a people easily given to belief in evil spirits. Surely the *Earth Mother* must have an explanation for this! And so the people prayed to their only important deity for an answer. The long oral history of their people held no clues.

One afternoon as Shk'al sang especially sweetly, the women in the pool listening raptly, a sudden gust of those terrible fumes arose from a cleft nearby and engulfed him. He screamed, began coughing desperately, and then fell unconscious. The weeping women carried him home. He died less than an hour later in his father's arms. Not even the most powerful insights could guess at the cause of his sudden death. But on that day his aunt, Pha'an, suffered painful voices and clutched her stomach. Only later did word come to her of Shk'al's death. And now, on this fateful night, at nearly the time the surge of hot water had emptied the village baths of their occupants, the sudden convulsion of pressure within the mountain forced a huge bubble of accumulated poison up through the widening conduits and into the open air near the cold-water baths, the waters bubbling and boiling at the intrusion.

The cool air of that night lay like a blanket over the grasslands. The dogs lay sleeping, snuffling and twitching in their dreams. Tina's father and older sister were just ladling out their evening meal into clay bowls. Neither heard nor sensed any danger. There was no warning until the campfire suddenly dimmed, its oxygen diminished. The dogs awoke and yelped in fear as they gasped for breath. The girl threw her hands out in front of her as if to fend off some threatening phantom. Her father tried to rise and go to her aid but fell forward, fatally stricken!

By the greatest good fortune that night, the blanket of cool, moist air upon the mountainside prevented the gases from descending lower toward the pine groves. Later in the night sea breezes would sweep up the slopes and dissipate the noxious cloud but not before wreaking more havoc among living things. Birds fell from their nighttime perches; small scurrying animals fell dead in their wanderings; delicate flowers and new, green buds withered. By morning a singed patina lay across the affected area, visible sign to the bamboo workers who climbed to their work the next morning that death surely stalked Sh'ham-Set! It was those men who, just after sunrise, discovered the bodies near the baths and later, four others of their workmates who had stayed overnight in order to begin work at the earliest hour.

The sudden and inexplicable deaths, which left no mark except expressions of panic on the victim's faces, instilled an urgency upon the Mal'lam which no amount of oratory by esteemed elders could inspire. The dogs were left where they lay while the bodies of the thatch-gatherer and his daughter were carried down the mountain with great gentleness. The family of the gatherer and his daughter were devastated. Sha'lat, Sh'tana and Tina were inconsolable. Pha'an held her counsel, although her grief too was great. Her *voices'* continued to warn her of impending horror. But also the urgency of the situation of the islanders required every hand be turned to the preparation to leave their beloved island as soon as possible - in but a few short days! The grieving wife and mother and her two remaining daughters looked to their responsibilities through weeping eyes. There would be no proper blessings of the dead nor mourning periods this time. A huge funeral pyre was constructed and set alight and the ashes and bones buried in a common grave, the villagers going back to their tasks immediately the fire was lit.

The bamboo harvesters who had found the sad remains returned as soon as possible to their task too. Aided by volunteers from other crafts, they quickly climbed to the groves of giant culms high above the grasslands. The long, heavy, often purposely-shaped lengths of bamboo were cut and carried back down the mountain for the construction of new rafts needed to carry the island's population safely away from this now-hazardous island. As they worked the men all fought the terrible fear of an unknown, stealthy enemy which had no name and no face.

Hourly it seemed, tremors rocked the island, some mild, some very strong. All were frightening. These worrying reminders spurred the bamboo-harvesters to complete their tasks as quickly as possible and quit this mountain of impending destruction. Seamen, those not immediately needed at the shore, were also dragooned into the great carrying task. Their discomfort at these unaccustomed heights was magnified by the same fear all shared. They fairly ran down the mountainside with their heavy loads.

The Mal'lam, inhabitants of a lovely paradise for over eleven generations, must now flee! These descendents of sea-wanderers must wander again in search of a home. Across the thirty sea miles the great volcano, Goro Votu, continued its eruption. Its spewing and booming, distant as it was, was but part of the holocaust which was approaching all the inhabitants of these beautiful islands.

There was a frantic rush by those involved in Herb-knowledge and horticulture to collect, wrap, and secure aboard the vessels those basic foods and other valuable plant materials for future propagation. Banana shoots, *taro* corms, Breadfruit suckers, fruiting shrubs and trees; so many plants to be carefully prepared for future planting. Paper mulberry suckers were also carefully dug up and packaged. A small, shrubby tree, the bark of which afforded the clothing of the Mal'lam, were wrapped in coconut fiber and leaves and set aside for loading upon the refugee fleet which would soon depart.

At a last moment, high above on the bamboo-covered slopes of the trembling mountain, a Herb-Master remembered to dig some viable roots of the great bamboos. These plants had their origins in a similar exodus so many generations ago. Other species of bamboos would likewise be dug up and readied for stowing. These islands had held no bamboos before the arrival of the Mal'lam. Nor was there breadfruit or banana or sugar cane. Indeed, so many of the staples of life for the Mal'lam had been imported with their ancestors that life in the future would seem unthinkable in a land which had yet to be found, should these staples of life be missing there! Al'an's great-uncle, Tal'ma, and his mother, Lana'ma-Herb-Mistress, supervised the packaging and storing of the valuable food plants. And so, day after exhausting day, the island's desperate inhabitants gathered and carried and loaded and constructed!

It would require eight days to finish the construction of the three new, large bamboo rafts. Normally, this process would require weeks of curing of the bamboos and many days of careful construction. Now was not the time for traditional craftsmen to insist on traditional craftsmanship. Green culms must suffice, even though in their green state they would support only half the weight of properly cured stems. As this work progressed, the large, beautifully constructed canoes were prepared for the coming voyage of salvation. Many were years old, but most were lovingly maintained and only minor repairs were necessary to make them fully seaworthy. These vessels, two matching hulls joined by a bridging deck of bamboo and hardwood, were to be the scout vessels and couriers between the huge but lumbering bamboo rafts. Added to this growing flotilla were three large bamboo rafts, which had already seen two seasons' trading. Still in decent condition, needing only minor repairs, these bulky, awkward looking vessels were never-the-less capable of carrying forty people and much other freight.

This fleet's destination was known however, unlike their ancestor's chance find of this archipelago, so long ago. They were going to join their clan cousins, members of a line which could be traced in their oral history back to the earliest sea-voyagers of the Mal'lam. While some less adventurous clans but followed the lead of these people, the Clan Sht'ah'ha, the forbears of this wing of the Mal'lam were always looking seaward, curious to the point of compulsion to see what the great ocean had to offer them. And now the vagaries of nature were to force this clan of people to recombine with their cousins on the island called Sht'ah'Lee. Sht'ah'Lee-Set lay far to the southeast, over three hundred sea miles. But the way was well known to the sailors of Sh'ham-Set who would be leading this journey, for they often sailed their large, double-hulled canoes there on trading voyages. And sometimes trade was simply an excuse to visit and enjoy the freedom and adventure of open-sea sailing.

The inhabitants of Sht'ah-Lee were renowned for their canoes. That island, by far the largest inhabited by the Mal'lam, held great forests of giant trees and the craftsmen there were the best among the islanders. The large bamboo rafts rarely made such a long voyage. Slow and not very maneuverable, these big vessels were usually confined to the closer, more northerly inter-island trade routes. The Clan-Sht'ah'ha were the uncontested leading sailors and traders among the Mal'lam. Other clans on other Set seemed quite content with a land-centered life.

While the people of Sh'ham-Set were engaged in their frantic preparations, small canoes arrived almost daily with tales of eruptions and earthquakes and even some destructive waves on other islands. It was no consolation. But what of their destination? Was Sht'ah-Lee also beset by this geological catastrophe? No one could know, for at this time of year the winds could be contrary. The seamen of Sht'ah-Lee usually spent this time of year in the repair of existing canoes and the building of new ones. Little voyaging was done to the north in this, the late Spring.

The people of Sh'ham-Set were near exhaustion. Although each tremor brought a reminder of the urgency, still both men and women dozed off at their tasks, even while standing up. Older children were in charge of their younger siblings and cousins and even they often crawled away to some shady spot to sleep, tired from their lesser tasks. On the seventh day since the emergency had begun, the packing and stowing of supplies was nearly complete. Plant materials for future propagation were stowed lowest in the open cargo bays of the rafts and extra wrappings designed to prevent the entry of seawater were secured around them. Smoked fish, fermented *taro* and breadfruit pastes were sealed into tightly woven baskets and additional wrappings added.

Basic tools and materials and an assortment of utensils necessary for the individual households were vetted and then stowed under the watchful, tired gaze of the canoe and raft-Masters. Chickens and pigs were gathered and put into clever cages of bamboo withes to be loaded aboard on the departure day. The little dogs would be tossed aboard at the last minute. They would be allowed to roam at virtual will about the decks during the voyage, being fed almost nothing for the duration to prevent too much smelly mess aboard. Pigs and chickens would contribute their share of that but the cages were designed for easy cleaning. Water was stored in both bamboo culms, with the internodes knocked out, and gourds of large capacity. More than likely, rain would fall during the journey, but no seaman ventured far from land without copious supplies of fresh water aboard.

And now, more than four hundred people would be crowded aboard the vessels. The water containers were all secured on the seventh day also. The construction of the new rafts had gone more quickly than planned, the skill of the builders exceeding even their own expectations and the departure was now scheduled for the morning of the eighth day. It had been hoped that a day of rest may have been possible before setting off, but the insistent shaking of the earth and the even more insistent urging of prognosticators like the venerable Pha'an, was driving wiser heads to leave *now*!

Each family packed only what it felt essential; then that list was shortened again. The Masters of the vessels, ever mindful of weight and space, excluded valued artifacts of appreciable size or weight. Tal'ma's remaining son, Enno Stone-Master, was not allowed to bring aboard his precious cache of obsidian. Only his tools could he bring. After all, Sht'ah Lee-Set had copious amounts of the valuable stone and it was his skill which was really important. Other craftspeople had to leave behind other materials equally as valuable to them. As the day of departure approached, it was another loss to endure, another source of near despair. And then the end began!

Day was fading into shadow and the great mountain above the Mal'lam shadowed itself as the sun sank low behind it. Bamboo decking was being laid over the storage area toward the bottom of the rafts and the decision had been made to load the pigs and chickens aboard this night before departure. Families, many of whom had been separated for most of the days of the preparation by separate tasks and areas of work, began to come together again. Mothers regained very young children and clasped them tightly, smothering them with kisses, desperate never to be apart again.

All throughout the now littered little community, the people were reuniting in preparation for one last meal ashore. And hopefully, some rest at last. But then came the shrill scream from a hut near the back of the village. All heads turned to locate its source. Again the scream, this time accompanied by the appearance of a small, bent figure staggering into view, one hand clutching her midriff, the other waving frantically at the gathering. Pha'an, her face twisted with pain and desperation, cried out words which made the hairs rise on the necks of all within hearing. They heard …"Aeiiii! It dies! It dies! Flee for your lives!"

The first to move was her daughter, Lana'ma. She rose from her seat of exhaustion and ran toward the beloved woman, her son Al'an quickly behind her. Tal'ma too, struggled to his feet but paused as the ground shook so heavily that he nearly fell. Nearby, once again with her mother and sister, Tina, with dark circles of fatigue beneath her eyes, suddenly put her hands to her head and her scream joined the old woman' laments.

"Flee! We must flee! The island dies beneath us!" In desperation, not knowing what else to do, her mother clamped a hand over her daughter's mouth. The slight girl struggled free with determined strength, faced her mother and shouted, "Mother! We must go! Now!" But above the hubbub of voices which the warning had caused came a sound which froze every islander where they stood!

Rushing down the opposite side of the great mountain, an area which faced onto a vast, dry, near-wasteland, rolled a huge cloud of smoke, steam and super-heated gases. That sound, which carried around and over the mountain, struck like a physical blow. A deep rumbling and then a heavy concussion which drove upward through feet and legs and bodies succeeded a high screaming roar. It was as if the earth had been thrust skyward by an immense blow.

All eyes turned to the mountain and saw an ugly grey-brown cloud rising on the opposite side, billowing upward with astonishing speed. Deep booms of explosion and heavy rattling sounds followed, as if boulders were being shaken in some giant fist. The ground moved sideways, upsetting many standing people, then it pounded up and down. Tree limbs broke free of their trunks and buildings began collapsing. The mountaintop, miles distant, now threw large boulders into the shattered air, trailing dust and smoke. One such boulder flew that distance and landed in the upper gardens where it rolled to a stop next to a thatched hut, smoking and making cracking sounds. Within moments the hut burst into flames.

Pha'an, her daughter and grandson now supporting her in her agony, received the order from her which they had dreaded for days. They must go now and leave her! There was no argument. Days before she had told her daughter, and a few other people close to her, that she would remain with her beloved Sh'ham-Set. This was her home in more ways than just to occupy its land for so many decades. Her soul was here and she could not leave. There was no recourse now left to her daughter. Pha'an had decided. No amount of pleading would avail. With a last, crushing hug from daughter and grandson, they turned and ran to the beach to join the retreat to the sea, A'lan looking back over his shoulder as he ran, tears nearly blinding him. His mother dared not look back.

Unable to make their voices heard above the turmoil of sound, the Elders and their younger lieutenants rushed among the people, shouting into their ears, "To the rafts! We must flee! Now go, go!" Adults grabbed any child within reach, lifted them and ran in desperation toward the beach. Last-minute parcels were forgotten. Scurrying Mal'lam poured down the grey sands toward the waiting bamboo rafts and canoes. Only the thoughtful planning of the Elders and the Sea-Masters, and the inherent discipline of the people themselves, prevented a fatal panic from developing on that terrifying evening.

One after another the great bamboo rafts were pushed and poled away from the beach, seamen aboard hurrying to raise the heavy sails while the crewmen of the canoes assisted - their own craft were to leave the beaches last. They gripped the sides of the rafts and waded and pushed until the water was too deep to push any more. In counterpoint to the madness of the rest of the scene, the graceful rise and fall of the huge, buoyant rafts over powerful surf gave courage and hope to those aboard and those still ashore.

The double-hulled canoes, the last to leave the beach, manned by the youngest and strongest seamen, carried the stragglers. One of those stragglers was Tina. Separated from her mother and sister, she collided with a large woman running at full speed and recklessly, the collision momentarily stunning the young girl and leaving her on hands and knees, gasping for breath. Around her, some of the older people, unable to keep pace with the frantic exodus, were picked up bodily in young, strong arms and helped aboard the last departing raft. Some others, the last raft finally out into the swell, were handed aboard from the canoes.

Tina, just getting her breath back, rose to one knee and was taken up in the arms of a young seaman and lifted into the hull of one canoe. She looked up into his face and he even managed a smile back at her grateful glance. Then he was gone, back up the beach to gather in one last straggler, a very old man whose face spoke gratitude as he too, was carried bodily to the last canoe on the beach. Only one person now remained ashore. She stood stoically on the top of the rise above the beach. Pha'an, her determination unfaltering, would not be persuaded, a weeping canoe-man finally leaving her and running back to his vessel. All argument had failed over the past few days. Pha'an would die with her island! To Pha'an this lovely Set, this rich, living island, was the only home she knew or would care to know. The psychic screams of warning, which had caused her pain for weeks, were silenced now.

Amid the shock and sound and movement, the old woman stood with serene peace in her soul. She also knew that some of that pain which had caused her to grip her stomach for so many weeks was from a physical cause. She had known for some time that she was dying. This sudden end would be a blessing. Her mind was now clear and composed as she stood watching all the people she loved struggling successfully to force their vessels through the surf and toward the safety of the open sea.

The last face she focused upon was not that of her daughter, who's raft was now far beyond the breakers, nor of her old friend, Tal'ma; he too was out of sight upon the same vessel. Rather her eyes locked upon those of a young girl sitting on the bridging deck of the last canoe to leave the beach. Tina. That sad, desperate little face held her whole concentration and her spirit, soon to pass away from this land, soared instantly over the sea to a far away location, to a distant and unknown soul of like sensitivity. She cast the thought to that distant soul: "Care for this child! She is unique. She is among the blessed children. Succor her!"

Way to the southeast, on another island called Sht'ah Lee, an even older woman sat up suddenly from her sleeping mat and acknowledged the call. She would ponder the meaning for many weeks until events revealed her part in this mystery. Such an event had never occurred with her before. She was called, The Vesa'tan. That young girl, Tina, sat disconsolately on the bamboo deck but her eyes never wavered from the receding face of that old women ashore, barely known to her. Distance and a gathering, smoky haze eventually broke the contact, but only visually.

Something within the girl had locked on to a source of unknowable power and settled itself into a corner of her mind, to be retrieved much later. Finally, Tina bent her head and wept. All her known world had disappeared. She was here on a vessel with people she barely knew, her mother and sister somewhere else, on another canoe or raft. She was alone and bereft. What would become of her? An aged, spray-chilled arm embraced her and she leaned into the offered embrace. Tina could only cry a child's lonely tears.

Pha'an smiled now, confident that her message had been received. She saw the last canoe make its way well beyond the surf and out into the wide passage, a distant island shining in the sunset, now colored bright orange by her island's last gasps of existence as the volcanic clouds covered the sky above. Pha'an was knocked to the ground by a jolt so massive that she was unable to rise. Above her a horrifying wave of grey smoke and gas descended at incredible speed down upon the last remnants of her island's life. Within it were temperatures hot enough to immediately destroy all living tissue. And so it did. Pha'an felt but little pain. Only release and peace accompanied her demise.

Chapter Six - The Voyage to Sht'ah Lee-Set

By the time the last canoe was well beyond the breakers and tacking steadily against the on-shore wind, the top of Sh'ham-Set was a boiling cauldron of smoke and ash and steam. Rock, from small gravel to boulder size, flew from the mountain and rained down upon the surrounding ocean, some large missiles narrowly missing the escaping fleet of rafts and canoes. The side of the mountain facing away from the villages had been torn away and was replaced by streams of molten lava. Had that explosion occurred facing the villages, not a single inhabitant would have survived. Then, as huge volumes of debris fell upon the once-verdant upper slopes, the grasslands and forests and bamboo groves bursting into flames, a great fissure began to open on this side of the mountain.

With a terrible rending sound, it released another gout of gas, smoke and steam, this time greater than that which had devastated the opposite side of the island. Traveling at nearly two hundred miles an hour it swept every living cell from existence. Within seconds the awesome, grey beast from the tortured interior of the planet had reached the seashore. Another explosion, this time the seawater's instant conversion to steam, sent a shockwave which rode out across the sea to the frantic little vessels. It was quickly followed by a blast of radiant heat which actually caused some burns to the skin of the refugees standing upright and facing the holocaust. The fleet was now tacking desperately. Paddles were wielded aboard the canoes and long, thick poles of bamboo aboard the rafts served as oars. Men and women, even children, pulled and stroked for their lives as the great conflagration drew cool sea air onto itself in a rush of wind almost cyclonic.

A'lan's mother, Lana'ma Herb-Mistress, watched through her tears as that greatest explosion of steam and smoke obscured her mother's island, and drew down over her death. A'lan sat beside her, gripping her hand while Tal'ma knelt behind them, his arms supporting both of them in their mutual agony. All around, aboard this raft and all the other vessels, similar scenes were repeated as family and friends tried to comfort their sorrowing fellows.

The sea was now bouncing and splashing like water shaken in a bowl, the wind shifting madly this way and that. Even the most experienced seamen had difficulty maintaining their balance aboard the crowded vessels. Slowly, agonizingly so, the little fleet and its four hundred souls pulled away from the brutal eruption and its terrible winds and heat. Across the archipelago, on any island within sight, islanders stood watching in horror as their cousin's island destroyed itself. Nearly all those people were of a certainty that none could have survived. Vessels at sea would in time dispel this certainty, carrying home the news that the people of Sh'ham-Set had escaped and that nearly all had survived.

One old woman, herself a child of Sh'ham-Set who had married off the island, sat weeping on a headland which afforded a clear view across the strait to the devastation there. She wept not only for her people there but also for the knowledge that, more than likely, her adopted island would itself suffer a similar fate. All Mal'lam, on all the islands within sight or sound of the eruption, shared this intuition. Even on the distant island of Sh'tah Lee, certain psychic individuals felt, heard or saw that something awful had occurred to the northwest.

Another old woman, who lived a lonely existence high in the forests of that island also sensed the catastrophe. It was she, The Vesatan, who had earlier been awakened by that strange communication from an unknown entity, entreating her to care for a certain child. Vesatan also '*saw*', in her mind's eye, a small number of canoes and rafts headed in her own direction. She gathered her few possessions and proceeded to jog down the darkening trail. So well did she know this route that not even full darkness hindered her progress. She must tell the people that their Clan-cousins, the Sh'ham-an, were coming.

The massive eruptions and seismic events among the northern islands of the archipelago were but a prelude to an uncommonly accelerated geological cataclysm. The faulted blocks of the earth's crust upon which these islands rested, always nervously, were in the process of rapidly building deeper troughs and higher crests. Swirling currents of magma deep below the crust had eroded and destabilized this area, causing buckling and subsidence of huge areas of this fracture zone. A geologic event usually requiring millions of years to evolve was only thousands of years old and accelerating. A terrible infant was being born! Some islands would be carried beneath the sea within a few short decades while others would explode; some would merely rise and tilt, changing profile and dimension. This present population, could they revisit here in their great-grandchildren's time, would find little that reminded them of home.

And 'home' was what would soon become the focus of many of this people's younger, more restless and adventurous souls. Most especially, among the seamen. The Mal'lam had for generations been a sea-people, seeking a home from which others could not again drive them. When they had eventually found these rich and varied islands, uninhabited and promising of a long stability and peace, many were willing to settle forever. But forever seems never to arrive and the promise eventually takes on another reality. Such was being proven again, now.

Their ancestors had, when first they left the old security of a mainland coast and ventured out of sight of land in their searching, headed more southwesterly. But soon the western seas proved inhospitable to them. Though rich and numerous, the tropical archipelagoes they explored had been made home by another people long before them. They were a fierce, barbaric people who took human skulls for trophies and were known to eat human flesh. They decorated their bodies with tattooing and seemed to thrive on warfare and killing. The early Mal'lam were horrified. In some instances they had to fight their way out of circumstances of entrapment or were pursued and attacked even while fleeing. A tradition of warrior-hood did develop for two generations among the Mal'lam, but soon declined when these present and presently dying islands were found and settled. Those dangerous peoples to the west would be remembered as the 'Itoi' and folklore grew around them down through the generations.

The prevailing winds and currents in that part of the great ocean usually made sailing eastward extremely difficult. This prevailing circumstance would inhibit that Itoi-lan, as they were collectively known, from moving eastward in their expansions. Rather, they would move ever southward to conquer rich lands and large islands with but few inhabitants. But in the Mal'lam's increasingly desperate search to the east, two contiguous years occurred in which the winds and currents flowed in their favor. And it was these years that brought their canoes to these islands. It was those traditions of experience upon the open sea, ever searching, ever gazing to the east and southeast, held in the oral traditions and kept alive by the institutions of the Seamen, which would help prepare the Mal'lam for the renewal of their seemingly endless quest for a home.

Of all the many crafts and skills which made up the wealth of the Mal'lam community it was the Sea-craftsmen who would dominate in the future planning. And this day it was the skill and courage of the Seamen which sustained a frightened and almost hopeless band of refugees, the majority of whom had never spent a night upon the open ocean. What a long and frightening night they would know! Behind the fleeing flotilla of vessels there shone the fiery demise of their previous home.

A dull orange glow succeeded the heavy pall of smoke and ash which had previously lay at sea level, blocking all view of their dying home-island. Freshening breezes from the east had carried much of it back toward its source. As the air cleared, to the northeast appeared a more distant glow, that of the great volcano, Goro Votu. That mountain's eruptions, having heralded the destructive collapse of the island of Sh'ham, continued unabated. Both destructing islands sent forth blossoms of fire and light throughout the long night, the stars obliterated by smoke and haze. And it was the seamen's knowledge which allowed them to utilize the relative positions of these known beacons, this night of skyward darkness, to gauge their course toward their cousins on Sh'tah Lee-Set.

To the south and southeast must the Mal'lam look for a new homeland! Little was known of those parts either; though many years before a large, paired-hull canoe from another island had ventured many weeks southward and returned telling of rich lands and great islands beyond the size of any now known. Those sailors had unfortunately perished in home-waters soon after returning, a sudden, severe storm leaving their stories but a mystery. One crewman, elderly now, had remained ashore after their initial return, due to an ailment. The experience and knowledge of the others died with them but the one survivor fired the sea-quest fervor of many a Sh'tah Lee seaman. This same desire for adventure burned as a live coal in the being of many seamen, not least in the hearts of the young men. Among these was the boy, A'lan, who had ingested the sea's seductive call with his mother's milk.

That boy, still trembling with shock and fear upon the open sea for the first time in his twelve years, would be among the pioneers. His name would be sung for generations in the oral sagas of his people. But this night, that boy huddled close to his mother, Lana'ma's arm around her only child's shivering shoulders. Tal'ma's figure lay curled near them, beneath the layers of fiber cloth made from the bark of the Paper Mulberry. The old man seemed shrunken and fragile as he lay snoring, these past days having invaded some last bastion of physical resilience within him. No voices sounded above the slap and rush of water around and between the bamboos of the raft's hull.

The night was dark and chilly and damp. Although the wind remained fair behind them, the seamen had to adjust sail frequently through the night, each movement of the crew bringing disquiet among some of the passengers: what was happening now? Finally fatigue claimed the consciousness of most and the small hours of the morning saw the added solace of a benign sea. As distance increased, those seamen and passengers still awake glimpsed just a glow cast upon the roiled waters between them and their previous home. Al'an began to cry, leaning into his mother's warmth."Mother!" he said quietly, looking up at her shadowed face, "When shall we come to our new home?" He had been asking that question of his great-uncle until the old man finally snapped at him in impatience.

Now he sought some comfort from the only other adult with whom he could comfortably converse. She answered tiredly. "A'lan, no one knows. We are all as anxious as you. You must wait as we all wait. Asking will not bring it closer. Be quiet now. Sleep my son, sleep." Sleep came quickly to the boy once he had lain beside his great-uncle's resting form. His mother freed one corner of the blanket which covered the old man and tucked it around her son. He fell to sleep to the watery sounds and the creak of ropes and bamboos and the hollow thump of the great sail above him. These sounds would etch themselves indelibly into his subconscious, reinforcing his destiny.

The following morning dawned with a weak, smoky light and barely enough wind to fill the big, woven sails. Startlingly, the sea around the canoes and rafts was not the deep blue of the channel waters. The sea was covered in what looked like gravel; grey and coarse and matted, with here and there patches of open water, or rather areas covered only in what looked like dust. What was this? Only a few Mal'lam had ever been upon the open ocean when it was covered in one of volcanism's more unique residues - Pumice! The grey, gravely stone was thrown so high into the air by the erupting volcanoes that winds actually caught it in its tons and blew it out upon the sea.

Pumice was a conglomerate of minerals which, super-heated and suffused with gases and air, congealed as it was rapidly cooled. As it flew through the air, the result was unique in the world of minerals. With gas and air trapped inside small pockets in the stone, pumice actually floated; and for a very long time. But this phenomenon was not from particles of the home island of Sh'ham-Set. The massive volcano, Goro Votu, that mountain which had first caused the panic on Sh'ham-Set, had been erupting with its own violence while the Mal'lam were making their desperate way out to sea and safety, their attention only upon the violence they were escaping. Now this buoyant mass lay upon the sea, its weight enough to dampen the waves and diminish the swells which normally would run strongly here between the islands.

As light increased, the view was still limited. Less than a mile. Smoke and haze from the two erupting islands laid a pall of dust which was now noticed on the very skins of the refugees. A grey ash, made sticky by salt spray, clung to everyone and everything. People's hair matted with the awful combination. The very sails of the vessels became covered also, prompting the various Sea-Masters to order men up the masts to flush down the sagging fabric.

The Sea-Masters had another difficult order to give to their passengers and crew also; in the panic to board the little fleet and make offshore as quickly as possible, the parcels meant for last-minute loading were overlooked. These contained ready-to-eat foods. Enough, it was hoped then, to suffice for the planned voyage to Sht'ah-Lee. Now the voyagers must do without a breakfast until foodstuffs stored below in the holds were retrieved and prepared and cooked. Even so, there would be very little to go around over the next few days. Few would eat this day! Water there was, but no food! Even suckling babies would suffer hunger pangs on this first, long and difficult day at sea.

As the sun rose and the smoky sky allowed but a weak imitation of morning sunlight, the people woke from their exhausted sleeps in bewilderment and not a little fear. Such were the extreme circumstances that men and women, few of either having experienced life at sea, shared the after-decks to relieve themselves into the sea. Modesty was forgone in the face of necessity. Attitudes may well have been moderated in this unusual situation, at least temporarily. The Mal'lam were a people who preferred to isolate the bodily functions of the sexes. Such separation made little sense, here and now.

Throughout the morning the scabrous coating upon the sea continued to absorb the attention of the voyagers. Who could believe that the whole ocean could be so polluted? Of course, not the whole ocean was; only about one hundred square miles of it! So massive was this pumice invasion that even experienced seamen shook their heads in wonder. By midday, those open areas between the dominant floating fields of corruption began to widen. From time to time a small school of dolphin surfaced and blew in these sheltered glades of muddied water, soon to dive and search for another such surface allowing breathing space. Still the Mal'lam retained their discipline: so deep was their faith in their families, their Elders and their wisdom, and their faith in the skill of their seamen that few grumbles were heard - and none recognized.

The grey morning wore away into a brighter afternoon. The wind began to increase and the swaths of pumice became the exception rather than the rule. Shortly after midday a huge whale surfaced between two vessels and its sudden blow of compressed air startled all those in the leading canoes. The rafts rode quite some way behind them. Quickly it submerged, then as quickly raised again, half its body above the sea, descending with an almighty splash and then disappearing altogether. "Hoosh!" cried the seamen, their word which included all cetaceans, regardless of size. Indeed, *hoosh* was the sound its exhalations made.

Through the day came more cetaceans, more 'hoosh', all seeming intent upon vacating these suddenly unfriendly waters, their murky surfaces offering too-little breathing room. And so that first day dragged on. The skies slowly lightened, the sea began to clear of its surface debris, the initial shock of what had befallen these people began to soften and the horror fade away. Bits and pieces of food were passed around, some vessels affording more than others, but no one feasted that day.

The Elders and Sea-Masters conferred in worried, small groups: what must we do? How will the people cope? They needn't have worried. As they themselves had dedicated their immediate future to the prospect of hardship, so too had their brothers and sisters. Land-bound and sea-ignorant as most were, the Mal'lam were unified in their sense of oneness. If the Seamen can go hungry, so can we! Someone on each vessel somehow found the bundles of sugar cane stowed securely below the decking platforms. Tough, not at all filling, the sweet juice never-the-less succored many an appetite, its sweetness even inspiring some jokes and lightness among its consumers. It was hard to keep a Mal'lam's spirits down!

By evening all evidence of those great conflagrations behind them had disappeared into a sunset of brilliant orange, attended by cooler, stronger winds from the north which allowed a solid run toward their southeasterly course. The little fleet increased speed as it made its way into darkness, a sliver of new moon greeting them in the western sky. Day two was much different. The day dawned clear, the seas deep blue and clean. The wind however, was fitful, having deserted its nighttime blow from the north. First from the south just after dawn, the breeze swung slowly southeast, effectively halting the progress of the Mal'lam. The big, clumsy, bamboo rafts had no semblance of deftness under these conditions and labored to swing their big sails in response to the vagrant puffs of breeze. Soon their Masters ordered the long sweeps of bamboo to be manned again. They were getting nowhere. And with this many hungry souls aboard the fleet, something must be done.

Some few among the seamen attempted to propitiate the Sea Gods. Few gave much credence to those deities' existence, let alone their efficacy in aiding men upon the sea, that great expanse which divided the realms of the *Great Earth Mother*. Most preferred to call upon Her to guide them back to Her realms and safety. Hour after hour did the sweating men and women tend the oars, the seamen aboard the double-hulled canoes equally engaged with their paddles? But late afternoon saw a blessing arise from the west! A gusting wind, almost cold to some, began to blow and oars and paddles were withdrawn from the increasingly choppy water. Sails which had hung negligently from their booms all day now filled with belated pride and the fleet regained its momentum. Southeast! Southeast again!

Through the brilliant sunset, the vessels rolled upon a following sea. The speedy canoes maneuvered between the great, ungainly rafts, some pulling close by. Here and there a woman leapt into the sea and was quickly pulled aboard a canoe. Her child, needing her milk, awaited her. Until nearly dark, when the danger of sharks precluded these transfers, some family members were reunited. Then the quiet of night returned and the wind continued fair and the Mal'lam lay down to sleep with greater confidence in tomorrow. All except those Sea-Masters with *sea-sight*.

One requisite for the role of Sea-Master was a very special sensitivity to some special phenomena which occurred at sea which very few people even suspected existed. Some few possessed a special sense of hearing which could alert them to the vague but important sounds of wind, sea and surf. A very few more had a visual experience of lines of energy which emanated from different directions, revealing themselves in colors which only those so gifted could discern.

This particular sensitivity allowed these men to determine the direction of the origin of these *light-lines*, leading always to a body of land. The color patterns varied with each island and in this manner could a gifted Sea-Master plot a direct course to a known destination. Unknown land and its emanations, however, would always pose a problem. The ability, and surely the experience, to decipher these myriad emanations marked a man of extraordinary talent.

This night every Sea-Master strained himself to his limits to predict their present and then their preferred course. Only two men were always unerring in their observations and predictions: the old Sea-Master, Telan and that difficult and mysterious younger Sea-Master, Tor'na. It was Tor'na's vessel which was last to leave the beach that awful evening of desperate flight, but now he sped ahead of all other canoes, impatient with the ponderous bamboo rafts. He would continually sail nearly out of sight and then come tacking back to rejoin the fleet. Although a master sailor and navigator, he was not a popular man. But that night both he and Telan found the pulsing shafts of greenish light they were hoping for. Signs of the existence and the sure direction of Sht'ah Lee-Set. Still indistinct to all but the very gifted, the distance could be calculated. Three days sail yet. They were making decent time now.

Rain and gusty wind woke the boy, A'lan, and he opened his eyes upon the third day's dawn. He awoke hungry, but there was little to be done about that. He stretched, shivered and stood, then bent and laid his part of the blanket over his mother, his great-uncle having already vacated their communal bed before dawn. A'lan bent and looked beneath the foot of the big sail and yes, there he was, sitting far forward with his old friend, Sea-Master Telan.

A'lan then moved aft to answer the morning call of nature, stepping carefully over sleeping figures. Sleep was a refuge from boredom for many of this raft's passengers. At the stern of the vessel was a narrow ledge fenced with rope, especially constructed for this purpose. He gripped a guideline with one hand and lowered himself down onto the ledge, grinning up at the tiller-man on the steering platform. Reaching one hand into the sea he splashed water over his face and then crouched to relieve himself into the raft's wake. "Hold on tight, boy!" the tiller-man called, "We nearly lost an old man overboard this morning."

From his awkward position A'lan looked up to see the man grinning mischievously. Completing his ablutions, A'lan clambered lightly back to the main deck and again stepped and hopped over supine bodies, pleased with himself at the nimbleness he was developing while moving about a sometimes pitching deck. Real sea legs! Stooping beneath the bottom of the sail he went forward to where Tal'ma and the Sea-Master sat, having just now been joined by another man. Telan glanced over Tal'ma's shoulder, saw the boy and waved him to come forward to join them. Such an invitation to an uninitiated lad was slightly uncommon and A'lan glowed with pride and surprise. Thus began the healing of the boy's fear and sorrow, the trauma of these past days washing away from his resilient young mind.

Others of the more than sixty people aboard the crowded raft were stirring now and the aft end of the vessel became quite busy. Seamen had to caution some men to go to the leeward side of the vessel to relieve their bladders. "Silly landlubbers!" some muttered. The bows were left to the three men and the boy. A'lan stood in deference to his elders and did not presume upon that initial invitation. With one hand gripping a forestay, he listened in on the men's conversation. The younger man looked glum. A'lan soon learned that his family was aboard another raft, a common story throughout this little flotilla.

The canoes had been busy that first full day ferrying nursing mothers to babies from whom they had been separated. One young mother, Ja'eel, a beautiful girl but self-centered and terrified of the sea, refused to swim to the child from whom she had been separated. Fortunately, aboard the canoe on which the child had been placed was another mother still nursing, with milk enough for the squalling little boy. This story will see more of Ja'eel. Many other people would remain separated for the duration of the voyage but none with so care-less an attitude.

The men were discussing the seas and the threatening weather and soon A'lan's attention drifted to that sea, the now regular swell rolling toward and under the raft, lifting and lowering the great construction which rode with a marvelous lightness. A'lan found himself drifting into a oneness with that movement, that sureness and balance which seemed to him the movement of a living thing. His depression faded even further as he swayed and flexed his legs in a musical union with the graceful flexibility of the vessel.

He thrilled to his exactness in gauging the timing and response of the raft's lift and fall as if he was commanding each movement. A sudden gust of wind pulled taut the stay which he clutched tightly, the plaited cords of coconut fiber stretching beneath his grip. A'lan was unaware of the Sea-Master's gaze upon him as the old man read his rapt concentration; the blossoming joy in that intelligent face. Knowing that the boy had never before been upon the open sea, and having noticed the boy's earlier bereavement, Telan was doubly impressed.

"There stands a sail-man, old friend!" he said quietly to Tal'ma. The boy's great-uncle turned stiffly, looked up at A'lan and slowly broke into a wide smile. "The boy has the *sight,* you know!" he whispered, looking to Telan for confirmation. Telan nodded in reply, his own observations melding with what others had said or implied. A'lan was oblivious of their conversation, his attention fully focused on the sea around him. "I understand he sees the *land lights.* We must wait to see if his vision penetrates the waters. It is not the same, you know." Tal'ma turned his stiff back to look again at the boy, the very one whose inability to function adequately up in the high country had so annoyed him.

A sudden vision intruded: all sight was momentarily wiped but that of a strange view of a tall man, bearded but with a long scar on one side of a fierce face. That man, long hair plaited in the fashion of a Sea-Master, gazed intently into some unseen distance. The form of the taut sails, two upon that vessel of which he was surely Master, were of a strange design. The man's face turned and looked out of the vision at Tal'ma who, for a moment, thought he recognized the face. The man smiled a crooked smile, a result of that scar, and then the vision faded to nothingness. Tal'ma shook his head and blinked but the vision was gone. Very strange! Tal'ma was not a man given to visions.

Ahead now and to the right of the raft a school of dolphin suddenly appeared. A'lan, whose eyes had been drawn to that very spot just before they broke the surface, felt a jolt of joyous excitement. That moment forever banished his childish fear and dependency. A'lan now knew himself to be, *of the sea*! Here was excitement and knowledge and a living thing - the sea itself! The splashing, leaping dolphins seemed to signal some vague promise to the boy. A'lan stood straight-backed and released his grip on the forestay. He stood unaided as the deck beneath him pitched and rolled. This was surely his *place.*

Telan, Tal'ma and the previously glum man, all stared in mild wonder at the boy whose presence at that moment exuded some special attraction of power. It was then that Tal'ma recognized the face in his vision of moments before. Yes! The boy, A'lan, would be that man! But what of that scar? Tal'ma looked at his old friend and their eyes met in understanding. Telan too, knew that this boy was special. He now had another apprentice, one of unique talent.

Leading the little armada of rafts and canoes, the vessels scattered but remaining within sight of each other, was one was named, 'Flee the Land'; a prophetic title in fact unrelated to any prescience on the part of its Master, Tor'na. Tor'na Sea-Master was a somber man in his early thirties, of medium height and powerfully built with a face that seemed never to have countenanced a smile. His eyes burned with some inner discontent. His personality was at best abrasive, at worst aggressive and threatening. As a young initiate he had always disquieted the Sea-Master Telan, under whose tutelage this man Tor'na had learned his craft. The mature man he loathed and barely tolerated.

Most Sea-Masters were of like mind about him. No one knew what exactly had transpired between the two men, but all knew Tor'na's demeanor barely disguised a general lack of respect for his elders. And he dismissed off-hand as nearly worthless those other craftsmen who had no link with the sea. There was a feral quality about the man which belied any trust or respect on his part. Over the nearly ten years in which he had mastered his own canoe, only two men had remained with him as permanent crew and these men too were strange and disquieting. It was said that Tor'na slept with boys. This practice was not a cause for concern to the Mal'lam, in itself, because sex was treated quite openly and freely. Only infidelity on the part of married partners was frowned upon. However, rumors of violence and strange practices persisted, and the man never spoke to women except with harsh condescension. But of one thing there could no denying; Tor'na was truly a great Seaman.

Closer to the water than the decks of the massive bamboo rafts, the joining decks of the canoes were wetter. The refugee Mal'lam aboard huddled miserably together as squall after downpour assaulted them on this fourth day of their passage to Sht'ah Lee-Set. This vessel, the last to leave the dangerous beaches of

Sh'ham, was now flying in the van of the fleet, sea-spray over its bows adding to its passenger's misery. This canoe held much more than just Tor'na's morose influence though.

The young girl, Tina, was one of those aboard and only a wise Fate could have ordained her presence there. Her sorrow was diminished by the passing days but her heart ached for the nearness of her mother and oldest sister, both making the voyage aboard another vessel. When she had been rescued, stunned by that collision with the big woman on the beach, she had looked into the eyes of the powerful young Seaman, and fallen in love, as young girls do, for the strangest reasons.

But another immediately filled her vision as she turned and looked back toward the beach. It was that old woman, standing alone and smiling, waving at her departing people. Even as that young Seaman joined another man in pushing the canoe into the waves, then leapt aboard close beside her, her eyes never left the old woman's face. Their eyes remained locked together until distance broke the view. But a powerful psychic connection remained, even as the death of the island claimed the old woman, Ph'an.

Of the twelve people aboard 'Flee the Land', six were vigorous young Seamen, Tor'na included. The other six were; Tina and a five-year-old girl, whom Tina nurtured protectively, that act salving her own sorrow, and two old men and two elderly women. Late in the afternoon of that fourth day at sea, one of the old men died, simply lying back and expiring without a sound. Tina had experienced death before, but this kindly old fellow's passing plucked at a hidden chamber within her. She clung tightly to the shivering child in her arms, proof against both the cold rain and the creeping chill within her. Would this voyage never end?

The old man who died was the grandfather of that same Seaman who had rescued Tina. Al'malan was his name. Al'malan wept openly and held the frail remains tightly against his chest, stroking the grey head, gently closing the staring eyes with trembling fingers. Tina reached out with one hand and stroked the Seaman's arm, desperate lest his grief should release her own tightly held sorrow. This show of grief annoyed the Sea-Master and he growled at Al'malan. "Enough now. The old die and that's all there is to that. Wrap the old man in a mat and let's be done with it."

Then he turned away, dismissing the event as unimportant to his, therefore everyone else's purpose. His eyes were now on the closest other canoe, a possible contender for the lead in the race which only he perceived. Tor'na saw nearly all of life as a contest in which he must remain the superior. In fact, the master of that nearest vessel had in mind simply to keep pace with 'Flee the Land', no thought of competition coloring his seamanship. Each morning's waking was another beginning to a never-ending race to Tor'na Sea-Master.

The old man's body was wrapped in a sleeping mat, too short to cover his whole, tall form, allowing his feet to protrude. Something about that sight appalled Tina, the weeping grandson deepening her gloom. She began to cry softly, burying her face in the child's soaking wet hair, her tears mixing with rain and salt spray. The little girl added her wails to Tina's sobs. One grey-haired old woman moved closer and tried to still the weeping children, glancing up at Tor'na's scowl. She looked away from his face as two Seamen lowered the body off the rear of the platform and gently consigned him to the heaving sea.

That old man had been a Seaman himself, most of his life spent on and around those big bamboo rafts in the inter-island trade. He had died where and how he would have wished, but he might have desired the formal prayers and salutations which by custom attended a burial at sea. But not a hint of respect or ceremony did Tor'na allow, least of all the lowering of the sail and the lying-to while the body was weighted and sent into the depths; a white banner should be raised on the mast to signal the passing of a Seaman to any other craft in the area.

The old man's other family aboard the other vessels would not know of his passing until landfall was reached. To compound the inappropriate, Tor'na cursed violently when the body swept back against the steering paddle which Tor'na was holding, nearly unbalancing him. That curse set smoldering a painful resentment in the heart of Al'malan and angered all but those two of the crew who had been his shipmates for so long and followed him with thoughtless devotion. The two old women now set up a wailing, clinging to each other in their distress.

Never had Tina known a more miserable day in her short life, worse even than the day of her father's and sister's deaths. She sat facing the stern now, glowering at Tor'na with a fierceness which did nothing to improve his humor.

He struggled to avert his eyes from hers and the weeping old women. He finally cursed again and commanded another Seaman to take over his turn at the steering paddle. He climbed forward, keeping as far away from the young girl's condemning gaze as the small deck would allow. He sat on the forward edge of the deck, his legs dangling into the spray, brooding, the woven matting of the sail but a fragile barrier between him and the force of thought emanating from the girl. All females angered him, even little girls. Only his own mother, now long dead, had ever held any claim on his affection, if in fact he was capable of such emotion.

The struggling people on the canoes and rafts behind 'Flee the Land' were now but a day's and a night's sailing from their destination. Tor'na's keen *sight* alerted him that night to the emanations beneath the sea which heralded the massive presence of land ahead of them. He stared with his usual morose anger into the depths while behind him the young girl's anger dissipated into sleep. She lay cuddled under the mat with her little charge, that child now developing a cough. A quartering moon shone its renewal high in the western sky.

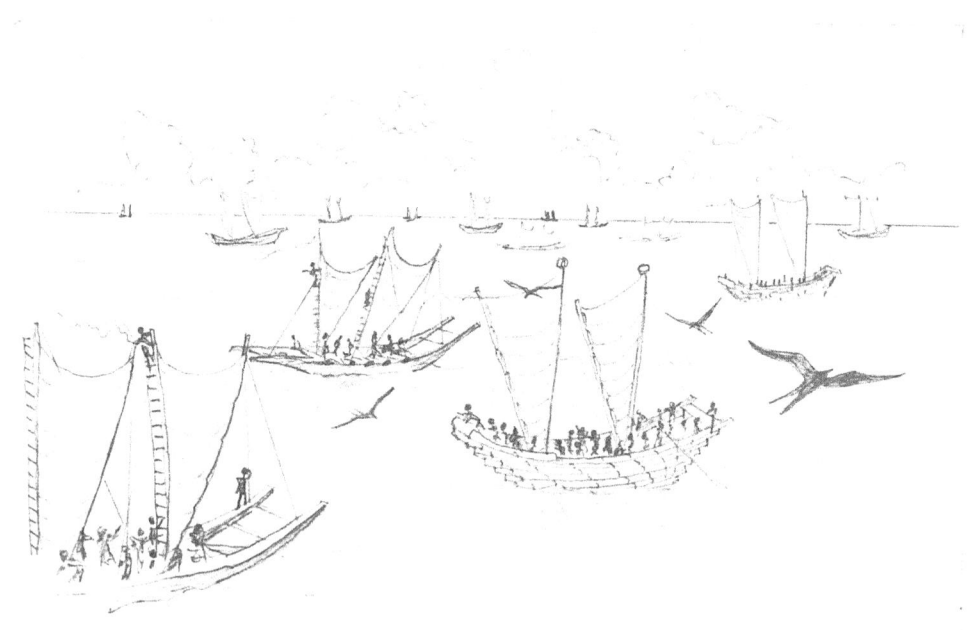

Research Notes: Impressions and General Observations

Subject: Tina Pua'lani Kaiser, Kaua'i, Summer 1972

It was early afternoon when Tina and I, our hands and feet shriveled from sitting in the water for over two hours, finally got out of the pool. The pool had warmed up as the sun got hotter, or maybe we just got used to the water temperature. Anyway, we sat on the grassy slope above the pool and decided to have some lunch. My head was still swimming with the tale she had told me. I took no notes while we were half-submerged because notebooks get soggy and hard to write on in mountainside pools. While Tina unpacked our lunch though, I quickly scribbled down some key words and phrases from her dialog. Tina was tired from all that talking too, but other than eating in silence, she seemed alright. But, Boy! A sandwich and a candy bar were like rocket fuel to that girl! As we got dressed again she turned to me and said, "D'you wanta hear about when they got to Sht'ah Lee?" Yes I did. And this time I had my notebook out and ready. She was off again . . .

Chapter Seven - Sht'ah Lee at Last

The sixth day was dawning. Seamen on each raft and canoe strained to see what lay beyond the dying night's darkness. Stars dominated the sky but to the southeast there lay a mass of lighter color. As the sky slowly brightened there began to appear a great volume of cloud piled high there. And then, with the first rays of sunlight, a shining, golden cone arose above the clouds. Volan Votu! The great mountain of Sht'ah Lee-Set! The sea resounded with the cries of joy and relief. Soon every man and woman aboard the vessels was awake and crowding toward the bows. The morning's breeze rose too and began fair from the north. It promised a steady run to their destination.

That great mountain, Volan Votu, continued to shine in the early sunlight as adjustments were made to the vessel's' sails. That northerly wind was strengthening and would now drive even the slow rafts at their optimum speed. The canoes could no longer be restrained and sped forward in joyous anticipation of this sought-after landfall. The island of Sht'ah Lee lay at the southeastern-most corner of this archipelago, which the Mal'lam had occupied now for over three hundred years. No sign of any preceding population had ever been discovered. They found and settled a virgin land. And such was to be the case for most of their Destiny.

The northwestern-most islands lay within the warm-temperate zone; chilly in winter, hot and often dry in the summer. Sht'ah Lee lay just within the sub-tropical zone, experiencing northeasterly trade winds for most of the year. Winter was short here, hardly deserving the name. Reliable rains fell throughout most of the year, creating the wide, rich forests on the windward side of the great volcano. That volcano had ceased its activity a few millennia before the arrival of the Mal'lam. Only periodic tremors and intermittent upwellings of steam signaled some residual life below.

The volcanism which had created all these islands had first established this island of Sht'ah Lee. Then it walked northward with giant steps, leaving this footprint of basalt, lava and ash far behind and undisturbed for thousands of years. The rumbling of the earth's fires sent only mild echoes south to Sht'ah Lee-Set and when the present conflagration began, only seismic-induced waves betrayed the cataclysm to the north. Some small damage occurred; vessels and some dwellings were destroyed by the massive waves which invaded only those sparsely settled coves of the dry, northwestern side of the island.

All in all, Sht'ah Lee seemed far removed from the plight of its cousin islands. When gathering its strength to leap northwestward, the great power of the volcano here stamped its fiery heels and created a land of substantial footing from which to launch its journey. Sht'ah Lee was long and triangular, high and rugged in the middle, topped with that towering peak, some of which held captive ice for all the year. Like a sail in the moist trade winds, its girdle of rock trapped the rains, drawing them down the mountainsides in cascades. These waters became streams and rivers which wound around ancient vents and cinder cones whose humps gave counterpoint to the general flatness of the coastal plain. Great forests and open grasslands painted the slopes of the mountain. Myriad leaves and blossoms raised skyward in seldom-denied confidence of cooling sustenance. Broad swamps of mangrove and scrub shouldered against sandy beaches.

The narrow end of the island, which pointed toward the progress of its successors, was rugged and sere with scrubby brush and stunted hardwood trees and grass. Rain was seldom, but sometimes came in flooding volumes which created deep gullies through the hard, dry country. Brackish wells barely sustained a few hardy fishing villages on the edge of the brooding, blue sea. The windward side of the island was host to most of the island's Mal'lam. There, drought was a seldom thing, springs and deep wells sufficing in extremity.

The Sht'ah Lee-an, as they called themselves, were rich in garden foods and the wild fruits and nuts of the forests and hills. The streams and the sea, plus their livestock, provided a wealth of protein. Also, they had the coconut palm. This invaluable plant thrived here on this island, whereas it barely survived, fruitless, on the northern Sets. Trade in the fiber of the coconut, mostly in the form of cordage, was the basis of this island's trade with its cousins to the north. That and the product of its skilled canoe-makers. Sht'ah Lee was truly a wealthy island.

And late that brilliant morning came the vanguard of the Sh'ham-an survivors, the double-hulled canoes racing for shore while some miles behind them wallowed the slow bamboo rafts, doing their best. The lead canoe, 'Flee-

The-Land', followed closely by a second canoe commanded by an older Sea-Master, surfed the swells at the narrow entrance to the 'Bay of Dolphins'.

This harbor, the largest and the center of population on Sht'ah Lee-Set, was today busy with a multitude of small canoes and two-man bamboo rafts. These tiny fishing platforms were harvesting the larger fish which had come to feed on the schools of sardines which every year at this time entered the large bay. Its narrow entrance was very deceptive for once past the portals of its headlands the bay widened into an expanse of deep and biologically rich waters, fed by underwater, freshwater springs, rich in minerals. Algae bloomed in this mineral richness; microscopic invertebrates feasted and became a soup of great richness for shrimp and other small, swimming creatures. Soon this wealth of food attracted the rest of the food chain, the sardines themselves being but another item on a larger fish's menu. The Mal'lam intervened with gusto to claim their share. Nets gathered sardines, hooks and barbed spears brought in larger predator fish. It was an auspicious day for these ragged refugees to arrive! It should have been more joyous, though.

A chant of welcome grew from those tiny vessels nearest the bay's opening, swelling in the distance as others took it up as they spied the approaching sails. "What news, my friends?" called an old man from one raft, his younger partner just pulling a net full of wriggling silver from the water. "Sh'ham-Set has been destroyed!" came the reply from the young Seaman, Al'malan, sitting to Tina's left. He and the other seamen were wielding their paddles now, Sea-Master Tor'na strongly gripping the large steering paddle at the stern of the port hull. As the steep swells pushed the big canoe through the bay's opening, Tor'na cursed under his breath at the fishermen who, eager in their concern and greeting, threatened to impede his progress.

Finally, having just missed one canoe, its two occupants paddling desperately to avoid the big hulls, Tor'na roared, "Get out of my way, you stupid fools!" So loud and harsh was that shouted command that immediately a corridor began to open as if by the force of that voice alone. No laughing banter and welcoming concern would greet this canoe in the future. Tor'na had violated the requisite ritual of arrival at a host island. The fishermen were shocked and scandalized! Tor'na's rudeness and recklessness, by association, mortified those others aboard 'Flee the Land'. Only his two long-time compatriots were unfazed. Not only had he refused to lower sail and enter the port entirely under paddle-power, reducing speed and preventing dangerous collisions, but he had called 'fools' his very brother Seamen, many of them his elders. The second canoe, some two hundred feet behind, dropped sail and began paddling. The wind and surf had drowned out Tor'na's folly and as these seamen approached the tiny rafts they were puzzled to encounter silence and scowls.

Still under full sail, 'Flee the Land' scudded through the fishing fleet and past, toward the black sand beach ahead. Calm heads prevailed, however, and as the second canoe proceeded carefully past the fishermen there came a shouted greeting, then another and another, reestablishing kindred regard. By now, Seamen in canoes not involved in the fishing left the beach and paddled toward the narrow channel of Dolphin Bay to greet the on-coming fleet. Ashore, dozens of people were making their way to the beach, waving and shouting greetings.

It was not other Seamen who had foretold this arrival, for no vessels had chanced upon the Sh'ham-an refugees. Rather, a strange, solitary old woman who had not been near the sound of the sea in over forty years predicted it, to the day. And the vision which had spurred her to a long trek across the face of the mighty mountain to spread the word was not of ships and crowded decks. It was that young girl's face and the words of another stranger which rang through her consciousness. That vision spoke of the dispossession of clan cousins and what would become a mightier exodus yet. Her people, the Mal'lam, were in great danger. By the time the little fleet sailed into safety, The Vesatan, the strange 'Wizard of the Mountains', had already returned there, back to her beloved forests.

The young boy, A'lan, stood upon the coil of anchor rope in the bow of the first raft to enter the bay. One hand grasped the forestay while the other rested confidently on his hip, his body swaying to the accelerated movement as the raft encountered the large swell now booming through the channel. He bent and looked behind, beneath the boom of the now-furled sail and again counted those sets of sail still to find this haven. Seven sets of sails were visible to him, the vessels beginning to form a long queue to enter the harbor singly. Turning to the front again he waved and called out to a dozen men who paddled a fast outrigger canoe, closing quickly on the raft from the starboard side. The low canoe disappeared momentarily in the trough of a wave and then quickly reappeared, a man standing now in the bow, leaning on a paddle for balance.

"Welcome, Mal'lam!" he shouted, "Our home is your home!" Another swell nearly hid the canoe and the man appeared to be standing alone on the water. And then that canoe was broadside to the huge raft, the paddlers stroking powerfully, the steersman turning the canoe and bringing them skillfully alongside, matching the raft's speed. Strong hands grabbed the side of the raft and held it, the canoe becoming a small appendage as the raft rose over the last large swell and coursed forward into calmer waters.

"What news, Seaman?" the standing man asked and then leaped aboard the raft in one easy movement, his outstretched hand taken in response by another Seaman." Sad news, my friend." Telan Sea-Master answered, coming up behind Al'an who moved aside to let him greet his old friend, Orn'ta. Orn'ta Sea-Master was a squat, powerfully built man. His long hair was plaited into two thick braids, one hanging over each ear; the Sea-Master's badge of authority. His hair was sprinkled with grey and his face was deeply lined from years at sea. Telan Sea-Master continued as the friends gripped each other's arms in a Seaman's greeting.

"Sh'ham-Set is no longer home to the Mal'lam! We have come as homeless ones, as did our forbears. We bless you for your welcome, Clansman." A'lan thought he heard the older man's voice nearly break with emotion. The native Seaman turned his eyes from his friend's face momentarily and looked among the other Sh'ham-an around him on the raft's deck, his own eyes sad. He placed his hand over his heart in a quick gesture, then turned back to Telan and smiled broadly. "Well, my old friend, your people are safe now. Soon you will lay your sorrows aside and feast with us."

He looked again at the exiles around him, and still smiling said loudly, "We are cousins and we have prepared for your coming. There will be no more hunger or thirst from this day forward!" With that he turned and with agility surprising for his age, leapt back aboard his outrigger canoe. He sang out to his paddlers, "Pull my brothers. Lead our kin to their new home!" This impressive Seaman, chief Sea-Master among the Sht'ah Lee-an, now raised his voice and led a paddling song, quickly taken up by his eleven compatriots. The canoe was swiftly steered away and with powerful unison its crew drove toward the welcoming black sand beach. With this song, A'lan was introduced to the new home which would nurture and direct him toward his very special Destiny.

As the fast canoe pulled away toward the shore, a large school of dolphin which had entered the bay to share in the feast of sardines, leaped and rolled between the two vessels as if wishing to add harmony to the paddlers' song. Tears of sadness, hope and relief flowed on the bamboo raft as it approached the safe haven of black sand. The eyes of the boy remained clear and wide, devouring the sight of a new land, a new set to the sun; all future, all possibility! And it was wise Fate again which brought this lad to this unique island at this time, for already a movement was underway among the Sh'tah Lee Seamen.

This part of the Clan Sh'ta'ha, when, those many generations ago, the Mal'lam had discovered this archipelago, continued their exploration until they had found this southernmost island. While their clan cousins found that now-destroyed island of Sh'ham most agreeable and immediately stopped and settled, the Sht'ah Lee-an were still restless. Perhaps some vessels continued on even after this big island was reached. If so, they were lost and forgotten now. But still the chants and songs of this people's history remained unchanged, a living reminder of the desire for the open sea and endless horizons. That spirit of adventure remained an ember, banked now for eleven generations. But recent events had breathed upon that spark and now it began to glow brightly in the hearts of the Seamen of Clan Sht'ah'ha. The arrival of their cousins, many of them also excellent sailors, injected urgency into the ongoing debate among the elder Seamen: should we return to the search of the southern seas? More often now the answer was, yes!

A'lan came ashore with a sudden reckoning. On his third trip to and from the bamboo raft, carrying goods and belongings, he paused before jumping down onto the black sand and stood looking up at the snow-capped mountain in the distance. Then his gaze swept the beach from left to right. There was what excited him. Double-hulled canoes of marvelous craftsmanship lay beneath thatched canoe-sheds or rode gently on the small waves reaching the shore. That great peak and deep forests were not his métier; indeed no firm ground would satisfy the desire which this recent, inflicted journey had instilled in him. A'lan would be a Seaman! He had not one doubt. He happily shouldered the last parcel which his mother had asked for. Precious herbs and plants they were, so carefully stored aboard the raft those many days ago. He would tell his mother soon of his decision and he was certain of her thoughtful response. He smiled again to think that convincing great-uncle Tal'ma would be easy. No more mountain climbing.

The Sha'ham-an were provided with temporary shelters among the groves of large-leafed nut trees which spread their cooling mantle along the brow of the black dunes above the beach. Piles of freshly cut poles and thatching and cordage for lashing were already on-site, that old forest-woman's warning having been heeded. Such was the Mal'lam's faith in their seers that no warning went unheeded. Other people with *sight* had added their predictions also. By late afternoon the last of the refugee vessels had landed and been unloaded. Curious islanders, most never having seen a bamboo raft before, the journey here too far for practical trading voyages by raft, gathered around to inspect them. These great constructions, now well cured by seawater, would be disassembled and utilized in constructing the new settler's homes, creating a new design for dwellings.

A total of four hundred and five people had survived the harrowing journey. Ten people had died on the passage. Mostly those were elderly, their hearts broken by the violent uprooting of their lives, the cold and damp causing many cases of pneumonia. One child fell overboard unnoticed and was lost, one young woman died in childbirth, no experienced midwife being aboard that particular vessel. In each case the tradition of lowering sail and hoisting a white pennant was observed. Each that is, excepting on Tor'na's canoe.

Word of that event and of his breach of etiquette upon entering the bay buzzed among the exhausted Mal'lam. Telan Sea-Master and a group of Clan elders strode angrily to where Tor'na and his crew and some volunteers among the native islanders were hauling his canoe up above the high water mark. Unlike the crews of the other canoes, these men seemed to ignore the needs of their fellow Sh'ham-an and tended only to their own.

Already Tor'na had absorbed the abuse of the master of the second canoe into the bay. Tor'na had only grinned wickedly, and ignored him with a malign subtlety. That Sea-Master had finally turned and marched away in disgust, unable to comprehend this mad Seaman's state of mind. This last behavior was all that the young Seaman, Al'malan, could tolerate. It was customary for a Seaman to attach a shell amulet, their personal identification and sign of rank as it were, to the gunwale of the vessel they were crewing on. After the other Sea-

Master had stomped away from the scene, incredulous, Al'malan untied and removed his amulet with an angry flourish. The memory of his grandfather's sorry death and sorrier treatment by Tor'na was now unbearable. He turned on Tor'na with a torrent of anger and condemnation.

While the other crewmen looked away in embarrassment, Al'malan poured his grief and frustration onto Tor'na. The younger man, a head taller and much heavier than Tor'na, seemed near to striking him in his anger. Tor'na stood with arms crossed, his body relaxed, confident, invincible in his arrogance. He said to Al'malan, who appeared near to tears, "Are you finished now? Good. Now hear me." And with arms still crossed, he leaned slightly toward Al'malan, his face a mask of grinning malevolence. "Your anger, your words mean nothing to me, boy. *You* mean nothing to me, you simpering piece of sea-slug shit!" Al'malan was seen to struggle mightily with himself to resist the urge to pounce on the man and smash him. Tor'na's two favorites moved a bit closer, anticipating violence. Without taking his eyes off Al'malan's face, Tor'na raised one hand and the two men stopped their advance. "So, go back to your mommy, you weak turd, and stay off the sea. You're not man enough to be a Seaman. You're only fit to suck your mommy's breast and whimper and cry!"

Few men could have withstood such abuse without striking out. And to deliver such a tirade was shocking. Tor'na was blatant in his attempt to force a fight with this young man. All of this was so *un-Mal'lam*. People simply did not abuse others in this manner. Everyone within earshot of this scene stopped what they were doing and gaped open-mouthed. Al'malan, however, suddenly seemed to relax, a curious half-smile replacing his red-faced fury of moments before. Some inner stability had returned. Neither defeated nor intimidated by the man's cold intensity, he gave a rueful smile and shook his head, saying, "Tor'na Sea-Master, you are an unfortunate man. You seek enemies when your only enemy lies within your own heart. I leave you in peace. This time."

Al'malan turned and strode away, swinging his small chain of shells around his finger as if he had no concern in the world. His stride betrayed neither defeat nor anger. His face registered no emotional involvement at all. He seemed to have confronted, borne and dismissed the conflict. He now proceeded to more important considerations. He had a wife and child to find on this crowded, busy beach. This trait of character would lead him to great adventure and responsibility, and no little sorrow. "Go! Get out of my sight!" Tor'na shouted after him, "You make me sick!" and he turned and spit onto the sand. In his unreasoning arrogance, Tor'na thought he had won a victory.

Tor'na's confrontation with the Elders, by contrast, was an anticlimax. To the stern words of the Master, Telan, he replied with a cold silence and haughty dismissal, busying himself with tightening lashings on his beloved canoe, casting mocking glances at the outraged Elders. When he turned away from them and urinated onto the sand, those Elders simply looked at each other and accepted the obvious: Tor'na was incorrigibly set upon a course of alienation from those of his craft and indeed, from his very people. The man had no living family which might help persuade him to sensibility. Indeed, when the great, terrible seismic wave of those years ago had taken his only relative, his mother, might that have been when his madness began? No, his truculence and antisocial behavior had been commented upon for more years than that.

The older Seamen walked away with sad resignation. Tor'na Sea-Master had gone mad! And so he would become known; 'Tor'na the Mad'! They would consult Elders of the other crafts but the consensus and outcome were inevitable. After facing a tribunal, Tor'na would face exile! Exile, for any sane Mal'lam, was soul-death. But Tor'na Sea-Master was not a sane man. Nor was he stupid and his sense of self-preservation was already at work formulating a plan for preempting the decision of the leaders of his Clan. He was already setting a new and irrevocable course which would see him sail against the tide of reason. But for now the Clan Seamen-Elders had other things to consider. Every end-of-voyage for Mal'lam Seamen was worthy of a celebration, and especially the end of this unique voyage. There would be feasting and joy tonight. Already fires were being lit on the sands. Soon earth ovens would be prepared. Six days of near hunger would be assuaged for the refugees.

Chapter Eight - Early, Dangerous Days

The young Tina, separated for long, miserable days from her mother and sister, waited anxiously for that last bamboo raft to be beached. She had been among the first to arrive on that hated man's canoe, "Flee the Land" and for hours she had run to greet each vessel, hoping to find her loved ones there. When finally the last big raft rode in on the afternoon swell, she could see her mother waving from the bow. She had clung desperately to them both, tears and wails matching many others on this bittersweet afternoon. Sht'ana Herb-Mistress and her oldest daughter hugged the child to them.

After so much horror and sadness, these tears began the healing. But even now, with love and relief overwhelming, Tina's special sensitivity reached outward to taste the emanations of this new land. Her proclivity for adventure and newness exceeded even her childish fears and the passions of the moment, pulling her on an unswerving course toward an early maturity. "Sweet child!" that voice within whispered, "I am uncle and aunt to your heart and cousin to your future. Find peace with us, for here will be your forming, your early destiny. Welcome, child of Sh'ham-Set!"

Tina shuddered at the strength of the message, mostly uncomprehending it. Mother and sister renewed their hugs, misinterpreting that shudder and the little girl happily surrendered to them. Her child's dependency and fragility was succored now and Tina allowed their solicitude to overwhelm her. Time enough to grow up. Similar scenes rendered tears from the native Mal'lam as they stood watching and their hearts melted into the pain of the refugees, helping to salve it. Mal'lam embraced stranger and soon there were no strangers. Laughter blossomed among the mingling group's sorrow, led by the squeals of young children as they discovered new playmates. What father, holding a giggling child, could resist this happy call for a confident tomorrow? Night beneath a quarter moon, full bellys and bone weariness saw most soon sleeping exhaustedly. 'Tor'na the Mad' slept fitfully.

The memories of these past days were dominated, for Tin-an, by that of that one, handsome young Seaman. He who had scooped her from certain death and set her into a canoe. He who had confronted the awful Tor'na on the beach, when she was within hearing. Al'malan Seaman was the girl's first infatuation and for days, seeing his powerful figure passing, her heart would leap and thunder within her thin chest. Mother and sister, seeing the signs, chuckled and passed knowing looks. The man was married and had one child. Tina discarded this knowledge and the distance in years between them, devoting herself to daydreams of 'one day'.

Only one person was able to confuse her devotion. A'lan. His presence too caused pubescent ardor to arise within her. Although the boy brushed aside her attentions, still too young to understand such fascination and considering her but another silly, giggly girl, still he was unfailingly polite to her. He just avoided her when possible. For her part, she found her dreams divided between the two. One morning, passing Al'malan on a path, she addressed him as A'lan, and immediately paled. So great was her embarrassment that she ran crying into the bush. The gentle man, never suspecting what lay in her heart and mind, shook his head in puzzlement. He continued on his way, vaguely hoping not to father any daughters.

The strange, internal voices which imposed themselves upon Tina at unbidden times, coupled with her infatuations, distracted the girl to the point where her mother decided that something must be done. Aware of the girl's sensitivity to the *sight* and fearing that her natural impishness might degrade into misbehavior, Sha'lat decided that she must now have her attentions diverted by some activity which would reinstate discipline. Sha'lat had sought out a woman of whom she had heard much to envy, were she an envious person. Instead, upon meeting Shen'ha Herb-Mistress, the two became instant friends. Shen'ha was a woman of quiet and powerful presence; slight and small-boned, her stature belied a strength of body as well as character.

Yearly, she led the arduous trek to the mountains to gather those valuable plants which grew only at high altitudes. These treks were just as Tal'ma had made for most of his life, on Sh'ham-Set. Shen'ha's fame sprang from her unique ability to properly balance the various properties of those rare plants and mushrooms and lichens; their use as catalysts in herbal concoctions was a very exacting science, requiring also a special intuitiveness. The slow growth and long-life of many of those plants assured a high concentration of their particular active ingredients. That journey was due to begin again soon and Sha'lat found no difficulty in persuading her new friend to allow her and her daughters to accompany her entourage.

Tina would soon find another distraction, this one imposed upon her. In spite of Shen'ha's talent for blending herbs and other healing ingredients, such skill did not extend to her abilities as a cook. Her well-fed son, Shen'ham, a boy of Tina and A'lan's age, sought most of his meals at the meal mats of kin or playmates' parents. Shen'ha only smiled sweetly at any comment on her lack of culinary skills. "Let those who enjoy too much spice and over-indulgence do so. They seem to come to me when their stomach hurts." So much for that. The two women shared many traits: forthrightness, especially with them both on one side of an argument or in remonstrance. They could be formidable. They also shared a similar sense of humor and it was chubby Shen'ham who often bore the brunt of their teasing when he was caught shoveling some other cook's creations into his greedy mouth.

When Tina was informed that she was now old enough to accompany her mother on the 'gathering', the child baulked and argued and even attempted tears. But her mother's firm, "You *will* accompany us child!", brought down the flimsy construction of reasons-why-not. With the minimum of pouting the girl worked herself into a genuine enthusiasm. Such was Tina's nature that reason, and her response to it, was always nearby. And no one could gather and exhibit enthusiasm like this young girl. Sht'ana Herb-Mistress, sadly now Tina's only sibling, would also accompany the herbalists up to the mountains. Sht'ana lacked a facility for the *sight*, such as possessed by her mother and sister, but she nevertheless possessed a strong personality in her own right. Always cheerful and willing, gentle and understanding of others, she was a welcome companion on gathering expeditions as well as in the everyday life of her village. It was her sweet nature and sensibility which had helped her mother and sister through their days of grief, shedding her own tears away by herself.

Aboard the raft, when some mothers were too seasick to properly tend their children, it was Sht'ana who cared for them both. It was also her industry and neatness which now organized their rough, temporary dwelling into a comfortable home. Tina's easily distracted energy and her mother's diffidence about the state of her house was more than compensated for by Sht'tana's quiet competence. It puzzled her mother though that no queue of suitors attended her oldest daughter. The girl's personality and character were carried gracefully in a comely body and shone from a pretty face. And yet, at the age of twenty years, when most girls were married or spoken for, she seemed to show no interest in finding a proper husband. Sha'lat knew that she had had lovers, as all young women did. She herself had instructed her daughter in the preparation of contraceptive potions, knowledge necessary for a Herb-Mistress, which had been Sht'ana's own choice of craft. Yet Sha'lat worried lest her daughter should extend her reluctance to mate for too long - too late to find a proper match. She need not have concerned herself. The young woman had her own plans which she kept well to herself. She also possessed a determination which in another person more demonstrative might have appeared fierce.

Nearly one month after the arrival of the Sh'ham-an to this island, the newcomers were settling in, difficulties few and disputes fewer. On the day when the sliver of new moon would appear, Herb-Master and Mistress cousins were busy preparing for their journey. Newcomer and native alike packed food, spare clothing, blankets and empty packs into cylindrical baskets which were used on this island for heavy hauling. Made from narrow strips of a thin-walled bamboo, they were both capacious and lightweight.

The three Herb-Masters would carry the heaviest loads, both up and down the long journey. As well, with their obsidian-tipped spears they would protect the company from the ever-present danger of wild pigs. These large animals, feral kin to their smaller domestic cousins found around the villages, were littering this time of year and could be extremely dangerous. Fortunately, they remained below the tree line, little food available for them in the heights. The trekkers would be free of that danger once they left the deep forests. On the open grasslands there was little danger except from lightning strikes and sudden, freezing storms. Yes, it was truly a yearly adventure.

Tal'ma Herb-Master, Chief Gatherer of the Sh'ham-an, sat watching the preparations, resisting his usual urge to direct, strangely relieved that he was no longer required. An insistant stinging had invaded his chest recently, actually its first pangs coming while aboard the raft on the long voyage. Tal'ma was resigning himself to an impending passing from this world and he nurtured few regrets. Each day in his morning meditations he called forth the quietness which had so well guided him for his long life. That stillness accompanied him now, sitting apart from the others beneath a large, shady nut tree. A cooling breeze wafted up from Dolphin Bay and whisked fine, grey hairs across his forehead. He didn't bother to brush them back but chuckled to himself that he should be grateful that he still had any there at all. As he watched the herbalists at their work he allowed no longing or sadness to block the blessings he silently extended toward them.

Sha'lat looked up at the old man, perhaps sensing his love, and smiled at him. She turned then and spoke to her youngest child. Tina looked toward Tal'ma, nodded, smiled and rose and came toward him with a gourd held in front of her. She stopped in front of him, a shallow bow it was, in deference to his age and position. "Mama says you might like some of this tea, Tal'ma Herb-Master." Formality of speech and address was impressed upon the young and followed throughout their lives. Tal'ma smiled his thanks, taking the proffered gourd and its cool contents with real gratitude. He drank quickly, then corked the container and handed it back to the girl. "Thank you Tina-an. That was most gracious of you and your mother." The girl beamed and bowed more deeply this time, then turned and skipped back to her mother's side. Sha'lat smiled again at the old man, her teacher and mentor in her craft, and returned to her work. Tal'ma sighed and leaned back against the coarse bark of the tree trunk and was soon asleep. His dreams were sweet and distant; scenes of Sh'ham-Set and a mountain which no longer existed.

Lana'ma Herb-Mistress visited the men and women in their preparations, chatting amiably with them, busying herself tying bundles for them. She would not make this journey, though she longed to explore the interior of this rich land. Her skills were needed here among the rest of her people more now than ever, now that her uncle was visibly ailing. It was her expertise at surgery and wound healing which might be needed at any time. The local people had their own herbalists who were as competent but now this island had four hundred more people to look after.

The health of the refugees was surprisingly good. Two other of the aged Sh'ham-an had died since their arrival but no younger persons or infants seemed to be in any danger. Her thoughts went back to that last conversation she had had with her own mother, Ph'an, only hours before the fatal conflagration and fearful exodus. "It is a venom emanating from the land itself!" she had said, "It was that poison which killed your cousin, Sh'kal-an. How it invades, I do not know. It is insidious, daughter, and it is well that our people leave this beautiful home at this time. Even though the mountain might not erupt. Which it will!"

But now Lana'ma allowed herself a cautious opinion based upon the revitalization of the Sh'ham-an on this new island. Perhaps that poison had lain only upon their precious Sh'ham-Set and that no such infection would follow them here. Even previously sickly babies whose lives were so severely tested on that long, cold voyage were thriving now. At least most of them. And most infants grew robustly, their mother's milk increasing in volume and richness. The thought comforted her and now she joined in the chanting of the women, a song whose origin lay somewhere in the dim past of these island's first settlers.

"Though far you be, and high and rare, we come for you with hearts free! Ascend, ascend we gatherers, to mountains 'neath the snowline!

Where air is thin and nights so cold, your magic grows upon the ground.

The healer's cup is but half full until your magic shares it's filling.

Sweet or bitter, by pinch or grain, your essence is our blessing!

We bless the land and cloud above which nurtures you, our loving cousin."

While Lana'ma Herb-Mistress sang, others sat in council elsewhere. A'lan sat with his new Sh'tah Lee-an friend, Shen'ham, beyond the circle of Seamen. The Sea-Masters sat in the inner ring, age and special competence determined the remaining distribution. Among those chosen to attend the inner circle was the young Seaman, Al'malan, recognized by the Sea-Masters as a person of note, one of special quality as a Seaman. A few Elders of other crafts sat outside the Seamen's circle, waiting to be called upon for their valued opinions. A year ago, A'lan's great-uncle Tal'ma would have attended, but now the old man was excused at his own request. They all were there to discuss the problem of the man, Tor'na Sea-Master. The process of censure was intentionally a slow one, hope being that the person in question would have acted in some momentary aberration and that sense and reconciliation would maintain. But even now the man continued to scorn the conference and its implications.

Two others also, his long-time crewmen, had been summoned but had also assumed their leader's intransigence, seeming to prefer Tor'na's fate. They too might be implicated and exiled for complicity in his arrogant affront. That three men at once should be in defiance of Mal'lam tradition was unprecedented. In the long oral history of the Mal'lam there did exist memory of convening's of the Seamen in which some individuals, refusing to conduct themselves in a reasonable manner, were dealt with severely and finally. If, after long days of consideration, during which the man might see sense and apologize and repent of his actions, that did not occur, then the offender was banished. Banishment, in the first case, consisted of being sent into the hinterlands, well away from the sea. No contact with any of the person's kin, nor anyone at all, was allowed for ten full moons. Should this sentence be violated, the result was complete and irrevocable banishment from the communities of the Mal'lam.

This terrible punishment consisted of the accused and convicted person being towed far out to sea in a single canoe, supplied with meager rations of food and water, and cast loose upon the swells, death being the sure result. Most had, according to legend, immediately plunged overboard and drowned themselves rather than suffer the total isolation of exile. But first, the individual who was sentenced to total banishment was dragged, usually kicking and screaming, before the whole of the Elders Council. His sentence was formally pronounced before all assembled and then a circle of shaped stone, heated to skin-scorching temperature, was pressed quickly against each cheek, marking for life the face of the offender.

The oral histories did mention a few men who became outlaws, preying on individuals and isolated communities. When apprehended, their end was swiftly brutal. The Mal'lam, for the most part of their history a peaceful people who sought solutions to disputes in a highly stylized form of mediation and debate, had been forced to apply means of controlling insanity with another insanity: institutionalized execution. But that recourse to fatality was immediate and unstructured, those men tracking down the offender and killing him suffering great pain and guilt themselves. Fortunately, the histories reported such aberrations as so remote as to be almost beyond consideration. Almost.

But on this day, the discussion included other considerations; in particular, the violent geological upheavals to the north. Should they continue, and vessels arriving within the past week from the north reported just such events, how would that affect the Mal'lam living here on Sht'ah Lee? Many more non-Clan refugees might well arrive here on this quiescent land. How would a sudden influx of people affect life here? Already, some individuals with clairvoyance were warning of further disasters. Such warnings were not to be taken lightly. Indeed, the Laws of the Mal'lam were not to be taken lightly, nor compromised by anti-social behavior.

This all led to a renewed call for the Mal'lam to seriously consider voyages of exploration to find a new home, one which could accommodate the estimated five thousand souls who inhabited this now- fragile archipelago. With this additional pressure upon the Elders, the need to reinforce the codes of behavior encouraged their usually long and convoluted discourse to rather quickly reach a consensus. Perhaps no more than two more days would be required for the Elders to reach a decision. But a shock was in store for those assembled: events were soon to occur, the repercussions of which would forever alter the social character of the Mal'lam.

Tor'na had been informed the day before that he would be called before the Council of Sea-Masters. Just what day and hour would be formally conveyed to him later. On the morning of this day he had risen at daybreak, leaving his two old comrades sleeping. Also still sleeping was one other, a native of this island named Mal'atan. That young man lay beneath Tor'na's own blanket. Considered strange and unbalanced by his own people, he had heard about the obnoxious Sh'ham-an Sea-Master and thought that he'd better look into this interesting person.

He and Tor'na shared an immediate attraction. The night of their first meeting they had lain together on a rough pallet far from the others. After their lovemaking they had spent hours discovering that they shared a warped vision. They pledged a singleness of purpose and a plan for action. Outcasts by nature and inclination, they conspired to defy all conventions and set upon a path of rule and conquest. They bared their mutual loathing for all women, the old, the presumptions of the Elders and, in general, the whole of their society. They spoke in earnest of bloodletting, rape and destruction in the midst of a world in which such things were terrible nightmares. Inconceivable! They finally fell to sleep together, to dream of unmitigated evils.

Mal'atan, nephew of Orn'ta Sea-Master, was by that man's urging convinced to train as a Seaman. He was a poor student. Since childhood he had been a worry to his kin. Inattentive and frivolous, he could be counted on to disrupt any gathering, no matter how formal and important within the context of his community. As an initiate to the craft of seamanship he was disrespectful of his tutors, applying an obvious intelligence and cleverness to causing uproar. Effeminate and shrill, his obvious homosexuality dominated his approach to most subjects. His aggressive sexuality and constant references to shafts and orifices, of which there are many on a paired-hull canoe, tried the patience of his teachers and alienated his peer group of budding Seamen. Their earnest attempt to learn their chosen craft was constantly compromised by Mal'atan's foolishness.

After a year in which he learned but little of how to handle a vessel, he was unofficially dismissed from the ranks of the trainees. He couldn't have cared less. And with no compunction to fulfill any discipline, he began to roam about the island, gathering a coterie of followers with similar proclivities. These boys and some young men older than he, he bullied and dominated, establishing himself as leader of a clique which caused much disruption and outrage across the island of Sht'ah Lee. Now seventeen years old, he was nearing the age when his community would begin to respond to him and his gang as adult incorrigibles. This situation could eventuate in some serious repercussions for the offenders.

He also developed a reputation for violence and was said to carry a beautifully crafted obsidian knife that had been stolen from a gravesite. This, if true, would be a shocking violation of a sacred institution. To disturb the bones and valued artifacts interred with them was tantamount to assault. But none could prove the charge. Although some claimed to have seen and recognized the knife, no one dared to desecrate a grave to find out if such was missing.

Mal'atan was indeed a clever boy; too clever for his own good and becoming even more blatant in his misdemeanors. He could no longer even claim the affection of his mother. That long-suffering woman had as much as disowned him, had there been such a legal precedent in Mal'lam society. This warped young man knew that his day of reckoning was approaching. The arrival of the Sh'ham-an and his now-beloved Tor'na was a stroke of Fate which even his vivid imagination had not conjured. He knew now that his Destiny was assured.

Tor'na had awakened after only three hours of sleep, too stimulated by this new experience of a kindred soul to complete his rest. He rose and with gentleness he'd never displayed to anyone before, laid his blanket over the sleeping form of his lover. Now he walked purposefully through the heavy underbrush behind the beach, leaving Mal'atan asleep at their trysting place. As he walked he began to form a plan which would forever confirm his madness and seal his doom.

Tor'na recalled with wicked glee how he had acquired the very special knife he now carried on his hip, the wooden sheath covered in sharkskin. It had been in the trading season, late summer, on the island of Shalan'la at the, 'Thieves Markct', it was called. Here gathered not only the traders of all the different Clans, but temporarily resided some of those few rascals which even Mal'lam society had to admit to. It was at a game of chance, played with shells and bones, that he had beaten an old Seaman of another Clan, time after time. Drunk now, on palm wine imported from Sht'ah Lee, the old man had bet his last item of value. It was an heirloom, carefully preserved in pristine condition by the aged Seaman. Double-edged, its handle was carved Sperm Whale tooth. The incisions on the handle, the old man explained, slurring his words and betraying tears as he handed Tor'na his prize, were very old. So old, in fact, that the meaning of them was lost even to the wisest of his Clan.

Tor'na had immediately decided that he had come into possession of not only a beautiful knife but messages of deep and mysterious meaning. Over the intervening years he had contrived his own meaning. To Tor'na, these were messages for him alone; some wondrous Fate had sent him confirmation of what he had always fantasized. Tor'na Sea-Master was destined to be a leader of his people; a great ruler! Those old, forgotten symbols spoke to him in a language only he could understand. And lately, voices had begun to accompany them. Tor'na was indeed sliding into madness.

Reaching the wide, black sandy strip of beach, he turned right toward the basalt cliffs which bordered the beach at that end. At the base of the headland he strode out onto the rocky ledge which extended some sixty feet into the bay. He stopped and picked up a partially burned stick from the remains of someone's fire. Then he went to a shallow rock pool set well back from the surf. The sea was calm this morning and within the confines of Dolphin Bay the water was like an inland lake, almost glassy, like the blade of his knife. He knelt and gazed at his reflection in a shallow pool.

Tor'na considered himself handsome, though his morose scowling had yet to convince any others of that opinion. Perhaps now though, one young man would agree. He again admired what he considered a perfect face. In secret, whenever possible, he had similarly sought out glassy water in which to admire himself. Now he finalized his plan to destroy that perceived perfection by his own hand. "I swear by the *'light-lines'* beneath the sea, that no Mal'lam shall mark my face in their stupid judgments!" Scenes of branding, of being forcibly restrained and having that hot piece of obsidian pressed against his beautiful face filled his mad mind's-eye."If I must wear the marks of banishment, then, by the Gods, those marks shall be of my own design!" Tor'na began to laugh in a hollow, chilling tone, causing a small flock of shore birds to rise in fright and fly off down the beach. Bending over the pool again he stared at his reflection for long moments. Then he rubbed charcoal dust onto his index finger from the half-burned stick. With the charcoal he made a black slash across his forehead, studied the effect in the pool, then with the other hand splashed water on his face to remove that first design.

Waiting for the ripples to flatten into a mirror again, he began a disturbed cackle, rapid and demented, devoid of any recognizable humor. Next he blackened his finger again slowly and deliberately, peering intently at his reflection, deciding. He inscribed a vertical line on each cheek this time. Just where the mark of the judgmental brand would strike him. "No!" And once more he washed away the charcoal, again chuckling madly as he waited for the water to still. The final test marks satisfied him. He had laid two black lines onto his face, one on each side of his nose, beginning at his nostrils and curving off diagonally down to the corners of his mouth. "Yesss! Yes. Yes!" A snarl of contempt would be forever inscribed.

Tor'na's eyes gleamed intensely as he considered how the ultimate effect would portray the power and threat of his being. He visualized the scars first as scabbed and swollen, eliciting sympathy from his two compatriots and now, his lover, Mal'atan. But more than sympathy; admiration for his courage in inflicting his own pain. And then, time would soften the wounds to a dark pink grimace, which would announce his terrible character to the world! "So it will be!" he shouted. Plunging the stick defiantly into the pool like a weapon, he rose and began to gather driftwood fuel for a fire. He built a small, hot blaze near the base of the cliff and waited for the coals to settle into a red, shimmering glow.

Tor'na had seen this type of surgical cut performed before, indeed had utilized the method once himself when a crewman had accidentally impaled himself with a barbed harpoon. That time he had heated an obsidian blade too much, causing it to shatter in half lengthwise. The resulting edge still attached to the handle though was superbly sharp. He had made the rather deep incision successfully, the hot stone cauterizing the blood flow. He must be very careful now not to repeat that mistake with this very special tool.

When the coals had reached their optimum heat, he was ready. With deep breaths and a quiet chant to an ancient Sea-God, he prepared himself. He knelt in a sand-filled hollow near the fire, laid the blade of the knife over a flat stone, the blade just over the glowing coals and sat back on his heels to wait a few moments. He knew that it must be hot enough to strike twice and burn deeply each time. Even in his demented state, he recognized a niggling doubt as to how much pain he could withstand. The branding must be quick and sure, with no time to reheat the blade; time in which his courage might fail him; time in which reason might prevail.

Closing his eyes he began a ritual taught to him by his Master, Telan, the man he now despised. He visualized the rays of light, those rays of 'sea-light' which only a few such as he were able to discern. The *sea-sight*. He drew those imagined rays into a focus which centered upon his navel; glowing, shimmering. He could actually feel their heat as he drew them up inside him, up his spine and into his chest. The power! The power was there. Solidifying his intent into a deed already done and finished, pain already borne, he opened his eyes. Looking up the beach he saw only a group of children playing far away. He glanced up to the top of the cliff where someone might be watching the bay for signs of fish. No one.

Tor'na took one deep breath, exhaled slowly and leaned forward and took the knife from off the flat stone. The carved handle was hot but not too hot and he gripped it securely in his right hand. He raised the blade toward his face, paused, and then struck. That scalding stroke from nostril to jowl was applied with almost inhuman control. Ignoring the shock of the pain but allowing himself a quick intake of air, he held that breath and pausing only a second, struck again. His control failed him on that stroke though, the sizzle and the stench of burning flesh forcing a shorter stroke. He now had two, uneven wounds which, when healed, would be a signature of the absurdity of the act.

Tor'na sat back on his heels again, his buttocks resting on them and he puffed and blew, willing his mind to ignore that searing pain. He visualized the act of penetration he had shared with his lover, recalled the strangeness of his gesture of laying his blanket over the boy, exalting in his victory over his life-long sense of loneliness and frustration. "No man such as I has ever existed!" he hissed, that prolonged exhalation carrying away the worst of the nearly unbearable pain. Tor'na, soon to be called, 'Tor'na the Mad' by his people, bent and swept sand over the coals. As he smothered the fire he was vaguely, distantly aware of some voice crying within him. Such dedication to establishing an almost inhuman uniqueness must exact a toll. Tor'na fought back the specter of madness.

He had always defeated that weak, disabling emotion before, and nearly every other emotion with it. He would succeed again. There was no place in his mind for love or compassion, least of all toward himself. Tears flowed uncontrollably from his eyes, bidden not by emotion but by physiology. He wiped his eyes repeatedly, his fingers venturing cautiously to his cheeks but retreating when they reawakened pain. Then he sheathed his precious knife, that tool which now more than ever possessed special qualities to this man. The insistent throbbing of that pain translated itself into an exaggerated swagger as he strode back up through the scrub toward where his lover, his beautiful Mal'atan, still lay sleeping.

Research Notes: Impressions and General Observations

Subject: Tina Pua'lani Kaiser, Kaua'i, Summer 1972

The shadows were long now and Tina was tired. So was I. I had writer's cramp and my ballpoint pen was nearly out of ink. My God! Had we really been here for six hours? Oh dear! Tutu Kinau would probably be furious with us. Especially me! We packed up our food wrappers and towels, put on our shorts and T-shirts and me, my hiking shoes. Tina remained barefooted. We set off back up the trail toward the road where Tutu had dropped us off. Tina seemed to regain her strength and soon I had to pick up the pace too. When finally the narrow trail widened enough for us to walk side-by-side, I caught up with her and glanced over at her face. She seemed deep in thought. I would have to hold off on those dozens of questions I wanted to ask.

When we came to the road, there was the old Chrysler and in the driver's seat was Tutu, a book propped up on the steering wheel. I expected a blast of impatience, if not anger. I braced myself but received a wide, white smile and, "Hello seestah! You girls have a good day?" Tina opened the back door on the driver's side and set her pack on the seat and climbed in after it. I went around to the passenger side and got into the front seat, mumbling an apology for being so long away. Tutu just laughed and said not to worry. She expected us to be many hours. "When my girl Tina start talkin' story, you know you goin' get an earful for a long time."

Tina immediately leaned forward in her seat and stuck her tongue out at the back of Tutu's head. What's this? But Tutu had seen the gesture in the rearview mirror and guffawed, half turning in the seat to face the girl. With a big grin, Tina then leaned further forward, put her arms around Tutu's neck and kissed her cheek. She said a few words to Tutu, in what I was to become familiar with as, Mal'lam. They shared a giggle and I couldn't help smiling too. Off we went, the forest shadows darkening the roadway. I was starving. I turned to Tina and asked her if she was hungry too. "I could eat Auntie's cat!" she replied and we all giggled and chuckled the few miles down the hill to the Kapuna's house.

Things were not entirely well when we got there. Warren had injured his back at work and some workmates had driven him home. They were still there, helping Warren drink his home brew and commiserating with him, rather noisily. Aunty Bev was not too happy. Warren had arrived shortly after Kinau had driven off to retrieve Tina and me, so she knew nothing of this little drama. Before I got into the house, having stopped to wash mud off my boots, I heard Tutu Kinau's voice at its most authoritative. "You buggahs better get goin' now. We got things to do around here an' you just in the way - an'gettin'drunk besides. Go on now, git!" Two red-faced men, one smiling wryly, made their way out of the house and down the steps, picking up their work boots on the way. One paused to give me the eye, grinned, and joined the other in the company vehicle they had driven Warren home in. They honked once, politely, as they drove off.

Aunty Bev came out of the kitchen, looking relieved, gave me a kiss on the cheek, then one for Tina, and said, "You girls gotta fix *kau kau* tonight. Kinau an' me gonna work on Warren's back." So much for an early dinner.

My new little *seestah* never ceased amazing me. My cooking skills extend to opening packets of prepared foods. Tina was right into it. She was soon ordering me around the kitchen, with a smile, and I was cutting and chopping, peeling and boiling. Then from the far bedroom, where we'd last seen Aunty Bev heading, came Warren's protesting voice, pain and pleading evident in the high tone he spoke in. Groans, gasps, even a shriek ensued.

"Know what they're doing?" Tina asked me. Did I?! I well remembered the Hawaiian massage my poor butt had received that time I bruised it on the hillside. Poor Warren. It seemed he had a back problem which put him off work from time to time. Tutu half-joked that it was his excuse to stay home and drink beer and read. But those sounds of suffering where for real. A lot of Hell to go through for a couple days off! The Japanese Shiatzu practitioners were pussycats compared to a couple of big, strong Hawai'ian women with hydraulic hands. It's called *lomi lomi*, a lovely name for a painful, but rehabilitating experience.

Anyway, soon the sounds of massacre subsided, Tina and I had the dinner ready and Tina went out to the beer-fridge and brought me back a cold one. Good girl! Half an hour later, Tutu, Bev and Warren came out to the kitchen. Warren looked done-in but he was walking straight-backed. His ordeal hadn't affected his appetite either.

We all sat around the table for a long time after Tina and I had cleared away the dishes. Aunty Bev said she would do the dishes. I protested. Kinau told me to hush up and asked to see my field notes … if I didn't mind too much. Ordinarily, that would have been a breach of my professional ethics, not to mention my personal privacy. But I didn't hesitate because she might be able to clarify some things I'd been wondering about. She glanced through them rather quickly of course; being a teacher, she'd learned to speed-read assignments and documents. Tina, meanwhile, had gone to take a shower, showing no interest at all in what I'd written during our long day together. Warren excused himself and hobbled off to bed, giving me a pat on the shoulder as he left. Nice man.

Early the next morning that nice man sat on the lanai, cup of coffee and a good book in hand while we four ladies cleaned up the breakfast dishes. Then it was off to the taro patch; weeding. If we'd been within sight of Warren he would surely have been giving directions. But Tutu said he needed a full day's rest. And no beer! He harrumphed a bit at that but accepted the prescription.

The morning was overcast and almost chilly, but a few minutes of bending, pulling and tossing, had us four ladies warmed up. At first it was all work; then I had to stick my two-cent's worth in.

"Tutu," I said, "what was the reason you named Tina, Tina?" I was still bent over, weeding.

Tutu Kinau stood up then, muddy weeds in both hands and replied, "The Mal'lam Spirits tell me. Tina still not born, you see. One day when I was up at the *heiau,* lots of voices came to me and said I gotta name the girl Tina. Whoa! I said. Her mama gonna name her baby, not me." Kinau tossed her handfuls of weeds away and bent back to her work, and paused. I too, pulled more weeds, waiting for her to go on.

"They told me then that the baby was gonna be mine to raise. I knew my daughter was gonna be a problem but I hoped she would get all right when the baby come." We had all stopped pulling weeds then, three women and a girl, mud splashed all over us, hands at our sides, dripping muddy water.

"I thought you already told her, Tutu!" Tina said. "No Baby. I was waiting for Katherine to ask, herself." Kinau looked directly at me now and said, "My Spirits told me that my Tina would know another Tina, a girl like her, someday when she was a young girl. I only told Tina when she began to hear her own voices." There was a pause and we all bent back to our work.

My mind buzzed with more questions but my attention was suddenly diverted by a glob of mud landing solidly on my left arm. I looked up to see who had thrown it. Everyone looked busy and intent upon their work. Must have been when someone was throwing the weeds away. Bend and pull, toss and bend again. Splat! Another mud missile, big this time, hit me on the shoulder. I looked up quickly to see Tina bending fast, a grin on her guilty mouth. I responded with a small glob of my own, then she threw another glob and then it was on! Aunty Bev threw a handful of weeds Tina's way, which missed and hit Kinau on the leg. Kinau chucked a big handful of mostly mud at me, her face a wide, happy mask. Minutes later, Kinau and I had fallen down into the paddy mud, water up to our waists while Bev and Tina were bent over laughing.

"Hey! What's goin' on down there? Don't you break my taro!" Warren's voice was distant but loud. Overcoming the giggles, Aunty Bev called back, "Neva mind, you. We havin' fun and gettin' work done too. Eh? You like another massage?" We all broke into giggles again. Warren remained silent. We four worked most of the day in the garden, Warren fixing us sandwiches and fruit for lunch, then retiring to have a lie down. We were covered in drying mud and dust with bits of grass and weed in our hair. Then Aunty Bev had a great idea. "Let's go to the beach!" she said, looking hopefully around at us. Yes! No argument. This is girl's-day!

We threw beach towels over the car seats before we climbed in, Aunty Bev brought a paper bag, which clinked like bottles and Kinau brought a cardboard box with some goodies. We were off to the beach.

Late afternoon and most of the traffic was downhill, tourists heading back to their hotels. Tutu Kinau's penchant for slow driving was slowly driving the following drivers crazy. After some polite honking, the beeps got more insistent. "Better pull over, seestah. Them *haoles* is cranky." Aunty Bev was always concerned about how others thought of her and got nervous in situations like this when she felt she was sharing in some breach of etiquette. Not so Tutu. "They's a place up ahead where they can pass." She said in reply, totally unconcerned. There *was* a passing lane and when the following cars accelerated around us we gathered some quite impatient looks. Tutu just looked straight ahead. After all, this was her road, wasn't it?

She drove to a far corner of the graveled parking area, beneath the shade of some big *kiawe* trees. The mouth of the Waimea River was broad and the water quite clear today. It hadn't rained up the mountain for a while and other local families were taking advantage of the cool, shallow beaches along its banks. Tourists didn't know what they were missing. Tina was out of the car in a flash, whooping and squealing. And then she was leaping up on one foot and holding the other in both hands. She had trod on a *kiawe* thorn; rather, a cluster of thorns which this big, spreading tree is notorious for. I still had my hiking boots on and ran to her quickly. As it was, some thorns stuck in my soles but didn't penetrate. She was obviously distressed so I picked her up and carried her back to the car. Tutu had her sit on the trunk of the car and took her foot in both hands to inspect the wound. With a quick motion she pulled the offending thorn-cluster out and threw it aside. Beads of blood quickly formed where the devilish spines had penetrated.

"No swimmin' for you, girl!" Kinau declared with finality. "Too much infection in this water today." Tina wiped tears from her eyes and managed to look brave. "It's alright, Tutu. Only little pin-holes." She took her foot in both hands and examined it herself. Kinau stood back, hands on hips, and gave the girl a big Polynesian scowl which contained whole sentences of meaning. Aunty Bev had a look at the wounds now too. Shaking her head she said, "Tina-girl, Tutu's right. We need to bind that foot up pretty soon."

Meanwhile, Tutu went to the trunk and opened it, taking out a cane knife, the big, broad-bladed machete used in the sugar cane harvest. That's a bit overboard, I thought. But instead of threatening Tina with it, she went to a small coconut palm and expertly hacked off two fronds. These she used to sweep a pathway through the thorns to the beach, about fifty feet away. Nature's broom. Casting a raised eyebrow above a little grin, Tutu reminded Tina, "Next time, girl, do this first."

Tina looked down at her wounded foot, decided this drama wasn't going to gain her much sympathy, hopped down onto the good foot and hobbled off toward the beach. The bottom of her punctured foot was now quite bloody but she soldiered-on almost as if nothing had happened. By the time she got to the sand she was even walking on the ball of the offended foot. Tough kid. The two women smiled to each other, Kinau winked at me and we carried the towels, paper bag and box down to the beach after Tina. Both ladies still watched where they put their feet though.

"Safe to swim?" I asked everyone, dying to get in and wash off the mud and dried perspiration. Aunty Bev nodded and smiled and in I went. Cool and sweet, the water. Ahhhh! Wearing their long *mu'u mu'us* , Aunty and Tutu were right behind me. Big splashes! Spluttering and blowing, ducking under water time and again, they joined me in this wonderful bath. Tina sat looking at us rather glumly, chewing on a candy bar, her bad foot sticking straight out in front of her on the sand.

We had a great couple of hours together. The clinking sounds were only bottles of Coke, darn it! The cardboard box had bread and sandwich makings and guavas and candy bars. But too soon it was getting dark and Tutu said it was time to go. Tina's foot was aching a bit now and Tutu said we'd stop at the drug store and get some salve and bandages. Aha! Now's your chance Katherine! Right next to the drug store was a Pizza parlor! My *haole* taste buds had been clamoring for a pizza for weeks. Boy, did I do the right thing or what? Yeah! Yeah! Everyone said - yeah! Aunty Bev said Warren just loved pizza, so I ordered four altogether. Tina got her foot bandaged while we waited for the pizza and Aunty Bev went up to the little corner store to get something.

By the time we got home it was fully dark, Uncle Warren was asleep in his chair on the *lanai*, a couple of empties beside him on the floor. I don't think he missed us ladies much that day. But didn't he wake up when Aunty Bev waved the pizza box under his nose!

Four days later, having said goodbye to Jiro at the airport, I sat next to Tina's bed at the hospital. Jiro had come over to see her after her surgery; a very doting Godfather was he. A piece of a *kiawe* thorn had broken off in her foot that day at the river and by the following night she had a red line running up from her instep to her calf. Blood poisoning! Hawaiian traditional medicine was not even considered here. Tutu had said, "Tina-girl, you're off to the hospital!" Tina was obviously a bit scared and as Uncle Warren, bad back forgotten, carried her out to the car with the greatest gentleness, I was further reminded of the warm regard which this whole family had for each other.

As children will, thank God, Tina was quickly on the mend. The doctor said she would have to stay in the hospital for three days, just in case. I readily agreed to spend most of the days with her, staying overnight with another family cousin in Lihue. Did I have a captive subject? I broached this with Jiro, who had read my notes, and he said, "Here's your chance to carry on with the story. Tina will be very pleased, not only with your company but with the opportunity to tell you more." And then he said something which quite amazed me: "That's why Tina Pualani was born, you know. She has a story to relate. That's her Destiny! And you are here to record that story." Jiro then started to join the passengers for the flight back to Honolulu, stopped and turned again to me. "By the way. Try printing. Your handwriting is atrocious!" With a final grin of utter mischief, he was gone. Do I hate him or love him? Bastard!

O.K., I'll try printing. I have a new ballpoint, plus a spare, a new notebook and Tina seems especially garrulous this morning, having slept well and been given her favorite breakfast; ' Wheaties.' Ready, my little seestah?

~ ~ * ~ ~

"I had lots of visitors in my sleep last night, Katherine. They want me to continue with the story of Tor'na and his madness. It's not too nice; I mean, it's kinda cruel. And the Mal'lam were never a cruel people. Except the mad ones! So, I'll begin where Tor'na has branded himself and is going back to his crazy friends . . .

Chapter Nine ~ A Rebellion is Born

Mal'atan woke to Tor'na's gentle prodding. He mumbled and reluctantly opened his eyes upon the wounded face. His lids lifted fully and he gasped as comprehension struck him. He sat upright and reached out to stroke Tor'na's jaw line, careful to avoid those awful sores, but lovingly as if admiring something of incredible beauty. Then he began a mad cackle, far back in his throat. It was a laugh of triumph. Tor'na, not understanding the real meaning of that laughter, added his own deep chuckle to the moment's madness. Mal'atan was, of the two, most sure of his triumph.

As the other two Sh'ham-an Seamen woke to their leader's urging, sleep-filled eyes opened wide and startled as they beheld the two angry slashes on the man's face. Already Tor'na's face was swelling in sympathy to the two deep, cauterized cuts, drops of lymph forming and beginning to scab. His eyes burned with a fanaticism more intense than they had ever seen. Both men were frightened; but then they were men who needed to be frightened, to be led by someone else's power of personality; to be molded to another's will. And here was a man who could command them with a powerful silence, intensified now by a fearsome countenance.

As Tor'na laid out his plans in detail for his two old comrades, Mal'atan stood behind him, arms crossed, smirking some secret satisfaction. None contradicted Tor'na as he spoke; on the contrary, the violence of his demeanor opened floodgates of suppressed violence in those others, making them quiver with anticipation. Soon he had to harshly quiet their enthusiasm lest they rise and rush out and do damage to those whom they accepted as the source of their leader's suffering. Mal'atan smiled again as he gauged the lengths to which these two silly men could be commanded.

They spent the early morning hours checking the lashings on the vessel 'Flee the Land', readying the canoe for what must surely be a speedy get-away. Mal'atan had minced away to coerce *his* band of followers to steal food and supplies needed for *his* voyage of liberation. He was to inspire two of those, one but a boy yet, one a grossly ignorant nineteen, to join the crew. Tor'na had given him prior permission to recruit extra hands. For all his expertise, Tor'na could not succeed in his plans with only three to help sail the canoe.

Tor'na

Mal'atan

By mid-morning all was in readiness to Tor'na's satisfaction. He instructed his two burly crewmen to arm themselves with short, water-soaked hardwood clubs but to hide them beneath their calf-length wraps, the standard Seaman's dress while ashore. Mal'atan rechecked the security of his fine blade which was secreted in the waist folds of his wrap. One quick twist of fabric and it would expose its handle to his grasp. Then Tor'na briefed them on what their role was to be. He alone was to speak, and he threw a special glower of command to Mal'atan. The pout with which the pretty lad responded made Tor'na quiver with desire, in spite of the pain in his face.

"No one is to say *anything*! No one is to answer any question. I will do all the talking. Do you understand me?" This was said with such force that they all looked away, nodding agreement. That force made Tor'na wince too, for by now his face rebelled at any movement.

"Then let us claim our freedom from these fools and begin to really *live*!" Nods became wicked grins which shouted aggression. Mal'atan stood again with his arms crossed, a wicked smile beneath his wispy, adolescent mustache. He winked conspiratorially at Tor'na. For a brief moment Tor'na felt a twinge of doubt about his pretty boy, but shook it off. At this hour, on this important day, he could not afford to entertain the least doubt; least of all about himself or his choice of co-conspirators. Just as the four set off to join their Destiny, a man and a teenager, followed by a group of small boys, arrived behind them carrying scruffy, hastily-wrapped bundles.

Mal'atan turned and approached them, looking over his shoulder at Tor'na, who nodded. Already these mad two had established a silent communication like two old acquaintances, or an old married couple, so similar were their mental afflictions. Mal'atan instructed the two new recruits to remain and guard the canoe, stow the food and supplies and make ready to launch 'Flee the Land' on a moment's notice. Their assent was enthusiastic and they both had the look of children about to embark on some exciting, new adventure. They would not remain child-like for long. The little boys who had, out of curiosity, accompanied the rebels ran now beside Tor'na and his three compatriots. One looked up at Mal'atan innocently and asked, "What happened to that man's face?" He received a backhanded blow from the mincing Mal'atan that knocked him backward onto his bottom. He sat looking after the four men, stunned. Upon regaining his feet, he began to cry. Soon all the little boys went crying to their homes. It had begun.

The young A'lan was the first to see Tor'na's group approach. His attention had wavered and then wandered as the debate among the Seamen-Elders droned on. Sitting next to his new Sht'ah Lee-an friend, Shen'ham, he had casually looked around and spotted the four men striding purposefully through the shady groves toward the huge council tree. Al'an nudged his friend and nodded his head toward them. Tor'na was a few steps ahead of his followers, they being line abreast directly behind. One, A'lan did not recognize; a thin, girlish-looking young man.

"Mal'atan the nuisance!" Shen'ham snorted derisively. His voice carried into a momentary lapse in the formal debate. Heads turned to locate the source of this intrusion by a youngster; this was a serious social gaffe. Then eyes began to follow to where the boys were looking. Orn'ta Sea-Master was the master of the canoe which had greeted the fleet of bamboo rafts. He was a strong-willed, decisive man, fair but strict in all Seaman matters; but to his chagrin, he was also uncle to the obnoxious Mal'atan. He was the first of the Councilors to rise to his feet.

A muttering grew among the Councilors and soon all were rising to confront this latest insult to the esteemed Council of Seamen. Tor'na, and he alone, was to wait to be summoned officially by an appointed representative. No formal charge had yet been agreed against the two crewmen. And what was that silly boy doing with them anyway? What Mal'atan was doing was declaring his membership in a small band of renegades. What no one suspected though was that he fully intended to eventually *lead* that band, in an expanded form and in the not-too-distant-future. Tor'na's lover was in fact a viper, patiently awaiting his moment to strike.

Tor'na now halted as he reached the edge of the crowd of murmuring Seamen, his followers stopping too, just three steps behind him. The two Sh'ham-an Seamen carried clubs at their sides, not too subtly implying their willingness to wield them. Mal'atan stood with his feet close together, his arms crossed over his outthrust chest, his usual smirk brighter and more malevolent than usual. "As you can see," Tor'na said loudly, "I have preempted your judgment!" His eyes swept around the assembly, lighting first on the old Sea-Master, Telan, then moving on to others he knew and abhorred.

The swelling of his face, gross now, had rendered his eyes into tiny slits from which hatred and uncompromising disdain gleamed darkly. All eyes facing him were on that distorted countenance, aghast at what they were seeing. Such self-mutilation was unknown among the Mal'lam. Only the feared Itoi'lan, so it was remembered in the oral history, scarred themselves in such a manner. "We have come to bid you all farewell … *Dear Friends*!" His irony was vicious and again he let his gaze fall upon each familiar face, saving the anger-clouded face of Telan for last. To him he addressed his next statement, leaning slightly forward toward the old man who had once been his mentor. "We could simply have been away in the night, sailing from this unpleasant encounter. However, I would not have had the pleasure of looking one last time upon your stupid faces!"

Tor'na let out a howl of demented laughter, but it was cut short by the protest of pain in his face. Tears of agony formed and spilled onto his cheeks, his body tensing against self-inflicted agony. He stood with feet wide apart, fists clenched at his sides as if anticipating some sudden aggression. His followers tensed also, trying to anticipate his next move. Except Mal'atan, who still stood motionless and smirking.

It was Telan who first gathered himself from within his shock. He took two steps toward this madman. In his whole life he had not encountered such a moment. Terrible storms at sea seemed but a light wind compared to this incomprehensible bad dream. Telan stood waiting for a gap in Tor'na's performance in order to speak to the man. While Tor'na continued his insults, some addressed to individuals, some encompassing the whole of the assembly, two within the crowd were able to wrench their attention away from this weird apparition; Al'malan-Seaman saw clearly the fragility of Tor'na's position. Coolly and without anger, he began sidling through the tight gathering toward the edge where he might have room to move should violence occur. Orn'ta, his eyes sick of staring at that warped nephew whose expression never changed, moved carefully toward the other side, his powerful body tense and expectant.

Of all those now held in thrall by this mad fool, Tor'na, only Orn'ta perceived that, somehow, it was his girl-man nephew whose perverse mind was behind all this. As Orn'ta continued to move slowly, unobtrusively toward where his nephew stood, that ugly smirk never changed. Mal'atan's attention appeared focused on the back of Tor'na's head, disregarding all else around him. It was as Telan was trying to find a pause in Tor'na's brutal soliloquy so that he could speak, that A'lan and his friend, Shen'ham, sidled slowly around behind the four conspirators, none of whom seemed to give the boys the slightest notice.

A'lan was burning with an uncommon anger pulsing up from within him and overcoming his natural inclination to avoid conflict. Still slim and boyish and a full head shorter than any of the four offenders, he never-the-less seethed at their effrontery, determined to fight them should it come to that. This impulsive response to a sense of moral outrage was to characterize the man whom A'lan would become. His new friend's motivation was simpler; he was moved to protect his friend of but three weeks, a brotherly bond having already formed between them.

"Tor'na-Sea Master!" Telan was finally able to interject, "You have not been formally summoned to this Council. Now, with not only your usual arrogance but accompanied by armed men, you further insult your people. I fear for your sanity, Seaman. What is your intent?"

Tor'na's face, which must have seemed to him a mask of burning pain, was too distorted by swelling to register any emotion. It was the heat of his dark eyes, squinted as they were, which portrayed his state of mind. The tenor of his voice betrayed the ferocity of his intent. "I spit on your Council of Elders to begin with!" And he did spit and the effect was as if he had done so onto hot coals. That hiss of outrage rebounding around the assembled men brought a heightened level of danger to this meeting, but still no one moved toward Tor'na. Impulsive, violent action was not a Mal'lam trait. But danger there was for this mad Sea-Master. A semblance of a grin forced its way painfully onto his face and tears started to well again.

Then he continued: "I have come here today to declare to you that I am now the Master-Seaman of all the Mal'lam, and soon, sooner than you will care to believe, I shall rule these islands and the seas which separate them." Tor'na relaxed his clenched fists and crossed his arms over his muscular chest, his chin jutting forward. The combination of his cruelly disfigured face and his appalling arrogance presented a hint of the ridiculous, lost to the man himself. But this last statement overcame the leniency of even the most forgiving of those assembled. The unspoken decision had to be unanimous; this poor man was indeed mad.

The Mal'lam had never, since leaving those distant shores to the cool north so many generations ago, submitted to an overlord. Theirs was a society ruled by consensus and by acknowledged wisdom, experience, competence and quite importantly, by the influence of those with *the sight*. But never, ever, had these people tolerated the self-centered egoism of any individual in determining the affairs of their society. Many uttered 'Itoi', the word meaning not only those legendary warriors of the western seas whom their forebears had encountered but any overbearing, aggressive behavior. In fact, the harshest reprimand delivered to an obstreperous child would be a growled, 'Itoi'. But Tor'na was no child and this word he absorbed as if it were a compliment.

"I tire of talk now." He said. "This moment begins a new age for the Mal'lam. You shall soon learn to respect me and attend to my demands. Whenever we meet again, be prepared to honor me!" These last challenging words met with a rumble of disbelief and outrage. Telan Sea- Master stood open-mouthed with awe at the sheer foolishness of such arrogance. Some of the younger men began to move forward with clenched fists, angered beyond endurance.

This eventuality Tor'na had planned for and with a quick gesture of one arm he signaled to his two long-time companions. The two moved forward to stand on each side of their leader, their heavy clubs raised to waist level and ready, faces flushed with brutal anticipation. Mal'atan whipped the hidden blade from the waist of his wrap and held it above his head, grinning challengingly, wickedly. The advance of the crowd halted and a sudden silence prevailed. It was into this silence that A'lan threw his wordless cry and lunged toward the armed men, coming from behind them, aiming for the legs of the largest of the two Sh'ham-an Seamen.

Mal'atan, revealing his acute awareness and exceptional reflexes, his insouciance a sham, swung his blade down and behind him without even looking toward the sound of the boy's rush. Mal'atan's smirk never wavered, nor did his eyes, which remained fixed on the developing scene before him. The savage blow by the keen blade caught the lunging boy just at the left corner of his mouth and ripped upward across his cheek to below his left ear. The angle of A'lan's lunge saved him from death, for the blade, though reaching bone, missed any major vein or artery. Specks of blood landed paces away onto the chest of the boy, Shen'ham, whose own following lunge he was able to halt just short of his friend's now supine body.

Al'an lay on his stomach, both hands clutching his face, blood flowing strongly between his fingers. Shen'ham stood momentarily, looking down at A'lan and then his body tensed to spring at his friend's attacker. Only the sudden strong grip on one arm prevented him from carrying out his own attack. He turned, furious, glowering with rage at whoever was impeding him. The vice-like grip remained. It was Orn'ta Sea Master, his own face a mask of anger, not at the boy but at the madness of the day. That one of his own family could have drawn blood, especially that of a child, was beyond his comprehension.

At this moment an all-out melee was immanent, definitely to the detriment of Tor'na and his little band. But others too would surely suffer. The crush of bodics had hidden the young lad's wounding from most eyes. Had the crowd known this at that moment, surely the crowd would have become a mob. As Orn'ta began to loosen his grip on Shen'ham's arm and prepare to launch his own assault on his nephew, a loud shout of, "STOP!" momentarily halted all action. It was the voice of Al'malan-Seaman and it contained so commanding a tone that even Tor'na searched the crowd for its source.

"ENOUGH!" that voice roared, and Al'malan stepped into a quickly widening space between the would-be combatants, his presence overwhelmingly persuasive. Tor'na, having to look up slightly into the face of the taller, younger man, knew instantly that his plans had been compromised in that unexpected moment. His shrewd mind however, reasserted itself instantly. He took one step back as if to see more clearly, his arms folded defiantly.

"Ah, Al'malan! How wise of you. I am very pleased that you have intervened. Surely to prevent any harm coming to these old ones." The edge of bitterness in his voice cut sharply, but no one moved, no one made to take advantage of what might be his moment of greatest vulnerability. "Stay where you are, everyone! And no harm will be inflicted on you." Again he was asserting his mastery over this drama, which was of his own creation. He raised his hand again in a signal to his followers, turned to the nearest to him and whispered, "Stay close to me. Back away slowly."

Mal'atan, still holding his knife aloft, began to slowly lower it, his face now set in a grimace of threat. He too began to back slowly away from the crowd, stepping deftly around the bleeding boy who now knelt behind him in silent agony. This sight, hidden before behind the legs of the four conspirators, sent a gasp of shock through the assembled Mal'lam. A number of men now ran toward the boy, disregarding Tor'na and his henchmen. Tor'na and the other three continued their measured retreat, stalked by angry young Seamen. Again

Al'malan-Seaman exerted a self-assumed authority. "Let them go, Seamen! They are already dead men. Let them go away from here. There are other things to attend to."

And then he strode powerfully through the crowd to where A'lan now sat, his friend Shen'ham's arms supporting him. Both boys were trembling, Shen'ham crying. Older men were patting and encouraging the wounded boy, one trying to examine the wound. Al'malan bent and gently put his hands beneath the boy's armpits and lifted him to his feet, some protesting that he should be carried. Al'malan said quietly, "No. He can walk. His courage will see to that."

The boy squinted up through tear-filled eyes and nodded, his hands still covering his lower, wounded face. Stumbling, he followed the big man's urging. Al'malan bent and whispered, "You are a brave man, young Seaman! Stay upright a while longer. We'll soon have you mended." In an attempt to further urge the boy, whom he knew aspired keenly to being apprenticed to the sea, he added, "Like a torn sail, Seaman, you'll soon be before the wind again. Good as new."

Shen'ham, himself weeping with shock and chagrin at not being able to help his friend, had the presence of mind to tear a corner from his own wrap and offer it to A'lan to help stanch the flow of blood. The tight group of men around the two boys led them up the hill toward the village and to the ministrations of the healers. A few of the Seamen, Orn'ta in the lead, followed Tor'na's retreating band, calling out threats and curses. Tor'na had turned away from them now, striding intently down the beach to where his canoe lay waiting for his escape. His companions still walked facing half-backwards, keeping close watch on their pursuers.

Mal'atan's face glowed with triumph as he tucked his blooded knife back into his wrap's waist. Soon he too turned and faced up the beach, extending his mincing stride to catch up with Tor'na. The two new Sh'tah Lee recruits were waiting as instructed by Mal'atan, having managed to shift the heavy hulls of the canoe a few feet toward the edge of a rising tide.

When Tor'na reached the vessel the men following them halted and watched as anxious and not-a-little fearful energy launched the gleaming hulls into the surf. Within seconds the outcasts were afloat. Experienced arms lifted the heavy boom to the mast, ropes were slung and tied and soon the tightly woven fabric of the sail was billowing in the early afternoon breeze. Tor'na himself stood in the stern of one hull, the heavy steering paddle gripped in his powerful hands.

When his comrades began to chatter and laugh in nervous relief, boasting of their victory, he roared at them, "Shut up! I need silence." What was really occurring in Tor'na's heart and mind at that moment was obscured from his crew as he faced aft toward the beach and the silent animosity of those left standing there. The pain in his face was not entirely responsible for the wetness in his eyes; pain, fatigue and relief were attended by a gnawing sense of failure and regret. The victory was an anticlimax. Where was that sense of conquest he'd been so sure of when he'd struck the hot blade against his skin? Where was the joy of prevailing against perceived enemies? Why did he feel so empty, so unfulfilled? Why did he have a sense of disquieting nervousness?

A hopeless yearning attended his view of the receding shore. The figures standing there had been his kin and Sea-brothers. What might he have been, had he remained and tried to accept their proffered mate-ship? What was really driving him? What was that sense of danger which seemed to emanate not from the shore, not from the hostility he would surely encounter wherever he now roamed among these islands - but from aboard this very vessel? 'Flee the Land' was his prideful home, his own creation, part of himself. What was wrong here?

Mal'atan stood alone in the peak of the opposite hull, one hand, that which had struck that bloody blow, clutching a straining forestay. His mind wrapped itself voluptuously around visions of such magnitude and magnificence that should those other fools aboard glimpse them, they would most likely toss him overboard. He smiled at his own cleverness, arched his back as if in response to some physical embrace and laughed out loud, but softly. Mal'atan's plans were right on schedule.

Lana'ma Herb-Mistress rose from her cross-legged position on the woven mat and listened, but not only with her ears. She had been wrapping food parcels in assistance to the Herbalist's up-coming journey when suddenly she was bidden by that internal voice of the *seer*. "My son!" she gasped. Emerging from the tree-line above the beach at the Bay of Dolphins came a crowd of men and in their midst, standing out on the screen of her special perceptions was her only child, A'lan. His handsome, boyish features were obscured by flowing blood, but his spirit, strong and no longer boyish, called out to her: "Mother! I need you!"

"A'lan!" she cried and began to run toward the approaching crowd. The other Herbalists around her looked up in surprise, saw the men approaching and, sensing the urgency of Lana'ma's sudden action, rose and followed her. Soon healers, Sh'ham-an and Sht'ah Lee-an alike, surrounded the bleeding boy. His pale, sweat-beaded face was quickly examined and the wound assessed. Had this event occurred one day later, he would not have had access to the ministrations of one of the Mal'lam's premier surgeons. That man was due to ascend the mountains for the annual gathering of medicinal plants the following morning.

But this day he sat cross-legged with the boy's head in his lap, holding him still while another wiped and cleansed the gaping wound. Pink-white bone gleamed from the depths of the gash and the surgeon knew that this wound would leave a vivid scar. Whether nerves had been damaged, only time would tell. Then he began his work with a quiet, soothing chant. One hand held in those of his mother, the other in Shen'ham's strong grip, A'lan would gasp and moan through gritted teeth but never once did he cry out. Tears streamed down his cheeks but were quickly swabbed away by an attendant healer who clucked encouragement to the suffering boy.

Al'malan stood nearby, watching the courage of the boy, noting the loyalty of his young friend, and measuring in his mind the potential of the two boys. He knew that they would soon be apprenticed to the Seamen and that he would be their mentor. Satisfied at last that all would be well with A'lan, he nodded to the boy's mother, smiled encouragement to her and turned to attend to other matters of importance. Al'malan Seaman knew within his heart that day that he would become a Sea-Master. Upon him would be laid great responsibility. Such certainty had nothing to do with egoism. The knowledge had come to him like the sound of waves beating their rhythm on the shore. And Al'malan's inner hearing was astoundingly accurate.

The Council was re-gathering, attended now by many other Elders than just the Seamen. While others muttered of revenge and retribution, Al'malan's mind was centered on more practical matters. His destiny was dawning on him in this hour. With a detached certainty containing no hint of guile or triumph, he accepted the message which had come to him the night before; a vision within a dream and so compelling that it had awakened him with a start. He would soon become the new Sea-Master of his Clan and would lead them on their quest for a new homeland! As he strode to where the others were gathered, a pair of loving eyes followed his passage. Sht'ana Herb-Mistress caught her mother's eye then. Blushing, she turned away. Sha'lat finally understood the mystery of her daughter's dismissal of all other suitors. She would have *this* young man and no other.

Research notes: Impressions and General observations

Subject: Tina Pualani Kaiser, Kaua'i, Summer 1972

Tina back from hospital now and feeling chipper. Doctor has her on a course of antibiotics though and orders to keep off the foot for a week. Hah! Imagine that. At least she has agreed to not swim or go into the water until the wound is totally healed. So, now I still have my captive subject. It's only three weeks until she goes back to school, so without crowding her too much, I've got to make good use of this time with her. Tutu Kinau has needed my help in the garden about half the day lately. Boy, don't things grow fast here. Especially weeds! Anyway, most afternoons I sit with Tina, either on the *lanai* or up in the guava orchard on the old bench and she continues her tale of the Mal'lam. Like now......

~ ~ * ~ ~

"The spirits, Katherine, tell me things, sometimes kinda disjointed, if you know what I mean. I kinda have to sort things out and rearrange them. Their idea of time is different from ours. It's hard to explain but I hope you can follow all of this. You see, the Mal'lam really are, or *were*, a peaceful people. Tor'na's madness, and that of Mal'atan, was almost impossible for the people to understand. Added to that was all the volcanic activity and everything. Pretty hard times for the Clan but they kept carrying on and having faith in each other and their traditions."

"Things were gonna get worse though, because the Mal'lam couldn't do anything about the earthquakes and volcanoes and in order to overcome Tor'na's craziness, they would have to do some things that were really against their nature. It's about at this stage of their story that I get to know more about my namesake, Tina. Tutu says she sees a resemblance between us, but I don't. Oh yeah, I talk to Tutu a lot about my spirits. And she tells me about hers too. You'll have to get her to tell you about them and their stories too. What d'ya mean, you've gotta learn shorthand?"

Chapter Ten - The Magical Mountain

As the sun rose over the wide plain to the east of the settlement, early risers gathered to wish the travelers a good journey. Two additional men now joined that group of twelve women and girls and three men. One was a huge man of nearly giant proportions, his gentle face wreathed in a wild beard, long hair pulled back and tied with a red-dyed cloth. His name was Joha'lan, a master wood worker and skilled canoe-maker. The other man, also a native of Sht'ah Lee, was older, smaller, but powerfully muscled and more somber of character. He was Ran'tar, Master canoe maker, famous throughout the archipelago for his superbly balanced craft.

Both of these men carried a woven bamboo pack, a water gourd, a small obsidian-bladed axe and a bedroll of layered *tapa* cloth. They, like all men on this island, wore calf-length wraps of the same material, covered in complex patterns painted with vegetable dyes. On this occasion, each also carried a heavy, stone-tipped spear. The Herbalists were happy for the additional armament. Two more spears were a welcome addition on the long trek through pig-infested forests. Joha'lan and Ran'tar would leave the company in the upper reaches of the great hardwood forest to search for trees for new canoe hulls. They had happily agreed to delay their departure by a day to join with the always-joyous company of the Herbalists whose lives revolved around an intimate knowledge of plants and healing. They would rejoin the herbalists when they made their return journey back down the 'Black Boar Track'.

The old Sh'ham-an Herbmaster, Tal'ma, always an early riser but lately given to sleeping in, urged his aching bones from his sleeping pallet and joined the well wishers. He went to the woman, Shen'ha Herb-Mistress whom, when he had last visited this island so long ago, had been but a child. Now this island's supreme Mistress of Herb Knowledge, she embraced the old man who whispered in her ear, "Take my love to the mountains, Herb-daughter. I shall make these journeys no more." Shen'ha hugged him and promised to remember him in her meditations upon the great mountain, 'Volan Votu.'

With the two Wood-Masters in the lead, the company headed toward the distant mountain, its sunrise-pink shades brightening into startling white. Long shadows ribbed the track through the orchards and gardens and the wet-taro patches. Early morning workers called greetings and the elderly among them, mostly there to tend to the young children, offered parcels of ready-to-eat foodstuffs; snacks for the trail. At the edge of the cultivated areas the trail narrowed and entered scrubby country, which, after a mile or so, thinned into grasslands dotted with fruit trees unique to this island.

"Are there poisonous snakes here?" asked Tina of a native girl who walked beside her. The girl, a year older and considerably larger than Tina answered, "Yes, but only one kind. The 'Vasa', but it's very small." Then she added, "And it's very shy. I've never even seen one." In turning to give Tina a reassuring smile, the girl stubbed her foot and nearly tripped over. There were sniggers and one older girl said, "There's a lot you don't see, Shana-lan!" Good-natured laughter tittered amongst the column of women and girls, the butt of the joke herself giggling, undismayed.

The premier Herbalists, Shen'ha and Tina's mother, Sha'lat, walked close together at the rear of the group. The men bearing the spears paused and waited patiently each time the women stopped to inspect some plant which the newcomer was not familiar with. The ecology of this southern island contained plants of which she had only vague knowledge. She had much to learn about this island's plant materials and her new friend was a patient teacher. The two older women were becoming close friends. The pace of the column was deliberately casual to accommodate this aspect of the journey and a short, vigorous jog would see the two women and their guards catch up with the others.

By midday the sun was hot, perspiration darkening the wraps and skirts of the herbalists, the bare breasts of the women gleaming with perspiration. The men had stripped to breechcloths, their bodies also dripping with sweat. At a creek crossing, a shady grove invited a stop for lunch and a rest. One of the men called up the trail to the two woodsmen who were out of sight beyond a bend. They soon returned to join the Herbalists, stopping to rinse their bodies in the stream.

As they sat to receive their share of the noon meal, Joh'lan endured the usual joking and teasing about his being given the food of two men. No one disputed his need for greater quantities of food than most and he good-naturedly returned the banter. His presence was always a happy solace in any company, children especially fond of the big man. He had no children himself, a secret sadness to a vigorous man of great gentleness. His wife of nearly ten years had but recently died of a stomach inflammation and yet he bore that sadness too with great equanimity.

Sha'lat Herb-Mistress rose and offered the unfinished portion of her lunch to the man who accepted and quickly downed the baked banana and breadfruit soaked in honey. There was something about this man which stirred curious but familiar warmth within Sha'lat. His size, his large quiet eyes, his easy, surprising grace of movement were not at all reminiscent of her own dear, dead husband. His memory was still a near and painful one. That loss of husband and daughter brought a twinge of guilt to erase the warm, youthful stirring deep within her heart. She went to the stream and rinsed herself a second time, the cooling water welcome and distracting. Joha'lan watched her and thought her very beautiful. The woman's oldest daughter, Sht'ana, smiled behind her hand, averting her eyes when his gaze turned to where she and the other women sat. Sht'ana Herb-Woman, patient and circumspect in her own affairs of heart, was especially sensitive to the hearts of others.

"Time to carry on!" said Shen'ha, rising and picking up her pack from the pile of bulky, coarsely woven carry-alls. As the company followed suit, the Master-Woodsman said warningly, "Stay close together from now on, all of you. We spotted pig-sign just up the trail. Joha'lan says he heard the squeals of piglets, and you all know to trust his big ears." Joha'lan made snorting sounds and the group giggled and tittered its way back onto the track. Ran'tar and his big companion took up the lead again, the three Herbs-men front, center and rear, their alertness increased, spears at the ready.

The land began to rise and fall now, the track winding up and over ancient lava flows and cinder cones, all quite heavily overgrown. These were the preface to the foothills of the mountains. The most demanding portion of this journey would not be the mountain itself, its slopes being long and gentle. It was the foothills which, eroded and very rugged in places, were cut by roaring streams and waterfalls. These would pose the greatest obstacles. The Herbalist's column began the climb in late afternoon, ascending into a thickening forest.

One steep gully was traversed by a log bridge, the single tree flattened on the top and each end resting firmly on expertly set dry-stone abutments. The structure was decades old and covered in moss and ferns and orchids. All around, the trunks of great trees rose like the legs of giant beasts; dark and immovable, the bases splayed outward like huge toes. It was here that Ran'tar and Joha'lan planned to rejoin the herbalists on their return journey down the mountain after they had completed their gathering. While here, the two woodsmen would survey the forests for new canoe timber. Now they decided to wait for the others to catch up. Pig sign was everywhere. They would spend the night with their friends at the first camp on the trek up the mountain.

The first day's march ended as the sun sparkled through the dense foliage and illuminated the great tree trunks with shifting spots of rose and gold. "Worst camp of the trip!" Shen'ha called out to her companions. The newcomer, Sha'lat, didn't quite know what to make of that statement. "It's the midges and mosquitoes!" said one woman, laughing. "Tomorrow we'll scratch ourselves for half the day!" A Herbalist added his assessment, in case the newcomers should miss the point: "And tomorrow night you'll freeze, up above the tree-line!" "No!" squealed another woman, "You men are to stay up all night and keep the fires going." Another giggled, "Or keep us warm on our pallets!"

And thus did the first day of the journey end, as it had begun, with humor and ribald teasing. While the people settled themselves into the camp routine, some gathering firewood, some unpacking for the evening meal, the often-used clearing in the forest murmured with chatter and laughter. Suddenly the shrill squealing of pigs fractured the gentle ambience of the happy gathering! From the nearby stream erupted a huge black and white sow and she was quickly followed by a litter of tiny pigs, all pink and hairless. Their own snouts waved in the air as did their mother's, high-pitched grunts and squeals congealing around her massive body. Following these were three other adult pigs, their tiny eyes gleaming above small, curved tusks. The lead pig, her own eyes spotting humans, gave a loud coughing grunt and wheeled in a sudden movement and lunged upstream along the bank, her brood and the other three adults following, trailing ear-splitting shrieks. As their crash and rattle and squeals receded, the five spear-bearing men relaxed their defensive stances and those women who had picked up stones at the first alarm, dropped their weapons. Smiles broke the tension and soon the evening's preparations resumed.

No Sht'ah Lee-an inhabited these dense forests, with their high humidity, insects and often gloomy, cloud-covered aspect. Nor did the Mal'lam anywhere within the archipelago tend to spend long periods within such confining jungles.

No dangerous animals plagued these forests, save the pigs and the furtive 'Vasa'. Bats of three species, rats and mice and numerous small reptiles rustled through the undergrowth. Many species of birds called through the forest, but little of substance could threaten humans here.

Altogether, these mountains presented a richly benign face to its vagrant human visitors. As it occurred, it was the human dimension which provided most of the human misery which these people encountered. And this was exceedingly rarc. From time to time a person such as Tor'na could arise, never before of such disturbing potential, however. These occurrences of madness were tolerated until tolerance found its limits. The Sh'ham-an were embarrassed that one of their own should have inflicted such intrusion upon their cousins, but the natives dismissed it as an uncontrollable aberration. That one of *their* own, that strange girl-man, Mal'atan, should have been involved in that regrettable incident seemed to balance the equation.

As the trekkers sat within the insubstantial shelter of their intentionally smoky fires, already slapping and scratching at the minute assailants of the evening, the Mal'lam spoke of yesterday's disgraceful behavior as if it was already receding into myth and the fog of distance. This was a proclivity of the Mal'lam; their tendency to forgive and forget, which so contributed to their general peacefulness. It was this same tendency, however, which would see them so ill- prepared for the outrages of their spawn. And this night's conversation around the smoky fire confirmed the tone of forgiveness as opinions were ventured as to what might become of the six recalcitrants now fleeing this land.

Among those listening, because of her age not involved in the discussion, was young Tina. She still clung to an emotion bordering on hatred and her elder's conversation stirred it anew. The misery of the flight from her island home and the subsequent open-sea voyage, compounded by that man Tor'na's seeming inhumanity was, to her young mind, more than enough reason for hatred. And then there was the wounding of her beloved Al'an! That was nearly insupportable. And why had no one done anything? And Al'malan. Her mind interpreted the event as shameful cowardice. The big ninny had apparently stood by and done nothing while Al'an was wounded! But as night settled around the herbalist party at the end of their first day's hard journey, her mind was once more invaded, but gently, by that *voice*; that mysterious, now soothing presence which whispered, "Be peaceful, child. Have no fear. Rest your heart."

Soon slumber gained on her and she began to slump against her big sister. Sh'tana wrapped comforting arms around her until sleep tugged at her own eyelids. When Tina finally fell asleep, Sh'tana gently lifted her to the woven mat and covered her with the *tapa* blanket. She then crawled beside her little sister and was soon asleep herself. Shortly, all were quiet and either asleep or drifting with the humming, chirring sounds of night creatures. An errant gust of breeze found the clearing, stirred the lowering fire into quick blaze, and then released it to ember and spark. The pair of eyes which peered from the forest were crinkled around a smile, the seamed old face intent but happy. Then the old woman turned and softly padded away into the dark forest, supported by her marvelously carved staff. Near one of the fires, but upwind of its smoke, a head was raised momentarily. Was that a twig snapping? Yes. The man smiled and lay back down on his pillow of folded pack, confident that this night was attended by one of his favorite people.

In the morning, as the women busied themselves with cleaning and packing after a light breakfast, the two Woodsmen sat alone near the trail, guarding against foraging pigs. In the background the others snuffled and scratched and cursed the night in this forest where no sane person would live. Having spent the night free of the wood smoke, the two Woodsmen only scratched. "The Vesa'tan was with us last night." Spoke Joha'lan, his voice matter-of-fact."Did you see her?" Ran'tar asked.

"No, I heard her. She grows very old now. Never before, even when seeing her, did I hear her movements. We must leave gifts for her, I think. Here, rather than above the pass. She may not follow the Herbalists up the mountain. She doesn't like the cold very much." Ran'tar nodded and rose to speak with Shen'ha-Herb Mistress. The two gathered small parcels of food, two clay bowls and a woven mat and lay them near the morning's fire. The Vesa'tan would certainly find them there. She would be expecting gifts.

The experienced among the group passed the word that The Vesa'tan was near. One explained to the newcomers: "The Vesa'tan is a witch who has lived alone here in these forests since long before I was born. It is said that she is the daughter of a wise herbalist and *seer* from another island who died here upon the mountain, struck by lightning. The Vesa'tan ... no one can remember her real name ... ran away from those who would protect her, even though she was still but a child. Somehow she survived and is now very old. She is very special to us all here on Sht'ah Lee."

The young woman spoke easily as she finished packing. She rose and motioned Sha'lat Herb-Mistress to walk beside her as they started out on the trail. She continued the story, smiling as if recounting a bit of old gossip. "She really is quite harmless, but it's best to stand upwind of her if you meet her. She doesn't bathe much. In fact, you see, she has warned our people on many occasions of storms or droughts impending. She's always been right." The woman looked meaningfully at Shal'lat and added, "She told us of your coming; of our cousin's tragedy and flight from Sh'ham-Set. That is why we were at least partially prepared for your arrival." The woman laughed playfully, then expanded on the strange character of The Vesa'tan.

"She is said to have a strange power over birds and reptiles, and sometimes, over people too. When the Woodsmen, like Ran'tar and Joha'lan, come up to the forests, she always knows when they're coming. She's very jealous of *her* trees and gets very cranky if men don't treat the forest with proper respect." A woman behind them laughed and said, "It's true! My brother is a Woodsman. Once he thought he'd be very clever and just leave her an old piece of torn cloth, instead of a full length of *tapa* for a wrap, as most groups of Woodsmen do. She got *really* cranky!" Another women behind her was listening to the story too, probably for the twentieth time, and laughed heartily, taking over the dialog.

"Yes, and her brother woke up the next morning at the Woodsmen's camp, which was a long hike yet downhill, to a nasty surprise. The Vesa'tan had returned his worthless gift overnight, folded neatly into his pack. It was full of pig shit!" Laughter rolled up and down the column of trekkers. Sha'lat-Herb Mistress had to grin. Yes, some men could be very stupid. Tina, walking behind her mother, giggled. Jokes concerning sex or bodily functions were nothing new to a Mal'lam child.

The morning was warm at first, the low sun gleaming through the treetops. But within only a few minutes a cool breeze began blowing down off the mountaintop, carrying with it a thick cloud cover. The trail began to be steep and rugged, a series of shallow switchbacks. The Herbalist men cut cane staffs for the women to aid them in the climb, their own spear shafts sufficing as trail-sticks. Pig-sign still abounded on the muddy, eroded soil of the track.

The forest undergrowth thinned as the girth and canopy of the big hardwood trees increased. These were the very trees which the Woodsmen had come to survey. It was here that the two Woodsmen took leave of their Herbalist friends and bid them farewell. The Herbalists waved goodbye and disappeared up-mountain. Ran'tar and Joha'lan were looking for six large trees, large enough to serve as hulls for the largest double-canoes yet attempted. Over many months the highly respected Woodsmen of Sht'ah Lee had discussed this project. Now, with the arrival of the Sh'ham-an and their own Seamen and skilled craftsmen, plus the spur of what seemed an impending catastrophe, the decision had been made.

Three great canoes, capable of transporting up to forty people each would be built. The project would require more than two years to complete, even with the added manpower of the refugees. Ran'tar, the most senior and highly regarded specialist in canoe construction, would lead the project. For an hour the two men sounded and measured trees, never having to move but a few paces from the trail, so great was the potential in this high area of the great forest. The Woodsmen were inspired, challenged men, speaking excitedly to each other as they moved among the massive tree boles. Neither felt any trepidation about the great task ahead. Neither considered any impediment to their eventual success. Neither saw the Vasa, which lay across their path and upon which Ran'tar trod!

"Aiiieeeee!" he screamed, as the small snake's fangs buried themselves into his ankle, the powerful venom injected directly into a large vein above the ankle joint. Joha'lan reached out instinctively to support his friend as the man hopped on one foot, his ankle held in both hands. Far below them, carried by the mountain wind, the scream was heard by an old woman. The screams of pain and fear increased, then subsided, but in the aural void there remained an echo of urgency. The Vesa'tan stopped and stood, listening. Then resting her staff against her shoulder she placed both hands over her ears and muttered silently. With eyes closed in tight concentration she took the staff in both hands now and began pounding the butt of the hardwood against the firmly packed soil of the trail. "Thunk, thunk, thunk!"

Tina and her mother looked at each other simultaneously, both in mid-step on the steep trail, nearly two miles from the incident. "Mother?" the girl queried, the sound within her head so loud that she was sure that all could hear it. Shen'ha, at the head of the column, turned and looked back toward the rear where her new friend and her daughter stood, both with stricken expressions on their faces. She knew of the woman's recent grief, her loss of husband and daughter and the additional strain of the recent weeks. Might not that subliminal alarm be magnified by residual, hurtful intensity?

No! Shen'ha herself now heard, rather, felt that sound. It was a pounding beat, which seemed to travel up her legs and to explode insistently inside her head. No! That woman, Sha'lat-Herb Mistress was a *seer* and if Shen'ha read the signs correctly, so was her youngest daughter. Perhaps even more sensitive. The girl's face was white with fear, her mother staring hard at her. There was certainly no local source for such concern. What was it?

"What is it, my friend?" Shen'ha called down to them, the others in the queue now stopping and looking back and forth at both women and the little girl. "Something …!" and Sha'lat closed her eyes and listened within. The pounding vibration there carried some awful message!

"The Woodsmen!" she cried, "Something is wrong with the Woodsmen!" In Sha'lat's mind surged a renewal of that recent pain in her own life. "What if that huge, sweet man - ?!" She shook her head fiercely, opened her eyes and looked up to where Shen'ha was now descending the trail toward her, her face too a mask of concern. "They are in need, Shen'ha!" Sha'lat called out, looking to all around her. "We must return to them!" Not the keenest ear in the world, man or beast, could have heard those screams from this distance, blown downhill as they were by the chilly wind off the mountain.

Those of the Herbalists who did not possess the *sight* stood wondering what was happening. That old woman's performance, mad if seen out of context, had in fact amplified the urgency of a scream, the meaning of which she had intuited in some mysterious manner. However, no wizardry operated here. Here was the focus of a very human ability developed over decades of unresolved yearning for oneness with her people that some psychic scar had conspired to deny.

The Vesa'tan's self-enforced aloneness had perversely given birth to an almost super-human sensitivity to her own kind, as well as to the plants and animals which dominated her surroundings. Exerting this sensitivity was the factor which prevented madness, prolonged her life and led her to these moments of oneness. She knew that she had been heard. After the last blow of her staff against the ground, she gasped and leaned for support upon the beautifully carved piece of hardwood, then slipped slowly to her knees uttering a prayer of thanksgiving.

"Go Healers! We are needed there! Run!" Shen'ha urged, and the column turned as one and sped back down the trail to where they had parted from the two Woodsmen. Her youth, strength and the strange urgings within her carried Tina to be first to the spot where Joha'lan held his friend in his arms. The big man's face was ashen with grief, tears streaming from his eyes. The victim's face was dead gray, an ooze of some ugly greenness drooling from the corner of his mouth. Joha'lan held Ran'tar to him as one would a stricken puppy; unbelieving, devastated and helpless.

Tina knelt beside them, her hands extending an instinctual comfort, one on Joha'lan's arm, the other to the stricken man's face. Within moments the others began to arrive and Tina's mother was first to kneel beside the two Woodsmen, urging her daughter aside. A sigh escaped her, knowing that it was not the big man who was in danger. As she knelt, one knee brushed Joha'lan's leg. She lifted Ran'tar's eyelids. Her heart plunged. Ran'tar would die! The others grouped around, all still breathing heavily from the dash down the track. Joha'lan reluctantly laid his comrade down on the cool, mossy ground, surrendering him to the ministrations of the healers. As those whose expertise was with toxins examined the wound and the man's condition, they each in turn shook their heads in resignation to the inevitable.

The snake's venom, having entered directly into Ran'tar's bloodstream, was eroding his body's autonomic system; lungs and heart were already badly affected. The man's face was taking on a bluish cast, his breathing becoming irregular and a greenish froth forming around his gasping mouth. His heart was fibrillating, fluttering like the wings of a wounded bird. Had those tiny fangs struck only skin or muscle, the poultices and herbs of the healers might well have saved him. Now, his vital signs were snuffing out like candles, one by one. With a final gasp, horrible to hear, Ran'tar died!

Joha'lan stood looking down at his closest friend, his massive shoulders shaking with sobs. He placed his great hands over his face and cried like a child abandoned. Others around him rubbed and patted his body in attempt to ease his suffering. One of the Herbalist men removed his wrap and laid it over Ran'tar's body, his own eyes brimming with tears. He tucked the fabric over and under the man's body and more hands assisted him. Then, from nearby on the trail came a shrill, keening wail! All heads turned to the source of this expression of pain. And there on the trail stood the frail form of an old woman, wild haired and wearing a tattered wrap which was fastened up under her armpits. Her face was hidden beneath bony hands; her equally bony shoulders shook with convulsions of weeping.

Few standing there watching the old woman knew that the dead man was The Vesa'tan's favorite of all the Mal'lam who visited her forest realm, Joh'lan a close second. Ran'tar had been her student, the one whose love of the forest and its great trees was deepest. Joha'lan too was her student but the man lying so still on the ground was someone very special to the lonely old woman. At first she had resented him, as she resented all who would harm her friends who grew in the forests. Over time she read his spirit, sensed his genuine empathy and slowly began to tolerate, then eagerly anticipate his sojourns up the mountain. Once she had led him to a great tree, which had been uprooted in a storm. Its timber was superb. His gifts to her from that time on had been most generous and thoughtful.

But now, as she neared the end of her long and mostly solitary life, The Vesa'tan was bereft. And it had been one of her little friends, the Vasa, which had taken this man from her. She was near to collapse with grief; the grief held within her for so many lonely years flooding out with this terrible catalyst. A number of the Herbalist women went to her, clucking and cooing in the particular manner of the people of this island. They wrapped soothing words and arms about her. This 'witch', this strange, forbidding old woman, was now but another grieving soul who deserved comfort and the healers did their best to provide it. One of the Herbalist men picked up her staff, which she had dropped on the trail. He marveled out loud at the magnificent carvings which ran up its length. He knew of only one carver who could have created such beautiful intricacies, such subtle yet powerful designs. Joha'lan.

That big man now seemed strangely shrunken in his grief. He sat alone at the top of a nearby embankment, gazing fixedly downhill. Shen'ha, with gestures and expressions, indicated to the others that he should be left alone for the time being. The other men, meanwhile, removed the generously loaned wrap which had been bound about Ran'tar's body, replacing it with the dead man's own woven sleeping mat. The Herbalist would need that wrap for himself, up on the cold mountainside evenings. It was Mal'lam custom to cremate the dead as quickly as possible, always considering the need to gather the families and friends first.

In this case, when the only family was two Seamen sons who were away at sea, and his many other friends were now two day's journey away, the ceremony would be carried out with dispatch. There were friends and admirers enough on this sad day to return his soul to the *Earth Mother* in a seemly manner. His bones, those that might survive the flames, would be taken back to his sons upon their return.

Ran'tar had been a widower for many years, his profession becoming his only passion. Now it seemed fitting that he should die here among the great trees which had been like life's blood to him. Joha'lan was first to begin gathering firewood and within an hour, a great pile of mostly dry material had been assembled for his pyre. Ran'tar's body, wrapped in the patterned mat which had been wound around with liana vines from the nearby forest, was gently laid on the top of the fire stack.

The company of Herbalists and Joha'lan stood in a circle surrounding the pyre. A small ceremonial fire was lit some distance away. Prayers and chants began, the old woman adding her voice, distant memory recalling the words of farewell, hesitantly at first but soon gaining full voice. One by one the weeping mourners took a burning stick from the ceremonial fire and placed it against the base of the pyre. Soon the dry grass and sticks began to crackle. The Vesa'tan was last to add her torch to the flames. Her tiny frame was taut and her face strained, but her eyes were dry now. Slowly, the fire grew and then blazed. People moved back away from the increasing intensity of the flames. A Herbalist began a chant which was joined by all assembled. Only the two young girls, Tina and Shana'lan, by custom, refrained from joining in. When they arrived at their first menstruation, then would they join fully as adults. The chant became a song:

"You came to us in pain and joy, old friend,

Your life enriched us all!

We rejoice in you, rejoice in you, rejoice in you!

"You left us in pain, old friend.

Now with joy we say goodbye,

Our sorrows turn to joy,

For now you are with our Earth Mother again!

We rejoice in you, rejoice in you, rejoice in you!"

The chanting song continued, verse after extemporaneous verse, extolling the singular life of this man. The flames now reared high toward the lower branches of the great trees. A drizzling rain began to fall and the Herbalists began to gather their packs to resume the journey back up the mountainside. Soon only Joha'lan and The Vesa'tan remained, each staring silently into the flames which rapidly began to recede to become a shimmering pile of coals, the heat still intense. Joha'lan sat cross-legged as near to the heat as he could tolerate. The old woman sat on her skinny haunches, her staff across her knees. One unbidden last tear fell upon the dry skin of her hand. She raised that hand to her lips and licked the tear away. Goodbye!

Joha'lan then stood up, arms crossed, facing away from The Vesa'tan as she still sat near the warmth of the dying embers. The sun was low and by now the Herbalists would be making camp somewhere up near the tree line. Joha'lan's gaze fell somewhere in the distance, beyond the thick forest which obscured eyesight. The Vesa'tan sat watching him as if reading his emanations, gauging his spirit. She had known this powerful man over many years now, since he had come as an apprentice to the Woodmen at the age of thirteen. Even then he was tall and exceptionally strong, with a keen intelligence. She knew that this long, silent vigil was more than grieving.

Joha'lan was thinking, planning, perhaps trying to distill some essence of his friend's own intelligence from the wafts of smoke from the dying funeral fire. Upon Joha'lan would fall the responsibility for the construction of the three new canoes. Not only their construction, down near the sea, but perhaps of greater difficulty and more trying would be the felling, hollowing and finally the hauling of the huge logs. The sea was many difficult and challenging miles away. Joha'lan knew that among the newcomers from Sh'ham-Set were many men skilled in woodcraft.

Although many of them were bamboo-raft sailors and builders, they nevertheless possessed valuable experience with canoes too. No one knew how long the first voyagers would require to reach new lands to the south and east, but surely beyond the reasonable life expectancy of one of the huge, awkward bamboo vessels. Besides, they were too slow. No! The canoes must be built. In the past five years, by some extraordinary fall of bad fortune, five … no, six, he reminded himself painfully, of the Clan's best canoe builders had died or become incapacitated. Of the remaining craftsmen, he was now the premier one. This was not just his opinion, for Joha'lan was a humble man, some would say too modest.

But modesty was an ego luxury his and his craft could not afford. It was accepted that should Ran'tar retire or die, Joha'lan would take his place as Canoe-Master. Joha'lan now berated himself for his indulgence in fine carving instead of attending more closely to this, the beginning phase of canoe building. "I should have spent more time up here with the really *big* work!" he grimaced. That expression was quickly replaced by a wry smile. His gentle spirit was in fact the product not of a happy accident of nature but more a result of a special patience and self-discipline.

To overcome the jibes and jokes he had absorbed since childhood, having mostly to do with his size, he developed a capacity to ignore the extraneous and insubstantial and concentrate quietly on his goals. And by way of this quality did he now cast away worry. His mother's words came back to him at this moment and he smiled. Ambitious for her only son, she had encouraged him always, reminding him that, "Humility is strength, son. Modesty is an indulgence. Never hide your light under a woven basket. It knows how to shine."

Joha'lan cast one last look at the dying funeral pyre, uttered a final farewell and turned toward the old woman. He had been unaware of her gaze upon him these past few minutes; her gaze *into* him. He walked to her, smiling. She returned the smile and struggled up from her cramped position, old bones and muscles protesting.

Joha'lan addressed her in a gentle voice, not as Vesa'tan, the witch, but as 'Forest Mother'! "Forest Mother, I need your assistance. My knowledge of the trees is not equal to Ran'tar's. In fact, my knowledge is unequal to the task before me. Will you lead me to those great trees which our people need? By way of an answer the old woman held out her hand and allowed it to be swallowed in his mighty clutch. She looked up into his eyes and sent her final question deep into them. Then, having made her judgment, she turned as he loosed his grip and walked toward where his and Ran'tar's packs lay. "First you have to feed me, big man. We will begin tomorrow. Come on! What have you got for me in those packs?"

A subdued sadness reigned at that night's camp on the slopes of Volan Votu. The Herbalist's conversations centered on their reminiscences of the man, Ran'tar. Sha'lat, Sht'ana and Tina were the only ones there with no stories to recount, barely having known the man. But the others addressed them directly, familiarizing them with the life of an exceptional member of their community, hoping to make his memory shine even more brightly in the telling. Their camp that night was but a yell from the edge of the tree-line, nestled among protecting boulders which reflected the big bonfire's warmth and glow, lightening the sadness. The air here was verging on cold and all available wraps were in use.

The two male Herbalists were doing the cooking tonight: dried fish marinated in coconut juice, fried taro flakes and mashed roots, collected along the way up here. The women managed to playfully grumble that the men should cook more often, so tasty was their effort. Tina and the other young girl in the group, Shana'lan, leaned sleepily against their mothers, both fighting to keep awake should they miss something interesting. Both soon failed in their attempts and were laid down and covered warmly. The adults remained up late that night. Important matters needed discussion. After the meal had been leisurely eaten, the conversation turned to tomorrow's gathering of the medicinal herbs and lichens and flowers. Shen'ha laid out her itinerary.

"We must contact the reed-harvesters first of all so we will know the places they have not gathered their reeds yet. Wherever they work, no more Mud Flowers are to be found. You three men can do that. And take the two young girls with you, since you are so much more fleet-of-foot than we mere women." This was met with considerable laughter and joking and then Shen'ha continued.

"Most of you will remember how cold and wet the Mud Flower harvesting is." Shen'ha then looked at Sha'lat and quickly explained that these valuable flowers, bulb plants they were, grew at the base of the tall reeds, which grew in the shallow wetlands. Even up here on the mountain, there was low-lying ground, which filled with the copious rainfall and in these basins grew the narrow reeds which were so valuable for fashioning rain capes and weaving basketry. "All that will take up most of tomorrow. Oh, and please remember; take only one egg from any curlew's nest you find. The Feather-Master says this year's breeding is low."

Another woman added, "My husband has asked that we count the eggs in any Ground Owl's nest we might find. Next year's feather-gathering depends on how many owls there might be to capture." Another said that they should be mindful of the number of storms and the time of day in which they occurred and so the minutes ran, the new moon drifting back down to the horizon and tired eyes fighting sleep as had the children's. Shen'ha then rose and, spreading her arms in a blessing on the assembly, bade them all a good night's rest. Soon the only sound was the cheery crackle of the bonfire and the gentle moan of the night wind through the pine trees. Tomorrow would be a busy day.

The dawn was crisp and clear, the thin air rich with the fragrance of foliage and flowers unknown below the mountain. Birds never seen at lower altitudes whizzed and chattered as they sought early-morning insects. Songsters chorused from the branches of the tall, slim pine trees, which had now replaced the forest hardwoods. No morning breeze had yet been born to the sun's heat and the breakfast fire's smoke rose in a thin vertical column from its source.

Through the sparse branches of the pines could be seen the dark blue sea, obscured the evening before by lower-level cloudbanks. Facing east, the sea shimmered gold and dazzling into the eyes of young Tina. She hugged herself, shivering in the cold morning air. No coughing or itching accompanied this morning's rising. Instead, shivering herbalists puffed clouds of steamy breath into the still air. They slapped and hugged themselves and each other, giggles and then laughter beginning amongst them.

This new day on the slopes of Volan Votu saw smiles. However, no one seemed too eager to have a morning bath in the nearby stream. Just one of the men tried it and soon ran blowing and grunting from the cold water, accompanied by outrageous but friendly, insults. Something to do with some bodily member having shrunk into obscurity. In any event, a morning meal was organized and a hot tea of herbs and spices soon put warmth into the group's bones. Tina, having but a short time before sulkily compared this morning with the worst night on that long sea voyage, now brightened and considered the warming world around her. Memories of chilly, but certainly not *this* chilly, mornings on her home-island, up that mountain with her father and sister on harvesting trips, returned.

Momentarily a sad nostalgia assailed her. She soon brightened though as a family of doves with whistling wings swept over the camp. Their iridescence gleamed joyfully in the rising sun as they quickly disappeared among the pines. Inside her began a lilting song; strange, yet welcoming. The mountain was greeting her, promising adventure and relief from the dramas of the past weeks. Fascinations to gladden a young girl's heart! Her new young friend, Shana'lan, came to her side, still sleepy-eyed but smiling. Tina knew she had found two new and true friends; one, a girl near her own age and another, ageless. This mountain, Volan Votu.

The threat of intruding pigs had been left behind with the lush vegetation of the forest. So too were the protective spears of the three men who now shouldered their empty packs. The heavy weapons had been stashed in the crotch of a tree at the edge of the forest. The men whooped and teased the women until Shen'ha finally ordered them to be off, like little boys too much underfoot. Tina and Shana'lan ran ahead of the three men as the five set out to find the reed harvesters. Above them shone the very tip of Volan Votu, gleaming in the rising sun, pink and white with shades of purple shadow.

The gentle roll of the mountain's massive slopes obscured all but that one intriguing glimpse of its true majesty. The two girls bounced and ran through the dew-wet grasses, startling birds which rose in protesting unity, their wings shimmering in the new day's light. The men smiled and chatted as they watched the youngsters gamboling ahead of them. One said with seriousness, "They say the little one is a *seer*!" "Yes", said another, "did you notice her yesterday? She and her mother both heard The Vesa'tan's call." The third man, always the joker, said, "And did you notice the hips on her older sister?" Laughter accompanied this dawning, always an auspicious beginning for the 'gathering'.

A narrow, gurgling stream, one of many which carried the snowmelt from high above, drew the two laughing girls. They drank and then splashed each other, squealing and giggling then running up a grassy knoll through knee-high pink flowers. At the crest of the knoll Tina stopped as if colliding with an invisible barrier! Shana'lan drew beside her, panting and still giggling with joy. She looked questioningly into her friend's face, then down the opposite slope to where Tina's eyes were focused. Below, in a grassy basin surrounded by rocky outcrops sat a man and a girl of about sixteen, eating their breakfast near a smoldering fire. Two dogs sat beside them, their bodies signaling the expectation of a handout. This ordinary vision of a father and a child attending the early-summer gathering of reeds was to Tina a painful reenactment of so many such mornings which she had shared, indeed, looked down upon from such a knoll on her home island. The girl was her sister's age when she had died. The man was short and stocky like her own father had been. Even the shaggy-haired little dogs could have been those she had raised from puppies. It was the dogs that broke the spell, releasing her from her sorrowful staring.

A stirring of early morning breeze wafted the scent of strangers to the dogs' keen noses and their alert protectiveness urged a burst of barking, hackles raised and stances braced to repel intruders. However, many generations had passed since one of these animals had been called upon to defend against anything but pigs. A Mal'lam was not a threat. Unless it was feast time. Then some dogs became part of the menu.

Man and girl looked up the slope to see what the ruckus was about. Tina's friend called down to the familiar pair, ignoring the half-hearted woofing of the dogs. The diminutive canines were now circling around the two young girls, still barking but hoping a few pats would be on offer, tails more active than their jaws. The man waved in greeting and motioned for Shana'lan and Tina to come downhill to join them. Shana'lan turned to Tina and beckoned her to follow and both girls plunged downhill through flowers and grasses, disturbed insects flying upward, the sunlight making varicolored jewels of them as they scattered.

The dogs, satisfied that they had fulfilled their guardianship, ran beside the girls, their barking now happy and playful. Still shaking off her sadness, Tina followed her friend and bent in stride to pat each dog as it came alongside to sniff the newcomers. The girl at the fire rose and called a greeting to Tina and Shana'lan while the man, resting on one elbow, picked his teeth with a straw and grinned at the scene."Good morning children!" he said warmly "Do the Herb-men follow you?"

"Three men come, Jash'na-an." Shana'lan answered. She used the familiar term of address allowed to cousins and the man nodded with enthusiasm. The reed-gatherers saw little of visitors and the anticipated conversation with other men was a welcome event. The man rose now and embraced his brother's niece, the daughter following suit with a wide grin of welcome. Tina, unusually reticent at the moment, stood a few paces away but she was warmed by her friend's next statement, her sorrow disappearing on another gust of morning breeze."This is my friend, Tina. She is of the S'ham-an. Her mother is a Herb-Mistress". The larger, stockier girl then turned to Tina and said in a voice filled with love and respect, "Tina-an is a *seer!*" the comment made even more appealing by her pubescent innocence.

Then, in rapid detail she recounted the tragic news that Ran'tar had died and all that had surrounded his demise. As the excited girl recounted her story, the harvester's daughter went to the cooking fire and retrieved two taro cakes and offered them solemnly to the girls, her brow knitted in a sorrowful frown. The moment had taken on a gravity which none of them felt comfortable with, but it was the frivolous dogs who injected a bit of lightness by engaging in a happy mock-combat with each other. They lunged recklessly about in their play, knocking into legs and knees, eliciting reluctant smiles from the recipients of bad new.

Then, as if responding to some clarion, the dogs reorganized themselves and rushed again up the slope, barking loudly in ferocious defense. The three Herbalists appeared over the crest of the hill, bending to pat the excited dogs and waving downhill to the encampment. The Harvester gently interrupted Shana'lan's tale of Ran'tar's death and then walked uphill to greet the three men. Shana'lan carried on with her story, addressing the man's daughter, all the while stuffing taro cake into her mouth. The older girl smiled indulgently and stood listening, casting furtive glances toward the new arrivals, trying to gauge which man might be interested in a sixteen year old girl.

Tina warmed to her new friend as she watched the girl's un-self-conscious behavior. Shana'lan's mobile features described with great clarity the drama of death and sadness and recovery. She even sang the first verse of the rejoicing of the dear, dead man's life in a sweet, strong voice. By then the four men had returned downhill. The father had heard the adult version of the story and now he spoke quietly to his daughter. "Bala'sha, take our friends to the big patch of Mud Flowers we saw yesterday." With a sideways glance at the three Herbalists he added, "And hurry back. We've much work to do today." The short, rather plain-looking girl smiled and nodded at her father, threw the Herbalists a coquettish grin and led the party from the tidy camp and away to the east. The sun was mid-morning high now and a brisk breeze had risen. Up toward the mountaintop the massive clouds formed and whirled and tore apart and reformed again.

Tina watched them as she walked, fascinated by this phenomenon unseen on her home island with its much lower peaks. They were definitely *much* lower now, she recalled sadly. In spite of the breeze, the sun was hot and the three Herbalists shed their wraps, tucking them into their carry-alls. They strode after the girls, now dressed only in their loincloths.

The shallow basin of wetland where the reeds had not yet been harvested lay but a half hour from the gatherer's camp. Growing bored watching the Herbalists' labors and not skilled or strong enough to participate, the two girls asked to be excused to return to where the women would be working. The men sent them off cheerfully, the jokester of the group already flirting with the harvester's daughter. The older of the men then suggested that the sixteen year old should return to her father. She did so reluctantly, following a different track home. The two young girls ran off together whispering and tittering about the other girl's cheekiness. Holding hands, Tina and Shana'lan skipped and jogged through the tall grasses and flowers back toward where they knew their mothers to be working. Away to the west the Herbalist women would be harvesting the Windflowers. These silky, waxy flowers, in shades of pink and gold, were an important catalyst in many herbal remedies. As the women bent and picked and stuffed the flowers into bags, they chanted and sang. It was their voices which would guide the girls to them.

The gentle swell of the slope of the mountain created a sense of impending surprise as one moved laterally around it. Large enough to create its own local weather patterns, Volan Votu this day seemed to be having trouble deciding the direction in which it wanted its headdress of clouds blown. The breeze rose and fell, switching this way and that, creating eddies which whipped the fields of flowers first one way, then another. High above a falcon jigged and flapped as it too tried to make some sense of the inconsistencies. The girls ran like puppies, filled to the brim with the marvelous energy of this beautiful morning. They crossed narrow streams in athletic bounds, dodged around ancient outcrops of lava and squealed in mock fright when startles of birds flashed up and away from their charge. And always, in the distance, was the deep azure of the sea, no clouds hiding its hugeness today.

"There! That way!" Tina shouted and her friend changed her plunging course to follow. When the bobbing bodies of the gatherers were in sight, Tina called out a challenge to Shana'lan. "Race you!" and down the last stretch of clear ground the girls flew, Tina's short, lean legs a blur of movement. The girls descended upon the women in gales of gasps and squeals, both claiming victory in a dead-heat. They were greeted with indulgent smiles, an event of minor reprieve from the monotonous work. The youngsters both fell gasping and giggling near Shana'lan's mother, the woman reaching out with a swift hand to deliver a light, loving blow to her daughter's head."Be careful girls! You'll crush the flowers!" Then she turned smiling back to her work. When she had regained her breath, the ebullient Shana'lan began to recount their morning's adventures: the finding of the harvesters, his cheeky daughter's flirting with the Herbalist men, the huge crop of Mud Mushrooms among the reeds! Shana'lan was a born storyteller. Into old age, she would regale new generations with accounts of adventure, discovery and very intelligent insights.

Below the sunny slopes where the herbalists gathered this season's harvest, a giant man walked slowly behind a tiny old woman, her tread small and weary. From time to time the old woman, The Vesa'tan, stopped and tapped on a massive tree trunk with her staff. She would then stand with her ear to the trunk, listening for the tree's secrets to rebound in echoes - whether it was sound or flawed, sometimes too young yet to be suitable. She directed Joha'lan to lay his ear against the smooth bark of one great tree, its nearest limb twenty feet above the ground and impressive in its own right. She smacked it once, twice, three times with her staff.

"Do you hear it, Joha'lan?" she asked, her voice a near whisper. Joha'lan's brow furrowed in concentration, listening hard to discern the message in the echoed response. "Yes! Yes, I understand!" he answered and stood straight, dwarfing his companion and seeming almost a cousin to these great boles of timber. Looking up into his bearded face she nodded with satisfaction. "Yes. You must listen for the high note. If it does not remain pure, you can be sure that there is some flaw." She nodded again, a confirmation of the accuracy of her diagnosis. The Vesa'tan entertained no doubts. She knew her trees!

"Come now. You must judge this next one yourself." And she set off at a pace of such vigor that Joha'lan smiled in admiration. He was certain, so great was her enthusiasm that this next tree was surely a test. This solitary, enigmatic 'Forest Mother' was not averse to playing tricks. She had once, when first instructing dear Ran'tar in the mysteries of wood, allowed him to go to the great task of felling a tree which he had chosen in spite of her subtle warnings. The tree had been flawed and could be used only for bridging a stream in a narrow, deep gully. She had chided, abused and insulted him. Then, duly chagrined and apologetic, Ran'tar was made to endure another embarrassment: the old women thanked him for bridging a stream which she found difficult to cross, reached up and took his face in both hands and gave him a passionate kiss on the mouth. She then disappeared into the forest, cackling in triumph. Ran'tar paid very close attention to The Vesa'tan's opinions after that. He was also known to flinch slightly whenever the imposing, somewhat smelly old woman stood too near him, a look of mischief on her wrinkled old face.

Joha'lan and his 'Forest Mother' walked for many minutes through the steamy forest until finally … "There!" she shouted, so loudly that it startled the big man. She pointed between two large trees. He bent to see beneath a large limb, paused, and then stood in awe. The trunk rose from buttress roots more than ten feet below them, its dark, smooth trunk gleaming dully in the dim light. Joha'lan identified the tree not by its bark but rather by looking up to the canopy where its leaves, tiny at that great distance, were of a pale green. Then, to make certain, he sought further proof on the forest slope beneath the great tree. Yes. The ground was littered with the distinctly pointed, now dry foliage.

It was a 'Kanta'Ab', the most prized of all canoe timbers, found only here in the high forests of Sht'ah-Lee Set. And it was huge! A tree of this size and age would have to have been growing here at least three hundred years; it would have been but a sapling when the Mal'lam first came to this island. Now, with the great journey to the south anticipated, this was surely the beginning of the immense project for which Joha'lan seemed destined. The Vesa'tan stood silently as the huge Woodsman climbed carefully downward to the base of the 'Kanta'Ab'. A smile of pleasure brightened her face as she watched him. Joha'lan could hardly spare a glance at where he was placing his feet, his long-handled axe thrust forward in support, his eyes glued to the bole of the tree.

Already in his mind ran the mechanics of cutting, hollowing, and then moving this great mass of wood to the seashore where it would become a masterwork of the Canoe-makers art. When he reached the tree he leaned into it, wrapping his powerful arms onto the smooth bark. It would have taken three men of his reach to encircle it. He then stood back two paces and looked up at the magnificence of it. It was fifty-five feet to the first branch, which was itself massive. Such a length of hull was what had been mooted as the optimum for the new vessels. Above, the wind was parting and waving branches about, allowing brilliant glimpses of the midday sun to further dazzle already intoxicated eyes.

Then Joha'lan remembered the old woman, still standing atop the embankment. And wasn't this tree surely a test? Was this giant really too old and probably flawed in its heart? Was she trying to confound him? He would see. He took up his axe and prepared to give the trunk a mighty blow with its stone head. He would strike those sounding blows which would tell him of its worth, and as well, return his mind to a professional stance.

"Noooo!" came the shout. "No, no, no! Never strike a tree with stone unless you are sure you are going to harvest it. It is a great insult to the soul of a tree." The Vesa'tan came stumbling down the bank, her staff supporting her, her face a mask of condemnation. Then she stopped a few feet from The Canoe-Master and waved her staff at him, the very one he had given her some years before. "You men are all alike! You're all fools! I don't know why I bother." She stood boring her anger into him and he looked down and away, unable to sustain the weight of it. He gathered himself to ask her, why this intense passion, this awful attack on him? And then she began to giggle. Giggling?! Now he knew she was mad.

Joha'lan tucked his axe back into his belt and stood with hands on hips, scowling at her. "Hee hee hee" followed by loud snorts of laughter as she leaned forward on her staff, one hand trying to stifle what was beginning to sound likes the joy of triumph. Finally she managed to say, "Awwww, wood giant! You should have seen your own face. Haw haw haw!" Joha'lan felt the heat of embarrassment rising in his cheeks, his puzzlement becoming irritation. He put his great hands together, then put them behind his back, and then wiped his sweating palms on his thighs, trying to shed the rising tension within. Finally he managed to reply to her tormenting, scolding and belittling laughter. "Well, old one. When you've stopped laughing, you might let *me* in on the joke."

The sight of him in his frustration drew another guffaw from her, then she stilled her mirth. She cleared her throat and said lightly, "There is no joke, dear Joha'lan. Never, ever, strike a tree with stone unless you are very certain that is the tree you wish to harvest. Take no life - threaten no life, unless the need is great." Joha'lan surrendered to the woman's now gentle smile and returned a sheepish grin of his own, looking down briefly like a naughty child. His potential for anger required more than one old woman's remonstrance.

"As I taught Ran'tar, so I must teach you, it seems." Her face was serious now. "To sound wood, strike with wood. And speak respect and love in your heart. I know what was in your mind, wood-giant. You were thinking men's thoughts. You were thinking of the muscle required, the power to be applied, the pain and sweat which would paint your pride with accomplishment." The Vesa'tan now climbed the rest of the way down the embankment with surprising nimbleness but still using her staff for support as she came. She stopped before him and looked up, smiling into his face. That strange warmth and familiarity wiped any insult or censure. He listened intently as she revealed further truths of the nature of trees, truths he had heard before but never truly absorbed. She moved past him then to the great tree, the focus of all her intensity. She placed one lean hand against the smooth, rippled bark and said as she cast a look of mild mockery over her shoulder at him. "Take no offence sister! He's only a man."

"But, not too bad a man." she added. Then she murmured beneath his hearing, not at the tree but *into* it. She straightened, gave a low gurgling laugh and slapped the tree trunk resoundingly with a sisterly intimacy and turned to her student. His face indicated full attention and a touch of awe.

"You must realize by now, you great mountain of muscle, that trees are female!" She lifted her staff toward his face and told him to look closely at it, his own loving work. "No man could carve with such beauty and sensitivity unless he carved with love. However, I'm not such a fool as to believe that your thoughts were only for me when your blades worked this staff." Her cheeky grin embarrassed him again and she poked his stomach with a boney finger, saying, "Pay attention now. A fine worker of wood must be a lover. He must make love to the grain and texture with the sharpness of his tools. He must allow himself to become intoxicated with its fragrance, the lovely nakedness of the newly uncovered flesh. This tree . . ." and she half turned and pointed up at the tree's height, "should you accept her as your lover, will test your manhood to its limits!" The Vesa'tan then took his right hand and thrust her staff into it. "Now!" she grinned impishly, "Give her a few kisses, Woodsman. See if I have not brought you to a grand love affair!"

The moon rose full behind the thinning clouds, the high wispy stratus clouds glowing with a pearly translucence. The night was chilly but windless, a nightjar calling mournfully from across the still grasslands. Around a large campfire sat the Herbalists, men and women, joined earlier that day by Joha'lan and The Vesa'tan, his 'Forest Mother'. The old woman sat wrapped in layers of blankets made of pounded fibers, thin but surprisingly warm they were. Her every need was attended to, every want quickly fulfilled. On each side of her sat the two premier women Herbalists, Shen'ha and Sha'lat. Never before had she joined in the evening gatherings of her people since she had so long ago fled to the forests, always remaining aloof and intent upon her own nocturnal mysteries.

But this night, at the urging of Joha'lan, a man she had now come to respect nearly as she had Ran'tar, she sat at ease as if it was a matter of usual course. This night's company regarded her with great respect, bordering on awe. Sh'tana Herb-Mistress poured a bamboo cup with herb tea and rose gracefully from beside the fire and went to the old woman, holding the steaming cup out to her with both hands, her two little fingers held outward in a formal gesture of offering. The Vesa'tan, not having engaged in this ritual since childhood but having observed it at other firesides as she watched from the darkness, hesitated momentarily. Then she remembered, extended her thumbs to touch the proffered fingers and nodded respectfully. She took the steaming cup and smiled at Sh'tana, looking deeply into the lovely young woman's eyes, reading.

Suddenly The Vesa'tan set the cup down before her. Sh'tana's eyes widened in surprise as The Vesa'tan reached out quickly and grasped both of the young woman's hands in hers. The surprisingly strong grip held Sh'tana in her kneeling position and the old woman stared into her face for long moments. Then she spoke, still holding the warm hands. "Prepare yourself, my child." The old woman whispered, the whole of the company silent now and listening carefully. "Your children will be few, your heartaches many. But you will have the love of the one you desire!" and then with a cackle which broke the rising tension, she slapped the backs of Sh'tana's hands resoundingly, and released her. "Not to worry though, my dear. You'll come through very well. And if you're lucky, you'll live to be as old and crazy as I am!"

As gales of laughter circled the group, Sh'tana rose blushing but smiling and returned to her seat beside young Tina. Her little sister had watched closely and now joined the smiles, trying to ignore the dim voice within her mind, which whispered, "Sh'tana needs much love, little one. Always be there for her. Remember!" Tina could not imagine her big sister, her self-assurance seemingly so complete, ever needing her own childish support. But Tina would remember, for those whispered voices became echoes which returned when need arose. And so the moment promised an evening which would congeal into an easy celebration.

That season's Gathering had been profuse and this night of the full moon was filled with rejoicing. Two bamboo tubes of palm toddy, kept secreted away until this night, were taken from a carryall and uncorked. The powerful brew was passed around the fire-lit circle. Only The Vesa'tan refused it, Joha'lan taking but one hearty mouthful, the women all took small sips. The three male Herbalists gulped big swallows. For Joha'lan this was not a night for inebriation. All evening long an electric discourse flashed between him and those beautiful eyes across the firelight. The direction this night would take for the two new lovers was mutually understood.

A flute and a three-stringed instrument were produced and soon sweet harmonies were sounded and baritone counterpoints added growing volume. Sparks rose from the bright fire as mineral salts were thrown on, blue and green flames erupting joyfully. Even The Vesa'tan hesitantly joined in as memory flowed back with words nearly forgotten for so many decades. Later, by hours, as the campfire glowed weakly, two figures walked quietly back into the sleeping camp, one huge hand enclosing a smaller, herb-stained one which glowed with warmth. The woman stood on her tiptoes and reached her mouth up to the man's bearded face. They kissed sweetly and long and as she hugged her body close to his, he wrapped his arms around her, enclosing her in a reluctant goodnight. No words were spoken. None could suffice on this night.

The woman then released him and padded quietly to where her two daughters lay sleeping. She turned and formed a kiss, sending it on warm breath. Then she lay down between the sleeping figures and fell into the soundest sleep she had enjoyed since before the death of her husband and middle daughter. Sha'lat was at peace. Joha'lan knelt beside the smoldering coals and poked a stick into them until it blazed, prolonging this special night. The blaze illuminated his bearded face and a pair of old eyes watched its gentleness, its strength. She watched him rise finally and go to lie beyond the fire's dim glow. She waited many minutes before rising and wrapping two of the gift blankets around her frail-looking body. Then she stole away into the chilly night.

Tired eyes woke to a heavy mist, cold and clammy. The first person up went directly to the fire and raked embers together, added kindling and soon had a cheery fire burning again. Many now stood with their backs to it, still blanket-wrapped, rubbing backs and stiff limbs. It was minutes before the absence of The Vesa'tan was noticed. Few were surprised. Some said they may simply have dreamed of her presence the night before, still so unusual was it. A light breakfast of baked quail's eggs and cooked tubers soon restored the Mal'lam Herbalists and then the serious business of final packing began.

A lively banter grew around the campsite and Joha'lan became the focus of offers to increase the ballast of his load, lest he should be unbalanced. He laughed and teased in return, the three heavy-headed Herbalist men absorbing the most pointed jibes. Joha'lan's congenial humor and deep chuckle were a welcome delight, especially to young Tina. She thought this big man especially wonderful and enthused about him to her friend, Shana'lan. Unaware of last night's first blossoming of a deep love, both girls chattered and dreamed ephemeral things.

By the time the sun had begun to burn away the mist, a chant had begun; a song of rejoicing and bounty which had been sung by generations of Mal'lam Herbalists. Packs were slung, the fire drowned and with Shen'ha in the lead, the company began the descent back to their sea-side home. Joha'lan brought up the rear, carrying nearly fifty pounds of compacted herbs and lichens and flowers. Sha'lat, at the front near her friend, Shen'ha, glanced back from time to time at the shaggy head which towered above the others. His eyes always met hers.

Within an hour they were among the sparse pine trees and scrub of the upper tree line. Birdsong gaily greeted them and flutterbyes and dragonflies animated the air. The third hour saw them entering the forest proper and the spears were retrieved from the crotch of the tree. The men Herbalists again took up their original positions in the column, armed now and alert. Joha'lan still brought up the rear, carrying both his and Ran'tar's spears. The air grew very still, heavy with retained heat and moisture. The forest birds called with bell-like songs or harsh chattering, sounding so near but seldom seen.

Near midday, Shen'ha called a halt at the site of Ran'tar's cremation and after packs were gratefully laid aside, handfuls of mountain flowers were cast over the ashy ground. Joha'lan, arching his aching back, stood looking thoughtfully at the site. Then he went to the low mound of charcoal and ash and began to run thick fingers through them, picking out tiny remnants of bone and placing them into a small, leather pouch at his waist. These he would present to the dead man's two sons on their return to the island. The Mal'lam tradition provided that the scant remains from the funeral pyre would be wrapped together with some personal items of Ran'tar's which had been of special importance to the man; his stone axe and a neckpiece had been removed from his body and wrapped for safekeeping before his body had been consigned to the funeral byre. These would be taken to a special hiding spot by his sons and buried with simple ceremony. Then the whole community would hold a feast in his honor; to celebrate and rejoice in the life of a much loved member of their Clan.

As Joha'lan stood looking through the forest, Sha'lat came beside him and rested her hand soothingly on his arm. He looked down at her with tearful eyes and managed a smile. From the group gathered beside the trail, Tina looked over and saw the unmistakable affection in their postures. She frowned, her child's emotions tugging and twisting within her. She glanced toward her sister, Sh'tana, who was also watching the two in their silent, personal moment. Sh'tana smiled at her little sister and came to stand beside her. She put an arm around the little one's shoulders and said quietly, "Mama has sorrowed long enough, Tina-an. Be happy for her." Tina thought and slowly her forehead released its frown. She looked up at her sister, nodded in confirmation and the two went to join the others as they all began unwrapping lunch- time snacks.

As Tina stood beside her new friend, about to begin their usual chattering, her eyes suddenly widened! Inside her, that familiar voice was commanding, "Go down the trail now, Tina-an. Alone." Moving as if mesmerized, she turned away from Shana'lan without a word and began walking toward the track. "Where are you going?" her friend asked, puzzled at her sudden action. "Uh, oh, I have to pee." Custom dictated that one relieved oneself in private. Shana'lan still thought this strange. There were many bushes nearby behind which to squat and pee. Why go down the trail? The girl shrugged. Her friend was sometimes rather mysterious. Then she turned and sought out some lunch.

Only Shen'ha's eyes followed her, suspecting, knowing that something was drawing her. The 'sight'. Sha'lat suddenly loosened her hold on Joha'lan's arm and turned to see her daughter round the corner in the trail and disappear. She too had sensed that indistinct peal of alert with which the 'seer' is blessed, or cursed, as the case may be. She felt no alarm but knew that something of significance hovered. Such events had often occurred in her life and she sent a silent wish of strength to her little girl. "What is it, Sha'lat? Is something wrong?" Joha'lan asked, growing ever more sensitive to this woman's moods and emanations. "The 'sight', Joha'lan-luv! The 'sight' is drawing my daughter! But, not to worry. She will be well." She smiled reassuringly at him and said, "Let's go eat before all those others leave us nothing."

He pondered quickly as he followed her, then said, "It will be The Vesa'tan. She is calling. Somehow I feel it." Sha'lat only nodded. She had already discerned the old woman's interest in Tina. When they sat to eat no one spoke of the matter even though the awareness of some important event had spread among the company on silent wings of thought. Such things were best left to take their own course, uncommented upon. Gossip and speculation might compromise the fragility of such happenings. Among the Mal'lam, the Herbalists were of the most respectful of the 'sight' and held 'seers', whatever their proclivity, in high esteem. Only people with corrupted souls, such as 'Tor'na the Mad', were considered 'sorcerers' and potentially dangerous. Herbalists spent much time devoted to quiet contemplation and meditation upon the workings of the human spirit. This was essential in applying their hard-won knowledge to the art of healing. All now ate in silence. Even Mata'ma, the company's jokester, resisted his usually irrepressible banter.

And so it was that on this day a child of the '*sight*' was followed by love and mental encouragements, willing her strength to reckon with the demands she would surely meet, alone on that well-traveled trail. It seemed to Tina that she would walk forever down the shadowy trail and yet, in footsteps, she had proceeded but a hundred paces. As she approached a bend, which was flanked by two trees of almost identical size, a chill ran up her arms, raising the fine hairs on the nape of her neck. She slowed, bending and peering around the corner, expecting … what? The voice in her mind spoke no words but only hummed its presence; comforting, encouraging."Come, little one! Have no fear!"

There came the words from all around her like an echo in a cavern. She stopped and searched for the source; not from within but from without; a human voice, someone near. Her skin seemed to prickle from head to toe. Childish fears flailed at her but still she moved forward tentatively, each step measured. A sudden breeze, cooler than the humid jungle would be thought to allow, blew at Tina's back, urging her forward again and thrust her around the corner between the flanking trees, standing like guardians before an altar. There on the track before her, on the moist and leaf-littered ground lay a carved staff. The Vesa'tan's! And over and around the length of wood lay the coils of a snake! Tina started, stood fully upright with her hands to her face, her eyes wide with alarm. She feared snakes, especially since the tragic death of Ran'tar. But as she focused on the reptile some strange familiarity, almost a remembrance, urged itself upon her.

"The creature is not venomous, child. Don't be afraid." came that voice again. She recalled now. This was not the feared snake which had killed, but this was a *Boota*, a placid and slow-moving plaything for some children. And then The Vesa'tan appeared. She was naked, emerging from the cover of a head-high shrub covered in tiny pink blossoms. She stood almost girlishly on the trail, her hands behind her, a wide, welcoming smile on her old, seamed face. Her body sagged as any old woman's does, her thinness accentuating the dry, wrinkled skin. But this woman's spirit seemed not to have sagged at all in a long and mostly solitary life. The twinkling eyes within that smile drew the girl like a beacon and Tina slowly, more confidently, approached the staff and its serpent minder. "I have a gift for you, Tina-an. When you receive this gift, your initiation will have occurred. The ceremony of 'The Warming Moon' will be but a formality."

Still smiling, she came close behind the staff and it's protecting serpent and knelt near them, extending one hand to stroke the smooth, shiny, newly-molted skin. The skin, grey-green with a bright green stripe running its length on each side, slithered against her palm in response. It moved along and over the polished wood, doubling back as would a loving pet beneath the hand of a master. The Vesa'tan held her hand still, the snake still running against the pads of her fingers, still sliding hypnotically along the staff.

The Vesatan began a breathy chant, Tina unable to discern the words, nor would she have been able to understand them if she had been able to hear them clearly. This was a personal tongue, evolved as much from the sounds of non-human nature as from the old woman's own spoken language. Tina found herself staring into a tunnel of concentration, her every sense drawn out and down and into the mesmerizing writhing of the reptile. Its movements, indeed its very body became more and more beautiful by the moment.

Tina could nearly sense the marvelous smoothness of its skin, the flicking tongue eliciting a wash of saliva in her mouth, her own tongue tasting some strange sweetness. She swallowed and heard a 'click' in her ears. And now she was sure she could hear the snake's belly scales shushing against the soft ground - the muted give of moss and soil. The Vesa'tan was staring hard into Tina's face but the girl's concentration was complete, inviolable. The Vesa'tan smiled, closed her eyes and uttered a silent song of invitation.

In the forest around them the birds ceased their busyness and calling. They too listened. Above in the forest's canopy, a strangely localized wind blew apart the covering branches, opening a window of strong midday sunlight onto that space in the trail where something awesome portended. Up the trail, the Mal'lam ceased their low buzz of quiet conversation and looked about them, also listening. The very earth itself was humming! A tremor, which rang beneath human hearing, was emanating from the forest below them. The child's mother closed her eyes and began a silent chant.

Tina was aware that perspiration was running down her body as if some sudden fever was boiling over within her. Her gaze un-diverted, she quickly undid her wrap and cast it aside, cooling air tingling against her bare skin. Her vision began to alter; the snake, the staff, even the moist ground upon which they lay began to shimmer with a beautiful translucency. The serpent's scales became no longer a clever camouflage but a transparent sleeve revealing a sparkling play of light beneath. Muscles and organs shone through, pulsating, fascinating. The long straight grain of the staff glittered in gold and reds, sparks leaping from crest to carved crest on the incised patterns. Tina's body answered some insistent pull upon it and she sat, cross-legged and straight-backed, her wrists resting on her thighs.

"Tina-an!" The Vesa'tan spoke. Her voice seemed disembodied, its source indistinct, echoing inside the girl. Tina's forehead wrinkled in concentration, her hands now gripping her knees. "Tina-an, of the Earth Discipline! You are truly a child of the land. Have no concern, little sister, for your destiny has been sung to me and I shall protect you, always! See what you see, hear what you hear and know it for the truth, for the truth is that your spirit lives within the '*sight*'! Where others consume the power of the mushroom or the herbs and incantations of their magic, you possess such vision as your natural birthright."

The old woman stood and stepped over the staff and its sinuous protector and stood before the girl. Tina's view of the legs before her was startling, fascinating! Old skin had become as clear as milky crystal. Vibrant energy glowed and danced beneath it, fluid and solid, both at once, color upon color. Tina's eyes shifted slowly up and her view was of a body lovely with youth and vitality, glowing with energy. But the face was without feature; rather, it shone almost painfully bright as if the sun glowed through it.

A vibrating hum began again and her taste and smell declared a leafy fragrance. Within her that familiar voice began again as a chant, the words but some unearthly call - pure sound. Her body became an integral part of the earth upon which she sat. She could feel the massive boulders beneath her, the rush of subterranean waters; and deeper still, a powerful heat welled up beneath all. As if with a detached eye she viewed the deep roots of the great trees around her, moving from tree to tree, reading the particular signature of each species, defined by color and combination of color. Each tree sang a different song and she found herself immersed in a joyous symphony of announcement.

"Stand, Tina-an, and take my hand." The voice again surrounded her. She stood easily as if her every movement was assisted by some outside force. She felt light, like she might lift from the ground and drift away. The hand she held was warm and dry and human yet possessed of an electric tingling. Still she could not see that face. It shone so radiantly that she looked away from it and into the forest. She saw not trees and leaves and branches but columns of shimmering green light and flat, waving plates of purple, glistening like ice. All around her the world she had come to know was transformed into an almost overwhelming environment of shifting, singing dimensions.

No longer just an observer of this, she was now truly a part of it. As she walked she was aware of this world's awareness of *her*! Every color, every sound, every sense she possessed, confirmed her oneness with this magical whole. The forest was welcoming her! Tina found herself standing in a cool flow of water which was not clear stream water but a blue swirl of light, with particles clinging to her ankles. She knelt, still holding The Vesa'tan's hand, and dipped her free hand into the blueness. It fell through her fingers with a tinkling like grains of sand on a seashell. She giggled with delight and dipped again and again.

"Sit, child. Sit in the water!" Tina leaned on the helping hand and sat upon the smooth, round stones, the water rushing around her bare hips and bottom, splashing blue sparks over her thighs. The Vesa'tan herself sat in the playful stream, releasing Tina's hand. Tina turned toward the woman and the intense glow which had obscured her features receded, revealing again the aged skin, the nearly toothless smile and eyes of an almost fearsome intensity. The rest of her body too was returning to its previous, familiar state.

Tina looked at her own hands, then at her legs and body. These too, were taking on the familiar tones of flesh. With a desperate, "Ohhhh?!" Tina looked around her. The familiar had all returned, only sparkles of fading intensity remaining. Her mind rushed outward, upward and then down toward the earth in a determined attempt to regain, rejoin that wonder! Her child's heart filled with tears of longing, the tears choking her throat. The old woman reached a warm, comforting hand to Tina's shoulder and cooed to her. "Don't sorrow, child. What you have seen and heard and felt is real! As real as this world you see now. And it is forever yours! Have patience now. You will see. Come!"

Taking Tina's hand again, they left the gurgling stream and returned to the trail. As they walked up the track, Tina tried to will the return of that world and was rewarded with furtive sparkles of light here and there, but all ephemeral and provocative. She felt very tired, as when a day of activity ended and her strong young body craved food and rest. The old woman's surprisingly strong hand was welcome support as she was led to the center of the trail once more, directly between those two perfectly matched trees.

"Stand quietly, child!" The Vesa'tan's voice was a whisper. The woman returned to where her staff lay in the middle of the trail. The snake was now lying loosely coiled and aside from the staff, its scales gleaming in the wavering, shifting spots of light let down from the canopy above. The Vesa'tan picked-up her staff and, waving a gesture at Tina with it, retreated behind the nearby flowering shrub. Returning moments later with her wrap tied up under her arms, she advanced toward Tina with something in her left hand. As she advanced she beat the butt of her staff against the ground, a dull marking of each step. "This is my gift to you, Tina-an - Earth Child!"

She opened her hand to reveal a shiny blue stone, highly polished and gleaming with streaks of green and gold. The stone was perforated with one hole through which ran a braided cord of almost transparent material. It was magnificent in its simplicity. "It is the sacred stone of the mountain, child. 'Volan Votu's Tear', it is called. The plaited cord is a year's shedding by our friend there" and she indicated with a nod of her head the snake lying just behind her. Tina had the distinct impression that the snake was smiling at her. Her tired mind accepted that smiling snakes might not be too exceptional on a day like this.

"Take it, Tina-an! This is your talisman, your door through which to enter the worlds of great knowledge!" Tina took the necklace in both hands and drew it close to her face, peering at the depth of color, the shine of the plaited snakeskin. She looked at the old woman's face, her own reflecting joy and wonder. The Vesa'tan's eyes misted with tears as she smiled at Tina, the warmth of triumph and completion nearly overwhelming her.

"Thank you, Vesa'tan" Tina croaked, her own eyes brimming. The old woman broke the moment's spell by turning and walking back to where the snake lay, her foot nearly touching it. She stood with both hands grasping her staff and leaned slightly toward Tina. The snake began to unwind and slowly, leisurely, slithered toward Tina. "Watch the snake, Tina-an. Don't take your eyes from it."

Tina stood with the necklace still held in her open palms, at waist level, a humming returning to that inner ear. Wisps of bluish light, like small lightning, began to play over the form of the reptile as it proceeded benignly toward her. The wisps congealed into a solid blue glow which enveloped its body and the humming became an ascending roar. That roar proceeded from her head downward and outward, filling her body and limbs and causing the stone in her hand to vibrate.

Then the snake coalesced into a ball of pulsating blue, transparent light, growing larger and casting shadows as it brightened. The reptile's body could still be seen writhing slowly, passively, within the glow. The sound filled and surrounded Tina, channeling every sense toward the light. Suddenly the ball of blue light leapt from the ground and hovered in front of her, at the level of her head. With incredible swiftness, it shot away among the trees, disappeared, reappeared, bounced against tree trunks, fell to the ground and bounded along the mossy cover. It then lifted into the air again and continued its mad flight. Its motion was pure joy! Tina laughed impulsively, delighting in the comic, madcap exuberance of its motions. She longed to join it, fly with it, share its joy! Back and forth and up and down the embodied glow flew, showering sparks wherever it struck. Gales of girlish laughter filled the scene, the old woman's cackling joining in.

And then, with startling abruptness, it flew to just in front of Tina, bobbing and swaying as if panting from its exertions. It pulsated in what could only be interpreted as a greeting. The roaring had receded to a high whistling like a night bird's call, staccato and insistent. She stood waiting - for something! The bright wide glow began to quickly draw in upon itself, shrinking in size while intensifying in color until it became a tiny point of intense azure, exactly the size of the bead which Tina held in her hand. Moving slowly, deliberately, it drifted toward Tina's open palms, paused, then with a movement so swift she was not sure she'd really seen it, it flew into the stone.

Tina stared into the stone bead which lay in her hand. A tiny gleam of light shone there for a moment and then winked out. The bead and its shiny, plaited string glowed with no more intensity than when she had first accepted it. It seemed altogether unchanged. Tina looked about her. The Vesa'tan was nowhere to be seen, nor was the *Boota* evident. Tina stood alone, the sound which had dominated was gone, the forest again rustling and twittering and chirping as normal around her.

Tina gripped the two clasps at the ends of the snakeskin tie and lifted the necklace up and attached it around her neck in an easy movement. A last sudden rush of sound rose, and then as quickly faded as she let the cool stone amulet fall against her throat. She was once more back in the world as she had always known it. Something was changed though, something she felt deep within her, beyond any of her five senses. She knew that she would never again know loneliness!

Voices! Human, familiar, comforting, came from behind her up the trail where she had come from. How long ago? She turned to greet her Mal'lam brothers and sisters. Sounds of laughter from down this trail had freed them from their quiet waiting. Sha'lat, her mother, was first to arrive, followed closely by sister Sh'tana and then the others. Soon all gathered about the girl, none speaking but all faces filled with questions. All eyes went from her tired little face to the gleaming necklace which lay upon her thin throat. It lay in such perfect balance that it appeared to have been born as part of her.

Shen'ha spoke softly to the giant man who stood behind the others. He nodded and moved through the company, stooped and picked Tina from where she stood swaying slightly with a sudden fatigue. He held her gently against his broad chest, her mother and sister moving to either side of Joha'lan, patting and rubbing the girl's arms, legs and body. Fifty paces up the trail and Tina lay against the man's shoulder, sound asleep. In her dream she heard an old woman's joyous cackling through a forest of emerald, sparkling trees. Around them all the forest sighed in wonder and fulfillment.

Research Notes: Impressions and General Observations

Subject: Tina Pua'lani Kaiser, Kaua'i, Summer 1972

Ten days of transcribing notes, going back to ask Tina questions, (and there were many), and struggling with a summer cold-in-the-head later, I finally got the story down on paper. So what arrived in the mail the next day? A small package, wrapped in brown paper and without a return address. The postmark was Honolulu. What's this?

It was a new tape recorder, the latest Sony version, small and compact and with ten blank tapes included! Inside was a short note from someone with a perverse sense of humor!: "Thought this might be of some assistance. Kind regards, Jiro." Talk about rotten timing! But, little did I know that that little machine was going to be absolutely indispensable in the coming weeks … after I'd finally learned how to use it. Who did I turn to to solve some of the technical puzzles of its workings? Tina, of course. She borrowed it for a couple of days when I had to fly back to Honolulu to attend a conference at the University. When I got back she had conquered the mechanics of the thing, and used up half the tapes recording everyone in the family and most of her friends. When she came with Tutu to pick me up at the Lihue airport, there she was, tape recorder held out to my face like I was a celebrity, asking for an interview, with the aplomb of a T.V. journalist! I remember grumbling under my breath that this kid would do all right for herself.

My trip to the University had been mostly a bore, compared to what I'd been involved in: it was dry, tedious, scholastic mumbo-jumbo, but one's attendance was noted on one's future assessment for a degree. Jiro came to the rescue though. He took me out to dinner at his favorite Chinese restaurant the night before I came 'home'. 'McCulley Chopsuey' was a local haunt of the University brigade. Like any good Chinese restaurant, it was brightly lit, noisy, crowded and served the most delicious food! It was that night that I began to know Jiro on a completely different level. He's not such a bad old bastard, after all!

Two weeks until school starts - for Tina I mean. Tutu Kinau and I go to Lihue to buy Tina's new school clothes. She's a freshman this year, first year of high school. A whole new scene! But, being who this young lady is, she's not much impressed. I think she'd be happier staying at home with her Tutu and me, hiking through the hills and recounting the stories her *spirits* tell her. Or maybe I'm just projecting my own prejudice. Subjectivity doesn't belong in a professional's field notes, I know. My project supervisor, Professor Jiro Yukihara, will of course edit this out. Tina has but six days to go before school starts now. All the little kids are excited about the new school year. Tina seems a bit withdrawn from the younger ones. Not cranky or anything like that but, somewhat distant. Tutu's eyes meet mine frequently in a mutual understanding: Tina needs to spend time with her story and me before school starts. O.K.! Let's do it girl.

Tina and I helped Tutu and Aunty Helen get the little kids ready for a pre-school picnic. They were like a litter of excited puppies. Finally they piled into

Tutu and Helen's cars and were off for the day. Tina and I looked at each other and sighed in relief. Silence! Then we packed ourselves a lunch and headed up the mountainside toward the *heiau*. It was a brilliant day, a bit windy but warm and mellow. We traveled fast through the forest proper to try and outrun those damned mosquitoes. Not fast enough! Itching and scratching, we made our way up to the grassy slope and the shade of the *kukui* tree. Tina had been chattering away over her shoulder to me all the way up. She was full of a new story and could hardly wait for me to get the tape recorder going. I took out my notebook and prepared to make additional notes as they occurred to me. I still wasn't completely confident of that machine, being something of a Luddite. She began to tell me about one of her favorite Mal'lam characters, and I was soon immersed in her story . . .

Chapter Eleven - Preparing for Change

Al'malan Sea-Master sat on the black sand in the early morning coolness, his infant son, Sahn'ta, playing happily near him. His thoughts had been on the coming initiation of the boys soon to be apprenticed to the sea and of his role as their mentor. A squeal of delight drew his attention again to the baby. The little one had discovered an innocuous shell, one of thousands which littered the beach, but he obviously found in it the amazement of discovery yet again. So like a child to find such pleasure in something so simple, thought his father and he smiled broadly as the tiny hand held the shell up toward him in triumph. This little boy was a great delight to his father and Al'malan often carried the happy boy around with him through the village and among the canoes and his Seaman mates. The baby's mother, Ja'eel, seemed more than happy to consign the child to his father's care.

Soon, Al'malan knew, he would be too busy to share these happy times with his son on a regular basis. Soon there would be demands upon him which would keep him away and fully occupied for days on end. And the *hewing* would be only the beginning of his obligations for he was now a Sea-Master and the master of one of this island's most beautiful canoes. He had been awarded the vessel of that dear man, Ran'tar, by the unanimous decision of the Seaman's Council. *Wa'Sho'la* was now his and it was as great a responsibility as it was an honor for a man so young. As the youngest Sea-Master, Al'malan was responsible for supervising the *hewing* of the young initiates who had chosen the sail-man's life. He must lead them by example through the strenuous physical ordeal of their training, an ordeal that the older Sea-Masters now avoided if possible. As well, he must instruct them in the songs, chants and dances which made up much of the lore necessary for the youngster's full initiation into the mysteries and wonders of the sea. Even now, sitting and watching his rambunctious son, he was humming and singing, sharpening his memory of those traditions which contained the collected wisdom of generations of Mal'lam seamen.

As Sahn'ta crawled about, collecting a thicker layer of black sand grains on his legs and hands, and now on his tiny mouth, that previously discovered shell was discarded and another white shard surrendered to his curiosity. Now something else caught his attention and that shell too was dropped. Al'malan watched in anticipation as the nine-month old Sahn'ta crawled on dirty hands and knees toward the just-discovered surf. Squealing delightedly the baby accelerated, sand flying in spurts from his rush toward that intriguing roll of water. Al'malan allowed him his investigation, rising and slowly following behind the fascinated boy.

When Sahn'ta reached the wet sand above the lowering tide's reach, he stopped to investigate this cool and firmer material. Quickly he snatched a handful to his inquisitive mouth. He turned and looked up at his father, a grimace of disgust on his face, half accusing him, so it seemed. Al'malan guffawed, and then said, "Tastes awful, eh, son?" Sahn'ta tried to spit the clinging sand from his mouth but only succeeded in drooling it slowly away down his chin. Then a crash of wave brought his attention around again and again he squealed and padded rapidly toward the shallow surf. When he encountered the first ripple of foam and cool water he stopped. Two quick slaps of his left hand sent a spray of salt water up onto his face and he squeezed his eyes shut and scowled. Another slap and the splash only reached his chest and belly. He giggled and pursued the receding wave, making a low growling noise, which brought a smile of delight to Al'malan's proud face.

The father watched with great concentration now as the next wave, ankle deep on Al'malan, surged playfully toward them. The baby knelt quietly, watching the foaming prelude to a deeper immersion approach him, fascinated. As the shallow front of water struck and shocked him, throwing a solid spray of water into his face, Al'malan held his breath. How would the child respond to this? His body tensed, ready to lean forward and snatch a frightened boy from this overwhelming experience. Then he roared with relieved laughter as Sahn'ta shook his head. The caked sand now washed from his beaming face by the force of the wave, he threw himself forward onto his stomach, and arms and legs flailing the escaping wave, shrieking in utter delight. Water held no fear for his son! No Seaman could experience a moment of greater pride than to know that his son found joy in the sea.

~ ~ * ~ ~

Autumn was the time of the *hewing*, when young boys twelve and thirteen years old were *hewn* to their lifetime craft. Most boys chose for themselves the craft to which they would dedicate their lives and in which they would find their own, individual status within their society. Some few, with no demonstrated leaning, or with slow wits which disallowed great concentration and ability, were assigned the stonemason's trade - not to impugn that craft, certainly. Great skill and mastery was required of the master stoneworkers, but the strong arms and backs upon which duller heads rested were always welcome in their labors.

The children of both sexes were allowed great freedom within the community, following their own predilections and engaging in unsupervised play. They never-the-less were required to assist in the necessary work of everyday life as a matter of natural affiliation. At planting and harvest time, or when fishermen brought in large catches, the sons and daughters of the adults engaged in such work attended those tasks alongside the rest of their family. Playmates from families whose chosen work differed might join a friend's family for a time, eating and sleeping with them, learning more and more about the interconnectedness of the different tasks which make up the world of the adults. As well, they would be exposed to the spiritual and ritual traditions attending Mal'lam life in its many intricacies. A parent, happy in their chosen profession and quite naturally desirous of their child following their lead, would be loath to force their child into a craft for which they were ill-suited or in which they showed no inclination.

It seemed that among the many crafts which constituted the technology of the Mal'lam, it was the Seamen craft masters who were most often inundated with boys seeking to be *hewn* of the sea. So strong was the allure of life upon the canoes and great bamboo rafts that every generation saw more and more youngsters seeking to be Sea-hewn. And just so were the traditions which had brought their forbears to these islands reinforced. So many people's eyes and hearts now turned ever more intently toward the horizon of endless sea and sky. This mood had always prevailed most strongly among the Clan Sh'tah'ha, the people now reunited here on Sh'tah Lee-Set.

When a baby was born, specially trained Herbalist women inspected the infant. They tested its reflexes, hearing, breathing and sight responses as well as the general soundness of its body. Should any deformity of significance be detected, anything which would likely make that child's life painful, restricted in large measure or sure to lead to an early death, the infant was immediately drowned. If within easy reach of the sea, the attending Herbalist diagnostician would wrap the tiny body in a white cloth. Accompanied by the other women walking in single-file behind her, quietly chanting a special dirge, she would immerse the infant in the surf until it had stopped breathing. The little body was then buried beneath the roots of a specially selected tree, chosen for this purpose. They believed the tiny soul would then return to the spirits of the *Green World*, the realm of trees and all green things from whence it had mistakenly entered the body of the child. It was believed that all deformities or stillbirths were the result of the errant wanderings of these spirits, drawn to the mother's womb in the mistaken belief that it was a portal to the living world of plants.

To the Mal'lam such a death was not 'killing' but the returning of a misguided spirit to its natural place. No stigma was attached to the mother or father; no sense of evil or violation accrued. It was simply an unfortunate mistake on the part of the natural forces, which, like humans, were sometimes less than perfect. Only the *Great Earth Mother*, the ultimate spirit that controlled the earth, was incapable of error. Though her manipulations of the earth and sky, and indeed the lives of man and beast and plant, were often unfathomable, the Mal'lam were resigned to both the joys and sorrows which resulted from Her breath upon the world. When a healthy child entered the world it was reason for great rejoicing within the whole community, for here was surely a special blessing from the Great Earth Mother.

Life flowed easily and freely for the children of the Mal'lam, their days filled with play, ample good food, good friends and the loving generosity of their whole community. In early childhood the few constraints imposed upon them were in the way of social strictures and conventions. Though numerous, they blended together to make a sensible design which the young minds could grasp and combine into an evolving and entirely livable whole. To break these conventions resulted in a harsh reprimand at worst. Usually a scowl and a slap of two adult hands together sufficed to bring an unruly youngster to order. Corporal punishment was never resorted to, not even a slap on the buttocks. A crawling infant might endure a snap of a finger for reaching for a dangerous object though.

Cooking fires and craftsmen's fires burned everywhere within a village and all little ones soon learned those dangers. Social convention among the Mal'lam had most to do with respect and reverence; reverence for the spiritual traditions and respect for one's elders. By the time one reached middle age though, a 'Grey-head' was allowed much greater leeway in expressing some irreverence. A common saying was, "Grey heads mean sharp tongues!" Children learned early on not to interrupt, contradict or inconvenience their elders but to respect and obey them, whatever their relationship. Staying out of the way of adults often proved the easiest option and children were most often seen in small groups or threes or pairs; seldom alone. There was so much to share.

The second major event in a child's life, after birth, was the *hewing* and *plaiting* when children, not quite yet adults, became focused on their path to adulthood and its responsibilities. For girls the *plaiting* was a festival of flowers and feathers and gaiety, preceded by a week of intense instruction involving chants and songs, which pertained specifically to their chosen craft. At the end of the formalities the loose hair of the girls was woven into a single '*plait*' which hung down the back of their neck and decorated with flowers and feathers. For the young women of the Mal'lam their initiation to their crafts and the mysteries of womanhood was leisurely and long, for it extended informally well into their early adulthood.

For the boys it was suddenly intense and severe, culminating in a ritual circumcision, the origin of the term, *hewing*! But after the *hewing,* their sense of self among the males of their community was assured. By enduring a series of demanding rituals and the pain of the removal of their foreskin, the boys were abruptly 'men'. The young men of the Mal'lam were still allowed the inconsistencies of youth for a couple of years. But the continual, reasonable discipline of their craft-masters gently saw them out of their adolescence and by their late teens most were fully occupied in the work of their chosen, or imposed, craft.

Few Mal'lam youngsters failed to meet the requirements of adulthood and the collective expectations of their society. That strange, and now estranged and banished Mala'tan, was a very rare exception among this Clan of the Mal'lam; indeed, among any of the Clans on the archipelago's many islands. Mala'tan had never completed his initiation. He had not been *hewn*, a very noticeable physical statement of his difference from all other Mal'lam males. Some of this season's initiates would be as exceptionally gifted as Mala'tan had been ill suited. Their best efforts and inspirations would one day be pitted against that one's clever vileness. He had been one of those boys for whom a craft had been chosen by the elders, for the boy had been sulky, arrogant and uninterested in any discipline or craft. It was because of his uncle, the Master-Seaman, Orn'ta, that he was placed with the seamen group of initiates. It had been a wasted exercise and after but two days among the initiates, he walked away from them, laughing derisively and calling them all fools. He was deemed hopeless and allowed to go his own, willful way.

Among this years' young *'new-hewn'* were two boys of limited intellect and no visible inclination toward any craft. They would both be *hewn* of the stonemason's craft. They would still have opportunity to share pride in the construction of weirs, water channels, house platforms and many other of the varied stone structures so integral to the built environment of the Mal'lam. In Mal'lam society, everyone was given a chance to fit in, to feel valued. One of these two lads already held claim to an adolescent fame, of sorts. He could heft a stone of as great a weight as most mature Stone-Hewn would care to risk their backs on, and did so frequently. He would be seen standing dumbly, legs braced wide apart, sweat coursing down his sturdy body for long minutes while his playmates urged him on. That he was otherwise quiet and amiable, childlike and dreamy-eyed endeared him to his companions.

He still endured some teasing and taunts however. Children can be cruel without being so tutored. His companion in the craft this year was a boy even duller of mind who tended to plod dreamily after his playmates, often distracted by a column of ants or a bird in a nearby bush, his friends leaving him to wonder where everyone had gone. That he was given to fits - convulsions of frightening proportion which terrified his mates - would, in time, lead him to the gentle solace of the Sht'ah Lee Herb-Mistress, Shen'ha. His name was Han. He would become Shen'ha's surrogate son and brother to that kind and gentle boy, Al'an's new friend, Shen'ham.

In all, twenty-two boys of this newly-rejoined Clan would be *hewn* this year. Among them, none was keener for the event to arrive, pass and free them all to take up their crafts than A'lan. A'lan's facial wound had healed well, thanks to his mother's loving care and skill. Twinges of nerve pain still assailed him from time to time however, especially in cold water or a cold wind. Had that fact been known to the Sea-Masters, it would not have boded well for his inclusion into a craft which spent much of its time in just such an environment. But such was the character of this lad that only his mother and his best friend, Shen'ham, knew the source of his glum expression on occasion, or the periods of testiness and aggravation he sometimes displayed. Pain had become a part of this boy's life and the distortion to his features which resulted from that scar, lent him a visage of seriousness and maturity beyond his years. Shen'ham, his quiet, gentle intelligence applied soothingly whenever A'lan was in pain, further cemented their friendship. A'lan grew to love him as any brother could.

The much-discussed ordeal of the *hewing,* especially the actual slicing away of that sensitive layer of skin, held no terrors for A'lan. He knew that that pain could in no way compare to periodic bouts of facial agony he already had to endure. In his own methodical and incisive manner of dealing with the quickly changing world around him, he developed an impressive and unique patience and forbearance. During the worst moments of agony, however, A'lan's mind flew back to the moment which had inflicted the wound and upon the perpetrators; then beyond, to the sickness of mind which had prompted such brutality. For one so young to have learned to bypass hatred of an individual and focus upon a state of mind, revealed an amazing capacity to reason in the abstract which few of any age achieve. That clarity of thought and his rapidly expanding understanding of the *sight,* which was growing ever more active and important in his life, was creating a young man of exceptional personality. A'lan-*un-hewn* was truly ready for his *hewing*!

Among the Sea-hewn, and couched in ribald humor, was an instruction to the initiates to stretch the foreskins of their penises in order to make the skin thinner and therefore less resistant to the not-always-keen edge of the seashell which would sever it. Most boys of course had been indulging in a similar exercise for some time. Each class of initiates seemed to invent their own unique set of jokes in reference to these instructions. The young girls, and even some of the women, delighted in joining in on the joke, teasing the young boys unmercifully.

~ ~ * ~ ~

For many joyful minutes Al'malan Sea-Master lifted and dipped his child into the water, standing now waist-deep in the gentle surf, his colorful wrap flowing around his hips. The child squealed with joy as again and again his father plunged him to shoulder-depth in the seawater. When finally his laughter began to subside, Al'malan ceased that play and bent and slung the boy, both hands supporting the fat little belly, into the surge of water, allowing it to cover and caress his shining body, careful to keep his head above the salty foam. Sahn'ta began making cooing, calling sounds, his body arched against those wide, supporting hands. His eyes followed each swell of surf as it approached, chubby hands occasionally slapping and splashing the water.

Their filial joy was interrupted when a small group of youngsters, all naked and sand-covered from playing on the beach, ran screaming and squealing into the surf near them. Two of the little girls, after their initial plunge, waded over to father and son. The girls asked to have the child, to include him in their watery games. But Al'malan was suddenly reluctant to release his greatest source of joy. Instead, he smiled and answered, "Not now, little ones. It is time he was fed." The girls accepted this reply with only a moment's chagrin and then turned and dove like seals and swam to join their playmates. Al'malan stood in the swirling water and was surprised when a flood of tears rushed from his eyes.

Never, ever, had he known a moment of complete love and acceptance such as this: his son's warm, wet body held against his chest, the boy looking into his face, grinning, the sea swirling about his body in some unexpected ritual of confirmation. Such a moment made a man. He bent and kissed Sahn'ta's forehead. The boy suddenly dropped his face against Al'malan's chest, prelude to sleep, uncomprehending but at this moment at one with his father. Thus was established another barrier against the man's fears and doubts. He knew that he was among the blessed and that the most urgent of his concerns was soon to be resolved.

Al'malan left the water with Sahn'ta in the crook of his arm, only to quickly return and submerge them both up to the boy's neck. The child had peed down his father's chest and belly! "Anymore surprises for me, Sahn'ta-luv?" the man asked, the initial frown relaxing into a grin. The boy only cooed and stuck his thumb into his mouth and laid a sleepy head on Al'malan's shoulder. He fell asleep even as he was being carried and, when his father laid him on a mat in the shade, he curled up, gave a shallow cough and slept deeply. Al'malan set about quietly cleaning up the area beneath the veranda. Dishes were washed, the whole area swept with a palm frond broom and the bedclothes hung up to air.

Domestic chores held no shame for a Seaman. Aboard a vessel, order and cleanliness was a necessity; so he had learned in his apprenticeship, so he still practiced it on land. Later that morning, the clean-up completed and Sahn'ta still sleeping soundly, his father sat cross-legged near him, fanning the persistent flies away. Al'malan often sat here early morning and late afternoon, watching the sea. He had intentionally sited the hut in this position so that he could sit beneath the overhang in any weather and meditate facing the rising sun.

Since his son had begun crawling, the boy would frequently find his way out to his father, long before his mother had awakened, and climb into his father's lap. Sometimes he would fall asleep again until hunger aroused him. Al'malan cherished these mornings and whatever worries might have been attending at first light, his son's warm presence melted them away. He felt that same sense of well being now, the busy work-a-day about him ignored. His attention was totally focused on the sounds of sea and wind, filtering all the many voices issuing from the people who passed by, none intruding upon the now-respected Sea-Master at his own home, his beloved son asleep in his lap.

Unlike most *sighted* Seamen, who saw and spent a lifetime learning to read those mysterious light-lines beneath the surface, Al'malan's gift, his *sight*, was aural. From childhood he had understood voices in the wind and surf where others only heard wind and surf. The scuffling of footsteps on sand he would often identify by sound before that person was in sight and he could pick the stride of one individual from within a group passing by. On the darkest, stormiest night at sea, when the *sight* of someone like Tor'na, when he had sailed with him, was powerless to read through the surface of the water, Al'malan could warn of a wind shift before it arrived or of a suddenly approaching rogue wave.

And curiously, his aural sensitivity extended to the human voice; what mood or intent lay within a word or comment. Al'malan could gauge truth and falsity while still very young and playmates soon learned not to tell lies in his presence. His wife, Ja'eel, had chosen to forget this strange capacity most of the time, secretly holding a small contempt for her husband. It seemed that it was his innate gentleness and concern for others, to her a sign of weakness, which caused her to consider him not really worthy of her beauty and uniqueness. When listening to that madman, Tor'na, at the dramatic encounter when he confronted the Sea-Masters gathering, it was the echo of the future in the man's voice which led Al'malan to say, "He's a dead man already!" It was not a projection of his own intent at all, but a conviction that within that voice he had heard a death-cry. He was spared the insight the he, himself, would one day initiate Tor'na's death. That was still months away.

Sahn'ta finally woke, a sheen of perspiration glowing on his body. The sun had moved to fall upon his sturdy, sleeping form. Waking hot and hungry, he groused and whined until his father laid a cup of cool water to his little mouth. He drank greedily, swallowing until he coughed and choked, Al'malan slapping him gently on the back to restore his breathing. Talking low and soothingly to his son, he set a ceramic bowl filled with chopped banana and cooked taro with honey before the child. Little hands plunged together into the proffered bowl and soon his breakfast was being smeared around his mouth; eight tiny teeth, four in each jaw, gnashed and tore at the soft food. Al'malan laughed and teased his son. "Boy … you'd eat my fingers if I got them in your way, wouldn't you?" It was when he was washing the finally satisfied boy's face that Ja'eel returned. She came around the corner of the hut and halted, watching Al'malan doing those things which a part of her guiltily confessed should be her duties. The other part of her bridled at the sight. She scowled, the enthusiasm of her recent, clandestine lovemaking fading, leaving a sour taste in her mouth.

"Have you only just fed him?" she asked, announcing her arrival. He had heard her footsteps moments before. The tone in her voice betrayed many things to him. She came to them and stood, hands on hips, glaring down at them both. Al'malan did not look up. This morning's meditation had revealed what this day would bring for them. Besides, her nearness brought the fragrance of sex to his nostrils. Her voice carried lies. Ja'eel reached down and snatched her son up with both hands, the baby's face registering a rude intrusion. He whimpered as she carried him at arms length to the open sand, well away from the hut. With one foot she dug a hole and plunked the boy down over it, bending over him, her hands roughly clasped under his armpits. Al'malan watched, one part of his heart aching at her roughness, devoid of motherly love; the other part hardened to a necessary finality.

When he heard the sounds of the boy's defecation, he rose and dipped a shred of old cloth in water and walked to where his wife held their son, her face a mask of distaste. He held the dripping cloth out to Ja'eel who took it and wiped the baby's bottom, dropping the cloth then into the hole. With a quick swipe of one foot she back-filled the hole and then held Sahn'ta out to his father. Al'malan took the boy and, seating him in the crook of one arm, kissed the fretting boy. "Shoosh baby … shoosh" he crooned. Then he turned a powerful gaze upon his wife as she walked with an air of dismissal toward the entrance to their home.

"Ja'eel!" he said, his voice even but containing a storm of undertone. She turned to look at him, her face still set in disgust. "Where have you been, wife?" he asked, his tone now betraying anger. She turned and stared back with annoyance but the intensity of his eyes caused her to look away. She replied with a hint of dismissal, "To my mother's house. She needed help stripping some *pandanus* leaves." Though her lovely face now spoke truth and guilelessness, Al'malan's inner hearing recorded the now-familiar gasps of sexual intercourse, of lies and mocking laughter.

Whether she suddenly remembered her husband's extraordinary abilities or rather some echo of guilt remained within her, she would never really know - or care. Ja'eel's beauty did not extend to her soul! Her attempt to once again deny her infidelity, her callous disregard for him and their son was pathetic. Al'malan felt his heart lurch with love for this woman with whom he had shared so much in so short a time. But he knew that that value was only of his own perception, not hers. They now shared only this one, painful moment.

"Ja'eel, you have lied to me since before our son cut his first tooth. You lie now!" The pause before his next words caused a cold rush of despair in the young woman. Some place within her signaled the inevitable and she shuddered, not with guilt or remorse but with a seething anger that her desires should be judged, her actions questioned. What occurred next was beyond her capacity to delay or deflect. No tantrum or flood of tears would ever again bridge this gaping chasm. In her husband's eyes a barrier rose, now forever impervious to her machinations. Ja'eel sagged in anticipation. She stood with her hands at her sides, fists clenched, and Al'malan finally saw his wife of two years in the totality of her immaturity. He tightened his clasp on his son but the boy thought it only affection and gabbled happily, pointing to a bird which had just landed on a nearby branch.

"Ja'eel, you are no more my wife! Nor are you mother to our son! You will leave this dwelling by sundown and return no more. If you challenge me, I will tell the truth of your infidelity and your negligence as a mother." He then bent and picked up a ceramic bowl from the low table of wood. With a movement no harsher than necessary, he broke the bowl over the edge of the table. Ja'eel's eyes remained fixed on the broken shards as Al'malan left with the baby. She didn't look up until they were well out of sight.

Just as drinking from the same bowl was part of a marriage ceremony, so too was the ritual breaking of a bowl the signal for the ending of that union. Among the Mal'lam, a people who by nature sought amicable solutions to disputes, divorce was unencumbered by complications of law. When one party decided that a union was no longer workable, this simple act sufficed as notice of divorce. A couple might break crockery in an argument but this intentional act was different.

Different too was this particular divorce, for usually children remained in the household of the wife's family. Sahn'ta would make his own choices in a few years but for now he would remain with his father and in the care of Al'malan's family. Ja'eel's behavior was well known among the Clan and many wondered how long Al'malan's patience would last. The fact that she was a poor mother to her son was also well known and even her mother despaired of her daughter's self-centeredness. Ja'eel would return to her parent's household until another man could be persuaded to take her as a wife. Her prospects in that regard were not good.

Ja'eel went into the hut and began gathering those possessions she considered her own; blankets of layered mulberry bark which she had made herself when quite young, wraps with embossed patterns, jewelry, all those odds and ends a woman begins collecting as a young girl. Only now did her eyes moisten, her face taut with emotion. She folded the blankets and all and placed them in the woven bamboo chest her father had presented to her so proudly when her son was born. She then stood in the middle of the single room, a cool breeze blowing from the sea. Through the entrance the curtain at the doorway flapped insistently, almost impatiently.

Ja'eel could not bring herself to mourn for that would have been to deny the sudden surge of freedom she felt. She gathered her belongings into one bulky bundle with an old blanket and dragged it out onto the veranda beneath the wide overhang. Her father would come and fetch it when she asked him. He always did her bidding and even though he was fond of Al'malan and admired him immensely as did all Seamen, he would commiserate with her, sadly agreeing with her complaints. She expected only quiet tolerance from her mother. She was a strong-minded and forthright woman who had often of late warned her wayward daughter of what her too-patient husband would do when finally he had reached *that* limit. Ja'eel had scoffed, certain of her ability to always distract her husband's anger and embarrassment with seduction. She now left the little hut without glancing back, still having learned little. On the way to her parent's hut she stopped to flirt with a young Woodsman.

~ ~ * ~ ~

A'lan and his friend, Shen'ham, paddled strongly as the little canoe slipped along the edge of the mangroves, tiny crabs waving claws from perches among the stilted roots. A grey heron squawked and labored up and over the water, flying on powerful wings upriver. A'lan, paddling in the front of the small dugout, watched the graceful bird's flight, marveling at such perfect control. "Beautiful, aren't they?" Shen'ham said, "We'll probably see him again, up ahead" A tree limb, large, with jagged branches like gnarled arms appeared ahead of them, floating swiftly downriver toward the sea. Shen'ham deftly steered the canoe away to the center of the river. "Look!" A'lan cried out, "What's that?" and he ceased paddling and pointed to something dark and wet atop the log. "A turtle!" Shen'ham replied and again he wielded his paddle skillfully and brought them back nearer to the floating timber "See him? He's a big one."

A'lan sat quietly watching the limb slide alongside. On Sh'ham-Set there had been no turtles, nor any rivers for them to live in. This was the first he had ever seen. With a sudden slash of movement the turtle lunged off its resting spot and disappeared into the brackish water. A'lan looked over his shoulder and shot a look of delighted wonder at his friend. Shen'ham had, since early childhood, a fascination with all living things. Neither the smallest insect nor the great whales which passed close by their shores in the autumn escaped his keen interest. And now to have a friend who shared this fascination was his great joy.

The boys were headed nowhere special, simply enjoying the freedom of their last days before the *hewing*. Already though, they were learning and practicing the songs and chants of the Sea-hewn even as they stroked powerfully through a narrowing of the Salt River, the water swift flowing and turbulent. The heavy growth along the river soon changed from salt-loving mangroves to the thick timber of lowland forest. The bird life here was changing too, though the grey heron continued its journey upriver ahead of them, flying from some temporary roost each time they came into its view from around a bend.

"Hey, Scout! What's ahead now?" Shen'ham called to the bird. In response it soared downstream toward them, low over the murky water. Then it pulled a sudden one-hundred-eighty degree turn, accompanied by a sharp, 'Squarrrk!' and flew back upriver again. "He's leading us now, Shen'ham!" A'lan said triumphantly, "Let's go after him." The boys again dug their paddles deeply and swiftly, the canoe speeding ahead, leaving a bubbling, roiled wake.

Around this bend the river straightened into a long, tree-hooded channel with swaths of bright sunlight like gold patches on a long piece of dark cloth. It glistened and beckoned. "Quietly now, Lan-an!" Shen'ham whispered, calling his friend by his boyhood mate's name. His friends in turn often called Shen'ham, Sha. "What is it Sha?" A'lan whispered again, both boys now paddling softly, their paddles executing an 's' turn as they drew them through the water without withdrawing them; the silent yet powerful stroke of the canoeist in stalking mode.

"Maybe Haw'lanks ahead!" was the reply. A'lan already had heard of the mysterious Haw'lank, a giant, water-living, air-breathing animal. They were secretive and few and were considered sacred, never to be harmed. Their flesh though, was said to be even better than pork! "Stop now!" Shen'ham whispered, and both paddles turned to stop the canoes' forward progress. The canoe slowed in the face of the current's flow and Shen'ham steered it toward the left shore and the cover of overhanging branches where shade predominated. Both boys now carefully withdrew their paddles from the water, each grasping an overhanging branch to secure the canoe against the current's insistent power.

Being as quiet as possible, their eyes searched the gloom of dark water beneath shadowy trees. Long minutes of buzzing flies and mosquitoes and yet the boys never moved, so strong were their intent. Sweat dripped from their faces. As arms clutching branches began to cramp, the river revealed its secret! Ahead, beyond the glittering patch of sunlit water was seen a misty explosion of spray, followed by a hissing, blowing sound. Then another, and again. And then, directly in the center of the patch of bright light a dark, shiny shape broke the surface. Another blow of mist and a quick swirl of water, closer to them this time. A'lan could scarcely breath, so great was his anticipation of observing a rare phenomenon.

"Haw'lank! See? See?" Shen'ham's excited whisper confirmed A'lan's own conviction. Straining muscles forgotten, both boys sat unmoving, eyes wide with wonder. All was silent on the river, only bell-like bird calls from deep within the bordering forest intruded, distant and seeming to mark the waiting seconds until … 'Sheeppp!' Another amorphous hump of wet blackness broke the surface, disappearing as quickly in a spreading mandala of ripples. Then another, this time so close that the spray drifted within reach of the two motionless, enthralled boys. The Haw'lanks were obviously moving quickly downstream, abreast of the canoe now, but the murky water betrayed no forms beneath the ripples.

Hairs rose on goose bumps and each boy fought down the niggling fear which accompanied this proximity to the mysterious, the sacred, and the utter magic of the unknown. Shen'ham, though having traveled this stream numerous times before, had never seen more than suspicious ripples on the water, only hinting at the presence of these sacred creatures. Now, on this first day here with his dear friend, the Gods of the rivers had blessed them with a glimpse of their most closely guarded secret. Tears blurred Shen'ham's vision and he turned his head to look at A'lan. A'lan returned his glance, his own eyes moist with the same understanding. He placed his hand over his heart and nodded his thanks for this marvelous opportunity. Much was said without speaking, a further cementing of a bond of friendship and partnership in seeking the unknown which would accompany these two future explorers for many years.

Another two almost simultaneous blows of spray brought eager gazes to the middle of the stream again. The boys watched and twisted their bodies to follow the progress of the Haw'lanks until they had disappeared around the bend behind them. As Shen'ham and A'lan unwound their cramped bodies and pushed off into mid-stream, the grey heron, surely the same one, flew low over the water from the gloom upstream. Powerful wings hushed their beat in the still air and it squawked three times, and then shat a dob of white manure into the water opposite the canoe. It continued its squawking flight downstream and out of sight, following the trackless departure of the Haw'lanks.

A'lan and Shen'ham dissolved into uproarious laughter. The canoe rocked from side to side as they swayed and beat on the gunwales, stirring a mixture of avian responses from the startled birdlife in the surrounding forest. Their joy receding into guffaws and chuckles the boys regained control of the canoe, which had swung broadside to the current, following its own joyous response to the power and magic of this flow of cloudy water. "Let's eat, Sha!" A'lan managed, before dissolving into giggles again.

Fruit, banana mush with honey and cold, fried taro satisfied their hunger but midges drove them from their picnic site some two-hundred feet upstream of where they had last encountered the Haw'lank. The sun was descending toward mid-afternoon and to return to the mouth of the Salt River, even moving with the current, would require two hours of paddling. And who knew what else of interest might intervene to swell this day's richness? As the boy's paddling and the strong current swept their canoe back down toward the sea, both of them saw this placid river not as a broadly-flowing, silt-filled drainage but rather as the rolling, tossing sea, demanding of alertness and physical strength. Young arms were glanced at as they worked the paddles, each lad hoping that only a short time would see these arms swell into powerful muscles. No impressive power yet displayed itself there.

Drive on! 'Someday I will have powerful muscles!' might have been their thought, but into that adolescent projection intruded, '*the hewing*'! A time of intense discipline and finally, someone was going to carve the living flesh off their penises! Paddle! Forget it for now. A'lan, because pain was a familiar attendant in his life now, worried less than most boys about the upcoming rituals. Although Shen'ham commiserated with his good friend and his recurring pain, he could not really know its meaning. He, like dozens of boys among the Mal'lam on the other islands, strove to overcome their fear, trying to focus on the end result; manhood!

When the canoe slid from the shadowy confines of the mangroves and into the wide estuary, the day was waning, shadows long and tired, like the boys arms felt. The tide had turned some time ago and flowed against their progress as the river's current had done earlier that day. Weary but still elated, they chattered together about the Haw'lanks, the heron named 'Scout', the moment the canoe had nearly capsized when they both foolishly leaned far over the same side - a day's adventure kept alive in the recounting. The Salt River spread out before them now as a wide, shallow lake of windswept turbulence; low waves undulated toward them from the river's mouth where the sea intruded. Other canoes lay about them, bouncing up and down in the increasing swell, two men in each casting and retrieving nets. On the incoming tide swam schools of Tilma, silvery fish with boney but sweet flesh which would fill eager stomachs tonight.

From a nearby canoe, rigged with one outrigger for stability in these bumpy waters, a fisherman waved and called to the boys. It was Orn'ta, master Seaman among this islands' many canoe masters. He was indulging himself in a rare pastime. "Hey, you boys! You had better get that canoe to shore now." He yelled. "There are dozens of sharks about today and the water is getting very rough." Indeed. The boys had spotted the ominous fins and flailing tails as the sharks fed on the schools of Tilma and both dug their paddles in urgently. A capsize here could mean the loss of a limb, or worse! A sudden gust of wind nearly accomplished that and it was only the quick reflexes of these two natural water-men-to-be which prevented a disaster. But it certainly frightened them. They ran their small vessel onto the grayish sand of the launching beach with gasps of relief, looking warily behind them for fins as they leaped out and pulled the canoe up onto the shore. Grins of relief and pleasure in a small victory lit their sweaty faces, the livid scar on A'lans's face causing a slight distortion to his mouth; a feature which would become more pronounced with age.

Soon the fishermen began returning to the beach, many with large catches of Tilma, most of the catch still alive in the ankle-deep water in the bottom of the canoes. The Mal'lam liked their fish as fresh as possible. A'lan and Shen'ham volunteered to bail a couple of canoes in exchange for some fish, though the catch would be shared throughout the community anyhow. It was the sharing of the task, the participation in a community venture which made an already adventure-rich day even more special. The boys had soon recounted their adventures.

The sighting of the Haw'lanks drew clucks of admiration for, although many fishermen had spent years fishing this particular river, not all had been privileged with a proximity to the 'River Pigs', the meaning of the word, 'Haw'lank'. The story of the 'scout' heron that shat in the water drew guffaws from many. All the while, the Sea-Master, Orn'ta, stood back studying these two young Seamen-to-be. His mind, not unlike Al'malan's, could discern fabrications. There was not even exaggeration in their story, he decided. And it was his experience that few people, especially such young ones, were acute enough and of the necessary sensitivity to unconsciously enlist the aid of one animal in finding another - dogs not included.

Truly, these two lads, soon to be *hewn* of the sea, would bear his special attention. Shen'ham he already knew well; son of his best friend, dead now, and his mother, Shen'ha, a dear friend also. He knew the boy to be self-sufficient and capable, unspoiled in spite of his overindulgence in food. Orn'ta himself had been a chubby boy. The newcomer-cousin, A'lan, his face severely scarred by Orn'ta's own nephew, carried an aura of quiet strength and determination which belied his age. He knew that the new young Sea-Master, Al'malan, had already judged the boy special among the prospective initiates. He would speak with Al'malan of this. Together, they must surely focus their attention on these two boys. And what was this? After bailing two other canoes, unbidden, between them they now carried a basket of fish heavy enough for two men. Already they were in tune with the basic lesson of *the hewing* which they were yet to experience: the co-operative endeavor of men of the sea for the welfare of their whole community.

Orn'ta smiled to himself as he hoisted nets and a basket of fish. "One worthless seaman, my own nephew, is replaced by two boys. Each worth six of him!" But deep within him, he still worried. Somehow, sometime, that strange, twisted young man was going to visit sorrow upon the people of the Clan. Tor'na, for all his brooding malevolence, was not the center of the evil which had burst forth that awful day. It had been Mal'atan, his own blood, whose emanations had glowed so menacingly among those four men. Tor'na had been but noise and bluster. It had been Mal'atan who had drawn blood, delivering undue violence upon a child. And there had been no hint of remorse, only that infuriating smirk!

As Orn'ta heaved his heavy load up the steep bank of sand toward the trail to the village, he recalled a nearly forgotten prognostication issued by the 'witch woman', The Vesa'tan. Many others had heard it too on that day."When the mountains of fire to the north of this island of Shtah Lee breath destruction upon those Mal'lam, this island will send forth its own creature of destruction. Beware, my people! Evil exists among you in the form of one now thought but ridiculous." Why had he not remembered or equated that warning before now?

Orn'ta scowled and silently berated himself. Ahead of him the two boys had set their load down and switched sides to relieve aching arms, the load really too much for them. But their movements and manner betrayed no appeal for aid or relief. They had committed themselves and neither was about to relinquish his assumed responsibility. Shen'ham, hefting his side of the basket said, "Squawk … Ptooie!" and the two strode on up the track, laughing and giggling, the fishermen joining in the merriment.

Chapter Twelve - The Thieve's Market

Off the island of Shalan'la, riding smoothly over an even swell, the canoe, 'Flee the Land', harbored five desperate men and a boy. The boy appeared totally disinterested in the situation which they all shared. Their food depleted to scraps, their water nearly gone, the master addressed his crew. "Now listen closely! We're all hungry and thirsty. Who's doing is that? Not ours!' he lied. "Those fools who presumed to limit us, confine us within their stupid rules, are to blame. We are warriors like our ancestors - men of vision and action! We are the future of the Mal'lam!"

Cheers of assent replied, his two long-time compatriots cheering loudest. Mala'tan only smiled, sitting separate from the others in the starboard bow, his usual position. He watched the backs of the thick skulls of the crew, Tor'na's face in full view to him. Tor'na's face had lost all trace of swelling now. The long weeks of healing since his self-inflicted wounding had resulted in two uneven slashes of cruel red. Almost exactly the result he had planned. The Sea-Master was fierce and imposing in appearance as he stood holding the steering paddle, haranguing his crew of misfits, stirring them to the inevitable; piracy!

When they had left Sh'tah Lee-Set that terrible day, contrary winds had impeded their journey to the northwest, the sailing time to the nearest Set a long, squally five days in which Tor'na suffered hellish pain, not only in his wounded face, but in his soul. They had beached 'Flee the Land' on the uninhabited end of a small rocky island. They spent a week there resting and repairing storm damage to the bridging deck between the canoe's hulls. Fruit, herbs and two snared wild pigs had fed them along with the plentiful fish in the seldom-visited inshore waters. In that week's rest, Tor'na regained his strength, attended by Mala'tan's solicitous nursing.

But a worrying restlessness soon reinvaded his mind. Already disputes had occurred, minor but potentially troublesome. He had imposed a harsh discipline then, harsher than his usual demanding presence required, and all had come to fear him then though he had not applied physical violence to anyone. Alone, those burning eyes and still-horrid features conspired to strike fear. Only Mal'atan was immune to Tor'na's outbursts, the strange young man able to calm Tor'na's violent moods and salve the feelings of the crew. Almost obsequious to Tor'na, Mal'atan nevertheless was patiently imposing himself between his lover and the other four men; one was little more than a boy but was quickly becoming hardened in this company. Mal'atan was carefully pursuing the plans he had formed in those first days in Tor'na's presence; plans imperial in scale which he held secret from all. Tor'na's suspicions amounted only to a subliminal disquiet which he could not identify; a nagging echo of danger which he always dismissed as the result of their perilous situation, and the dangers inherent in his plans. But termites of doubt were already nibbling, slowly eroding his mental balance. Now, after another weather-assaulted voyage to the sparsely populated island of Shalan'la, Tor'na decided that there could be no more delay. If he did not now commit his followers to action, he felt his authority would begin to wane and the renewed impetus would be lost. And so would they all!

Shalan'la-Set lay at the junction of the busy trade lanes which served the central group of islands of the archipelago and was an often-used layover stop for the crews of the big bamboo rafts. At this time of year when crops were being harvested and the farmers busy with their urgent chores, the Seamen loaded their vessels with those items of manufacture which had been assembled for trade among the islands: coconut fiber cordage and twine and palm toddy from Sh'tah Lee; obsidian tools of fine craftsmanship from Bal'lal-Set, that island providing most of that valuable stone for all the Mal'lam; dried meat and fish, herbs and root vegetables, fermented taro and breadfruit as well as fabrics made from the pounded bark of the mulberry tree.

The end of summer and early autumn was the season for this trade and at this time the small, quite dry island of Shalan'la was the scene of a busy market: it was widely called, 'The Thieves Market'. Theft was not common among the Mal'lam, though certain Clans produced more thieves than most others. No bands of ruffians or thieves were tolerated, yet here on Shalan'la-Set during the great trading time, men and women of questionable ethics tended to congregate. It was here at this time that hoarded items, sometimes stolen and unsafe to traffic at home, appeared blatantly in the ramshackle bazaar in the main port of the island. Precious stones and gold and pearls in small quantities, rare and often proscribed feathers and items decorated with them, finely carved chests and utensils and tools and high-quality ceramics … all could be found in relative abundance in the busy lane called, 'Sh'ul'shem', the 'Thieves Market'.

As each year's trading came to an end, most off-islanders returned to their home islands, leaving the native people to regain their quiet lives as farmers and fishers. Some few, however, by preference or circumstance, remained and most of those lived marginal lives, scratching subsistence wherever and however they could. Every few years, when these people had reached numbers and behavior intolerable to the locals, an appeal for inter-island cooperation was called. Clan heads from throughout the archipelago would travel to the beleaguered island attended by a large number of burly young Seamen and convene a council of elders. Clan cousins among the resident expatriates would be persuaded to return to their own communities, sometimes under some duress.

Most often, in the long tradition of the Mal'lam, the influence of and the respect for the elders, the grey-headed men and women of the Clans, brought reluctant but reasoned acquiescence. Those few who defiantly remained, if peaceful in their refusal and gaining at least three local referees among the local Elders, stayed on within a much reduced and now subdued society of traders, entertainers, prostitutes and some thieves. Some corruption surely accrued in 'persuading' a local referee, deepening the impression of incipient depravity on this somewhat compromised Set. The security and peace of mind of the local populace would be somewhat restored. The next trading season would see a still-seamy, but much subdued confluence of traders and adventurers. Sometimes a whole generation would pass before another such remedial council was required.

This year however, was a year of upheaval! The destructive volcanism and the resulting social dislocation had stirred the human broth and upon this beleaguered trading post descended those least able to combine with their own communities in the struggle necessary for communal survival. These flotsam and jetsam of Mal'lam culture assembled in unprecedented numbers here, and by the time the six renegades aboard 'Flee-the-Land' reached the port, theft, assault, rape and even murder were rife. No authority existed capable of containing such anarchy; reason and respect were the first casualties here. It was into this poisonous brew of fear and dissipation that two uniquely inspired egos sailed, each with private yearnings but both with an inspired dedication to a common, unified, immediate goal. With them rode four others, limited in mind and spirit, fired by a mad demagoguery unique in the history of this people.

It was mid-afternoon when Tor'na ordered the canoe pulled up above high water mark. The thin, wasted-looking boy and Mal'atan pushing and pulling as hard as the others. Mal'atan was arrayed in regalia he had never before worn, except in the esoteric gatherings of young miscreants he had led on Sh'tah Lee; secret, erotic trysting places where group fantasies were played out. His long hair was worn tied on one side of his head with a seed necklace, another necklace of seashells and red seeds around his neck. In one pierced ear, common between both sexes, he wore a long, skillfully crafted pendant, stolen from the burial site of a long-dead elder. In the other ear - men had only one ear pierced - hung a gold and coral chain which fell upon his neck and down over his collarbone. Stuck into his oiled, dark brown hair were feathers and seashells attractively arranged. He had smoothed scented oils over his arms and upper body, his lower body wrapped in a skirt of fine fiber with brilliant red and yellow designs on a white background. Woven bands of black-dyed hair circled each ankle. In the fashion of a bride, his eyes were darkened with mascara, his lashes too were darkened and his lips painted red with oil and oxide. Tor'na stood watching his inamorata swing his lean hips up the wide path toward the distant noise of the village bazaar. With eyes misting in lust, he forced his attention away and ordered his two stalwart companions to follow him toward a scrubby knoll above the beach. They carried the materials for their own uniquely different costume.

In train to the exhibitionist Mal'atan followed the tall, awkward man and the skinny boy whom he had recruited to join this company. They had not been his favorite choices but time and circumstance had dictated there inclusion. Anyway, they were what he had to work with and his confidence mounted as their devotion to him grew to an almost slavish degree. The tall man, sharp featured, effeminate, ungainly in his movements and possessed of neither the theatricality nor the decorative artistry of his mentor, nevertheless followed obediently. He wore what finery he possessed with what panache he could muster, clumsily trying to copy Mal'atan's insouciance. With a nod of encouragement from Mal'atan, he soon warmed to this role as a public spectacle and stood happily to his full height as he walked. The boy wore only a Seaman's wrap and no decorative accoutrements. His role was to remain innocuous within the crowds and indistinguishable from many another young seamen who roamed the bustling, noisy bazaar.

Groups of men and women, many obviously inebriated, passed the three, all commenting and cat-calling ... all ignored by Mal'atan. Most were headed for the huge, beached, bamboo trading rafts aboard which private parties were being held. As the numbers of passing people increased, more comment flowed about the two opulently, strangely dressed newcomers. There was something about the really fancily dressed one; something stranger than the usual strangeness of this places, this day.

The Sh'ul'shem, the 'Thieves Market', was a sandy, dusty lane lined with crude huts and stalls. Dozens of Mal'lam flowed up and down the concourse, groups of hagglers here and there. Others circled around busking musicians, conjurers and jugglers, with the occasional food stall. The sound was a rich mix of flutes, stringed instruments and percussion, voices buzzing and occasionally shrill. A hint of decay and carelessness assaulted one's nostrils: the smell of urine and un-washed bodies and food-gone-off. A very un-Mal'lam smell! Drunken people staggered and belched and collided without an 'excuse me' and there was an unsettling, but to some exciting, debauchery to the whole scene.

Mal'atan raised one garlanded wrist to signal his two followers to halt. His cold, keen eyes swept the length of the scene, perusing the emanations of sordid energy which surrounded him, coming to rest on a gaily-decorated hut at the end of the pathway. "Yes!" he smiled. "That's the place." With his left hand he motioned the boy to his side, bent and whispered in his ear, then straightened and continued his promenade as the skinny lad disappeared ahead into the crowd. His remaining companion, his interest captured by a nearby event of foreign uniqueness, gasped and stumbled paces behind Mal'atan, hurrying to catch up. Mal'atan's presence became a focal point of interest as he paraded down the dusty path. Heads turned to stare and his own glimpses captured those curious eyes ... challenging, distant yet demanding of recognition. He flirted with his eyes and mobile, painted eyebrows, with pretty boy and homely man alike. Hardened, homeless women followed his progress, some cursing, some admiring. "Who is he?" was the question on many lips. Who, indeed! Soon they would know.

Halfway down toward that hut which he had decided was his goal, a small group of naked, unkempt boys ran into the path before him. One, smaller and filthier than any, stood with his hands on his hips, his bright eyes challenging. Mal'atan stopped and looked down at the boy for a moment and smiled, his painted face beaming with feigned friendliness. In that dirty face he recognized his own pubescent wildness; the insolence and aggressive disrespect which had marked his own childhood. Then the smile faded and Mal'atan's eyes glared at the boy with a malevolence the child had never seen. "Get out of my way!" he growled. The boy jumped with fright and turned and ran, the other children scurrying after him. Mal'atan tossed his head in dismissal of the grubby hoodlums and resumed his theatrical tour of the bazaar, his awkward companion, Joom'ta, still behind him, managing a silly approximation of Mal'atan's exaggerated swagger. The boy accompanying them reappeared, caught Mal'atan's eye and nodded affirmatively, then stood in the shade of a small tree.

The smells of the food stalls intoxicated the boy and his stomach grumbled with hunger. None of his band of rebels possessed the polished, perforated pebbles and rare pink shells which served as currency here, the Mal'lam equivalent of ostentatious wealth. He resolved to obtain some of these chains of shiny, functionless baubles. He glanced down at his faded, threadbare wrap and seethed with the injustice of his loneliness and poverty, that feeling of separation which had plagued him, inexplicably, since early childhood. Sh'ul'am was his name, or rather, nickname. It meant 'little thief', for he had developed a light-fingered attitude to the possessions of others at an early age. It was he who had presented Mal'atan with the knife which he always kept hidden in his wrap, a bribe allowing him entry into Mal'atan's 'tribe' of rascals back home on Sht'ah Lee-Set. It was he who ferreted the burial sites and desecrated them for whatever he considered of value. Sh'ul'am knew no shame, held no values save a blind loyalty to the haughty Mal'atan. And it was his mentor who now, with a meaningful glance, summoned the boy.

Sh'ul'am hurried to him, dodging among members of the milling crowd and stood expectantly, looking at Mal'atan. Mal'atan didn't look directly at the boy but keeping his haughty smirk intact, spoke quietly and commandingly: "Do you see that hut at the end there?" The boy nodded, the movement seen out of the corner of Mal'atan's mascaraed eye. "Go and find out what it is and who is there. Take your time and don't be obvious about it" he added. Needlessly, really, because Sh'ul'am was a consummate sneak. As if to prove the point, he suddenly disappeared into the crowd with a quick stealth. Mal'atan glanced about but the boy was nowhere in sight. He smiled appreciatively and continued his own parade-within-a-parade, swaggering to a stall which displayed finely designed wraps. Joom'ta hurried after him again, lifting his wrap skirt-like above the dust.

Sh'ul'am had quickly worked his way through the crowded laneway to near the end, where the gaily-fluttering banners on poles designated that large hut as a special place. At its entrance stood two burly, glowering men. A plainly decorated curtain hung loosely, blocking the view to within. Not far from it, on the right side, was a stall with a small fire burning, a large ceramic pot resting on stones steaming above it. The smell of the fish soup grabbed at the boy's throat, his hunger now acute. An old woman appeared from behind the stall, struggling with a heavy basket. Sh'ul'am's response was immediate. He ran to the old woman and grabbed hold of the basket."Here, grandmother! Let me help you!" The wide, generous smile he offered was met with a suspicious scowl but she released the basket to his grip. "Where would you like it?" he asked, his eyes wide with innocence above a big-toothed grin. She continued to scowl but pointed to a corner of the small lean-to. The basket, filled with blue-shelled mussels, rattled as he set it down, glad to be rid of its weight. He looked at the woman, still smiling at her, and said, "Can I be of any other help to you, grandmother?" A quick, furtive glance at the cooking pot gave his true motives away. The old woman's scowl dissolved and her face softened, some maternal memory stirring within.

"No, boy." She answered, hobbling on what Sh'ul'am now noticed were crippled feet. She sat herself awkwardly down near the fire, squirming to adjust her arthritic body into some semblance of comfort. The boy remained standing, pretending a respect which he did not feel, quick eyes returning again and again to the steaming pot. "Are you hungry, boy?" she asked, the sudden gentleness in her voice unsettling him, causing him to answer honestly, "Yes, grandmother!" The old woman gazed at him a moment, wondering; just another unattached mongrel who stole and damaged?

She couldn't guess yet, so, leaning forward she took a clay bowl and ladled it full of the thick soup. She took a none-too-clean wooden spoon from a small basket of similar ones and held the whole out to the obviously famished lad. "Sit here boy," and she indicated the sand near her. He took the bowl and nearly fell into a cross-legged position beside her, the spoon already plunging into the hot liquid. Too hot! He blew and slurped on the spoonful, trying to overcome the heat. She watched his eagerness with a distant sadness. Once she had lived in a community in which no child knew hunger. Now, here in this pigsty of an island, hungry children roamed in numbers. Born hungry, she thought. How had she not seen him before? He must have just come in on one of the trading rafts, son of some negligent, drunken Seaman. Before she could ask, the boy, between gasps and gulps of hot soup, began his own subtle interrogation.

"Grandmother, what is that place there?" and he indicated the mysterious hut with a toss of his head. "I am no one's grandmother, boy. My name is Mar'tah Leaf-Plait." Her voice was level, her eyes betrayed no condemnation but Sh'ul'am was careful, always, and continued his pretence of respect, addressing her with a child's familiarity and guilelessness. "Wonderful soup, Mar'tah-an. I thank you." He smiled around a hot mouthful, his chin wet with spilled liquid. She smiled too and accepted the compliment, confident that it was true. That she was an accomplished cook was the reason her stall had been sited at this place, near to that building. "That is the house of Rohr'rit!" she said. "Do you not know his name?" The boy shook his head as the last spoonful of soup disappeared, his eyes asking questions. "Rohr'rit is now *master* of Sh'ul'shem!" She looked around her quickly and then spat meaningfully on the ground and continued. "He's from my island, you see, from my Clan." She leaned over the pot and motioned for the boy's bowl, took it and ladled it full again, handing it back to him. She nodded at his 'thank you', this time a genuine response.

"He's always been a hard man; hard on his crews, hard and mean in his trading. Last year, somehow, he became rich! He began trading in obsidian, all he could get his hands on. He had a lot of gold and pearls and fine cloth, some say it's stolen from grave sites." Sh'ul'am winced but not from hot soup. She continued: "He didn't leave here after the trading, as most do. He stayed here like those of us who no longer have a home and began bossing people around. Me, he told to move my hut to his place and cook for him. He frightened me. He still does!" She was staring at the big hut, Rohr'rit's home, but then turned away quickly as one of the men at the doorway looked in their direction. Her voice lowered to almost a whisper but she continued with her story. The boy finished his second bowl of soup, belched politely and leaned forward, his elbows on his thighs, in order to hear her better.

"He began gathering men around him, some women too but they're all whores!" She spat again. "Some of the local people, they're all of another Clan here, got into an argument with Rohr'rit about this; about how the men he calls his 'crew' were stealing things and annoying their women. They got into a fight, a bad fight. One of the local men was killed, two more hurt badly!" The old woman's voice was becoming shrill and she checked herself, glancing over at the two guards at the hut.

Neither was taking any notice so she continued again, quietly, "Anyway, things got worse for everyone after that. People got beaten for no reason. Rohr'rit took to swaggering around like he owned everything and everybody, but always with some of his 'crew' around to protect him." She again paused to modify her tone and leaned closer to Sh'ul'am. "But he's a coward, really, you know. When *real* Sea-Hewn come here, he's as nice as can be and orders his people to behave themselves. But no one trusts him. He's a bad man and some of his 'crew' are even worse - just stupider."

Mar'tah shifted her painful joints to a new position and groaned. "I've got to stew these mussels for Rohr'rit's dinner soon. You boy, maybe you'd be so kind as to help me?" She looked hopefully at Sh'ul'am and was not disappointed. His belly full now, the boy was happy to remain with this talkative old woman for a while. That was what he was here for; to learn what was going on and report back. While he helped with the cleaning and shelling of the mussels, Mar'tah-Leaf-Plait continued her lament about the terrible state of affairs on Sha'lan'la-Set. How could she know how much worse things were to become?

It was well after dark when Sh'ul'am made his way along the beach to the canoe, 'Flee the Land'. Tor'na and Mal'atan were there, the others up the slope at the campfire in the scrubby vegetation which bordered the beach. Mal'atan, sitting swinging his bare legs from the platform, leaned forward and extended his hand, his lean fingers running teasingly through Sh'ul'am's hair. In his mock-sweet voice he purred, "Did our clever boy discover anything of interest today?"Tor'na, leaning on the edge of the platform near Mal'atan, snorted with humor at his lover's performance. Warmed by what he interpreted as concerned interest, the boy related all that he'd learned, speaking quickly, being asked to slow down, to repeat, until the other two were satisfied they had learned all he had to tell.

"Alright Sh'ul'am, you've done well, very well. You'd better go and get some sleep now. We start early tomorrow. Tomorrow is the day we've all been waiting for." To Sh'ul'am's surprise, Tor'na clapped him on the shoulder in what could only be described as a brotherly gesture, so unlike Tor'na, and the boy walked away toward the firelight on the rise, his mind swirling with a sudden sense of comradeship, of importance, of participation. He was greeted at the campfire with what passed as warmth from the two big men and a hearty greeting from Joom'ta. The plans for tomorrow were recounted to him. He finally fell asleep two hours later, with fear in his heart. It was too late now to run away.

The next day dawned cloudy and gusty, showers threatening from a grey, rumpled sea. Approaching the now-crowded beach was yet another bamboo raft, a small trader nearly too late to catch the full tide. Sh'ul'am sat alone watching in the dim light, the others of the company still asleep, the beach deserted of other people. Eighteen rafts he counted and only two other paired-hull canoes like 'Flee the Land'. The majority of those fast vessels had left the day before, their small cargoes already traded for, the crews anxious to return home, their duties performed.

This year, due to rumors of injustices and disruption on Sha'lan'la-Set, canoes were sent here from many of the Clan centers, their crews of vigorous, dedicated young men to assure the peace and safety of the trading. Rohr'rit had wisely seen that nothing untoward occurred; his crew of louts and whores remained subdued and law-abiding. Most of those young peacekeepers had sailed for home satisfied that all was well at the 'Thieves Market'. The remaining crews were to depart with this morning's outgoing tide. What amounted to a law enforcement agency in the world of the Mal'lam would be gone from Sha'lan'la by midday. Too few righteous men and women would remain to prevent what was impending.

In the oral traditions of the Mal'lam existed the sagas of the valiant seamen-warriors who had forged a path from a drought-seared and enemy-invested homeland to the new home here in these islands. They had fought some vigorous battles on the way, indigenous inhabitants understandably reluctant of their encroachment. It was only when they searched the western seas, the home of the legendary 'Itoi', that they were routed completely, every incursion bringing retreat with few survivors. From the memories of those scarred survivors came down the fearful tradition of an implacable foe; men horrid in appearance, vicious in battle, brutal in victory.

For generations the young boys had sat at the feet of storytellers with wide eyes and raging imaginations, absorbing every word. Among that generation of boys now in their mid-thirties, having heard those tales but put aside their enthrallment for more contemporary concerns, there existed a few still in thrall of the imagined world of victorious ancestors and horrible foes. Tor'na Sea-Master was one of those men. The visions his active imagination had contrived lived as vividly to this day. He had, since one stormy night in the dim light of a storyteller's hut, painted a portrait of a valiant warrior in his mind. It was through this picture that was superimposed on his psyche that he saw himself and that he built his concept of who Tor'na really was.

When the rest of the people around him saw a different boy, and then a man, than he perceived, he convinced himself that all about him were blind to his true persona. His isolation began that night, relieved but in part by finding a like-soul in his beautiful Mal'atan. But even Mal'atan, his slight, almost feminine body precluding the might of a warrior, could but watch admiringly as finally this very morning, that compilation of historical hero and mythical 'Itoi' emerged as *'Tor'na, Master of the Mal'lam'*! With that first daub of paint, a dark grey mixture of charcoal, lime and oil, he was inscribing his own tragic demise.

Gathered about Tor'na at the smoldering campfire, four of his followers copied his actions, trying clumsily to recreate the pattern and effect he was applying to his face and body. The old tales were replete with detail: how the 'Itoi' tattooed and painted their faces and bodies to frightening effect; how the ancestors had bound their arms with blood-red bands, trapping blood in veins and muscles, swelling and accentuating them. Years of recalling, redesigning and modifying had created the patterns Tor'na now directed his company to paint upon themselves. All except Mal'atan. Such masculine exaggeration did not suit him - was not pertinent to the special purpose Tor'na had perceived for him since first they met.

Mal'atan sat slightly apart, as always, a special mixture of paints on a slab of moist bark nestled between his legs. A large, shallow wooden bowl was propped on a stand of twigs in front of him, the still water which brimmed the container mirrored his reflection each time he bent over it to guide his slender fingers as they applied red, yellow and white ochre's to his face. His hair this day was tied behind his head in the male fashion but it was decorated with the small jaws of a deep-water fish with long, nasty-looking teeth. Over his forehead were tied the jaws of a small shark, framing his thin, subtly voracious features. White painted lines expanded the effect of the teeth onto his face while a broad band of bright red, beginning at his lower lip and extending to his throat, gave the impression of his just having feasted on blood. He was now applying dots of yellow pigment in some esoteric pattern, carefully spacing them, daubing away any smear with the end of a chewed twig such as one used to cleanse one's teeth.

Joom'ta, the gawky, effeminate Sht'ah'Lee-an, still pouting at not being allowed his own cosmetic creation, nevertheless studied Tor'na's lead, painting the face of the boy, Sh'ul'am. The two burly seamen likewise took turn-about with each other's faces and bodies, eager to replicate the emerging dramatic persona their leader was creating as he worked over his own bowl of mirrored splendor.

Even Mal'atan, in his secret contempt, straightened and stared in admiration when Tor'na finally stood and silently presented his transformation. A man of stocky, muscular build, of medium height, he now seemed to tower above them all. His black hair shone with oil and he wore a shark's upper jaw on his forehead. His upper face was painted solid black to a line just below his eyes, a dark grey below with an unpainted gap surrounding the still-vivid scars which ran from nostril to jaw, one side incompletely formed. From the corners of his mouth ran a line of bright red, bordering the square-cut section of beard which was all that was left of his once flowing facial hair. At the juncture of each shoulder with the bicep was a blood-red band of plaited fiber with small shells interwoven, a strangely feminine accent. Horizontal stripes of black ran across his chest and each nipple was outlined in red. A red spear-shape rose upward from his navel, surely a symbol of rampant sexuality.

Years of resentment, of subliminal hatred and aggression shone forth in fearsome array. No one, not even his despised trainer and mentor, the Sea-Master Telan, would recognize Tor'na today. A new man was born of this, Tor'na was absolutely certain. Could he have seen the totality of himself in a mirror he would have been even more pleased. He did not even deign to glance at Mal'atan for approval, so sure was he. Here was a warrior! A 'Master of Sea and Land', the embodiment of all that was truly majestic in Mal'lam tradition. Tor'na's ego soared on painted wings!

An hour later, still unobserved by anyone, this company of misfits and madmen rose in unison from a kneeling prayer to the Gods of retribution, Gods long asleep in Mal'lam memory, and they strode toward the clamor and avarice of the 'Thieves Market'. Sh'ul'shem was in for a rude shock. Marching from the beach entrance to the trader's lane, the group headed single-mindedly toward its end and the hut of Rohr'rit. Those first traders and other citizens saw but a small group of painted entertainers, jugglers perhaps. Then the clubs in their hands were seen and the emanations of menace caused the crowd to part before them.

A mutter of surprise and warning grew and all heads turned, all barter forgotten. In the lead was a huge ... no, a big ... well a powerful man who carried a broad-bladed club edged with shark's teeth!

Behind him was a lean, incredibly costumed man. Yes, it was a man! He carried no obvious weaponry but shone with an eerie strangeness; all sharp points and blood! Behind him was a taller, somewhat awkward looking fellow, also gaudily painted and he carried a heavy club and looked eager to use it. Behind him, and side-by-side, were two burley, ominous looking men also bearing edged weapons. Last was a small man. No, really but a boy, but vicious looking too and also carrying one of those terrible looking, shark's tooth-edged weapons which no one there had ever seen before. No one in the crowd which followed them followed closely; they were all looking about nervously, wondering, whispering.

Surprise and shock were the components of this maneuver which Tor'na and Mala'tan had agreed was essential for success. So far, so good. Word of something momentous ran ahead of the crowded people along the laneway but the usual guard at the door of the still sleeping *master* of Sha'lan'la, Rhor'rit, were themselves complacent. A riotous debauch the night before had rendered them only half-awake. The two men only roused to attention when the nightmarish visage of Tor'na appeared before them on a wave of crowd noise. Then it was too late! "Kill them!" Tor'na commanded, his voice high pitched with excitement and tension. The two old companions sprang forward to the hut's entrance. Two blows carrying the weight of inspired aggression landed on two, too-slow heads. One had managed to raise a defending hand, its fingers severed as the edged club carried on to his skull. The other died with an expression of uncomprehending shock.

As Tor'na and the other two pushed aside the drape at the entrance to the hut and plunged inside, Mal'atan stepped between the two dead men, their blood still flowing. He knelt with knees together and patted each head in exaggerated commiseration, rose and glanced at his hand. Seeing a dab of blood on his thumb, he put it in his mouth and licked it clean. A shuddering groan of disbelief rose from the crowd but instantly subsided as the remaining two of this nightmare's coterie turned and raised their weapons threateningly. "Itoi!" someone muttered. It was the old woman, still sitting beside her cooking fire.

The body of Rohr'rit was dragged from his hut by the two Sea-Hewn who were now murderers. Two terrified, naked women fled out the door after them. Tor'na had hoped for the satisfaction of a short confrontation, a personal victory, ego against ego, power against power. But the man could not be roused from his drunken stupor. Killing Rohr'rit was no more satisfying than clubbing a fish to death. Tor'na seethed with frustration. He had planned that his entry into the annals of greatness would have been one of prevailing over an enemy in combat. Now, all would know it was but bloody murder.

But his mind was still ordered enough to reckon his next move carefully. In the format of the paint and fish teeth, his grimace shone with such evil ugliness that, could he see it, even he would have been shocked. Joom'ta had hauled himself up to his full, skinny height and looked more than ridiculous, even in this terrible circumstance. The boy, Sh'ul'am, his weapon swinging freely at the end of his arm, had in the past minutes shed his boyhood. Though he had struck no blow, he considered himself as much a murderer as those who had actually killed. More than his boyhood had died this day. Neither excitement nor inspiration attended his thoughts. He was simply an observer, a cipher, and an uninterested participant in someone else's drama. He cared for nothing nor anyone involved, yet was willing to do as he was directed. He too, had become a very dangerous man.

To his left, still seated, the old woman choked back a sob. She recognized him now. For one brief day she had dared hope that a boy might have truly wanted a 'grandmother'. She could see that the boy had died within that small frame and wondered fearfully at the terrible, cold spirit which now occupied it. He glanced toward her and she shuddered and looked away. His eyes were nearly as devoid of life as those three dead men lying there. Mar'tah Leaf-Plait closed her eyes and began chanting silently, her body rocking back and forth; a prayer for the dead.

By that evening, five violent men and a boy had established their control over a population of more than two hundred. Knowing he had not the manpower yet to prevent the traders from launching their great bamboo rafts and sailing home, he gathered men with the unsubtle threat of violence and directed them to assist the traders in launching their vessels. The sooner they were away, the better. He was quick to consolidate the advantage his first, shocking appearance and actions had gained, confronting anyone who balked or protested at being ordered about. Always domineering and intimidating, his appearance now, and the brutal killings earlier, made him awesomely overwhelming. No living Mal'lam had ever seen such men, had ever experienced such measured brutality. Their shock and fear overcame any will to resist. That would come later when Tor'na's intent became apparent, and that his ambitions did not end here.

Among the masters of the last bamboo trading rafts to leave the beach that day was a Clansman of the Sh'tah Lee-an. He had recognized Mal'atan and Joom'ta and knew Tor'na by previous reputation. Though a rough and independent trader himself, the arrogance and butchery of that morning had kindled a fierce rage within him. He stood looking aft as the big vessel wallowed over the breakers and out toward the open sea. He struggled with contending thoughts; why should he concern himself with such madness? He had valuable cargo aboard, commitments to fulfill; and Sh'tah Lee was a long, hard sail away and the weather now would begin to be very contrary.

But, were these hoodlums not his clansmen and did not their piracy compromise his own name? He looked over at the two men struggling with the steering oar, then to his bulging pile of trade goods, then to the mast-top pennant, which stood out significantly toward the south. "Steer for Sh'tah Lee!" he growled, and turned and walked forward to the bow. The steersmen looked at each other in surprise, then shrugged and leaned onto the heavy rudder, obeying. The master shouted orders and the great boom swung on its mast, filling with a provident wind. The southern island of Shtah'Lee must be alerted.

Research Notes: Impressions and General Observations

Subject: Tina Pua'lani Kaiser, Kaua'i, Fall 1972

Things are a bit tense around here this week. Tutu Kinau is on the warpath and I'm trying to keep a low profile, busy typing, and also dodging leaks in the roof. Pots and pans and old cans all over the place. Can't repair the roof until it stops raining. Jeez! Tina came home from school this last Monday quite obviously 'stoned'! I'm sure that Kinau had anticipated this because 'pot' is everywhere. Yes, I've tried it, once. And, yes, I inhaled. And, no, I didn't like it. I may have stated before that I'm known as a control-freak and marijuana is not very conducive to full control. I was really sorry to find out about Tina's experimentation but I'm also sure, knowing her as I do, that she'll survive this little drama.

Kinau read the riot act to Tina on the day and has carried that 'Polynesian scowl' around for the past two days. She's pretty imposing when she's cranky!

Update, following day:

Tina came with me for a long walk and a talk this afternoon after school. Things seem o.k. Now. We both had a little cry and a hug. She doesn't like school much this year. She thinks a lot of the kids are rude at high school. She'll be alright though. I remember feeling rather like that myself at 12 or 13. I've been helping her with some homework, Tutu Kinau is no longer scowling (thank God) and I've had lots of time to compile and record the stories about the Mal'lam. I've bought a new portable typewriter. Hopefully, no more grousing from Jiro.

Kinau and I sat up late tonight chatting. She was so upset with Tina because she knew that drugs could jeopardize her sensitivity. Kinau said *her* own voices had warned her about that. She said that what seemed to get Tina back on track was her understanding that smoking pot or taking any drug might break the 'connection', especially the possibility that her 'Daddy', grandfather Willem, might not be able to get through to her. I hadn't thought about that myself. Dummy! Also, Kinau told her that she wouldn't be able to get *there*. I had to ask where *there* was; she told me, with a serious look, followed by a smile. *There* is wherever her destiny wants to take her. Remind me never to question that woman's wisdom.

Update, the weekend:

Rain, rain, rain! The kids are housebound and I've firmly refused to go mud sliding again. Salvation! Aunty Helen is taking all the kids to the movies in Kapaa and then out for hamburgers at McDonalds. Tina keeps insisting that her 'voices' want to tell her more of the story. Right now! Ah Kinau, my good *seestah*! She's taking Tina and me down to Helen's place in Hanalei so we can have some peace and quiet when the screaming horde returns.

Update, following week:

The tape recorder, and my note pad, got a real workout last weekend. After helping clear up some last minute homework for Tina, she immediately sat back on Helen's big couch and began with another installment. You've heard of automatic writing? Well, she's an automatic talker. It has taken me three days to write all of this down.

Chapter Thirteen - Farewell the Vesa'tan

The rhythmic beat of heavy stone blades rang through the forest, counterpoint to the subliminal death songs of the huge trees. The Vesa'tan sat as she always did when her beloved trees were being cut down; far away and sorrowing. She had reluctantly attended the ceremonies, conducted by Joha'lan, when the Woodsmen sang songs of respect and appreciation to the trees. Each man cut a small chip of sapwood which Joh'lan's ring-barking had exposed. Each used the sharp edge to draw a drop of blood from one hand, symbolically sharing in the death of the great forest monarchs.

The felling and transporting of the huge logs was a difficult and dangerous task and the vengeance of unassuaged forest spirits was a possible complication not to be presumed upon. Therefore, simple ceremonies attended the beginnings of the cutting of each tree. The Vesa'tan, too far away to hear the cutting and felling but still aching from the wailing within her inner acuity, attempted to assuage her own feelings with a feast of greasy pork. It was part of the beast sacrificed for the occasion, another tradition of the Woodsman's work.

Nearly toothless, she sucked, rather than gnawed the ribs. This was the only meat she ever ate, and only on occasions like this. She would take the life of no animal to sustain her own life. She lived on the generous produce offered by the trees and shrubs and herbs which formed the roof and walls and floor of her forest home. Pigs, she hated! They uprooted and trampled and destroyed in their gluttony and were the only living thing in the forest, save a thoughtless human or two passing through, whom she could not communicate with. Not even the venomous 'Vasa', if she were careful, would threaten her. But those damned pigs!

She allowed her diminishing hunger to help salve the great hurt and soon, tossing the bones away, she wiped her hands on her wrap. Her years of solitude had worn away the fastidious habits of personal hygiene common to all Mal'lam. That she stank nearly as much as her hated neighbors, the pigs, never occurred to her. She had ceased bathing in the cold streams in middle age. A comb was a useless encumbrance to her and as she scratched at her perpetually itchy scalp, she sighed and laid back on the new blanket which Joha'lan had recently presented to her. She slept often and long these days and each rising was a struggle against protesting muscles and reluctant joints.

The Vesa'tan knew that soon she would not awaken from sleep. One day, and this the forest had promised her, the spirits of the 'Green World' would collect her and absorb her into its everlasting beauty. Each time she closed her eyes lately, she vaguely hoped it would be for the last time. One thought, however, one vision always intruded just before sleep overwhelmed her; the child, that little girl, Tina. How the forest had sung that day! And still the echoes of the girl's power tinkled among the green. Oh, what joy she had brought, that innocent yet so-knowing child. And what of the other? That unknown but now familiar face - an old woman like herself - she who had spoken to The Vesa'tan in a dream.

It had been oh, so many months ago. "Protect our daughter!" the vision had pleaded, "Guide our sister-luv to her destiny." Such a burden it had seemed then, not knowing who, or when, or why. But she had known immediately, unquestioningly, when she had watched the herbalists that night at their camp in the forest. The child had shone from within, as did the mightiest of trees! Green light and earth-fire! So taken had The Vesa'tan been that she had clumsily snapped twigs as she moved around the periphery of the camp, seeking a better view of the young one. Joha'lan had heard her. Dear, giant man, silly as all men are, but so *whole*! So very warm.

"Ah, Kal'lan!" she spoke her own name aloud. "Ahhh that my days should end with such bounty, such precious friendships". The Vesa'tan slept. And the spirits clad in green crept silently, carefully, lovingly to her resting place. The time had come! Far away among the rebounding limbs of trees, abused by the fall of the first huge log, a giant man heard not 'crash' or 'boom', but , "*Kah'laaaannnn*!" For the rest of his long life he would silently utter that sound in moments of birth or death, never really knowing why.

That same sound brought the girl, Tina, to a halt in the midst of her play with some friends. Her eyes lost outward focus and a sudden sense of loss deluged her senses. By now, however, the girl could most often wrest her emotions back from the demands of that *other reality*. Tina! What's wrong?" her friend Shana'lan asked, looking intently into her playmate's face. She still did not fully understand Tina's periods of strangeness. Tina shook her head and regained herself and smiled. "Oh, nothing; just voices. You know." She then returned to her play. The sound, the name, if that is what is was, continued to resound but it echoed away in diminishing reverberations.

Tina's hand went to the stone which lay upon her throat. It was cool and comforting. The last fragment of that sound seemed to reside within the stone. Tina was learning to use her talisman and that dying old woman's name hushed to a cool glow in her hand. She smiled innocently. It just felt right. The answers would come later.

The Vesatan

Joha'lan walked beside the length of the huge log twice, once on each side, inspecting the timber, frowning in concentration. Returning to the severed butt he smiled and those sweating men around him smiled in response. It was a good log! One down, five to go! Moving from the large butt up to the crown, twelve men hewed at thick limbs, careful to cut obliquely so that those huge structures, when they fell to the ground, would not tear wood from the main timber. Then, beyond the hacking nearby came the crash of a second tree, two hundred feet away. A cheer rose from the men culling the limbs of the first log. The work was going well.

Joha'lan's tall figure moved from cutting-site to cutting-site, the intensity of his concentration more imposing even than his physical size. His mind struggled with this huge task; a craftsman's duty new to his experience. All the while, a niggling sense of loss interposed. Joha'lan knew that his 'Forest Mother' was gone! He now stood alone in his responsibility, accountable to all but with no one to assist. This giant man had never really seen his surroundings from a point of advantage. As a boy and as boys will, he engaged in wrestling matches, and he always won. But his ego never strayed beyond the gentler restraints of his humanity.

Those broad, powerful hands which wielded carving tools with such exquisite sensitivity now clutched the heavy handle of an adze. With powerful strokes he stripped away the bark from beneath where another Woodsman had severed a limb of the second tree. There was a discolored stripe beneath, signaling some damage to the timber. He stood back and called, "Grash'an! Measure to that first limb." The order was but a momentary ruse to cover his indecision. This second tree had labored in its plunge, twisting and lurching in its reluctance. What damage could that dying dance have done internally? Had the integrity of the huge baulk of timber been compromised? Had the shearing of one limb toward the top weakened the lot?

Never had Joha'lan known such stress of decision. He had contrived his professional life to allow his preference for the minute, the tiny detailed sculpture, while still maintaining his authority as the foremost successor to the rank of Canoe-Master. Again he berated himself, absorbing again the guilt of not attending enough to the discipline of his craft which Ran'tar had gently, constantly, urged him to do. As he strode along the cutting-path, a sudden spring of a cut-through branch swept toward him, a workman standing between.

Lunging forward with instinctual alertness, Joha'lan's hands struck that man's legs behind the knees, causing him to collapse onto Joha'lan's own arms. The wickedly swinging branch passed barely above the cutter's head. With a final splintering sound, the heavy limb fell upon the two with almost apologetic gentleness. The Wood-Hewn rolled onto his belly and looked back into Joha'lan's strained features; then his face exploded in a white-toothed grin and soon Joha'lan's booming laughter joined in. Both men lay, head-to-head, uproariously venting the shock and the passed danger. When they had recovered from their fright, Joha'lan continued his inspection of the tree trunk. No damage! It was still sound!

Once a tree trunk has been painstakingly incised to a certain depth, the cutting must continue. If left standing overnight a wind gust might cause it to fall in an unwanted direction. Worse still, the trunk might split, rendering the whole exercise a waste. By twilight the sixth chosen tree remained standing and all the cutting crews gathered around it. Turn on turn, the strong, broad-backed men cut at a furious pace until near collapse. Others quickly replaced them. All these men were near exhaustion, having swung the heavy stone blades since early morning. Only a few inches to go, the up-hill side now the focus of their efforts. Two men, one swinging left-handed blows, the other right-handed, their faces livid with the strain, cut and chopped until the cracking sounds began. "Ho'aaaaaahhhhh!" the shout came, warning all that the moment had come.

Men ran to each side of the estimated path of the tree's fall, desperate to be out of the way. The under-cut, that slice taken from the down-hill side and acting as the pointer for the tree's fall, was so precise, so well-judged, that this great giant too fell exactly where intended. The silence which followed the last clattering of branches as the great log finally lay still, reigned with soul-pinching intensity. No true Woodsman could experience the death of a tree without feeling that mortality within himself. For many seconds no one spoke. Then a fatigued cutter coughed; then another, and a tired, almost reluctant sense of victory began to murmur among the men.

"Well done, brothers!" Joha'lan's deep voice boomed through the forest. "Who is hungry? Who would like a bit of palm toddy?" He stood smiling as the dozens of tired men shouldered their tools and trudged toward the camp, each casting grins and comments at the Canoe-Master as they passed where he stood, reflecting their triumph with his own smile. When the Woodsmen had passed out of sight toward the encampment, Joha'lan stood alone until darkness drowned the scene of this day's mighty effort. He sorrowed for this day's losses: the death of The Vesa'tan, of this he was sure. And the surrender of six, huge volumes of living timber to his purpose, his responsibility. The proper utilization of that was a burden as great as fatherhood. Such fatherhood! He felt the full weight of all that timber upon his soul, his shoulders slouching forward in response. Joha'lan struggled with those doubts which attend all beginnings, if those beginnings signal even greater effort. His mind reached forward in time and hesitantly stroked the concerns of his future; his mind's hand grasping and weighing, testing resolve. He sighed and turned to wend a darkened path to the encampment when a sudden sound penetrated his worried awareness like a splash of cold water. Joha'lan stood still and suddenly alert.

"Twee chit chit!" it came. "Tweee chit chit!" It was the 'Night-Singer", a bird so rare that no description existed; half-seen movements against starlit skies rendered this creature almost mythical. Hairs stood up all over his body and a cool embrace of mystery and wonder caressed the back of Joha'lan's neck. "Tweee, chit chit." Closer now! "Where are you, little one? Let me see you." A partial moon and starlight offered little chance of this. Still Joha'lan insisted. "Come little one. Let me see you." The calls came closer now, tantalizing. Joha'lan breathed deeply, worry and weight-of-concern dissolving on the bright tones of a fascinating uniqueness. Joha'lan stood transfixed. Few ever came close to these night-songsters, but all recounted magical involvements; momentary flights of spirit into the seduction of nocturnal mystery.

"Twee chit chit!" even closer now, and Joha'lan hunkered down onto his heels, his hands braced on the cool earth; not to spring forward but to receive whatever was coming. That song suddenly changed and Joha'lan settled into a comfortable crouch, waiting. "Chee tit tit!" was repeated for many moments until he was certain that the bird could only be but paces away now, level with his body. Joha'lan slowly settled back onto his buttocks and sat comfortably, ready to accept whatever might occur. His mind was unfocused, open.

The call now became high-pitched, a repeated, "Tseeet, tseeet, tseeet!" which ran up and down his nervous system like a gentle massage. His powerful body relaxed in response. And then the light! That pale, shimmering blueness! This blue light cast no shadows as it intensified and Joha'lan, eyes wide open, knew it was not his eyes which perceived this mounting glow. Emotions and echoes of emotions; some obscure, some even sensual, pervaded his thoughts. What is this? Warmth in his groin, a surge of sexual power; a sweet memory? a lover? Sha'lat! Her lovely face, all blue and smiling and warm arms embracing, not from lust alone but from love - love all embracing! Afterglow! And a loving smile, and whispers he couldn't quite hear. Then there was more.

That other face; a child, limbs and love wrapped around mother and himself, powerful in their youthful strength yet gentle in their caress of wisdom and gentle age. Tina! It was Tina, smiling at them both as they clung lovingly to each other. And yet another! Sweet, soft, yet solid-as-stone. Sh'tana! Three pairs of feminine arms now embraced, now pulled and pushed, now led him to a great log of wood, which glowed with an inner fire. Those arms and hands now loosed him and he stood alone before the timber. The timber sang to him yet frightened him. He turned and still those three stood, love in their faces like sunrise on water.

"Yes! Yes!" Joha'lan took the final step toward the challenge of the wood and it too embraced him with soft arms, gentle laughter now behind him. "The tree is a woman!" "Twee -chit chit." And the vision burst and coalesced into the toothless grin of an old woman, her eyes ever young, burning with promise and love. "Forest Mother!" Joha'lan gasped and as that light quickly faded and starlit darkness prevailed, he felt the light brush of fingers through his hair. The forest around him applauded with fluttering leaves and clacking branches. Joha'lan sat now, breathing deeply and purposefully as he accepted this sudden return to what-must-be-done. The song of the bird receded into the dark forest and Joha'lan sighed a goodbye. "Oh yes!" he said out loud, but softly. "Oh yes. I know." He rose then and resumed his march to the campfires of his responsibility. "I know too well, you charming schemers. I am eternally seduced!" The Night-Singer sang a faint and distant chuckle.

~ ~ * ~ ~

Sahn'ta giggled and squealed, the eight tiny pearls of baby teeth exposed in glee. Cradled in his father's lap, he kicked and squirmed as Al'malan poked a tickling finger at his taut little tummy. This was the last morning of such freedom for father and son. As the rising sun warmed his shoulders, Al'malan smiled with quiet resignation. Today would begin the '*hewing*' and his involvement would be nearly as intense as that of those twelve nervous boys. They would all surely be awake by now, their mothers making last-minute preparations. This would be the last morning they would attend those sons as boys. When next they slept under parental roofs, they would consider themselves, *men.*

Al'malan rose in an easy movement from his cross-legged position, the baby snuggled against his father's chest, still making delighted sounds. It had been two weeks since the mother, Ja'eel, had left this house and in that time had shown no interest in her son. Nor had the baby exhibited any sense of loss, his father's kind and loving attention fulfilling the infant's needs. Today though, he must go to be cared for by his grandmother, Sh'ta'et Feather-Plait, Al'malan's mother. A quiet, gentle woman, 'Mistress-of-the-Feather' due to her great knowledge of bird lore and her rendering of the beautiful feather capes worn by the girls at their '*plaiting*', herself was up early preparing for the arrival of her grandson. Sh'ta'et had kept to herself her misgivings of her son's choice of wife, weeping privately when his growing unhappiness became evident. She knew this day would arrive long before the 'breaking of the bowl'. She hummed and sang cradlesongs, nearly forgotten now since this was her only grandchild. Her husband, Lon'sho Sea-Hewn, had smiled his own excitement as he had left for his day's fishing. He too looked forward to returning home to the presence of a little one.

The woman busied herself with rearranging the interior of her cheerful home, its walls hung with the vivid products of her talented fingers. There were capes and stoles of iridescent feathers, intricately sewn onto a finely woven fiber background. Also there were marvelous decorations made by Al'malan's father; constructions of shell and fish scale and carved wood. All were temptations which must be placed out of reach of tiny hands. The tiny crèche in the corner was tidied for the tenth time. Standing near the doorway she surveyed the room, sure that something had been forgotten. Oh, how wonderful it would be to have a child at home again! How she had delighted in her own son, how proud of his strength and gentleness and intelligence, even as a boy. And now *his* own son showed signs of being so like him, even as an infant. Her daughter's impending motherhood would mean more babies to love and cuddle. Oh, life was full and rich and Sh'ta'et smiled and hugged herself in anticipation of it all.

"Good morning, mother!" Sh'ta'et turned quickly and ducked through the doorway."Little messy-bottom has come to see his gran!" Al'malan's smiling face above the baby's sent a jolt of exquisite happiness through the woman and she hurried to them, reaching up to kiss her son's face. Then she took the grinning baby from his father's arms and smothered it in kisses, cooing and clucking mother-sounds as she carried Sahn'ta inside. Al'malan followed, carrying the bundle of baby-things he'd brought with them. He gazed around the reorganized room and chuckled; "Father's peace and quiet has gone, I'm afraid!"

Suddenly he felt strangely awkward, almost sad, and even lonely here in his parent's newly built home. For most of his people from Sh'ham-Set, settling down to life on a strange island had been difficult in some ways, though their Clan cousins showed them every hospitality and consideration. He shook off the feeling. He needed to be away, busily attending to his duties. His mother made it easy for him, so involved was she with her grandson now. He bent and kissed the baby, then his mother and left the house to the sounds of a happy reunion. As he walked from beneath the upward curve of the building's awning he stopped and turned toward the soft footsteps approaching from his right. Around the corner stepped a young woman whom he'd known all his life, but until this moment had not recognized her beauty. Sht'ana Leaf-Plait stood with one hand holding a large shell filled with flowers, the other a large fruit. A delicate *lei* of pink shells hung around her neck and fell upon her lovely breasts. A large flower rode upon her glossy hair.

She smiled shyly and said, "Good morning Sea-Master Al'malan. I've come to see if I can be of any assistance to your mother today." Her smile was warm and guileless but his special hearing detected another, hidden meaning. As if aware that he might hear the secret in her heart, she suddenly blushed and looked away, then called to Al'malan's mother and went to the doorway. As he turned to go, suddenly realizing that he'd neglected to respond to her, he stopped and looked again at the doorway. She had turned too and looked after him and their eyes met and meaning sung between them, which gripped his heart with gladness! "How have I never really noticed her before?" he asked himself, carrying his own boyish blush away to his man's work. Behind him came the sounds of warm, happy greetings and the chatter of his beloved son.

Chapter Fourteen ~ The Hewing

'*The Place of the Hewing*' was far from the settlement, hidden within the towering culms of the sacred bamboo grove. Already it rang with adolescent voices chanting the ancient wisdoms in time to a solitary drum. Seated in rows were the initiates, wearing only loincloths on this cool, cloudy morning. Their skin was anointed with scented oils. Perspiration ran in beads over their glistening skin, residue from their long, hard run on this first morning of their '*hewing*'. In each row were arrayed the initiates of each craft; twelve boys who would become *hewn* of the Sea sat in the first row; six for the Wood-discipline in the second, one for the Leaf, then three for Stone. Their intent faces displayed not fear but an understandable anxiety. The details of the '*hewing*' were always kept secret; from generation to generation no *un-hewn* knew much at all about the rituals. All knew of the circumcision ordeal but no clue was given as to when and where it took place, giving rise to considerable speculation and not a little unease when a new function began in the training schedule. Certain songs and chants the boys picked up from listening to the craftsmen in the community but the secret knowledge of each craft remained a mystery to them.

Arrayed before the boys were their mentors, the chief craftsmen chosen by their fellow practitioners for their expertise and, most especially, for their encyclopedic knowledge of the oral histories of their Clan. Most Mal'lam knew by heart the broad history of their people; the long journey of their ancestors, the development of the Clan structure represented by six distinct groups. These groups, or Clans, represented the order in which various segments of the early Mal'lam arrived here in this archipelago. The Sh'ta'ha-an was the first to arrive. Naturally, among them were people who possessed the various skills necessary to sustain their society. Seamen of course, and wood-craftsmen were foremost in importance in maintaining the long passage, but knowledge of growing food crops and gathering valuable plant materials came second. Tools must be fashioned, protective fabrics woven or layered, utensils of wood and shell and to a very limited extent, ceramic items.

The skills required formed a body of knowledge passed on to succeeding generations through a series of guilds. When the Clan Sh'ta'ha, the first group to arrive, settled on their respective two islands, the people of Sh'ham-Set, for various reasons having mostly to do with sheer relief at finding a rich and hospitable land, stayed there. Those others who became the Clan cousins, the Sh'tah Lee-an, decided to forge on further southward. Maybe even better lands were on offer here! But fatigue of travel, many pregnant women and not least, the beauty of this marvelous island surmounted by its great, snow-covered mountain, inspired a halt to the forward progress of those of the Clan. This would do! For now.

'For now' had extended for three hundred years. But always, especially among the Seamen, lived and breathed the wanderlust of their forebears. The Clan affiliation remained also. To the northwest, on the island of Sh'ham, those Clansmen had no huge timbers from which to hew great canoes and time and wear saw their vessels of arrival slowly deteriorate. But always among them were many with a deep and abiding devotion to the sea. Large-diameter bamboos, both cuttings and roots, carefully husbanded for many hundreds of miles across open sea, became the source of the Sh'ham-an's technology of large, sea-going rafts. Thus was the Seaman's tradition extended on that northern island.

Over time, trading allowed the Sh'ham-an to obtain large-diameter logs for their own fast canoes and within a generation they had re-established a regular contact and intercourse of trade with their Clansmen to the south. During that generation, the last of the Mal'lam groups succeeded to this archipelago and established their own Clan destinations on separate islands. But none of them continued to foster that intense interest in the far horizon. It was the great bamboo trading rafts which established the Sh'ham-an sailors as the pre-eminent seamen among the northern island groups. But now, those fragile, ephemeral vessels of bamboo could not reach the challenge of the great open wastes of sea toward which the Clan was focused. And so it was that the lads of this hewing, especially the Sea-hewn-to-be, dreamed of double-hulled canoes coursing ever southeastward. They saw their futures aboard the new canoes, which were now to be constructed, and no anxiety about their *hewing* could impede those dreams.

After two days of intensive instruction and repetition of the history-chants of the Clan, the boys were led from the confines of the creaking, sighing bamboos and went in separate groups to the sites of their individual craft training. The to-be-Sea-hewn of course, jogged in single file, chanting songs of the sea and were led by Al'malan. The young apprentice Woodsmen were led into the surrounding forest; the stone quarries awaited another group. The single apprentice to the skills of plant and herb knowledge followed his mentor up the Black Boar Track to the slopes of Volan Votu, a cold and harsh journey this time of year.

While the ten lads of the land-crafts went inland, A'lan, Shen'ham and their ten mates were plunged into the rigors of the sea. The autumn waters were becoming chilly now, the days often cloudy and with brisk winds blowing. These conditions did nothing to lessen the difficult trials of the initiates. From daybreak to dark the boys literally ran from place to place as the tall figure of Al'malan led them from boat-timber grove to headland, to beached canoes, on and ever faster. From bamboo rafts holding two trainees and a number of large stones the lads learned breath control. Grasping a stone to their chests, they dived overboard, the weight of the stone taking them to the bottom. There they released the stone and the lungful of air which had accompanied their dive and swam strongly to the surface again where they gasped and shivered and climbed back aboard the small raft to take up another stone.

Though all could swim with seal-like fluidity from early childhood, they all learned new ways of surviving and working on the sea: they treaded water in pairs for what seemed like hours, taking turns to hold one another up for a few moments rest. Al'malan swam continuously between the pairs, attentive to their individual condition and safety. Other Sea-Hewn rode in small canoes around them, ready to assist should a boy get into difficulty. None did. For A'lan and one other boy with the *Sea-sight*, it meant cold, wet nights in the bows of paired-hull canoes at sea, learning to read the ephemeral and mysterious lines of radiance. Shen'ham, as strong in spirit as he was in body, led his mates in most endeavors save running, his propensity for lots of rich food betraying him.

All boys lost weight now though, their diet proscribed and meager compared to their usual ravenous consumption of anything edible. They fell onto their sleeping mats and succumbed to a deep sleep within moments after downing a scanty but nutritious meal. Most would not even recall dreaming, so deep was their fatigue. Al'malan, little more than twice their age, sought his pallet with similar relief. He must teach them to be seamen by his example. Thus it was that most mentors during the *hewing* were themselves quite young and vigorous. The older, more experienced seamen would add their own example later, when the young apprentices had been *hewn* and assigned positions aboard various vessels.

In the quarries the Stone initiates learned to shape rock; they made rough blanks of adze blades for the professionals to complete, ax blades too were roughed out and techniques of reading a stone's structure began to be learned. Likewise did the Wood-Hewn teach their students to begin to really know wood; its grain, its strengths and weaknesses, how to properly and safely fell a tree and prepare it for use. All this and much more. They attended exercises designed to strengthen hands and arms and backs for the particular stresses which their craft demanded of their bodies. And the lone but not lonely, to-be-herb-hewn lad, found great satisfaction and fulfillment on the rugged climb to the highlands. He was truly destined to this role and he and his mentor were becoming soul mates. It helped that his mentor was also his father.

On the twelfth day the lads and their craft mentors reassembled within the seclusion of the bamboo grove. Nearly all the boys, and many of the men, sported abrasions and bruises from the days of intense activity. The time had come for the intentional bloodletting! As weary as the youngsters were, fear stirred tired minds and tensed their bodies. As various speakers began the final ceremony, eyes that were supposed to be centered on their mentor sneaked glances to where an old man sat, monotonously honing to razor edges a basket of thin seashells. This night, as the moon rose to its fullness, the '*hewing*' would be complete.

To lessen the rising tension of the initiates, a grey-haired Wood-Hewn, this session's 'Master of the Hewing', led them in a long mantra of humming. Raising his arm slowly to guide their inhalation, he then dropped it slowly and breathed out an exhalation of, 'shooooooooo!' Soon all were repeating the sound with eyes closed; 'shoooooooo!', all except that older man who kept up his monotonous honing, an ever present counterpoint. The chanting lasted for half-an-hour and as the moon rose from behind the waving tips of the bamboos, all the boys had resisted the tendency to fall asleep and opened their eyes on the cool glow of the globe above them. Some few fell into a renewal of anxiety but most of the boys had entered a mind-state of quiet resolve; fear far removed, some even were anxious for this final, painful act to occur and be past. A'lan and Shen'ham were among those bravest of boys.

The campfire, allowed to recede into glowing coals during the mantra, was re-ignited and soon blazed brightly. From its flaming branches were laid three other smaller fires enclosing a square of open ground which was soon covered in a large woven mat. The mat was decorated in esoteric patterns and in its center was a shallow platform like a sleeping pallet; room for one slim boy to lie. A'lan un-hewn was first to be called. He stood and walked proudly to where the group of Elders sat around the pallet, all of them naked and their bodies painted in white, black and ash-grey with strange whirls and concentric circles in red.

A'lan untied his loincloth and dropped it on the edge of the mat. He lay down quickly but his movements hinted a last-moment fear. It was only as he lay back on the mat and a pair of hands clasped his shoulders, other hands gripping his feet and hands strongly, that a rush of adrenalin brought a sheen of perspiration to A'lan's scarred face. He closed his eyes as instructed and gritted his teeth, waiting for that inferred agony! What he felt first was fingers gripping his flaccid penis. It had withdrawn as far as fear and cold air could inspire it. Then icy-cold drops of some thick liquid were applied to the glans penis and the foreskin was allowed to return to cover it. Forever moments passed during which a tingling numbness grew there. Another movement of fingers and there was a sharp stinging which made him flinch involuntarily. Only a sharp intake of breath betrayed him and the Elders attending him nodded or smiled in satisfaction.

The bodies of the men who knelt around A'lan blocked from view the surgery taking place there in the firelight and anxious young eyes could not see what was awaiting them. What was happening was a perpetuation of generations of a fraud! So long ago that the origins of circumcision had faded in the collective memory of the Mal'lam, the technique of anesthetizing the foreskin had been developed by an equally obscure Herb-Master. Generations of boys had been deluded into believing that a great agony awaited them. Generations of 'hewn' men continued the misconception. Generations of wise women guessed at the truth and 'women's talk' evolved a source of scathing reproach to be used in the face of male bragging. Yet, they too played the game and so the gentle balance of the war-of-the-sexes continued.

The combined essence of the three herbs involved, one actually the sap of a tree whose fruit was commonly eaten, imparted a short-term nerve deadening effect on the tender foreskin, at the same time acting as an antiseptic. The fluid, when in contact with the mucus membrane, caused a foaming to arise. When the foaming ceased, it was time to cut. The foreskin was pulled up hard and cut around with the sharpened edge of the seashell. The dexterity of the practitioner was all-important!

There existed in jocular tradition tales of men who had lost the tip of their penis due to a tremor in the hands of '*hewing*-Masters', who were too old for the task. In fact, the worst pain of this final act of the '*hewing*' was that stinging ache that would accompany the newly initiated boys for but a few days. The scab and soreness dropped away within short weeks. The shell, which had separated the boy from the man, was packed with a glob of crushed leaves, a poultice in effect.

The lad was instructed to clasp this over his wounded member to stanch the bleeding and further soothe the growing pain of it. When the twenty-two new *hewn* stood in the flickering firelight, left hands clasping the soothing bundles to their crotches, right hands loose against their thighs, the attending adults were once again assaulted by the inescapable humorous quality of the scene. Eyebrows clenched, eyes glazed, many of the boys seemed stunned; not just by this last event but also by the cumulative effort of nearly two weeks of intensive commitment.

A Grey-Hewn of great age who had entered the circle of firelight only moments before, having observed the proceedings from the shadows, stepped forward. His leathery body was wrapped in a long cloak against the night's chill. In a quavering voice he began to address the boy-men. "New-Hewn!" he intoned, as if he had made this same speech many times before and secretly hoped it would be the last. "You have all endured. You have all succeeded in your trials. You have conquered a man's first involvement in a world of men!" The younger men around him, Al'malan included, all nodded gravely.

"Your mentors have instructed you in your beginnings as men and shall continue to instruct you in your chosen crafts." He continued, his tone stronger, now more controlled and he sounded younger and began to warm to his task. Again the younger men around him nodded but now grins were being guarded against, faces more purposefully taut. They knew what was coming.Sentence after meaningful sentence followed, the old man speaking quite rapidly now, his back arching with some residual fervor. Just as all the boys were swaying with fatigue and most struggling to feign attention, he finished with, "And as you all stand now holding your penises, temporarily in pain, soon the young girls will want to hold you. And there will be no pain! You are now *men*!" He delivered this last with such ironic gravity that it was many moments before first one and then another boy guffawed, sniggered, giggled or snorted.

Soon the circle of fire-cast shadows lurched and swayed and the circle began to chorus with laughter. Sea-Hewn and Wood-Hewn and Stone Hewn and the one Leaf-Hewn mentor advanced and embraced their charges. Backs were slapped and private words of congratulation were whispered within the rising sounds of relief and celebration.The following feast, with copious amounts of food, and wine for the older Hewn, created a scene of merriment. Much laughter ensued when ravenous youngsters kept dropping their healing shells as they reached for food. The revelry continued until the silver disc of the moon fell beneath the circling bamboos, their culms and leaves now silent in this windless night. One by one the boys went to their pallets, exhaustion overcoming the pain in their groins, full stomachs easing them soon to sleep.

Joha'lan, Wood-Master at these ceremonies now, sat in conversation with Al'malan and Orn'ta-Sea-Master. "Two of my boys have shown exceptional potential." Joha'lan said. Orn'ta nodded in agreement as Al'malan replied, "Three in my group are quite gifted. And those two," and he nodded to where A'lan and Shen'ham lay sleeping close together, "are quite special lads. But we must work them hard and not allow them to become complacent and too full of themselves. What is planned for our people is our responsibility. What becomes of our venture will depend upon *them*. We must work them hard - but wisely."

Al'malan and Orn'ta exchanged glances of agreement then both looked to Joha'lan for a reply. His heavy features betrayed none of the concern which his new responsibility must surely be imposing upon him. Joha'lan read their meaning but paused and looked into the fire before replying, his face both shaded and highlighted dramatically by the nearby fire. The two Seamen waited patiently. It was important that a man compose a reply to such important discussions; unhurried and thoughtful. And then he embarked upon a monologue of uncharacteristic length.

"As you will have heard, The Vesa'tan is thought to be passed from us!" The firelight illuminated a glitter of moisture in his eyes. "It has been revealed to my heart that her spirit lives on in one of our young ones. A girl, Tina, Tina-unplait, of the Sh'ham-an. You may also have heard that her mother, Sha'lat, is to become my wife." The Seamen had not heard of that yet and they exchanged glances of surprise, then looked even more intently into Joha'lan's face as he spoke.

"All has gone well with the felling of the trees for the canoes and in two days we shall return to them. I wish the two of you to accompany me." It was customary for the future Masters of canoes to attend the initial shaping of the newly fallen logs and indeed, to lend his back to the labor involved. In such a manner did a Seaman imbue the wood with his own spirit, the beginning of a long and intimate relationship. Joha'lan looked steadily into the darkness surrounding them, into the wall of bamboo as if he sought something there. Speaking slowly and carefully as he chose his words, he uttered them with a certainty and conviction that impressed the Seamen.

"It will require every available man and lad for a period of many weeks to haul the logs to the construction sheds. The sheds are completed now. The logs have been de-limbed and stripped and two of the hulls roughly hewn. Two weeks will see them ready for transport. We will transport them in stages, keeping the crews together. There will be less risk and the load will be easier to handle." Joha'lan looked directly into their faces and grinned broadly, exposing his joy. "You will be amazed by the size of these logs!" Then he turned again and gazed into the shadows beyond the fading firelight. "Custom will be followed as the histories direct. We will feast on pork and fish the day before we depart. After that we will eat no land-flesh, dried fish only, and the children will keep us supplied with fresh fruits and greens. The women will cook *taro* and breadfruit daily but no man will sleep with his woman during this time. The women will camp away from the men while the work progresses." Again a mischievous smile and he added, "Another reason to hurry, if you know what I mean?" He continued as they chuckled, "Some voices spoke to my spirit, just yesterday. These voices said that you two must go to the village of Manala'wan and see an old man by the name of Jo'lo'tan." Orn'ta nodded vigorously. He knew that man.

"Something important awaits you there. By the time you return, the feast will be prepared and then you can come to the forest with us." Suddenly Joha'lan paused as if listening to something, his head cocked slightly to the left. The two Seamen looked in that direction but neither saw nor heard anything. The big Wood-Master then nodded slightly as if agreeing with an internal thought and turned again to his companions. "A vessel approaches Sh'tah Lee-Set. Wait for its arrival before you go. It carries bad news from the north.!"

When, after two minutes of silence, Al'malan said, "Thank you, brother. Now, I am done in. I'm going to go and sleep." The others followed suit and silence lay gently upon the last night of the '*hewing*' like a soft blanket. At sea the sinking moon shone brilliantly on the huge sail of a large bamboo raft, stranger to these southern seas. That same illumination made the snow of Volan Votu shine like a beacon of pearl, guiding the vessel's master with cold vigilance. "The southern island must be alerted!"

Research Notes: Impressions and General Observations

Subject: Tina Pua'lani Kaiser, Kaua'i, Winter 1972-73

Well, Christmas has come and gone and I'm back in Hawai'i, back at Hanalei with Tutu Kinau and family. I've had a wonderful holiday with my parents and brother, caught up with lots of friends and managed to contact my other project advisor at the University in L.A. For some reason, he seems a bit nonplussed at the direction in which my research is headed. Can't imagine why!

Jiro met me at the airport and I stayed at his sister-in-law's place for four days while we compiled my transcriptions of Tina's story to date. He asked me, "Are you sure you want to continue with this?" The thought of not being with my Hawai'ian family again and especially, not following up on Tina and Kinau's stories nearly brought me to tears. I thought for a moment that he was trying to tell me that I wasn't doing the job. He reached across the table and gently pushed my jaw closed. "You've got to get a sense of humor, my girl!" he grinned. Grrrrrrr! He got me again!

Tina has settled into high school quite nicely, it seems. Her initial reluctance was just a bit of stage fright, I think, and now she has a few good friends about whom she often talks … endlessly! Was I like that too, at thirteen? But Tina has no difficulty in re-establishing contact with her Mal'lam spirits and in the few days before school recommenced we had many hours for her to tell me of more peaceful goings-on in that world of long ago . . .

Chapter Fifteen - The Itin

Orn'ta' Sea-Master's vessel, the sleek, paired-hull 'Hoosh-im'wa', the 'Dolphin's Tail', beat heavily against the wind and sea as it ran on tack after tack up the western coastline. The very wind which had swung about and allowed the cumbersome trading raft to quickly reach Sh'tah Lee, now confronted 'Hoosh-im'wa as it battled its way toward the northern fishing village of Mana'la'wan. The big, triangular sail allowed for little windward progress in these conditions and what would have been a day's sail in Trade Wind conditions now was a voyage in its second morning. And still most of the morning to go!

A'lan Sea-Hewn and Shen'ham Sea-Hewn - they both still glowed at being so addressed now - sat cross-legged on the bridging deck along with A'lan's cousin, Faldo'in Sea-Hewn, named after Great-Uncle Tal'ma's long-disappeared son, Faldo Sea-Master. Faldo'in had been born the month after his uncle had been judged missing and likely dead. The three newly *hewn* boys were on their first fully-fledged voyage as seamen and although they were consigned to menial chores, as now when they sat plaiting new lines, all three saw the world through new and excited eyes.

These boys were the brightest, most promising of the Sea-Hewn initiates and they would spend much of their time in the company of the most skilled seamen. In spite of their obviously favored positions among the younger lads, there was little jealousy among their peers or among the slightly older trainees. All the Mal'lam held competence and gift in high esteem. As well, and most importantly, young egos were not allowed to get out of control when boys such as these were put in positions of favor. They were worked harder than their less-illustrious achievers and any hint of arrogance was immediately quashed by the glowering intervention of an elder.

It was remembered by the Sh'ham-an seamen that Tor'na-the-Mad, as an initiate seaman, had constantly to be reprimanded for his incipient arrogance. That remembrance was invoked often but no comparison to this group of youngsters was relevant. Tradition and common sense did prevail here, and these three youngsters were protected from innuendo and misinterpretation by the simple fact that they smiled a great deal. Those who knew Tor'na-the-Mad as a youngster held no recollection of a smile from that brooding face, let alone the spontaneous gaiety and humor of this class of young seamen. It was these factors which Al'malan, Orn'ta and two other ranking seamen discussed as they sat near the aft end of the vessel's bridging deck. The news had been bad! Shocking, but not altogether surprising. "Three killed, many bashed and everyone threatened!" had been the trader's statement. "He nearly didn't let us go. We were last out. But I ordered my crew to draw their knives and he backed off." The trader had hawked and spat in disgust, then added, "The crazy fool had the gall to wish us a hearty voyage and said that he'd see us again soon and that we would then address him as 'Tor'na-the-Magnificent'! The man is truly mad!"

One of the younger seamen, tending a steering paddle but listening closely to the Master's' conversation, interjected with, "I spoke with two of the man's crew, rough rascals all of them, and they said the skinny, girlish one was really scary. Something about him, they said, something really evil!" The young seaman shuddered, accenting the story. Orn'ta looked down at his callused hands and imagined that skinny, girlish one's scrawny neck clasped within them. His sense of pride and familial responsibility still stung any time Mal'atan was referred to. He looked into the faces of those senior Sea-Hewn squatting or sitting about him and left each with the truth of his words: "Tor'na is bad enough, my friends. But his madness will surely destroy him. Mal'atan, however, is truly evil! That is not just my opinion. *Seers* have warned of him - they still do. Fear undoes many a man. Fear is running rampant now, rushing from Set to Set in the north and in time we here in the south will have to confront it also. It is my belief that we must invoke the old warrior's methods, sooner rather than later. We must gird ourselves against fear and its products, our own as well as that of others."

As if to accentuate his message a sudden powerful gust of wind struck 'Hoosh-im'wa'. The heavy sail swung abeam and a sheet parted, then its opposite line broke as the sail swung uncontrollably to leeward. The three boys sitting forward looked up at the booming rigging with a start. The sudden surge of the bows to windward unbalanced the two steersmen, one being knocked off his feet by the vessel's violent turn. The windward hull lifted clear of the water, splashed down again, and then rose once more, threatening to capsize the canoe.

Just as an experienced Seaman lunged to the mast and the halyards to drop the sail, all the senior Seamen were now on their feet and scrambling to assist. Shen'ham, his mind still fired with the intensity of his initiation ordeal but his inexperience misdirecting him, lunged upward and caught hold of one flailing sheet. His instinct was to pull the sail back to balance the heeling vessel.

Another big gust of wind caught the sail and as it swung again to leeward, shouts of, 'Windward hull!' resounded and crewmen leaped to lend their weight to re-balance the craft.

Before the sail could be released and sent plunging in a controlled fall safely to the deck, it billowed outboard again, this time followed by Shen'ham, clinging still to that broken line. He gripped the rope in desperation as he rebounded at the end of the arc of his swing over the cold, swirling sea. No sooner had he been submerged in the water than A'lan, followed closely by his cousin, Faldo'in, dived to his rescue. Al'malan, Orn'ta and the other Sea-Hewn looked on in horror as the three boys disappeared into the surging waters! The sail was now safely on the deck but a large section of it blew away again overboard, acting as a sea anchor, pulling the canoe's bows back around.

A Seaman recovered his wits and quickly threw a line overboard to where the boys had disappeared. Shen'ham still clung to the rope which had propelled him overboard but his young mates, their heads now above water and looking about desperately for him, slid astern and into mortal danger. Faldo'in was first to grasp the lifeline. He threw one arm out to grasp A'lan's extended arm but their hands missed by inches. Faldo'in turned tortured eyes behind him to watch his cousin slipping astern. A'lan's mouth was wide and shouting beseechingly. Terror clawed at his mind, but only briefly.

The boy whose face was increasingly dominated by that awful scar felt the cold invading his vibrant strength and at that first signal of alarm, his mind retreated to the training of his *hewing*. "Concentrate your strength in your belly!" it had directed him, on that miserable day when they had been commanded to tread water for hour upon hour in waters not unlike these. He watched with an inborn detachment the movement of the canoe away from him. Away from salvation.

It was then that the first onset of pain struck him; that pain which only in later life was he able to equate with any other. Like a severe toothache it was, but not in his jaw. The pain shot across his cheek and to his nose, searing and causing his left eye to close sympathetically. He grabbed at his face as if to brush away the stinging tentacles of a jellyfish. But there was nothing there to be felt but the long, pink residue of scar tissue. He rubbed frantically, but to no avail. It became worse and dominated the whole of his concentration, wiping away the fear which moments before had bordered on panic. This pain was an old adversary and he knew how to deal with it. Cold seawater was as nothing compared to that pain's insistent humiliation. Automatically, his legs and arms continued a strong treading motion, keeping his head above the constant invasion of the waves. And now began the strange process by which A'lan survived that pain. He became angry, and that anger brought a shout, half-smothered as a wave struck his head. The canoe was coming-about now, the Seamen having taken to their paddles and digging into the waves desperately. But the vessel was still far away. So far away!

A'lan's mind blazed with resentment and that resentment flashed from vision to vision in his mind; he saw again the disdainful back of the man who had wounded him and his anger flailed at Mal'atan's figure. Anger struck out at the sorrow and misery of his mother as she endured the death of his grandmother in that great conflagration on Sh'ham-Set. It flew across the deep sea to Sha'lan'la-Set, the island cringing before Tor'na's wickedness. And finally, it whipped upon the choppy waters between him and the canoe and he struck out with his mind, his legs and arms joining in with powerful strokes. Forgotten was the cold, the fear; all that existed was the ridiculousness of his situation and his determination to alter it. He would survive! He would not only escape this pain, he would extinguish it!

"A'lan-Sea-Hewn will not die!" rang in his head now, and aboard the canoe the frantically paddling Sea-Hewn watched in admiration as the boy breasted wave after wave, his arms moving in wonderful rhythm as he came toward the plunging vessel, to be hauled aboard by glad hands. Coughing and gasping, he knelt on the coarse mat on the deck and pressed both hands against the left side of his face. "What is it boy? Are you hurt? Let me see." Orn'ta knelt beside A'lan, trying to pry the lad's fingers away from his face, expecting to see another wound. But there was only that other, now-pale streak of shiny flesh, which ran from lip to ear. The boy's left eye kept closing involuntarily as Orn'ta held A'lan's hands away. Nothing! And yet the boy was obviously in great pain. He knew then, and looked to the others around them, some nodding in confirmation of his unspoken thought. The sudden immersion in the cold water had set off a reaction in those damaged nerves that ran out of control and only warmth would still it.

Orn'ta called for a blanket and as he waited he held his own, warmer hands against the lad's face. Through gritted teeth, A'lan hissed and blew, the anger and focus gone now, pain slowly subsiding, and cold and fatigue beginning to conquer him. Soon a dry blanket was wrapped around him and he was led to the low, covered shelter amidships and encouraged to lie down. His two young friends knelt solicitously near him as the men withdrew back onto the open deck. The re-sheeted sail was back up again and the course was being regained. Al'malan and Orn'ta were engaged in an intense conversation on the forward edge of the platform as A'lan fell into an exhausted sleep.

Neither had thought yet to reprimand the three boys for the reckless, foolish actions they had performed. What was being discussed was the glow, bright and blue, which Orn'ta and another *sighted* Sea-Hewn had observed surrounding A'lan as he swam so powerfully toward them. Al'malan reported hearing singing in the air, his eyes not possessing that other *sight*, and the words, 'Hoosh'dwan!" The 'Hoosh'dwan' was a legendary black whale which traveled in great numbers, only seldom seen and then only far out at sea. How could the Masters be angry with the boys in the face of such occurrences? These were truly strange times. Many yards away, unseen in the choppy sea, two large, black, bulbous-headed whales blew, inhaled and dove away to the depths, their mission of guardianship completed. They weren't needed this time.

~ ~ * ~ ~

Mana'la'wan was a tiny village and it reeked of drying fish this day as the big canoe glided into the small bay. The rain and gusty winds which had challenged 'Hoosh-im'wa' on the voyage were gone now, replaced by a gentle Trade wind which allowed the canoe to navigate the narrow opening without effort. The small cluster of well-built dwellings, low-roofed canoe shelters and store huts obscured the dozens of drying racks which glistened with their loads of thousands of small fish. Tall stands of coconut palms surrounded the village and extended well beyond its perimeter. Besides dried fish, coconut fiber twine and rope were the basis of these outlier village's commerce. On the far end of the yellow sand beach was that which they had come here to see. Al'malan spotted it first, his brows lifting in surprise.

The two Sea-Masters helped to beach the canoe and then strode toward the village, the fisher-folk descending the sloping sands to greet them. Leading the group of adults, the children already running up the beach like happy heralds, was the man they had come to see. Jo'lo'tan was crippled, but his lurching limp was no more demanding of recognition than was the beaming, gap-toothed grin which dominated a sea-worn face. He waved heartily with both arms as he lurched down the slope, the other villagers remaining a few steps behind, all smiling and calling greetings.

The children by now had reached and were clambering aboard Orn'ta's canoe. It was larger by far than any which this modest, dry-side community possessed. A'lan and his young mates had been instructed to remain aboard 'Hoosh-im'wa' for the time being, to prevent curious and possibly acquisitive little hands from damage or petty theft. These villagers were not 'Clan'; not part of the Sh'tah'ha, but descendents of the last wave of those ancient forebears who straggled among the now-occupied islands of the new home of the Mal'lam.

Many generations had passed before the last of these stragglers had crossed the dangerous distance from the dry lands far to the north. And these tardy groups had scattered and settled, for no known reason, on the least hospitable parts of many of the Set. Perhaps the marginal nature of their experiences had inculcated some preference for the extremes of dryer lands near deep waters. During that long period, they had developed dialects which, though based upon the general Mal'lam speech, varied enough to require some skill and patience for proper understanding between the two groups. That they were the best fishermen and most courageous coastal seamen there was no doubt.

Their vessels, though well constructed, were small due to the lack of large trees in the areas they inhabited. Also, they were known to be light-fingered and cunning while still genuinely openhearted and humane. They were a puzzle to the Clan but a general, if grudging, respect for them prevailed. Among the Sea-Hewn, genuine friendships endured with these singularly independent and somewhat mysterious folk. It was their villages which had born the brunt of the seismic waves produced by the volcanism to the north. Yet after each disaster, they doggedly rebuilt and reestablished themselves as if the great waves were but another, harsher, change in the seasons. They too accepted the benign but mysterious benevolence of the *Great Earth Mother*.

Their speech was somewhat grating to Clan ears yet perfectly understandable after a short time. So too was their art basic and un-demonstrative yet curious in its simple, animistic quality. The dyed patterns on their roughly-layered *tapa* cloth wraps, traded for the product of their major occupations - fishing and coir production - were of fish and other sea creatures. Missing were any more abstract design elements common among the other Mal'lam Clans. Their Clan neighbors called these people the 'Itin', a corruption of the word 'Itoi', the name for those mythical and fearsome enemies of the Mal'lam ancestors.

They were neither fierce nor threatening nor 'of us'; they were simply different. Their appearance differed somewhat from the usual Mal'lam though. They were slighter in build but nearly as tall. Mostly lean and muscular, their faces revealed the inter-breeding which had occurred among their forebears on their way to these lands. Their cheekbones were more prominent and a more slanted cast accented their dark eyes. But they too, had dark brown to black, slightly wavy hair. Among the Clan Sea-Hewn there existed a light-hearted acceptance, indeed a brotherhood between these two groups of sailors. That sea-born brotherhood was being celebrated at this moment.

"Orn'ta-Sea-Hewn! You son of a horny dolphin! What brings you to this smelly village?" Jo'lo'tan's grin was irresistible and the two Masters embraced as two old friends will. Al'malan was introduced to the old man and likewise embraced, Al'malan unable to discern if the smell of over-ripe fish came from Jo'lo'tan or from the nearby drying racks. All were invited; a feast was being prepared. How convenient. Surely, someone here knew of the Clan's representatives' approximate arrival. Al'malan sensed the presence of *sight* in this whole coincidence. People who live on the fringes of material well being sometimes develop a sense of smell for opportunity. He waived any personal judgment. He must get to know these people better.

Following the Itin Grey-Hewn up the slope to the village, Orn'ta paused only to signal to the three young initiates aboard his canoe to remain there until relieved. Jo'lo'tan chuckled at seeing the sign out of the corner of his eye. He lurched up the sandy slope with a bit of extra effort, chattering still. His infirmity was not congenital. It was the result of shark-bite! As a young man he had been mistakenly, but severely, bitten by a small shark which thought it might have a seal snack. One testing bite had been enough. Tendon, muscle and bone had been severed and the healers of this village had not possessed the skills of their Clan neighbors in healing such wounds. Infection they could stave-off, but surgery was not within their ken.

Jo'lo'tan's right leg bent outward at a radical angle and those calf muscles had long-ago atrophied, leaving him with a limb controlled only by the muscles of the thigh. His body swayed to the right at each step, his whole frame having warped and bent in response. Yet he never winced or complained but wore his wounds as a badge; a living talisman of his power and strength. He was supreme among a tribe of survivors and a man of inestimable wisdom ... and cleverness.

The meal, in spite of the predominant sight and smell of drying fish, was fowl. The birds were wrapped in layers of herbs and *taro* leaves and cooked in an earth oven. And *taro* was the preferred starch here on the dry side of the island. It was of a type which grows well in dry-soil conditions rather than requiring inundation in paddies. A sauce of hot, spicy herbs in coconut cream, which caused sweat to pop out on the foreheads of the uninitiated diner, was served with the fowl. And all was ladled out of wooden bowls onto shallow, carved wooden trays, rather than served on banana leaves as was the Clan custom.

Here among the Itin the custom was for men and women to eat together, all seated cross-legged around a long, shallow, stone-edged platform. Their children ate separately and earlier than the adults. Now, with visitors in attendance at the feast, the children sat around behind their elders, giggling and whispering. Also in attendance were the ubiquitous, short-legged, barkless dogs whose breed had been kept pure by the Itin, unlike the more usual mixed breed mongrels found in Mal'lam settlements. Many people found them quite succulent when served up at a feast. The meal was a leisurely one, the Itin a people who valued guests and the opportunity to catch up on gossip about the wider world. And this day there was much to learn about.

A gregarious folk, in spite of their strange ways, they laughed and joked with their Sea-Hewn friends. Al'malan felt immediately at home here. A young woman, quite handsome until her smile betrayed missing front teeth, flirted constantly with her eyes, apparently believing this big, handsome Sea-Master might just be available, if only for a night. Al'malan managed to discreetly ignore her, another young woman on his mind; indeed, in his heart.

Food had been taken to the three young Sea-Hewn still standing watch
aboard the 'Hoosh-im'wa. The Itin thought it all a good joke that they were there
to guard against possible misbehavior on the part of their own youngsters. They
took no offence at the implication that their children might be thieves. A casual
observer might assume that these people took little very seriously. But one had
only to carefully observe the quality of their dwellings, the meticulous
cleanliness of the grounds in and around the village and the fine workmanship
on their canoes. These were especially finely crafted, equal to any of the larger
Clan vessels. They possessed a special refinement of design which gave them

the appearance, as they rested on the beach, of great impatience to once more be free upon the sea.

Living for generations on drought-afflicted shores of their own choosing, no substantial timber sources readily available to them, the Itin treated every scrap of wood with reverence. Their firewood was mostly the tough, stringy branches of a low-growing scrub tree, useless for much else. Palm fronds and other scraps of generally useless vegetable material were also burned. However, it required a sharp tool, such as the coveted obsidian axes which the Mal'lam produced, to harvest this wood and other timber species endemic to this dry side of Sh'tah Lee-Set.

Obsidian, a volcanic, glass-like stone, was never-the- less rare in these volcanic islands and one of the most valuable trade items. The stonework of the Itin was also unique. Their dwellings rested on raised platforms of the most wonderfully crafted stonework, much of which was actually tediously hammered and shaped to fit together. Mal'lam stonework was more massive and it must be said, rather rudimentary in comparison. The gnarled hands of many of these lean, wiry men testified to years of such labor. Generations hence, in an island chain far to the east of these islands, other voyagers in this oceanic world would marvel at such work. The Itin descendants would leave a mysterious legacy in a far land.

Necessity had led to many inventions among the Itin; one being the double-outrigger which kept their light, shallow canoes upright in heavy weather. Only now, after more than two hundred years, were their Mal'lam cousins beginning to adopt this innovation on their smaller fishing canoes. They had for that time doggedly insisted on double-hulled vessels. But what the Sea-Masters this day had come to see was not a canoe but what drove it.

Chapter Sixteen - Impressing the Sea-Masters

The leathery Jo'lo'tan belched loudly and stretched his upper body, apparently a sign that he was finished with his meal. He threw the chicken bones from his platter over one shoulder and immediately the small dogs rushed in to claim them. He nodded his head at them, indicating to his guests that they were free to do so also. A feast for the canines too. The women then rose from the banquet table and began removing empty bowls and platters, shooing the squabbling dogs out of the way and indicating that the feast was over. The men remained, burping and picking their teeth and chatting. Jo'lo'tan showed no inclination to get up and go anywhere just yet.

The latest news from the north was related to the Itin men and their obvious response was one of shock and disbelief. Al'malan spoke at length of the need for the Mal'lam to arm and train themselves for martial activity. It seemed obvious that without active intervention, the depredations of Tor'na-the-Mad and his partner would only become more horrible and more threatening to Sh'tah Lee-Set. It was Orn'ta who broached the subject of training. His long acquaintance with Jo'lo'tan and his family had informed him of the existence of a small group of Itin, on this and other islands, who still practiced a form of stylized martial art, primarily as a competitive form of dance-cum-exercise routine. It had its origins in the misty past when the Mal'lam and the Itin were making their way slowly through the myriad of island groups to these, their present home islands.

Too long ago for any living Mal'lam to know for sure why, their part of that great migration had abandoned all such martial arts. The Itin professed similar ignorance about their own people's retention of these practices. It was just enjoyable exercise, it was suggested. Laughter accompanied the suggestion that women were attracted to men who were proficient in this art form. Jo'lo'tan responded to this idea by lifting his game leg and waving it over the low feasting table. With a brazen grin he declared, "Well, if that's the case, tell me how I came to have had three wives and seven sons … and maybe a few more, here and there!?" Even his sons, sitting near their father, doubled up with laughter.

One son though, the eldest, his name was Ch'am'lo, rose and went behind his father and knelt to speak in his ear. Jo'lo'tan listened, nodding seriously, and then he broke into a grin. Ch'am'lo stood up and reached down a hand to assist his father to rise. The old man grunted with the effort but was now on one good foot and ordering the other foot to follow. Without comment he motioned his guests to follow him too and he lurched off through the small village to a sloping grove of coconut palms, children and dogs in train. The Sea-Hewn followed, not knowing what to expect.

Jo'lo'tan called a halt in the shade of a tightly grouped cluster of palm trees and settled himself again into a sitting position, signaling his guests to do likewise. As Al'malan seated himself in the shade and rested his back against a coconut tree trunk he looked around, curious as to where that son, Ch'am'lo, had got to. Jo'lo'tan was telling a humorous little tale of when he was young and not yet shark-bitten and himself quite adept at this martial art, which he called, 'Shan'. Suddenly a blood-curdling scream came from behind them! Everyone, except Jo'lo'tan, turned, startled, to see what was happening.

Up the slope from the village came the figure of a man carrying some large, circular, flat object in his left hand and a long-shafted spear in his right. As this apparition, now obviously that missing son, Ch'am'lo, came into the roughly circular grouping of men in the palm grove, he stopped quickly and lay down the spear and that other strange object. With a formal bow toward his father, this lithe young man began a series of startling maneuvers which held the Mal'lam Sea-Hewn in open-mouthed thrall. Had these people any familiarity with the animal family, *feles*, that is how they would have described his movements; 'catlike'!

From a standing position he arched his back and threw himself into a backward somersault, landing on his hands and then walking on his hands for maybe eight feet. This time he somersaulted forward and landed on his feet, gathered himself for less than a half-second and leaped into the air and twisted to his left, his left leg withdrawn and then thrust outward to full extension in a movement not only swift but shockingly powerful. Had anyone been standing within the scope of that thrust, they would have been dealt a damaging, possibly fatal blow to the body.

As he again landed in perfect balance on both feet, this time with his arms held closely to his body, fists held upward, a series of outward thrusts by those fists exhibited the same aggressive power as had that extended leg. Al'malan saw the power, the implied intent to damage, to kill! Then came a lull as Ch'am'lo stood quietly, arms at rest beside his thighs. He stood but two feet from the long-hafted spear which he had earlier laid down. With another sudden movement he bent and retrieved that shaft, lofted it to head-height in an easy movement and grasped it with his right hand near its mid-point of balance. With a scream more death inferring than earlier as he had come up to the coconut grove, his body twisted around with that spear held aloft and as quickly loosed it toward a distant palm trunk. The missile struck the very center of the tree and the long shaft undulated for many seconds, releasing its residual power.

Just when this exhibition might be thought to be finished, another shout of aggression resounded behind the gathered onlookers. Another of Jo'lo'tan's sons ran uphill, a brutal-looking, shark's-tooth-edged club held high over his head. As he rapidly bore down upon his older brother in what looked to be a serious assault, Ch'am'lo quickly bent and took up that circular object which he had earlier discarded with the spear. Split seconds saw the younger man bring down the awful weapon toward his brother. This seemed not to be a choreographed event but rather a serious attempt to kill! Both Orn'ta and Al'malan gasped, sure they were about to see murder done.

Up came that shield, for that is what it was, deflecting the cruel weapon's blow and in the same movement Ch'am'lo's right leg swept around and knocked his brother's legs from under him, the toothed weapon landing harmlessly on the ground as its bearer too fell with a resounding thump on the dusty soil. Ch'am'lo quickly went to his downed sibling to see that he was all right. Grins greeted each other and the two quasi-warriors stood up together and bowed to their father, who had sat impassively through the whole, sudden exhibition. Both those brothers then went to their father and took his hands and helped him to his feet, standing aside as he gathered himself. The two young Itin stood impassively behind him, their faces betraying neither victory nor ardor. They both held themselves in a mood of relaxed readiness, calm and confident should more be required of them.

Orn'ta, who thought he knew these people well, had never witnessed such a dramatic exhibition of these men's potential. Al'malan listened intently to the subliminal. He heard nothing which disturbed him. These were indeed exceptional young men. And exceptional young men were sorely needed at this crucial juncture of Mal'lam history! Jo'lo'tan came forward to the Mal'lam Sea-

Masters, a twisted grin on his face, not really a smirk but an expression of, "I thought you'd be impressed!" "Does that offer any ideas to you?" he asked, serious now.

Al'malan was first to reply. "Yes brother-seaman. You have my full attention. Our people must surely work together now. We need your skills. We cannot proceed without them." Jo'lo'tan gazed into Al'malan's eyes with great intensity for a few moments, coughed and looked away, then back again. "You and I have far to sail together yet, young Master!" With a glance toward his old friend, Orn'ta, he added, "But it is my sons with whom you will sail the farthest. Today is not over. Hold your opinions until you have seen what you came to see. Let's go to the beach."

The whole of the village, it seemed, followed in procession as Jo'lo'tan led the way to the sandy slope above where the fading tide gently washed the beach. On the way to the wet sand lower down, easier walking for the old man, he waved and shouted to the children still scrambling around and on Orn'ta's vessel. They all leapt off and ran toward the village as if a hive of hornets was after them. Whatever words he had shouted, and none of the Mal'lam quite understood them, the youngsters obeyed that command with a quick discipline which surprised the Clansmen. Once on the hard-packed sand, the old man moved toward where a group of small fishing vessels were parked, his stride energetic enough to inspire the Mal'lam Sea-Hewn to step out to keep pace. Al'malan mused that he must be as old as Telan Sea-Master, but much fitter.

Among the traditionally rigged canoes, their stumpy masts rising above bulkily stowed boom and sail, were three other canoes; one, a paired-hull vessel of approximately thirty-two feet in length which displayed a unique, still standing set of two sails. The two smaller canoes had but one mast each. The sails, so totally unlike anything the Sea-Masters had seen before, were rigid panels of finely woven material, pandanus leaves from that strange, prickly-leafed tree. When its leaves were properly aged and treated, they produced a very strong and long-lasting woven mat. Mal'lam sailors most often used it also.

But these sails, about four and a half feet wide and maybe twenty feet tall, were held rigidly from their masts by curved booms which rose vertically, parallel to the mast. Lashed to the boom and the mast with many loops of rope, these sails rose beside and then curved slightly over the mast. From their tips fell, waving in the mild breeze, long, feather tell-tales which seemed to beckon to the sailors to join them in a last, late-day sail on the falling tide. The panel-sails rode freely in the breeze, swinging in response to every change of direction, offering no resistance and demanding no response from its host canoe. They simply sat there in their vertical majesty, awaiting the whim of some seaman.

"What are you seeing?" Jo'lo'tan asked, standing with his hands on his hips, right leg askew, looking up at his creation. Al'malan's eyes traveled again up and down the length of these weird sails. That thin, long, vertical member curved gracefully into the mast at its bottom where it was ingeniously lashed with a system of over-lapping knots. The upper end extended well above the top of the mast itself, the woven panel cut in a curve complementary to its bottom. The long tell-tales of white seabird feathers would signal every wind shift, day or night. "That's not much sail for a vessel of this size!" Orn'ta added doubtfully. The old Itin Headman guffawed and looked away to where a group of young men were seated about another canoe.

"Ch'am'lo, Ran'ra! You boys! Come!" he shouted, his tone unmistakably commanding. The response was instantaneous. Seven muscular but slightly built men of various ages from late teens to about thirty leapt laughing and shouting and ran to that largest canoe. They were obviously there just biding their time, waiting for this order."Climb aboard!" the old man offered, "We'll see what we'll see." As the Sea-Masters and but one of their own crew, a senior Sea-Hewn, moved to help launch the canoe into the surf, Jo'lo'tan said, "Don't bother. My boys will do it."

The visitors heaved themselves aboard, then the old man humped himself up unaided and the seven Itin began pushing. The sands on this beach were high in clay particles, unlike the coarse, black sands of Dolphin Bay. The added slipperiness allowed the hulls to free themselves more easily from the land, a narrow band of muddy water near the shore revealing this helpful soil condition. The young men leaped aboard in turn, two remaining at the prows to give that final push. Then Jo'lo'tan's canoe, the largest in this village, still smaller than the big Mal'lam canoes but equally well constructed, was afloat and underway.

"They're all my sons!" Jo'lo'tan shouted proudly, his arm making a sweeping motion around the deck. Then even louder he added, "All worthless, lazy louts they are!" The seven responded with grins and laughter but moved to their tasks with consummate professionalism, hauling lines and taking up paddles as the canoe backed into the deeper water. The Clansmen seated themselves where Jo'lo'tan indicated, between the two masts, and proceeded to call out orders in tones of harsh demand, which Al'malan had not heard since sailing with Tor'na. Yet no reproving glances occurred; grins and powering muscle was the response, pride and affection glowing among them all. Then the old man began a sail-man's chant, as all masters did as their vessel separated from the shore. The sons took up the call:

"Welcome us, spirits of the sea,

Know our love for you!

Challenge us as you will, but return us free!

Sailing, sailing, sailing on.

What will you reveal this day?"

The onshore breeze, light and variable in the late afternoon, barely rippled the waters of the small bay. 'Crab's Claw' it was called, the two rocky arms of the headlands coming to sharp points as they curved around to enclose the sheltered harbor. Beyond the mouth of the bay were two low islands, bare even of brushy scrub. These flat wastes of rock further sheltered the harbor as they intercepted the swells that rolled in from the expanse of blue water beyond. But that buffering created a tricky current and leaving 'Crab's Claw Bay' could be hazardous.

Missing on this vessel was the flap and thump of the big triangular sail traditional to Mal'lam canoes. The whole of the unfolding maneuver was exceedingly strange to the visitors. The only sound was the gentle creak of rope upon timber as the tall, rigid panels were expertly shifted to catch the wind. The eyes of the Sea-Hewn moved back and forth, up and down in fascinated attention as this revolutionary sails-manship progressed around them. Jo'lo'tan sat alone on the aft edge of the bridging platform between the hulls, calling out orders, keen eyes constantly moving.

From time to time an arm pointed toward a line which needed loosening or another tightened. The sturdiest of the sons manned the single steering oar off the back of the platform near his father; Mal'lam canoes too were steered by a large paddle off the stern of each hull. The Itin dialect was becoming less difficult to interpret now for the less experienced Mal'lam but Orn'ta had known these seamen for many years, so when he heard Jo'lo'tan's next order he said to his companions in amazement, "To windward?!" His vessel, 'Hoosh-im'wa', when it left this secluded harbor, would have to be propelled by paddle power, the big triangular rig useless against the wind in these tight quarters.

This vessel however, sprang forward now, the big panels nearly at right angles to the hulls. The steering oar was laid back deeply into the water to keep the bows pointing high. Beyond the points of the claws at the harbor's entrance the crosscurrent caught the canoe and began pushing the vessel sideways, the steersman straining to keep it pointed directly at that nearest rocky island. On the canoe struggled, approaching the rocks at speed. Al'malan tensed, as did his Sea-Hewn mates. Grounding seemed imminent.

Then a shouted command, a word that sounded like, "Come about!" in Mal'lam, but somehow different. Instantly, the sheets, which held the panels to the breeze, were let go and the steering oar was lifted from the water momentarily. As the wind against the hulls slowly turned the vessel to the right, the panels were repositioned to catch the breeze at another angle and the great steering oar went amidships again. The canoe now picked up speed and began to run parallel to the shore, the current helping carry it out of danger and toward the open sea. The Mal'lam seamen breathed out in a simultaneous blow of relief.

Jo'lo'tan got up from his position of command with an awkwardness which his age, and an already long day, were beginning to accentuate. He hobbled forward to his guests, all three of them with looks of surprise and wonder on their faces. He grinned his private triumph, reflected in the faces of his sons. "Well, Sea-Hewn! How did you like that, eh?" He extended his stiff, bent leg and lowered himself onto the heel of his left foot, plunking down beside Orn'ta. Relinquishing the sailing of the canoe to his oldest son, Jo'lo'tan recounted the events which inspired this innovation, this radical development, which already had Al'malan's head spinning with its implications.

"About two years ago, this time of year it was, my oldest boy and my youngest and I were in an outrigger, there off La'chun-Set." He pointed toward a small, dark green island away to the north and just on the horizon."There was a strong sou'easterly blowing and the seas were big but we were catching lots of big, fat 'Stoman' and we figured we'd load up with them and head into La'chun-Set for the night if we had to. We got greedy, you see!" and he laughed, "We forgot to watch the seas closely. Stupid! But there you are. Shit happens. Anyway, a big wave and a heavy gust of wind hit us at the same time and even though we were pretty low in the water, what with our heavy cargo of fish, over we went." He laughed again as if it was all an hilarious adventure.

Al'malan was beginning to appreciate the uniqueness of these dry-side cousins. "None of us was hurt. We just swallowed a lot of water is all. But the boom and sail and all but one paddle took off on their own course, leaving us behind. The boys were going to swim after them, it wouldn't have been very far away, but the sharks stopped us. The bastards were feasting on the 'Stoman' we'd lost and there we were, three turtles floating on a log, trying to keep our legs and bodies out of the water." The old man rocked back and forth with mirth as if he'd heard the funniest joke of his life. The two sons involved, one on the steering oar, chuckled along with him.

"The current took us toward the island. We floated all night and the sharks kept coming up and grinning at us." The Sea-Hewn were chuckling too now, discovering a new dimension to this almost legendary seaman. "Well, we managed to swim and push the canoe along the shore, once the sharks went away, until we got it beached. The canoe was pretty beaten-up. The outriggers were all askew and there was hardly anything left inside it. All we had left was our sleeping mats, some fishing line and hooks and our personal knives and some pretty soggy food. No water though." One of the boys interrupted then to point out that the wind was shifting and should they head back? "Not yet," he replied, after a quick look around at the sea and sky, and continued his story. The Sea-Hewn noticed how quickly the canoe was speeding along, straight out to sea. The late afternoon sun shone gold on the top of Volan Votu in the distance.

"There's lots of good bamboo on that Set, so we weren't too worried about being able to rig something up. We didn't have anything to cut it with though. We'd lost all our adze blades when the canoe overturned. My boy, Ch'am'lo, the ugliest one there," and all joined in the laughter as Ch'am'lo threw a mock-threat at his father, "he worked it out. There's no obsidian or other good tool-rock there so he found some big shells and sharpened them and managed to gnaw off some good lengths. It was our mats which saved us though. We sewed them together with the fishing line. We had just enough. We used some vines and bark strips to tie things together and thin strips of bamboo as stays and shrouds. But fixing the sail we had fashioned to the mast and controlling it was still a problem. It was a pretty weird looking contraption, I can tell you."

Again Jo'lo'tan enjoyed his own joke loudly, then coughed and continued. "Ch'am'lo, in spite of having no brains, came up with the idea of lashing the sail to a long, curved piece of bamboo, attaching one end of that to the bottom of the mast and with some lengths of split bamboo, we could swing the sail one way or another. Well, we mucked around with the silly thing for about two days, all of us getting skinnier; nothing to eat but some bitter berries and our fishing line was tied up in the sail. 'Didn't get thirsty though. It pissed down rain the whole time!" And again he collapsed into mirth. "Well, to cut a long story short," and Al'malan saw one son raise his eyes to the sky in relief, "we finally got it rigged and figured we could get something out of it. The weather cleared up but the wind was still blowing from home. We had only one paddle and that was needed for steering and it would have been a long pole home with just lengths of bamboo to row with."

Jo'lo'tan looked up at the sky, out to sea, back to land, then called, "Come about boys! Best we head home now." And with marvelous facility, the double-hulled canoe, with only one steersman, turned and headed back toward land without even re-setting sail, again facing at an incredible angle to the wind but much more slowly now. Such a maneuver would not have been possible with a Mal'lam canoe's rig. "Anyway, it worked!" he beamed. "If it had been stronger, it would have worked better. The bloody thing came unstuck a couple of times but we managed to get home on the fourth day. We've been experimenting ever since. This rig here," and he pointed up at the finely woven pandanus-leaf sail panels, neatly secured to that radically curved bamboo boom, "is the best yet. I reckon those big canoes you plan to build would sail real well to windward with this kind of rig."

Jo'lo'tan looked intensely into Al'malan's eyes and said, "If it wouldn't be too insulting, Sea-Master, my stupid son there, Ch'am'lo, might be willing to give you a hand." He sat back a moment and looked over at his old friend Orn'ta too, gauging their level of interest and intent. Satisfied with what he saw he added, "I think we can do a deal, don't you?" Al'malan's keen inner hearing sensed no mockery or conspiracy in the old man's voice. He glanced around and Ch'am'lo was gazing steadily at him, anticipating the answer, calculating his own new adventure with the Mal'lam and a wider world than the little village he'd known all his life.

"Alright," Al'malan finally answered, "but one more thing. I would like Ch'am'lo to also help to train our people to fight. I've never seen such maneuvers as he performed earlier today but I can see how valuable they could be to our men. We need the help of our Itin brothers." He spoke with a sincerity and honesty which Ch'am'lo accepted without question. His father hesitated, himself reading again this very young Sea-Master's emanations. It was Al'malan who now came to the point of the business. "It will be a year before the first vessel is completed and rigged and ready for sailing. But we must begin our preparations for seeking out and stopping 'Tor'na the Mad' immediately. Ch'am'lo could return to the 'Bay of Dolphins' with us tomorrow. What is your price?"

Jo'lo'tan, a crafty trader himself, was somewhat surprised at this young man's directness. He looked at his son, Ch'am'lo, who nodded with a quick, shallow movement. Then he looked around at his other sons, stared for some moments at the approaching landfall of his village, then suddenly his face lit with glee and he cleared his throat and replied, "Twenty obsidian axes, my friends!" He included Orn'ta, gesturing with a nod of his head, "And paid in full by the next full moon!" Al'malan shared a glance with his Sea-Master brother, paused a moment and then answered, "Alright, twenty axes it is. If your 'very special' son there comes with us right away!" Al'malan looked to that young man now, seeking his most important approval. It was there in his eyes. Jo'lo'tan held a closed fist toward Al'malan, the gesture copied by the younger man and they bumped their knuckles together in agreement. "You should be a trader, Jo'lo'tan-an. You'd be rich by now!" Al'malan added, using the familiar term which their new friendship now allowed.

"I am rich!" the old man fairly shouted, grinning widely, "I have seven, ugly, stupid sons to take care of me!" He cast a glance of genuine fondness about the deck of the canoe and absorbed its return from the eyes of seven quite extraordinary young Itin. As the wind died away those young men took up their paddles and propelled the vessel back toward shore. Laughter and shouts carried across the still water of the little harbor to A'lan's ears. The boy had remained aboard Orn'ta's canoe, his sense of duty stronger than Shen'ham's hunger. The other two had gone up to the village in search of more of that good, spicy food and none of the Itin children had dared return after that curt order issued an hour ago by Jo'lo'tan. A'lan sat alone and happy, watching the approach of the Itin canoe under its strange contraptions.

The setting sun had laid a glittering carpet of gold across the still water. It faded quickly to rosy-yellow, then pink. As A'lan watched fascinated, his *'sight'* revealed another light, not part of the sun's fading gift. The craft approaching the beach now appeared suspended, not on water but on a blue oblong of pulsing brightness from which white flashes shot away in all directions. Those vertical sail panels shone with some internal power and the whole vessel glowed in their illumination. A sense of familiarity flowed from that canoe to some receptor within him; he *knew* this vessel, *those* sails! Somehow, they were already a part of him. It was like remembering what he could not possibly remember: the future!

A'lan stood up, paused, then jumped down onto the sand and began running as if responding to some voiced command. As the hulls of Jo'lo'tan's canoe nosed onto the beach, A'lan was there to greet it and he joined the crew in pulling it up the slippery sands. One lad, the youngest, a year or two older than A'lan, said, "Well, Sea-Hewn, what do you think of our weird canoe?" A'lan replied with a silent grin, speech somehow inappropriate at that moment. The other boy looked questioningly at him for a moment, then shrugged and leaped back aboard to begin stowing gear for the night. Other brothers ran up the beach, hauling lines to anchor the vessel.

A'lan stood now, still dumb-struck, his inner-eye still registering the strange light which pulsed from the craft. Al'malan, Orn'ta and the other Sea-Hewn alighted, followed by the old Itin headman. "It's quite amazing, Sea-Hewn!" Al'malan said, smiling at A'lan. Jo'lo'tan then limped up and stood before the boy, staring into his eyes. Silence surrounded the group for a moment or two and then the old man said softly, "One day you will sail on such a vessel, my boy. And you will command it!" A'lan finally spoke, his enthrallment broken. "I know." he said, his voice even and self-assured. Jo'lo'tan studied his face again. He gave a brief smile and nodded his head. "I know that you do." He glanced at the Mal'lam seamen standing behind the boy, nodded and then turned and limped away back to his village. As he progressed out of earshot ahead of them he chuckled under his breath, "Twenty axes! I thought they'd only go for ten. I must have balls of stone after all!"

Chapter Seventeen - Blessing the Canoes

When the huge log rolled off its chocks, only the quick thinking of a few Woodsmen prevented a disaster. Some well placed poles, quickly jammed into the ground and up against its bulk, stopped its threatened progress down a slope. The group of imperiled men below looked up wide-eyed at the still-trembling mass of timber which had threatened to crush them. Overcoming their fright, they quickly ran to help their workmates up the slope, pushing cut-off limbs under the log to further stabilize it.

Joha'lan stood white-faced, only now taking a deep breath, shocked as if that dreadful weight had but barely missed himself. Men were looking toward him now, expectantly. He must respond. "Well done, Wood-Hewn!" he managed and forced a broad grin. But the words sounded hollow and inadequate to him. He should have seen to those braces himself. He should not have relegated that duty. But then, he must, mustn't he? Six of these massive timbers were being worked at once; most were widely separated from each other. He could not be everywhere at once. But those four men seated below that log, honing the adze blades! If not for that quick reaction …?! He shook his head and slapped his hands together, the act freeing him from his paralysis. Carry on!

One more week of shaping and hollowing and the logs could be called hulls, ready to be slid and rolled and lifted those many miles down the mountain to the sea. More than once had Joha'lan invoked the memory of his friend, Ran'tar Wood-Hewn. Though no direct sign of that man's spirit occurred with Joha'lan, strange events did occur among the crews; inspirations of craftsmanship which echoed that man's exceptional qualities. Joha'lan still sorrowed at his loss. This giant and gentle man suffered a loneliness which had but little to do with this enforced separation from the woman he now so loved.

Each night at the camp within the forest he sought the companionship of the Sea-Hewn who also attended the work, Orn'ta and Al'malan especially. It was these men to whom he felt the greatest responsibility, the deepest commitment, for the hulls which he and his skilled crews were now roughly shaping must suit a very special task. Upon their shoulders, as well as his, would fall the work which Joha'lan must learn to understand without ever experiencing, for he was not himself a sailor. He must come to understand the subtleties of hull balance and wetted surface and lift and all the other esoteric elements of hull design which he had neglected for so long. And there were no texts of instruction to inform him; there were no texts at all. Empathy and keen attention to the Sea-Hewn must suffice as his source of learning. And these new hulls would require even more than traditional knowledge: the new sail structure would demand subtle differences of hull shape which no one yet quite understood. Though no man could wield an adze with greater subtlety and precision, shaving a hull to incredible exactness of thickness, Joha'lan lacked a full understanding of *why*!

Each night as they sat facing the glowing fires, slapping at mosquitoes and midges and rubbing sore muscles, the three men commented, examined, discussed and argued until sleep finally insisted. As usual, the one-hundred-fifty men around them were all snoring peacefully by the time these three turned in. On the night before the final roughing-out and preparation for transport of the first pair of hulls, Al'malan sat deep in thought, slightly apart, and he was allowed his silence by the other two men.

"No!" he finally said and scooted himself over to join Orn'ta and Joha'lan. They looked questioningly at him, so definite was that, "No!" "Look!" he said, reaching for the carved hull-model which Joha'lan held in his lap."See! We've been assuming that our traditional hulls would work as well with the twin masts. But Joha'lan mentioned that he felt something was not quite right. It's obvious!" He smiled half-apologetically at Orn'ta. "We both should have seen it sooner. Joha'lan didn't because he's not had the long, open-sea experience we have. It's the taper to the bow and the deeper stern, which will be the problem. The hulls must taper equally toward both ends. Deeper, considerably deeper in the center. And yet the bow must be more full than the stern! Do you follow me?" and he ran his fingers over the model, indicating the correct curvature. He looked back and forth at the other two, Orn'ta's expression indicating that he understood. But Joha'lon felt that he was back again where he had begun; lost! "Alright! Yes, of course." Orn'ta said, reaching out for the carving. He held it out toward the Wood-Master, pointing.

"You see, Joha'lan-an, the two masts must be in equal balance. They must be an equal distance from the stern and the bow with the deepest part of the hull in the very center between them. The hull must curve equally from end to end. Simple!" He smiled and slapped his forehead, indicating his foolishness in not seeing this before. Joha'lan shook his head at both men and though he feigned disgust and frustration, he was unable to hide the grin which tugged at the corners of his mouth. He *was* beginning to see, of course! "They have to work their way through things just as I do. And they can stumble over the obvious until it bites them on the ass just as I can." Somehow, as they would struggle through and reach the right conclusions, so would he. He took the finely shaped hull model from Orn'ta, stood up and looked at both men and said, "I'll start anew tomorrow night. You two have worn me out. Go to bed!" His tone was a false command. They grinned widely at his retreating back as he dropped the now-useless model into the fire, sending a shower of sparks rising into the chill night air.

The following morning saw a lively discussion concerning how to proceed with the final roughing-out of the logs; whether or not to shape the hulls now, to the contours discussed the night before or to leave them in the relatively flat-bottomed configuration they now possessed? "Less weight to control!" was one side of the argument. "If we round the bottoms and taper the ends, they'll tend to rock back and forth when they're underway, making them hard, and dangerous, to control!" was another side to consider. Someone had to make a final decision and of course, that really fell to Joha'lan as Wood-Master. He took a long look around the huge work area; men swinging adzes here, axes there, others plaiting the big ropes made of bark for the hauling. Their safety was equally as important as the logs themselves, certainly; and there was danger enough in using the old, tried and trusted methods of moving the partially hollowed timbers with their nearly flat bottoms. All right. Decided!

"We will move them as they are, or soon will be. And instead of using only half the men on each log and moving both downhill at once, we'll use everyone on one log at a time. With logs this size, there will be many times when we'll have to use both crews on one log anyway. No, it will be safer and probably faster in the long run. One log at a time, that's it!" and he smiled at the Sea-Hewn and Wood-hewn senior men who were standing with him. Al'malan, anxious to get the huge logs down to the seashore and to see the final stages of their transformation begun, hesitated. "Will we take them all the way, one at a time?"

"No, Sea-Master." Joha'lan replied. Understanding his friend's sense of urgency, he reached across to where he stood and slapped him encouragingly on the arm. "We'll stockpile them all on the flat ground, just at the beginning of the *taro* paddies. After each one is down there we'll all have a day and a night off work. Then back to it again. How's that?" He spoke loud enough to be overheard by a number of men working nearby and the word quickly spread. Already high in the esteem of the Mal'lam men assembled, his reputation had just gone up a notch.

Another day of shaping saw the first big baulk of timber ready to move downhill. The inner bark of a low-land, fast-growing tree had been stripped by the hundreds of yards and laboriously hauled uphill; three big rolls of it were slung on long poles and a dozen rolls at a time were carried up the mountain by rotating crews of Sea-Hewn volunteers. Kept wet, these plaited ropes of bark were extremely strong. Now they were attached to the logs at strategic locations and the labor began. On level ground the big logs were rolled over smaller logs, younger or smaller men given the task of placing them under the leading edge of the advancing canoe hull. As the hull rolled onward, the logs left behind had to be lifted and carried forward again and placed in front.

This was heavy and tiring work, especially as the temperature continued to rise as the project descended down to lower altitude. When a steep slope was encountered, and most of the track downhill was steep, a different technique had to be employed. Standing trees were utilized as anchors for the thick hawsers used to slowly lower the big logs in a controlled manner, the ropes being controlled by up to thirty men at a time. Tough work! But then came the raising of the log up another, possibly even steeper slope to another ridge. This was hardest of all. The streams which wound down the mountain were all too small to allow floating the logs. The steep terrain in the canyons was dangerously rugged and boulder-strewn so that avenue was not possible.

Experienced older Wood-Hewn, after many years of this work, had already scouted the best route. Joha'lan too, walked the path they had laid-out and could only concur; this was the best way. If only logs had wings! One steep canyon however, provided its own, easier solution. On its slopes were numerous large trees, useful as anchors and tie-points for ropes but also there were two large trees which, when felled across the gully side-by-side, created a bridge. The big logs could be turned broadside on the downhill side and quite easily skidded across. A clearing had to be made on the other side to accommodate swinging the log around again to point uphill. This required a whole day. But every other of the five remaining logs would pass here with ease.

Some slopes were so steep that every man involved had to strain on a rope to control the ascent and descent of the great weight. Once, a plaited hawser broke and for a terrible moment Joha'lan saw the immanent death of members of his crew. The bow of the canoe however, lodged against a tree and stopped before any damage could result. He leaned against a tree trunk and stood for a while, gathering himself again. Eyes closed, sweat running in rivulets down his body, he thanked his old friend Ran'tar. He had no doubt that the man's spirit had somehow been involved in the miracle. And also, *that* word hummed in his mind: "*Ka'laaaaan*!" She too was here! The Vesa'tan!

Finally the last of the six hulls was only a half-mile from the village. The double-row of men pulled the long, heavy ropes; younger men and boys now ran back and forth, alternating the log rollers which allowed the rapid progress of the hull. The whole of the settlement had turned out for this momentous arrival. The songs of the haulers, beating each step to a slow, powerful chant, was counterpoint to the chant of the onlookers - women, children and men too old to assist.

Standing among them were two special old men, side by side, whose long years of friendship seemed to them to culminate in this one event. Their reedy voices sang the 'canoe song' with all the power they could muster. Tel'an Sea-Master, whose strength had begun to falter after that confrontation with Tor'na-the-Mad, had relinquished all involvement in marine affairs, spending most of his time seated under the great beach-nut trees, watching his memories dance with the waves. His dear friend, Tal'ma Herb-Master, had likewise ceased his herbalist's craft, offering advice to others only after the intercession of his niece, Lana'ma-Herb-Mistress. He usually sat near Telan, but his view was always toward that great mountain, Volan Votu. And so the two old Masters spent their days waiting for death, wrapping their age in youthful recollections, their every need attended to by solicitous family and neighbors.

Among the Mal'lam existed an ancient tradition: one of announcing one's death before acute illness even arrived. Some old people, their involvement with life no longer of a quality which they felt sustainable, would announce the day and the hour of their passing. They would nearly always quietly die at that self-appointed time! Without mutual knowledge, these two old men, on this day as they sang the beginnings of a future they could never share in, each had decided that their time for passing from this life was near. Tears glistened in tired eyes as they watched their people concluding the first part of a great task which would lead to another exodus; hopefully without terror and violence attending. The huge, roughly shaped canoe hull, the sixth and final one, passed them. The crowd coalesced behind it and continued the song of greeting. A song of the sea:

Earth Mother, Earth Mother, hear our song of gratitude.

Earth Mother, who gave us the mountains,

Mountains, who gave us your forests,

Forests, who gave us your trees,

We honor you all with our love and our lives.

Earth Mother, who gave us the sea,

Guide our hearts and our hands,

Share your wisdom and strength as we set forth again.

As Telan and Tal'ma stood alone alongside the dusty, trodden path, Telan leaned on the walking stick which he now found necessary to help him move around. Tal'ma, still reasonable steady afoot, suggested that they follow the procession which was now moving away down the slope to the beach. As if to reinforce his suggestion, a small group of children rushed back from the crowd. Their little faces flushed with excitement and enthusiasm, they all spoke at once, jumping up and down in a circle around the old men.

"Dear Old-Hewn, please come to the blessing. Please! Please!" Warm little hands wormed their way into dry old palms until gap-toothed, aging grins signaled surrender to such youthful love and respect. Two of the children ushered the men slowly and gently, the others bolting away, returning and running away again, exhilarated by this great celebration. By the time Telan and Tal'ma had reached the beach and the high, long canoe sheds, the whole community had gathered around. The songs and chants had ended, the chatter and buzz of the crowd infecting the two old codgers with an enthusiasm neither had felt for too long.

Banners of colored *tapa* cloth and streamers of feathers and rattling chains of seashells danced in the fresh breeze. That wind was cool, one of winter's last gasps, but the crowd of celebrating Mal'lam was unperturbed. The sun was warm on their skins and the Clan-Sht'ah'ha was rejoicing in their perceived uniqueness and the challenge they had accepted. Now was a grand new beginning! The histories were coming to life again. Soon, very soon, the Mal'lam would set forth upon a new adventure and the Sht'ah'ha would lead them as they had led their forebears centuries ago.

While Telan Sea-Master's mind embraced this greatest of all the canoe blessings he had experienced in his long life, his full heart momentarily denying his commitment to death, his comrade smiled in spite of his sadnesses. How good it was to see the Clan so united and how relatively smoothly it all had happened. Only that business with the mad Sea Master, Tor'na, had marred the merging of the two wings of their Clan. The great sea-distance and all those years had not diminished but rather somehow enriched the unique traditions of these people of the sea. What seemed foreign and somewhat disturbing to Tal'ma however, was the level of excitement; the commitment and almost fanatical devotion to a dangerous mission.

The young Sea-Hewn all had a strange, feverish gleam in their eyes, especially his young, great nephew, A'lan. Always polite and considerate, as were most youngsters, he was now somehow remote, detached from all but his intense study of seamanship. And his friend, Shen'ham, growing before one's eyes into a powerful young man, that baby-fat hardening into muscular bulk. He too seemed inordinately committed to his craft. Tal'ma mused that, in his day, even after the *hewing*, boys remained boys until they were at least sixteen. Now though, they all were so serious! Ah well, he would not have much longer to ponder such things. And he was really quite glad of it. One day soon he would begin his fast. That last, fateful withdrawal from this world would occur within this year. He had decided!

The massive, partly shaped logs lay bottom-up, two to each shed, room enough around each for the teams of Woodsmen to chop and shave and finish the exterior dimensions. Then the hulls would be turned over and the interiors cut away, leaving an exacting thickness from stem to stern. As had been determined by Orn'ta, Joha'lan and Al'malan after long debate, there would be little to distinguish bow from stern during the basic shaping stage. Only the keenest and most experienced eye would detect that slight bulge forward or the equally subtle taper toward the stern, both innovations developed by the man who had thought he knew little about sailing.

Joha'lan Canoe-Master continued to amaze his Sea-Hewn brothers with his insightful creations. When the canoe was completed, there would be large additions to both bow and stern which would be designed to break the force of wave action at both ends of the vessel. These would strongly define fore and aft to the average eye and embrace differences in design which would identify each canoe from some distance. The two Sea-Masters had decided upon a radical, and only partly proven theory. What that eccentric Itin Seaman had begun would find its completion and success here among the Mal'lam's best sailors and craftsmen.

There was considerable grumbling among some of the greyer heads, however. Hadn't their forebears journeyed successfully, thank you very much, with that old tried and trusted system of design? And here they were, risking the largest project in memory to the questionable invention of that 'Itin' rascal, Jolo'tan. "We must watch for signs from the Sea Gods!" some whispered. But, and all had to agree in the end, they must put their trust in the stable and reliable Orn'ta Sea-Master and the brilliant young Seaman, Al'malan. The decision had been made in council and would not be revoked.

Today these roughed hulls lay upon heavy baulks of timber and adorned with garlands of colored cloth and leaves and flowers. Upon each hull rested a beautiful, ornately woven mat such as was used on the big bamboo rafts to make more comfortable the resting areas on the tall decks. The women from Sh'ham-Set had woven each of them; that craft a tradition on their home island, their expertise not matched by the local weavers. Each had a different pattern, immediately discernable. Its purpose was to imbue the hull with special qualities and to lend guidance to the craftsmen as they worked: representations of birds such as the frigate bird, the gannet and the albatross, highly stylized and evoking lightness and speed: sea turtles, their hard shells lending strength and resilience to the hulls. And scattered among these were stars of the constellations, illuminating the path to southern seas. Some of the symbolism was of obscure origin, abstractions whose meanings were derived from the distant past but lovingly reproduced in the intricate and colorful weaving in pandanus leaves.

When the time came for the expedition to depart, Orn'ta Sea-Master would not be aboard any of the craft. Though still vigorous, not yet fifty years of age, it had been his decision to remain as mentor to the upcoming young seamen, yet to be *hewn*. The events to the north, the rumors of Tor'na's further depredations, the continuing volcanic activity which was already seeing refugees of other Clans making their way to safety on Sh'tah Lee-Set and the pleas of many of his Seaman compatriots helped to persuade him.

However, it was the recent birth of his twin sons to his young, new wife, which finally decided his future. They would be too young to make the journey and he could not bear the thought of being long separated from them, perhaps never to see them again. And to leave his beloved wife was unthinkable. Al'Malan would be leader of the expedition and, as Voyage-Master, it was he who conducted this ceremony. The sound of voices faded around the canoe sheds, replaced by the sweet trilling of flutes. The traditional musical instrument of seamen, they played in soul-stirring unison one of the oldest, most loved songs of the sea. And song it was, for a Sea-Hewn of middle-years joined in with a rich baritone, reciting the love song to the sea which all initiates learned in the first days of their *hewing*.

When this music ended, silence surrounded the whole area, broken only by the odd cough or fussing of a small child. Al'malan strode solemnly through the crowd toward one set of hulls. He was resplendent in a highly decorated seaman's cape, his legs bound at each knee with fish-leather bands and a stock of fish scales and shells hung upon his chest. His dark brown skin glistened with coconut oil scented with herbs. On his head was a woven cone of coir string, covered in the white feathers of the gannet. A strap under his chin, which was laced with cowrie shells, secured the headdress. From shoulder to shoulder, supported by the cone-shaped headdress, stood out a fan shape of the long tail-feathers of the red-tailed tropicbird.

He climbed onto a bench of carved timber, his head now towering above the crowd. Every movement caused the white and red feathers to jiggle and wave as if there rested on Al'malam's head a living creature. And just so was that headdress designed to represent the living strength and wisdom of its wearer. This crown of great honor and responsibility, he wore with grace. Raising his arms to the sky he began to intone an ancient chant of blessing upon what would become, "Wa'Ran'tar',

"From the sky,

From the mountains,

From the Earth Mother's green creations

Come these logs.

Listen,

Listen,

See,

See.

Know the canoe which is being born here.

Its name is Wa'. Wa' Ran'tar!

Ran'tar Canoe-Master,

Here is a new home.

Come home,

Ran'tar!

Welcome!

Then two seamen approached, carrying a small basin of seawater between them. Al'malan dipped both hands into the salty water and sipped a mouthful, turned and spat the water onto the two hulls. Where that water landed Al'malan placed his hand and smoothed the rivulets onto the roughed outer shell of the hull. At each hull he bent and spoke quietly, privately, making understated gestures which were his alone, his own ritual. This was his vessel; this new and radical invention born of necessity and inspiration was to be his upon which to lead the voyagers.

But beyond that was the inference that, honors and respect aside, his whole future as a Sea-Master had yet to be tested. That beautiful woman who waited in his future faded momentarily to a warm, hazy remembrance. Now! Now is the moment! His whole life started anew, right here! The future of his people, of all the Mal'lam, rested upon the energy of this moment! And behind him strode his greatest ally, his own blessings flowing outward on the beat of his long-handled adze as he followed his friend, sounding each step on the sand with the tool's heavy head.

Joha'lan Canoe-Master was truly the key element in Al'malan's dreams for the coming exodus of his people from these increasingly troubled islands. Wa'Ran'tar now properly blessed, Al'malan moved on to the next canoe shed to bless those new vessels; 'Wa' Olon' and 'Wa' Boton', both the names of departed and revered Sea-Masters. The quiet, reverent crowd followed, the space between held by Sh'tana, his wife-to-be, glorious in a halo of flowers and feathers as she cast blossoms and herbs onto the various logs. Her's was a sacred position, chosen by he who officiated this ceremony. All attending understood their relationship and each toss of flower petals brought a loving hush of applause. The love of these two young people, their stability and devotion, were the anchors upon which the people must now depend.

The two Sea-Masters who had already been chosen to command these other two new canoes stood beside the upturned hulls with pride in their faces. A 'sighted' Seaman, one Sh'ban'al, a native to Sht'tah Lee, would command 'Wa'Olon'. The other man chosen as captain was one with familial ties to the Itin. He too possessed that visual peculiarity. An extremely competent seaman, his name was Ham'sha and his choice signaled a growing awareness among the Mal'lam that the Itin were indeed part of them. Ham'sha Sea-Master had but one eye.

This ceremony of the blessing of the canoes ended with an abruptness which was almost anticlimactic, as did many such events with the Mal'lam. The emotional slack was almost immediately taken up by celebration. Within minutes the crowd had returned to the village where a feast lay waiting. Only the Sea-Hewn, all eighty of the first-class seamen and young initiates who would be involved in the expedition, remained. They all assembled cross-legged on the black sands below the canoe sheds, arrayed in three concentric half-circles around a growing fire. Al'malan addressed his compatriots in informal language and mode but his authority was unmistakable.

"Brothers," he began, standing across the fire from them, "the work on our canoes will begin tomorrow. 'Wa'Ran'tar' will be completed first. As many workmen as is efficient will be applied to it. The new style of rig and technique of sailing will take place on 'Wa'Ran'tar' while the other two vessels are completed. Each Master and his crew will train first on 'Wa'Ran'tar'." Al'malan paused now to remove the rather cumbersome apparel of his office and then sat down, still opposite the other Sea-Hewn.

"However," he began again, "unlike in the past when all Seamen focused on the development of new canoes, there is other work to do; very important work! As you all know by now, 'Tor'na the Mad' has commandeered two canoes, and committed murder to do so." This last intelligence had reached Sh'tah Lee but three days ago, resulting in a lengthy debate among the Elders and the senior Sea-Hewn. All knew of the Council's discussion but as yet their decision had not been formally announced.

"It has been decided by the Council of Elders and Sea-Hewn that we must prepare ourselves, Seamen and landsmen alike, to fight Tor'na and his henchmen. We must all learn new skills; skills once applied by our ancestors on their way to these islands."

A murmur ran through the assembled men but Al'malan's raised arm quickly quieted it. Al'malan stood up again, the firelight highlighting his features and painting a face of strong lines and deeply shadowed eyes; a sense of drama was not beyond his utilization. His stance and the powerful figure of the man in the firelight was impressive. "Like most of you, I have neither participated in nor witnessed a fight in which a man was badly injured or killed. A'lan's wounding the only exception." He nodded to the young initiate who sat in the back row, the scar on his face evident in the bright firelight. The air was becoming chilly in spite of the heat from the fire and there was a rustle of activity among the seamen as they drew their woven rain capes around them. An assembly such as this usually implied hours of discussion and rhetoric and most had come prepared. That Al'malan was not given to long discourses gave encouragement to the seamen; the smells of food being prepared up the hill at the feast tugged at their attention.

"It has been nearly eleven generations since the Mal'lam have known warfare." He smiled pointedly at a few of the young men before him across the fire, "Of course, I know that some of you consider yourselves battlers - good at the occasional brawl on Sha'lan'la-Set during the trading!" Gibes and laughter followed as the young men accused one another, Al'malan watching closely those at whom fingers were pointed, registering the faces and names for future consideration in the martial training. "A punch-up is one thing, brothers. Spearing or stabbing or clubbing to death another man is something entirely different!" His words laid a silence upon the men gathered before him, eighty minds trying to grasp the horror of that event. "This is what we may be - in fact, most certainly *will* be faced with in the near future. The *seers* have predicted it. I believe them!" This time there was no murmuring or joking or light-hearted pokes in the ribs. Every face now registered solemn attention.

"Our fighting traditions exist only as empty words in the histories we chant. We are weak, defenseless lumps of muscle. Men like Tor'na can cut us up and have our livers for breakfast!" The response pleased Al'malan but he kept his expression severe and unfathomable. Scowls and rebuttals and faces flushed with anger reproached the very idea. He took heart now, this very subject had increasingly kept him awake these recent nights; worrying, desperate for some solution.

Now he sat again, the movement quieting his audience once more, all eyes burning toward him. He knew that they could but agree once their male egos slipped back into reason and he waited before continuing. In the back row, Shen'ham as always seated beside him, A'lan Sea-Hewn rubbed his face, tingles of insipient pain responding to the chill air. Anger was rising in him, but his mind was steady on the revealed threat and he struggled to find his own solutions.

"Who among us possesses the experience, who has the slightest idea of what to do when another man thrusts a spear at our belly? Who among us knows how to fend off a fatal blow? Or a stab? Surely, ten of us could overwhelm a single madman but at what cost? There is history, as recent as the memory of our oldest Grey-Hewn, of a man who went feral in the northern islands and was captured and killed. But he killed three men in the fight! Three good men to one madman! These are not the odds which we can allow." Al'malan was roaring now, the passion of his message beating into his fellows. Pausing for some moments, he lowered his voice, preparing them to accept the only viable solution to their great lack.

"Those of you who have had dealings with our neighbors, the 'Itin', will know that for sport and entertainment they indulge in a mock-combat which is quite marvelous to watch. They call it 'Shan'. It was taken up by the 'Itin' generations ago when they had to fight to survive as they followed our people's journey to these islands. Unlike we peaceful, and so it appears, negligent Mal'lam, they retained the knowledge and practice of a warrior's ways. And yet, as we know, they too are a peaceful people. But after seeing them practice their 'Shan', I very much wish to keep them as good friends and neighbors."

Al'malan took notice of his audience's reactions; nodding heads or expressions of dismissal of those 'poor-cousins-who-stink-of-fish'. His own nature and its reaction to that one, short experience with the 'Itin' had left him with a sense of kinship and admiration. But he knew he must work his own conviction into his audience's awareness carefully. Prejudice there was among his people and in some, a denigrating denial of any worth to be attached to those barren-land dwellers. He had been impressed by the deep respect, yet good-humored rascality with which the Itin treated each other.

For a long time now, Al'malan had the growing conviction that the Mal'lam were beginning to become 'soft'. His months sailing with Tor'na, before that man became 'mad', had inspired him to believe that discipline, coupled with rigor and dedication could create a 'toughness' in his people which their ancestors must surely have possessed. His role as 'Hewing-Master' for the young seaman initiates had solidified that belief. The same vigor and intense dedication which those boys had, and still do show ever day, must manifest itself again among the 'Hewn" of all craft, most especially among the Sea-Hewn.

He looked hard across the fire at the faces there, flickering shadows and highlights giving them all a surreal appearance. He worked on instinct now, his inner hearing aiding him. "They, the 'Itin', are the friends we must turn to to assist us Mal'lam in regaining the capacity to defend ourselves. We shall not become as the old 'Itoi' of the ancestor's days, but we must and we will become Mal'lam warriors again. If we do not, our own lives and the lives of our loved ones may be given up to madmen!" Again he waited and let the meaning sink in, then he concluded with, "Think on this. Deeply! In two days there will be another Council. The decision will be made then as to how we are to proceed. But now, let's celebrate, brothers! Tomorrow you can think while you rest your sore heads!"

Research Notes: Impressions and General Observations

Subjects: Tina Pua'lani Kaiser, Tutu Kinau Kaiser and Jiro YukiharaKaua'i, Winter 1973

What a heck of a week this has been! The transcribing of Tina's tapes: the last batch has taken a month, what with colds and flu, broken tape recorders, Tutu's car crapping-out and the ever-reliable 'Unka Teddy' down with appendicitis and he can't get under the car for three weeks yet! Thank God for Aunty Helen! Thank God for my Hanalei family!

Jiro asked me to come to Honolulu to meet with a colleague of his, Richard Snakenborg, a professor of linguistics and apparently a close friend. I had made a recording of Tina and Kinau speaking Mal'lam, interspersed with some Hawai'ian and pidgin. Jiro asked me to meet with Richard off-campus; where else but at the 'McCulley Chop Suey' restaurant? Richard is quite attractive, even suave, and really knows his business. Unfortunately, his wife and kids think so too!

Richard… 'Dick', he asked me to address him … had been very interested in the tape and had spent considerable time investigating the ramifications! Between the dim-sums and the short-soup we had established that what he was hearing was 'Old Hawaiian' and local pidgin and the most interesting melding of at least three linguistic traditions which were of particular interest to him. We ordered another beer and when the lobster Cantonese arrived he laid a bomb on my dinner!

"Frankly, Katherine, I think this is really a most clever hoax!" I didn't know what to do: barf on my plate!? Plead with him to reconsider!? Go to Jiro's house and kill him!!? Fortunately Tutu's presence, away there on Kaua'i, interceded. I thought of her and held my temper. No blood or other obnoxious fluid was expelled that evening and Dick and I had a most enlightening joust of pseudo-academic posturing. Both of us, of course, knew that we were dealing with a subject which the scientific world was certainly not yet ready to entertain as plausible.

There was the recent information about a people, 'Lapita' the name given to them, who had certainly inhabited the south Pacific long before Polynesians came on the scene. So what? How could this reflect on the establishment of a pre-Hawai'ian culture? There was no physical evidence to indicate even the necessity to investigate the possibility. I was grinding my wooden chopsticks together on my lap, sharpening them, considering using them as a last measure to bring this man to his senses. It wasn't Kinau, there on Kaua'i, who interceded in this case though, but Dick's wife, Clarice! Ah, Clarice! Thank you! A rather boozy night came to a pleasant end when Clarice and Dick waved me off in a taxi to a good night's sleep. The driver had to wake me up when we arrived at Jiro's sister-in-law's place. She is another great character!

The next morning Jiro rang me at my hideout, asking if I'd had a good discussion with Dick. Gritting my teeth, I told him what had transpired. The bastard laughed! I nearly hung-up on him! With his usual gracious interjections though, he managed to assure me that I shouldn't worry. He *is* good at that!

Jiro reassured me that Dick only knew the bare bones of what I was involved in and that my study there on Kaua'i was purely speculative. Speculative?! But he had told me that as the flight back to Kaua'i was announced for final boarding. He gave me a warm kiss on the cheek, whispered, "You're doing wonderfully!" then turned and left me standing alone in the line of waiting passengers.

When I got back to Hanalei it was as if I had fallen again into Paradise! Noisy little kids all over the place; another litter of puppies shitting all over the lawn; the rain couldn't find a place in twenty-four hours to take a breather and best of all, there was a leak in the roof above my bedroom! I knew that I was home! Recorder on . . .

Chapter Eighteen - The Evil Grows

The Clan Bal'lat huddled miserably on the two headlands which enclosed the tiny port of the community, 'Wan'Bal'lal'. On this small island, Bal'lal-Set, the home of the Obsidian Masters, the survivors of another holocaust of volcanic activity now waited for relief to arrive. Their faces smudged with soot and sweat, they sat upon bundles of belongings which were last-minute retrievals from now burned-out homes. The smoke from that last great conflagration which had raged for two days hung low and choking. The sea around them was flat and brooding, looking like hammered red timber beneath an orange, smoke-filtered sun. Those huge waves which had roared parallel to the shore, spilling frighteningly into the little harbor but causing really little damage, had passed hours ago. Now an ominous stillness surrounded this rocky little island. What more could happen? What worse than having homes and crops destroyed?

For three days the volcanic eruption on the north end of the island had boomed and fountained, streams of molten lava spilling into the sea amid thunderous clouds of exploding steam. The heat had drawn air onto itself in howling gusts, further drying the already drought affected land. When the eruptions had suddenly ceased, the sea-winds blew with cruel insistence, igniting first the scrub near the lava flows and then growing in intensity as it swept into the ragged forests and out onto the croplands and orchards.

Homes and farmsteads and fishermen's huts were overrun, sometimes only bare minutes after the inhabitants had fled. Now only small pockets of green existed on the ravaged Set; tiny havens of shocked humanity and their few possessions and animals, many of those scorched and singed. The main village of Wan'Bal'lal, site of the Clan's source of wealth, its workshops and stores of fine obsidian, survived untouched. But the storehouses and granaries which had been located further inland were gone - burned to cinders.

The wealth of stone remained, as it had for millions of years. But the scant productive agricultural lands and the trade wealth of their craftsmanship, which had always sustained the Clan Bal'lat well above subsistence level, was now totally degraded. As in those first years so long ago when these people had settled here, the specter of famine lay across their future. The Bal'lat-an must send for help. A people of the land who waited for the sailors and tradesmen to come to them, they had never developed a vigorous tradition of seamanship.

Small canoes for inshore fishing were the extent of their seaward excursions. Not one Sea-Master existed among the Bal'lat-an. The first off-islanders to arrive were six small canoes of Itin from a nearby island, Lat'lan. Having watched the smoke on the horizon for these past days, they finally braved the headwind-seas and arrived at Wan'Bal'lal harbor at sunset on the sixth day after the eruption began.

Fishermen readying their fragile vessels for launching on the morrow, courageously planning to make the same voyage themselves, met them on the beach. The Itin, after a night's rest, would turn about and spread the alarm that yet another Set was in danger, its inhabitants in dire need. Within five days the whole of the central group of islands were informed and Sea-Hewn raised sail to travel south or east or west to tell the whole archipelago that the home of the Obsidian Masters had been devastated. One fast canoe sped southward to inform the Clan Sh'ta'ha on Sh'tah'Lee.

Those messengers would spy other columns of smoke in the distance. Among the islands of the archipelago there were no less than five volcanoes in various stages of activity. On the island of Sha'lan'la, word also reached the mad Sea-Master Tor'na and his partner, Mal'atan. Both were immediately inspired with a plan. To assist those desperate souls on Bal'lal-Set? Certainly not!

The control of that island's wealth of high quality obsidian and the products made from it were the source of those Clan people's wealth and respect. Only coir rope and twine and a few food items rode higher in the Mal'lam economy. Tor'na and Mal'atan shared the same thought, which immediately became an active plan: they would conquer the Obsidian-Masters and control all their wealth for themselves. Then it would be on to the south, to Sh'tah Lee, and their control over all the Mal'lam would be complete. Truly, no such men had before existed among the Mal'lam!

In the short months since 'Tor'na the Mad' had established his incredible suzerainty over the island of Sh'lan'la, he had assembled a pack of sixty outlaws. Mostly these were men already in conflict with their various Clans. Some, caring only for their own lives and welfare, had stolen vessels and fled their own people's travail on their home islands and come to this gathering-place of the marginal; the 'Thieves Market'. Tor'na's strange power to inspire aggression and accent instability had easily recruited those who sought adventure but cared little what form it might take. From among the late Rohr'rit's band of ruffians he selected the most venal and brutal and assigned them the task of enforcing his will among the populace. Mal'atan, meanwhile, busied himself with his more subtle plans, quietly choosing a few young men, most of whom shared his proclivities, and formed a small core of adherents to his own peculiar bent. Tor'na, totally convinced of his own power and a limitless future of more of it, still remained blind to the threat which shared his bed each night, coiled and well camouflaged.

Mal'atan insisted that the 'followers of Tor'na' should be arrayed in some uniform manner, distinguishable on sight as members of the force which one-day would rule the Mal'lam. He spent hours and days and then weeks preparing this theatrical transformation of a polyglot and often-grubby conglomeration of misfits. The rhythm of the clacking of the *tapa*-makers dominated the background sounds of the now-motivated village of the 'Thieves Market'. Their hardwood beaters worked overtime, flattening the bark fabric, melding strip onto strip until the wide swaths of creamy-white fabric were complete. Every Mal'lam village resounded, almost daily, to this happy, musical cadence of creativity.

But here and now there was a frenzied, discordant rush of hammering. The dozens of women making *tapa* were working under duress. This entire island now vibrated with fear. Mal'atan would have his new uniform clothing, no matter what the expense. He had ordered every grain of red dye powder be brought to him. And when the volume of bark cloth was ready, he had produced for him great lengths of fabric; half the width dyed red, the remainder the natural off-white. With this he would clothe, ostensibly, all of Tor'na's people. But for his own recruits he selected out the very best quality in fabric and color. Tor'na never noticed. Mal'atan's plot was developing apace. So subtly and insidiously was he working that Tor'na suffered less and less from that former disquiet, that itching anxiety that something was amiss nearby.

Tor'na and Mal'atan sat in private council in the now-expanded building in which Rhor'rit had met his end. The smell of food wafted through the open doorway of the bamboo and thatch structure from the small stall at which that same crippled old woman sat cooking. The five men who always accompanied Tor'na wherever he went now stood guard outside. No one dared approach too closely lest a blow remind them that this man stood out above all others;

inviolate! Mal'atan's personal guard sat quietly nearby, beneath the shady awning outside the door.

The one who had recently been but a boy, Sh'ul'am, and the gangly, awkward Joom'ta always attended Mal'atan. And another young recruit now joined them by the name of Jan'shor. He was a pretty-faced lad of sixteen, a native of this island and as devoted to Mal'atan as were the other two. He was Feather-Hewn and he came to Mal'atan's attention not just because of his beauty but because he kept and carried with him a falcon. Perched on the lad's arm, which was wrapped in a sharkskin gauntlet, the raptors keen, coldly intense and ferocious eyes reminded one of Mal'atan's as it swiveled its head constantly, wary of all intent except his master's. The boy's eyes, by contrast, were small and very pale for a Mal'lam and they betrayed no hint of what lay behind them. He seldom spoke but when he did it was only in a whisper. Boy and bird seemed strangely of a kind; both potentially vicious.

Tor'na displayed no jealousy of Mal'atan's dalliances with other boys. Indeed he seemed relieved of the former need to accede to his lovers' voracious sexuality. He also apparently was not concerned about the growing coterie of young men about Mal'atan and their obvious, slavish devotion to him. No timidly offered warning by others was tolerated, not even from his two long-time compatriots. And Tor'na's mind was too absorbed now with this latest bit of news and what it offered him, to consider treachery within the ranks.

No, the news from Bal'lal-Set was what he had been waiting for. Here was a victim with its throat exposed, demanding his attention! Almost as if he could spy the future, Tor'na was prepared for this eventuality. The broad plans for conquest, which fired his existence, dropped the necessary elements neatly into an ordered progression of activity. First he must organize three canoes with full crews, men whom he could trust to follow orders without question. These he had; twenty seamen besides his own five bodyguards who were now parading about the village dressed in their new uniforms. *Strutting*, might have better described them, as they exuded a fierce aggressiveness.

He knew he must soon channel that aggression or it might become a danger to him also. Already squabbles were occurring between some of these men as they vied for influence within his cadre. Tor'na was conscious of having created a monster, which, unless he kept it firmly leashed, might turn on its creator.

Treading a dangerous path of his own design inspired an almost gleeful excitement in him, which exhibited itself not in lightness and companionability - it made him fiercer, inflexibly determined and his face and body radiated a dynamic energy which was infectious.

Ten days later, shouts of, "Tor'na! Tor'na! Master of the Mal'lam!" rang out along the beachfront as his three canoes were pushed with exuberance into the afternoon surf. The mad Sea-Master stood in the center of his vessel's bridging-deck, his face and upper body painted and glistening with oil. Shells decorated his two side-plaits, unmistakable insignia of his rank. The masters of the other two canoes were allowed to decorate their faces only. Rusty-red pennants stood out in the rising onshore wind, held rigid by bamboo rods along their top edges. They swung inland in the breeze, pointing back toward land like warning fingers, the lowering sun turning the natural reddish dye of the banners to blood red.

Mala'tan rode separately in his own vessel, 'Wa' Pa'La'Ta', 'The Canoe that Severs'! His own choice of name, applauded by Tor'na as apocryphal. His was the canoe which was acquired at the cost of two lives, a source of perverse relish to the younger madman. His retinue gathered about him on the bridging deck in their gaudy wraps while those few men with any skill at seamanship manned the vessel. Mal'atan himself never deigned to lift a hand to the sailing of the canoe; never pulled on a rope or ventured a command. Just as well. Mal'atan's only skill lay in being 'Mal'atan the Beautiful'. And plotting!

Joom'ta, too, had few skills to offer except his obsequiousness and devotion to his beloved Mal'atan. But in spite of his silly awkwardness, in a fight, especially against the unsuspecting, he could be vicious and deadly. He had proven that when this very canoe had been stealthily invaded in the dark of night and the two crewmen left to guard it had been killed. One had died by his hand. The only other member of this group who exhibited any tolerance, perhaps even a vague fondness for Joom'ta, was that strange lad, Sh'ul'am.

Both accepted the new boy, Jan'shor Feather-Hewn, as an equal because Mal'atan insisted on it. His secretive quietness was quite like Sh'ul'am's and the gregarious Joom'ta was often so frustrated by their lack of conversation that he would complain to Mal'atan: "Dear One. Why do they not like to talk with me? There is so much of interest to discuss … like we do!" Mal'atan could offer a surprisingly insightful response, if so inclined; "Dear Joom'ta. You are my ears beyond my head; listen more, speak less. I depend on you to tell me what is really happening around us." This always salved Joom'ta's hurt feelings and his skinny chest would swell with renewed pride.

As the small flotilla left the shore the curious onlookers, locals and expatriates alike, watched the departure and wondered what now would happen to them all. Among them was the old woman, Mar'tah; she who longed to be friend, yes, grandmother, to that strange young man, Sh'ul'am. She watched his slim figure fade with the rest of that vessel's crew as twilight descended on the misty ocean. The few of Tor'na's group who had been left behind to govern the local population renewed their swagger in red and white, arrogant policemen in a captive society. Surely these horrible men would return from whatever mischief they were embarking upon and when they did, how worse might things become? How much greater might their arrogance be?

Far to the south, and several weeks before, the final days of Tal'ma's dying were nearly done. He had lain on his simple pallet, warm wraps of bark cloth and finely woven pandanus matting keeping him warm, tucked up under his chin. A'lan Sea-Hewn and his mother, Lana'ma Herb-Mistress, sat on each side of him, the small hut illuminated by a lamp of 'candle-nut' fruits skewered on a thin stem of split bamboo. The smoky flame spluttered and rose and fell in brightness, the black residue from its smoke a feature of many a house interior here in these islands.

Tears flowed from Lana'ma's eyes in long tracks down her still face. But no sobs escaped her. Her body was relaxed, resigned to the inevitable. Uncle Tal'ma had willed his passing to the day and the hour and this was the hour. His gentle snoring was suddenly broken by a cough. He cleared his throat and opened his eyes, looking briefly puzzled as if he didn't know where he was. Blinking, he gathered his focus and looked in turn at his niece and then to the young, scarred face of her son. Blinking and clearing his throat again he managed to speak, his voice weak and hushed. "Is he coming?" he asked.

"Yes uncle - Al'malan comes now." And she reached one hand to wipe away her tears and then laid the other onto the sinewy old arm nearest her beneath the blankets. A'lan leaned slightly forward to better hear the old man's voice, then straightened to look toward the door of the hut as the Sea-Master Al'malan entered, crouching under the low door frame. He stood for a moment, looking intently down at the old man beneath the blankets, allowing his eyes to adjust to the dim light within the hut. A'lan rose to his knees and moved around Tal'ma to sit beside his mother. Al'malan knelt and sat in his place.

"Greetings, Grey-Hewn!" Al'malan said softly, "You sent for me?" The dying man struggled to open his eyes as if deep sleep was tugging at his mind. He licked his dry lips and looked up at the young Sea-Master, eyes focusing but reluctantly. "I have had a vision, Sea-Master, and you must listen closely!" Al'malan leaned his head closer to the old man's, his eyes focused on a middle space, mind open and alert. Visions were to be noted, especially those of the dying.

"I have seen - I have seen a man killed!" Tal'ma swallowed and sighed deeply, then continued with a stronger voice. "It was you who bore the weapon - you who killed the man!" He was looking intently at Al'malan now and the younger man met his gaze. Al'malan's brow furrowed as he listened, both eager yet strangely reluctant to hear the rest. "Do not fear or sorrow, Sea-Master. It must be done!" Tal'ma suddenly began a fit of coughing, dry and brittle was the sound, and his niece placed a hand beneath his back and lifted him to a sitting position. After his convulsion had passed she gently laid him back down again, A'lan lending his hand to ease the old head down upon the carved wooden headrest.

Moments passed as the Grey-Hewn regained his breath. Then he reached a weak grasp up to Al'malan's shoulder and said, "You must go soon - very soon. You must sail to the north. Evil grows there and my son is in danger. And - and you must take this lad with you. He has a destiny to fulfill, as do you!" With his other hand he reached toward A'lan, but the gesture never succeeded. A sudden stiffening of his body, eyes wide in a stare into an unknown space, and then he collapsed with a long, wheezing sigh.

Lana'ma Leaf-Plait gave a sharp cry and covered her face with her hands. A'lan looked across at Al'malan through tears. The Sea-Master bowed his head and grasped the dead man's hands in his own. "Farewell, old one. We rejoice in you! Farewell!" He then laid Tal'ma's hands back onto his chest and rose to leave the hut. Pausing, he turned and said very quietly, "A'lan-an. Do not repeat his last words to anyone … for now." Then he was gone and moments later the sound of mourning rose from outside the hut. The young Sea-Hewn put a strong arm around his mother's shoulders and pulled her to him, absorbing the shudders of her weeping. His eyes were fixed on that faint, diaphanous light which hovered over his Great Uncle's body, now fading - dimmer, dimmer, then gone.

Al'malan Sea-Master stood with Orn'ta and four other masters, apart from the crowd that had gathered around the funeral pyre. The flames were towering now, the roar and crackle of the fire nearly drowning out the chant of remembrance which had begun minutes before. There was much about this old man to be remembered, much of him to be rejoiced in. In the front rank of the mourners, steadied by friends and family was Tel'lan Sea-Master, himself embarked upon his own dying. He was weak and shrunken yet had been insistent upon attending his old friend's funeral ceremony. His own fast had begun six days ago and all knew that he would not see another six days.

Al'malan gazed thoughtfully at the old man's figure. Another valued Grey-Hewn soon to make the long journey back to the *Earth Mother*; another beloved mentor and friend to be mourned. Al'malan shivered in spite of the intense heat from the fire. "What awaits me?" he thought. "Surely that old man's vision, the killing of another man by my hand, was to be believed." No wise Mal'lam could discount such a warning. But how? How to proceed without directing such a destiny? That was always the problem with such things; how to carry on as if such foreknowledge didn't exist, yet be prepared for it when it did eventuate. Oh, how heavy a burden *knowing* could be! And how must he now act upon this warning without revealing to others its true import? A'lan, of course, already knew and he trusted the youngster's discretion. But how must those words have affected him, too?"

Al'malan's reverie was interrupted when Orn'ta asked, "And what of Tal'ma's son, Enno Stone-Master? Why was he so intent on traveling to Bal'lal-Set, I wonder?" Al'malan took his friend by the arm and led him away from the gathering, their presence properly fulfilled, sorrow and respect genuine. But tomorrow's necessity was pressing. Enno Stone-Master had gone to Bal'lal-Set after those twenty axes had been created under his direction and sent off to the Itin village headman, Jolo'tan. The autumn winds now were cool and the seas spawned sudden storms.

But word had reached him that the Stone-Masters of Bal'lal-Set had discovered a new source of another hard, workable stone on their island and invited him to come and work with them. The vessel which had brought that news was to turn around and return to the north in just a few days. He must be on it. That his father, Tal'ma Herb-Master, was failing and might soon pass away was a source of great conflict for him. He loved the irascible old man and as his only surviving son, assuming that his older brother, Faldo Sea-Master was indeed lost forever, he had a special obligation to his extended family. But his father had made it easy for him. "You must go, Enno! There can be no question." He had stated. "I shall not be here when you return. We will say our goodbyes on the day you leave."

And so that day had come and the heavy clouds mirrored the sorrow in Enno's heart. They had exchanged gifts and then Enno had hastily boarded the canoe, hurrying really to hide his tears. The old man's small, blanket-huddled form stood unmoving in the drizzling rain on the black beach until rain and mist and distance erased the last glimpse of the sails. Enno wept unashamedly and had sat looking back until darkness fell. His dreams that night as he lay shivering beneath two woven mats were visionary. Tal'ma chanted warnings; dark-faced, fiery-eyed men, vaguely familiar, screamed threats while glowing embers singed his face. He awoke with a cry!

Enno Stone-Hewn, the Master stone-craftsman of the Clan, was a quiet, introspective and quite solitary man of almost sorrowful mien. In his late thirties, long-separated from his wife and childless, he displayed no interest in starting another family of his own now. Enno worked long hours at the small hut where he fashioned the most perfect stone tools. His knives, spearheads and axe heads of obsidian were superb, while his adzes of another; dense, grey stone were unmatched. He nearly always insisted on fixing these tools to their handles, a masterly skill in itself. The Clan cousins on Sht'ah Lee accorded him profound respect, the local craftsmen eager to emulate his techniques. Generous and patient, he sat quietly at his work as his more garrulous work-mates chatted and joked amid the clatter and hammer of their trade. He seldom participated in gossip or idle chatter but always responded willingly to serious inquiries as to method and technique.

Then on that first morning at sea as the grey light crept up dimly from the eastern horizon, he sat in meditation alone, forward of the mast. No visions attended his concentration on infinity. The squawk of a seabird held no message nor did the gurgling passage of the hulls through the water speak any wisdom. Enno had been left with a deeper sense of aloneness than that which so often attended him. He opened his eyes fruitless minutes later to look into the face of a young Sea-Hewn, a new initiate on his first long voyage on the open sea. He was one of those in A'lan's *hewn* group, now smiling widely and holding out a bamboo cup of warm, spiced tea, the seaman's morning heart-starter. The boy's warmth and obvious respect brought sudden, inexplicable buoyancy to Enno's unhappy heart.

Enno accepted the cup with a nod and the boy responded with a shallow bow and lightly strode away on the swaying deck. Memories of his own youthful ease and confidence flooded back upon him and he mused as he drank the sweet-tart infusion. "Why must I be so silent and alone? I am becoming too withdrawn. I even neglected to thank the lad!" With a quick gulp he drained the cup, rose and staggered on yet-unaccustomed legs aft to where the other Sea-Hewn sat. He greeted them with a smile and sat among their group. The rest of the voyage to Bal'lal-Set passed with surprising speed for him, his shipmates remarking among themselves on the man's unusual garrulousness. As the canoe glided to a rasping halt on the sand at Wan Bal'lal, a mood of foreboding descended upon him; some prescience apparently shared by many others aboard, this bright morning. The crew was hushed as they leapt to shore to pull the heavy canoe up onto the beach.

It would be but a few days before that destructive eruption would begin at the far end of the island. The Bal'lat-an jogged down the beach to greet them and to assist in the securing of the vessel. While exuberant in their greetings, there also rang an uncommon sense of impending … something! Those native to this Set who possessed the '*sight*' had issued warnings, vague as to what and when but *bad* and *soon* was strongly implied. Thus did Enno Stone-Master find himself upon an island soon to be terrorized by two cataclysmic events: one, of nature's design, one of design by some of nature's most complex creatures gone mad!

It was late morning and the fires across the island were finally, belatedly quelled by the autumn squalls. The air was clear and crisp and visibility good. Then on the horizon came the sight of the great sails of two bamboo rafts. Relief was on the way! Word had reached neighboring islands of the plight of the Bal'lat-an. Victuals, seed plants and cuttings, a few animals, household items and tools, all had been hurriedly loaded aboard vessels only recently retired for the season.

The contrary winds of autumn slowed the passage of the always-ponderous great rafts, adding time in passage, which allowed three fast-moving canoes to precede them to their destination. As thankful, eager Bal'lal-an gathered enthusiastically on the small harbor's beaches and headlands, three more sails suddenly appeared from around the island. Their approach from the east was un-noticed by eager watchers searching southern and western waters. Cheers of greeting erupted as the vessels approached the mouth of the little bay but they soon faded into wondering chatter when the canoes, instead of proceeding shoreward with a fortuitous wind and tide, dropped sail.

The three canoes were now maneuvered by paddle and held stationary in line abreast, across the harbor's mouth. Most strange! Men, dressed curiously in bark-cloth wraps of white and red then began feeding what looked like a thick line between the canoes. The canoes moved apart with the heavy rope between them until their formation nearly spanned the bay's entrance. What was this? They were creating a barrier, but to what possible effect? The two still-approaching trading rafts were far off the entrance yet but the on-shore wind was picking up and they were approaching more quickly now. The rafts needed that strong run of wind to safely penetrate the harbor's mouth without having to use its long oars. If those canoes remained where they were then the rafts would have to drop their sails and anchors and stop completely.

Enno Stone-Master stood with his compatriots in the same mood of incomprehension. Then a sudden recognition struck him. That was Tor'na's vessel, 'Flee-The Land', there in the middle of the three canoes. He knew that unique shape of the bow structure. What in the name of the Sea-Gods was he up to? A group of islanders walked to the foremost point on the highest headland and called out to those seamen in the canoes. "What are you doing?" Neither word nor gesture answered them, and surely those men down there heard their voices of inquiry. For a time the calls from shore grew louder and more shrill, but when Enno's recognition of who these seamen were spread among the watchers, silence slowly settled over the harbor.

An hour of tiring paddling while station keeping, maintaining their barrier to the rafts, finally saw the first raft approach within hailing distance of the canoes.

Shouting across the closing space the Master of the raft called out, "Bear away, Sea-Hewn! Give us passage to the harbor!" But no passage would be allowed just yet and in reluctant response both rafts lowered sail and dropped two huge stone anchors overboard, six fathoms of line running after them until the bottom was reached.

Curses and threats issued from the rafts, suddenly ceasing as the canoe crews were seen to be pulling that heavy hawser across two of them and into the third. The large mound of coir rope was piled onto the bridging deck and suddenly those uniformed men took up their paddles and surged toward the stationary rafts. Forty-two men, all dressed similarly in red and white wraps, drove a final, challenging, muscle-straining hundred yards to the rafts, Tor'na's canoe and one other went to the nearest big vessel while the third went on to the second raft.

Waiting for the third canoe to reach its goal, Tor'na ordered silence among his crews. Bracketing the first raft, they were unresponsive to the queries, indeed, invective shouted down at them from the higher decks. When the third canoe was in position alongside its quarry, Tor'na let out a roar so loud and violent that its awful intent froze those manning the rafts and those ashore as well. With a final swirl of paddles the attackers brought their canoes against the sides of the rafts. Then, issuing terrifying screams and cries they leapt and clambered aboard the layered bamboo hulls.

It was over almost before it began! With clubs and shark's-tooth-edged weapons, Tor'na's men laid about them wickedly, striking viciously, indiscriminately. There was no intention of sparing lives. Tor',na, with Mal'atan's connivance, ordered that their attack must once and for all convince the Mal'lam everywhere that there was no resisting his dominance. There was no resistance but five men of the victim crews had the presence of mind to dive into the sea and swim for shore. One of those died from a spear in his back. Eighteen Mal'lam Sea-Hewn and two women passengers had been aboard the rafts.

Those ashore now looked on in horror, trying not to believe what they were seeing. Finally men and a few boys from shore dove into the water to assist those four escapees who swam for their lives toward the beach. By the time the survivors were safely ashore, their dead companions had joined the sea, sharks gathering in cautious circles about the bleeding bodies. Tor'na now stood on the bow of the nearest raft, resplendent in costume and gore. Mal'atan and his crew aboard the rearmost raft waved their bloody weapons and jumped and shouted in mad glee.

Mal'atan turned slowly to gather-in the scene aboard his conquest. Joom'ta, his face ugly with grim pleasure; Sh'ul'am, blood-spattered and emotionless, his gory weapon held casually in both hands, dripping blood. Jan'shor Feather-Hewn, eyes seeking his falcon there on the deck of the canoe below him, anxious of its welfare, showed no interest in the dead who lay about him.

Mal'atan looked across to where the lead raft swarmed with those costumes of his design and smiled horridly.

There too had blood-lust reigned and he raised his own defiled hand to wave at his partner. Two great vessels laden with food and supplies meant as relief for the desperate Bal'lat-an were now under their control. Both knew that those people would offer no resistance when, come tomorrow morning, their leaders would be called to parlay with 'Tor'na the Magnificent'. He would be generous with them. No more violence would accrue unless they resisted. They would be free to continue their generations-old tradition of stonework and tool making, and he would be their only representative in trade. All this would they learn tomorrow morning. Now the rafts must be moved inside the mouth of the harbor and re-anchored. Tor'na's pirates would need a night of rest before landing and securing their second island conquest! Enno Stone-Master sat with his head clasped in his hands, weeping with horror and shame. Another Stone-Master leaned down to comfort him and all around them voices raged and shouted in impotence.

Chapter Nineteen ~ Justice, of a Kind

Through that night the sea was moderate and the wind fitful. Low cloud dimmed a quarter moon to a dull glow. The three canoes and the two captured rafts bobbed in the glow of torches, guards on each vessel keen to spot any intrusion upon their conquest. None occurred, but a furtive venture was being undertaken on the opposite side of the southern arm of land which partially enclosed the harbor. A fishing canoe of single hull and two outriggers, only seventeen feet in length and recently repaired after the conflagration, was being readied for launch. Carried on the shoulders of a large group of desperate, determined men, Enno Stone-Master among them, the canoe was set into the light surge of a small inlet half a mile from the harbor. Four seamen, all coastal fishermen with little open-sea experience had volunteered to sail and paddle the frail craft to the nearest Set and spread another, greater alarm.

The tide was on the rise now, the night dark beneath the thickening cloud cover. The sea beckoned the courage of these men whose minds were still brimming with the horror of the day just past. With powerful unison the four seamen drove the craft through the narrow, rocky enclosure and out onto the swell beyond. Enno and the other men remaining stood knee deep in the surf, sending prayers after those brave men until they had disappeared into the gloom. Then they returned to the village. The only lights visible that night were the torches in the distance at the harbor's mouth, their glow an evil track upon the intervening waters. In the darkened village grim features watched fearfully through the night, half expecting an assault from 'Tor'na the Mad'.

Two hours saw the tired paddlers beyond sight of even the keenest of watchful eyes, on or near Bal'lal-Set. It was safe now to raise the flimsy mast and sail. Providentially, the clouds began to clear and the wind rise and a guiding star became visible. While one man steered toward that star, beneath which lay that island goal, the other three tried to snatch some sleep beneath woven mats. The night was chill now on the open sea and spray dowsed all aboard. The morning's sun would rise behind that nearest island, but dawn would offer closer ears for their tale of murder and piracy.

Al'malan Sea-Master sat in morning council with three other Mal'lam Sea-Hewn and the Itin Sea-Hewn, Ch'am'lo. A'lan and Shen'ham sat nearby with twelve other young men, some of them landsmen who had volunteered for this expedition. Six men were on duty at the steering paddles or stood by to handle the sail. These men and boys, and the twenty-one would-be warriors on the other double-canoe sailing close abeam of them, had been training for five weeks for what might occur if success sailed with them.

All had attended daily training sessions conducted by the rather awesome Itin, Ch'am'lo. He had drilled them in the use of weapons and how to defend themselves: Shen'ham had become the most outstanding practitioner of the sling, able to send a stone into a man-sized target time after time with great accuracy and rapidity; A'lan and a number of other lads lifted rocks and wielded heavy pieces of timber to strengthen arms and shoulders for the use of heavy, hardwood clubs, some with terrible shark's tooth or obsidian-chip edges.

The sling was a widely used toy among the boys of the Mal'lam but now it became a fearsome, long-range weapon. Most men could use a spear, but the enemy now was not a wild boar. Shorter spears with long stone points and heavier shafts were the new weapons Ch'am'lo instructed them to use. For close-in fighting, all would carry daggers of fire-hardened wood, pig's leg bone or obsidian. Old mats were stuffed with grasses and fashioned into man-sized targets and they steadily disintegrated under the improving marksmanship of the trainees. Muscles, which ached for days under the rigorous regimen of exercise and repetition, slowly became stronger and more supple. The minds of the trainees, men and boys, were subtly being altered: Ch'am'lo was indeed a gifted teacher as he slowly began to create a small force of males with a warrior's intent.

"How are we doing, Ch'am'lo? Tell me honestly." Al'malan had asked the Itin martial artist one afternoon of the fourth week of their training. Ch'am'lo, typical of his people, answered with total candor. "I am impressed, brother! Some of these men, and boys, are learning very quickly. And I want you to know that I insist on accompanying you when you finally go after that madman. I will stand with them in a fight with no hesitation. Only …" and he looked cagily out of the corner of his eye at Al'malan, "I do hope you get better soon with the spear."

Al'malan, a head taller and thirty pounds heavier and himself rather awesome when wielding the weapons in practice, looked down at his new friend and nodded. "Alright teacher, let's have a little contest! Are you game?" The two walked smiling to where a number of spears lay on the ground about thirty feet from one of those disintegrating targets. Bending and picking up the heaviest, Al'malan tested its heft and balance, raised it above his shoulder, took a step foreword and threw it with a mighty heave. It struck home, passing nearly through the packed grass of the target. Ch'am'lo pursed his mouth, nodded and threw Al'malan a look of mock-admiration. Then with a mischievous grin, he reached one foot out to the pile of spears, lifted one into the air with a quick movement, caught it and threw it from a standing position, feet close together. It too struck home exactly, right beside Al'malan's spear.

Ch'am'lo presented Al'malan with a look of innocent guilessness, reminding one of his father, Jo'lo'tan. Then he burst into a loud laugh and slapped his compatriot on the shoulder. For many minutes they threw spears, but by the time all had been heaved away. Al'malan, having missed the target twice, gasped, "Alright, teacher! You've beaten me." Ch'am'lo walked to in front of Al'malan and stood with hands on hips and looked meaningfully into his friend's face. "Sea-Master, you are as ready as you need to be. When the hour comes you will cast your weapon with all the accuracy that's demanded. You are indeed a warrior; greater than you know. I will follow your lead, my good friend. Hmmmm! Do you have a thirst such as mine? A bit of palm toddy perhaps?"

With that they strode together downhill from the training ground, following the other young, and not-so-young warriors. Orn'ta Sea-Master also took part in these sessions, as did another four Sea-Hewn who were no longer young. Their efforts too were great, their achievements perhaps gained at greater cost to body and mind than the youngsters. But their experience and wisdom added a meaningful depth to this rapidly maturing force of protectors of the Mal'lam. And very importantly, these men now considered their Itin neighbors truly as brothers. Ch'am'lo had bridged whatever gap may have remained between these neighboring Clans.

Now, as the freshening breeze negated the first glow of the sun's warmth the Sea-Hewn listened with rapt attention to their leader's words. Pulling their rain capes about them more tightly for warmth, they shared the added chill of anticipation. Combat! The very meaning of the word still but an abstraction and a mystery. What would really happen? What was it *really* like? What was it to kill another human being? What was it like to die? No one there knew. All would soon learn at least some of the answers.

The Sea-Masters of both Mal'lam vessels held council with their crews; Al'malan on his canoe, 'Wa'Bo'ton' and Orn'ta on his 'Hoosh'im'wa'. Al'malan was telling his crewmates in definite terms that theirs' was a journey from which some would surely not return. Grim faces and nodded heads encouraged him. At least no one was expecting child's play; no more exercises and games with weapons. "We don't know their strength yet," he continued, "but we can be sure that they will resist mightily. I can offer you no more than my confidence, brothers. I possess no more experience than any of you here." He looked at his friend, Ch'am'lo, and said, "This man whose expertise we have been depending upon to prepare us for this venture is himself a novice to actual combat. But his presence here with us should give us all great heart. He is here with us because he has confidence in you all. Should my judgment fail or should I be killed or wounded, look to Ch'am'lo to guide you. Most importantly, protect your brothers and stay aware of what is happening all about you, as much as you can. And keep in your hearts the courage of our ancestors. So long ago, they fought and won their last battles, else we wouldn't be here."

Al'malan stood up then and signaled his compatriots to stand. He was about to lead them in a song which they had learned during their martial training; it was a song taught them by Ch'am'lo and came from the long tradition of his martial art form. But then came the cry, "Sail! Sail to the northeast!" The same alert was heard shouted from Orn'ta's vessel and all moved to look where the lookout up the mast was pointing. A sudden chill ran up Al'malan's back. "Are we ready to fight them here - now?"

The morning's wind carried the warning cries across the water to the tired helmsman on that small canoe and he called his friends awake. Soon it was seen by the big vessels that what was approaching them was but a small, lone fishing canoe "Quite small to be so far from land!" Orn'ta yelled across to Al'malan. Both Sea-Masters ordered a course change to take them directly toward this surprise visitor. Within a few minutes Al'malan ordered sail to be dropped and both big canoes came to a slow halt in the moderate swell of that day.

The little fishing vessel closed with them and soon lines were thrown and Al'malan's crewmen pulled the smaller craft gently alongside 'Wa'Bo'ton'. Orn'ta brought his vessel alongside Al'malan's and soon joined him to meet these intrepid sailors. These four, tired, still-frightened men unburdened their tale to the Mal'lam warriors, all the while taking long drinks of fresh water and hungry mouthfuls of the proffered food. Their tale would rouse some fear in the minds of the listeners, all eager for news of their enemy. But as well, the horrible events solidified these warrior's intent. Cold determination now dominated the shifting emotions of those who heard the tales of that deadly intervention on the island of the Bal'lat. One message was of reassurance; Enno Stone-Master was unharmed and on the island and the canoe which had brought him there had left the night before Tor'na's arrival.

Al'malan ordered that long bamboo poles be lashed between both large canoes, a temporary, flexible anchorage system which would allow both vessels to remain as one for the interval needed. What was needed now was to bring together the information provided by those brave fishermen, combined with Orn'ta's knowledge of the port at Bal'lal's harbor, and formulate a plan of attack. A seaman is constantly involved in strategy: ship against the sea; ship against the land; ship against the weather. Now, all three of these ingredients must join another set of unknowns never before encountered by the Sea-Masters of the present-day Mal'lam.

What would Tor'na's response be to their approach to that violated harbor? It was Ch'am'lo who offered the most cogent advise. "Allow me to speculate, brothers." He said, his manner quite demanding of attention. "From what we have heard from our Bal'lat cousins, Tor'na has three canoes but barely enough men to sail them efficiently. He is depending on surprise and ferocity to achieve his objectives. He appears to have no depth of manpower. He also has two large rafts filled with goods most valuable to his cause. He will protect these with vigor. He will be expecting more vessels to arrive to aid the Bal'lat-an in their hour of extremity and he expects to overwhelm them with the same ease with which he had earlier succeeded. Here is what I propose we consider as a plan of attack on the man and his allies, who may well be much less awesome than he would have us believe!"

Only an hour was necessary for Ch'am'lo to convince his comrades of a viable plan of attack. Orn'ta's crew rejoined their vessel, uncoupled the two canoes and both then got underway, Orn'ta's canoe towing the small fishing vessel, two men aboard to steer it. The clearing skies and the drift of the current had now brought the highest point of Bal'lat-Set into view. No more than two hours away now. The big, smooth hulls cleaved insistently through the waves, speeding toward Bal'lat-Set with heightened confidence and greater urgency. In one bow of Al'malan's canoe the young Sea-Hewn, A'lan, stood gripping the forestay and gazing at the blood-red shimmer beneath the surface. Only his special vision was capable of discerning this glow in broad daylight. He shivered in spite of the sun's increasing warmth on his back. He fought his fear and uncertainty by beginning a Seaman's chant, quickly taken up by the men behind him:

"Challenge me, sea and wind and night and cold,

Test my strength and feel my resolve!

Mal'lam am I, born of the blue deeps.

On! Child of warriors under sail.

Attend me, ancient ones,

Share your courage with me

As I share my life for your memory.

On we sail. Never alone! Never alone!

"Mal'laaaam!" came the shout at the chant's end and fear and fierceness assembled a tighter bond between these men and boys; among these innocents. Above circled an Albatross, his feathers dulled and shredded by the storms of his own encounters. His sharp, quick call saluted the figures upon the swaying decks below him and then he swung away into the wind and sought his own destiny. He left behind those strange creatures on their chunks of driftwood to follow their own shadows upon the sea.

Tor'na, his appetite for advantage whetted by yesterday's triumph, looked eagerly seaward as the two sails grew larger in his view. His experienced eye counted two large double-canoes, their still-hidden hulls described by those big triangular sails held out on their long booms. Vessels from a nearby Set, of this he was sure, and bound here with more relief supplies. More booty for ransom and perhaps crewmen too, should any have the sense to join his crusade. Just in time had the call of; "Sail ho!" come from one of his mast-lookouts.

He had been about to call to those cringing people ashore to send out their headman and other representatives to parlay with him; rather, to take orders from him! There was plenty of time for that and now this impending confrontation, and conquest, would double those people's respect for "Tor'na the Magnificent"! But the potential problem of two more canoes under his control niggled at him. He barely had enough men, and silly boys, to sail the three he already had. Oh well, he could always hold them here and negotiate for their transfer of ownership at a good profit. His arrogance had been offended by the reluctance of Sea-Hewn to join his band before though. Damned fools! Fear would bring them, this was his certain fantasy and no one could dissuade him of it, least of all his beloved partner, Mal'atan.

And that other disquiet was peering over his mind's shoulder again too. What was Mal'atan up to? His canoe, 'Wa'Pa'La'Ta', rather the one Tor'na had presented him with, was now totally occupied by Mal'atan's personally chosen group of adherents, and a silly lot they were too, he thought. Not a good sailor among them and none with the *sight*. But Tor'na turned from these worries and called out orders. The thick hawser would not be used again this time. It had proved to be heavy and unwieldy and took too much time to undo. And these canoes would be approaching much more quickly than had the bamboo rafts. No, this time it would be an aggressive frontal attack, timed to catch them as they dropped sail and proceeded under paddle-power.

He must leave crews to protect the rafts too, in case those cowards ashore gained enough courage to try to retake them. That meant he would have only his canoe, 'Flee-the-Land', and one other. 'Yes, that's all right', he muttered to himself.. He would assign three of his best seamen to Mal'atan's canoe to help with handling it and leave the rest to guard the rafts. Two of his best, meaning nastiest, fighters, he would keep aboard 'Flee-the-Land' with him. They would take over one of those approaching canoes, then proceed on to the second to assist Mal'atan and his crew, if need be. At least they were good at killing, even if they couldn't sail well.

The wind was shifting now and both his and the arriving vessels would have beam winds but Tor'na knew that his expertise was greater and before those fools out there knew what was happening, he would be upon them. "There will be blood again today, comrades!" he called across to Mal'atan's vessel. Cheers and growls of intent called back to him across the swell at the mouth of the little harbor. Ashore, those words brought added fear and loathing to the blockaded people on Bal'lal-Set. Among them, Enno Stone-Master secreted his fathers returned gift, a long-bladed knife, beneath his wrap. The man's quiet demeanor and phlegmatic personality were undergoing a sudden change. But all they could do now was watch. Renewed horror seemed inevitable. Those two unsuspecting vessels were too far away for any warning to reach them. Women wept quietly while some muttered their frustration at their men's haplessness. Misery and depression lay cloud-like over the beaches and headlands of the devastated island. But another brutal destiny was unfolding there on the rolling seas beyond the bay.

Tor'na set forth from the harbor's mouth with only two canoes this time, so sure of his conquest was he. The third vessel lay unmanned, secured to the side of one of the captured bamboo rafts. The late-morning wind was increasing, an along-shore breeze playing steadily abeam of Tor'na's two attacking canoes. Perfect! He shouted across to Mal'atan to approach the second canoe on its right side. He would approach the lead canoe on its left side and they would clamp the two hapless vessels between them. It would not even be necessary to throw grappling lines. These foolish, tradition-bound Mal'lam would soon drop sail and take to their paddles and enter the bay at a leisurely pace. Then he would strike!

His two canoes raised sail and utilized the wind only long enough to get under way and achieve good speed. Then, in four minutes, down came the big, woven triangles again. Too much speed might carry him beyond those vessels and his crewmen, who should be getting ready to board and attack, would have to apply paddles as brakes. No, he would wait for his quarry to come to him. Eagerly, impatiently, the livid twin scars on his face beneath the painted patterns glistening with sweat, Tor'na waited for the rapidly closing distance to bring his victims foreward. His paddlers grunted with the strain of gaining speed again as the quickening breeze was slowing them too much. Tor'na stamped one foot loudly on the bamboo deck in time with their strokes, urging them, commanding them. Soon those canoes would drop sail.

Yes. But too soon! Stupid idiots! The lead canoe was now taking to its paddles, a small crew it was too. This will be easier than he'd thought. The second canoe was quickly drawing abreast of the first, sails pulling at peak efficiency. What clumsy seamanship! Too late did Tor'na Sea-Master, 'Tor'na the Magnificent', he of the *sight,* recognize what these strange maneuvers spelled. Too late did his natural wariness puncture his arrogance. He now recognized the second canoe as belonging to the Sht'ah Lee Sea-Master, Orn'ta. Suddenly the mats, which surely must have covered the relief supplies on the bridging decks, were thrown back and from beneath them scrambled many men and likewise, from the hulls beside the decks rose more who had lain hidden. And, oh, by the Gods! They were not only armed but they carried flat, oblong shields. Shields! Why had he not ever thought to employ such defenses?

Those shields of tightly woven bamboo lathes covered in sharkskin were painted in the abstract symbols with which he was vaguely familiar. The old Mal'lam warrior's symbols; grotesque faces with long fangs; circles and dashes of bright colors and the spears and other weapons carried there were likewise painted in bright colors. It was he who was ambushed this time! For a moment Tor'na thought that he might escape this danger but before he could order the sail to be raised to drive them beyond the approaching canoes, a shout came from that lead vessel; 'Grapples!" and four men aboard Al'malan's canoe ran forward with a pair of hastily contrived assemblages of stone and sharpened bamboo staves, tightly bound together.

With mighty heaves they threw them outward toward 'Flee-the-Land', both landing accurately on the bridging deck and biting into the bamboo decking with a '*clunk*' of finality. Powerful arms gathered to haul on the attached lines and they were quickly attached to strong points on Al'malan's canoe. Trapped between the two surging enemies, Tor'na's canoe was brought to a halt, swaying back and forth as the hulls clashed loudly. The sail on Orn'ta's canoe was dropped quickly and untidily. No time for that now. One grapple was tossed successfully from 'Hoosh'im'wa' and now all three canoes lurched and jerked, lashings and timbers squealing and groaning in protest. Hull banged against hull and then they were joined!

One of those throwing a grapple had been A'lan Sea-Hewn. He stood for a moment, his eyes burning their hatred toward that powerful, painted, costumed figure of Tor'na. In that moment their eyes locked and with a roar of rage the mad Sea-Master launched a spear he had picked up from the pile on the deck. So swiftly did that spear fly that A'lan had time only to duck sideways. His friend Shen'ham, always beside him, reflexively held out his shield to protect

A'lan. The spear glanced and twisted away, the butt of it landing a stinging blow on A'lan's face, on that vulnerable scar, as it spun harmlessly away overboard.

By now, sling stones were raining upon the deck of Tor'na's canoe, Shen'ham among the marksmen, and those stones were directed first at the men scrabbling desperately to tear loose the grapples. Bones broke, nerve and muscle were paralyzed and one man lost an eye to a ferocious blow from one of Shen'ham's missiles. Tor'na's oversight, the neglect of that obvious element of combat, the shield, now was costing him dearly. A'lan had screamed, momentarily overcome with the pain of that glancing blow. But now *he* overcame the agony. He reached down for an edged weapon and shield, aided by his friend's lift under one arm, regained his feet and screamed in rage.

That scream carried him in a mighty leap over the three feet of distance between the two contending vessels. He landed upright and ready to attack, just as behind him came Al'malan's cry of, "Board them!" The Itin Seaman, Ch'am'lo, was right behind A'lan, followed instantly by twelve others, spears, clubs and shields in play. One of the first to follow was the fifteen year old Sea-Hewn, Tal'tan, but his landing left him momentarily off balance, a moment which allowed Tor'na to lunge forward and thrust a spear into the boy's chest. The first of the Mal'lam warriors had fallen! A'lan's advance was blocked now by one of Tor'na's old crew-mates, a man of power and viciousness. That man swung an edged weapon at the lad but A'lan's reflexes deflected the blow with his shield. Just as he tried to counter with his own weapon, the Itin warrior, Ch'am'lo, leapt clear over A'lan's crouched figure and brought down his own club onto that man's head.

All about the bridging deck of Tor'na's beloved canoe, 'Flee-the-Land', his men fell dead or badly wounded. Most, to their credit, fought bravely but numbers and ferocity now overwhelmed them. Realizing his situation, Tor'na chanced a glance away from his foes to where Mal'atan's vessel should be closing to join the battle. His eyes widened in disbelief! "No!" he screamed. "No! Come back!" Mal'atan's canoe was altering sail and coursing away to the east. His beloved serpent had finally struck!

And at that moment too, Al'malan took two steps forward, his heavy spear raised above his shoulder, the warning of that old man, Tal'ma, flashing through his mind. With a heave of such force that the spear penetrated Tor'na's chest and thrust a hand's width out his back, Al'malan fulfilled the vision's destiny. Tor'na had kept his eyes fixed on the betrayal, the fleeing friend, the only loved-one, even as he died. Blood gushed from the mad Sea-Master's mouth as he fell backward into the arms of his men.

Until this moment Tor'na had remained uninjured, lashing out repeatedly and causing wounds, his ferocity encouraging his henchmen. But now his death brought a moment of hushed silence, heavy breathing and some groans the only sounds. Whatever that horrible awareness had been which so distracted Tor'na, the effect of it combined with their leader's death conspired to collapse their resistance. "No! No!" one shouted, looking back at Mal'atan's cowardly retreat. This distraction lasted only moments and then the Mal'lam warriors brought the battle to an end.

None of Tor'na's men remained alive on his canoe. 'Flee-the-Land' lay rolling in concert with its captor's grasp, the beautifully constructed and maintained vessel leaking blood into the sea like a dead whale. The Mal'lam warriors stood on that gory deck, bodies drenched in sweat and splashed with blood, their weapons now hanging listlessly or tossed aside. In those last moments some enemies had raised futile hands in supplication. No quarter was given. A'lan Sea-Hewn had been one to bring his weapon down in a killing blow onto a defenseless head. That act would remain as an insidious infection within his psyche and would one day mark the course of his future as a 'Master of the Sea-Hewn'. No Mal'lam warrior that day escaped scarring. Killing demands an accounting! That accounting would come, if only on one's deathbed.

Panic reigned aboard the captured raft where Tor'na's remaining henchmen stood watching the approach of the three canoes. The 'Wa'Bo'ton' and the 'Hoosh'im'wa' still held captive between them Tor'na's 'Flee the Land'. On its deck lay the sprawled bodies in their red and white wraps, most now more red than white. By the time that abandoned element of Tor'na's force discovered that it was truly isolated, the man in charge, one of the madman's oldest, most trusted followers, totally lost control over his duty. He stood gazing at the approaching canoe on which he had so faithfully served these many years.

Then he looked eastward to where Mal'atan and his crew were fleeing. That vessel was still being badly handled but the following wind was allowing it rapid progress regardless. The dissolution of his world showed in the man's face, in his stance and in the dimming of life's light in his eyes. He had already accepted his death. "What should we do!" came the desperate questions, the others of this crew frantic for some guidance. Then another shout and he turned to see the harbor creased with the slim wakes of two dozen small bamboo rafts and one small fishing canoe. From behind the three big slowly moving canoes came scudding that brave little vessel which had been towed to near the island and let loose beyond the headland.

The men of Bal'lat were in full rage; the spur had been their women's silent insistence, an onslaught of meaningful stares and conversely, the refusal to look their men in the eye. They had to do something! When the engagement beyond the headlands had begun, a wave of resolve solidified and without direction, men ran in twos and threes to those fragile little craft and launched their own attack. Enno Stone-Master was among them, one of three men to launch the one small canoe. Because of its quality, it was the first craft to reach the side of the big raft, quickly followed by the little bamboo fishing platforms.

The years of sublimated anger at minor frustrations coupled with the recent outrages against defenseless people had freed a ferocious resolve in that mellow, quiet craftsman. Now as the little canoe came to the big raft's side, he freed the sharp weapon from the waist of his wrap and prepared to board the big craft. Within his mind rang the last words he had exchanged with his father on that cold, rainy morning: "Have no fear, my boy!" his father had said, "Your spirit shines like the products of your hands. You are a man of quality! Here, my son. Take this with you. I will have no more need of it." And he had handed back to Enno the gift he had made to Tal'ma many years before. "It shall defend your memory, father!" was all he could reply.

And nor did this man of quiet consideration now throw his anger upon the enemy recklessly. Two spears hurtled toward him and the two men with him but each was fended off with a paddle or an arm. Shouts and curses assailed the big raft upon which Tor'na's remnant force ran back and forth in utter panic, their former brutal omnipotence evaporating with each breath. Closer came the flimsy craft until they crowded and bumped all around those high sides. Men who the day before had committed willful murder now whimpered and pleaded and sobbed for mercy. Men now began climbing the bamboo sides of the raft, almost unopposed. Enno's blade claimed the first victim, plunged deep into the chest of a man on his knees, begging for mercy. Around him swept the terrible vengeance in which ten men died and not one of the avengers was even bruised. Enno fell to his knees and vomited. Terror works in both directions. Leadership, or its lack, most often makes the difference. Yet no leader could be identified among the Bal'lat-an for all seemed to proceed upon some spontaneous ideal: revenge for an outrage with no known parallel. A cleansing force of brutal quickness was at work here. The remnants would be disposed of that very day.

A great fire had been laid around that canoe which had carried so much terror among the islands of the Mal'lam. 'Flee-the-Land' was to become a funeral pyre. It had been pulled high up on the sands of the little harbor and all available fuel had been collected, enough to set alight the timbers of the canoe itself. The bodies of Tor'na and his murderous band were laid inside the hulls along with the combustible materials. Fish oil and coconut oil were liberally splashed over the whole and the fire was lit. Then all the islanders and those off-islanders who had come to their rescue moved well away uphill to watch from a distance. The wind was offshore now so they would be spared the stench of this mass cremation but all simply wanted to be as far away as possible.

Al'malan, Orn'ta and a number of other warriors sat with the Itin, Ch'am'lo. The shade of the big tree was welcome as the late day was surprisingly hot for this time of year. The effort involved in moving that big canoe also added to their discomfort. All were near exhaustion. As well, all were grieving for their lost comrades; the young Sea-Hewn, Tal'tan and the Sea-Hewn cousin of Orn'ta, Or'ma'lat, both slain in the battle. Since not enough firewood could be found at short notice on the day of their deaths for their own ritual incineration, the Mal'lam survivors held a short ceremony celebrating their lives. The people of Bal'lat buried them in the sand.

That afternoon or the next day, after the canoes had left in pursuit of Mal'atan, these traumatized people would perform that last rite themselves. Another Sht'ah Lee man would remain on the island, too badly wounded to join his shipmates. "I think we can be sure that Mal'atan will return to Sh'ul'shem, brothers." said Al'malan. Most nodded agreement. Orn'ta, frustrated that he had missed the opportunity to apprehend his despised nephew on this day, replied, "I agree. And I think we must pursue him as quickly as possible. We don't know how many supporters of him and Tor'na may still be there at the 'Thieves Market'. Surely some would have remained to keep the people of Sha'lan'la-Set under their control."

The pyre was now blazing awesomely. Another time would have seen celebration of the dead. Silence accompanied this cremation. Al'malan's sensitive ears searched his surroundings and heard only silent grieving and unresolved hatred. Others would hear only the roar of the fire and the wind in the trees around them; most would still be deaf to the truth of their own thoughts. The warriors would seek a good night's sleep, a few succeeding, for tomorrow's dawn must see their departure. One lone figure still stood on the hillside, looking down on the dying fire. Gusts of wind stirred bursts of sparks, which rose like final comments into the night sky. Finally Ch'am'lo turned and strode inland to seek some rest. "What have we done? What have *I* begun?" he asked himself. Others that night would also ask the *Earth Mother* to forgive them.

Chapter Twenty - Return to Sha'lan'la

The canoe had been named 'The Canoe that Severs' by its new master, a blatant allusion to Mal'atan's goal of raiding and pillaging. This night the canoe carried a cargo of fear and frustration. Half reefed, the big sail flapped and struggled to hold the wind. Still the vessel wallowed clumsily through the cold squalls. The awkward, obsequious Joom'ta softly sang a love-song of his own composition while Mal'atan sulked. They huddled together beneath the small thatched shelter in the center of the bridging deck; the night's chill biting deep.

The emotionless Shul'am sat cross-legged at the hut's entrance, a club resting on one leg, one hand clutching a knife. Danger lurked aboard tonight in the form of three resentful men who believed themselves captives of treachery; unwilling partners in an awful betrayal. It was the three men whom Tor'na had ordered aboard 'Wa'Pa'La'Ta' to bolster its compliment of Sea-Hewn who muttered most dangerously. Their curses were recorded in the mind of the young Feather-Hewn, Jan'shor who, with his falcon, had sat shivering just beyond the huddled group of rebels. As silently as the glide of a bird he rose and carried the news to Mala'tan, whispering in his ear. Then he returned to his former position. The falcon peeped and squealed nervously, perched on the sharkskin-covered arm of its master. "Shush my sweet! Shush. Soon you will have food."

The night wore on with bitter endlessness. Helmsmen struggled with their steering paddles as ill-tuned sails flapped and swung in the blackness. Mal'atan slept little, for sleep brought dreams and the scarred, fearful face of Tor'na Sea-Master haunted all those dreams. That man was un-lamented by Mal'atan but his ghostly presence remained. "Tomorrow!" he thought, "Tomorrow is critical! I must consolidate. And I must start now!" And then in the darkness a toothy, shark-like grin spread over his face, the drying paint flaking around his mouth.

Joom'ta, himself still awake, stirred in response to his master's unseen emotion. "Joom'ta!" Mal'atan whispered and that man leaned close to hear. A hushed order, an encouraging pat on the shoulder and Joom'ta was sent on his mission. Pausing at the hut's entrance he knelt and repeated the words of his master quietly to Sh'ul'am. The thin, cold-faced lad eased off his damp rain cape and rose with his weapons at the ready. Without stealth or sign of their intention, the two moved forward on the deck, one on each side. In the hulls below lay eight men trying to sleep as spray and rain swept over their lightly covered bodies.

A distant flash of lightning lent a momentary illumination and the two saw their compatriot, Jan'shor, sitting at the base of the mast. His falcon was now perched on the top of a basket, hunched against the rain. A knowing smile flashed over his usually placid features and he rose to join them. A smile, a whisper, a nod toward that place in the starboard hull where the three suspects lay sleeping and the three assassins moved quickly and brutally. The consolidation had begun.

After much discussion in the early morning hour, the leaders of the Bal'lat-an agreed to accept the remaining canoe of Tor'na's fleet. No one there actually knew what it had been named, for no one survived except Mal'atan and his crew who would know. Orn'ta was sure that it had once belonged to a Sea-Hewn whom he knew but vaguely and it had carried the name, 'Wa' Pan'Lat", 'The Flying Canoe'. So, 'Wa'Pan'Lat' it was and so Al'malan did formally rename it in a short ceremony held on the beach, far from the still-smoldering, still smelly funeral pyre.

As he stood in his Sea-Master's regalia, chanting the age-old ceremonial words, few could suspect the disquiet within him. He bore himself with his usual unassuming dignity; however, inside he held many doubts. Too many mistakes had been made, oversights which could have spelled disaster for his men. He had completely lost track of Mal'atan's vessel's movements when they boarded 'Flee-the- Land. That could have been disastrous had Mal'atan joined the battle. His deep sense of responsibility gnawed at him. And the escape of Mal'atan was a heavy burden which must be attended to, and soon. As soon as this nuisance ceremony was done with. Tor'na's former possession, quite possibly gained with bloodshed, had been ritually doused with boiling seawater and prayers of healing banished any residue of that previous owner's spite.

It's new, and maybe original name was chanted at length. Its new master would have to be chosen from among other visiting Sea-Hewn since no qualified man lived on Bal'lat-Set. The two big bamboo rafts likewise would be claimed by the Clan which had sent them, the few survivors too few to sail even one. What had been intended as an early morning departure in pursuit of Mal'atan was extended by ritual and traditional requisites to a late afternoon sailing. With them would sail Enno Stone-Master, insistent that he should take part in the expected fight. Al'malan again commented on the change in the man.

The memory of that first battle still sickened Enno though and so he told the Sea-Master, "We do what we must, Al'malan-an. You know that. I see in your eyes the same shadows of horror as you must see in mine. Let's not speak more of it."

With a thin smile and a nod he turned away and hefted a heavy basket containing his tools and some stone. His young Sea-Hewn nephew, Faldo-in, carried his other belongings and they clambered aboard Al'malan's canoe. Enno felt himself to be a bit of flotsam on a raging sea of uncertainty. He was surely not alone in his bereavement, for all around him men and women looked within themselves for some sign of certainty. Some delayed that search and focused on the present. The present demands were enough to think upon.

Sea-Master Al'malan suffered no doubt now. He had shed his chagrin and, listening to his inner acuity, discerned the course ahead as clearly as any chart could do. A'lan Sea-Hewn likewise suffered no doubts. His blooding, in which he had taken two lives, had lit a determined fire within him. He stood now in his usual position aboard a canoe when not needed elsewhere, in one or other bow of the twin-hulled vessel. And again his exceptional vision pursued that same red streak beneath the sea's surface. It pointed to Sha'lan'la-Set. As if they too could read that glow which pointed to the southeast, two seabirds flew in tandem along its track and disappeared into the evening's gloom.

'The Canoe that Severs' was paddled quietly onto the beach at the foot of the village, 'Sh'ul'shem', 'The Thieves Market', in the dark before dawn. It arrived with three fewer crew than when it had fled that disastrous battle three days ago. None aboard though, spoke of their demise for Mal'atan simply refused to recognize that they had ever existed aboard his canoe. They died with Tor'na in the treacherous ambush which had destroyed all but Mal'atan's courageous crew! That was the story. In the hours before landing, Mal'atan had ordered his crew to don clean wraps and paint themselves anew in that deceased leader's manner. He himself applied his own garish patterns and mounted his fish jaws in his flowing hair. Sh'ul'am was to perform a recce of the village and report back before sunrise. His slight figure disappeared quickly into the scrub lining the sand dunes above the beach.

Sh'ul'am, dodging among the trees which skirted the village, kept to the downwind side and managed to avoid alerting any of the many dogs which inhabited the village. He came at last to the tiny hut which the old woman, Mar'tah the cook, lived in so that she could rise early and begin her day's duties. Yes, she was awake, just returning to her mean little shack from a patch of nearby scrub. "Mar'tah!" the whisper came and she stopped and peered into the gloom of the underbrush. "Mar'tah, here!" the voice familiar in its cold harshness yet welcome to her ears. "Mar'tah, it's Sh'ul'am!"

The woman looked intently around her. Satisfied that no one was stirring yet, she hobbled painfully on her arthritic feet toward the clump of bananas where the only person here for whom she felt any kinship waited. She held her hands out into the shadows and her heart leapt with gladness when two warm hands grasped hers and drew her into the cover of the banana leaves. In hushed tones she answered his queries about the status of the village in his absence, where certain individuals were likely to be at dawn, etc. Ten minutes later, with a muttered thanks and a squeeze of her hands, which he had continued to hold, he faded soundlessly away, leaving her alone but filled with pleasure at her 'grandson's' return. It was time to prepare breakfast for her masters. She had not been told of Tor'na's death nor anything else of what was happening. She didn't ask. To see Sh'ul'am safely returned was enough.

Mal'atan and his band marched into the now-stirring village in full regalia and with weapons at the ready. Their leader's harangue had imbued them with a new confidence, a sense of purpose. They strode with the arrogance of conquerors, a pretense which became, to them, a reality growing with each step. Mal'atan was a master of subtlety and persuasion of almost mesmeric quality. Yet on this morning he harbored doubts; fear that someone had tried to usurp Tor'na's, and consequently, *his* suzerainty. He was prepared for a fight.

Sh'ul'am's recce had revealed that there had been dissention among those left behind to control the island. There were abuses and fights but no deaths. The old woman had said that the very night before had seen a drunken orgy and that many, most importantly the most dangerous, would awake with sore heads and dulled wits. How like Mal'atan's first, shared conquest of the 'Thieves Market'. Their return was met with much barking and howling by the village dogs. Then tosseled, fretting heads began to emerge from doorways and soon the whole settlement was abuzz with anxious curiosity.

By midday the whole of the island knew that 'Tor'na the Magnificent' was dead and that 'Mal'atan the Beautiful' was in charge. "Mal'atan the Beautiful'?! Was there no limit to this young man's arrogance? And two men had died violently today! They had been Tor'na's recruits who had asked too many questions and protested too much. Sh'ul'am's weapon had dispatched them. Rumors abounded and gossip flew in all directions. The most persistent rumor was that Mal'atan was planning on leaving this island, sailing away to a more likely site where he could establish a new realm. There was hope in that! One rumor, which found few ears willing to pass it on, was to originate that day too; that 'Mal'atan the Beautiful' had not long to live.

No one yet dared to speak publicly of that. That rumor was the product of one with *the sight*. His message had been, "The man shall fall to one who now licks his feet!" So great was his confidence now that even had Mal'atan heard the prediction, he would have laughed it away and forgotten it. It probably would not have alerted him to danger for his nemesis was not a plotter nor a person with ambition and would not have been within his scope of suspicion.

Joom'ta was first of Mal'atan's retainers to rise next morning and after his own toilette returned to the quarters of his loved-one with a cup of hot tea, brought from the fire of that old woman, Mar'tah the cook. He gently roused Mal'atan who, on waking, moaned and rubbed his jaw. He was suffering from an emerging wisdom tooth and Mal'atan did not enjoy his own pain. Sh'ul'am, sleeping on a mat at the foot of the big bed, roused too and sat up, Mal'atan's moan a spur to his protective instincts, which seemed to embrace his master only. Even Joom'ta could never be sure of his younger mate's real loyalty to anyone else. Joom'ta offered the tea to Mal'atan, a wide smile of subservience on his features. Mal'atan took a sip and then spat the liquid with a grimace of disgust and roared, "Yaaaagh! Vile!" The spat liquid sprayed half on the bed covers and half on Joom'ta and in that man's eyes flashed a momentary outrage.

Immediately his demeanor assumed a motherly concern. The next few minutes passed with Mal'Atan throwing a tantrum; moaning and weeping dry tears of pain, his retainers standing by helplessly, confused and unsure of what to do. Never had they seen their beloved Mal'atan so distressed. Joom'ta roused enough courage to lay gentle hands on the flailing arms and speak soothingly and passionately; "Dear one. Please, what can we do?" Mal'atan swept the consoling hands aside with a violent gesture and whirled and ducked through the building's entry with such violence that he tore the drape half-off the doorway. Glowering bitterly he stamped to the base of a large tree nearby and ripped aside his loincloth and urinated on its trunk, his manner one of intentional insult to the innocent tree.

Finished relieving himself, Mal'atan turned and walked back toward the building. His face was somewhat softer now, the pressure on his bladder gone and those first twinges in his jaw subsiding. "Would you like some breakfast now, Mal'atan-an?" Joom'ta asked hopefully, his shoulders as ever stooped in a manner of servility. Mal'atan threw him a reproachful glance and brushed past him, saying, "What? Idiot! With my mouth in terrible pain?" Mal'atan passed through the doorway and disappeared inside. Joom'ta, in his weaker moments suspecting that not even his sweet master truly loved him, glanced at his only other hope. Sh'ul'am, who stood guard near the entrance, ignored Joom'ta's plight, if indeed he recognized it. Only those expressionless eyes answered his desperate question. With a last hope Joom'ta asked, "Shall I bring some food, Sh'ul'am-an dear?" As if finally reckoning his mate's distress, Sh'ul'am replied, even attempting a slight smile, with a nod. Then he went inside the hut to better keep guard over 'Mal'atan the Beautiful'.

Joom'ta and Sh'ul'am sat together near the doorway cleaning the last of their breakfast from their banana-leaf plates when Mal'atan called from within. "I'd like something to eat now!" The two looked at each other and Sh'ul'am's nearly blank eyes managed to convey an order upon Joom'ta. Mal'atan's call had contained a distant and commanding order. Joom'ta took the empty banana leaves and wadded them up for disposal and rose with ungainly speed and strode toward the cook's shack. He returned moments later empty-handed and with a face struck with sheepish reluctance, leaned through the doorway of the hut and announced to Mal'atan that, "The old woman is warming your breakfast. She's adding something special too!" he added desperately, waiting to cringe at a negative, even abusive answer. It was thankfully mild. "Alright Joom'ta. I'll wait!"

Joom'ta withdrew with a sigh of relief but within his heart something was giving way; something to do with blind loyalty and unrequited love. A cold chill of determination began mentioning the unmentionable, the unsustainable. Impatient minutes had passed but finally Mar'tah had organized the serving of steaming food. Breadfuit and honey, coconut sauce and as a special treat, fried prawns with salt. She laid a leaf of banana over the serving to keep the heat in and the flies away and hobbled toward the master's abode. Her eager eyes searched the pale, expressionless face of the guardian as she approached but his eyes avoided hers. Even that look-away was a confirmation to her.

Mal'atan meanwhile, his tooth no longer aching but his appetite replacing that sense of urgency which his warped psyche demanded at all times, swung his legs out of the bed and stamped toward the doorway. "Where is my breakfast?!" he shouted. That shout ran like a hot ember through Joom'ta's nervous system but still following a life-long tendency, he quickly rose to pull back the drape over the doorway. Sh'ul'am had given a quick nod of assent to the old woman to proceed in delivering the still-steaming food. Her arrival on limping legs coincided with Mal'atan's rush through the doorway. The two collided; the old woman knocked off-balance and shoved backward by the force, the hot food splashing forward onto Mal'atan's legs and feet. He leapt backward into the doorway and issued a howl of pain, his arms flung upward above his head.

Joom'ta, momentarily caught between a strange urge to laugh and the compulsion to reach out to his master, only sat slack-jawed and looked up at the evolving drama. Sh'ul'am reached down to assist the old woman. Mal'atan, his legs and feet twitching with pain, jumped forward and kicked at but missed the old woman. Snarling with rage he reached down to rub his scalded legs and screamed at Sh'ul'am, "Kill her! Kill her! Kill the stinking old hag!" Joom'ta sat paralyzed with fear; fear that the screaming within himself would explode upon this suddenly mad love-of-his-life! Sh'ul'am rose above the stricken old woman, his tooth-edged weapon gripped in both hands, looking down at her wide, terrified eyes. Mal'atan's right arm whipped outward and slapped a stinging blow to Sh'ul'am's back. "Kill herrrrr!" he screamed!

Eyes that had not for years betrayed emotion bored into the old woman's and something sparkled and rippled between them. Sh'ul'am took one step backward and raised his weapon to shoulder height, never taking his gaze from Mar'tah's wide, horror-stricken face. Mal'atan saw that horror and smirked in triumph, straightening now to watch his order carried out. Sh'ul'am leaned back upon his heel, tensed his body powerfully and swung the vicious weapon around and behind him, slicing Mal'atan's chest at heart level, rending rib and muscle and artery. It was a blow meant to kill, and kill it did! Mal'atan's eyes widened in amazement and then life flickered and died in them. He fell backward in a spray of blood which layered the seated Joom'ta in gore. That man's mouth opened in a shrieking scream and his hands flapped in crazy denial. Others around had seen the blow and now many others were drawn by Joom'ta's screams. A crowd quickly gathered.

Sh'ul'am looked down at his master's motionless body, his eyes again dead of expression. Then he turned away as if dismissing the existence of the man, their previous relationship and his death. He bent and helped the old woman to her feet and together, she repeatedly glancing up at his face, passed through the murmuring crowd and slowly walked off into the scrublands. No one followed, Sh'ul'am's bloody weapon still hanging from his hand a reminder of the lad's madness. Still the screams of Joom'ta continued, growing ever louder, emptying his soul of its life-long grief. The sound sent chills through everyone within hearing. Suddenly the screams stopped. A killing blow to halt a spreading madness simply signaled the beginning of another form of mind-out-of-control!

And so began a day of murder as factions fought each other for power until no one group remained with enough numbers or will to prevail. Then into this vacuum of madness crept, and then rushed, the indigenous people of the island of Sha'lan'la. Fishermen and farmers and trades people wreaked a bloody revenge for the two years of virtual slavery which they had endured. Survivors of the internecine struggle between Tor'na's and Mal'atan's devotees that day soon discarded their identifying red and white wraps as the vengeance of the locals began. All those previously identified with the 'Magnificent' or the' Beautiful' cowered in whatever brush-covered hole they could find, red and white garments lying strewn at random around the 'Thieves Market'. Just before total darkness Sh'ul'am and his 'grandmother' were found. The young man presented himself with weapon in hand but didn't raise it. The two died with her protestations of innocence falling on ears deafened to reason. It was done! A falcon, trailing its leather thong of captivity, rose and flew into the night, abandoning the body of its young master. Free at last!

Research Notes: Impressions and General Observations

Subject: Tina Pua'lani Kaiser, Kaua'i, Spring 1973

Spring at last! Boy, what a wet winter it has been here on the Windward side of Kaua'i. I understand now why the old Hawai'ian populations where so large on the Leeward side of all the islands. They liked the sunshine too! Oh yes! a P.S, in case you missed the rumors: Jiro and I ran away and got married (yes, to each other!) on Maui last Saturday. I'm so happy, I'm finding it hard to concentrate on this entry. Jiro! Stop that!)

Tina has received her grades from her first year at high school. I'm as proud as if I were her Mother! I bought her a brand new Sony tape recorder for all her good work. And her Godfather, Jiro, bought her a brand new Sony tape recorder for all her good work. Anyway, she has two back-ups in case mine craps out.

Recordings:

I have spent very many hours transcribing a series of long recordings of Tina's story. These sessions were more difficult than the earlier ones because Tina more often speaks in Mal'lam, directly relaying what her *contacts on the other side* are saying to her. I have to stop her from time to time and say - "In English please!" She just giggles and starts over again. I'm quite worried! I'm beginning to learn some Mal'lam! And according to Bill Snakenborg such a language doesn't exist.

Speaking of the Snakenborgs; Clarice Snakenborg and I have become fast friends, *seestahs* even! Amazingly, to me at least, Clarice is a *channeler!* Yep, wife of a scientist (who I think is becoming a begrudging believer), and a teacher and a researcher. She is Chinese-Hawai'ian-Portugese-English and Hawai'i born and bred. Now *that's* an Hawai'ian! Over the winter I have gone over to Honolulu a half-dozen times for professional duties (it's called, sitting-in-the-sun- at-Wai'kiki-and-getting-the-mold-off-one's-skin, therapy) I stay with Clarice and her family now when I go over. Bill and I have our little discussions and try to avoid mention of the Mal'lam language. But he has referred those earlier recordings on to a colleague in Indonesia. We'll see what comes of that.

Tina, because she is part Hawai'ian and a good student, has been offered a scholarship to the Kameha'meha School in Honolulu. This is a great opportunity for her. We all have most of the summer to think it over. I'm included in the thinking process because, in the Fall, my grant runs out and I'll be attending classes at the University again. If Tina is in Honolulu too, we can at least spend some time together on this project. Tina, bless her, also considers it *her* project.

We now have about a week together here in Hanalei before I have to attend a seminar on the Mainland. My *little seestah* is such an angel. Rather than going camping and swimming and whatever with her new friends from school, she's nagging me to sit down and do some more recording. O.K. One more time before we take a holiday, Tina! Which recorder do you want to use?

Chapter Twenty One - The Urgent Months

'Wa'Bo'ton' and 'Hoosh'im'wa' approached the island of Sha'lan'la from the east, the side of its main port where the 'Thieves Market' lay. The setting sun glared their vision as the now-blooded crews sought some view as to what might be happening there. Columns of smoke became visible as clouds covered the lower western sky for a few minutes in a dark-grey backdrop. Al'malan Sea-Master turned his inner ear to the land. What he heard was disturbing. He turned away and walked to the port side of his vessel and called loudly across to Orn'ta, master of the other canoe: "Ornta Sea-Master! I feel we should heave-to for the night! Bad things are occurring over there now but I feel we cannot be of any true assistance. It will be full dark if we land and we will be totally without guidance as to what is happening!" A few moments passed and then the reply came, "Yes brother! I concur. Dawn will be soon enough. Let us set lights so that we can maneuver for the night and come together again at just before dawn!" Settled! A final wave from Al'malan in the gathering gloom and the two vessel's crews relaxed into the routine of standing offshore until morning. Only Orn'ta, his hands still clasping and un-clasping, that scrawny neck their goal, really felt reluctance. The rest of those men had had enough of battle and killing and dying. Tomorrow was soon enough!

Tomorrow rose with high wind from the northeast, allowing the two canoes to make a hasty run ashore. The fires of the night before had burned out and the low clouds and cold wind made for a gloomy arrival. Few people seemed to have noticed the landing of the vessels but when word spread as the crews struggled to beach their canoes, suddenly many people began to arrive. Some few ran down to assist with the hauling-out but most villagers stood looking on suspiciously. Al'malan could still hear those murmurs of disturbed minds, the signs of which others began to see on the faces gathering around. Suspicion had turned to curiosity and three men who had once been the village Elders came forward to speak with the Clan Sea-Masters. Orn'ta knew one of the men quite well and began questioning him. It was soon apparent that the newly proven warriors would not be needed. Orn'ta at last could stop clenching his fists and imagining Mal'atan's neck within them. Al'malan sensed his relief and put an arm around his friend's shoulder. "It appears that we can put aside our warrior's weapons and get on with living now. By the *Earth Mother's* smile, we can go home!"

And home they went, on the lowering tide that afternoon. The wind had shifted more northerly and was increasing, a reef having to be taken in the big sails. But it would be a voyage of considerable stress and bother and the two big canoes returned to Sht'ah'Lee-Set nearly four weeks after leaving. Violent storms had forced them to run for shelter on two occasions and to lie ahull in raging seas for three days. Blown far off course, it was the keen sight of the young Sea-Hewn, A'lan, which guided them unerringly back toward their Clan island. Orn'ta's eyes were much less cognizant of those sub-sea lights which had for so long guided him across these seas. The acceptance of this lessening of his powers of observation both saddened and pacified him. His decision to remain while the adventurers sailed into the unknown was further strengthened and supported by this occurrence. But he grumbled loudly, making sure all would know of his chagrin, his reluctance to accept this inevitability. But once back on shore, his loving young wife hugged him with renewed ardor. He would remain her man now; no Sea-Hewn's wanderlust could take him away from her.

No Sea-Hewn aboard the warrior's canoes had ever experienced a more dangerous voyage. The vessels were battered and barely sea-worthy, as were the crews. When one morning's rising sun glistened on the snow-capped peak of Volan-Votu, a cheer of thanks rang between the canoes. Home! It was the canoe, 'Wa' Bo'ton', it's Master standing far out in the bow of the port hull, that came first onto the sands of Dolphin Bay. It was his sorry duty to call loudly to his people, gathered excitedly, expectantly, rushing forward to help with the landing, that there was terrible news! Two of their young men had been killed in the battle with Tor'na; another had been badly wounded and left behind to recover among the Bal'lat-an.

Worse again was that one man had been lost overboard in those terrible seas on the way home. Two other crewmen had been badly hurt in the storms. Healing hands reached up to the decks of the arriving canoes and carefully lifted down the injured. Wailing rose from the beach as word of those dead spread among the gathered throng. But, for most, this welcome arrival brought unspeakable relief. Upon the upper slopes of the beach stood two women and a young child; one the grandmother, the other the prospective wife who held little Sahn'ta tightly to her chest, his arm pointing down to the sea where the boy's father stood so tall and proud in the bow of that canoe. Another, Lana'ma Leaf-

Plait, likewise wiped away tears to better see her son, A'lan, as he alighted from the vessel.

Near her stood her good friend, Shen'ha, Shen'ham's mother, her face streaked with tears of gladness. There he was! So big now, as if he had grown to manhood in these few weeks. But his emanations worried her. He was wounded where no spear or knife could penetrate. With a quick glance to her friend she turned and raced downhill to embrace her son who still stood in the surf, helping with the unloading. Lana'ma quickly followed and they joined a joyful onslaught onto the black sands. Cries of greeting, of pleas for more information about the missing, of general thanksgiving, made the scene almost one of chaos.

But it was not quite that. The Clan Sht'ah'ha had turned a corner of its existence. The past was irrevocably withdrawn now; too much had been lost in the past two and a half years. Only the now and the future remained to the majority of the Mal'lam. Only those relative few among them clung to a past which could never be other than wishful thinking. Ja'eel, ex-wife of the Sea-Master Al'malan, stood well back and beyond the crowds, her heart filled with loathing and disgust for what she was seeing. A quick glance brought her son, Sahn'ta, into her view but her gaze quickly dismissed his presence and moved along to judge the whole scene. Here was potential, she thought! Masses of people with their emotions exposed, their hearts vulnerable. She must think on this.

Along with the joyousness of those not now grieving was a growing awareness that something about these men and boys now disembarking was changed. It was in their eyes. A look none of them had ever seen before. Though Lana'ma hugged and kissed her son and he returned her affection, she no longer held a boy. Something had altered him forever. His mate, Shen'ham, stood slightly embarrassed as his mother held him at arms length, studying his strong features. She inspected the still-infected gash on his thigh; it would need her skills. Then she kissed him again and resigned herself to now being the mother to the man.

To Sh'tana's delight, Al'malan, as quickly as he could, relinquished his responsibilities on the beach and ran quickly uphill to his son and his lover. No pretense of dignity or position restrained his whoop of joy as he picked up her and the child she held and swung them around, all the while kissing and hugging them both. His father and mother soon joined them and lost themselves in the rapture of reunited love. Another who observed this arrival from a distance, unwilling to intrude on familial emotion just yet, was the big Woodsman, Joha'lan. He stood leaning against a tree trunk, which nearly hid his big frame and cast his own special sensitivity down toward where all those returned warriors were interacting so vibrantly with their people. His woman, Sha'lat-Leaf-Mistress, had briefly gone to welcome the man who was ostensibly her son-in-law, and now came to join Joha'lan in his semi-hidden location. She took one of his big arms strongly in her own, squeezed, and said; "Now it begins, eh?"

"Yes, my love!" he replied, drawing her to him, "Now it begins in earnest. I feel that they are seasoned like good wood; tough but pliable, with scars and cracks which time and love will bring to a brilliant finish. They are ready!" Sha'lat urged him forward now to join in the greetings. He had dear friends who now needed his council and the comfort of his growing wisdom. Only she realized the depth of this wisdom fully: another had an insight approximating her own.

A half-day's journey away, alone but unafraid, the slight girl sat beneath the great tree, her eyes closed but her mind filled with sight and sound. Tremors of joy and sadness vibrated up from the ground beneath her and she smiled and sighed with relief. They were home! And among those returned she felt the strong vibrations of three to whom she was most sensitive. She could almost see their faces; A'lan so much older, so serious, that scar's meaning inching deeper into his being; Al'malan, his power so increased; and Shen'ham, dear, funny, gentle Shen'ham … with blood on his hands and agony in his heart! "Oh dear one! Don't mourn your Fate! Be brave, sweet one. You've done what must be done."

The girl placed her hands flat upon the cool earth and into her palms rose messages readable only by one such as she was becoming. Tina-Earth-Plait opened her eyes on a darkening forest, sighed deeply with satisfaction and lithely jumped up and trotted to her campsite. Hungry! Start the fire! Oh, those taro fritters and spicy herbs lovingly formed and patted flat between preserving leaves by her mother! The evening's chill within the damp forest urged her hands to rapidly rub hardwood against the softwood from her fire-kit. Moments later, blowing softly but urgently into the fibrous peelings and pitch-wood shavings, she was laying a growing fire which cast a crackling and joyful light as it blossomed.

Nearby in the quiescent undergrowth sang the trill of that unseen night bird, an echo of the Vesa'tan's presence. Tina felt complete and fulfilled. Her day's meditations and communing with the land and all which grew upon it, had removed the doubts and vague fears which had pursued her here two days before. Tina wrapped the layered *tapa* cloth blanket around her shoulders and stared into the light of the fire, the fritters now beginning to bubble and steam on the thin, stone cook plate over the fire. Tomorrow would see her return to her people and share their continuing joy in the return of the warriors. Warriors? Never had she heard that word applied to the sailors and landsmen of her Clan except in the tales about the ancestors. Bloodshed in mindless violence had intruded and it would stain her people for ... who knew how long? Too soon to know and besides, she was ravenous!

Shen'ha extinguished the fish-oil lamp and pulled the blanket more tightly around her. She sat gazing at the still form of her son. His description of the voyage was told, not with boyish enthusiasm but with the weary objectivity of a world-saddened traveler. Knowing him as she did she realized that much of his despondency would quickly pass away. He was too bright and too determined in his own quiet way not to recover that admirable buoyancy of spirit. But still she worried. Taking another's life, even in such extreme circumstances, must have been a terrible burden to one so young and so sensitive. She must speak of this with his friend, A'lan.

Dear A'lan! He too seemed so changed; yet he seemed less remorseful, less wounded by their ordeal. The sign of great power was already upon the boy - rather, the young man! Many had so remarked and by all accounts he had been ferocious in battle. Some said like a madman! How fortunate that when they had arrived at Sha'lan'la-Set, no further battle was necessary. Mal'atan and his henchmen had all been slain. And that was worrying too. Some had said that those local people had appeared somehow brutalized themselves, suspicious and with an underlying aura of violence; hard-eyed and vicious.

Yes, these were indeed bad times! The convulsing earth, the spewing eruptions, has unleashed some terrible disease of the spirit. Is it a disease, as some have suggested? Some poison? Perhaps it *is* time that the Mal'lam *do* leave these islands and find a new home. A peaceful home. Shen'ha sighed again and wiped a hand across her eyes as if to dispel a painful vision. She bent over her sleeping son and tucked the blankets around his shoulders. He stirred and rose on one elbow, startled and alert. "What? Oh, mother! It's you."

She whispered, "I'm sorry, Shen-an. Forgive me. Go back to sleep." and she quickly added, "All is well, my son!" His smile, barely discernable in the darkness, brought a wave of renewed hope to her and she rested a hand briefly on his shoulder as she had done since he was a child. "Goodnight mother." he mumbled and was soon asleep again. Shen'aha now went to her own bed, acknowledged the spirits of the world and the Great Earth Mother and soon drifted away to dream of happier days. Han, the slow-witted, epileptic boy whom Shen'ha had adopted as a surrogate son, rolled over and muttered in his sleep upon his mat in the far corner of the hut. Devoted to both her and Shen'ham, his presence had brought her solace during her son's absence. And in her healing presence the boy had suffered fewer and less severe seizures of late. The night outside welcomed the wan, cold light of an old moon rising and the Clan Sh'tah'ha slept, some with sorrow in their hearts but all, in peace.

Al'malan, Orn'ta Sea-Master and a number of senior Sea-Hewn had sat for most of the morning with Canoe-Master Joha'lan, discussing the progress on the six new hulls. The work for the rest of the winter was planned. And it had been a wet and windy winter so far, colder than most could recall and those with the *Weather-sight* pronounced more of the same to come. The rain-swollen streams and flooding rivers had delayed the harvesting of certain timbers required in the construction process. Crews were even now struggling back toward the coast with the hard, straight logs of Folo'ab; these would be the cross-arms which would wed the two hulls of each vessel. And Talat'ab bark; rolls of the stripped fiber would be soaked in seawater and then plaited into immensely strong rope.

Dozens of men too old to join the mountain harvesting sat under wide, thatched shelters, rolling coconut fiber into cordage and rope. They laid the tough fibers from the husk of the coconuts across their thighs and with the palms of their hands rolled the growing strings back and forth. No old man had any hairs left on his thighs after a day of this work, jokes abounding about their smooth, baby-like skin. Certain other trees, multi-branched and of soft wood, were marked with ribbons of *tapa*. In the spring, as the sap rose, their sticky resin would be tapped, boiled and applied as glue and sealant for the hull planks.

Even now the straight, golden-grained timber of P'sa'ab was being split with careful wedging and painstakingly adzed to a perfect thickness as planks. These flexible lengths would be lashed ingeniously, edge-to-edge, to build the sides of the canoes to nearly head-height. Effort was being concentrated upon those two great logs which would become Wa'Ran'tar, Al'malan Sea-Master's vessel. Already the Sea-Master was experimenting with the revolutionary new sail system, in smaller scale and under the tutelage of Ch'am'lo. The results were proving more than satisfactory.

In the cold highland quarries Stone-Hewn huddled beneath makeshift shelters, grouped around warming fires, shaping the adze and axe blades of shiny obsidian and a tough, grey, local stone nearly as valuable as that volcanic glass. Not as sharp when broken, it nevertheless could be ground to a fine edge. Unlike obsidian, which could not be ground but had to be chipped to a new and often inferior edge, this grey stone was becoming the favored tool-stone of the wood workers. Hundreds of such tools were being consumed on this mammoth project. Only the finest work was rendered by the Wood-Masters, Joha'lan supreme among them, utilizing that special grade of obsidian from Bal'lat-Set.

Enno Stone-Master was a very busy man. He had a group of seventy men working with him. His task was to provide those special tools for the special skills of the Wood-Masters. But the formerly quiet man of phlegmatic demeanor now chatted amiably as he worked. He even told a joke now and then. It had already been decided by the Councils that this man would accompany the voyagers. He worked hard to tutor the most promising of the younger men, determined to leave behind a wealth of talent and experience that could carry on this important work.

When the three new canoes and their two older, smaller escorts left for the unknown, many more canoes must be built here on Sht'ah Lee; for even should the explorers not return, a new fleet would eventually follow in their unknown wake. The Elders, Hewn and Plait, had begun a quiet assessment of their people; individuals were discussed in the context of the needs of the voyage. Already the Sea-Hewn grey heads had short-listed the Sea-Masters and the senior Sea-Hewn and even now three of the youngest Sea-Hewn had been unanimously chosen. The other crafts were still under discussion for the most part. It had been agreed that no pregnant woman, no child less than nine years old and no one with a disabling physical impairment would be included.

Already too, painful separations were being anticipated, not least by the leader of the expedition, Al'malan Sea-Master. His beloved son, Sahn'ta, must remain behind and now such a mother and son bond had grown between him and Sh'tana Leaf-Plait that he feared the parting day doubly. Sh'tana may also be pregnant. Al'malan must leave his loves behind. But that was all yet to come, a day of mixed joys and sorrows, still far away. The Clan Sh'tah'ha had much to occupy their busy hands and to focus their minds upon in the present.

So heavy and persistent had the winter rains been that considerable havoc fell upon the intricate system of weirs and channels and viaducts which provided summer irrigation for the crops and orchards. At times even the Sea-Hewn and busy Woodsmen were called from their work to rescue flooded dikes and crumbling stonework. Without a large harvest this coming season, there would be inadequate provisions for the voyage. Not even the most eager young adventurer could contemplate a journey into the unknown seas without proper victuals. Winter had fallen even more heavily upon the Mal'lam's northern islands.

Although for the most part quiescent for some months, the volcanoes continued to writhe and rumble deep in their molten hearts while above, especially cold winds and storms lashed the frantic islanders. Heavy snowfalls deepened upon the mightier peaks, creating a new potential horror for the islands. Flash floods and mudslides of immense proportions would inundate the streams and rivers and valleys. Flood and minor earth collapse had been shaping these islands for eons but now was introduced a combination of elements never before experienced by humans here. With the spring came a period of clear skies and hot sun. Quite naturally, snowmelt would occur and streams would fill with water and some spring flooding would occur.

Unnaturally though, this year saw the minor explosions of a half-dozen volcanoes throughout the islands, occasioning great clouds of dust which found their way to fall upon the deep snowfields. The dark-grey dust drew in the sun's heat. Snow and ice rapidly melted, coursing down the hillsides in great volumes which overwhelmed the streambeds, riverbeds and all the man-made irrigation channels. Sodden soil gave way under gravity's insistence and chased the flowing waters downhill. Thousands of tons of mud overwhelmed the natural drainage fields and the glutinous mass ran heedlessly down onto the Mal'lam farms and villages. Earth tremors further weakened the compromised, saturated soils.

Within two weeks, two of the remaining occupied islands in the north had been made uninhabitable. Farmlands were buried, bamboo groves but scarred wreckage on the hillsides. Whole villages were buried. But for the timely warnings of the *sighted*, those villagers would all have been buried too. As it was, one village of reed gatherers chose to ignore the protestations of their own gifted *seers.* All seventy souls perished.

Surely these events were awful enough? Oh, no! The very earth seemed determined to dislodge its peaceful occupants and if it could not drown or crush or bury them … it would starve them out!

The prevailing winds which blew from the northeast to the southwest over this once-beautiful archipelago now conspired with the loosened bowels of the volcanoes to lay upon the islands the final, irresistible disaster! Near the northern end of the central group of islands burst the mightiest eruption yet, a conflagration of such magnitude and duration that it would end all hope of further habitation by the Mal'lam, save those far to the south upon Sh'tah Lee-Set. On Sh'tah Lee, the young Earth-*seer*, Tina-un-plait, awoke in the quiet hours before dawn and screamed! Her scream was an echo of the tortured shout from the earth's crust some six hundred miles to the north, in that hollow center of a recently active volcano.

That volcano had, with its most recent convulsions, weakened its very walls until but a few feet of fractured stone formed a precarious dam against the cold seawater beyond. The lava plug at the volcano's base had been eroded by the seething, surging magma until, with a horrendous blast, it surrendered and sundered and gave passage to the liquid fire below. At a speed near that of the sound it made, this furious fountain of gas and molten rock shot upward through the mountain's throat and vomited its blast into the night sky.

As the first voluminous gout shot skyward, the force of its passage shattered the last desperate semblance of integrity of the seaward wall. When the gaseous lava reached its apogee it fell back upon itself to gather for another, more powerful escape upward. The fragile barrier collapsed and thousands upon thousands of tons of cold seawater poured through the rift and down the gullet of that incurable inflammation. Instantly upon contact with the magma, the seawater became steam and that steam, under pressure from the weight of the descending sea built to a pressure of thousands of tons per square foot. When the stasis between weight and pressure, a function of no more than three seconds, was succeeded by the hellish power of the steam, there followed a blast of such magnitude that it carried away the whole of the island.

Having once given birth to its island child, it now carried it away in an instant. The seismic shock raced through the earth's crust at incredible speed. On the islands near and far, men and women, and a young girl, awoke in horror. The unimaginable force of this phenomenon instantly recruited the ocean to its drama. Seismic waves, moving at a speed of over four hundred miles per hour, rushed outward. These emanations passed beneath vessels at sea with hardly a noticeable bump but on encountering land beneath the surface, they began to throw up huge surface waves which grew and grew until they finally plunged upon shoreline and reef and cliff and land-living things with awesome devastation.

On some islands the waves rushed inland for a mile or more, crushing and drowning nearly all life before them. On other Set, the side away from the approach of the great waves hardly noticed the catastrophic events. The convulsion of subterranean forces continued for hours and waves continued to arrive in ever diminishing height and destructiveness. The loss of life to the Mal'lam was enormous! Yet as horrific as this cost was, the final accounting was yet to be read. Their loved ones taken from them, their only means of escape, the canoes and rafts, crushed and broken in the harbors, they could only seek the solace of the one thing remaining to them; the summer crops and the autumn harvest. Only this growing season would feed and succor the survivors in their separate isolations. A seeming conspiracy of unfathomable scope operated against them still.

The terrible volcano which had spawned this catastrophe now changed tactics. No more evident explosions, no earth-shattering, sky-splitting demonstrations. Instead, for months on end it would emit constant clouds of smoke and ash. The conspiracy of earth and sea and weather brought the final blow and ended the peaceful habitation of this archipelago, Sh'tah Lee and its tiny island neighbors the only survivors. Now began the slow, insidious finale to this happy, peaceful people's reign. The normal cycle of fifty-year weather change which had brought the colder and wetter than normal winter also brought the weakening of the trade winds and long intervals of shifting breezes, or no breeze at all.

The gas and ash from the great volcano lay over the whole of the sea and land to its north, east and west, reducing light levels so low that plants withered and perished. Localized rainfalls were often so acidic that they poisoned even the inshore sea-life, the desperate people's only other source of food. Swine and fowl and dogs perished and illness plagued even the most robust survivors. Forays northward by the Clan Sh'ta'ha brought news of the catastrophe and chance contact with a few vessels carrying survivors who sought a final chance at life on that southern island.

Many didn't arrive as weather and sea and improvised craft conspired to defeat their journey to salvation. Those who did reach the sub-tropical shores were welcomed with Mal'lam hospitality and graciousness but the expected flood of refugees did not eventuate. Fewer than one-hundred survivors struggled ashore on Sh'tah Lee-Set after that terrible spring and summer. A further hundred had arrived earlier, nearly as traumatized and seeking some foundation for a continuing life. That strange young woman, Ja'eel, could be seen daily up on the headland to the north of the entrance to Dolphin Bay, counting the arrivals, judging their condition, planning their involvement in her own peculiar destiny.

As autumn neared and the healthy harvest on Sht'ah'Lee was ripening, the second great canoe was nearing completion. As each canoe was made ready for sailing, more craftsmen, all highly experienced by now, were available to concentrate on the next. There was hardly enough room for all the Woodsmen who now focused their skills on that last big vessel, the 'Wa'Maton' and its completion would be accelerated. When the Trade winds began to resume a more obliquely eastern and cooler flow and the nights began to demand another layer of *tapa* cloth blanket, the Elders of the Clan Sh'tah'ha convened a gathering which was to include the newly arrived non-Clan Mal'lam refugees.

Long, carefully contrived formal speeches, with all the requisite pauses for decorum, droned on, preceding the important matters to be discussed. In the center of a twelve foot open area, a small, nearly smokeless fire burned, primarily to illuminate the features of the speakers. Grey-Hewn men assumed the inner circle, some of them unknown to the host Clan but accorded traditional respect. Women Elders made up the second ring and behind them were the various trade Masters. The majority of the younger generations made up a loosely organized ring beyond. They too, listened quietly, reverently.

Accepted now as unquestioned Sea-Master of all the surviving Mal'lam, Al'malan sat among the Grey-Hewn in the inner circle. His attention was focused not on the drone of the formal speech making but on the faces in the firelight around him. So much sadness, so much sorrow and hopelessness was reflected on those illuminated faces that his own heart wept. His inner hearing, that acuteness which allowed him to hear the truth within a voice, was now an almost unsupportable burden. That massed sadness was of nearly physical form, heavy and oppressive and he involuntarily squirmed as he sat, trying to shrug it away. With a great effort he applied his special powers of mind to the most important element now; action! What action must be taken? What course must he, as one of the leaders of his people, now lay out and how must these 'crewmen' respond? As usual with Al'malan, the answer came almost as soon as the question echoed away. He swung his gaze to the old Herb-Hewn master of these ceremonies and nodded a silent request. The bald man with the wrinkled face nodded in return and when the present speaker had finished and had sat down, the old Master-Herbalist signaled assent to Al'malan and held out the speaker's staff to him.

Al'malan rose and gathered his special cloak around him, the feathers which formed the multi-colored patterns on it shone iridescently in the firelight. The heavy stock of fish scales and shells which lay on his chest gleamed and drew all eyes toward his bearded face. He had recently taken to parting his beard in a fork, which gave his lean features a more pronounced impression of determined strength. He held the intricately carved and inlayed staff lightly in his left hand, its heavy butt resting in the sand. "Mal'lam-an!" he began, his position of respect and authority allowing him to use the term of familiarity to all. "We gather in sadness. We gather with hearts heavy with sorrow for our lost brothers and sisters." That reminder caused many to drop their heads or look away into the darkness and sobs were heard anew among the gathering.

He continued with tears in his own eyes but his voice remained clear and calm."But I tell you that we must swallow our sorrow now! We must put aside this great burden and be as children are; so full of life and the *now* and the *future* that our great, shared sadness will melt away like the mountain snows in the summer. Watch, all of you, how our children rise to greet each day. Cast away what is done and cannot be undone!" Al'malan paused and looked among the faces of the northern survivors; non-Clan Mal'lam who's only future now lay with their new acquaintances, brothers and sisters who but a short time ago were mostly strangers. Their attention now was fully on the young Sea-Master, his manner so assured, his mind so obviously clear and centered. Al'malan ended the compulsory pause, a long-held custom of oratory which allowed, encouraged, the speaker to frame his address succinctly. It also inhibited long-winded diatribe and hyperbole. He rested both hands on the staff now, cleared his throat and continued:

"For the time being at least, it seems that the Earth Mother shall spare our beloved Sh'tah'Lee-Set. But when might She unleash Her power again and this haven for our people also suffers earthquake and fire? None with the Earth-*sight* will venture such a prediction, wise and gifted as they may be. The consensus among our *wise-ones*, declared this day, is that we Mal'lam must pursue our goal of seeking new lands for our future generations. I, in conference and agreement with the Sea-Hewn Masters and the Canoe-Master, have determined that the three great canoes must be seaworthy and our Sea-Hewn trained for the voyage to begin in the month of 'Hoosh', when the whales pass to the south. The other two, older canoes also must be prepared. There will be five canoes in all for this first voyage to the southern seas." The finality of this decision was firm in his words.

After months of speculation, when a natural conservativeness, reluctance even, was apparent within the ranks of the Grey-Hewn and Plait, there would be no more hesitation. The Mal'lam must commit themselves. The message elicited smiles of satisfaction and anticipation among the younger Sea-Hewn. Their youthful impatience had been tried continuously, tempered for a time by the need to attend to the refugees. But now a new sense of urgency reigned. Only five more months before Hoosh! "Therefore brothers and sisters, as Master of the canoes I request the whole of our people to contribute to this urgent task. We've little time and much to do. Free your hearts and lend your hands. Stand and join our voyage for it truly begins now, at this moment, upon these very sands."

Al'malan raised the speaker's staff high with his left hand and with the other urged his people to stand and begin the journey with a song. His mild demagoguery had been more than adequate. Young, strong sea legs were first to respond, quickly followed by young and old of all crafts of Hewing and Plaiting. Grey heads rose with measured dignity, some helped to stand by younger hands. A chant began, hand clapping and foot stomping and from somewhere in the shadows two drums began a beat. Then the ancient song of Mal'lam brotherhood rose in volume, an ancient homage to a lineage which included and superseded all Clans. Far into the night the bonfire was kept blazing as the very young played and danced themselves into exhausted sleep. Their elders gathered in groups, discussing how best their skills must be applied to the urgent tasks before them. Dawn was seen in by very few.

Among those few, A'lan Sea-Hewn and his friend Shen'ham sat near the still-glowing coals of the night's big fire, its warmth easing the chill of the morning breeze. Neither spoke. The night had been full of talk and now, before they went to their homes for a few hours of sleep they shared the sunrise and the promise which the future held for them. One other watched the two young men from a distance. Tina-un-plait sat huddled in a blanket near the top of the beach's sandy rise. Her love sang out to both of them. She loved them equally, devotedly, but hers was the love of a woman whose wisdom belied her youth. Through her body vibrated the song which the earth spirits sang; a song of hope and courage, but daunting challenge.

Although many months of planning had already defined the imposing task before them, the Sea-Masters and Hewn of other specialties murmured in awe at the final list of logistics this great endeavor would require. On long knotted strings, in tightly clustered bundles of esoteric meaning were held the count of all the items needed for their survival upon those unknown seas to the south and east. Added to these were all those elements of the future settlement, wherever that would be, which would be required in order for the Mal'Lam to carry on and re-establish their material culture: dried fish, wrapped in near-airtight bundles to feed the approximately ninety souls aboard the voyaging canoes; the It'in had pledged their bounty already. Trade and profit no longer held any meaning in this crisis and besides, one of the canoes would be commanded by one of their own ... Ch'am'lo Sea-Master.

Dried fruits and berries and a fermented paste made from breadfruit would likewise be sealed and stored in the final weeks before sailing. Seeds, plant cuttings and rooted plants; food, fiber and wood in seminal form were to be similarly packed in layers beneath waterproof coverings. Rope and twine, finished and roughed-out stone tools and a limited weight of rough stone; steamed and shaped bamboo utensils and containers, lighter and less fragile than ceramics. On and on the list grew, weight and space limitations demanding the rediscovery of the ancient's packaging and stowage skills. Cherished household items with no immediate use would find no room aboard, nor would pet chickens, pigs or dogs. The animals would be specially chosen at the last moment. The lands they sought would surely be much warmer than Sht'ah Lee and winter comforters of layered *tapa* cloth, stuffed with soft grasses, would be left behind. The deepest sorrow though, would not be for abandoned *things*. Sorrow was welling in the hearts of all by now, for every person knew that a terrible parting loomed, a wrenching separation that would see loved ones left behind, perhaps forever.

Al'malan, the expedition's leader and now recognized warrior-captain, would share this sorrow, for in spite of the intensity of their love and devotion to each other, he and Sh'tana had agreed that she would remain to care for his son. Besides this consideration, her body now held a new life within; a child would be born but a few months after the scheduled departure of the voyagers. Her expertise as a Herb-Mistress would be needed here on Sht'ah Lee. Her mother, Sha'lat, would accompany her now-husband, Joha'lan Canoe-Master.

It was important that he visit whatever new lands they eventually found and assess the timbers and other materials there for future canoe building. That she was one of the Clan's most accomplished healers made their joining a most fortuitous pairing. To most families came such painful realities, such dreaded partings. All braced themselves for that fated day. Another person torn by this impending sorrow was Shen'ham Sea-Hewn. His mother, Shen'ha Herb-Mistress had declared her intention to remain. A sensible decision, for the refugees had in their number few survivors with such advanced knowledge. Also the boy, Han, whom Shen'ham felt was his own vulnerable, sweet brother, would not survive without Shen'ha's loving care.

Those Mal'lam whose birth deformities or weaknesses did not become evident until after infancy were accepted as 'wounded birds', the Mal'lam word, 'Tan'dar'an', imparting a sense of tolerant acceptance and, most often, tender care. Shen'ham's wounded spirit was mending, as his mother had known it would and although his friend, A'lan, had taken on a new, sometimes almost arrogant impatience as an aspect of his character, his patience and understanding always extended to his best friend. A'lan could wring a chuckle, a laugh, then hilarity from Shen'ham, each intake of breath healing and restoring the lad's vision of the world and his place in it. And part of his healing was coming to terms with the almost universal trauma of parting.

Shen'ham   A'lan   Tina-an

Chapter Twenty Two - The Leaving

A strange silence lay upon the settlement on Dolphin Bay this evening. Instead of the noisy revelry of the previous night, the Mal'lam spoke in hushed, solemn tones. On this night before the leaving even lovers acted less in lust than in an almost desperate confirmation of love. The mood infected the children as well; their usual rowdy, early evening games were forgotten as they sat in quiet groups. The dogs of the village, which always accompanied the youngsters in the evenings, lay quietly by, uncomprehending but attentive, expecting something unusual to occur. The late autumn warmth lingered this day, the evening ripening into soft night. The full moon was rising now, ascending from behind Volan Votu's silvery peak. Beyond the circle of village structures, beneath the thin branches of a fruit tree, sat the slight figure of a girl.

Alone in the moonlight which reflected off the *taro* patches, Tina's eyes glittered with tears. Through her body resounded the '*voices*', strong and insistent. The blue stone which hung beneath her neck shone with a light not wholly reflected moonlight. Tina had for days now dreaded this night of goodbyes. But rather than attending friends and family tonight, she had come to this spot with its view to that great mountain, to say farewell to someone. Although she would remain here on Sht'ah Lee, someone else was leaving, but not aboard a canoe. For many minutes she sat listening to the *voices:* words of caution, words of love and eternal support. They rose and fell upon her inner hearing. But it was another voice she waited for ... eagerly, impatiently in her young girl's manner. Her tears betrayed her sadness and apprehension. Then ... *she* was there! Not a disembodied, hushed whisper more felt than heard but a living voice which carried across the glittering paddies to her.

She leaned forward, trying to source the sound. "Tina-an, come to me!" the voice commanded and Tina leaped up and broke into a run which carried her trustingly toward that voice in the brightening moonlight. "This way, girl!" and in response Tina turned up a muddy path toward the voice's urging. As she ran the stone necklace bounced upon her throat and collarbones and she became aware of its brightness now, growing brighter as she closed the distance to the source of the voice. And then she was there. Tina halted abruptly on a small mound over which the path ran and upon the mound stood ... 'The Vesa'tan!'

Forgetting, Tina leaped forward to embrace the old woman's figure, but her outstretched arms met nothing. The figure still stood, just beyond reach.

Before her embarrassment could express itself the Vesa'tan's voice spoke a chiding, chuckling warning; "Silly child! You know you can't touch me with your hands. But, will this do?" The figure never moved but Tina felt a very real touch of lips upon her forehead and the almost-real sensation of leathery arms embracing her. The girl stood enthralled, a grateful smile spreading over her moonlit face. A welcome wave of chills and goose bumps signaled the presence of a Spirit. "Sit, little one. I have things to tell you, things to show you, and not much time." Tina had the impression that this appearance was very difficult, very stressful for the old woman. She still understood but little of the world of the *Spirits* but instinct demanded that she obey and listen carefully. The Vesa'tan might just disappear at any moment!

"The Mal'lam are of two parts now," she began, the words echoing like two people speaking from two different directions. "Those who go beyond our horizon and those who remain here on this island. Yet these two parts will not, must not, diverge. For what is discovered there beyond the sunrise cannot support the discoverers without the growing wisdom of those of you who will remain. And so you see child, separation is but in the mind; a creation of that part of us which refuses to accept the obvious: we are always but of the one! So don't grieve for your loved ones who must leave you. They will return. Know that while their bodies are away from you, never so their *Spirits*. Though sunrise and sunset shall see our people upon different seas and lands, our people are always one. Always! Just as our people strive and suffer and rejoice on their great journey, so too must you who remain strives and suffer and rejoice. For one day, one day still within your youth, Tina-an, our people will rejoin and great healings will occur. Great joy and harmony will result and the Mal'lam will follow a different Destiny. Someone new, they will be, yet made of the old. There will be a continuity for which your own Destiny has declared its part. You, Tina-an Earth-Mistress, will become the binder, the welding force which will call together the two parts of our people and help set them upon a path yet to be described."

Tina's attention was riveted to the words and their meaning. She was aware of neither the rising moon nor the cold, muddy ground beneath her, nor of the sounds from forest or village. And the meaning of The Vesa'tan's words was deposited within the blue stone of Tina's necklace, soaked-up for later perusal and the understanding which escaped her at this moment. It was given her as a repository of word and wisdom which the young girl had yet to divine the keys to. That would come. That much of the '*voice's*' promise she accepted without question. "Your sister, Sht'ana Herb-Mistress, will be in need of you, little one. Much more than just tomorrow's parting and a long separation will cause her sorrow. You must keep yourself available to her and support her."

Tina shuddered with apprehension at the Vesa'tan's words. There was greater meaning there, an undertone which spoke to a prescient receptor within her; another hinted mystery. "I must leave you soon now, my child!" The words rang of a finality, which made Tina stiffen and lean forward, protest on her lips. "No, Tina-an. There is no appeal. I must leave you now and we shall not meet again in this manner. However," and the old woman's voice carried a soft, reassuring laugh, "I shall always be with you, never fear. Our Spirits are eternally joined. Sisters are we. Whenever you need me, whenever you require the assistance of the *Spirit,* only hold your talisman and utter these words; 'Mal'lam'la'so!' Remember that; 'Mal'lam'la'so'. Farewell now, my dear one. It's time to rejoin our people. Farewell!" And her appearance and voice faded into the moon-shadow.

Tina's eyes filled with tears of denial. "No, Vesa'tan! No!" But then she forced her incipient sobs to transform themselves into a rueful smile of gratitude. Grasping the necklace stone in one hand she murmured, "Mal'lam'la'so", and a tiny sparkle of blue answered from the moon-shadow. Quickly gone! Again she uttered the word but knew it was but an indulgence and that she must put away her childish dependency. She squeezed the stone and then let it fall softly onto her throat. "Goodbye, Vesa'tan. Goodbye for now. Thank you." Aware now of the cold, muddy seat upon which she had been resting, Tina rose and stripped off her wrap, went to the nearby stream and rinsed it. She wrung it as dry as her small strength could manage. Rearranging its cold wetness about her hips and giving a loud blow of discomfort, she turned back up the pathway to the dim and distant lights of the village to rejoin those others whom she loved. Tomorrow would be a day of parting and she would need to rest some to prepare for it.

The Mal'lam stirred and rose, even before the cock's crow or songbird's trill. Sleep had been but a stopgap between retiring and rising; some had not slept at all. Al'malan was one of those. He had lain long with Sht'ana's head upon his chest. Later, she had turned in her sleep and cuddled her back against him, his son's soft breathing adding to that night's sad music. He allowed his tears to flow as silently as he could, choking back the insistent sobs of his sorrow. What Destiny was this that allowed such long, painful hours of waiting? What sense could one make of such pain? So strong was the longing for tomorrow and release from this endurance, and then flight from it upon the great quest. How strange it was, this questioning, this struggle between the sweet known and cherished and the fearsome unknown. And, of course, it did supersede the known and cherished certainty of home and loved ones. What extraordinary foolishness we find ourselves involved in! Why does the Earth Mother test us so?

Before his tears allowed entry into self-pity, Al'malan rose quietly from the pallet, gently removing his arm from under his new wife's body, careful not to disturb her deep sleep. Sahn'ta made a small sound and repositioned his little body, as if in response to his father's movement. Moments later he resumed his regular breathing. The Sea-Master drew his wrap about himelf against the early morning's chill air and ducked beneath the draped opening of the little house. He gazed up at the familiar stars of this last night in the lands of his birth. Then he sat with his back against the doorframe and bade his meditation, the practice of a lifetime. His inner, exceptional hearing opened to whatever message the dawn would bless him with. Very long minutes produced but one message; "What you do is right. Proceed!" Not the powerful inspiration he had hoped for. He smiled as he thought; "There is nothing new, you silly man! Your life is aimed as truly as a rocky headland; unyielding, predetermined, unquestionable. Proceed, indeed!" Al'malan wiped the moisture from his face, tears they were, and rose again. This time he strode down to where the five canoes lay, the starlight gleaming on their polished hulls. There was always one more thing for a canoe's Master to check before sailing.

Even as the first dim glow of dawn chased the starlight from the sky the Mal'lam were on the move. Lovers clung to each other on their pallets one last time; children were gently woken; dogs roused and stretched and shook themselves as they heard the sound of human activity. Belatedly, cocks began to crow, officially heralding the new day. High on the black sand beach lay the three huge, new canoes, pride of this tiny fleet of voyagers. Their polished and oiled hulls gleamed with vibrant life in the dawn's rose and yellow flowering. There was 'Wa'Ran'tar', Al'malan's vessel, its stern closest to the waves, first to be launched. 'Wa'Olon', commanded by the Sea-Master Sh'ban'al; 'Wa' Botan', under guidance of the Itin Sea-Master and warrior, Ch'am'lo.

Near them but further along the beach lay two older vessels; smaller double-hulled canoes which had once been among the largest and proudest of the Sht'ah Lee fleet. One was 'Hoosh'im'wa', Orn'ta's pride and joy, which he had so magnanimously contributed to this voyage of discovery. The last of the five was the beautifully decorated Wa'Sa'lat, a canoe which had been donated by an aging Sea-Master of another Clan. Quite new and now rigged with the radical sails of the new fleet, it rested uneasily on its sandy bed, eager to be set free once more and fly on new wings.

But even sitting still upon the shore these vessels projected a proud majesty. The tall masts with their narrow sail panels edged with those curious, curved booms swung gently in response to this morning's undecided wind. All but last minute items, like the animals and personal gear had already been loaded the previous evening. Cages of woven bamboo were now lashed to the decks, ready for the pigs and fowl. The little, curl-tailed, barkless dogs would be lifted aboard last of all.

Overnight, the close friends, A'lan, Shen'ham and Faldo'in had slept aboard 'Wa'Ran'tar'. Actually, they had slept little, their excitement too strong to allow more than a doze or two. The boys and slightly older Sea-Hewn had spent most of the night chatting, hardly able to contain their enthusiasm. 'Hoosh'im'wa', that vessel which Orn'ta had donated to the adventure, would be captained by the one-eyed Sea-Master, Ham'sha. An intense man, some would say humorless, he was nevertheless of great talent. His one eye was still blessed with the Sea-*sight*, the other having been lost to accident. He, of all the Masters, eschewed a last night in a familiar bed and had slept soundly aboard his new vessel. Orn'ta also slept aboard; one last night with his beloved canoe!

The canoe 'Wa'Sa'lat', donated by the Clan-Weron, was ostensibly mastered by the old Seaman, Gra'sha'lon. In reality it was his son, Val'on, who would command it. Gra'sha'lon had been the one who had survived that long-ago voyage to the south which had spurred the hopes and dreams of the young sailors of all Clans. Having been taken seriously ill while aboard that canoe on its return voyage, he had been left on Sht'ah Lee while his shipmates carried on to their home island, anxious to impart the story of their adventure to their Clan. They had never reached their island. It was thought that they had been sunk in a huge typhoon which had struck many of the islands. Only Gra'sha'lon's version of that voyage remained. Unfortunately, his illness while aboard their voyage home prevented him from memorizing the star route on the return. All knew that he would likely pass away on this renewed journey, he more certain than any. His age and infirmity and obvious inability to physically contribute to the management of 'his' vessel was waived in the consideration of the Sea-Hewn Masters. He was like a living talisman; a bringer of good fortune by his presence alone.

As the dawn rose, Volan Votu shook off its attendant cloud and beamed the sun's reflection down upon the gathering Mal'lam. The tall, narrow sail panels shone in response, standing like proud emblems of this people's hopes and courage. Now early morning breezes danced with the long, feathered tell-tales suspended from the mast tips. From outlying settlements and farmsteads, groups of people began making their way seaward to join the throng assembling along the black sand of Dolphin Bay. The full moon was just making its dive into the western sea, leaving the day to an autumn sun still full of warmth. It was going to be a clear and beautiful morning. Sound began to dominate the senses. Mutts began barking excitedly as they chased around human legs, human voices were raised in pitch and volume as excitement grew among them too. A bustle of back and forth movement seemed increasingly chaotic but was in fact a disciplined and orderly progression.

The tide was perfect now for departure and would remain so for only two more hours. All must be loaded and ready and the big canoes underway within that time. So little time! Too little time for every last goodbye, every unspoken sentiment. Regrets would sail with the voyagers and sit with those left behind on the black sands. Regret and sadness, but also joy and exuberance, especially among the young men among the crews. The responsibility of the youngest seamen was much like that of any apprentice; they got the monotonous, mundane work such as seeing to the cleaning chores aboard, and with the fowls and pigs aboard each vessel, that could be onerous; wet the ropes and sails when they sagged and slackened, keep the coals smoldering in the fireboxes, on and on the list went and in between these jobs the Sea-Hewn elders made certain that each day included formal tutelage in the many seamen's skills. And that's when the youngsters would truly excel.

On this morning of departure however, it was all-in for loading and stowing those items of personal gear brought aboard by the non-Sea-Hewn passengers. As well, there were the woven baskets of fodder and feed for the animals and coconuts, both green and ripe. The dogs taken aboard were of the type which could survive handily on a vegetarian diet, and coconut meat was a staple for them, as well as anything else they could get down their throats. Small, compact and very docile, these carefully bred descendants of those barkless dogs which the forebears had sailed with, would again take to the sea. The other mongrel breeds picked up along the way to these islands were too noisy, boisterous and difficult to feed for sea travel.

The pigs, but two aboard each vessel, were young, pregnant sows. They were small yet and also quite docile and happy to feed on anything available. These animals were together in a single cage on the deck, a mesh floor of split bamboo over the well-spaced timbers below allowing for easy cleaning. Two cocks and twelve hens would travel aboard each canoe, similarly housed as the pigs but additionally protected from extremes of weather with screens of woven fiber. The crow of the cocks would add an incongruous but mostly welcome sound on an empty, endless sea, though a few two-legged passengers might complain of these serenades.

As when the Sh'ham-an had fled their home island … was it really but three years ago? … Sea-Hewn and lands-people were severely restricted on what they could bring aboard on the voyage. It amounted to no more than what was required for personal hygiene, protection from rain and spray and cold, some few small items of adornment and, of course, those tools and basic materials of an individual's craft. Enno Stone-Master argued until the last moment to be allowed to bring a larger store of obsidian. With a final shrug of acceptance he lifted up just the two wooden boxes of his tools to the waiting seamen and climbed aboard, following them to make sure all was properly stowed. On each canoe similar small dramas occurred, but soon last minute rushes up the beach to deliver a last kiss, a message nearly forgotten or a last hug for an elderly loved one - the little flotilla was ready to sail. The tide would begin to turn in but half and hour. It was time to launch. It was finally time to say goodbye!

The sun was now halfway up the morning sky, high enough to catch and make glitter the tears which coursed down hundreds of unashamed faces. Mostly men, but many women too, wishing to maintain a last grasp upon those hulls which held their loved ones, strained and pushed and lifted the massive weight of the double hulls until each canoe rode free upon the morning's light swell. Ropes were hauled, paddles wielded with determined strength and one by one, the big canoes preceding, the voyagers separated from their land.

A chant began now, a song whose origin lay in a long-forgotten past. It rose in the throats of the Mal'lam left standing in the surf, upon the sandy beach and out upon the headlands. Out on the bay, from the many small Itin canoes which had made the journey to witness the departure, rang the same song, the accent only slightly different.

"May the Sea-Gods smile upon you, voyagers!

May the Gods of this land not forget you!

Sail for far lands, sail for new lands,

May the Earth Mother bless you all!

May we meet again soon, voyagers,

Carry our love with you, voyagers.

Return to us,

Return to us.

You carry our hearts with you!

The Sea-Hewn were the most fortunate this day, their duties offering them an escape from the emotional intensity which all the others must endure without relief. Quick glances ashore while hauling lines or wielding paddles or steering oars or, as among the young apprentices, trying to look properly busy, too busy to look shoreward, helped keep the tears at bay. Nearly every seaman would leave behind loved ones whose bonding tore at their hearts. As the canoes passed the Itin canoes, those people threw flowers and leaves upon the water, blessings meant to follow the vessels on the receding tide. All were weeping.

Ashore, among the many still standing in the rolling surf, stood one whose heart overflowed not with sorrow or grief but with animosity and unwholesome vengeance. Arrayed in an outlandish fashion of her own design, shells and feathers and colored *tapa*, Ja'eel waded out to thigh depth, carrying a struggling chicken by its neck. Shrieking loudly the incantations dredged up from the depths of her own disturbed mind, the still-beautiful young woman cast curses upon the departing fleet and all aboard it. All around her the Mal'lam stood in wonder at this apparition. Wonder turned to horror as she quickly pulled a long-bladed stone knife from her waistband and with one savage swipe, separated the chicken from its neck. The flapping body foamed the water beside her, its blood spreading around her legs.

Sht'ana Leaf-Plait stood but twenty feet away, little Sahn'ta clutched tightly to her chest, the child still looking out to sea where those big canoes were passing beyond hearing range. Sht'ana's eyes widened in terror as the seemingly mad Ja'eel turned toward her and threw the chicken's head and neck absently in her direction, insult very much intended. Turning once more toward that receding fleet of voyagers Ja'eel screamed one last epithet: "I curse you, Al'malan Sea-Hewn! May we never see your stupid face again. I curse you and the Sea Gods that will swallow you! That I promise you!"

Along with dozens of others within hearing and sight of this performance, Sh'tana stood in the surf and stared unbelieving. She clutched Sahn'ta even tighter to her, causing him to protest, those vibrations of malice now growing around him making him whimper with fright. All around people gaped in disbelief. Ja'eel turned and with a last rude gesture toward the departing canoes, waded ashore, blood still mixing with the innocent seawater in her wake. Ashore she was joined by a small group of women and men who gathered around her. They turned with her and proceeded away up the beach as if formally escorting someone of great importance. Sht'ana's eyes followed the retreat of the mother of the child she held protectively. She looked around her at those nearby, searching for some denial of the fear she felt. Some coming nightmare, some new horror such as these people had but months before rid themselves was again festering here in their midst.

What Sht'ana saw there in those other eyes was a shared prescience. She shuddered again and now her tears of sadness and parting became tears of fear. Sh'tana swung around, the waves now growing higher and wetting both she and the child, looking desperately for some support. She looked to that place high on the sandy slope where her sister, Tina, so often sat alone. That girl's power was growing so greatly, Sht'ana knew, and now she needed her, badly! Yes! Up there! Sh'tana's eyes locked onto that small figure within the crowd. In another instant Tina clutched the talisman around her neck and ran with reckless speed through the crowd and down to where her sister was struggling up out of the surf. Her ears had not heard the offending sound of Ja'eel's voice nor had she seen the offensive, parting gesture but her inner acuity had bade her, "Go to your sister now! She needs you, Tina-an!"

On this morning of hope and sorrow, Tina's task truly began. Contending personalities were now embarked upon a collision course. Neither party understood, even suspected what had begun. One, a willful sensualist who had recently discovered a special ability to persuade weak-spirited individuals to her purposes; the other, a child-woman who was but beginning to understand the powers bequeathed her. Sht'ah Lee-Set was to soon endure a catastrophe of purely human dimension while the earth beneath rested peacefully, benignly, and patiently. The many refugee Mal'lam, forced now to this last bastion of their people's homelands, were wracked with grief and bereavement.

Many among them, in all-too-human a reaction, sought solace and hope in the form of Gods and spirits whose particular, and often frightening qualities had been nearly forgotten. Those generations of peace and harmony had left behind the Gods of vanity … until now! Into this gap which fear had created stepped the warped soul of Ja'eel. Many would eagerly submit to her seductive power. By sunset of that day the tall masts of the canoes had long disappeared from the view of even those who climbed to high vantage points. The voyagers were truly gone now. Not even those sorrowing the most believed that tomorrow's sunrise would reveal them again. Sht'ah Lee-Set must now contend alone with its own adventures, its own dramas.

Research Notes: Impressions and General Observations

Subject: Tina Pua'lani Kaiser, Honolulu, Christmas 1973

Another wonderful year about to change to yet another wonderful year! Jiro and I are very happy together, living in his (our) lovely home up Manoa Valley. Tina has settled in well at Kamehameha School. All the family on Kaua'i are well but they're missing Tina, and maybe even me? The past Summer and Fall have seen a huge amount of recording of text from Tina and I have only just transcribed it. Phew! The story has progressed now to when the Mal'lam finally set sail for the unknown and their first few months on the voyage. A lot of important things were happening back on Sht'ah Lee too. Sometimes Tina's Spirits come across with simultaneous stories and both of us have a job sorting it all out. They have a very different concept of time over there on the 'other side'.

My friend the linguist, Bill Snakenborg, has discovered some similarities to the Mal'lam language. He says he's found words very similar among some of the indigenous people on the islands south of Taiwan. It's still all very tenuous though and he's not about to commit to anything yet. Typical scientist. I guess that makes me a very un-typical scientist, or a bad one! Tina and I and Tutu Kinau are working on a comprehensive recording of the language. Jiro advises us to keep all of this under our hats. Marriage hasn't mellowed him … he's still bossy! But loveable.

Bill Snakenborg and his wife Clarice took us three out sailing with them last week. There was more than just fun involved. Tina had never been out on the sea before and she wanted to see what it was like to be under sail and out of sight of land. We went northwest up the chain of islands to Nihoa and back; four days of great sailing weather and many hours with nothing but the horizon of blue.

Chapter Twenty Three - Becalmed

The mass convergence of the big, black, bulbous-headed Hoosh'dwan began where the sea so often lay in repose. Into this area of hot doldrums came, first, the big males in bachelor pods of from ten to thirty. Then began the arrival of the females and calves and adolescents in even larger groups. The view from sea level was of an horizon-to-horizon parade of rolling, blowing black bodies, sharply curved dorsal fins rigid in salute. Beneath the calm, sun-bright surface the sea rang with clicks and whistles and rumblings as thousands of these Hoosh'dwan vocalized their joyous reunion. The annual convocation of this dolphin species preceded their journey to the cooler, richer waters north of the Equator. They would travel in consort now for weeks. Their eons-old ritual and progression up that liquid highway, guided by an infallible, subliminal imprint would bring them through the many channels which divided that archipelago that was now bent on dramatically reordering itself.

Very different creatures, once native to those tragic islands, now sat in awe and wonderment upon their sun-baked vessels as around them for as far as the eye could see, the waters seethed with black bodies. The mist of those thousands of exhalations filled the air with a not-unpleasant fishy-briny odor. First sighted at dawn, still they came at midday, swimming casually in procession close by and all around the becalmed canoes and still filling the sea to the horizon. It was neither size nor any remarkable individuality which had caused the Mal'lam to consider this species, of all the many whales which traversed their home waters, as unique; it was their numbers!

"Like La'hourn, they are!" a Sea-Hewn would cry, comparing the great schools of squid to the day-long passage of the Hoosh'dwan. And suddenly, as the shadows of the tall masts rode long upon the glassy water, the awe-inspiring phenomenon ended. An almost comical anti-climax occurred when, as the last of the big, black cetaceans disappeared into the haze, a small school of dolphin appeared. Short-bodied and densely spotted they leapt dramatically into the air and spun wildly until splashing down again and submerging. They hurried on past the little stationary fleet of canoes as if late for an appointment with their larger, black cousins.

The disappearance of the cetaceans into the northern seas brought with it a welcome change in the weather. Almost as if that magical, powerful presence was to be replaced with a parting gift from those creatures, a cooling breeze began to blow. For most of eight days the little flotilla and its gasping occupants had endured a terrible becalming. No breath of wind rose, day or night. The long, feather-light tell-tales hung dejectedly from the mast tops while ropes and halyards grew dry and slack. Only at dawn, just before the brutal sun roared up from the parched eastern sky, could the passengers collect the cool dew which lay heavily over every horizontal surface. This was but temporary relief, but relief just the same.

Nor did the flat, blue, inviting sea around them offer any succor in the form of a cooling bath. Large white-tipped pelagic sharks, accompanied by their black and white striped retinues of Pilot Fish, paraded insolently around and between the canoe hulls which had been tethered together to form a slowly shifting, gently swinging little village upon the sea. From dawn to dusk, and surely all night too, these deep-sea raptors cruised with patient malevolence. No Mal'lam dared a plunge to cool their sweating body. Some of the youngsters though, small enough to be quickly swung by their arms, were dipped under the water and then quickly pulled back up. A little bit of excitement to break the monotony!

The long hollow bamboo water containers, as well as the large brown gourds, were being emptied at an alarming rate and the vessel's commanders were forced to impose a strict ration upon their shipmates. With the enervating heat and lack of strenuous exercise which being under way required, even decreased appetites were disappointed when food was rationed too. No one on this voyage had sailed this far south except that one old man, Gra'sho'lon. That long-ago voyage, of which he was ultimately the only survivor, had known kindly winds here near the Equator. They had attended in both directions on that passage.

When the amazing, whale-filled day was ending and the cool northwesterly breeze seemed to lay the canoe's shadows even longer upon the rippling water, hawsers were loosed and each canoe prepared to regain its independent way. "Let us follow the wind for the night, brothers!" Al'malan Voyage-Master shouted across to the Sea-Masters of the other four canoes. Gestures and shouted agreement answered him and the voyagers began preparing for a most welcome run before the strengthening wind. Young Sea-Hewn apprentices scrambled up the masts, containers of seawater in tow to moisten, and subsequently tighten the ropes and sagging sails panels. These had developed puckers and folds in the long days of dryness and were at risk of tearing should a sudden strong gust put too much strain on them.

A'lan Sea-Hewn clung with one arm about the foremast of 'Wa'Ran'tar', Al'malan's personal vessel. His friend, Shen'ham, clung equally precariously to the aft mast. Their job of wetting the sail panels and ropes completed, each was enjoying the invigorating cool breeze and the increasing movement of the vessel beneath them, accentuated by their height above the deck. To the east-southeast, the course their now bounding canoe was headed, a deep mauve and gold light was beginning to dominate that sky. To the west spread the more dramatically hued impending sunset; rose and gold and bright pink upon shades of blue and incipient greens. So near a deathly nothingness had those doldrums seemed. The boy's very hormones were tied to the vigorous movement of these powerful vessels and all the young lads on this voyage felt themselves to be an integral part of them. They watched entranced as their brother-vessels' sails swung to accept the wind.

Each canoe was moving steadily away from the others, creating safe-way between them to accommodate the coming darkness and the increasing possibility of mischance and collision. Fellow apprentices, similarly ensconced upon other vessels and their perilous perches, waved to brother seamen; a brotherhood renewed and strengthened over the rapidly lengthening distances. Cool breeze; perhaps a shower or a squall? Surely a good night's run beneath starlit skies and surely stronger winds and more exciting sailing tomorrow. Sailing forward, ever forward! Then the young Sea-Hewn called greetings to the approaching night and climbed hand over hand down the masts' ladders, back to the decks. Again tonight they would sit with their tutors and scan the moonless sky and along with those older seamen, discover unfamiliar stars as they revealed themselves in the southern heavens. New ones would lay beneath that horizon, of that all were certain. The sharks were left behind now to seek other prey.

That evening's observance of the stars was short-lived. Heavy cloud followed the northwesterly wind. The growing breeze swung southward until it blew strongly from due west. Beneath the surging hulls the sea grew lumpy and confused, eventually sorting its wind-driven swell into the more orderly ranks of white capped waves as squalls began to appear out of the darkness. The clammy heat of the past days was rudely replaced by wind and stinging rain, cold like ice upon bare skin. The light, woven, leaf-fiber shawls of the Sea-Hewn now appeared and those other passengers not involved in the sailing of the big canoes scuttled for cover. The deck shelters were soon crowded with laughing people.

Many Sea-Hewn, their watches coming later in the night, crawled beneath the water-shedding covers in the hulls and lay down to sleep until they were roused for their turn at the steering oars and ropes and lines. A'lan was one of those who scuttled for cover in the starboard hull. He quickly picked up a roll of *tapa* cloth and rubbed his head and face dry, protection against chill which might bring on the neuralgia in his scarred face. Nearly three years had passed since that wounding which had left a glowing scar from the corner of his mouth to below his left ear. Still its sensitivity to cold was undiminished, perhaps even more sensitive now, here upon the sea. But A'lan took great pains to hide his pain. He worried that his elders would find this to be a weakness. He would countenance no threat to his chosen lot in life; his Destiny was to forever sail these unknown seas! Of that he had no doubt.

He prepared to lie down and cover himself with his seaman's quilt; three layers of *tapa* cloth sewn over two layers of soft grass, one layer treated with coconut oil for water resistance. Suddenly, clumsy feet dropped near him and thudded heavily upon the bamboo platform which served as a bunk, deck and storage shelf. "Be careful!" he said loudly, not knowing who it was who had nearly landed on him in the blackness. "Sorry, Sea-Hewn!" came the reply. It was his dear friend Shen'ham and the two exchanged a joking repartee' for some minutes until sleep quieted them both.

Chapter Twenty Four - Land at Last

"Do you see them, Sea-Hewn?" Through chattering teeth A'lan answered, "Yes ... y, y, ... yes!" A'lan's *sight* was growing ever keener. The boisterous, cold night and surging waves could hardly diffuse the tell-tale emanations which flashed beneath the plunging hulls. Their source lay to the southeast and the blue and blue-green shafts of light were spawned by land. And that land was somewhere close! On this late watch, the two hours before dawn, the elder Sea-Hewn had awakened from a dream whose strong afterglow urged him to rise from the cocoon of warmth beneath the covers in one hull and go on deck. He had greeted the younger seaman and the elder watch-master and gone forward to sit near the bows. There they were - those glowing lines of fluorescence which pulsed and wavered but ran ever true. On the other vessels, now widely separated again because of the weather and the night's darkness, other *sighted* Sea-Hewn were also noting the phenomenon. But rather than vision it was hearing which brought the Voyage-Master Al'malan to join his shipmates. He had awakened suddenly from a deep sleep to the sound of roaring surf upon a reef. He leapt from his special sleeping platform in the forward part of the port hull, certain that 'Wa'Ran'tar' was about to run aground. He looked in all directions, frantic to establish where that threatening surf was.

As he moved abeam on the bridging deck to join those faint figures in the bows, he realized that it was his *inner* hearing, not his ears, which had alerted him to this sound. That clarion call subsided as he ducked around the forward mast's boom and hailed his crewmen. Silently he marveled at how his special gift could sometimes be a bloody nuisance! "Greetings, Sea-Hewn. It seems land is not far away!" All those there turned toward him in recognition, some wondering at his perception of this occurrence when he himself did not see the *sea-lights*. Ma'hon'ah informed him that, by consensus, the *sighted* ones aboard had agreed that so vivid were the shafts of light over which their vessel rode that land could not be far off.

"A'lan!" Al'malan called to the lad, "Light two flares and suspend them between the masts. We must call the other Wa to us as soon as possible."

That agreed signal to come close to the Voyage-Master's canoe was seen by many keen eyes within the fleet. Soon one, then another, then a third vessel of the little fleet answered with their own lights; tightly wrapped bundles of fiber soaked in fish oil and stuck onto tall lengths of bamboo served as torches which would individually burn for up to half an hour. Al'malan, noting how distant some of these lights were, determined that from now on, weather permitting, each vessel must burn a torch continuously at night. One canoe's faint light would have been over a mile away. They must all assure that they do not become too widely separated. By daybreak the five double-hulled canoes had returned to formation, Al'malan's 'Wa'Ran'tar' leading the wedge; the new, large canoes, 'Wa'Olon' and 'Wa'Boton' aft and abeam on each side. The two smaller, older vessels, 'Hoosh'im'Wa' and Wa'Sa'lat' brought up the rear, one on each wing.

High on each ship's mast clung a lookout, sharp young eyes searching south and east for signs of land. This early morning the sky was dotted with puffy, fair-weather clouds and no haze lay over the sea. Perfect weather! Then a cry from vessel to vessel, "Birds! Birds to the east!" Sure enough, a scattering of gannets flew toward them, bouncing up and over the swells, wingtips just skimming the water. It was difficult to see them as one looked into the eye-stinging glare of the sun, still low over the sea. "We haven't seen birds in twenty days!" commented one person and the awakening passengers began an excited buzz of speculation.

It was the keen eyes of a young Sea-Hewn aboard 'Wa'Olon' who first raised the next cry; not of an island seen but of a faint greenish glow along the base of a large cloud to the southeast. The long, puffy formation had anchored itself to land and some shallow body of water near it was reflecting its color upon the belly of the white cloud. All eyes strained in unison and fingers pointed at the faint revelation which many landsmen had difficulty in identifying at first. Al'malan signaled a change of course to due southeast. The tall, narrow sail panels were shifted slightly to catch the beam wind and all five vessels turned smartly. Ninety Mal'lam chattered in excited anticipation. Could this be a new home?

To those aboard the canoes who were not avid sailors, the slow approach to land seemed interminable. Later in the morning a series of line-squalls obscured this promised destination causing some to fear it would not reappear when the rain cleared away. Other doubts and fears accompanied the voyagers within the prevailing enthusiasm and excitement. Some few feared that this land would not be found to be suitable and that they would be forced to endure more weeks of cold, wet, seasick misery. Some of the younger Sea-Hewn, among them A'lan, feared that this new land would be *so* suitable that their voyaging would end here; too soon, far too soon!

As the day progressed the squalls continued, allowing only momentary glimpses of their destination. When finally the skies cleared there appeared a looming dark mass filling half the southeastern horizon, its crown of cloud piled high in salute. Orange of a sunset hue lit the towering cloud. It was late afternoon when it became apparent that this was not one large island but at least three separate islands. Two smaller bodies of land lay in the foreground while a mountainous hump rose some way beyond. Showers could be seen falling on its upper slopes so surely there was abundant water there. All the canoes drew closer in consort now, within easy hailing distance. The masters shouted across a professional and dispassionate conference. It was quickly decided that the eager little flotilla would endure one more anxious night at sea. There was not daylight enough left to properly scout this new set of shorelines let alone effect a landing. Disappointment muttered away to resignation and the Mal'lam prepared themselves for the last night at sea on this first leg of their great voyage of discovery.

The cooking fires in their stone-edged beds of sand on the bridging decks glowed and flickered, the smoke drifting away on a now fitful, weakening breeze. The order of sailing for this night was line-astern, 'Wa'Ran'tar' in the lead. Small torches were lit and carried on the sterns of all but the last vessel in order to facilitate an ordered separation between the canoes. A course was set for well offshore that would carry them around to the eastern side of these islands. No one knew if more islands might yet lie further to the south. The moon was nearing its fullness but would descend well before dawn. The darkness before dawn would require alertness as sudden reefs or shoals might block their way. All prayed for a cloudless night with light winds. The large frame of the Canoe-Master Joha'lan threw a long shadow on the hull cover. He stood grasping a shroud as he relieved himself into the sea, gazing at the setting moon, not quite awake yet. He had risen after sleeping soundly next to his beloved Sha'lat. Being Wood-Hewn rather than Sea-Hewn, he was allowed to sleep next to his woman while under way.

Mal'lam custom disallowed sex while on a voyage; for seamen, that is. Landsmen and women were allowed however, but Joha'lan and his wife had decided to share their Sea-Hewn friends' celibacy. Most other non-Sea-Hewn would also. Sex aboard a vessel at sea was thought to weaken the resolve of a sailor, make him less willing to endure those unavoidable hardships of sailing. The voluntary sharing of celibacy, for a reasonable time, was another characteristic of the Mal'lam sense of communal responsibility. It also surely affected the birth rate. Always a pre-dawn riser, this morning was more than special to him. His dreams and half-dreaming states had offered him communications again. As he had matured, these events occurred more often while fully awake. It was *that* sense which had informed him of the death of The Vesa'tan, his great friend. 'Forest Mother', he called her. And could it be that these same demanding, yet comforting emanations were a message from that same dear old woman? All these days and weeks at sea, away from her mountains on Sht'ah Lee? His musings were broken by a fond greeting from the young seaman, Shen'ham. His features were outlined by the fading torchlight.

"Good morning Canoe-Master! This will be a special day!." The lad's sincere enthusiasm brought a joyful laugh from Joha'lan, fully awake now. "May I bring you a cup of tea, Joha'lan-an - it's just fresh? Allowed by tradition, now that he was initiated, *hewn*, the young seaman smiled his question using the familiar suffix, *an*. Close friends and family used this term and life aboard a sailing canoe made everyone a family member. Joha'lan smiled down at the sturdy young man in the dim light and replied, "Yes, Shen'ham, I would like a cup of tea." With that the lad turned and loped off to the fire-box aft of the hut amidships. Joha'lan moved forward onto the bridging deck and approached the other men on watch. There were six men there along with Voyage-Master Al'malan. He had not slept at all that night, never leaving the deck except to fetch his seaman's wrap as this morning's darkness held a chill.

"A good morning brother!" Al'malan said, rising easily from his crouch and laying a hand upon the big man's shoulder. "We've come around the back side of the big island now, Joha'lan. We're sailing back up the northeast side. The wind has shifted to southeast trade, as if it was waiting for us." Shen'ham arrived with the cup of tea for Joha'lan and the Voyage-Master paused to let his friend take a sip of the hot brew. "I have a deep feeling, brother," Al'malan continued, "that these islands will suit. Not end our voyage, but be most agreeable to some of our water-weary passengers."

Joha'lan nodded, his mind divided in its attention, *that sense* still speaking within him. "I … well, I think I know what you mean. I too feel something is, mmmm, special about this place!" He chuckled deeply, then said, "Strange, isn't it? We haven't even really seen these islands and here we are predicting what they'll be like. Maybe we're all just a bit *sea-happy*?" Others in the group chuckled too and then, a call from astern and all heads turned to look back at 'Wa'Olon'.

"Wa'Ran'tar!" hailed the strong voice from that following canoe, "there are lights ashore! Look to your port side and forward!" All the Sea-Hewn and Joha'lan quickly strode to the port side of the bridging deck and searched the dark mass of the looming island away there in the pre-dawn gloom. Yes! There it is! There's another! Two more! A'lan Sea-Hewn was first to voice the obvious. "There are people there. Look! More lights further on to the right. See?" That subliminal humming of awareness grew in Joha'lan's mind but a sudden rising wave of voices around him brought him back to the common consciousness. The sleepy passengers and resting crewmen aboard all five canoes were alerted and the decks were now crowded with eager and excited Mal'lam. Who could those people be? Surely not Mal'lam! Would they be friendly, or like in the old tales of the ancestors, might they be aggressive? The speculation became a loud murmur, a strange sound upon these dawn waters.

Water-shedding covers had been removed from the canoe's hulls and paddlers took their places, ready to begin their powerful strokes to the chant of the chief paddlers. Each vessel had let go the lines to their aft sail panels and allowed them to swing idly to the whim of the morning's steady, easy breeze. The foresails continued their strong pull until they too were let go and the paddlers became the canoe's propulsion, slower but more controllable in these potentially dangerous circumstances. The flotilla was skirting a wide reef, unlike any the Mal'lam had seen before. The crystal clear waters revealed a myriad of colors and brilliant fish in great numbers were seen cruising or darting beneath the hulls. Large sea turtles surfaced briefly here and there, many of them. The Mal'lam were experiencing their first big coral reef. The big island loomed dark green and steep beyond that reef. Coconut palms were seen massed along the island's foreshore. On this morning the swells rolled gently and moderately from the northeast, growing to nearly five feet in height before unfolding in a white explosion upon the oddly colored rocks below.

High above 'Wa'Ran'tar's' decks experienced seamen, one foot jammed onto a rope-wrapped bamboo sling and the other braced against the mast, one arm hooked strongly for security, waved and pointed directions to the steersman below. "Come starboard. Yes, more. No, No! There is a large boulder coming up! Go Port, hard!" Moving well ahead of the rest of the fleet now, Al'malan's responsibility was to see the little fleet safely through this maze of multi-colored boulders and flat pans of strange rock. With the sun behind them it was easier as the depth of water was more clearly judged. But these unfamiliar conditions posed potential trouble for the Mal'lam Sea-Hewn and Al'malan stood tensely near the steersman, looking up at the man at the masthead until his neck ached.

Ghosting along now in a very light breeze, one hour became two and still no adequate breach in the reef could be found. A wide sandy beach lay tantalizingly near but between it and the canoes the surf continued uninterrupted. All the while, eager eyes searched the shore for some sign of the island's inhabitants. Surely they had been seen! Rounding a point of the island, bringing the wind more directly abaft of them and creating a more dangerous potential for grounding should the wind rise ... there they were! There appeared off another long beach a small canoe, moving swiftly seaward beneath a strange, oblong sail. It looked to have but three or four people aboard and it was tacking directly toward the breaking surf ahead of the course of the canoes.

The Mal'lam gazed with excitement and much comment as the little craft skipped easily across the shallows and toward the foaming breakers. Figures were visible moving about the beach. A second, then a third canoe was seen being launched. With paddles flashing wetly in the late morning sun these canoes raised their sails too, which tilted oddly on short masts. Al'malan Voyage-Master ordered a steady course along and well outside that strange reef with its many colors. He was waiting to see what these native canoes would do, all the while calling for reports from his masthead lookouts. What would happen now? The Sea-Master struggled to contain his own excitement among the babble of those around him. "Faldo'in!" he called to the young apprentice, "Bring weapons on deck, quickly! The lad plunged into the already opened locker toward the bow of the port-side hull. He began passing slings, stones, spears and shields up to other crewmen. Best to be prepared for anything, was the thought!

Ashore, amidst a murmuring crowd of short, dark-skinned people stood a taller, brown-hued man with grey hair tied in a knot on each side of his head, reminiscent of the hair style of a Mal'lam Sea-Master. His grey beard was neatly trimmed and braided down the center. Beside him stood another man of similar appearance, but older and apparently blind. Both his eyes were a cloudy grey-blue and his left hand rested on a thin staff. The first man was missing the lower part of his right leg and he too leaned upon a straight shaft of wood but his had a wide crotch which tucked up into his right armpit.

"Who do you think they might be, Faldo-an?" the blind man asked, turning his head searchingly for his friend. "I can't even guess, brother. I've never seen craft like these. The sails seem to be rigid, held stiff by a boom around the outside edge. The three vessels in the lead are huge. I can't quite make out the hulls yet."

An elderly, black-skinned man now joined them and spoke to them in another language. "Do you know these canoes, Fa-do? Are they your people?" and addressing the blind man he said, "They are very big canoes, Mah'tah. And there are many men aboard them." His face, like polished old leather, beamed with excited wonder. The man with the braided beard answered in the black man's language, "No, my friend. These canoes are strange to me." A chill of fear grew within him as the childhood memories of a people called the 'Itoi' came haunting through his memory. "I know who they are, Faldo-an. They are our own people. Believe me!" Faldo Sea-Master looked into the older man's blind eyes and wondered, then remembered.

Out on the reef's edge the husky young black men powered the fragile looking little dugout canoes through the rearing swells toward a wide break in the surf which had only now appeared to the Mal'lam lookouts. Those strange little craft were moving slowly their way, still far off to the left. The islanders' dark skins glistened with spray and sweat as they paddled furiously, assisting the pull of the canted sail on its stumpy mast. With final bursts of strength they fought their way over the last surge of wave and through the gap in the reef. No weapons or hostile intent rode with them, only excitement and innocent wonder!

Other than the two, fairer-skinned castaways who had lived among them for so many years, kind and brotherly men both, these people had never seen a stranger. Now that first and largest of their canoes, with three young men and an elder aboard, had passed through the gap in the reef and was sailing quickly toward those wondrous big vessels. The world of their experience was benignly beautiful and their society a cooperative and peaceful one like the Mal'lam. No word for war or hatred existed in their musical language. They killed only for food. All life was precious to these people whose population was small and growing inexplicably smaller.

The Mal'lam were about to meet a people even more innocent and guileless than themselves! A'lan it was, as usual perched as far out on the bow of one hull as he could get, who first saw the wavy, crystal-blue shimmer beneath that fast-approaching little craft. At first he thought it was a trick of sunlight and reflection. But then an older Sea-Hewn near him said quietly, "Do you see it, young Sea-Hewn?" and A'lan turned to face the man's intense eyes. "Yes. Yes, it's very strange. As if the canoe was floating on light." "Yes!" replied the *sighted* one, "I've seen it twice before. Both times in company with a Hoosh and its baby. It's very strange, yes, but it makes me feel peaceful inside. Quiet and peaceful." He looked deeply into A'lan's questioning eyes. Then he turned and walked back to join those seamen who were holding weapons, ready to repel an attack. He spoke quietly to them and they began to lay their burdens down on the bamboo decking. Al'malan turned and looked at them, started to speak but paused as if listening to something, then turned back without comment to watch the approach of that first canoe.

The dark-skinned elder in the canoe was first to raise an arm in greeting. Al'malan strode across the deck to the starboard side and returned an open-palmed wave as the little craft came even with 'Wa'Ran'tar' on the seaward side. Wide-eyed and smiling, the young crewmen in the canoe scrambled to drop their strange sail, all turning to gesture and wave as they worked. Soon unintelligible words were shouted at the Mal'lam and inadvertent smiles broke out all over the big vessel in response. When the native crewmen paddled their craft to the looming side of the huge canoe, 'Wa'Ran'tar', Mal'lam seamen offered hands and ropes down for them to secure their little dugout. By now the other three small canoes had passed 'Wa'Ran'tar' and were approaching the following big Wa, in line behind their leader. In the spreading excitement, Al'malan had to loudly shout orders over the babble, running astern to send orders to the following canoes of his fleet. There was danger here in the foaming surf of the reef and he ordered the vessels to steer clear and round-out to sea, well beyond any sudden current which might trap them.

It was an hour before the first Mal'lam vessel breached the opening in the reef and sailed toward that inviting white sand beach. It was preceded by three of the little native canoes, the crews singing and waving their paddles in the air between strokes. The Mal'lam arrival had taken on a definite festive quality for all involved. The sun was well past midday when the last of the five voyaging canoes were safely beached high up on the sand. The small islanders showed great enthusiasm in helping move the big hulls, their white teeth shining in constant grins. No one of the different peoples could understand each other, and it didn't seem to matter … gestures were sufficing. And then came the Mal'lam's huge surprise! As the last of the canoes was drawn up and secured, there came two men and a little dark-skinned boy from beneath the shade of some spreading nut trees, such as were native also to Sht'ah Lee.

Enno Stone-Master could not believe what he saw! There he came, stumping as quickly as one leg and a crutch would carry him, strange but so familiar too. Could it be? That man's face was alight with ecstatic joy, his voice screaming out his happiness. Many steps behind him, led by the little boy, was another, older man who was surely also Mal'lam. The child was bouncing and laughing as they came. Enno, standing on the deck of a canoe, helping to unload, slumped to his knees. How could this be? Faldo Sea-Master had disappeared more than fifteen years ago while on a voyage south to Sht'ah Lee. He and his vessel were never heard of again. And yet … yes! By the *Earth Mother*! That was him!

Then that man was surrounded by other Mal'lam, three of whom had known him and their incredulous greeting soon blocked him from Enno's view. One in that group turned and looked toward the canoes and searched the decks with eager eyes, saw Enno and signaled to him to come. Enno regained his feet with tears streaming down his face. The group around the crippled man parted, hands still patting and rubbing his shoulders in warm greeting. Two pointed to where Enno stood. He saw the glow of recognition on Faldo's face as he followed their gestures. With a surge of joy Enno found his strength again and leapt from the edge of the hull and landed running. Alternately they embraced, held each other at arm's length, then embraced again, both men crying and laughing simultaneously. Tal'ma's two remaining sons were reunited again - the wonder of miracles!

Behind them a similar scene of reunion was occurring as the blind man was embraced by a sobbing daughter. She had been but eight years old when this man, Mah'tal, had sailed away with his captain. The little boy, Mah'tal's carer, caught up in the emotion of the moment, hugged both the legs of his dear, blind friend and his daughter, tears in his eyes too. She instinctively included him in her embrace. Others who had known this older Sea-Hewn arrived to join in the joyous greeting.

The sense of strangeness and dislocation which attends any arrival ashore after a long voyage, coupled with the introduction of a strange people and the reincarnation of two of their own people, caused many Mal'lam to consider this day as a surreal dream. Most moved about in a happy daze with a constant grin on their faces; faces which soon began to ache with all the smiling. But no one could stop. Black children, their frizzy hair bleached almost blond by sun and salt water, ran and dodged between adult legs. The few youngsters among the Mal'lam began to make new friends, language little barrier, their utter strangeness drawing them together like opposite poles.

When the animals - pigs-chickens-dogs, were brought ashore there was pandemonium among the native people. These people had no animals. Their protein was solely from the sea and from the seasonal nesting of seabirds. Fear became fascination however. It would not be long before these animals, especially the dogs and pigs, began to disappear. Not into a cooking fire. No, the natives would sit for hours watching the strange antics of these wonderful creatures, often rolling around in hilarity. A little girl ventured to pick up one of the little dogs and received a wet lick on her face. Still she held it to her and from that day it was *her* dog.

The little people of this island, which they called Tara'tor, inhabited only eight of this small archipelago's islands. They called themselves the 'Tarbara'ut'; 'The People', it meant. They were small in number as well as stature. Short but well proportioned, they all had black, kinky hair, except the children. Men and women were nearly the same height and all were athletic and active. The men wore only a slim breechcloth of a coarse fabric similar to *tapa.* The women wore skirts of grass which extended down to their knees. Children mostly went naked.

Their dwellings were little more than thatched, conical huts supported on thin posts with woven pandanus mats as screens, windbreaks and rain shields. Like the Mal'lam, they cooked in earth ovens. However, they ate much of their fish raw. Unlike the Mal'lam though, they were not gardeners. Coconuts, fern shoots, some wild nuts and fruits and small yams, apparently gone wild many generations back, sufficed for their vegetables. Sea turtles were reason for feasts and the shallow sea around the islands abounded in them. That clear, blue-green water also abounded in voracious sharks.

This largest island, Tara'tor, held one of the smaller populations though. Only one passage through the coral reef existed and during storm seasons it could be impassable. It was also obvious that they were strictly an inshore people. Once they would have had to be oceanic sailors, their very presence here proving that. But now their small dugout canoes with their high prows and awkward sails, and no outriggers, revealed a contentment to remain within the sheltered confines of this immense coral reef.

These high, volcanic islands of great age were home enough for these unique people whose origin was a mystery. Even their myths gave no solid clue as to their original homeland. They were a very gregarious folk. If one island group gleaned a large harvest of fish or turtle or perhaps bird's eggs, they would quickly load up their canoes and make off to another island to share their largess with their friends and family there. They might stay for days until all the food was eaten, all the gossip shared and maybe a marriage organized. But how would the sudden incursion of ninety strangers with big appetites affect these peoples' limited economy. Some among both parties were even now considering this impact. But for now, it was time for the Mal'lam to relax and unwind.

By dusk the five canoes were secured and unloaded, all the Mal'lam's possessions stashed neatly back among the coconut palms and covered with matting. The chickens and pigs were corralled into temporary pens, curious Tar'bara'ut already gathering around to watch them. Empty bamboo water containers, many twelve feet long, were taken from the canoes and incorporated in the construction of temporary shelters with coconut frond thatching. Water aplenty flowed down through the beach sands from streams inland. The five Sea-Masters had a busy time overseeing this first day's settlement, Al'malan moving among the groups, chatting, giving encouragement, discussing this coming night's ceremonies with some of those who would organize it. Every landing of canoes upon some foreign shore required a convocation of the leaders and all the crew in order to give proper thanks to the *Earth Mother* and the Sea-Gods for a safe arrival. The Mal'lam's first night on tropical shores would be most exceptional.

Chapter Twenty Five ~ The Castaways' Story

At the convocation of Sea-Hewn that evening, all Mal'lam in attendance, the men seated in their usual half-circles of age and position, it was the long-lost Mal'lam seamen who held everyone's attention. The large bonfire's light illuminated Faldo Sea-Master and his fellow castaway, Mah'tal. *Leis* of white shells were strung around their necks because they were special personages. All could see the resemblance between the two brothers, Faldo and Enno. Enno sat beside his brother, a courtesy of the Sea-Hewn, and the other seaman, Mah'tal, sat with them at the center of the row. Everyone wanted to hear the tale of their disappearance and their survival on this welcoming Set. The obligatory chants and songs of thanksgiving were duly performed with great sincerity and then Al'malan remained standing as all others sat down.

Wearing his regalia as Voyage-Master he turned and addressed the two castaways. "Well, Sea-Hewn. Please tell us your story. Our hearts wait with joy and our ears with curiosity." He then lay the speaker's staff on the sand in front of where they both sat, mindful of their separate infirmities. Faldo's one leg would surely tire before such a tale as was expected could be related. Mah'tal Sea-Hewn looked too frail and tired to remain standing for long either. Both were urged to sit comfortably while speaking. Faldo Sea-Master turned to his blind companion and laid a hand gently on his knee. "I think my brother seaman, Mah'tal, would be better at telling this tale. He sees only what is in his mind, therefore his memory is perhaps clearer and more unadulterated. The richness of sight will surely have compromised my perception of all which has occurred since last we met." Turning to look at his sightless friend he said, "Mah'tal?

Mah'tal smiled somewhat ruefully and replied, "Alright, Faldo-an, I'll do my best." He paused long, in the manner of formal address, his cloudy eyes aimed at the firelight as if some vestige of sight might remain. A dim glow perhaps. Then he began: "The wonderful joy of this day is attended by a profound sadness too, having heard of those terrible events in our homeland. But I will recall to you all that I remember. And Faldo-an, please interject if my memory fails me." He turned sightless eyes toward his left. A quick squeeze on his knee reassured him. He drew himself up into a comfortable, cross-legged position and continued: "We left as we always did, as some of you will recall, with song and speech and ceremony. And some tears too." Surely his thought was for his daughter whom he knew to be sitting back among the shadows, intently listening.

"Our destination was Sht'ah Lee-Set, with three other Set to visit on the way. It was when we had completed our business on Hom'ha-Set, which I have been told has been destroyed by a volcano, that we set sail for Sht'ah Lee. On the morning of the second day out we were overtaken by the most awesome storm from the North any of us had ever witnessed! Our vessel's Master, my brother-of-the-sea, Faldo-an, ordered us to drop sail and secure for the worst. And the worst it was! For two whole days we struggled to survive, our canoe being turned over and broken apart on the afternoon of the second day. The port hull disappeared when we were capsized by one huge wave. Faldo-an and I managed to surface next to each other; Oh, it seemed like minutes! Three other Sea-Hewn succeeded in surfacing and we helped them to momentary safety. Moments later another of our crew surfaced close to us, gasping and struggling and we swam to help him. He had been badly cut on the head and face and he was bleeding terribly! It was a while before we could recognize him; it was young Ch'al Sea-Hewn from Sht'ah Lee, only sixteen years old."

From the background in the crowd came a gasp followed by a low wail of renewed grief. That lad's sister was one of the women among the voyagers. Mah'tal paused in his story out of respect for that sorrow. Then he cleared his throat and continued. "The starboard hull, with much of the deck still attached, bobbed up almost underneath us all. I had the sudden vision of a great whale surfacing. It was frightening, as if we weren't already terrified out of our wits! For the rest of that day and all of a very long night we clung to that hull and the wreckage. Broken bamboos and timber were another danger to us as the waves thrashed them around us with great force. Huge waves washed over us repeatedly all night, one really big one turning the hull upright again. Even though it was filled with water and barely afloat, still we were able to climb inside and find some protection. There had been six of us when darkness fell; only four of us at dawn. Young Ch'al was one of the missing."

Mah'tal then recited the names of the eight lost crewmen and again, moans from the assembled Mal'lam. Mah'tal motioned with an upturned hand and the young black boy, who was nearly always with him serving as his eyes and general help-mate, passed a small gourd of water into his hand. He drank deeply, then again, finally holding the gourd out for the always-smiling boy to retrieve.

"That day the storm passed away from us. Fortunately for us, rainsqualls continued and we were able to collect rainwater. Our supply of drinking water had been torn away as had most of our food. But it was the cold which caused us much suffering that day. We huddled together like four little pigs, trying to keep warm. Only the next day did the clouds retire and the sun come out to slowly reawaken our shaking bodies. One of our companions had become unconscious and we couldn't wake him. He died that night. We gave him a seaman's burial, as best as we could. Finally we bailed the seawater out of the hull and at last could be dry. It took hours and exhausted us."

"Under Faldo Sea-Hewn's direction we rigged an outrigger. We used one of the crossbeams and some lengths of bamboo. There was still a lot of rope floating about so it was quite strong when we finished it. All the paddles were gone but I was able to make a steering oar, of sorts, out of bamboo and a broken hull panel. We had no idea where we were. The sea had never seemed so vast and empty. And then another, smaller storm was upon us and we had another day and night of high winds and rough seas. When finally the skies cleared, the night revealed stars to the south which were unknown to us. We must have been caught in a powerful current to have drifted so far south. We knew that we were far away from Sht'ah Lee. Even the water was now warmer!"

"Dear, old Fan'sha Sea-Hewn, our remaining crew-mate," and here he bowed his head in deep reverence, his gesture repeated all around as an exceptional seaman was remembered, "although a Grey-Hewn, he was strong and vigorous and so skilled that he made for us a sail. Bits of matting he used, sewing them together until we had one strong piece the height of a man and as wide. We rigged it to a stump of boom timber toward the front of the hull. Actually, it looked a bit like these little sails that our friends, the Tarbara'ut use. In a decent breeze we could maintain the speed of a casual walk. Since we were being carried on a southbound current and the wind was nearly always from the northwest, Faldo-an decided that we could only continue on this course. The wind and sea now decided our Fate. No seaman's skill could alter the course the Sea Gods had set us upon."

"Water became a problem again. We had no rain for seven days. Again our Grey-Hewn friend came to the rescue. With a spear of bamboo he caught fish for us everyday. It was their blood and the moisture of their flesh that kept us alive. For eighteen days we journeyed thus, each day the sun beat down hotter than the day before. A line of squalls would appear, tantalizing us, then disappear into nothingness before our tiny speed could take us there. Finally one night it rained so hard that we had to bail the canoe. The rain was both a blessing and a curse because it came with such a rush of wind that it tore our little sail to shreds before we could lower it.

Then we entered a place of strange stillness. For three days we sat and endured a stifling calm, the sea so smooth we felt almost that we could walk upon it. Even the nights were hot and clammy; the stars themselves seemed to project heat. And no fish offered themselves. The water was again running out and we wondered at the waste of bailing after that last rain." Mah'tal paused again while he shifted his body, easing the strain on his back which apparently pained him frequently.

"On the third night a cooling breeze developed but died before dawn. Faldo-an said then that we had no choice; weak and shriveled as we were, we would have to propel ourselves. 'Better to die trying than to die sitting idly!' he declared and he forced us by his will to do something. We fashioned two long oars such as are used on the bamboo rafts. Bare poles of bamboo they were but they did get us moving. And then Fan'sha-an took another pole and began sculling from the stern of the hull. One hour at the oars, one hour at the scull and one hour to rest. Taking turn-about like that we were able to make some headway. We all lost track of time. We all began to hallucinate. Fan'sha died while rowing; he cried out and simply fell forward, dead. Faldo-an and I buried him in the sea, wrapped in the remnants of his sail. Then we both lay down and slept.

It was nearly dark when we were awakened by rain and, a miracle again! Three flying fish had thrown themselves into the canoe. We ate them without even cleaning them. More of these morsels flung themselves toward us, chased by some bigger fish I'm sure, and again landed within our reach. The rain poured down. "We drank and drank and channeled the rainwater into the empty bamboo tubes until all were full once more. All that night we clung to each other for warmth. We had no more mats to even act as rain shields. The sea began to get bumpy and spray kept us wet even when the rain eased up. Oh, such a cold, dreary night! Only Faldo-an's courage and encouragement kept me from dying of despair." Mah'tal paused and momentarily appeared pale, even in the yellowish cast of the firelight. Shortly he was able to continue, his voice sounding more strained.

"Morning greeted us with a special warmth. The wind had shifted easterly, gusty but mild, ruffling the sea with little whitecaps. Then we saw the birds!" With this, Mah'tal's face lit up in a smile of such animation that laughter grew in his audience. "Away to our south, then more to the west, then a flight of twenty or more flew right over us. They all came from the southeast. There must be land there!" Mah'tal again requested water, the boy quickly responding. Though he could understand none of the words, he seemed as intently involved in the man's story as were the Mal'lam.

"Faldo-an immediately took up the oars and I struggled to the stern to begin sculling. Our joy gave us strength which we thought we had lost forever. 'Slow and steady.' he ordered and slowly and steadily we moved our battered canoe, and our battered selves, to the southeast. By midday we both could see the clouds piled high on the horizon, cloud masses such as are indicative of islands beneath. Again flying fish sacrificed themselves to our hunger; one of us ate while the other rowed, turn-about. All day and until well after moonrise we rowed. It was I who collapsed first, in the stern. I simply lay down and went to sleep. Faldo-an could endure no more either and he fell asleep at the oars. It was rain again which woke us both. The sky was solid overcast but the rain clouds were thin because the full moon glowed through, casting a queer light upon the rather smooth sea.

Though neither Faldo-an nor I had the *sight*, it was a mutual conviction, which we discussed excitedly, that directly off our bow lay land. And as dawn came and the sky began to clear … there it was! During our exhausted sleep an advantageous current carried us as unerringly as could we have done, sculling and rowing. The Sea Gods did not want us to perish, this we now knew. We sang our songs of thanks to them all. All that morning, as we eagerly drove our canoe forward, the sea and sky joined in our songs of rejoicing. Dolphins leaped and dove all around us while huge flocks of seabirds dove and splashed and fed on some great schools of fish. Whales we'd never seen before, twice the size of dolphins, joined in the feast, one actually coming so close that I struck it accidentally with my oar as I sculled.

In the early afternoon we were close enough to these islands to make out the surf on the shoreline and, in spite of our fatigue, we still rowed on. It was my Sea-Master who saw the canoes first. We were passing between the far side of this island we're on now and two smaller islands, Jun'tee and Aht'tee. These people believe those two islands to be man and wife. Anyway, I was sitting rowing and he was standing and sculling. He shouted to me to look to the port side and forward. There were two of them with odd, square sails that looked as if they had half fallen off their masts. 'They've seen us!' Faldo-an shouted and he began waving his arms at them, completely letting go of the sculling oar, which went overboard." Faldo Sea-Master looked at his old friend and grinned, not in the least embarrassed by this revelation of inept seamanship.

"The rest happened very quickly. The canoes, each with four Tarbara'ut aboard, came quickly toward us. Soon they were beside us. Never have I known such joy as when these strange-looking little black men, their eyes wide with the same wonder as we both felt, grinned and waved and called out to us. They pulled their canoes beside us and reached out to touch us and pat our arms, all the while laughing and exclaiming wildly. They exhibited not the least reservation about two salt-encrusted, wholly mad looking strangers. They welcomed us with the greatest warmth and generosity which has never failed in all these long years we have been here!"

Mah'tal Sea-Hewn reached a hand toward the Tarbara'ut child who sat beside him. The little boy placed his own hand into the Mal'lam's and smiled up at him.

"This boy - his name is Kuk'toh - is my adopted son. I love him as I loved my own son." A shadow passed over his face momentarily, then his features regained a rueful smile. That son had died in the combat with Tor'na, a fact he was still trying to accept. When told of this madman and what horror he had spawned, Mah'tal had gaped, unbelieving. It took long minutes of denial before he could accept that the peaceful world from which he had been torn by *Earth Mother's* unfathomable sense of humor, no longer existed. Mah'tal suddenly appeared very tired, his features paling again in the golden firelight. He grimaced and leaned toward Faldo Sea-Hewn and spoke softly to him. Faldo nodded, patted his friend's arm and began speaking in the formal manner of the storyteller, as had Mah'tal.

"My brother seaman is not well. He asks that he be excused from this assembly now." Al'malan, as senior Sea-Hewn, rose quickly and signaled to two seamen sitting near the ailing man. They both quickly moved to assist Mah'tal while Al'malan said, "We thank our brother-seaman for his words. Go now, and rest well, Mah'tal Sea-Hewn."

The little boy continued his grasp of his adoptive father's hand and accompanied him as he was helped away to his rest. His long-lost daughter followed as the shadows closed quietly around them, the Mal'lam full of great respect for this hardy survivor.

Faldo continued: "My brother seaman's illness comes and goes without warning. It is the result of an unfortunate accident; of unavoidable ignorance really. One day in our first year here he caught and ate a poisonous fish. He nearly died then. He lost his sight at that time and now suffers relapses of his malady; more frequently of late. I fear he will pass from us soon." A long pause ensued, formality observed, and then he continued with *his* story. Pointing to the stump below his right knee he grinned and said, "I know that some of you are curious as to how my leg got short and useless." A mutter of laughter followed that comment, Faldo squinting around at his audience with a storyteller's expressive eyes.

"Well, I guess I'd better tell you. A shark ate it!" Ooooh's and Aaaah's answered him. His voice had risen to match the rise of his expectant eyebrows and he grinned mischievously at the enthralled audience. His brother, Enno, sitting beside him, now recalled with love that irresistible sense of humor which had so lightened his life those many years ago. At that moment Enno Stone-Master realized that his depression had begun when that sense of humor had disappeared and only now was it returning to its home.

"Yes!" Faldo roared, "And an ungrateful wretch he was too! He tried to eat my other leg also, but my gallant Tarbara'ut friends resented his gluttony and they had *him* for a feast instead." Tears choked Enno's throat as he listened to the laughter around him and he looked toward his beloved brother with renewed respect.

"I was fishing on the outer edge of the reef with my friends. I didn't understand their language too well then and I didn't know what they were trying to tell me. They were trying to tell me to hop back into the canoe because a big shark was headed for me. The way they were carrying on, I thought I'd offended them or something. So I stood there, hip deep in the water, looking rather foolish. The next thing I knew, I was underwater and the water was turning pink and my right leg hurt a bit. Someone grabbed me by the hair and pulled my head out of the water. Someone else grabbed my arm and began lifting me out of the water and into the canoe. Just as I was hauled rather roughly aboard, I looked back down into the water and saw a big fish lifting its big head toward my left leg. It was then too that I noticed that my right leg didn't have a foot attached to it and there was blood spurting out of my leg. Coward that I am, I fainted!"

More laughter now and a macabre story took on the air of a comedy. The seriousness of the night was dissolving around this man's talent as a storyteller. Faldo paused to take a quick drink from the water gourd left behind by Mah'tal, wiped his mouth and then continued.

"I woke up hurting really badly. I felt as if my leg had been torn off. Then I remembered that it had been! My black friends got me back to shore pretty quickly. There I was, lying on the sand and they were standing around me chatting as if they were discussing their latest catch of fish. When I later learned their language better, that's exactly what they were doing. You see, shark-bite is pretty common here among the Tarbara'ut islands. There is one really nasty shark around that we Mal'lam aren't familiar with at home. Here, its called the 'Striped Shark' and the ugly brute has a habit of not announcing himself. Up he comes out of nowhere and gives you a big chomp! Well, another nearby canoe harpooned that shark for whom I'd been good bait and they brought it ashore too. They dragged it up the beach and left it, still squirming, about ten feet from where I was still squirming too.

Faldo Sea-Master's gestures and facial expressions had his audience giggling and guffawing. A young seaman arrived out of the darkness and threw a great armload of wood on the bonfire. The column of sparks and the flash and crackle signaled a return to the old times when such nightly storytelling was an integral part of Mal'lam culture. Fatigue and the wearying demands of this strange day of arrival and reunion dissipated in the sparkle of laughter and firelight. All about him his audience bent forward to hear the continuation of Faldo's story.

"Well, you see, since shark-bite has left quite a few of our friends limbless, over time they have developed a knowledge of how to effectively treat such traumatic injuries. I was fortunate in that this island's main healer of such wounds was herself upon the beach when I was brought ashore. While my fishing mates discussed the division and distribution of the monster's flesh, and I lay there bleeding, that old lady - Sek was her name - and one other nice person began to work on my leg. My cowardice kept surfacing and my consciousness kept submerging. I do not possess the '*sight*', but I still vividly recall her placid face as she attended to my wound.

This lady I speak of has passed from us now, some two years ago, but her skills have been passed on to others. This lady 'glowed' from some inner light which even my eyes could discern. With the greatest gentleness she stopped life-blood from leaving my leg. Not being fond of my own pain, I fainted frequently, which I'm sure made it easier for that good lady. Awake, I recall screaming a lot." Faldo took time out to clear his throat and perhaps enjoy the chuckles from the crowd.

"It took many weeks before I was really up and about again. One day when I was sitting on the beach, feeling sorry for myself, a canoe from another island landed. It held eight people, a big canoe among the Tarbara'ut. One of the people who got out was a man like myself, short on one side. He pulled a stick out of the canoe, tucked it up under his arm and hopped quickly up the beach behind his friends. Well, from that day I have been hopping around this island like that man did. He was an inspiration to me." Faldo's manner and voice changed now. He shifted his sitting position, took another quick drink of water and wound down his story.

"Before Mah'tal became blind, he and I planned to rebuild the canoe we came here in and sail back home. When he became ill however, I knew that we could not sail alone together. Losing my leg sealed our fate. We resigned ourselves to living out our days on these lovely islands among these lovely people. Our old canoe hull is now on another island, being used there, but rotting away." Faldo Sea-Master ended the story of the castaway's adventures with what wiser heads among the Mal'lam had already, on this first day, begun to consider. He gently warned that if the whole of the voyaging Mal'lam, let alone more of their people who might come after, settled on these small islands, these native people whom he loved would be terribly compromised.

Would the Mal'lam, the miseries of their homeland still keen in their memories, extend a compassionate understanding to these small, smiling black people? After all, their own ancestors, in their quest for a new homeland, suffered many casualties in attempting to displace indigenous people. And how cruel would it be if, like a human volcano, the Mal'lam destroyed another people's lives? As the voyagers dispersed along the moonlit beach and lay their exhausted bodies down to rest, from the shadows among the trees not a few small black men and women looked on … worried!

Chapter Twenty Six - Respite

Days of rest, fresh food and the balmy air of this land of perpetual summer allowed for a calm, thoughtful approach to serious questions. Humming absently to herself, Sha'lat Herb-Mistress sat in a shady nook beneath a copse of small trees unwrapping the valuable plant materials they had brought with them on the voyage. As senior Herb-Mistress among the voyagers, it was her responsibility to oversee the propagation of these most valuable food plants, herbs and other growing things so necessary to the Mal'lam culture. Two other women assisted; younger Herb-Plait who had initially been tutored by Sha'lat during their initiation and on-going schooling in the complex world of horticulture and healing.

They too sat sailing among their own thoughts, the initial task of unwrapping and sorting requiring no special expertise. They all carefully unwrapped the valuable parcels, some containing cuttings, some seedlings or just seeds and some actual rooted cuttings such as the varieties of bamboo. There were failures too as moisture had penetrated some parcels during the long voyage and unwrapping revealed just a gooey, grey-green sludge. It was to be expected and so far Sha'lat was not discouraged by the percentage of spoiled goods. In the sunny open space behind them lay the contents of the parcels, spread neatly onto woven mats, drying in the morning sun. Some green shoots were evident and those would have to be quickly planted into the island's obviously rich soil. Just behind that open area was a large pen constructed for the pigs.

A local variety of bamboo, hitherto unknown to the Mal'lam; narrow but thick-walled and very strong, it served nicely to enclose those animals whose nature it was to wander and forage. The chickens too, were now held in long bamboo cages, four-foot high panels brought together on one side to form a triangular shaped enclosure. Tarbara'ut children sat or squatted by the cages, feeding flowers and seeds and greens to these unique birds, giggling and chattering all the while. These little ones seemed to find the Mal'lam's animals much more interesting than the Mal'lam themselves. Probably their familiarity with the two Mal'lam castaways already among them was the reason for that.

Among those plants so important to establishing the horticultural basis of the Mal'lam's material culture were: Pandanus, for woven mats, baskets, canoe sails and many other uses. Fortunately, pandanus also grew native to these newly found islands, as did the coconut palm and that was certainly of great importance. The coconuts they brought with them on the voyage would nevertheless be planted also because the nuts of the local trees tended to be smaller than those from Sht'ah Lee. The plant which gave them their *tapa* or bark cloth, the Paper Mulberry, grew from root cuttings and fortunately most had survived the journey. Like the bark cloth plant, the Breadfruit tree was propagated from root cuttings and they too had mostly survived, but wanted planting immediately.

Yams, traditionally a staple starch for the Mal'lam, and *taro* likewise, had come with those forebears so many generations ago, along with bananas. The voyagers would have to begin immediately to construct wet-paddy environments for their taro because most varieties required permanent immersion to grow well. Fortunately, among the ninety voyagers there were four expert Stone-Hewn who, on their second day on the island, began to scout for likely sites for these growing areas.

Other trees too were represented in the collection now being unwrapped. The Candlenut tree, its hard nut providing a condiment and a source of lighting as well as its valuable timber; the nuts of the Kon'ta'ab, the hardwood favorite of the canoe makers. However, it would be many generations before those seeds yielded useable timber. The Beach Nut Tree, a large-leafed shade tree with small but nutritious nuts, fast growing and eventually large and providing good building and canoe timber. The list went on, some trees small and with esoteric medicinal qualities, others, their barks and roots for dyes. Sha'lat Herb-Mistress and her Herb-Plait friends could look out from their little clearing on the slopes through the coconut fronds to the sea beyond.

Shal'lat, responding to a twinge of pain in her stomach, low on the right side, straightened her spine and rested in her labor for a moment, looking out onto the blue-green of the shallow reef waters. There was a serene beauty about this island, as little of it as she had seen so far, and her thoughts flew back to that other lovely Set, Sht'ah Lee, where her two daughters remained. Her oldest, Sht'ana, would now be well advanced in her pregnancy. These thoughts grew from that monthly discomfort in her own stomach. Still of child-bearing age, Sha'lat's hormones continued to signal her femininity, nuisance that it was now that she had long ago decided to bear no more children. Mood changes also occurred. Since the deaths of her beloved husband and middle daughter, so long ago now it seemed, she had been assailed by periods of mild depression.

Her new husband, that darling man Joha'lan and their intense involvement, combined with the other involvements of the past three years had allowed her to escape the worst of these periodic afflictions. This day it was her daughters whose memories were most keen and a nagging sadness began to grow in her. Here she was, a world away from a mother's prime responsibility, sailing off on an adventure with a new lover as if she was but a girl with no other obligations. Obligations? Wasn't her present occupation responsibility enough? She was the one person in charge of all of her people's most important requirements for their survival! It was up to her to see that all these plants survived and were propagated. 'Oh, *Earth Mother,* why have you chosen me?' A gloom was setting in and Sha'lat Herb-Mistress found herself sinking into its dark seductiveness.

All of a sudden from down the slope the loud voice of that rascal Herb-Hewn, Sal'lo'lat, rang out. "Sha'lat-an! Come see what we have found!" The Herb-Mistresses' assistants, glad for a break in their monotonous sorting, responded with questioning looks at their mentor. The men had returned from a foraging expedition and may well have found something of importance, were their expressions. "Let's go see what new plants they have discovered!" one young woman said, looking hopefully at Sha'lat. At first Sha'lat's inclination was to deny them this respite but then felt guilty at even the thought. She too needed a break, she allowed, then smiled reluctantly and stood up, another twinge of minor pain in her side.

"Alright," she said, "but we must get back to our work soon. Let's go see." She grumbled to herself that it was the men herbalists who so often seemed to be the discoverers while the women accepted these more mundane chores. She led the way down the slope with a burden of blackness in the back of her mind, totally unknown to any other around her. It was then that the little black children decided that chickens were not quite as interesting as pigs. Led by a boy of about seven, the children ran giggling past the three Mal'lam women, smiling up at them as they passed. "Aren't they cute?" one of the Herb-Plait said, looking back at their childish enthusiasm. "Not a worry in the world!" answered the other young woman.

The children only glanced back at the retreating Mal'lam women and then ran on to the pig's pen. They moved all around the enclosure, peering through the bars at the young sow and her newborn litter of fascinating, tiny pigs, still just able to totter on strengthening little legs. One child in the group, of course a boy, eager to exhibit his courage and mastery, un-did the flimsy cord latch on the enclosure's gate and gravity assisted in letting it swing widely open. The sow, her litter fussing close to her legs and comically colliding with each other, raised her snout and sniffed the freedom offered by the open gate. Tentatively she stuck her head through the opening, snuffed loudly and backed up and turned around, the piglets trying to follow. Then again she explored the gate's enticing possibilities. Two steps forward through the gate she came and the children scattered in a tittering flock, hiding behind the square corners of the pig's pen; watching, wondering, waiting!

Sha'lat led the two Herb-Plait down to where the Herb-Hewn were squatting over a pile of what looked like wet weeds. With them was Faldo Sea-Master and two Tarbara'ut women. Faldo-an looked up and greeted the Herb-Plait with a broad smile. He and Sha'lat had known each other well as children and she was warmed momentarily by his kind attention to her. "Sha'lat-an, come see for yourself! These two women …" and he introduced the two shy but beaming Tarbara'ut herbalists.Sha'lat had to force herself to focus through the encroaching darkness threatening to overwhelm her.

Faldo-an began a running interpretation of those women's description of what was revealed as seaweed; species which were commonly collected inshore here on these islands and of both nutritional and medicinal qualities. The Mal'lam Herb-Hewn and Herb-Plait where enthralled, chattering away, repeating the native names over and over, trying to remember them. Sha'lat heard mostly echoes of voices, her hand went to that ache in her side but she had no limb to caress that other, growing agony! She glanced uphill; something of urgency was calling out from there but in her growing confusion she couldn't quite make out its message.

With a huge, painful effort Sha'lat took two steps backward, managed to clear her mind enough to absorb what was happening with these other people and with a tone of finality which caused the other Mal'lam to look toward her in surprise, said, "This all must wait. We have important work to do now. Please thank our sisters of the Tarbara'ut, Faldo-an. We shall meet with them again.

Please excuse us now." And with that she turned and strode back toward the slope where that *something* was drawing her!

The two Herb-Plait hurried after her, casting questioning, worried glances back at the men and the puzzled Tarbara'ut women. On arriving at a cluster of coconut seedlings forming a dense shelter, Sha'lat stopped, something besides her bladder speaking to her and said, "You two go on. I'll be right with you." and she stepped into the cover of the palm fronds, hiked her skirts up around her waist and proceeded to relieve herself. The two Herb-Plait could only look at each other, sharing their puzzlement which had now become worry, and walked back uphill.

The always-hungry sow had discovered the packets of plants and seeds and her snuffling became an excited grunting, her piglets following her every move, just being piglets. The Tarbara'ut children, more courageous now that they had become somewhat accustomed to these strange creatures, crept closer to watch more intently. That same mischievous boy who had opened the gate now ventured close enough to reach out and grasp a tightly wrapped package of herbs and throw it just in front of the sow. She hesitated, took a suspicious look at the boy, then advanced on the offered food. Soon valuable plants were disappearing down the greedy throat of a nursing pig, her babies trying to emulate their mother but just adding to the growing carnage without gaining any sustenance. They were only four days old.

As Sha'lat started back up the track to the clearing, her time-out to pee having allowed her to somewhat collect herself, shrieks and screams assaulted her! She broke into a run, lifting her long skirt above her knees. Once she arrived, the horror of the scene before her was insupportable! The psychic wounds which the deaths of her husband and middle daughter had inflicted, combined with a life-long tendency to assume fault upon herself in spite of her proven capabilities, fused with an ego screaming to assign guilt. And she accepted the guilt with a heart which cried out to die!

The love of her husband, Joha'lan, was nowhere within her reckoning; nor was the deep respect, fully earned, of her people. Only a black abyss beckoned her. Her mind screamed incriminations! 'You have failed your people! You have neglected your duty!' Sha'lat surrendered to madness! She stood gazing at the ruin of all she had accepted as her duty. Plants and seeds and cuttings were spread around the torn mats with an abandon which hissed guilt at her and signaled the death of her last reserve against that madness. Sha'lat let out a soul-wrecking scream which froze her two compatriots where they stood. Hands over faces, the two women could only burst into tears of confusion and helplessness. What is happening?

As if some malign entity roared above with sadistic laughter, a sudden rainstorm, common in these parts, poured down upon them, soaking the dumb-struck women and the remaining hoarded treasure of plants. In the background the sow and her piglets sought the shelter of their cage, trying to escape the cries and shrieks of the humans, uncomprehending such behavior. The children too had fled. Unaware that she had fallen to her knees, Sha'lat struggled up again, took a last painful look at the source of her chagrin, her condemnation, and turned and ran blindly down the path toward the beach. As she ran, heedless of the branches and thorny limbs with talons which reached out to tear her skin as she sped past, she sighted the blue horizon. 'The sea!' her mind screamed at her, 'There must you end your stupidity! You must die, you stupid woman! You incompetent, worthless woman!'

Turning a corner in the trail she stumbled and fell into a large shrub. Scrambling desperately to her feet again, she failed even to notice that her wrap had been torn off her body and lay upon the brambles, a flag indicating her frantic passage. Down she fled, ever downward toward the beach and the waves which would swallow and absorb … and maybe absolve her. She was unaware that all the while her mouth was wide open, releasing the screams of her tortured soul. Sha'lat finally reached the beach, its sands burningly hot, the heat totally unnoticed by her.

As kind chance would have it, the beach was occupied by those who loved her. Joha'lan, her husband and her son-in-law, Al'malan Sea-Master and a number of other Mal'lam were engaged in various chores, most standing on the cooler, wet sand near the water's edge. All heads turned to seek the source of those skin-prickling screams which were rapidly approaching from just behind them. "What is happening?" a Wood-Hewn asked out loud. And then the naked figure burst into view.

"Sha'lat!" Joha'lan called out, her familiar body immediately informing him of 'who' but not 'why'. Heedless, indeed unaware of anyone else in her crashing world, Sha'lat's madness gathered a last burst of strength and commitment and drove her recklessly toward oblivion. Those on the beach were frozen with shock. This could not be happening! Then the cries of the Herb-Plait who had tried to catch up to her were heeded. "Stop her! Please, someone stop her!"

Those cries brought a belated response and a flurry of action. It was Al'malan, lighter and faster than Joha'lan, who first gained his feet and reckoned the situation. Joha'lan was quickly behind him. They plunged together across the hot sand toward the woman whom both loved so dearly. Stop her they would. In the shallow surf, but waist deep when they grabbed her, it was all the two powerful men could do to subdue the screaming, flailing, convulsing woman.

Close behind them now, wading as quickly as she could, followed an older woman, a Herb-Mistress in her own right. This woman, Ka'lat'lan, was a woman of very special skills. Most knew her as a skilled healer but few really knew of her extraordinary powers. As Joha'lan and Al'malan struggled to hold Sha'lat still, her frenzy frightening both men, she continued to force her body toward deeper water and the death her tortured mind sought. Coming beside the struggling threesome, Ka'lat'lan reached out both hands to Sha'lat's neck, now extended in a horrible scream. The older woman's fingers formed a strange configuration around Sha'lat's neck, clamped powerfully, and within seconds Sha'lat collapsed into the men's arms, unconscious but alive.

~ ~ * ~ ~

Sha'lat had lain weeping and crying out from a semi-conscious state for two hours. She had been carried to a hut on the beach by her distraught husband. They were followed by Al'malan, the Herb-Plait Kal'lat'lan and others of her group of healers. A screen of woven panels was hurriedly erected around the hut to provide shade and a modicum of privacy. Concern and sadness masked every face. Word spread quickly among the Mal'lam and within an hour nearly all had gathered on the beach.

The people sat in a wide circle around the hut, keeping vigil on this beloved woman. A low crooning chant began, a sound not unlike a lullaby, for it was known now that Sha'lat Herb-Mistress must be born again into this world. It was actually a heartfelt call to her Spirit to return to her rightful home among her people. Healers knelt inside the hut; some massaged her arms and legs while others gave gentle treatment to her torso and head. Then Kal'lat'lan asked for complete silence and that was signaled to those outside also. Just the soft rustle of the wind through the palms and a hushed, almost apologetic splash of surf could be heard.

With a nod Kal'lat'lan signed the other healers to move back and give her room. Joha'lan did not move. He knelt with his wife's head resting on his thighs. His face was set in an impassive stare down at her face. His eyes, blinking tears, were all of him that moved, even his breathing seemed suspended. Kal'lat'lan reached out a hand and touched his arm. He looked up and she smiled at him. Her nod this time meant that he could stay where he was. It was as well, for nothing and no one could have moved him away from Sha'lat at this time.

Kal'lat'lan then straddled Sha'lat's legs and lowered herself gently onto the woman's knees. She began to hum; a low, solemn sound which brought a prickle to the skin. She leaned forward and with both hands, gently grasped Sha'lat's head. Closing her eyes, her humming growing softer, she began to enter a trancelike state, rocking slowly back and forth. Many others around them also closed their eyes and the silence was only nudged aside by gentle breathing and from time to time, a low moan from Sha'lat. Joha'lan too was trying to still his worried mind. Suddenly, Kal'lat'lan hissed a harsh, spitting sound and Sha'lat's body convulsed. Joha'lan responded by grasping her shoulders to hold her down while the Herb-Plait woman's weight on Sha'lat's knees held her lower body still. Sha'lat screamed.

The crisis lasted only moments and then that psychic fever broke. Bathed in perspiration now, her body slowly relaxed. Her features relaxed also and she appeared to fall into a deep sleep. Kal'lat'lan released her patient's head, looked up at Joha'lan's strained face and smiled, rose and left the hut. It was over! Sha'lat's healing had begun. Not a word had been spoken to bring about this catharsis. Joha'lan carefully moved back from Sha'lat's sleeping form and sat in a corner of the hut. He wept quietly in relief, love and hope. The two were left alone now and word quickly spread that Sha'lat is well again. 'Thank you for your prayers.'

Research notes: Impressions and general observations

Subject: Tina Pualani Kaiser, Honolulu, Spring 1974

We had a bad week last week. Tutu Kinau went into hospital. Big scare, it was! Then, after extensive tests, conducted here in Honolulu because there wasn't the proper facilities on Kaua'i, the results came back. Tutu is diabetic! Could have been cancer, or worse, whatever that would be. She is now on insulin, daily, and has to change her diet, big time!

She's been staying here with us and Tina has been by every afternoon to see her. Tina wants to go back to Kaua'i so that she can care for her Tutu, go to school there and, I think, really misses Kaua'i. Jiro, Kinau and I have had long conversations about this and finally, we've had to resort to some strange thing called, democracy! We asked Tina for her opinion. Well! Didn't she get political real fast? She said she'd already told us what she wanted to do and how come we're still jawing about it? 'I'm going home!' she said. O.K.! Does that downright pig-headedness ring a bell? Tina's namesake, that long-ago person way over there in the Western Pacific, seems to be hanging around here too.

Jiro and I have helped Kinau straighten out her finances and insurance, Kamehameha School has graciously accepted the situation and even agreed to pay a not insubstantial sum to further Tina's schooling when she graduates from high school.

Tina will finish this semester here in Honolulu, then back to Hanalei where she will re-enroll at Lihue. She's still an 'A' grade student, enrolled now in a sailing class and I think, may just regret her decision next year. But who am I to say? She still insists on our sessions with the Sony tape recorder and is well into another phase of the Mal'lam story.

Oh yes, one more thing. I'm pregnant!

Chapter Twenty Seven - Decisions To Be Made

Two days after Sha'lat's ordeal with her rampant ego, this morning was beginning with these islands' usually tranquil ambience. The local inhabitants would surely have found the crowing of the cocks a challenge to get used to since the local birdlife was considerably quiet at this hour. Nevertheless, they too were early risers and the Mal'lam voyagers greeted the Tarbara'ut with a genuine and growing regard.

One of these little black people was but a boy and he was holding the hand of an elderly, obviously ailing Mal'lam. It was little Kuk'toh, gently guiding his adoptive father on an early morning errand of great importance. The boy was obviously a bit uneasy. He kept looking up at the sightless face of his good friend, wondering just what the meaning of this very uncharacteristic visit to the camp of the Mal'lam must mean. Mah'tal had attempted to explain it to him but the language difference and the boy's youthful innocence of the world of adults just left him puzzled. Mah'tal finally bent and kissed the little fellow on his frizzy head, patted him on the back and said, in Tarbara'ut, "Take me now to the hut of the Mal'lam lady who was very ill the other day."

Arriving at the dawn-lit encampment of his people, no one yet stirring, Mah'tal asked the little boy to find the hut with a staff with an adze hanging from it. The requisite symbol of a Canoe-Master was indeed hanging from an ornately carved staff and the boy described it in a hushed tone, remarking at how beautiful it was. Mah'tal smiled. He had known Joha'lan since he was a child and that this symbol of his rank would be exceptional was to be expected. He now felt totally justified in his early visit and what importance it presaged.

Like all little boys, Kuk'toh's attention span was relatively short, except when it came to caring for his beloved Mah'tal. Mah'tal spoke softly to him and told him to go back to his family now as breakfast would soon be available. "Yes, yes. Go home now, Kuk'toh. Your mother will be wondering where you are. Thank you, my dear boy. I will be with you later." Kuk'toh rose and walked, then trotted, then ran back up the beach to the little settlement of his people. He was hungry!

The boy, having only been asked to lead his dear friend to the hut of the 'unhappy woman', could not know of the Mal'lam custom of not approaching a residence at the front of a dwelling in early morning until the occupants had had opportunity to complete their morning's ablutions. Mah'tal's blindness, and perhaps those long years away from Mal'lam society, had led him to forget that.

He sat quietly, waiting for Joha'lan to awaken and come out to greet him. Therefore, when Joha'lan emerged sleepy-eyed from the hut and urgently about his morning's business, he was momentarily taken aback by the figure of the elderly Sea-Hewn seated there upon the cool sand. "Excuse me, Mah'tal. I'll be back with you shortly." With that, and his short length of bamboo with its one end cut on a slant, the toilet spade, he quickly hurried off into the scrub uphill from the beach.

For Sha'lat he had thoughtfully left behind bunches of soft foliage and a basin of water for her own morning needs. Covered in bruises and scratches from her ordeal of two days ago, she was loath to present herself openly just yet; an understandable feminine vanity which itself signaled a healing, a recovering of self-esteem. Inside the little hut she dug a deep hole in the sand in which to relieve herself, then carefully backfilled it. Crabs and other organisms would soon remove all trace of it. From the basin of water she rinsed her mouth, washed her face and attended to those natural preparations of the early morning.

Hurrying back to the hut, some other people now moving about, Joha'lan sat in front of Mah'tal on the sand and said, "What brings you here so early this fine morning, my friend?" Mah'tal cleared his throat, forced his aching back into an upright position and said, "Canoe-Master, I have come on behalf of your good wife. May I speak with her? It is quite important!"

Joha'lan gazed briefly at the blind man's face, considered, then replied, "Give me a moment, brother. I will speak with Sha'lat." With that he rose and entered the little hut, letting the door flap fall back into place behind him. Moments later he emerged and asked Mah'tal if he would come into the hut. Sha'lat would prefer to speak with him there. "Of course." Mah'tal replied and began to struggle up from the ground. Joha'lan quickly reached down to assist him and gently led him to the entrance to the little dwelling, holding aside the door-flap and guiding him inside. There was a moment's awkward silence as the fragile old Sea-Hewn followed Joha'lan's guidance to be seated facing the woman whom he could not see, but for whom he had a most important message.

"Greetings, Mah'tal-an." She said when he had settled and reached her hands out to his, grasping them softly. She was a little nervous still, wondering what others might think of her sudden, but thankfully brief spell of madness. Besides, her reckoning of the world was still a little shaky, a bit hesitant. "Thank you for coming to visit. Is the little boy with you also? He is welcome too." Mah'tal coughed a couple of times, wiped his mouth with the back of his hand and then smiled and answered, "I sent him home, Sha'lat-an, after he had guided me here. He's a growing boy and he needs his breakfast. Someone will help me return to my home later." Mah'tal was gratefully confident that should he appear to need assistance, any number of people would be glad to help him, Tarbara'ut or Mal'lam. In both societies, the elderly were well looked after, especially if they were at all handicapped. Courtesy and good manners fulfilled, Mah'tal came quickly to the point of his visit.

"I would not impose upon you at this time, Herb-Mistress, were it not of great importance to us both. Joha'lan-an, this involves you too, most certainly." Coughing and clearing his throat, he again shifted uncomfortably, his old back obviously paining him."You see, since I lost my sight and suffered a terrible fever in that illness brought on by stupidly eating the wrong fish, something else occurred which I would never have expected. I have developed a certain '*sight*' which does not involve my eyes. Only my good friend, Faldo-an, has any knowledge of it."

"Last night as I lay in my bed, unable to sleep, the sounds and visions came to me as strongly as I have ever experienced. I was informed very gently, so as not to frighten myself," and here he chuckled briefly, "that I would soon pass from this world. Well, *I* knew that! You must understand; my visions and voices have a strange sense of humor which I have tended to adopt myself."

Both Joha'lan and Sha'lat appreciated the old man's humor because it eased the rather awkward circumstance of his being here. Sha'lat especially, since more puzzlement was not what she really wanted to deal with.

"It has been given to me, this final capacity before I go to join the *Earth Mother*, to carry with me from this world the sorrow and burden of your own Soul. It is not a burden to me since I have no knowledge of it. I have been asked to simply carry it away from you and the *Earth Mother* will dispose of it. You, Sha'lat Herb-Mistress, have much yet to contend with and much of value to give to your people. You will soon voyage back to our homeland and be rejoined with your daughters. You, Joha'lan, have much yet to accomplish for your people - and you will!" Mah'tal was visibly weakening as if this last testament was draining his remaining strength. He wiped a hand over his face and requested a drink of water. It was within Joha'lan's reach and he put the water gourd into the old man's hands. Sha'lat was weeping quietly, her hands now resting on Mah'tal's boney knees. She looked into his sightless eyes and wished that through them she could speak her heart's message.

"I am trying to understand, Mah'tal. I accept what you say as the message of your heart. Forgive me if I do not thank you properly, if I cannot find the right words …!" Sha'lat choked out a sob, composed herself, never releasing her grip on the blessed man's knees. "Thank you, dear friend. I wish I had known you long ago." Wiping the water from his lips, Mah'tal managed an impish grin and said, "I wish I had too. I hear you are quite a beautiful woman!" Joha'lan had carried the dying man back to his little hut beneath the palm trees, a crowd of concerned Mal'lam and Tarbara'ut following. Mah'tal passed away that night, quietly in his sleep, the little boy, Kuk'toh sleeping unaware but a few feet from him. In spite of her genuine sorrow, Sha'lat secretly rejoiced in a wonderful sense of rebirth!

~ ~ * ~ ~

As the weeks passed the Mal'lam remained active in spite of the enervating heat and humidity. They were adapting to the mild discomfort and strangeness of these tiny, rock-girt islands. So thick was the jungle growth that to climb to the topmost lookout meant near-exhaustion. The more adventurous, which always included most of the younger men, had soon explored all the islands, learning to sail the little dugouts which sufficed for travel between the various islands.

One young Sea-Hewn however, rarely ventured far inland, even Shen'ham's urgings to explore could not persuade him. A'lan was intent upon the refit and testing of the Mal'lam canoes, working toward the day when they would again set sail for the unknown. He and Shen'ham had made friends with two young Tarbara'ut lads, Jun'tee and Ah'tee, themselves keen boatmen and commonly possessing many a young man's spirit of adventure. The four boys quickly devised a pidgin language of sign and sounds, often resulting in bouts of laughter among them as they tried to make themselves understood. Their Mal'lam friend and fellow Sea-Hewn, Faldo-in, divided his time between them and his new-found uncle, Faldo Sea-Master. Those two had formed a fast friendship, both rejoicing in having another blood relation near them.

Faldo-in displayed a talent for learning another language and with coaching from his uncle, was soon helping his Mal'lam friends understand their hosts better. Similarly, people of the other crafts advanced their exploration of 'things Tarbara'ut'. When those first intense days of the meeting of these very different people had begun to relax into a more casual mode, both groups naturally found themselves working side by side. Water had to be fetched from the same spring: the Tarbara'ut collected water in the old shells of sea turtles, rope handles looped through holes at both ends, two people carrying. The Mal'lam used both bamboo tubes and large gourds. The gourds were wearing out now but newly planted seeds were already sending up shoots in this warm, wet climate. The Tarbara'ut thought gourds were quite wonderful so a generous quantity of seeds were given to them, but they showed little enthusiasm for tending any kind of garden. They gave the seeds back, asking for gourds instead. Some ideas were obviously going to take time in the sharing.

Fuel for the fires was not a problem for the Mal'lam. With their sharp, stone axes and adzes they were able to cut plenty of wood. The Tarbara'ut built small fires mostly, except when cooking something large like a turtle and their cooking fires were most often fueled by dry coconut palm fronds. Since they ate many of the fish they caught raw, they seldom cooked in the earth ovens so common to the Mal'lam. Culinary proficiency was not an important part of the Tarbara'ut log of skills.There were no bees on these islands, therefore no honey. The only sweet things were the seasonal flowers of a few species, little treats for little children.

When the Mal'lam offered a taste of sugar cane to a couple of Tarbara'ut adults, they made bad faces and quickly handed it back. One Mal'lam Herbalist said to another, "At least we know they won't be pulling up the cuttings very soon!" Many of the Tarbara'ut cutting edges were not of stone but of seashell. Although these volcanic islands offered numerous types of hard, workable stone, these people seemed to prefer to shape and grind shell to a sharp edge. Only for heavy work such as constructing their dugout canoes did they go to the trouble of fashioning stone adz heads. Enno Stone-Master always had a large audience of small black men around him though when he began experimenting with local stone, and he found some of it quite satisfactory. A couple of them had taken to sitting near him, copying his techniques. His natural patience as a teacher resulted in some new and warm friendships.

Enno, however, did not possess his brother's or nephew's facility with language but the Tarbara'ut were proving to be good copyists in this craft of stoneworking. Soon they were producing an improved tool to the one they had always used. Enno felt right at home. Faldo Sea-Master was kept busy working as an interpreter for the Mal'lam, most of all with the Herbalists. The complexities of herb-knowledge and healing skills required considerable effort on the part of all concerned. Faldo joked that soon he would be *'hewn'* as a Herbalist and his one remaining 'sea-leg' taken off him. "At least," he added, "they can't *'hew'* anymore off me!"

To the puzzlement of the Mal'lam, these little people had no formal institutions for imparting skills and knowledge such as their own *'hewn'* and *'plait'* traditions. Rather, so it appeared, any of these people could flow easily from one craft or skill to another with surprising alacrity. Only physical strength inhibited some women from some male activities, such as canoe building. Women, however, sailed their fragile little dugouts with aplomb. Sometimes one would see three or four Tarbara'ut women launching a canoe, no men in sight, to spend an afternoon fishing on their own.

Enno Stone-Master was surprised one day to have a small, black women join in on a session of 'flint knapping'; shaping one of the local types of stone to a sharp, fluted edge. She was good at it. Enno asked his brother to translate his enquiry as to why this woman was so adept at a skill of which so few evidences existed in the Tarbatra'ut tool-kit. Enno saw the woman's expression when Faldo-an asked her and he had the impression that she was replying, "Silly man! You know I'm a healer and a surgeon. I sometimes need a sharp blade and these men here can't be bothered to do it for me, so I have to do it." "What did she say?" Enno asked his brother. "She said, 'Silly man! You know I'm ...'"

It was to the wonder and delight of the Mal'lam healing crafters that the Tarbara'ut population included so many people with marvelous skills in pharmacology and the healing of serious injuries. Faldo-an's experience was proof enough of that. Almost daily people came from the other islands to see and meet these incredible newcomers and this led to those invitations to visit the other islands which gave the Mal'lam the opportunity to further explore their new surroundings. They soon noticed and confirmed what Faldo had told them about the number of victims of shark bite. It was quite astounding! The sharks of this archipelago were especially rapacious. And yet the Tarbara'ut displayed only a mild regard for the danger which swam ominously through the shallow, blue-green waters around them. A jolly, gregarious people for sure, they also possessed a fatalism which exceeded even that of the Mal'lam.

Sha'lat, nearly completely recovered from her breakdown now, journeyed to all the other inhabited islands, and a couple of uninhabited ones, along with many other Herbalists. There was so much to learn. There were very many trees, shrubs, grasses and other plants totally new to their experience. For the Feather-Hewn and Plait there were glorious new birds to discover, only one or two familiar and they were migratory seabirds. Joha'lan, ostensibly along to search for valuable timber, still kept a watchful and loving eye on his wife. She was aware of this and even as she grew more confident and secure each day, she was grateful for his benign presence. What Joha'lan Canoe-Master was discovering was that even the uninhabited islands abounded in coconut palms, the rich source of fibers for all the rope and twine the Sea-Hewn would need to repair and restock their vessels.

Three Sea-Hewn on this voyage had been bamboo-raft sailors from Sh'ham-Set. They discovered another species of bamboo on one of the islands which had a wide girth quite like the species they had used on their home island. These bamboo culms tended to naturally lean outward from their mother grove in long, graceful curves. Soon they and some Wood-Hewn were harvesting this rich possibility, constructing a test vessel with a shallow draft which might just be ideal for moving materials and people between the various islands, over the shallow coral reefs. The Tarbara'ut looked on in wonder at the energy and incessant busyness of these newcomers. On the day of the third new moon since their arrival, the Mal'lam leaders met in Council to take stock of their situation. As convener, Al'malan Voyage-Master sat with the councilors in a half-circle facing him, the speaker's staff standing upright in the sand before him.

"Ham'sha Sea-Master, would you please give us a report on the work being done on the canoes?" The One-eyed seaman nodded assent but instead of rising and taking the speaker's staff he remained seated. This was a very informal session."Thank you Voyage-Master. Yes, I'm very pleased to tell of our seamen's progress." This very able sailor and navigator was a difficult person to gauge sometimes. His manner tended to be very formal on most occasions, even here in an informal setting. That he was missing an eye, the result of a childhood accident, was quite evident as the eyelid had been badly scarred. He had developed the habit of turning his head and cocking it slightly toward the person he was conversing with, giving him the appearance of exaggerated attention, slightly disconcerting to someone who didn't know him well. He smiled rarely. Ham'sha was a very serious man. However, with a few bamboo cups of palm toddy in him, he could be downright garrulous. But this early evening he was speaking in his usual monotone, his expression almost grave. What he had to report though was most gratifying and boded well for the continuance of the voyaging.

"Three of the canoes, the large ones, are now seaworthy. One of the older canoes, 'Wa'Sa'lat', still has some splits in the hull to be mended but that should only take a few days yet. Of course food supplies are the problem now. I believe it will require some months before all the canoes can be totally outfitted for voyaging." He sat back, apparently relieved that he had completed his part in the discussions. He now sat looking down at his hands in his lap, deep in thought. Al'malan gave a short smile and a second look at Ham'sha. Funny kind of fellow!

"Joha'lan Canoe-Master! What have you been up to?" Al'malan's question was half in jest, the two men having established a very close rapport and manner of joking with each other. "I have been chasing after the Herbalists, all around these islands, getting absolutely nothing of importance done." He spoke around a huge grin, everyone knowing that he had indeed been very busy and had found some interesting timber. "Well, I have found a tree on one of the other Set which shows great potential for further canoe building. Some of the Woodsmen will begin falling two of them in a few days and we will see what results. The wood is quite resinous and I believe we may have to soak the logs in a stream for some time before we begin trying to shape them into canoe hulls." Minutes of discussion later, all were agreed that work should continue apace on refitting the canoes but only Al'malan and Joha'lan shared the knowledge that one canoe would indeed be sailing again soon. That decision would be shared in but a few days.

The Herb-Mistress Sha'lat described the activities of her group; how many interesting and potentially valuable plants had been discovered; how many people were actively engaged in planting out the seedlings, cuttings and seeds which they had brought here with them and the progress with the *taro* paddies. She also broached the idea that the Mal'lam who had definitely decided not to go to sea again might be persuaded to move to a most amenable, presently uninhabited island at the far western end of the chain of islands. Already food was becoming in short supply here on what the Mal'lam considered the 'main' island of Tara'tor. This proposal found great interest and Al'malan asked one of the Woodsmen present how the work was going with their experiment with the big bamboos. "Could your rafts carry a number of us to that island; tomorrow perhaps?" he asked.

"I thought you'd never ask, Sea-Master!" the Wood-Hewn spokesman answered, his grin broad and continuous. "We have two rafts ready now, another being built. They work really well. We've even rigged a small sail on one of them. Now we just need some of you Sea-Hewn to show us how to sail them." His impish grin just got broader as Al'malan feigned surprise and insult while others tried to hide their own grins. It was known that these innovative craftsmen had already sailed successfully from the island on which the rafts had been constructed. Ham'sha Sea-Master, not known for his sense of humor, actually did look annoyed at this jibe at the Sea-Hewn's expense. Chuckles conquered the moment however and soon the planning for tomorrow's two-raft excursion to the island of Tara'Bet was organized.

The following morning's journey to Tara'Bet was well attended. As well as the majority of the declared land-lubbers, Al'malan, Joha'lan, Sha'lat and three other Herbalists, three Wood-Hewn and four Sea-Hewn joined the excursion. They were escorted by three canoe-loads of happy Tarbara'ut and Faldo Sea-Master riding with them to explain what the Mal'lam were considering. Another reason for the local people to be so happy. It was strongly suspected by many Mal'lam that they were beginning to be a considerable burden upon the Tarbara'ut's capacity to continue their previous hospitality. It had been Faldo-an who had first mooted this prospect of some of his people occupying an unused island. And his choice had been carefully considered.

The breeze was light and steady, the bamboo rafts low enough in the water to allow canoe paddles to be used to propel them. One raft, its small sail pulling quite efficiently, moved ahead of the other, the other raft's paddlers struggling to keep up. The Tarbara'ut canoes glided ahead across the multicolored reef. Deep holes were evident here and there and a few coral heads showed above the surface. The water was crystal clear and hundreds of fish of many varieties could be clearly seen flitting among the coral and stone features below.

Ahead of the course the canoes were setting was their goal. 'Tara'Bet' the locals called it, but as the Mal'lam came closer, another name was now bandied about as being quite apropos: 'Young Woman-Set'! Indeed, two nearly identical mounds rose from the center of the island, land sloping away, long on one end, more abruptly on the other. As they drew nearer they could make out thick forest on the flanks of those two mounds and a heavy skirt of coconut palms all around and close to the shoreline. On this very beautiful morning the mood of expectancy was high and laughter and joking sounded across the crystalline waters. Al'malan commented, "The Tarbara'ut canoes seem to be stopping. Maybe they're fishing on the way."

Sure enough, up ahead the three small dugouts had come together and as the rafts approached, it appeared that some intense discussion was taking place, Faldo Sea-Master in the midst of it. Faldo turned from whatever that vigorous debate was about and waved to the Mal'lam rafts, urging them forward more quickly. It was then that another Mal'lam said, "Look at all the eels! There are dozens of them!" They weren't eels. They were yellow-banded sea snakes and there were surely dozens of them. As the rafts closed with the Tarbara'ut canoes the voices of the black people were loud and high-pitched and much arm waving and grimacing could be seen. The canoe in which Faldo sat pulled away from the other two and came quickly beside the lead raft, Faldo reaching out to grasp an anchoring hand upon the bamboo sides. Grinning up at his fellow Mal'lam he said, "You'll have to take me aboard with you now. I'll explain later. Just give me a hand up."

Al'malan looked at the faces of the Tarbara'ut paddlers and saw genuine fear and an obvious anxiety to be away from here. Faldo was helped aboard, only one working leg making it a bit difficult for him. He started to chuckle as he swung around on his buttocks and looked up at those standing near him on the bamboo deck."The Tarbara'ut are going home now." he said, waving his big smile at the quickly departing little black canoeists. A couple of them waved in return but most had their focus on the water and its increasing content of writhing sea snakes.

"What in the *Earth Mother's* world is all this?" Sha'lat asked, moving a step more inboard, Joha'lan following. Both of them were remembering the terrible death of Joha'lan's dear friend, Ran'tar Canoe-Master, the name-sake of Al'malan's canoe. Faldo Sea-Master still sat on the deck, laughing and gesturing toward the bright water now littered with those swiftly swimming reptiles. Looking around and up again, he finally realized that his Mal'lam brothers and sisters all had horrified looks on their faces!

Moderating his humor he began to explain the unique phenomenon they were witnessing. "Well, alright, I think I'd better explain. First of all, don't be afraid. Those snakes won't come aboard and attack us. They live in the sea all their lives … except for a time like this. This event has only occurred twice before since I've been in these islands." For a people who had neither seen nor heard of sea snakes before, this was small consolation. But he continued in spite of their obvious reluctance to carry on sailing toward their island goal.

"You see, they come ashore once every few years and lay their eggs on land. Then they're gone again in a few days. When the eggs hatch, the little snakes immediately go into the sea and everything is back to normal!" He looked around at them again, grinning broadly, hoping he had salved their shaken nerves. No! Not yet!"See that island over there?" and he pointed to the south where a low hump of green lay on the water. "The sea snakes go there too. But it's so small that they're all over the place when they go to lay their eggs. Even I, crazy as I am, wouldn't step ashore at a time like this!" Again he looked around at his audience and was disappointed. A glimmer of inspiration driven by his irrepressible sense of humor led him to say now, "Al'malan Sea-Master! As ranking Sea-Master on this special voyage, I order you to command your crews to proceed to our destination!"

He looked hopefully at Al'malan, not knowing what else might work to release the Mal'lam from their fear-ridden stasis. The bamboo raft without a sail had by this time caught up with this vessel and were questioning: what was happening? Al'malan looked down at the seated Sea-Master and could no longer resist his good natured appeal. Surely this man knows what he's talking about.

Still standing well inboard himself, Al'malan called over to the arriving raft and said, "Let's keep going, brothers and sisters. Faldo-an has much to show us yet."

With a wind rising now and in the right direction, the bamboo raft with the sail and the dominant Mal'lam leaders aboard made swiftly for their destination. Less than half and hour later they landed on a stretch of open, white coral sand. No snakes!

"The sand's too hot here, now." Faldo stated, "The snakes go ashore where the shadows cool the sand. There won't be any snakes near us now as we go ashore. Just watch those in the water!" The exodus off the deck of the bamboo rafts was highly athletic and quite comic; women raising their wrap skirts up above their knees and leaping outward with controlled desperation; men broad-jumping down onto the serpent-free sand and running inland with the anchoring ropes, all the while searching about them for wriggling threats. None were there.

"There is a good stream with sweet water just up the slope to the left." Faldo announced. "Everybody have a good drink and a relax. There are no more snakes anywhere after here!" It was at this time that Faldo Sea-Master truly understood his role. He was absolutely indispensable to his people in their adjustment to and understanding of this, and perhaps, many other new lands. Youth gone and some semblance of good sense prevailing, he congratulated himself on being one-leg-short but a day-ahead in anyone's reckoning. He grinned up at the two Mal'lam who helped him dismount from the bamboo raft. They grinned back with what he hoped was a mutual understanding.

This island, which was called 'Tara'Bet' by the locals, was to inspire great enthusiasm this day. Two miles long and nearly a mile wide at its widest, it rose to approximately six hundred feet at the tops of its twin peaks. As the explorers moved inland past the hundreds of coconut palms they were greeted with rich bird song. There were no trails to follow. Few Tarbara'ut ever came here. 'Tara'Bet' meant 'Snake Island'! The Tarbara'ut might laugh at sharks, and eat them, but sea snakes terrified them. No land snakes existed on this archipelago, to the relief of the Mal'lam, but the highly venomous yet generally inoffensive sea snake lent a certain wariness about their newly found home. Joha'lan, of course, was on the lookout for big timber and he and Al'malan, with two other Wood-Hewn, climbed up the crest of a ridge to look over the land.

The ridge was eroded and mostly covered with short grasses, allowing an unobstructed view over one side of the island. Between the flanks of the one peak on which they stood and the other peak was a wide, sloping valley. At the head of that valley could be seen a large stand of big trees, heavy grey branches towering over the tree species below them. The men climbed up the ridge to the stony peak, all of them panting from their exertions as they reached the top. The view as well as the climb was breathtaking."I didn't realize there were so many little islands!" Al'malan said, letting his gaze sweep in every direction. Joha'lan added, "Yes, and look at the wide reef. It seems to encompass the whole island group. See? There aren't many openings in the reef either."

The view truly was magnificent, Joha'lan wishing that Sha'lat could be up here to see it. But Sha'lat Herb-Mistress was enthralled by her own observations. She watched as a Herb-Hewn took a stick and dug down into the soil. The reddish volcanic soil was rich in humus here beneath the forest cover and obviously full of nutrients. Their group was proceeding up the valley which the men on the ridge had identified. They passed over and through numerous small creeks, some with quite large rock pools. Irrigation was going to be no problem.

The soil was also rich in rocks lying on the surface and one of the explorers, a Stone-Hewn who had definitely decided not to go to sea again, exclaimed enthusiastically about the wealth of material for building weirs and water channels. Large stands of a bamboo with a small diameter were common. These slopes would be perfect for the many varieties of this valuable timber which they had succeeded in bringing with them. They came upon a wide open, grassy area, possibly cleared by a fire long ago, A few saplings were taking root and some shrubby plants grew in clumps. The Herb-Hewn again dug into the earth and again discovered its richness. "Bananas will do well here." one Herb-Plait said, her mouth watering at the thought. No Mal'lam had tasted a banana for these many months.

In their enthusiasm to explore, the men up the mountain had neglected to take water with them. The day was hot but a brisk breeze was blowing from the southeast so it was some time before they began to feel thirsty. By this time they had proceeded across the ridge between the peaks and climbed to the top of the second one. The view from there revealed another surprise. The northern end of the island was widely rounded, the end near where they had landed came to quite a narrow point. And the deep blue of open sea came ashore here in crashing breakers. There was no reef at all. This would require more exploration, another time.

Thirst and the fact that the sun was well past midday now urged the men to descend to where the others would be, down in that big valley. Along the way they tasted some berries on low-growing shrubs. Astringent but pleasing, they all helped themselves to handsful and ate them as they followed Joha'lan's lead downhill. They proved to be quite thirst quenching but soon a stream appeared and they were able to slake their thirsts properly. A Wood-Hewn with keen ears said he thought he could hear voices. Joha'lan stood up and gave out a long, KOOOOEEEE!, a woodsman's call; a sound which travels well through forests. An answering KOOOEEE! rose up from the wooded valley below and within a few minutes the two groups were reunited within the cool shade of this richly promising island's interior.

Faldo Sea-Hewn, meanwhile, had been sitting quietly on the beach beneath the shade of a small coconut palm, not yet dangerous with a load of heavy fruits. Dozing in the growing heat of the day, he nevertheless was subliminally alert for creepy crawlies. To his far left the sea snakes were coming ashore in large numbers, crawling with some difficulty in this unaccustomed environment, the palm grove's shade now extending over the water and offering them a cool entry to the land where they would lay their eggs.

The beach upon which the two bamboo rafts had landed was wide and its outer edge would remain in strong sunlight until very late in the day. Therefore, this beach was essentially free of the serpents now gravid with eggs. And so it remained. But certainly the Tarbara'ut name was warranted. The Mal'lam, however, would find another name for it in time. And in time so would all the other islands bear Mal'lam names, Mal'lam culture and society. And the Tarbara'ut would be benignly, but totally, eclipsed. This inevitability was on Faldo's mind constantly but he knew that not he nor anyone or anything would prevent it. And then he fell asleep until his people, the Mal'lam, returned from their explorations.

~ ~ * ~ ~

On the night of the fourth full moon since their arrival, Sha'lat sat alone beneath a small palm tree, gazing out upon the sea. It shimmered wonderfully in the moon's rising glory. Soon she closed her eyes and began humming her mantra of meditation. A warm breeze was rising, enveloping her. By contrast the cool, clean light of the moon bathed her in almost liquid presence. Her uncle, Tal'ma Herb-Hewn, had visited her in a dream on the very night of her breakdown. He had bade her meditate on such a night as this for the moon was her special envoy of thought and dream.

This, her third such meditation since his bidding, was now different from the others. Those had been only partially successful. She had not been sure if she was experiencing wish, dream or vanity. But tonight she knew it was not overheated emotion. Her mind was calm and open; even her mantra had faded away. With a startling jolt, almost physical, her awareness was invaded by a sweet sense of presence. An electric tingling had begun to spread all over her body. Every sense was alert - sparkles of white and blue light formed although her eyes remained closed. Sound! The high, girlish giggle of little Tin-an rose within her. 'Be calm', her consciousness reminded. No words came with that sound, only a gentle murmuring spoke to her.

Now light became scene and the scene was of an infant, itself bathed in moonlight! It moved its tiny arms and legs while a woman's hand extended to gently caress the baby's tummy. The infant was a girl. Suddenly her daughter Sht'ana's face glowed briefly before her mind's eye, lit with the smile which only a new mother smiles. And then both were gone, blinked out in a sparkle of time! Stunned by the intensity of the experience, Sha'lat sat shivering. Opening her eyes she stared around her. Shadows had moved from where they had been when she sat down. Clouds now swept over the moon causing its light to rise and fall. "Al'malan!" she cried out, "Oh, Al'malan!"

Sha'lat rose, stumbled briefly as cramped muscles protested her quick movement, then she gathered herself into a run and set off for the encampment where her son-in-law slept. She choked back the urge to shout, to sob, to cry out her joy. Breathless when she reached the group of thatched huts, she searched bright moonlight and deep shadow for the place where the Voyage-Master slept. Yes! There! The staff of the Voyage-Master stood like a sentinel outside one hut.

She hurried forward, ducked under the fringing thatch and dropped to her knees beside the sleeping man. Still gasping from her long run she reached out a hand and gently prodded his arm. He grunted, gasped and rose on one elbow, a Sea-Master's instinctive response to what might be an emergency. "Ah - who? - What?" he managed. "What is it?" Taking a deep breath, her joy and excitement barely containable, she sat back on her heels and said in an almost girlish voice: "Al'malan-luv. You have a daughter! And she is beautiful!" Sha'lat was rocking back and forth on her knees, unable to resist the urge for movement, for expression.

It was some moments before his sleep-muddled mind could fully grasp it. 'Was she going mad? Was she having a relapse? What?' And then it came together. This was full moon night. Al'malan himself had sought solitude and meditated at moonrise and had seen Sha'lat walk alone away from the encampment. That was one, maybe two hours ago. 'Ah! Of course! She has communicated with Sht'ana - we have a child - a daughter! Oh, thank you, *Earth Mother*!'

"She is well, Al'malan, she and your baby. My granddaughter!" They laughed and embraced and woke those nearby. Campfires were stoked and singing, chanting, handclapping and cheers soon had the whole of the Mal'lam awake. Sha'lat's vision was confirmed by another with '*the sight*'; a Feather-Plait who had herself seen an infant, but the face of her daughter Tina instead of Sht'ana's.

Loath to diminish the joy of this impromptu celebration, it was the following evening when she came to Sha'lat and Joha'lan and revealed the full message she had received. "Your daughter and granddaughter are both well, Sha'lat. So is young Tina-an. But there is trouble on the island! That silly woman, Al'malan's ex-wife Ja'eel, has been gathering a coterie of other silly people around her. I saw it, but only briefly." She said almost apologetically. "But there is evil afoot there. Ja'eel has threatened to reclaim her child - Sahn'ta, isn't it? Yes, Sahn'ta." The woman paused, trying to remember more but there was no more to recall. "I will try again, often, be sure, to learn what more I can." She reached out and touched the couple on the backs of their hands, a Mal'lam gesture of sympathy and regard. Rising with a smile she turned and ducked under the door cover and was gone.

Joha'lan placed his great hand on Sha'lat's clenched fists, squeezed firmly and said, "We must tell Al'malan. The time is near when the Council must debate our next actions. You know that some insist on staying here and now we have found a perfect island for them all to call home. Also, some wish to return home." He looked intently at her and she nodded. "And I know that you wish so also, my dear wife. So do I. Most, of course, want to be off to sea and to further the voyage. And so they shall too, when the time is right. But now, immediately, we must visit Al'malan and tell him what we've heard. We know him very well and he would not forgive us if we did not." Sha'lat did not hesitate. "Of course my dear. We have many Sea-Masters among us. Granted, none will surpass Al'malan's talent and leadership but there is skill and wisdom enough for them to carry on." She looked into his eyes with a question but did not voice it. He read that question with his special perception, nodded and smiled and they both rose to go out and find their Sea-Master friend. Sha'lat was fully healed.

~ ~ * ~ ~

The Convocation was held on the night of the next full moon, traditionally the time for making decisions affecting the future of the whole community. Enough time had elapsed since preceding events for people to discuss, argue and decide. The major question this night was, 'Who stays, who goes back and who voyages on?' Al'malan was again the convener as he had been since he assumed the mantle of Voyage-Master. Arrayed before him in concentric half-circles were the Plait and Hewn craft Elders. The younger newly initiated sat randomly in friendship groups behind them.

A'lan, Shen'ham, Faldo-in and the other young seamen sat behind the group of Sea-Hewn Elders. All but Shen'ham were certain of the outcome of tonight's discussions. All - everyone indeed - would agree to sail on to new and wonderful adventures! Oh yes, there were those who would remain here with the Tar'bara'ut but they were not really voyagers. They even got seasick! The almost fanatical focus of the young, in consort with their peers, can be most one-eyed. How could anyone want to return to Sht'ah Lee-Set, let alone remain here on these insignificant little islands and never sail into blue water again? Impossible! Yes, this night would see the great adventure continue and it was A'lan Sea-Hewn who led that chorus among his young mates. The night might bring perplexing surprises for him.

The only Grey-Hewn among these Mal'lam was Gra'sha'lon, the sole survivor of that long-ago voyage to these southern waters. His age and experience granted him the speaker's staff this evening. Al'malan was unadorned with his regalia of office now and but one among the number of Sea-Hewn leaders. Al'malan handed the staff to Gra'sha'lon and resumed his seat within the half-circle of seamen, the old man smiling graciously. Gra'sha'lon helped himself to rise to his feet with the speakers staff, a new one , beautifully crafted by Joha'lan during those dreadfully long days of the doldrums.

Joha'lan   Al'malan   ch'omilo

It was to his son, Val'on, the actual master of the canoe, 'Wa'Sa'lat', that he first assigned the office of speaker. A tall man, nearly as imposing as Joha'lan but leaner, he had spent much of the day composing the speech which he would now deliver in the formal manner. "My brothers and sisters. Please consider these words which spring from my heart." Val'on's voice was a deep bass and loud and he spoke more quickly than many would this evening. He was a no-nonsense, sometimes abrupt man-of-the-sea who always chose his words carefully. To the delight of so many Sea-Hewn, and nearly all of the young seamen, Val'on spoke of his desire, indeed his personal commitment to continue the voyaging, to finding a new home for the Mal'lam.

The inference of course was that these present islands were of insignificance compared to what lay just there, beyond the horizon. Were cheers and applause allowed at such meetings, A'lan and his mates would have been on their feet leading the hurrahs. But this was a solemn and crucial night of discourse and debate and decision. The young seamen made do with winks and nudges. Many older seamen nodded and whispered in agreement as Val'on ended his address with the formal, "Know that I have spoken fully and truly on this matter!"

Next to speak was a woman, Win'ne'ha, a Feather-Plait of renown wisdom, one with '*the sight*'. She too had received warnings from their homeland. Her plaits were wound around her head and white feathers adorned her hair. They shone wonderfully in the combination of firelight and moonlight. Her message began with support for those who would go beyond the southern horizon, praising the courage and dedication of the seamen. Then she brought another consideration to the discussion. There were more than a dozen men and women who had declared their absolute refusal to voyage on. 'Never again!', had been their declaration and it was now accepted that they would move to that beautiful little island where, from time to time, the snakes came ashore.

They would remain there, hopefully establishing a way-station of supply of food and other goods for further Mal'lam excursions involving these islands. And there were surely many more Mal'lam to sail this way in the near future. With the invaluable assistance of Faldo Sea-Master as interpreter, the Tarbara'ut, ever the epitome of hospitality, had agreed to accept the settlement of these strange people among themselves. Faldo would remain on the island where the Mal'lam first came ashore since this island, Tara'tor, was the only island on which a large enough passage through the surrounding reef was offered. This would be the first outpost of the Mal'lam's new era!

Finally the woman asked for the Council's decision. Actually it was a de facto situation which required only a formal, but lengthy acknowledgement. Her power of personality, as she stood resplendent with her white feather crown, certainly urged a bit of hurry-up among the deciders. A buzz of hushed conversation, the decision makers leaning left and right to canvass their peers and then a predominance of nods settled on the obvious conclusion. It was Al'malan who now stood and took the speaker's staff.

"Brothers and sisters." He began, "We as a council accept and support the decision of our loved ones to remain here with our friends, the Tarbara'ut." He turned and looked to Faldo Sea-Master. "Brother, please convey our heartfelt gratitude to our new friends!" Faldo nodded in return, acknowledging what he had already sought and received in consultation with those people who had given him succor and life for fifteen years."This decision is most fortuitous for our people."

Al'malan resumed, "These islands can function as a supply and rest stop for our voyagers - going both ways, to and from Sht'ah Lee." A shallow gasp ran around the assembly as the implication sank in. Return? A'lan's face was one which registered amazement. He had somehow not heard of or had simply ignored the rumors that were flying about the beaches to which he mostly confined himself. So centered on his own confident picture of the future was he that it was not unlikely that he simply dismissed what he did not want to hear: both a strength and a weakness in great leaders, which he was Destined to become!

"In consultation with many of our brothers and sisters, it has been agreed to request this Council's support for a return of some of our voyagers to Sht'ah Lee-Set. I, myself, would command just one vessel on the return journey!" The muttering and whispering rose in volume until Al'malan raised his staff in a signal for silence. When order had returned Al'malan recounted the messages and visions which those with 'the sight' had reported over the past few weeks.

A great danger had developed on their beloved Sht'ah Lee and some of the leading members of their present company must return to solve this growing, frightening problem at 'home'! Yes, indeed his own family's welfare was directly involved. But did that not mean that, by extension, all families were in danger in this mutually supportive society? Of course! No Mal'lam could imagine abandoning a part of their people to evil, especially, a home-grown corruption such as they had but recently overcome; the madness of those two, Tor'na and Mal'atan. But no, he reassured them, this would not mean the end to the present voyages of discovery. That must continue! Only the gathering of sufficient foodstuffs and the reorganization of the command structure remained. The canoes were nearly ready to sail on into the unknown.

Another hour of consultation and discussion later and finally a decision was made. Yes! One canoe, 'Wa'Ran'tar', with Al'malan in command, would return as soon as possible to the home island. The following two days were granted for a final decision as to who would sail with 'Wa'Ran'tar'. Some had already firmly decided: Joha'lan and Sha'lat; the Sea-Master, Ham'sha, presently commander of 'Hoosh'im'wa' and twelve other Sea-Hewn. The Itin Sea-Master, Ch'am'lo would also return to his people. Even one or two of those who had forsworn sailing again thought, 'home again? Maybe.'

A'lan and his mates left the gathering-ground only as the eastern sky was lightening. They had remained after all the others had retired. Now they renewed their enthusiasm for voyaging on. With spirits buoyed by the certainty that they themselves would be voyaging on, they gabbled and giggled sleepily toward their huts. A'lan, Shen'ham and Faldo-in shared a leafy shelter and all three fell onto their beds exhausted. Shen'ham Sea-Hewn decided that he would wait until the following day to make known his own, personal decision.

As he fell asleep he tried to conjure the face of his mother, as he did every night. Shen'ham would not be sailing on with the adventurers, not just yet. First he had to return home. He had finally decided but moments earlier as his head hit his sleeping pallet. For days he had struggled with an overwhelming sense that he was needed back on Sht'ah Lee.And there was another consideration which he had held close to his heart, sharing it with no one. Not even A'lan's anticipated arguments would sway him. So be it! Shen'ham's determination was unequivocal.

Chapter Twenty Eight. - Sht'ah Lee Again

Tina Earth-Plait, the name which the whole community had accepted was her proper title now, strode quickly down the Black Boar Track toward her village. Behind her the great mound of Volan Votu shone in the early morning sunlight.

Her most recent visitation to the summer highlands had been most rewarding, but it was also a time of some consternation. Tina had, just two days before, begun her first menstruation. Alone and away from the support of her sister or any other woman, she had greeted the expected but still somewhat frightening event with her usual recourse to her Spiritual guides. The Vesa'tan's Spirit had responded to her call for comfort with muted chuckles, felt but not heard. Tina still muttered under her breath at the old woman's lack of sensitivity; her own sensitivities ruffled a bit by what she perceived as her mentor's lack of consideration. After all, were she in the village now there would be celebration among her family and friends of her age. Tina Earth-Plait was now a woman!

Then a small pig broke cover in front of her and in her present mood, she bent and picked up a rock and threw it at the startled porker. Her aim was true. The indignant pig squealed in protest, hesitated, then rushed for cover among the heavy undergrowth alongside the trail. Still grumbling under her breath, Tina strode past the place of the pig's retreat without a glance. Tina did indeed have a cranky side to her nature, not unlike that old woman, The Vesa'tan.

The past eleven months had passed with amazing speed for most of the Mal'lam who remained upon Sht'ah Lee-Set. In the initial days after the little fleet's departure most people resorted to busyness in order to overcome the painful sorrow of the leaving. The daily, ordinary tasks became the focus of great exertion, even heightened skill as people sought escape from that dull emotional pain. Slowly though, life became truly normal again. It was harvest time once more, the Herbalists had returned from the Gathering on the high mountains and herbs and medicines must be sorted and stored and applied as needed. Also, the 'hewing' was approaching and men like Sea-Master Orn'ta and the other hewing-Masters were preparing to initiate yet another class of young boys into the mysteries of manhood. But beneath this apparent return to normalcy there stirred an insidious corruption; a heresy which aimed at altering the very nature of the Mal'lam!

Ja'eel sat on a cushion of finely woven pandanus leaf stuffed with coconut fiber. It lay upon a large mat liberally sprinkled with flowers and scented leaves, nearly covering the raised, stone platform which was her 'throne'. To her left sat her father, a *lei* of fragrant flowers about his neck. He held a fly whisk made of carved wood and the fine fibers of a tree valued for its soft, inner bark. Further away on her right sat a big, burly man, a refugee from the island of Sha'lan'la, 'The Thieves Market'. He had been involved in that day of bloody murder when the islanders had rid themselves of the remnants of Tor'na's and Mala'tan's band of ruffians. The hardwood club which rested across his knees denoted his role as bodyguard. That club had already claimed lives.

Ja'eel herself, 'The Mistress' she liked to be called, wore white seabird feathers in her hair. Unlike most initiated Mal'lam women, she wore her hair loose and long, like a young girl's. Her full breasts were bare and her beautifully decorated *tapa* cloth wrap she wore tucked up just beneath them. A thick garland of white shells surrounded her neck and lay upon her breasts. Each ankle, too, was wrapped in white shells which tinkled when she moved. In her hand she held the wing of a Gannet, white with black tips.

She sat with back straight, shoulders slightly pulled back as if to accentuate her breasts and her legs were not crossed but rather she sat on one hip, one leg pulled back beside her. She presented a lovely, impressive figure there beneath the shading branches of a nut tree as around her in a semi-circle sat all her followers, perhaps sixty in number. Most of the men wore some decoration; a neckpiece; one earlobe with a spiral shell piercing it; some with white *tapa* cloth turbans and some men from one Clan whose island had provided Red Tropic Bird feathers for armband decorations. Some of the women emulated Ja'eel's long, loose hair while others maintained the customary coiled plaits, worn in a bun-like fold on the back of their necks. All wore flowers or fern leaves in their hair and various necklaces and armbands of shell and fish scales. It was a very warm afternoon with little breeze and fly whisks and fans were much in evidence, the movement of these objects adding a curiously festive element to what was declared to be a most serious address by 'The Mistress'.

Her audience waited with intense expectation for Ja'eel to begin another of her long monologues; another exposition of her brilliance as an orator; one more chapter to the growing mythology she was constructing around her own personality. But what was it which had drawn this audience, these devoted

Mal'lam men and women who every day were behaving less and less like Mal'lam? What collective similarity did they share and how did she succeed in not only holding their devotion but increasing it?

Ja'eel's career as a manipulator began early, firstly with her own father. She failed in the attempt to always get her own way with her mother but that was one of her very few failures in this regard. As a child she had a special sensitivity to a person's little weaknesses, little habits and addictions. She had learned to exploit these characteristics to her own advantage, or sometimes just to prove to herself her ability to know what a person might be thinking in regard to herself. She was a conniver soon after she learned to walk!

Ja'eel's relationship with her father, Sho'sha'lo Sea-Hewn, had for years induced gossipy speculation among the community back on Sh'ham-Set. His overweening attention to his daughter's every stated wish brought constant strain between her parents. He would never discipline his headstrong, selfish daughter. Naggingly prompted by his wife, he might try to be severe with Ja'eel. A coy smile, a giggle, and as she grew older, a sudden hug and a kiss, her pubescent body pushing meaningfully against his, would leave him blushing and muttering in helplessness. Whether or not their relationship ever really became sexual, no one knew. Her mother refused to discuss the possibility with even her closest friends. End of story!

But there was no doubt that Ja'eel Feather-Plait stood alone among her young peers when her initiation time arrived. She was indeed skilled with her fingers and could produce decorative items from bird's feathers which most adults could only but admire. But collection of feathers out in the bush or on the windy headlands among the seabird rookeries and their mess and smell was not for her. Ja'eel had no close female friends, but boys and young men flocked around her like dogs in heat. Even before her first menstruation she was sexually active and only her mother's stubborn insistence on adhering to the pharmacopeias of the Herbalists prevented her becoming pregnant in her early teens.

The handsome young Sea-Hewn, Al'malan, became the target of her desire when she was but fifteen. Casual lovers at first, as were most Mal'lam of that age, she nevertheless set herself the goal of claiming him as husband. For a long while her aggressive promiscuity put him off but by seventeen she had truly seduced him. They were married; he nineteen, she a self-centered seventeen, demanding and to him then, irresistible woman of not only great beauty and sensuality but of commanding presence. It made them, together, a notable couple among their community.

But Al'malan's happiness was short-lived. Even during her pregnancy to him he had reason to believe that she was unfaithful. To the Mal'lam, marriage included faithfulness in all matters, sex included. Al'malan's divorcing her so finally and uncompromisingly, including the assumption of total guardianship of their son, carried this young woman of undoubted intelligence but fragile ego, over the edge. Who she had been, was no more! Ja'eel would become an *other!* When the island of Sh'tah Lee became the refuge of many dozens of terrified and homeless Mal'lam, outcasts from their homelands due in no part to their own doing, Ja'eel perceived a feast of human suffering which she could mould to her own insistent will.

By the time the refugees from the north began arriving she had already gathered about her eighteen Mal'lam of her own Clan, both from her home island and of Sht'ah Lee-an natives. She had drawn first some young men to her for she was always on the prowl for new lovers. Then gradually young women were drawn to her, and some of them became her lovers also. She began to sense her own power to attract and direct the actions of others. With her father's help she organized the construction of a small group of dwellings in a clearing in the scrub forest, two miles inland from the main Mal'lam village.

Already she had decided that neither she nor those around her would have anything more to do with the sea. One young Sea-Hewn, strongly devoted to Ja'eel, was made to declare his rejection of seamanship. He became her carpenter, stoneworker and gardener. Two women were experienced in farming and she had other willing hands to help, but she deigned to dirty her own. Soon crops were planted and the tiny village began to take on the appearance of any other Mal'lam settlement. But there the resemblance ended.

Ja'eel's older cousin, Jana'la Feather-Plait, she who could not, or would not, speak, and had been silent since early childhood, was recruited to Ja'eel's following too and she immediately became 'The Mistress's' handmaiden. There was no precedent for this role in Mal'lam society. Having lived alone for most of her adult life and having no other family still living, Jana'la was grateful to be part of something beyond her own loneliness. She was also not averse to joining in the orgies which were a signature function of Ja'eel's 'new society'.

In Mal'lam tradition, sex was a casual and normal human activity with few strictures attached. Infidelity in marriage and public displays of sexuality were the only sexual activities which garnered social condemnation. Homosexuality too was free of castigation, although not widely practiced. Community celebrations usually culminated in wild drumming, dancing and general merriment with all but the youngest children joining in. Young men and women, their natural exuberance and excess hormones combining to spur sexual interest in each other, would drift away from the public activity in pairs and disappear into the shadows. That was the Mal'lam way of sex.

But wild drumming, dancing and liberal amounts of coconut palm wine among Ja'eel's followers always led to an open and very public licentiousness. And this very activity, formalized by 'The Mistress' and most often led by her, was one of the main attractions for many, if not most of her adherents. Outraged by this gross behavior, most Mal'lam condemned it and those who took part. Clan members were urged by family and friends to distance themselves from what was generally perceived as wicked and foolish behavior. Few of Ja'eel's devotees heeded this advice.

As quickly as Ja'eel could purr and smile and entice, just as quickly could she fly into a rage if someone or something displeased her. Her father encouraged her in the use of the smile and frown as replacements for the whip of green brushwood which she often used to bring her devotees to her way of thinking. Slowly she learned the wisdom of his advice and practiced different types of 'purrs' and 'frowns', all subtly constructed to suit each individual as she came to know them well. And there lay her greatest strength as a controller of people; she had an uncanny capacity to read what lay in the eyes of all those whom she addressed or conversed with. Both reckless and cunning, 'the Mistress' kept everyone guessing, but happy to do so - to be involved in this seductive game in which she made sure that all felt they were important to her and their fellows. And all kept in mind the next exciting orgy!

'The Mistress', Ja'eel, now shifted her position on her stone dais and sat cross-legged, allowing her greater freedom of movement with which to emphasize her words. "I welcome you all here this afternoon. This is a most auspicious day!"

Auspicious because one of her followers had told her the day before that the season of storms up on the great, dormant volcano was due to start. Ja'eel was depending on some sky-borne theatrics this afternoon. "The ancient Gods have bade me address you on their behalf. They wish me to explain to you the truth of what has been occurring among these islands and what must be done by you, the chosen people of the old Mal'lam Gods! No longer must you think of yourselves as Mal'lam. The 'old Mal'lam' were, and unfortunately most still do consider themselves, people of the sea." Her voice was level and controlled, no hint yet of that shrill emotionalism with which she so often addressed her followers.

"But the Gods who have blessed me with their presence and guidance have declared a new awareness for us all to attend. They have banished the Gods of the Sea!" She waited a few moments for this to sink in, leaning forward slightly when she continued. "Yes! That's right! The Gods to whom the 'sea people' are so devoted are now dead - banished forever by the power of the ancient Gods of the sky and the land. Those fools now searching for new lands far from this blessed island no longer have assistance. Their prayers will go unanswered when the storms and waves come to claim them. They will all perish!" Now her voice began to gain that shrillness and her face clouded darkly. She brushed hair from her face as an errant gust of wind swept across the gathering place, noting the expressions on the faces of her audience, gauging their level of acceptance of her meaning.

"And hear this and know that I tell you truly: The first God to be banished was the *Earth Mother*!" There was much muttering and some grimaces of disbelief. The humorless bodyguard beside her tightened his grip on his club, distrustful of any expression of dissent or argument, even rightful questioning. "You think not? Think of this then; where was that *Earth Mother* when this horrible catastrophe began. That kind and benevolent Goddess was utterly useless then and is of no use now because *She* is no longer on this earth -above or below it! She never did exist!" Ja'eel fairly shouted the words and some in her audience winced at the impact of the meaning.

"The old Mal'lam, the 'sea-people' as they are now to be called by all of us here in this blessed place, have deluded themselves for generations. They nearly deluded us too, didn't they? Yes. But for the generous intervention of the old Gods now being reborn, we too would still be living in ignorance. But the Gods who visit me and speak their wisdom to me have promised that all those who follow their commands will find lives of joy and plenty here on *our* island - *our* Sht'ah Lee-Set!" Ja'eel's devotees broke into applause, a few with expressions of ecstasy both on their faces and in the tone of their chanted response: "Mistress Ja'eel! Mistress Ja'eel!" Ja'eel let the wind again cover her face with her long hair, partly hiding an insipient smirk of victory. A raised hand quieted the chant.

"Why did the Gods of sky and earth ever abandon us, so long ago? Well, they did not abandon us. They have been waiting. A year is but a second to the Gods. They simply breathed deeply and waited. For a moment they looked upon Tor'na, but Tor'na was mad. He neglected his duty to his people and so the Gods let him be destroyed." Ja'eel had secretly admired the insane Sea-Master for his initiative and daring but recognized long before his demise that he had overlooked the most important element which might have brought him to power: he forgot to gather a wide base of adherents and when finally confronted, lacked the manpower to defend himself. Also he kept a traitor close to him, and he was unable to appreciate the fact. He had trusted someone even more mad than himself. Ja'eel promised herself never to allow such a mistake to be repeated here.

"Because my devotion to you all is complete, the Gods continue to encourage me, to speak to me every day, every night. And they tell me many things which I must keep a secret to myself until the time is right. But what they wish me to tell you this day is very important to us all." Ja'eel paused for effect, again brushing her long, glistening hair from her face in a gesture so feminine, so casual, and so sensual that her lovers among the small throng squirmed in remembrance. Then she stood in a single, graceful motion, her youthful body still strong and flexible, although beginning to put on extra fat. "Listen!" she said, bending forward slightly, one hand to an ear. A distant rumble was fading, unheard by most there. Then another deep booming, far in the distance.

Ja'eel straightened and grinned widely. "Do you hear? Do you?" She was displaying great excitement now and that excitement raced around the crowd like a cheer. "She is calling to me! Yes! The 'Goddess of the Skies' is calling to me at this very moment. *Ja'jan of the Skies* has come among us!" Every face around her glowed with the excitement, the wonder of it all; all except the face of the dour bodyguard. His eyes just continued to sweep restlessly back and forth over the crowd. It was only thunder, after all. Just ordinary thunder. But 'The Mistress' had transformed the perfectly natural, and very timely, arrival of the season's mountain storms into the signal for some divine appearance. Ja'eel now raised both arms above her head and looked skyward, gazing intently into the darkening clouds which were swiftly descending down the mountain toward the lowlands.

A bright flash, another and soon after that the grumbling of the answering thunder. "Hear what *Ja'jan of the Skies* has to say!" Ja'eel shouted, her voice powerful and demanding but no longer shrill. Every ear was tuned. "*Ja'jan of the Skies* brings us gifts! She brings us a new future!" Ja'eel waited for nearly thirty seconds while many tried to hold their breaths the while. Still she looked up with arms raised, obviously listening to divine words while the thunder rolled ever closer behind the crowd of her devotees. Beside her, her father Sho'sha'lo ran a sweating palm over his face, the urge to smile almost irresistible. His adoration of his daughter was now enriched by the recognition that she possessed powers of persuasion not even he had guessed at.

"Yes! Yes, dear Goddess, I hear you!" Every follower was now unconsciously leaning forward, mouths open, waiting ... waiting! BOOM! BOOM! CRASH! and the storm was truly upon the village and the rain began to pour down."Go now, my loved ones. Go to safety. I will speak to you again tomorrow. Oh, such good tidings we have!" And with that Ja'eel's bodyguard stood and raised a large *tapa* cloth over Ja'eel to protect her from the downpour. He continued sheltering her while she stood now with her arms at her sides, eyes closed, a look of ecstasy on her rain-drenched face.

Even Sho'sha'lo finally rose and ran for cover as the lightning flashed and crashed about them but Ja'eel never moved from her place on the rain-soaked dais. Even the burly bodyguard flinched at one close lightning strike but 'The Mistress' never wavered. She remained until the storm had passed away and darkness had claimed the steamy woodland gathering place. When the man could finally lower his arms, shaking with fatigue from holding the cloth above Ja'eel, she turned to him with a wide, mischievous grin. She reached up and kissed him on the lips, wrapped her arms around him and pulled him irresistibly down onto the wet platform and demanded his body. Such excitement always inspired a voracious appetite in this woman. No one was any wiser. No one had heard or seen the gifts. But no one doubted. Truly, these people were no longer Mal'lam!

As on many a beautiful late summer morning like the next day saw, groups of Mal'lam craftspeople gathered up their work in baskets and trekked to the rise above Dolphin Bay. There they lay out their materials and tools beneath the wide shade of those big-leafed nut trees, Feather-Plait and Hewn assembling their colorful headbands and capes and decorated baskets with the myriad colors of this island's rich birdlife. Herbalists sorted and bundled the results of this year's journey to the slopes of Volan Votu. Even some Wood-Hewn carried timber and tools to the hill of black sand and soon woodchips were scattered and the fragrance of newly hewn wood filled the air like perfume. Potters lugged their heavy clay and water gourds and joined the growing crowd. Chanting and singing began and the counterpoint of the hammers of the *tapa* makers joined in. Below the rise, the waters of the bay were calm and blue, only wavelets sloshing onto the sand. Sea-Hewn in their canoe sheds attended to the constant maintenance of their vessels while children ran and played and dove and swam. Dogs and puppies added their rowdy voices to the general cacophony.

Sht'ana Herb-Plait sat with Shen'ha Herb-Mistress and others, chatting happily as she nursed her new baby girl, La'teel. This year she had not accompanied the 'Gathering' up to the great mountain. She was kept too busy with her step-son, Sahn'ta, and of course the expected arrival of a new child. Sahn'ta was presently spending the morning with his grandmother, Sh'tah'et, Al'malan's mother. Sht'ana could see him clearly from where she sat, gleefully attempting to grab handsful of feathers from his Gran's work basket, glancing up at her teasingly. Her mock-scowl did nothing to dissuade him. She was having as much fun as he was. Other babies and children sat, crawled or toddled from one fascination to another; some simply lay down where they were and napped. Many of the older children, those soon to be *hewn* or *plait*, lent themselves to the skills of their choosing, assisting adults in their work.

This was a scene of total peace and tranquility and no sense of harm or danger intruded. Midday passed and some adults made their way to the water to cool off, some to cleanse themselves of the dust and sweat of their work. On returning to the welcome shade of the trees, many brought out small parcels of food. The Mal'lam did not indulge in a formal midday meal, rather they snacked whenever the mood took them, usually leftovers from yesterday's evening meal. On this day, which was becoming quite hot, a number of Sea-Hewn climbed up to the shady knoll to join their families and perhaps enjoy some food themselves.

Foremost among them was the Sea-Master Orn'ta, eager for a visit with his twin sons. The timing of the seamen's arrival was most fortunate. Orn'ta's decision to remain on Sht'ah Lee instead of joining the Voyage was never a source of regret for him. His young wife and twin sons were a constant source of rejoicing for this man approaching middle-age. His tenure as most respected Sea-master was secure for many years yet. His only mild regret was the generous contribution of his big, double-hulled canoe to the Voyage. Sometimes he sorely missed taking to sea on his beloved vessel but then there was hardly anywhere to sail to any longer; most of the northern islands of the archipelago were destroyed or uninhabitable now.

All the Mal'lam who were able had fled here to this southernmost island many months ago. Only one small Clan remained intact besides his Clan, the Sh'ta'ha, and even they seemed a shattered and demoralized lot. Many of them too were gravitating to that woman, Ja'eel, and her crazy followers. Orn'ta sat now, cross-legged on the sand with one of his twins in his lap, the other asleep, and was feeding the baby a banana. He chatted easily with his wife and two other women who sat nearby.

Gradually an awareness grew that there was a silencing of conversation from the inland direction. Something was drawing people's attention away from the usual easy chatter of this day. Ever alert to strange occurrences, the habit of a good Sea-Master, Orn'ta relinquished his son to his wife and stood and looked to where a silence was developing; a psychic rumble of some significance. Then a low murmur of real voices began to hum and soon others were standing and looking questioningly toward the source.

Sht'ana Herb-Plait was among those closest to the inland edge of the gathering. She had been lying back, resting on one elbow, her baby sleeping beside her. Not possessing the '*sight*' she nevertheless responded to some inner clarion of warning and shifted to a sitting position. Then she picked up her child and rose to her feet with many others around her. What she now saw emerging from the back side of the hill of sand chilled her to the bone! It was the '*Ja'eel'lo'an*', the followers of Ja'eel, led in procession by that woman herself. Since that painful day of the Parting when the fleet of canoes, led by her husband, Al'malan, had left these very sands, Sht'ana had lived with a subliminal fear bordering on terror.

As she had stood waist deep in the surf, his son Sahn'ta on her hip and a child in her womb, that woman's vicious curse had penetrated her very marrow. Ja'eel's growing following had only increased her anxiety. She ran with her child to where her step-son played in the company of his grandmother and a group of other women. Somewhere, there must be protection from what she feared was about to occur! Orn'ta Sea-Master, his own sensitivities now focused on the approaching drama, could almost taste the similarity with that terrible confrontation, three years ago now, with Tor'na and his own despised nephew, Mal'atan: that terrible day when violence and aggression had prevailed over the sensibilities of the Mal'lam.

"No more!" his determination announced and he began to stride toward the on-coming spectacle which the woman Ja'eel and her company presented. As he moved forward he signaled to his fellow Sea-Hewn and some Woodsmen to join him. Most did. A few moved to the periphery of the crowd, expecting something, they knew not what.

Ja'eel Feather-Plait, former wife of the Voyage-Master, Al'malan, was, early in her young adult life, known for her seductive, erotic appeal. Surely by this appeal did she seduce the young, idealistic Sea-Hewn. But as powerful as her seductive energy was, her understanding of the basics of societal responsibility and adult conduct was non-existent. Her infidelities scandalized her husband's family and only his too-forgiving nature reconciled their marriage for as long as it had lasted. The birth of their son, Sahn'ta, seemed only to further remove her from the expected, dedicated activity of a young mother. Ja'eel was hopelessly subservient to her own sensuality. She knew this and now played upon this reality as a means to gaining personal power in an environment which held many frightened and spiritually bereft individuals, refugees from the holocaust of the past three years of traumatic events.

Over the past year she had gathered about her a like-minded group of sensualists bent upon establishing a new identity for themselves. Most hoped to find a mitigation of their fear and uncertainty within an active assembly of others seeking someone to lead them to their salvation. So much of Mal'lam society had disappeared, utterly abolished by a cruel natural phenomenon. The

Great Earth Mother was held responsible by so many who could not comprehend a God who shows such utter disregard for human life. But as one God is discarded, many seek an immediate replacement. Into this chaos of human emotion stepped Ja'eel, waiting patiently like a gorgeous raptor, ready to succor her appetites by throwing out the bait of new Gods!

She had arrived that mid-afternoon resplendent in garish finery; layers of shell necklaces and wristlets, her ankles bound with polished shell and bone and upon hcr hcad was wound a crown of flowers. Her breasts were bare and glistened with scented coconut oil and her wrap was of the most intricate, painted design. Behind her came her entourage of men and women of all ages, equally over-done by Mal'lam standards. They carried themselves with an arrogance which many in the crowd saw as reminiscent of the followers of Tor'na and Mal'atan. Orn'ta's hackles rose in anger and shame for he saw in that approaching procession the utter rejection of all that he held dear. Here again was madness!

He moved instinctively to stand near Sht'ana Leaf-Plait, her mother-in-law Sht'ah'et and the children of his great friend, Al'malan. Ja'eel was headed directly for them. Other Sea-Hewn were now in position behind Orn'ta, ready to lend forceful assistance if necessary. From where she had been sitting with a group of other Feather-Plait, Ja'eel's now- estranged mother rose and walked to intercept her daughter and the mission which she had rightly guessed at. The cruel argument in which they had been engaged had estranged not only Ja'eel and her mother but mother from husband. Sho'sha'lo was Sea-Hewn but in recent months, at the insistence of his daughter, had eschewed any contact with his brothers-of-the-sea. His devotion to his daughter could only be called infatuation; another strange and very questionable manifestation of this woman's power over others. Since Ja'eel harbored an explicit hatred of the sea and all who worked upon it, the Sea-Hewn of other Clans who were drawn to her beliefs also surrendered lifetimes of association there.

The woman who had born Ja'eel now disowned her; despised her in fact. Doubling the hurt was her husband's desertion of their home and marriage of many years. He would now follow Ja'eel's campaign. What campaign? Ja'eel proposed a return to the worship of Gods whom most Mal'lam had long ago discarded as manifestations of a well-forgotten barbarity in the distant past. Those were ugly, jealous Gods who demanded sordid rituals and frightful sacrifices, concepts which the Mal'lam could not countenance. Even the sacrifice of an animal such as a chicken for any purpose other than food was incomprehensible to them. And Ja'eel's father's devotion to her was perceived as more than strange; incest, was the gossip.

The flamboyant appearance of Ja'eel and her retinue carried with it no sense of celebration; rather there was a disturbing inference of threat. What was she doing? "Go back to your filthy encampment, Ja'eel! You have no place here. You will not take my grandson!" It was Ja'eel's mother, Ma'tea, whose shrill voice raised hackles on necks. The older woman positioned herself in the center of the only path through the crowd of incensed Mal'lam. She stood with legs spread and braced, as if expecting a physical assault, her hands clenched at her sides. The glare of hatred in Ja'eel's eyes was indeed like an assault. However, she halted her advance, her followers stopping in lock-step behind her.

"Get out of my way ... *dear mother*!" Ja'eel hissed, her fists also clenched at her sides as the two women faced each other in deep animosity. It was then that Orn'ta Sea-Master intervened. Coming up behind Ma'tea he said softly but firmly, "Go to your grandson now, Ma'tea-an. All will be well. I promise you!" Ma'tea Feather-Plait turned to see who spoke, then immediately returned to her defensive posture. "Do you know why she is here, Orn'ta?" She never took her eyes off her daughter, returning glare for glare.

"Yes." He replied quietly, "Everyone does. It will be alright." Ma'tea gave her daughter a last, withering stare, relaxed her stance and turned to obey Orn'ta's direction. Orn'ta's eyes met hers briefly. There was such pain there, along with her righteous anger. By the time she had walked the few paces to where Sht'ana, Shen'ha and two other women stood protectively near little Sahn'ta and his infant sister, she had covered her face and was sobbing. Sht'ana herself was trembling with fear, her baby clutched tightly to her with one arm while with the other she held Sahn'ta firmly against her thigh. He was whimpering, the heavy vibrations of human maladjustment beyond his comprehension.

"You have been directed by your Council of Elders, Ja'eel, to remain away from this community. Your behavior and arrogance, and that of those who attend you, will no longer be tolerated among us!" Orn'ta's voice conveyed an unequivocal demand. Other men around him began moving forward a step or two, their presence in support of his authority. All waited for her reply. Her once-lovely face was now becoming a mask of darkness. Then she bared her teeth in a hideous grin and her body began to jiggle with a rising, bitter chuckle. For long moments she returned Orn'ta's stare. Then, with a loud laugh of dismissal she turned and walked through the small group of supporters with whom she had arrived. They bunched around her protectively, glancing nervously around them as they went. Hissed epithets of, 'Itoi!' followed them. They were being likened to those mysterious, almost mythical savages who had so terrorized their ancestors. As Ja'eel's group left the edge of the assembled Mal'lam she suddenly turned and shrieked, "I will return for my son! And any who dare oppose me will die! The Gods have been awakened and they will destroy all who reject them. All who follow me will be saved! All who reject me are doomed!"

A terrible chill ran through the crowd as she turned and strode slowly away to the small village which her devotees had established two miles inland, far from the hated sea. Ja'eel knew quite well how to instill fear; fear and lust being not too distant in character. She left behind creeping doubts in a few simpler minds. Sht'ana broke into tears and was immediately surrounded by loving and concerned family and friends. Orn'ta Sea-Master gathered some of the community leaders there that afternoon and declared the need for a convocation of the Elders. Soon!

~ ~ * ~ ~

Late afternoon shadows latticed the pathway as Tina jogged through the fruit orchards, only two miles from the home village. She was tired. Only the downhill run kept her from stopping to rest, gravity assisting in keeping her going. Earlier that day as she had paced herself to arrive back home right on nightfall, this trip having been made numerous times now, she had received that message through her talisman which hung kindly around her neck. There was urgency in that emanation of energy which presided in the blue stone at her throat. There was also a subliminal reference to her sister, Sht'ana. "Return home now!" had been the message. Tina Earth-Plait pushed against her fatigue and increased her speed. No greater obligation did she recognize than that to her older sister.

Tina waved in return to the greetings of other villagers as she neared her sister's abode, the home of Al'malan's parents. Dusty and disheveled, her knapsack flapping against her back, she stopped her long run just in front of the doorway of the neat hut. From inside came the lusty cry of her niece, little La'teel, and murmurs of adult conversation.

"Sh'tana!", Tina called out, slipping the loops of her knapsack and letting it fall to the ground. There was an answer from within and she was met at the doorway by Al'malan's mother, Sh'tah'et. Sht'ana followed her, the baby in her arms. Both women embraced Tina, rubbing her arms and back in greeting and smiling gratefully at her safe return. They all worried at her long absences, not fully understanding her motivations. Still but a girl, lean-hipped and lanky and with a little girl's infectious laughter, she was never-the-less earning a reputation for eccentricity.

At that moment they were joined by Shana'lan, Tina's closest friend who joined in the hugs and smiles. Shana'lan, a year older than Tina, born and raised here on Sht'ah Lee-Set, was without the gifts of 'sight' or any obvious psychic abilities. But her joyous and creative nature and her gentle acceptance of Tina's eccentricities endeared her to all who knew her. She was also already a gifted storyteller. Small children gathered around her in the evenings, eager to hear her tales of animals, birds, Forest Spirits and all manner of other fictitious characters. Tina loved her like another sister.

Tina was ravenously hungry. She quickly stripped off her muddy wrap and stood gasping as Shan'lan poured cold water from a gourd over her dusty head. Tina was not terribly fussy about her appearance at the best of times and now, as she toweled herself off with a scrap of *tapa* cloth, she went naked inside the hut, looking for food. Combs and unguents and scents and a clean wrap could wait. Sh'tah'et stood back, arms crossed, looking on in bemusement, smiling tolerantly. As she ate, Tina listened to the recounting of the day's drama, told with great gravity especially by her young friend, Shana'lan. Finally finished with her copious meal, Tina took her little niece into her lap and sat gently rocking her as the conversation continued. The little boy, Sahn'ta, crawled over and rested his head on Tina's thigh and was soon asleep. He too, loved his 'aunty'.

The following day was abuzz with rumor and gossip. The Elders had gathered again at the grove of Beach Nut trees, although it was overcast and threatening rain. Those with some measure of clairvoyance were called upon first to report any visions or inspirations they may have experienced. One elderly Wood-Hewn spoke first, having waved an insistent hand at the convener.

Having received the Speaker's staff he rose and leaned on it and said, "I have seen things, this last night, which disturb me!" He stood more erectly now, warming to his pronouncement. "It has come to me that Ja'eel and her followers," and here he paused and spit on the sand, "are moving their settlement. They are going somewhere beyond the fruit orchards. I saw the Black Boar Track and some huts being built. One hut was very large." He paused, in the formal manner and then said, "That's all I have seen." He quickly passed the staff back and sat down again.

Next to speak was a middle-aged woman, renown for her accurate prognostications. A Leaf-Plait and respected healer, she too took the Speaker's staff and began: "Many words have I heard and many scenes have I witnessed. My *Voices* kept me up half the night." She sounded a bit peevish. "And things are not well!" This woman, Val'lat by name, seemed always to prolong her pronouncements, rather irritatingly.

"I am told, as we have already heard," and she nodded toward the previous speaker, "That Ja'eel is moving her people further inland, away from sight and sound of the sea. There is another sinister reason for this." Again her formal pause and the clearing of her throat three times caused some to roll their eyes in impatience. "Ja'eel and her people intend to impede the High Gathering next year as well as prevent the Wood-Hewn from harvesting timber for new canoes." This statement brought a growl of anger from the assembly, faces displaying both unbelieving shock and an aggressive denial of this occurring. Orn'ta Sea-Master waved a signal for silence and nodded impatiently to Val'lat to continue. Val'lat saw the gesture and wisely heeded its import. Orn'ta was not one to tolerate too much theatricality.

"This much, too, was imparted to me." She continued, "Sht'ana Leaf-Plait must find safety away from this settlement, far from here. Ja'eel fully intends to reclaim her son. She also means to harm Sh'tana, her mother Matea and Sh'tah'et! Worst of all," and this time it was honest emotion which choked her voice, "she means to take away Sh'tana's daughter." There was a momentary, unbelieving silence, allowing Orn'ta to rise and take the Speaker's staff. He called for any further announcements, hoping there were none. Enough bad news already. But a final speaker rose and with no hesitation, or even taking the staff, she spoke of her message which was at least of as great import to the Mal'lam. "My visions have called to me for days now. I have hardly believed them. Yet, they are most insistent and true. Our voyagers, some of them, are returning to us! They know of our worries and the increasing threat to our people. Voyage-Master Al'malan leads this return!" The ooh's and aaah's of the assembly drowned out Orn'ta's own gasp as he choked back a sob of relief. For weeks he had been imploring the *Earth Mother* to answer his pleas. "Bring back our best and strongest to us. We are in great danger here and my strength is insufficient!" He *was* a man of great strength but if he thought it insufficient … so it was! He feared for his young family, he feared for his people. His fear could undo him.

A vigorous debate followed and finally a consensus was reached: word of the return of some of the voyagers under Al'malan's command was to be kept secret! Strictly! And within a society such as this, in which discussion and consensus prevailed, it was a chancy ruling at best. Orn'ta again rose as convener to insist on this silence. Here, in this instance, he held no doubt as to the adequacy of his powers of persuasion. No word did escape this assembly, although many must have bitten their tongues to the point of bleeding! Orn'ta called for another gathering, this one just Sea-Hewn, separate from the now-dispersing Convocation.. There he canvassed his constituency as to their willingness to collude in a plan to spirit the threatened woman and her children away to some safe haven. All agreed that the safest haven could only be with their cousins, the strange people of the Dry-Side of the island; the Itin.

The village of Bant'la'wan, on the far northwestern end of this island was the obvious destination. It was known that great respect reigned between that settlement's leader, Jo'lo'tan and Sea-Master Al'malan. Surely he would accord that man's wife and children refuge. But first, an envoy must approach Jo'lo'tan with this proposal. There was a system of ritual to be adhered to here. Immediately, a young Sea-Master with his first canoe volunteered to make the journey. Here was an opportunity to really test both his canoe and its crew on the sometimes difficult sail up the coast. His offer was accepted. He too was doubly imbued with the necessity for silence. This young man, actually a cousin of Al'malan's, could not have been better chosen. Equally well chosen was one of the least reliable gossips in the community!

A rather silly man, often under the influence of palm toddy, he was a Stone-Hewn who usually worked by himself, doing minor repairs to the area's irrigation systems. He lived in a small village away from the main settlement, toward the north. His name was Kal'to'lot Stone-Hewn. He was allowed to overhear, actually was intentionally given the information, that Sh'tana and the children would be taken to a hideout not far from his village. He was sworn to secrecy. How un-Mal'lam this subterfuge was! Who had thought this conspiracy up? Most certainly he would see that this intelligence reached the ears of Ja'eel. Who was it? It was Herb-Mistress Shen'ha. She had had enough of all this indecision. Anyone, she reckoned, could see what was coming.

As much as she respected Sea-Master Orn'ta's leadership in the community, much more insight into the machinations of a warped female mind was required than even his experience could provide. Who better to understand a woman than another woman? And a secret, carried to her in a small, hushed whisper, told her that her son, Shen'ham, would also be returning. "Time!" she said quietly to herself, "Time is needed now. Time to gather our best people to combat this mad woman's ambitions. Oh Al'malan, Joha'lan, my sweet son Shen'ham; please return to us."

Research Notes: Impressions and General Observations

Subjects: Tutu Kinau Ho'opai Kaiser and Tina Pua'lani Kaiser

Lots to report this time: We're back on Kaua'i for a few weeks vacation. Jiro is off to London the first week in August to present a paper at a convention. Me, I'm staying here because my doctor doesn't want me to fly at this stage of my pregnancy. And I'm only five months along! Actually, he's afraid my great bulk will bring the plane down. God, but I'm big! When we got here last week I hardly recognized Kinau. She's lost so much weight! She's feeling fine though and is quite proud of herself. Has her schoolgirl figure back, she says. Her diabetes is well under control now and she's even more energetic than when I first met her, and that's saying something!

Tina is a bit less insistent on staying here on Kaua'i for the upcoming school year. She may go back to Kamehameha. She knows her Tutu is quite well and can manage without her. She did very well with her grades again but instead of another tape recorder as a present, we bought her a new surfboard. You should have seen me trying to give her surfing lessons! Me, with this big basket of laundry in front of me, trying to stay on my board while giving her pointers on how to stay up on hers. I spent most of the time in the water, trying to get back up and standing. Doc says it's good exercise and I should keep it up. Thanks Doc.

Uncle Warren and Aunty Bev Kapuna are staying here for a couple of weeks. Warren's on vacation. He brought his home-brew kit with him, of course, and he and 'Unca' Teddy go out fishing (read, beer drinking) most afternoons. Aunty Bev is a delight as always, and she's been helping me with my study of Hawai'ian. She speaks a very old and pure language, coming from Ni'ihau, and there are actually a few words which sound Mal'lam. Could just be my imagination. But when I mentioned it to Tutu, she just smiled inscrutably and said, "Keep studying." She and Jiro are a lot alike, I'm discovering.

A colleague of ours has recently returned from a field trip to New Britain and we had a fascinating conversation about his work there. His group has been working with some pottery artifacts found at various places in the South Pacific, all with unique and similar decorative patterns. They are calling this type of pottery, *Lapita*, named after an area in New Caledonia where these pottery shards were first identified. Dating procedures indicate that these Lapita people, whoever they were, settled in a number of areas of what is now called Melanesia. But apparently, judging from the style and quality of the pottery, it was not produced by Melanesians but by another group. And that unknown group of people pre-dated the Polynesians. Aha! she said! Were the Lapita people really the Mal'lam?

Maintaining my studious objectivity, and heeding Jiro's raised eyebrows as I nearly opened my big mouth, I didn't mention the Mal'lam to this fellow. But another door of possibility has opened. Only time will tell. Summer vacation is here and Tina has lots more to relate of her 'voice's' on-going tale of the Mal'lam. Someday I'll have the proper perspective on this whole thing and write a thesis on it. I'll probably be an old granny by then. Grumble, grumble! But then, here's more . . .

Chapter Twenty Nine - Prepare to Sail

It took A'lan Sea-Hewn a few days to get over his anger at his best friend, Shen'ham.That his friend would even consider returning to the known when the unknown held so much promise was still beyond his understanding. Yet it was testament to his basic sensibility that on that afternoon that they were put together to work on some replacement matting for one of the canoe sails, he lowered his shield of anger and disappointment.

Shen'ham, stung and disappointed by A'lan's attitude, had kept to himself after their first argument, even moving to another hut to sleep. Now, bent over some cordage, the day very hot and humid and making any work a sweaty task, he was about to stop for a drink. A'lan was feeling the same heat and thirst and had been first to pick up the hollow bamboo tube and uncork it, pouring the cool water into a half-gourd container. "Want some water, Sha?" A'lan asked, using Shen'ham's nickname. 'What?' Shen'ham answered peevishly and stood up … only to receive the gourd-full of water squarely in his face! Spluttering and gasping, he recoiled at first. Then with a roar he charged at A'lan. A'lan backed up running, pouring another serving of water which again caught Shen'ham full in the face. Then they were locked together, the water tube and gourd gone flying as they rolled together on the sand. Punches became jabs in the ribs, became tickling, became pushing and pulling. Growls of anger became grunts, became chuckles, became giddy giggles as they eventually both dissolved into gales of laughter. Boys again. Friends again and forever!

A scowling senior seaman stood up from his own work, about to shout at these reckless youngsters when Al'malan, who had been standing nearby, held his hand up to halt the seaman's remonstrance. "Let them be, Wen'lat. It'll soon pass." He walked away grinning. The lads returned to their work with the tension of the past few days forgotten, chatting away as they always had. What they were working on, the replacement of a panel of woven pandanus fiber, required not only skill but very strong fingers and hands. Both were quickly developing the requisite skill. That they had strong hands and grips could not be questioned. All Sea-Hewn had tough, gnarled hands by the time they were but two years into their apprenticeship. They were now joined in their task by the Itin Sea-Master, Ch'am'lo. This Itin seaman and warrior had formed a warm relationship with many of the Mal'lam Sea-Hewn, these two youngsters among his favorites. He unrolled the tough cordage of coconut fiber from a skein and fed it to A'lan as he threaded it through the spaces in the woven panel which Shen'ham was opening ahead of him. Three sets of hands made this task much easier and as they worked they talked.

"Do you know yet which Sea-Master will take over 'Wa'Boton', Ch'am'lo-an?" A'lan asked.

"No," the Sea-Master answered, "That's yet to be decided. As you would know, the Council will have to debate the question. I might not learn the answer to that before I leave." A'lan frowned briefly, still not reconciled to this valuable man deciding to return to Sht'ah Lee-Set. He could envision the man's martial skills being of great importance should the on-going voyagers run into man-made trouble. Such were his thought processes; already planning well ahead into the unknown. "Have the Sea-Masters decided when the voyage will resume?" Shen'ham asked, just as curious as A'lan."No, again! There are still too many things that need to be organized. Food will be a big problem, we all know that. As well, more Sea-Hewn feel they may be needed here to help support the people who remain to settle 'Snake Island'. Frankly, I think there will be but three canoes fully manned to set off." The three then turned the big panel over to sew from the other side, a task requiring some grunting and blowing - it was heavy.

Beginning again, they settled down to repeat the rather monotonous task. "Have you been practicing with your sling, Sea-Hewn?" Ch'am'lo asked Shen'ham. He was impressed with the lad's expertise with that toy-become-weapon."Yes, Sea-Master. And I've been teaching a couple of our Tarbara'ut friends to use it. One of them is getting good at it. We were hunting some of those little birds that can't fly. You know the ones?" Ch'am'lo nodded affirmatively. There were many of these flightless birds here on these islands, found mostly deep in the forests where sling hunting was most difficult. "The boys and I kept snagging our slings up in the branches. We spent most of our time laughing our heads off!"

"Well," Ch'am'lo said, "You'll have plenty of opportunity to practice on the trip back home. I suggest you load a lot of sling stones onto the canoe. We don't want you getting bored or losing your edge." He followed with a serious tone. "That skill may be needed, Sea-Hewn. The *seers* are still giving warnings; daily, almost." All three were quiet with their own thoughts for some minutes then. Finally the task was finished and they stood looking down at the completed work, rightfully proud of a good job done. Even for young bodies, the work required cramped positions and strain which caused stiffness and aching muscles. Ch'am'lo, older and feeling it perhaps more said, "Alright lads. Time for some exercises. Come, I'll show you how to limber up quickly."

Standing straight he arched his back, moving his spine sideways and back and forth, leaned forward slightly, then he swung both arms forward briskly and somersaulted backward, landing squarely on both feet. The two youngsters' jaws gaped in awe. "Try that!" the Itin master of martial arts said, grinning like a teenage show-off. The boys looked at him in disbelief. Ch'am'lo chuckled and grinned at them again, more generously now. He'd had his fun. "Another time, my friends! You might really hurt yourselves without proper preparation. But do this . . . !" and he led them in a series of exercises of stretching and bending, reaching and thrusting which took them back to the training he had conducted before that horrible combat with' Tor'na the Mad'.

A'lan knew that he was going to miss this unique man's presence on the upcoming voyage to the southern sea. In the days, hopefully, weeks before their departure back to the home island, A'lan determined to spend as much time as possible in the company of this man. He knew that one day, probably not too distant either, he would need to know much more about martial arts. A'lan had killed before. The experience still haunted him. But he had a strong sense of the power inherent in the ability to kill if necessary, or simply imply that ability to cause a potential adversary pause in his reckoning.

Later that day A'lan Sea-Hewn sat working alone in the shifting shade of the coconut grove, a brisk wind waving the fronds in a rustling whisper; a background to his private thoughts. He was plaiting cordage into stronger, small diameter rope for use in temporary lashings aboard the canoes. It was solitary, monotonous work, requiring little concentration or skill, but it needed doing as great lengths of this cord were required on each vessel. His mind was centered on the upcoming voyaging; actually, little else occupied his keen brain. He was running through the list of logistics involved in preparing the big vessels for sailing:

Certainly, 'Wa'Ran'tar' would soon be sailing but outfitting that canoe would be less demanding than had its first sailing to these islands been. The return voyage to Sh'tah Lee-Set would not require the shipping of the pigs, chickens and dogs. Therefore, no fodder would be required either. No plant materials for starting new gardens, no herbs, no bamboos, no plants whatever since this vessel was returning to where all those originated. With the exception of food and water and the minimal personal items and spare materials for maintaining the canoe while underway, 'Wa'Ran'tar' would run light and free on winds of whatever set. A'lan liked that idea, except that that canoe would be sailing in the wrong direction for his designs.

And who would be sailing home to Sh'tah Lee? Well, that much seemed to have been finalized already. He now accepted Shen'ham's reasons for going, although he knew he would miss his dear friend badly. Why Joha'lan and Sha'lat were returning was becoming more obvious all the time; their dear ones were in great danger! There would be thirteen Sea-Hewn making the return voyage, more than enough to safely sail the canoe. Al'malan's plan, of course, was to push his vessel as hard as was reasonable and return home as quickly as possible. Two other Wood-Hewn would be aboard too, two Herb-Hewn, two Clay-Plait and three Herb-Plait making up a total of twenty-four aboard. Certainly there are many imponderables involved, not least of which would be weather and current. But now at least they knew the course home.

A good seaman watches that part of the night sky which recedes behind him as well as a new sky approaching. This was certainly done and the path to this archipelago was memorized on the way here and would be doubly checked as the course home was taken. That was one reason for Sea-Master Ham'sha insisting on being aboard. A bit difficult to understand sometimes, a man of no close friendships and no wife or children, he was nevertheless well respected as a seaman. His one good eye served him well for he even possessed that 'sea-sight' which set him among a small, elite group of Sea-Hewn.

Sensitive to all aspects of the vagaries of sea and sky, Ham'sha also catalogued in his expansive memory the paths of seasonal seabirds, fish, turtles and whales. A casual question by someone just passing the time of day might result in a long dissertation on some vaguely related subject. His dedication to the on-going voyaging was no less than any other Sea-Hewn's. Ham'sha simply had a deeper grasp of the requirements of the up-coming, two-way traffic between these islands and their homeland. Only two of his crew aboard the 'Wa'Boton' had chosen to follow his lead and return to Sht'ah Lee, both for similar reasons: to assure a depth of talent that the Mal'lam could depend upon.

The inescapable reality of continuing the onward voyage was that, one; not enough foodstuffs were available yet. The most ambitious estimates put that eventuality at least twelve to sixteen months away, even given how quickly things grew in this climate, two; that the makeup of the on-going fleet and its command structure had yet to be determined. The solution to the first problem was inescapably obvious: Sea-Hewn would have to become farmers and fishermen, gathering smelly lots of fish for drying and preservation and getting their hands dirty and developing aching backs from agricultural toil! There was no way around it. Grumbles were plenty.

Only the prospect of the open horizon managed to sustain their commitment to the distasteful inevitable. That second problem would require long and thoughtful working out. That was just as well, for the Mal'lam tradition of conciliation and compromise needed time to properly apply itself. A solution would be found while open-sea sailors sat in small dugout canoes and fished and chatted; others would find the solutions while stopping to wipe away sweat and mud while working in the paddies and gardens. They were still a sensible people who lived by the inevitable, sensible flow of nature. It was a form of democracy, one might conclude.

~ ~ * ~ ~

Al'malan and Joha'lan sat together on the coral sand beach in the light of the rising, nearly full moon. Soon the other two Sea-Masters on this voyage, Ch'am'lo and Ham'sha would join them. The eve of a sailing was always a tense and worrying time for the master of a vessel, especially this vessel and at this time. In a sense, they would be sailing to a destination of unknowns as much as would the other voyagers, months from now. The visions of clairvoyant *seers* were never substantial enough to provide certainty. That some very serious disruption threatened their people back on Sht'ah Lee was a message often enough repeated that that much could be relied upon. But just what, how, where and many other questions would find no answers until these returnees reached home. The weight of this not-knowing now displayed itself on the moonlit face of the Voyage-Master.

Joha'lan had been surreptitiously watching his friend's face and body language. Finally he reached out a hand and slapped Al'malan on the thigh. "I think we will have adequate time in which to prepare ourselves, brother!" he said, "Sometimes, my friend, you do worry just a bit too much, eh?" Al'malan turned to answer but just then Ham'sha Sea-Master arrived - looking worried! He sat down quickly, facing both men so that he could see their faces clearly. Without ado he began to unfold his concerns.

"My brothers," he began, his fingers playing among themselves in a dance which displayed his nervousness. "We are to sail tomorrow. We are still short of sixteen tubes of drinking water! Where will we find those bamboo tubes before launching time?" He hardly paused for a breath let alone an answer. "And where are the two young crewmen who were to join us? What are their names? Oh yes. Shen'ham and Shal'tan?" Al'malan composed his face with some effort, darkness aiding in hiding his near-grin. Ham'sha had been like this the night before their little flotilla had left Sht'ah Lee.

On that night too, almost exactly a year ago now, he had been dumb-founded to discover that one of his Masters was acting like a silly little girl! He worried about every little detail which had already been attended to the day before. By now Al'malan was quite used to his comrade's fuss-budget dramas on the eve of sailing; he had spent all the daylight hours doing the same thing. He just listened patiently as Ham'sha finally ran down like a top. When finally he had finished his discourse and adjusted his posture, no longer leaning forward to accentuate his intensity, he peered one-eyed at Al'malan with great intensity, expecting to be mollified of his concerns. He was.

Al'malan simply took a deep breath, leaned confidentially toward his second-in-command and said, "These things were taken care of just a short while ago, Ham'sha-an. Sorry brother, I simply hadn't had time yet to inform you. Thank you for double-checking." Ham'sha straightened up, made a serious face, nodded with grave satisfaction and said, "Good. Thank you Voyage-Master." With a sniff of satisfaction he then rose, nodded at Al'malan and Joha'lan and padded away into the night to catch a modicum of rest. Not a night for levity,

Joha'lan nevertheless sniggered quietly as Al'malan reached across and thumped him on the thigh, his own chuckles discreet little snorts.

From among the shadows behind them, just beyond their sight, came the clearing of a throat; someone politely requesting recognition. "Come." said the Voyage-Master, quite expecting a visit from this person tonight. It was A'lan Sea-Hewn. Al'malan would have been greatly disappointed in fact, had this young man not come to speak with him on this important evening.

"Sit, Seaman of the Mal'lam. We are pleased that you join us!" Al'malan's gracious invitation ran like warm water through A'lan and he quickly sat across from his Sea-Hewn Master and that other man whom he greatly admired, Joha'lan Canoe-Master. These two men represented to the young seaman the epitome of what he had aspired to most of his short life. And now, on this sad occasion, both would sail away from him before the morning's sun was fully into the sky. How could he express his deep regard for them without betraying his quiet dismay at their decision to return to the homeland? No young initiate, with the possible exception of Shen'ham, would have presumed to approach his Elders on such a special night simply to tell them that he wished they would change their minds! Not even the other Sea-Masters, those remaining behind, had felt it necessary to intrude upon these two head-men on a sailing eve. But A'lan Sea-Hewn had already made his mark as a dedicated, fiercely determined individual whose quick mind and exceptional intelligence was matched by a growing capacity with his *sea-sight'*.

Al'malan regretted not having A'lan with them on this voyage; yet he knew that A'lan's Destiny lay upon unknown seas and adventures which he, himself, would not encounter. Al'malan Voyage-Master had his own Destiny to fulfill and it would most likely be years before these two sailors greeted each other again. A'lan was momentarily taken aback when Joha'lan asked him, "Have you come here tonight to persuade us to change our minds about sailing?" There was a vague note of censure in his voice but in the darkness A'lan could not quite read the man's eyes. Undeterred he replied, "I must admit, Canoe-Master, that I would surely prefer that you remain and continue the voyage of exploration. But truly, I do understand why you must go."

To escape any further admonition from his esteemed elders, A'lan quickly shifted course and asked that Al'malan carry A'lan's love to his own mother and also his blessings to Sht'ana Leaf-Plait, the new baby girl and to Al'malan's son, Sahn'ta. And then almost forgetting, he added that he sent his best regards to Tina-an, now Joha'lan's step-daughter. A few moments of awkward silence later and Al'malan chuckled quietly, his wide grin gleaming in the moonlight. "Thank you Sea-Hewn. We are indeed grateful for your coming here tonight and for the good wishes which we will indeed carry home with us. I, personally, will miss your mate-ship upon 'Wa'Ran'tar'. You are a fine seaman already, A'lan-an, and our people will prosper from your presence on our voyaging canoes. May the *Earth Mother* and the 'Gods of the Sea' watch over you." With that Al'malan reached both hands out to the young man and they sat sharing a moment's special regard. Joha'lan then did the same, adding his own quiet blessing to the moment. He was himself secure in the belief that A'lan Sea-Hewn would be a most exceptional man; perhaps even great, whatever that might be! Greatness was not a concept much discussed in this society.

A'lan suddenly became aware of a glow which suffused the air around these two men; mist-like it was, of a rosy hue and shifting to a reddish-yellow, then gold … then gone! The men sat in silence as the lad rose and bowed slightly and disappeared among the night's shadows.

"Good evening, brothers. What a beautiful night!" It was Ch'am'lo, as usual full of energy and good cheer. Both Mal'lam grinned widely as the slight, muscular Itin Sea-Master sat down in that easy movement which his martial training had created as a signature of the man's physicality. "You're late, Sea-Master!" Al'malan said, trying to sound grumpy and authoritative. Joha'lan added his own grumpy harrumph, which actually came out sounding like a frog croaking and soon all three were cackling and giggling. Ch'am'lo had been sitting very quietly in the deep shadows not ten feet from where Al'malan and Joha'lan had spent the past forty minutes and had observed the comings and goings over that time. He wasn't spying! Actually, the two Elders had plunked themselves down for the evening without even seeing one of their most valued seamen sitting in a meditative state beneath palm fronds only a few steps away.

"Well, Ch'am-an," Al'malan said, using the familiar and informal address allowed among friends. "are we truly ready to set sail tomorrow?" Ch'am'lo paused and considered his reply, then finally squeezed a retort from around a building gale of laughter, "Wellll! Noooo! We are about six women short for a voyage like this one - don't you think?" A handful of cool sand flew his way from Al'malan's hand and Joha'lan reached out and grabbed for the man's arm but he was too slow. Suddenly Ch'am'lo was on his feet and bowing deeply, and sincerely, to his two friends. "Gentlemen, if you're half as tired as I am, it's time we wise and wonderful Elders got some sleep. Otherwise, we'll all three be stupid and half-awake when our canoe leaves the beach." He began chuckling wickedly, "Can't you just imagine that?" Another handful of sand flew his way and missed its target. He was gone, totally out of sight, flitting among other fleeting, wind-driven shadows. Al'malan and Joha'lan retired to their respective beds for those few hours of rest which the short night still afforded.

~ ~ * ~ ~

A'lan Sea-Hewn was busily attending to fiddly little items aboard 'Wa'Ran'tar' as the first rays of the sun began to lighten the sky. With him was his dear friend, Shen'ham. They spoke in a near whisper, aware that there were three Sea-Hewn aboard still sleeping in spite of eager restlessness. This was the day! 'Wa'Ran'tar' would sail on this morning's lowering tide and begin the journey home to Sht'ah Lee-Set! In unspoken harmony both young seamen turned together to face the rising sun. They stood silently, arms relaxed, hands empty and watched as the orange ball glowed into existence through a thin layer of cloud. That cloud lay just above the horizon, a flimsy last bastion of night. Within an hour those clouds would move on over the horizon, surrendering the sky to an awesome blueness which would prevail throughout this special day.

Other seamen now began to arrive and there was a general stirring of activity on the beach. Last minute bundles of personal belongings were being stowed in the niches among the bundles of foodstuffs, rope, gourds and other cargo. Two hundred freshly harvested ripe coconuts were now stowed aboard and one hundred green, drinking nuts. These green nuts would be consumed first as they would only retain their freshness for a few days. Stones for ringing the fireplace on the open deck and the sand and coral gravel to act as a fireproof floor for the fire were laid out in front of the canoe's low, thatched shelter.

The six women passengers saw to the stowing of their own parcels and baskets and then sat themselves near the little hut, out of the way of the Sea-Hewn as they made last minute preparations. Shen'ham's own bundle had been stowed the night before. He now rolled and gathered his wrap up just above his knees and cinched the woven fiber belt around his waist. From that belt hung his personal seaman's knife, its obsidian blade and carved hardwood handle resting in a smoked pigskin sheath. All Sea-Hewn so adjusted their clothing when preparing for going on duty, freeing their legs for maximum flexibility and extension. A'lan, out of an acquired habit, nearly followed suit but smiled sheepishly at his friend, accepting that this day, he would remain ashore.

Hardly a word passed between the two as they worked side by side in helping prepare for launching.The heavy hawsers of coconut fiber ropes, three plaited together, were untied from their palm tree anchors and coiled on the bridging deck. Later, when safely at sea, they would be stowed below in one of the hulls. 'Wa'Ran'tar' now floated free of any restraints with only the very front of the two hulls resting on the coral sand. The long tell-tales which danced from their mast tops made the tall masts and sail panels look animated; the vessel had the appearance of a creature waiting in anxious anticipation.

These new sails, well proven now on the long voyage to these islands, required less muscle power than those cantankerous triangular sails which the Mal'lam had depended upon for so many generations. The thirteen Sea-Hewn aboard, plus whatever assistance might be offered by the other passengers, assured an efficient, twenty-four hour run under sail; assuming no heavy storms or calms interrupted. Chants and songs now began and combined with the rising general clamor, aided by the cheers and chatter of the Tarbara'ut.

Their musical language was a liquid babble compared to the more clipped, glottal sounds of Mal'lam. Faldo Sea-Master, his brother Enno standing beside him was attempting, for the twentieth time perhaps, to explain to the little black people why these Mal'lam were going away. These people had no recollection of such an endeavor. It had been very many generations since the Tarbara'ut had set forth on the open sea. These people had been so content to remain where they were, here on these few islands, that it boggled their comprehension to witness such frenetic activity.

Faldo-an had determined months ago that he would join no voyage, ever again. Rather, as the only Mal'lam with a knowledge of the Tarbara'ut language and society, he was absolutely essential to the ongoing residence of the Mal'lam in this archipelago."That rotten shark must have known somehow that my Destiny lay here with these beautiful islands. What spirals of Fate and energy the *Earth Mother* does weave around us!" Faldo's philosophizing ended abruptly when questions again assailed him in the language of the Tarbara'ut.

Why are there so few women aboard that canoe?" asked one elderly black islander. "They will be exhausted by all those men wanting their bodies. No?"

Faldo could only smile in reply, adding that when the Mal'lam were sailing on a long voyage, lovemaking was not allowed: he mumbled something about conserving energy, preventing jealousy, preventing pregnancies which might culminate in Mal'lam children being born on unfriendly shores. He might just as well have saved his breath. It was impossible for the Tarbara'ut to comprehend why anyone would want to set sail for the 'unknown beyond' when here was solid land and security, and willing women any given day. Strange, these newcomers! All the natives could do was roll their eyes in wonder.

The activity on the beach now was at a climax; last minute additions of almost-forgotten parcels or tools which had escaped even the most thorough itemization of those responsible for such things were being handed aboard. Shen'ham had remained ashore until the last moment. Loath to part from his dear friend, A'lan had held him in a long embrace. He whispered to Shen'ham, "Give my love to my mother, to your mother and to Tina-an. Assure them that I *will* see them again. And you, brother, take very good care of yourself. We will sail together again!" With tears in their eyes the two young men let go of each other and Shen'ham turned and ran and leaped aboard 'Wa'Ran'tar' as the dozens of helpers gathered around the vessel to begin pushing it into the waiting sea. The songs of parting then began:

"*Return to us, brave voyagers . . .*"

Chapter Thirty - The Voyage Home

Twelve little Tarbara'ut canoes, their crews paddling hard to keep up with the big double-hulled vessel, finally had to relinquish the struggle. The tall broad sails of 'Wa'Ran'tar' now caught the rising wind and her own paddlers stowed their paddles and began securing the woven mats as covers over the open hulls. This morning the wind was fair, out of the south with a touch of easting. The big canoe rode easily over the smooth swells ever more swiftly. Noticeably lighter than when it had arrived, it danced joyously over the deep blue waters beyond the reef. The helmsman felt the difference too. 'Wa'Ran'tar surged ahead with less control needed on the long steering oar, less muscle needed to maintain the course. To those with a great sensitivity to sailing vessels, it was obvious that this one was eager to get home!

The keenest eyes aboard could no longer make out the beaches, the surf breaking on the reef or the little square sails of the Tarbara'ut canoes. Only the high, green hills of the islands were visible and they were becoming obscured in a late morning cloud cover. All aboard were reminded of the sad day of departure from Sht'ah Lee-Set but that day the massive height of Volan'Votu had remained visible until after sunset. Now here they were again, fighting back tears as they left behind loved ones. Shen'ham Sea-Hewn remained perched high on the aft mast until cramping muscles drove him back to the deck. His heart bore sadness but his eyes were dry. He was going home and the joy of that prospect overrode his loneliness for friends left ashore behind him.

Another, very special reason for returning made him smile. That first day's running boded well for this voyage. Though the wind kept shifting northerly, the tall sails needed only minor adjustments to continue pulling at their maximum efficiency. A direct northerly would certainly require tacking but that maneuver with this vessel was so much easier than with those old, bulky, triangular sails. These sails had now become and would for generations remain, the unique signature of a Mal'lam voyaging canoe. And these southern seas would eventually count thousands of such sightings. All aboard 'Wa'Ran'tar' this day shared a strong confidence. Sea-Master Al'malan, like most captains, gave little away of his inner feelings when under sail. But his very *being* rejoiced with the same enthusiasm as those around him displayed. A quick glance at his great friend, Joha'lan, revealed that the big Woodsman shared the same joy.

Still within the range of seabirds which roosted on the islands of the Tarbara'ut, late afternoon saw large groups of them returning to shore, flying over or near 'Wa'Ran'tar'. "These will be the last birds we're likely to see from now on, until we near Sh'tah Lee." said the Sea-Master, Ham'sha, standing beside Al'malan in the afternoon's fading brilliance. "Yes, brother." Al'malan replied, the days emotions and a nearly sleepless night before beginning to weigh heavily on him. Turning to the one-eyed seaman he asked, "Can you take the first watch tonight, Ham'sha?" The ever-diligent Sea-Master replied with excess gravity, "Certainly Voyage-Master!" He drew nearer to Al'malan and spoke in a near whisper, "I know how trying this day must have been for you. Please rest now. I shall supervise the night watches … if you wish?" That tone of obsequiousness made Al'malan uncomfortable. Tired as he was, he registered this for future consideration. But now, he did need some rest. It had been a very long day and the sun was only now beginning to set. His inner hearing, that special sixth sense, recorded a long, fading echo of the man's parting words as Al'malan went into his sleeping quarters in the covered space in the port hull. "Be watchful!" was the inference of his inner acuity. He slept deeply, dreaming of lovemaking with his sweet Sh'tana.

~ ~ * ~ ~

The winds had been strongly from the east southeast for twelve days. 'Wa'Ran'tar' was making wonderfully fast headway on a course just west of north. Storms had passed away to each side of that course but only sporadic showers were encountered. Rainwater was gathered whenever possible and the sun beat down brutally. Everyone was thirsty and Al'malan was seriously considering rationing their drinking water when, on the afternoon of that day they encountered a series of line-squalls which more than replenished their supply.

Sunset was celebrated in the sea around them too. A group of six massive, majestic whales, three on each side of the canoe, came from behind them, their exhalations rising many feet above. "Hoosh'im'la'lat" Sea-Master Ham'sha cried. And so they were; the second largest whale ever to live, their black backs displaying a large, curved fin as they dove back under the water. They slowly overtook the speeding canoe and passed it. One whale raised its great head momentarily, scanning this strange floating object and then it too dove and continued on. With awe and admiration, all the Mal'lam watched the whales disappear into the hazy sea ahead of 'Wa'Ran'tar' "Hoosh'im'la'lat are considered a very good omen by my people." said Sea-Master Ch'am'lo. He, Al'malan and Sea-master Ham'sha had been sitting together at the front of the vessel's bridging deck. Out of the corner of his eye Al'malan saw a pucker of what might have been disdain momentarily flash across Ham'sha's face. He was already aware of the man's almost forced camaraderie in Ch'am'lo's presence but had never heard nor suspected an active prejudice in him. Al'malan's sensitive inner ear had nothing to judge by in this instance but he would pay close attention in future.

"I am amazed at how fast they are!" Al'malan said, hoping to lighten the disquiet he still felt. They returned to their previous discussion having to do with the stars. With night approaching, all three would be on deck again, memorizing the heavens in relation to their present course. Ham'sha would again sit alone most of the night, applying his *sea-sight* with his one eye, searching for any long, sinuous lines of light beneath the surface. That special sense would be their first indication of land anywhere near them.

Ham'sha explained to them that every body of land had a specific signature, a complex of colors and intensities which were emitted by that one island alone. Even in the confused light-show beneath the sea when in proximity to a group of islands, each one spoke its own identification. Ham'sha Sea-Master, one-eyed or not, was a master of this craft. What his experience did not inform him of however, was the existence of seamounts, still deep below the surface but massive enough to generate those light signatures. Extraordinarily, that archipelago which was their original home saw every ancient volcano reach the surface of the sea. Some eroded into stony reefs just below the surface but no deep-water mounts existed there which would send out their own signature.

With a softly spoken request, Canoe-Master Joha'lan approached and asked to sit down with the Sea-Masters and was immediately included. The big man sat quietly and listened, simply enjoying the mateship of the warm evening. They were soon joined by Sha'lat Herb-Mistress and another Herb-Plait, Ven'ana. At this, Ham'sha excused himself politely and went to get something to eat. Sha'lat sat next to her husband, one hand resting on his knee, Ven'ana beside her. "I have words you should hear, Voyage-Master!" Ven'ana said softly, leaning across Sha'lats legs toward Al'malan. Ch'am'lo stirred as if to rise and leave them but Ven'ana said, "Please, Ch'am'lo-an. These words are for your ears also." He shifted himself on his buttocks to more squarely face the woman and hear her message.

"Al'malan-an, my Spirits inform me that events at home on Sh'tah Lee are becoming very serious. Sht'ana, your son Sahn'ta and your daughter - La'teel is the name her mother has chosen for her - are all under threat from Ja'eel!" The woman looked away from the stricken faces before her, her powerful psychic abilities sometimes a terrible burden when having to impart such painful information.

"Sea-Master Ch'am'lo," and she now looked directly into his eyes, "Ja'eel has cursed all Itin. She declares that your people must all die because you do not recognize her Gods!" Ven'ana sat waiting for a reply which she knew would come from this exceptional man. "All I can say to that, Ven'ana-an, is that my people and I have no knowledge of her *Gods*," and he spat the word out like a sour fruit, "and she has exposed herself as a great fool." He shifted a bit as if some small itch needed scratching. "The time will come, soon enough I think, when that silly woman will have to answer to herself for what she is about!" Ch'am'lo looked directly into Al'malan's eyes now with all the strength of their friendship. "Brother Sea-Master, we must get home as quickly as we can. Unless I'm mistaken," and he grinned mischievously, "you have no special power over the Sea Gods, whoever they might be, so I suggest that we all give a special thanks and appeal to *Earth Mother* to allow us smooth passage back to our home island."

"Dear Ch'am'lo," Sha'lat said, and she reached out to give the back of his hand a convivial slap, "you are indeed a valuable friend!" The five of them closed their eyes in unison and sent their individual prayers to that power beyond any of them, unknown to any of them, hoped for by all of them.

~ ~ * ~ ~

On the twenty-seventh day of their journey, the winds having remained kind and co-operative from the southeast, 'Wa'Ran'tar' rode over high swells emanating from some great storm to their northwest. Shen'ham Sea-Hewn was aloft as lookout, his feet firmly but tiresomely resting on the loops of rope tied around the bamboo rung for this purpose, one arm gripped around the mast and keen eyes focused on the horizon from port to starboard. It was near midday and his right hand shaded his eyes from the hot sun's glare. Directly below him on the deck, by the foremast, Al'malan Voyage-Master stood leaning on the rope-wrapped timber of the mast. The heat of the day produced a somnolence among most of the crew and passengers; nodding heads of crewmen fought to maintain awareness as the regular surge of wave coincided with the gentle, complimentary roll and plunge of the vessel. So it had been for days now; both monotony and acknowledgement that they were finally nearing their goal. The Sea-Hewn aboard were in agreement that the doldrums which has assailed them on their journey southward had been passed.

Nevertheless, the midday heat saw most of the passengers lying beneath the shelter of the small hut amidships, the screening panels at both ends open to allow the breeze through. Most were sleeping or adrift among daydreams. Ch'am'lo sat in the scant shade of the aft sail, discussing martial movements with the young Sea-Hewn, Shal'tan, Shen'ham's initiation-mate. Roll after roll of regular swell raised 'Wa'Ran'tar' up and over the mesmeric rhythm of this day's sea. The assistant to the helmsman, seated near him, cast a cluster of coconut shells lashed to a long line into the sea, drawing up cooling seawater with which he dowsed himself and the man on the steering oar; temporary relief from the heat.

A sudden, larger swell, coupled with a strong gust of easterly wind, caused the foresail to swing against its restraining sheet and the sheet parted. The rigid, upright sail swung in response to these forces and moved suddenly aft, the ropes securing the woven sail to the mast, upon which Shen'ham's left-handed grip rested, momentarily opened in response. And as quickly and forcefully those ropes closed over the left hand of the lookout, crushing his hand beneath the force of the sail's recovery. Al'malan looked up reflexively in response to the shriek of pain from above him! What he saw was the body of the young Sea-Hewn swinging by his left hand from the mast, his right hand reaching out desperately to grab hold of something to support him - something to relieve the pain which ran down from his left hand and filled his whole body with its agony!

That cry of pain woke most drowsing Mal'lam, most looking about for its source. Shal'tan Sea-Hewn, even more quickly than Ch'am'lo, scrambled to his feet and ran forward to where Al'malan stood, momentarily helpless, trying to assess the situation. With astonishing reflex, that young seaman swept past his Sea-Master and leaped onto the mast, grabbed hold of the circling ropes and began pulling himself upward toward his suffering friend. Shen'ham's cries of pain and calls for assistance continued, sending chills of foreboding through the gathering people below.

Al'malan ducked sideways and grabbed a loose coil of rope from the deck. "Shal'tan!" he shouted upward to the lad, "Take this. Tie it under Shen'ham's arms, tightly, and loop it over the upper stay. We'll lower him down when you've done that!" Al'malan tossed the loops of rope upward, missed, recovered the rope and tossed again. This time the young seaman caught it and scrambled with amazing agility up to his friend. By now Shen'ham had caught hold of a rope-wrapped rung with his right hand and his legs had found a hold around the swinging mast. His left hand remained trapped beneath the tight ropes around the mast, blood pouring down his arm and falling in crimson droplets onto the deck below. Ch'am'lo Sea-Master was soon up the mast behind the young seaman, both of them quickly close beneath the stricken Shen'ham. Shen'ham, his face pale with pain and fear, looked down upon his rescuers with pleading eyes. Shal'tan now moved upward to support his friend with his own body, pushing forcefully to ease the weight of Shen'ham's body which was increasing his agony.

Al'malan shouted to another crewman to secure a strong line to the boom to replace the broken one; another swing of the mast might be disastrous! While this was occurring, Ch'am'lo had worked his way up and partially over Shal'tan's body to see what the situation was with Shen'ham's left hand. Aghast, he hesitated only moments. Shen'ham had his face pressed against the mast, his right hand gripping a rung. His left hand was still wedged tightly beneath that rope which wound around the mast. Bare bones stood out starkly against blood-smeared wood and rope.

Below, Al'malan again shouted to a crewman forward to secure the boom with yet another line. His face and chest and arms were spotted with Shen'ham's blood. Ch'am'lo said, "I'll support you, Shal'tan-an. Put the rope under Shen'ham's arms and tie it tightly." Ch'am'lo now had his left arm clasped tightly around the mast, his right hand gripping the ropes, his shoulder pushing upward on the young seaman's buttocks, his legs clamped to the mast by the Sea-Master's chest. The long, high swells were quite regular and Ch'am'lo was able to adjust his body to the sway of the mast as the vessel rode up and over each wave. His mind raced: what now? What's the next move?

Then he turned his head downward and shouted to the deck, "Joha'lan! I need your sharpest adze. Get it quickly. I'll send the end of this rope down. Tie it to that." Shal'tan Sea-Hewn now had the rope wound around Shen'ham's chest and up under his arms. Cham'lo's own arms and legs were burning with the strain of essentially supporting both young men's weight. "I've got it tied, Sea-Master. Now what?" The lad's voice was tense with strain and fear. No sounds were coming from Shen'ham. "Now wrap the rope around through the sail loops", Chom'lo replied, "Here's the end - and get Shen'ham tight against the mast so that he can't slip down."

That maneuver took what seemed ages as it was difficult to push the end of the rope through. Joha'lan called up that he had the adz ready. Everyone on deck was craning their neck upward, even the helmsman found it hard to look away and focus on the approaching swells.

"Shen'ham?" Ch'am'lo called. The lad answered, his voice weak and frightened. "What I want you to do is hold on tightly with your right hand while Shal'tan tightens the rope around you. Can you do that?" Ch'am'lo's own voice was high with tension.

"Yes - yes I can." Shen'ham replied and his young mate quickly cinched the rough coconut fiber around Shen'ham. "Done!" he said. Ch'am'lo was near to exhaustion but called up all his reserves of strength. "Now, Shal'tan, I want you to slip beneath me and climb down. Take the end of the rope down with you and tie the adze to it. Alright?" Without answering, the young seaman wrapped his arms onto the mast, fingers clutching for a hold, and began to worm his way beneath Ch'am'lo's body.

Trusting the lad's rope work - he had no choice - Ch'am'lo reached upward and altered his grasp on the mast until he was pressed full length against Shen'ham's back and legs. With his head close behind the suffering boy's he muttered to him, gasping for air as he did so. "Shen'ham, do you know what I have to do?" The boy's head nodded and he grunted acknowledgement. Good! This lad has courage, Ch'am'lo thought. What had to be done was to amputate two fingers from Shen'ham's left hand!

The rope which had trapped his fingers between it and the hardwood mast had stripped the flesh from all of his little finger and half of the finger next to it. The rope lay over the knuckle and still clamped his hand firmly. That pressure was in itself a blessing. It had eased the bleeding to a trickle. But the exposed bones of those two savaged members lay pinned beneath the rope and there was no way to move the rope away except to cut it; and that would mean that the line securing the sail to the mast would immediately begin unraveling and the wind's pressure on the sail would quickly rip the sail away from its moorings. To prevent a potential disaster, a Sea-Hewn was about to make a mighty sacrifice.

"Don't think, just do!" Ch'am'lo said to himself, forcing that steadiness of mind and focus of intent which his years of training had instilled in him. A tug on the rope from below brought him back from his concentration on his breathing. He looked down, saw Joha'lan holding up the adz with its handle tightly wrapped in the rope. He hauled it awkwardly up with one hand, the other needed to hold on to the mast. Shen'ham's body was slipping downward, the rope around him cutting painfully into his side and back but he only groaned faintly.

The tool now grasped in his right hand, Ch'am'lo carefully shifted position until his head was at the height of that trapped hand. He found purchase for one foot on a rung, slowly worked his left hand into a tight grip on another, higher up and steadied himself. Shen'ham turned his head to look at Ch'am'lo but the man said, "Look away, brother. I'll be as quick as I can. Then we'll get you down from here. I promise you."

Ch'am'lo took a series of deep breaths, paused to judge the movement of the canoe as it rose over a wave and slipped gently down its face. Then he struck. The sharp stone blade separated the two fingers from the hand, barely missing the rope and the weight of Shen'ham's quivering arm pulled the knuckles from their entrapment. Blood flooded out, splashed over the Sea-Master's chest and fell down upon those looking upward. Ch'am'lo fought against a rising urge to vomit. Shen'ham's body now collapsed fully against the rope holding him to the mast. He had fainted.

Ch'am'lo felt someone touch his foot and looked quickly downward. It was Al'malan, his face and chest smeared with the boy's blood, his face twisted in a grimace of concern, fear and intense concentration all at once. "Can you tie this around his wrist, Ch'am-an?" he said, holding a length of cord up to Ch'am'lo. Ch'am'lo took it and as quickly as he could without letting go his own precarious hold, looped a pre-tied knot over the boy's limp arm at the wrist and cinched it tightly in a tourniquet. It took more agonizing minutes to re-thread the rope through the mast ties and drop the free end down toward the deck. Then that end had to be tied to another, longer rope but finally Shen'ham's unconscious form was slowly lowered downward. Al'malan and Ch'am'lo worked their way downward beneath him, Al'malan supporting Ch'amlo while Ch'am'lo supported Shen'ham.

The group of Mal'lam who gathered at the base of the mast, faces contorted in shock and fear, were asked to move aside as the three seamen finally reached the deck. It was Joha'lan who picked up the limp form of the young seaman as the rope was unwound from him and Sha'lat Herb-Mistress who immediately picked up his arm and investigated the wound. She winced inwardly while maintaining a calm exterior and still holding his arm, led Joha'lan toward the protection and seclusion of the little hut amidships.

Shen'ham began to come around as he was being laid onto a pallet, his eyelids fluttering open and then squeezing closed against the reborn pain. A soft roll of matting was placed beneath his head and he was offered a drink of cool water. He drank deeply, coughed and spluttered and lay his head back down, still awake but with eyes closed.

He knew he was in capable, loving hands now, could do nothing for himself anyway and tried to relax into his personal mantra of meditation. Therein lay some release from that terrible ordeal he had now escaped. A damp cloth was placed over his eyes and forehead, a double thickness of tapa cloth draped over his shivering body and his left arm brought out to rest on Sha'lat's lap. This work would require all of this gifted woman's experience and skill. Holding the injured hand gently in both of hers, she closed her eyes and sent prayers to the *Earth Mother*. She would need special help here.

The pharmacopoeia of a sailing canoe would have been inadequate to the task of repairing this ghastly wound; a brutal cauterization would have been the only recourse. But this day this young Sea-Hewn had the good fortune of the presence of one with inspired brilliance as a surgeon. Four hours later, Shen'ham slept deeply with the aid of some herbal concoctions prepared by another Herb-

Plait. That other Herbalist, Ven'ana, had blended a powerful sedative which made the ordeal less painful for the patient; indeed, it rendered him nearly unconscious throughout. Sha'lat lay beside her patient now, sleeping off the exhaustion of her work. This was the customary practice among Mal'lam healers; to rest with their patients, sharing in the healing process.

~ ~ * ~ ~

And where was Sea-Master Ham'sha during that drama earlier today? With all the attention focused upward toward the mast top and the duty crewmen scrambling about, trying to keep the vessel running smoothly over the swells, no one now seemed to recall seeing him during the whole drama.

It was twilight now, often a magical time of the day aboard a voyaging canoe in good weather. Al'malan and Ch'am'lo sat together at the forward end of the hut, Joha'lan and the Herb-Plait, Ven'ana inside keeping watch over the injured lad and the exhausted Herb-Mistress, Sha'lat. "Frankly, Ch'am'-an," Al'malan said, "I'm concerned about the man. One would have thought that as second-in-command, he would have been in the thick of things. And I've been noticing small things which, together, are a bit worrying."

Ch'am'lo answered gravely, "I know what you mean. I've always had a bit of difficulty communicating with Ham'sha. I thought he might be prejudiced against me because I'm Itin." He looked meaningfully at Al'malan, the fading light still allowing his features to be accurately read. Al'malan nodded and replied, "Yes, I have considered that but I think there's much more to his recent behavior which comes from somewhere deeper inside him than a bit of peevish jealousy. That's what I think his attitude to you reveals, by the way, not that you're Itin."

Al'malan shifted his position so that he could face Ch'am'lo closely and speak more intimately. "I have noticed that he seems a bit unsteady on his feet at times. It's hard to describe. He seems to reach out to steady himself often and sometimes he bumps into guy ropes and even a mast. Now, I can understand him not seeing something close to him on his right side, but he often collides with things on the side of his good eye."

Both men looked around the vessel, the mutual impulse being to spot where Ham'sha was now. This was his watch. Ch'am'lo even rose and looked to where their seated view was blocked. No Ham'sha!

"Perhaps he's ill and no one has noticed. Let's go see." Al'malan said and they strode to the rear of the port hull where his small compartment lay. "Ham'sha! Are you there brother?" Al'malan called quietly. No response. Both men went immediately to the mats covering Ham'sha's sleeping compartment and pulled them back. Nearly dark now, still they could make out the man's form lying on the light-colored sleeping mat. He was curled up in a fetal position on his left side, facing outward. He didn't move even as Al'malan stepped down into the cramped space and knelt beside the still form. He knew the man was not asleep. What was this? He must be very ill. He reached out a hand and placed it on Ham'sha's shoulder. It was warm and the man moved slightly in response. Al'malan turned and motioned for Ch'am'lo to join him, squeezing aside in the narrow hull space.

"Who is it?" came the first sign that the man was conscious, but he didn't turn his head toward them. He lay as still as death, his voice sounding disembodied. "It's Al'malan, Ham'sha. Are you ill brother?" Al'malan was bent over him now, bracing himself against the vessel's motion with one hand against the hull frame. "How can we help, my friend? What can we get for you?" Al'malan's concern was evident in his voice and he knelt completely now in the cramped quarters, ready to be of assistance.

"Nothing can be done, Voyage-Master. I am a dead man!" This was spoken so softly that Al'malan resorted to his inner hearing to try to divine the truth of what the man was saying. Still Ham'sha had not moved. Just then a large wave was encountered and spray rose over the hull's edge and splashed into the compartment, it's cold intrusion causing Al'malan and Ch'am'lo both to flinch and gasp. Ham'sha, likewise splashed with seawater, still didn't move.

Al'malan's hand was on the man's shoulder and would have felt the slightest response. It was as if the man *was* dead and only his Spirit was replying to Al'malan. A chill not caused by cold water ran up Al'malan's spine. "Can you sit up, brother?" Ch'am'lo asked, himself aware that something very strange was occurring. "Can I get you a drink of water?"

"I am dead! I need nothing. Go away now." Again that disembodied, creepy voice responded from the sleeping platform. Al'malan rose to his feet and motioned to Ch'am'lo to do the same. "Ch'am-an. Go fetch Ven'ana please. Hurry!" The Itin seaman leaped quickly upward and was on the deck and on his way in three seconds, disappearing into the dark of this moonless night.

"Can you tell me what is in your mind at this moment, Ham-an?" Al'malan thought perhaps the term of familiarity and friendship might rouse the man somewhat. He waited and in the near total darkness saw movement on the pallet before him. Ham'sha coughed once, twice and Al'malan could see him struggling to sit up. He reached out to help the man, fumbling in the darkness to find an arm or hand with which to assist him. He caught hold of an arm and felt Ham'sha raise himself into a sitting position, his back would have been resting against a bulkhead of timber slats.

Over the sound of sea and wind he could hear Ham'sha panting with his effort. He let go of the man's arm and sat back, allowing him freedom in his movements. Just then Ch'am'lo and Ven'ana arrived, their figures silhouetted against the night's stars. Ven'ana it was, who felt her way into the tight confines of the compartment, kneeling beside Al'malan and asking in a hushed voice what was happening. "Our friend," he said loudly, "is in some distress, Herb-Mistress. Perhaps you can offer some assistance to him. He believes he is dying."

"I *am* dying! And no one can alter the fact. It is time Ham'sha-the-fool was away from this world!" The words were spoken with such bitterness that none of the three witnesses of that utterance could support it. Here was a man whose expertise was widely respected; a Sea-Master of renowned ability which, in spite of his sometimes strange behavior, was trusted and relied upon among his fraternity of seamen. Al'malan listened with his inner hearing and concluded that the words truly reflected the man's state of mind. It was not Ham'sha's body which called for death, but his mind!

Herb-Mistress Ven'ana reached out and took the man's arm, slid her fingers down to his wrist and felt the peripheral urgings of his heart. They were strong. The temperature of his skin was within the range of normality, slightly damp with possibly a slight fever. But the wet night most probably caused that dampness. While performing this clandestine assessment of the man's physical condition, her psychic antennae searched for other symptoms. Yes, the man was ill. Dangerously so!

"Ham'sha-an, my friend," she said quietly, "excuse me for a few moments. I will be right back. You just relax and talk to Al'malan Sea-Master." She patted his wrist with warmth. There was a sense of demand there also. Ch'am'lo assisted the women up out of the narrow quarters and followed her away into the darkness. Al'malan's sensitivities were flooded with this poor man's inner conflict; almost a physical pain could he feel. "Please tell me, my friend," he said, "When did you decide that your life was no longer of any worth?"

As he said this his right hand fumbled around in the darkness to find the layered *tapa* cloth blanket which he knew must be close to hand. Finding it, he pulled it open and leaned forward to place it about Ham'sha's body, noticeably trembling now as the night's cool air became colder. His own chilliness he ignored. Ham'sha remained silent for a long time, Al'malan afraid that he had asked the wrong thing. Finally the suffering Sea-Master replied in a hoarse voice in which Al'Malan could hear tears and pain.

"My sight has left me, Al'malan. My one eye has betrayed me, as I always knew it would. Nights ago - oh, it would be twelve or so - as I sat in the bows watching the *sea-lights*, I saw the most different, interesting array of purple light rays. They were from the northeast, exactly on our course. Land! I knew it was land, but it wasn't Sht'ah Lee. The signs were totally different. I didn't tell you - or anyone. It was so strange that I couldn't be sure of what to predict. Do you understand what I'm saying?" Al'malan again reached a comforting hand out and laid it on Ham'sha's own arm and left it there. His mind was being flooded with the truth of this ailing seaman's sentiments.

"For two nights it grew stronger until on the third night it radiated around us as if we were sitting on top of it. It was so powerful!" Ham'sha broke down into sobs, choked them back and regained himself enough to continue. "And then that very night, and I sat there for hours repeatedly asking the crew if they could see any sign of land, they all said, no! Not even signs of clouds attaching themselves to the breast of an island; no surf, no sound, nothing! And the moon was still bright."

The chill of the night was finally demanding some protection and Al'malan searched blindly about the compartment again, seeking the layered rain cover which every seaman wore on such nights. Finally his fingers recognized the soft grass covering and he retrieved it and pulled it over his shoulders. His attention was hardly divided though and Ham'sha continued his narration, unaware of Al'malan's movements.

"The following night, Voyage-Master, those emanations came from behind us! We had passed the island, or whatever it was, and were now sailing away north from it. I knew then that something was very wrong with my *sea-sight*!" What Ham'sha could not know, his experience and his past teacher's experiences could not know, was that beneath 'Wa'Ran'tar' had lain a huge seamount, the peaked remnant of an ancient volcano which had not succeeded in reaching the sea's surface.

This mass of stone emitted a powerful radiance of its own, quite like an island's would, but different again because it lay deep below the surface. Ham'sha had been betrayed by nothing more sinister than ignorance. It was then that Ch'am'lo and the Herb-Mistress Ven'ana returned. Al'malan could smell the infusion the woman had prepared; sweet and acrid at once, inviting in its uniqueness. Ven'ana climbed carefully into the cramped compartment, Al'malan lending a guiding hand. She sat herself on the edge of Ham'sha's sleeping platform, reached a searching hand until she had found his right arm and pulled it toward her.

"Here, my friend, please drink this. I assure you it will make you feel more at ease." She had now managed to locate his palm in the darkness and persuaded his hand to accept the warm bamboo container filled with her medicine. It was not a soporific, meant to ease him into sleep but rather a stimulant, meant to raise his spirits and help him overcome his depression. He grasped the bamboo cup and mumbled a thank you, placed his other hand around it as if savoring the warmth there and then tipped it up to his mouth and swallowed the whole contents at once. Gasping and coughing, the liquid slightly too hot for such gusto, he nevertheless overcame its heat and then laid back against the bulkhead timbers again and sighed.

"I can do no more for now, Sea-Master," she whispered, "Call me if I can be of further assistance. He should become a bit talkative in a few minutes, and then fall to sleep. I believe he has become overwrought about something; something to do with his past perhaps. I don't know. We will see." And with that the Herb-Mistress stood up and was assisted by Ch'am'lo to regain the deck and return to her vigil at Shen'ham's bedside. What a strange day! What a strange night!

Sporadic showers doused the canoe but the seas remained quite constant and moderate. The evening's crew change was occurring and some curiosity was developing about what might be occurring back there in Ham'sha's territory. Ch'am'lo saw to it that curiosity was diverted. This was his watch now and he put crew to work on minor items, far forward of the port stern. He himself remained away. He knew that Al'malan could handle whatever transpired back there.

Ham'sha suddenly resumed speaking, asking Al'malan a puzzling question. "Do you remember when I lost my eye, Al'malan?" Al'malan couldn't possibly, for he was from Sh'ham-Set and Ham'sha was from Sht'ah Lee and some years older. "No, brother. I wasn't there when that happened. What did happen?"

"Well, I'll tell you!" Ham'sha replied, his voice taking on a slightly tipsy tone, as if he'd had a cup or two of palm toddy. "My mother got angry with me one day, for some reason I've forgotten - she often got angry with me - and she threw a clay pot at me. A good aimer, she was!" His chuckle contained not a trace of humor. "The pot hit me right in the face and shattered and at the same time I fell over something trying to back away from her. Then she threw another pot at me!" This time his statement was followed by a sound which Al'malan's special hearing read as a child's scream of fear, disguised as a chuckle. What a strange, one-way conversation this was, he thought.

"She hit me in my right eye again, almost as if she had been aiming for it! Oh, *Earth Mother!* Why did she do that?" Ham'sha choked back sobs and Al'malan wished he could somehow reach inside the man and drag away that awful memory from his tortured mind. The subject changed as swiftly as it had begun. "Do you know why I couldn't help when Shen'ham was in trouble up there on the mast yesterday? Hah! I couldn't see him! That's right, Voyage-Master ... I couldn't even see up to the mast. My vision has been dying for days. I bump into things that I should see. I had to cling onto the deck edges to find my way here to my little hole in the deck while all of you were helping save the lad!" Ham'sha's voice was rising in pitch and volume and punctuated with quite horrible-sounding guffaws; self-mocking and cruel. Then there was a pause.

Al'malan was grateful for it because it allowed his sensitivity to translate the truth from those words edging on madness. And that's what the interpretation was; the man was going mad!

Ham'sha remained silent after that last outburst and Al'malan recalled Ven'ana's statement that Ham'sha would soon become sleepy and rest would come. "Ham'sha?" he ventured. No reply. In the darkness Al'malan felt for the man and adjusted the blanket around him, gave him a pat on the shoulder and rose stiffly. How long had he been crouching there? He ached. Climbing onto the deck he carefully replaced the covering mats and their light fasteners. 'He should sleep now. Tomorrow we can talk again.' Al'malan's own fatigue was nearly overwhelming now. He must rest.

~ ~ * ~ ~

Ch'amlo had gone with a small torch, its flame spitting sparks across the deck as the night's strong wind threatened to extinguish it, and checked on Ham'sha every hour of his watch. Each time, the man lay in another sleeping posture, unresponsive to the dim light. Good! He would sleep well and tomorrow was another day. When his shift had ended he climbed into his own bed, utterly exhausted from the long day's travail and immediately fell asleep.

Ham'sha had awakened shortly after his guardian's retirement, his mouth dry, his mind again aflame. With blind direction, his eye still betraying him, nearly useless as it would have been in this night's utter blackness anyway, he pushed back the covers over his sleeping compartment and pulled himself up and onto the solid supports on each side of the entry. The wind was cold but his body sought a deeper immersion.

Finding the edge of the hull he threw one leg over and paused. That voice resounded again, that same voice which had haunted him for so long: "Why are you so ugly, Ham-an? Why did you make me throw those pots at you. It was all your fault, you know!" Ham'sha took a deep, last breath, exhaled completely and let his legs slip down into the sea which was much warmer that this night's wind; warm and inviting, so smooth on his skin. He let go his grasp on the hull of a canoe which had been like so many others - his only fortresses against his anguish these many years. He submerged and inhaled the balmy liquid which had beckoned to him now for days.

Chapter Thirty One - An Interim Island

Joha'lan Canoe-Master had cut away the outer husk of one of the last ripe coconuts and had passed it and the small adz to Voyage-Master Al'malan. Al'malan was wearing the full regalia of a Voyage-Master; shells and fish scales and a tall headdress, his ankles and calves were clasped in fish skin circlets and the white marks of mourning were on his chest beneath the wide cape of shell.

All aboard on this bright morning were gathered to say farewell to one of their own. No funeral pyre would there be and there was no body to bury in the sea. Ham'sha had simply disappeared into the black night, discovered missing just after dawn. Walking to the edge of the deck on the starboard side, the wind behind him, Al'malan held the coconut over the edge and with two hits, cracked the tough inner shell and allowed the juice inside to flow down into the sea. "Ham'sha Sea-Master," he proclaimed in a loud voice, "Wherever your soul now resides, we know you are with the *Earth Mother*. We rejoice in your life! We rejoice in you!"

The crowd on the deck took up the cry and in unison their voices sent a genuine rejoicing of that man's existence among them. Al'malan then threw the drained coconut into the blue water and with a silent, personal blessing, watched it float away behind the canoe, soon lost in the wake. This was a particularly sad end to a sea-brother and respected Sea-Master, regardless of his many peculiarities. Suicide was a very un-Mal'lam recourse, bar that tradition of the elderly willing their own passing at their own bidding. Had the Mal'lam not lost that knowledge of the existence of seamounts and their sudden but ephemeral signature visible to those gifted few Sea-Hewn, Ham'sha might well still be alive. He had been stricken with hysterical blindness; rare but particularly devastating to a one-eyed man. Ah well, dear brother of the sea, you are at peace now!

~ ~ * ~ ~

Shen'ham sat in the shade, leaning back against the wall of the little hut on deck. His left hand was wrapped to the elbow with soft, clean *tapa* cloth, unguents and a poultice of crushed herbs caressing that terrible wound. His arm was supported in a cloth sling, the hand raised high beneath his chin. It ached badly but Sha'lat Herb-Mistress had dosed him with soporific drugs and he now spent this beautiful afternoon dozing and daydreaming. Around him the easy ritual of fair weather sailing allowed for conversation even among those on duty at their posts at the steering oar or on the lines controlling the sails. The sun still beat down with a tropical ferocity but then it was summer here in these latitudes. Even on Sht'ah Lee it would be hot. Ah, Sht'ah Lee! How the people aboard longed to see its great mountain come into view.

"Land! Land, Sea-Master! Over there to the left, forward. See?" The Sea-Hewn on watch up the forward mast had cried out with great excitement which quickly brought everyone to their feet. Even Shen'ham shook himself from his reverie and struggled up, leaning heavily on the wall of the hut. Al'malan, Ch'am'lo, Joha'lan and Sha'lat were already sitting, chatting, on the forward deck and were the first to repeat the cry. Yes, there *was* land there! On the clear horizon, the blue of the sky reaching unbroken to the sea all around, there lay a mound of white cloud, stark and definite. Al'malan called for a change of course and seamen rushed to obey. The lines which held the sail panels were adjusted and 'Wa'Ran'tar' swung gently to the left and pointed its twin bows at that cloud mass. No, certainly it was not Sht'ah Lee. This was another, unknown land. It would be very much smaller than their home island but the excitement it aroused was great. None of the Sea-Hewn were surprised that whatever island this was had not been seen on the voyage south. The sea was vast and just a few miles more to the east and they would have missed it entirely this day.

Al'malan was more than joyous about this happy occurrence, but being master of this vessel, he must maintain a calm composure. Really, he would like to jump and shout and hug his shipmates. He did so silently, looking about him at these people whom he loved so dearly. Joha'lan gave him a big hug and a slap on the back, grinning mischievously, knowing of Al'malan's need for reserve. Rascal!

The Herb-Hewn and Plait immediately began to chatter about what wonders they might find here on this new land. Joha'alan and another Wood-Hewn were discussing the possibilities of timber there. Ch'am'lo and Al'malan stood separate in the bow of the port hull and wondered out loud if this, or perhaps, *these*, islands, like those of the Tarbara'ut, might be populated. As the day wore on the bank of cloud began to reveal its anchor. A dark green mass beneath it was seen to rise into the cloud and disappear. A high island it would be, and that promised fresh water. Would it too have a wide, multicolored reef surrounding it? The next few hours were filled with speculation and growing anticipation. However, like their arrival at those islands to the south, nightfall would prevent a landing until tomorrow. The skies boded well for another day of clear weather tomorrow but the coming night would be moonless. 'Wa'Ran'tar' would have to remain well off this gift of land throughout the hours of darkness and keen eyes would have to keep careful watch until dawn again revealed this new destination.

Joha'lan sat with Al'malan until the sky was entirely dark, save for the brilliant array of stars. His watch coming up, Ch'am'lo joined them. On this night, perhaps an omen of some import, meteors began to flash across the sky with increasing regularity. Zipping across the velvet blackness from all directions they created a rare and awesome light show which many Mal'lam sat up to watch, many finally curling up to sleep on the dew-damp deck. The bank of cloud above the island dissipated almost entirely as the night wore on and near the midnight hour Ch'am'lo ordered a tack and a reversal of course. Al'malan, too excited to do more than doze, climbed back on deck as he felt the movement of his vessel change considerably. "What's happening, brother?" Al'malan asked, knowing the answer of course.

"It's time to run back upwind, Voyage-Master." Ch'am'lo replied, "The wind is steady, still from the south with a bit of east thrown in. The north end of the island is now visible and I think we should reverse so that we'll be off the other end near dawn." Al'malan agreed, went to the edge of the deck and peered hard at the dark mound about ten miles away. No sign of any lights. But then, who would be up and around at this time anyway. He kept trying to extend his sensitivity onto that island; read its emanations, feel its character but all that came to him was a sense of calm and peace. Well enough! He returned to his pallet and dozed again until just before dawn. That dawn's sky was dappled with small, fair weather clouds and as the sun rose it painted them in shades of pinks and orange. Already the island was reclaiming its bonnet of cloud and it was closer now by a few miles, details of the land itself becoming clear as the light level rose.

Deep shadows marked a series of steep valleys and red, volcanic soil showed along the ridges. Too soon to define any detail along the shoreline though. From the lookout where the Voyage-Master himself had climbed to scout the land and shore could be seen a constant line of breakers exploding over some barrier reef. Whether it was rock or coral he couldn't yet tell. "Come right and make for the shore, steersman. Ch'am'lo, would you climb to the other lookout, please." Al'malan called down other orders to his crew to alter the sail settings and prepare to run cross-wind, straight at the island. He needed a much closer look. All the while the Sea-Hewn, Shen'ham, his hand still aching continuously, watched and recorded all that was occurring, filing every little detail of the proper handling of a vessel. From time to time, like a doting mother, Sha'lat would come to him with a drink of cool water, admonishing him to drink often. "Your body needs water to heal properly!" she would say, then give his arm a squeeze and leave him with a smile which reminded him so much of his mother. "What a momentous day!" he thought then, "ouch!" as his wrist collided with a rope as he turned a corner.

Joha'lan too was waving his internal antennae toward this new landfall. Like Al'malan, he recorded only passive and gentle soundings. Now he strained his eyes to survey the upper slopes of the island, this windward and certainly wetter side which may afford some good timber. As far as he could judge, the cloud around the island's apex was still obscuring its totality. This land was approximately seventeen-hundred feet high. High enough, he reckoned, to afford rain falling at least on this side for much of the year. He looked up to where his friends hung from their tiring perches and hoped they would decide to round the island and have a good look at the other side. That is exactly what they did.

The wind was shifting more southerly and Al'malan decided that now was the time. "Helmsman!" he shouted down, "Take us on a course back up the island to the right. We are going back up and around to the leeward side." The helmsman, a qualified Sea-Master himself, called out orders to the deck crew to shift sail. The deck was momentarily alive with movement, non-seaman passengers ducking out of the way. He and Ch'am'lo carried on a running conversation from their respective positions at the mast tops, just over sixteen feet apart. Both were enjoying the view, both outward toward the island and downward onto the decks and the other people moving about there.

"You wouldn't be dead now for anything, would you?" Ch'am'lo said, grinning widely in almost adolescent enthusiasm. "No brother!" Al'malan grinned back at him, "But don't tell anyone we're actually having fun." That exchange was heard from below and guffaws and jokes followed. All the Sea-Hewn were sharing in this greatest of a sailor's joys: landfall! One hour became three as the canoe, 'Wa'Ran'tar', finally rounded the northern end of this promising new land and turned left again. The wind had again shifted and the sky was changing color. A very high overcast was moving in from the north, long fingers of thin cloud stretching out to offer another set of sea conditions. Time might now be of the essence. The high island diverted the wind noticeably as the canoe sped down southward again. But Al'malan and Ch'am'lo, both tiring from their long service up on those precarious and uncomfortable perches, agreed that it was time to change shifts and allow another two seamen to replace them. Both badly needed a pee.

The leeward side was proving much more promising as far as a landing venue was concerned. Yes! There, just a few hundred yards ahead - a break in the surf and a long, grey, sandy beach behind it. Al'malan looked to the growing clouds above, changing now from thin and high to lower and thicker … and greyer! Time to take the chance! The two Sea-Masters climbed down as quickly as cramped muscles would allow and went to the leeward side of the deck to relieve themselves, chiding comments accompanying them. Such was allowed, within reason, just to remind a Sea-Master that he too was just another Mal'lam Seaman!

"We'll have to make a sharp turn between those two rocks!" Al'malan stated, his focus concentrated on that inviting passage through what was obviously a reef of rock and not coral. He ordered the covers to be removed from the hulls and the paddling stations opened and ready. Volunteers such as Joha'lan Canoe-Master slipped onto the seats and prepared to lend a hand in what might be a crucial maneuver. The Mal'lam women too stood by to lend assistance wherever they could. This canoe's population was a tightly organized team. A deep roll of thunder from those rapidly approaching storm clouds spurred the whole crew to be ready. The wind was increasing in velocity and shifting steadily to the west. Good! Now, if they could just gain that opening in the girdle of rock which seemed to nearly surround this island, before the storm hit ……

'Wa'Ran'tar' was now moving rapidly, the swells coming regularly from the starboard quarter. Al'malan stood forward of the leading mast, Ch'am'lo at the stern ready to assist the helmsman. Seconds now, to make the final decision, to commit his vessel to a landing. He turned and looked up to the mast lookout and called out one last time. "Jo'shan! What do you say?" The Sea-Hewn's gaze was focused on that inviting opening and the water just beyond. He could see no impediment. "Go, Voyage-Master! It's clear!" Al'malan waited a few seconds more then shouted, "Hard to port. Leave the sails as they are. Paddlers! Do your job!" Ch'am'lo grabbed hold of the long, heavy steering oar and he and the helmsman pushed hard to the right. Riding light and high, 'Wa'Ran'tar' responded immediately, both tall sails still pulling at their maximum. A large swell sweeping into the mouth of the little harbor lifted the canoe high and added its momentum. Fourteen men and women dug their long handled paddles deeply into the frothing water. They were through!

And just in time, because the sky opened up with a barrage of lightening and thunder and followed up with a deluge of rain. The wind was ferocious now and without waiting for the order from their Sea-Master, the crew on deck loosed all lines to the sails and allowed them to swing forward. The tall, narrow panels no longer collected the wind but let it pass parallel to them. Still the vessel's momentum and the straining paddlers were driving it directly at the shore. The rain was so heavy that it was like trying to see through fabric. The beach became invisible. It was now that Al'malan's special hearing came into play. Above the roar of thunder, wind and surf, he was able to discern the distance to the beach with great accuracy. Still running blind, the canoe began to slow as the impetus of the swells diminished. "Paddlers stop!" Al'malan shouted at the top of his lungs.

Still the rain poured down and the lookouts on the masts held on for dear life, anticipating a sudden collision with the sandy beach. Everyone else aboard too was bracing themselves, except Al'malan. He stood now beside the foremast, on the opposite side from the sail, his arms crossed, looking almost nonchalant. 'Wa'Ran'tar' slid softly up onto the sand, nearly square with the beach, then the starboard hull caught up with its mate and the canoe was firmly aground. The following waves inched it even higher and now the storm was abating; passing over the island and out to sea from where the vessel had come.

"Secure the vessel ashore!" Al'malan shouted, and six seamen picked up the heavy hawsers and leaped overboard from the bows and ran with them inland. As quickly as that fierce storm had begun, it moved away and blue sky began to reclaim the scene. The sun broke through the residual mist and, like a spotlight, shone onto the water around 'Wa'Ran'tar'! Safe! Slowly the anxious Mal'lam regained themselves. The mast-top men climbed quickly down, the paddlers stowed their paddles and the men ashore were tightening the hawsers around the nearest trees. Al'malan walked aft and joined his number-two, Ch'am'lo, and the two Sea-Masters began chatting as if this was something they did every day. Sitting at the forward door of the hut with the Herb-Plait, Ven'ana, Shen'ham Sea-Hewn, arm still in a sling, turned to her and said, "That's why he's a Voyage-Master, Ven'ana. That was one of the most skilled landings I've ever witnessed." He grinned and shook his head again in admiration.

It was as if no storm had been here at all. The only sign of its short-lived ferocity was the sparkling sheen of moisture on rocks and trees, glittering like a million jewels, there to greet these strangers. The land rose steeply behind the beach, which was much wider than it had appeared from out beyond the breakers. Heavily forested, the green landscape rang with birdsong and smelled of foliage and humus. But there were no coconut palms in sight. Perhaps no one had ever lived here. But no time for much exploring just yet. Al'malan ordered that all bedding and mat coverings be brought ashore and hung on temporary drying racks.

Foodstuffs too, were to be brought ashore and given a check-over for rot. Ropes and cordage likewise needed drying out and an inventory of everything was to be recorded on those knotted cords whose esoteric meaning was the responsibility one seaman. By early evening, all these tasks having been completed, the Mal'lam gathered around a large fire and prepared for a celebration. A meal was prepared but there was discouragingly little to add to the earth oven's contents besides some dried fish, some *taro* and questionable breadfruit paste. Food was definitely foremost in Al'malan's mind. They were close to running out!

A drum was produced, a couple of flutes and a small, three-stringed instrument and then a chant began. This was an evening of thanksgiving. Two hollow bamboo tubes of palm toddy, carefully hidden away beneath other stores, were opened and passed around. Song and laughter grew and the tension and sadness of the past weeks began to fade. At the height of the evening's celebrations, Joha'lan and Sha'lat held hands and walked into the shadows together. They were back on land now. Free to make love.

~ ~ * ~ ~

After all the important tasks involving the canoe had been attended to - scraping the hulls of their accumulation of sea-growth, minor repairs to the lashings and the replacement of some worn wooden fittings - the Sea-Hewn joined the rest of 'Wa'Ran'tar's' compliment of Mal'lam voyagers to explore this new-found land.

This island, seen from its long, nearly flat top, was twice the size of 'Snake Island', where at this moment other Mal'lam were busy exploring further and setting up residence. Over the next seven days the twenty-four voyagers spread out in small groups, climbing steep ridges, descending into steeper ravines, trekking along the long, convoluted shoreline. This was an island as different again as were the Tarbara'ut islands from Sht'ah Lee. At a latitude still far south of Sht'ah Lee, this subtropical island, attended by a series of smaller, mostly rocky islets, was rich in vegetation. The Herbalists, led by Sha'lat Herb-Mistress, were constantly surprised and pleased to find familiar plants, many of them valuable to their practice. Joh'alan, as he climbed into the heavy forests with the other Woodsmen, sought and indeed found trees of familiarity. A few he deemed possible canoe material. There were both hardwoods and softwoods, vines for lashings and tough barks for making rope. Two species of palms were found, their wide, fan shaped fronds certainly suitable for thatching dwellings. And streams flowed fresh and clean everywhere, even on the leeward side.

The almost table-like structure which formed the island's apex acted as a reservoir and it shared its collection of rainwater with great generosity all around its slopes. And the bird life! How could all of these different birds have found this little island here in the middle of the wide sea? There were seed-eating birds of many shapes and colors, food in abundance for them everywhere. High in the trees small flocks of honey-eaters whistled and twittered, bright colors predominating, feeding on the flowers of the many varieties of tall trees. On the ground, totally unafraid of these human invaders, were at least three species of flightless birds, one larger than a chicken. These proved just as delectable as any fowl the Mal'lam were familiar with.

Insectivores and omnivores flitted among the vegetarians, this fecund environment promoting large populations of insects and invertebrates. And also two kinds of hawks, small in size, were seen flying on various occasions. There were no Mal'lam here now whose specialty was birdlife but so wondrous was it that many became serious birdwatchers. No snakes had yet been found, nor had keen eyes seen any discarded snake-skins anywhere. Small lizards were everywhere though. Some were bright in color, but most were well camouflaged and visible only when they moved. The lizards, at least some of them, gave out chirping or clucking calls during the night, adding a welcome sense of mystery and delight to the sea-tired Mal'lam.

Along the seashore was found a wondrous wealth of readily available food: oysters in huge fields of grey and white shells lay just above low-water level. Mussels too were in wide patches all along the shoreline and along the deepening edge of the rocky shore were clouds of fish in huge schools. Every day the Mal'lam reported seeing groups of dolphin close inshore, a sure sign that huge schools of fish were common here. There was no sign of the coral growth which had so uniquely signaled a wholly new environment when the Mal'lam had reached the islands of the Tarbara'ut. The waters here were much cooler than those southern islands, perhaps too cold for any such colorful reef as had amazed the voyagers those long months ago. But the inshore waters held at least as many varieties and numbers of fish. This was truly a rich and promising piece of the *Earth Mother's* creativity! One plant sorely missed though was bamboo. Not a single species had yet been found. High on the mountaintop, however, in the swampy low areas which really amounted to a shallow lake, there grew a solid-stemmed cane. This promised utility as a thatching perhaps. But a long haul down the mountain.

The acknowledged leaders of this seaborne community, Al'malan, Ch'am'lo, Joha'lan and Sha'lat, went together one morning, Ven'ana Herb-Plait and Al'walla Herb-Hewn attending. Some serious discussion was required. They hiked along the foreshore for a mile, finding a pleasant, shady spot overlooking three small islands in the distance. Al'walla, a vigorous, animated man nearing middle-age, had discovered bushes loaded with edible berries. Bringing up the rear of the procession he had caught up with the others with his wrap filled with the reddish-yellow, tart-sweet berries. Helping themselves, the others quickly ate their shares and Al'malan suggested that they take a big harvest of them back to the others at the encampment when they returned.

Ven'ana chided Al'walla like a wife would, pointing at the stains on the man's *tapa* cloth wrap. "Just like a woman!" he said, his berry-stained mouth in a wide grin. "See!" and he turned his wrap inside out to show how he could quickly rectify the problem. His expression changed to one of chagrin though. The stain had come through the other side. He quickly brightened and proclaimed that he had discovered a new dye and that the women should be most grateful. Ven'ana chucked a stick at him and told him to sit down and behave himself. Al'walla was always good for a laugh, Ven'ana often acting as straight-woman for him. The two were old friends and some said, lovers. The group chatted casually, Joha'lan tossing stones into the water in front of them like a small boy would. Finally Al'malan stated, "I think we are all quite aware of the problem we face now." He looked around the group and quickly had their sober attention. "Food for the journey!" Sha'lat said.

"Yes," Al'malan replied, "and we need to make some decisions very soon. It would appear that there is a plentiful food supply here on this island. What concerns me is that I don't think we can organize enough preserved food to support all of us on the continuing voyage to Sht'ah Lee. At least not for many months, and we haven't got that much time. We need to return there as quickly as possible."

Ch'am'lo added, "Al'malan and I have gone over the counting of supplies which were loaded on the day before we left. As best either of us can recall, everything was accounted for." Ch'am'lo, among his many talents, had a head for figures. For the Mal'lam these figures were recorded, not in any written form but with knots tied on long strings. The knots were given meaning by their grouping on a single string and numerous strings together could compile considerable information. It was an art form really, and many Mal'lam practiced it. Sha'lat added her opinion quickly too. "There are not many medicinal herbs and plants left aboard. Shen'ham's injury consumed many of them." With a broad smile she added, "But now we've found many of the plants we traditionally use, here on this island. *Earth Mother* has been very kind."

It seemed to be left to the Voyage-Master to broach the most difficult subject. He visibly squirmed, straightened his back and began.

"It is my firm belief that at least eight people must remain here on this island!"

Only Ven'ana and Al'walla expressed surprise, the Herb-Hewn's mouth dropping open. "What?" he said, his eyes wide with surprise. Regaining himself he asked, "Who must stay? And who is to decide?"

Joha'lan, having held his piece until now, replied gravely. "*Who*, must be decided in a council of all of us, everyone aboard. But among those chosen to stay will not be our Voyage-Master, naturally. We all know of the predictions and messages of our *seers*. Something dire is threatening our loved ones at home. Most of us aboard will be returning to family members who require our assistance. However, some of us do not have such urgencies - yourself, as I understand, Al'walla?" He was looking at the Herbalist with great intensity, his eyes demanding the greatest honesty. Al'walla returned the gaze and spoke with that frankness, a little grin of his usual mischief at the corner of his mouth. "I see, Canoe-Master. You are asking me to nominate myself as one to remain here?"

Before Joha'lan could reply, he had his answer."That's alright, actually, Joha'lan-an. Only last night," and here he looked over to Ven'ana and reached out a soft touch to her arm, "Ven'ana and I were talking about just this. We both said we wouldn't mind having a year or two to have a really good look at this quite wonderful island." Suddenly he sat bolt upright and looked around at each person there. "Oh, by the way! Don't you all think it's time we gave it a name?" Laughter eased what was threatening to become a rather tense discussion. Al'walla to the rescue! "Ven'ana?" Sha'lat leaned toward her Herbalist-sister, the tone of the question all that was required.

"Yes. I would not at all mind staying here. Even if this nuisance man stays too." She said it so lovingly that all there knew the truth of their relationship. Al'malan sighed a silent expression of relief. 'Two down -six to go!'

"Do you two know of anyone else among us who might be easily persuaded to remain here until the whole of the Mal'lam return for them?" Ah, what a shrewd person you can be sometimes, thought Sha'lat, listening to Al'malan's persuasion. She knew that it might be three years before the whole of the Mal'lam society voyaged southward. And if something terrible happened to 'Wa'Ran'tar' on the final leg back to Sht'ah Lee, this island may never be found again! Would the inherent trust in their society be adequate to overcome those very thoughts which the eight people left behind would certainly harbor? They could only hope so.

Ven'ana answered equivocally, screwing her face up with some slight doubt. "Well, Bal'lee and Sho'lat Clay-Plait have been enthusing over some clay deposits they have found. I haven't seen it yet but they say there is really good quality here. And I know that those two prefer to spend most of their time together. Perhaps they would stay." Al'malan and Joha'lan both spoke of men who might be so inclined to stay while Sha'lat mentioned one other Herb-Plait. This would not be a decision brought about by lottery. It was incumbent upon Al'malan, as Voyage-Master, to devise the proper and just solution. If that failed, he would have to fall back on the Sea-Hewn tradition of the vessel's Master being the final arbiter. He shuddered at the thought of that responsibility.

~ ~ * ~ ~

The Convocation was held four days later, late in the afternoon and beneath a hastily constructed shelter. Rain had set in and gave no hint of going away for a while. By now everyone of the twenty-four Mal'lam knew what was to be discussed. The young Shen'ham Sea-Hewn was probably the most nervous person there, bar his Voyage-Master, Al'malan. Young people did not in fact have the same weight in community decisions as their elders. Shen'ham, his hand still aching, free of infection but painful in its healing, felt that he would most probably be among those chosen to stay. His value as a seaman was still greatly restricted because of that injury. He was really worried. The thought of not returning to be again with his mother and that beloved little rascal, Tina-an, brought him to the verge of tears throughout that day. But he neither spoke of nor gave any other signal of his stress. He simply sat quietly among the group of Sea-Hewn at the inner circle before their Voyage-Master.

Al'malan wore none of his office's finery this late afternoon. No adornments at all. Rather he was dressed almost as one would at a funeral; *tapa* cloth wrap below his knees, no belt, necklace or hair decoration. Actually, a few of the women in this group found him especially attractive in this guise; younger looking, somehow vulnerable but strong. Most of the men saw him as an equal brother in their life's commitment - sailing! Sha'lat smiled to herself as she had that day along the seashore when he had plied his will with great subtlety with but two of those whom he hoped to convert to his reasoning. And she knew that the man's special ability to hear the truth in one's words would be powerfully focused.

"You all know the reason for this council today." He began. "It is imperative that we continue the voyage back to Sht'ah Lee as quickly as possible." Al'malan looked each person there solidly in the eye and then continued. "As you'll remember, we were all getting worried about the food stores before we sighted this lovely island. Well, we have even less to carry on with now." Nodding heads revealed general agreement and again his eyes sought each person's face. "So the fact is, 'Wa'Ran'tar' will not be able to support all twenty-four of us for the voyage back. It is my decision that only sixteen people can be supported for our journey. As it is, we must try to gather some foodstuffs from this island; fresh food which will last for a few days of sailing before we have to start using our stores again." Al'malan shifted position, leaning back on his arms, legs still crossed, furthering his guise as just another Mal'lam seaman. It was also a signal that others could now ask to speak. Formality still pertained.

Two Sea-hewn raised their hands simultaneously, looked at each other and the younger dropped his arm in deference to his elder. It was Mool'lem, the eldest of the Sea-Hewn, not of the Clan Sht'ah'ha but of Clan Wa'sho. His Clan had been among those few survivors to reach Sht'ah Lee and one other of his Clan was a crewman here.

"Voyage-Master, I thank you for the time to speak. I will be brief. My cousin here," and he nodded to the young man who had also raised his hand, "Well, we have discussed this between us as well as with our Clan Sh'ta'ha brothers. May I speak for you, Sho'ja?"he asked his younger cousin. A nod and Mool'lem continued. "We both have little to return to, as you know. Our people are few now and the generosity of the Clan Sh'ta'ha has already begun to absorb us. We both feel as true brothers to your Clan." Al'malan's inner hearing detected only genuine emotion. "We understand the situation very well." Then he smiled and said, "Personally, I was getting heartily sick of voyaging rations!" and chuckles echoed around the Mal'lam. Al'malan was especially grateful for this break in the tension. "So, Voyage-Master, my cousin and I are quite willing to remain here and eat well while some of the rest of you arrive back on Sht'ah Lee, skinny and drawn." Again laughter swirled around the assembly and Al'malan knew that he had already won his case. "*Earth Mother*, you have given me the very best of the Mal'lam for this journey!" was his earnest thought. Four down, four to go!

Sha'lat watched Al'malan's face as the rest of the meeting progressed. She could tell that he was quite amazed at the ease with which his intention was being fulfilled. The two Clay-Plait, Ba'lee'an and Sho'at, quickly threw their lot in with the two Sea-Hewn, followed by the Herbalists, Ven'ana and Al'walla. And then, to everyone's surprise, the young seaman apprentice, Jo'shan volunteered to remain. Somewhat embarrassed by speaking at a formal assembly for the first time, he stated his reasons for wanting to remain. "Voyage-Master, like Mool'lem Sea-Hewn, I too like to eat well." He wasn't trying to be funny but he got chuckles anyway. Now he did look embarrassed. He looked over to his initiation mate, Shen'ham, for moral support and Shen'ham too was giggling. No help. "Anyway," he croaked, "I and my Clan Wa'sho brothers, we think the people staying here on this island will need canoes and Sea-Hewn to build them and sail them. Mool'lem can build canoes and with Sho'ja and me helping, we can make a canoe soon." Jo'shan had run out of words and with gestures of continuing embarrassment, indicated that he was finished with what he wanted to say. Seven down, one to go! Al'malan was confident now that someone else might have been thinking of similar things and perhaps with some persuasion, might also agree to remain here. More surprises!

It seemed that, known only to very few, there were two romances which had blossomed over the past months and those people were here. It was not the men, however, one a Sea-Hewn, one a Wood-Hewn, who stood to declare their intent. It was their ladies, both rising together, smiling shyly, who spoke now of their desire to remain on this as-yet un-named island. And the most startling revelation came when the young Herb-Plait, Shena'sha, announced that she was pregnant! Well! That ended the formal proceedings and Al'malan was left sitting on the sand, dumb-struck, grinning like he was drunk.

"Oh my dear!" Sha'lat said, coming over to Al'malan, a delicious hint of mockery in her tone. "You have done a wonderful job of organizing this. Well done!" Joha'lan stood behind her, his big grin beaming down at his friend. Al'malan lowered his head, held one arm up in the air and Joha'lan grabbed it and lifted him to his feet. No one else noticed this because everyone was gathered around the budding mother, swamping her with congratulations. A baby, here on this new island! Oh, how wonderful! But Al'malan would not be outdone; he was Voyage-Master after all. "Everyone! I have one more thing to say to you!"

Grudgingly, the crowd quieted down and turned to face the Master of this community. "One important thing has been overlooked here today." he said loudly, asserting his position of authority. You will all know how happy I am at those generous decisions by the eleven of you. All of our people on Sht'ah Lee will know of your generosity and courage. But now is the time for me to act in my office of Voyage-Master! Shena'sha Herb-Plait," he addressed the pregnant girl, "please come forward." The glowing young woman paled and looked a bit frightened but stepped up to stand in front of Al'amalan. She knew this man to be kind and understanding but she couldn't imagine why he was calling her forward to stand before everyone.

"Shena'sha Herb-Plait," Al'malan said , now in a soft and loving tone, smiling down at the girl. He reached and took her two hands in his. "This island has not yet been given a Mal'lam name. It is within my authority to do so." He leaned forward and kissed Shena'sha gently on the forehead, still holding her hands. "In honor of the upcoming birth of another of our people, I name this beautiful land, 'Win'no'hi-Set'; 'Island of New Beginnings'! May the *Earth Mother* bless this island forever!"

~ ~ * ~ ~

Three weeks later 'Wa'Ran'tar' was ready for sailing. Every lashing, every join of wood to wood, every support member and the whole of both hulls were scrutinized and repairs effected wherever needed. Fortunately, enough spare coconut fiber cord and rope had been brought on the first leg to fill these needs, with spares left over. Four ripe coconuts, hoarded from that first part of this voyage, were ceremoniously planted on the fertile soil just above the sand of the beach. It would be eight to ten years before they bore valuable fruit but already strong shoots were growing from each and a couple had roots beginning to extend. One day this island, 'Win'no'hi-Set', would have coconut palms.

Large quantities of fish had been caught, dried, smoked, salted and packed away in water-resistant containers made from a local bark. Some breadfruit and taro pastes were left from the earlier passage and remained viable. These were re-wrapped and stored aboard. Long, straight, hardwood poles were cut and de-barked and laid aboard for possible use should the vessel incur storm damage. Every eventuality was considered and provided for as thoroughly as time and materials would allow. However, many of the bamboo water tubes had cracked and were no longer serviceable as were a number of the gourd containers. Water would be an ongoing source of worry should a drought occur on the way. Some of the cracked gourds were sealed with tree gum but no one knew how long those seals would last. They would be consumed first.

The voyagers themselves were practicing another survival method unique to sailors. They were putting on as much fat as they could! The two varieties of flightless birds on the island were in the first stages of extinction. They were totally unafraid of humans; no other predators did they know here except the occasional hawk catching a young bird and the Mal'lam were able to actually run them down and wring their necks. The voyagers of the 'Wa'Ran'tar' ate them nearly every day, the bird's flesh full of fat and high in nutrients. They also gorged themselves on oysters and mussels and fish. There were two species of tree ferns on this island, growing in large groves, and their new, curly shoots were sweet and most edible when boiled. While the work on the canoe continued, the Herbalists scoured the hillsides for edible plants, bringing back more nutrition. Those remaining on the island were quickly becoming aware of just how rich their new environment really was.

When not required to work on 'Wa'Ran'tar', Joha'lan spent time with the two non-Clan Sea-Hewn and the Clan seaman who were to stay behind. Together they had already cut down and transported a sizeable tree to just behind the beach and set up a canoe shed over it. He gave them a few of his own woodworking tools to use; "Just a loan, you know. I'll be back for them." Comforting words for men who were about to see their friends disappear over the horizon.

There was good tool making stone on the island fortunately and with a bit of trial and error, the seamen and Wood-Hewn would learn to fashion suitable tools on their own. The two Clay-Plait ladies were already experimenting with the island's varieties of clay and were very enthusiastic. It seemed that they had recruited the Wood-Hewn to be their supplier of firewood for the open-ground kilns they traditionally used. They were going to keep him quite busy. The storm season was beginning in these waters now and the air temperature was noticeably cooler all day. Extra coverings had to be installed to protect the food supplies aboard 'Wa'Ran'tar'.

The night before the 'leaving' however, was clear and pleasantly warm. The Mal'lam gathered on the beach and lit a large bonfire, broke out the musical instruments and proceeded to have a party. Shen'ham Sea-Hewn, his wounded hand healing well and much less painful now, sat with his Sea-Hewn mate, Shal'tan and the other seamen who would be remaining. Shen'ham had been contributing to the preparations as best he could, one-handed, and had even begun to practice with his sling again. His aim was still unerring and his mates joked that his nickname of 'Sling-stone' should be changed to 'Three Fingers'! He didn't mind. As usual, this young man seldom took such things very seriously, even when Sha'lat joked that really, his nickname should be 'Chubby', as it had been when he was a boy. He had made sure that he put on plenty of fortifying fat before the voyage.

Al'malan was in a thoughtful mood this night, feeling a heavy responsibility not only for those aboard with him on the return trip but for those remaining behind. His acute sensitivity to the meaning behind a person's words was well in play tonight. He made a special effort to speak individually with all eleven of those who would remain on 'Win'no'hi-Set'. He was encouraged by what he discovered. Ven'ana Herb-Plait had been his recommended and ultimately chosen Elder to act as community head-woman. He heard some little nervousness in her conversation with him but he reckoned that to be quite natural. She was a wise and intelligent woman. Her *sight* was her most important attribute for this small community. Besides her capability as a healer, that special talent was vital for that continued psychic contact with her wider Mal'lam community. It was this link which would help sustain the morale of the people on this island for those busy but anxious years to come before once again Mal'lam canoes were seen on the horizon.

This night's revelry ended early. The full moon was directly above when the last person fell asleep. Dawn would see a full tide beginning to drop at sunrise, perfect timing for departure. And dawn broke with the sky still clear and a fair breeze blowing from the northwest. It would require a hard paddle to exit the little harbor but allow a swift release from land once the corner had been turned. Last minute provisioning, last minute hugs and goodbyes, and all hands pushing for all they were worth to launch the heavy vessel; 'Wa'Ran'tar' was again afloat! The small community of 'Win'no'hi' stood together on the beach and sang the departing songs, tears and some trepidation there. Return to us, indeed!

Shen'ham, his good hand gripping the steering oar while his wounded arm wrapped around the hardwood shaft in support, was assisted by Sha'lat and the only other woman aboard, Tela'wana Herb-Plait. Between them, their strength would have to suffice to guide the canoe through the bay's opening. All the other men, Al'malan included, would have to paddle. The tall sails rode freely on the mast, offering no resistance to the wind, their sheets lying loose and ready on the deck. Al'malan led the paddler's chant. His voice boomed out loudly and ten paddles dug deep and with a powerful rhythm. Past the big rock mounds which framed the entrance to this island's only harbor, over the sea's waiting swells and into the open sea they ploughed, the now even-lighter vessel ready for its ultimate propulsion. Al'malan called out the order, "Down paddles!" and in seconds the sails were clutching the increasing wind, the bows lifting in response, eager to be away; eager to be going home.

Research Notes: Impressions and General Observations

Subject: Tina Pua'lani Kaiser, Honolulu, Late Summer 1974

Yes, Tina will be returning to Kamehameha School this Fall and we're very happy for that. She has just turned 14 and is a real little Miss (in the best sense of the term) I wish I had been as mature and downright nice at that age.

I have had lots of time to spend with her and record our sessions together with her Spirits. She is as anxious for our baby to get here as I am - for different reasons. She's looking forward to being an Aunty! I'm looking forward to getting this kid off my belly! Only kidding, really. Some medicos are saying that within a few years we will be able to determine a child's sex, without invasive techniques, well before birth. Jiro and I are enjoying the suspense, thank you very much. He wants a girl, since he already has two sons, one of whom is only a year younger than I. He's a dirty old man! But he's *my* dirty old man and I adore him!

On the more objective side of things: Bill Snakenborg (bless his cotton socks) has asked for the tapes of Tina's and Kinau's recordings of the Mal'lam language. His colleague in Asia is doing further study of what some are now calling, *Proto-Polynesian* languages, and I think that's a pretty good phrase. Of course I won't be taking on any full-time teaching or advisory work at the beginning of Fall Term. Our little one is due in about 7 weeks. I have promised to take on part-time work at the U.of H. at the beginning of Winter Term, in February.

Tina is just now returning from a day's sailing with the Snakenborgs. She loves the sea, especially sailing.

Chapter Thirty Two - Conspiracy Aborted

Al'malan's younger cousin, Chom'shul Sea-Master, guided his new canoe 'Wa'ma'lan', up the west coast of Sht'ah Lee-Set. This was the second such voyage he had made in three weeks; first, to negotiate with the Elder of the Itin village of Bant'la'wan, Jolo'tan, for a safe haven for Al'malan's wife and children. This voyage was to deliver his cousin's family to that hospitable haven. The Autumn storm season was upon them yet the wind this day was mild and agreeably from the east. This newly-made vessel, rigged with the same upright sails as had been invented by Jolo'tan and his sons and which now served the discoverer's fleet, was the great pride of its young master's life. Not resembling Al'malan Voyage-Master physically, he possessed many of his cousin's attributes. That one so young, but twenty-four, would be given such a responsibility was uncommon; as uncommon as had Al'malan's own advancement been. But like Al'malan he was a gifted seaman. And he was '*sighted*'! His *sight* was of the lights beneath the sea and as uniquely powerful as was Al'malan's special hearing - or A'lan Sea-Hewn's sight!

Chom'shul was stocky of build, powerfully muscled but as yet his face did not produce a beard! Very unusual among Mal'lam men. He did manage a wispy mustache which he assiduously attended and encouraged to some semblance of length and thickness. But his appearance was one of a youth with a position beyond his years.But those who served on his vessel knew better. He sat beneath the foremast, his little cousin, Sahn'ta, on his lap, explaining to the little boy what the different parts of the canoe were. The child tried to form the words for 'mast' and 'stay' and 'bow' and 'stern' but soon both of them fell to laughing as Chom'shul abandoned the lesson and began tickling the boy. Sht'ana sat behind them, her daughter, La'teel, nearly asleep in her lap. For the first time in many weeks, Sht'ana began to feel some sense of relaxation. How horrible it had been! That awful woman, Ja'eel, and her strutting minions! That curse which had begun the months of terror; that day when her beloved Al'malan had left! Now she felt that she could take a deep breath without inhaling that terror. She turned as she sat and reached a hand out to her little sister. 'Dear Tina-an! What would I do without you?'

Tina Earth-Plait had been watching the shoreline pass. The heavy swells crashed in insistent sequence upon the rocky shores, the land becoming drier, the trees and shrubs there sparse and stunted. This was a part of this wonderful island she had not seen before yet it held as much fascination for her as did the forests and jungles. This island of Sht'ah Lee was her home. How could she ever leave it?

"Sail, Sea-Master! Dead ahead! It's Itin, for sure." the mast-head lookout had called down. Chom'shul reluctantly released the charming little boy back to Sht'ana's care and rose to respond to this journey's need. That they were nearing the Itin village he knew well from his initial journey up this coast. That great headland, looking very much like a man's profile, had been passed a half hour ago and he knew they were now within Itin waters. That little sail ahead, a single panel on a small double-hulled canoe was not on a fisherman's duty today. He recognized the black, abstract pattern painted on the sail. It was Jo'lo'tan himself come to greet them and how in this world did he know we would arrive on this very morning?

Having followed Jo'lo'tan's lead back to his village's small port, 'Wa'ma'lan' slid softly onto the slippery sands of the beach. A dozen Itin ran to assist in the beaching of the big canoe, grinning renewed greetings to their Mal'lam cousins. Jo'lo'tan himself, right leg askew and his body lurching along the beach toward them, opened his arms wide in greeting. The leathery old patriarch had divined this morning's approach by the 'Wa'malan'. No one knew how, but in such things his prescience was unmatched. "Greetings, young Sea-Master! Greetings to you all!" the old man shouted and his call was repeated all along the shore as now all the village's inhabitants made their way to the beach. A couple of dozen children of all ages ran ahead of the crowd, intent on joining the arriving Mal'lam.

Chom'shul Sea-Master was first to leap to the sand and embrace the old head-man of the Itin. Then he turned to introduce his passengers who were standing on the edge of the deck, preparing to climb down themselves. Chom'shul reached up and took the boy, Sahn'ta, set him on the sand beside him, then reached for the baby, La'teel. Tina jumped down of her own accord and took the baby from him while her sister climbed down more gracefully. Jolo'tan stepped forward and held his hands out in greeting to Sht'ana. He gazed into her eyes, gauging what might be this young woman's true spirit. He saw a tiredness there, and traces of fear. Then Tina stepped close beside her sister and handed the baby to her. Tina was still shorter than Sht'ana but the two had begun to resemble each other facially. Her hands too were taken in the tough leather of the old sailor's palms and her eyes were read. He blinked once, then again. "What have we here?" he thought. There is power in those eyes; a strange kind of power! Tina-an was doing some assessing of her own and immediately decided that she liked this rough old fellow and that they were going to become friends. Mal'lam and Itin seamen began unloading Sht'ana's and Tina's baggage and other items which had been sent as gifts for the Itin. A happy throng surrounded the Mal'lam, baggage and supplies finding many hands to carry it all up to the Itin village. Sht'ana and the children, Tina-an close behind, were taken immediately to their new quarters, Chom'shul and Jo'lo'tan bringing up the rear, deep in conversation but smiling and laughing.

Six Itin ladies, dressed in their finest and sporting sea-bird-feather headdresses, were waiting in front of the neat, new little hut, each with a shallow, woven basket filled with flowers and herbs. Their welcoming smiles brought tears to Sht'ana's eyes and it was all she could do to keep from weeping in relief. For the first time in many months, Sht'ana Herb-Plait felt safe. Little Sahn'ta had by this time been commandeered by some of the Itin children and was being lifted, carried, tickled and kissed as the children all followed in train behind the adults. The love and respect which emanated from this little population flowed over and around Tina's awareness and her Spirit sucked it up like a sponge. The *Earth Mother* truly resided here as benevolently as She did anywhere and Tina-an Earth-Plait rejoiced in this discovery of another manifestation of Her blessings. Tina's hand went to her necklace and the blue stone vibrated gladness into her palm. Her thought now was, "Oh Al'malan! Do hurry home!"

When finally the greetings and celebration had begun to fade into a general acceptance of a new relationship between strangers-become-friends, Sht'ana sought the cool, shaded interior of their new but temporary home. Their personal belongings laid carefully along the walls of the hut, the baskets of aromatic flowers and herbs set near the door, Sht'ana finally sat and wept. Tina was now holding her niece on her lap, the child sleeping quietly. Tina-an laid a hand on her sister's arm and it was immediately covered by both of her sister's hands, gripping strongly as her sobs shook her. So grateful was she! So lonely was she for her husband! So determined now was she that soon, this nightmare of Ja'eel's madness would be overcome. That terrible emotion bordering on hatred was beginning to recede. "One must never hate! Hatred brings a blindness of Spirit!" So had that strange woman, The Vesa'tan, told her sister? And Tina-an had more than once reminded her sister of that truth. Sleep! Sleep and restful days were the prescription now. While Tina-an sat holding her child, Sht'ana lay down and fell into the deepest sleep she had experienced since the night after her baby's birth. Tina covered her sister in a light blanket and went in search of a wet nurse. Little La'teel was hungry but her mother's rest must not be disturbed just now. Healing was taking place!

Chom'shul and his Sea-Hewn mates turned about and set sail for home within the hour of their arrival. No time for celebrations. Their dawn departure had been clandestine; Sht'ana, Tina and the children had boarded the canoe in the dark of pre-dawn to avoid anyone discovering this deception. Only a small group of trusted Elders and those Sea-Hewn involved knew of this voyage. Again, it had been the inspiration of Shen'ha Herb-Mistress to remove the threatened mother and her children to the distant protection of the Itin. Sea-Master Orn'ta had equivocated at first, unsure of the wisdom of removing these refugees from the protection of his own community. Shen'ha had finally convinced him that distance must be the protecting warrior at this time. She knew that her other machinations would add support to the deception. The first layer of that deception was the misinformation given to that silly man, Kal'to'lot Stone-Hewn, he who lived on the far outskirts of the Mal'lam villages and could be counted upon to leak the desired information to anyone who might question him, especially if lubricated with a bit of palm toddy. And who would question him on the day before the secret departure?

Kal'to'lot Stone-Hewn set out on his own that morning, working solo as he often did. There were minor repairs to be made to the weir on the inland irrigation system. Over the years his inability to bond closely with his workmates was really a result of his constant foolish patter and practical jokes which at times constituted not only annoyance but danger to his workmates. This brought him to a solitary daily existence. His personality had adjusted accordingly but his loneliness only increased. He tried to compensate for this estrangement by becoming an agent of rumor and gossip; anything which might make others think of him as worthy of a listen.

Unmarried and sexually frustrated, as few Mal'lam men ever were, Kal'to'lot liked to work naked when laboring alone, as was usually the case. While he lifted and adjusted stones and packed earth behind them, his mind often left his work to an automatic efficiency and focused on daydreams of sexual prowess and of women coming unbidden to him for gratification. These daydreams, in spite of the intensity of his work, often resulted in an insistent erection. The morning was proving quite hot for the season and Kal'to'lot's body was covered in a sheen of sweat, his fantasies inspiring a rigid response from his penis. As he knelt with a heavy rock in his hands, preparing to insert it into the opening which required just this very stone, a shadow fell over his efforts; a real shadow cast by a real person!

Startled, not expecting any visitors to this far end of the taro paddies, Ka'to'lot looked up into the sun. As his eyes adjusted to the intense light, the features of that person casting the shade became evident. Kal'to'lot looked up into the grinning face of Ja'eel! No fantasy could have been more intensely fulfilled! Her buxom figure shone with the morning's heat, her wrap low on her hips and with a toss of her head she revealed a sensuous wrapping of tiny seashells which circled her neck in a thick cord. Ja'eel's gaze was not on the man's face but on what stood rampant from his groin. Neither did this sudden intrusion dampen that sexual insistence or persuade any embarrassment on his part. He stood stock still, his mouth slightly open in amazement as he watched Ja'eel take those few steps down the bank of the stream to reach him.

"Good morning, Stone-Hewn!" she purred and with a quick movement reached down and grasped that member which had been a major focus for all of her adult life. Still too amazed to move, this action brought his mouth open in a loud gasp. Keeping her soft grip on him, Ja'eel used her other hand to undo her wrap. She looked quickly aside, chose the shallow, grassy slope beside his work area and pulled him down with her as she descended to her knees. She cast her wrap in a practiced throw and it fell nearly open onto the grass. "Lie down Kal'to'lot. That is your name isn't it?" Of course she knew his name and she was not here at this hour, alone, just for sex. Sex she could have anytime of day or night. It was her major tool of persuasion. And Ja'eel could be very persuasive.

Kal'to'lot's eyes never left the woman's face as she urged him with little nudges and whispers to lie down on her wrap, on his back. Still she didn't loosen her grip on him but rather began to squeeze with a practiced insistence. Ja'eel then straddled his body and lowered herself deliberately, slowly, that grip of her hand releasing only as a softer grip succeeded it. She was in charge here and the bewildered man surrendered with a moan. Half an hour later, lying next to the sated, exhausted Stone-hewn, Ja'eel rested her head in the palm of one hand while she ran the fingers of her other hand through his hair. Both their bodies glistened with perspiration, little rivulets of sweat making muddy tracks down his dusty ribcage.

"Of course you know that I came here to speak with you, Kal'to'lot. I mean, I really did need to ask you some questions. What a nice surprise you gave me!" and she giggled, sounding like any young girl. "I am looking for someone. Someone very important to me, and I think you just might know where I can find this person. Hmmmm? You do know who I mean, don't you!" Her tone allowed no denial; neither demanding nor harsh, just with a definiteness he could not deny. He gulped and coughed. Did he tell someone what he had overheard and which Shen'ha Herb-Mistress had made him promise not to repeat? Well, only one person … maybe two!

As if to stir his memory, that hand which had been stroking his hair moved downward and began another manipulation which elicited a moan of anticipation from him. "Please tell me, sweet man. It's very important to me!" A squeeze of her hand broke the tissue-thin resolve of a man not accustomed to holding his tongue.

"Well," he cleared his throat nervously before continuing. He was committed now. Ja'eel knew that and the hand ceased its insistence and withdrew. "Well, I only over- heard this when I was sitting talking to a friend near where the Elders were having a conference. Shen'ha Herb-Mistress told me not to tell anyone. She was very insistent, actually kind of angry with me. But I hadn't done anything - I was just sitting there! She can be a bit bossy, if you know what I mean." Ja'eel's expression didn't waver but she had already measured this man's worth and judged him as a bit of a fool. "And what did you hear, Kal'to-an?" she purred familiarly. Ja'eel had now sat up, looking down on her recent lover with eyes growing a bit darker with insistence.

"I heard a couple of the Elders talking about Sht'ana and her children and how they were going to find a place away from the village where she could be, uh, umm," and here Ja'eel smiled and filled in the blank; "Away from me?"

"Uh, well yes. That's about what they said." His face was flushed now but not from sexual activity. How could he deny this woman the truth as he saw it; as she demanded it! "Well, I heard them say that Sht'ana and the children would be taken to the northern village, where I live … somewhere around there." Kal'to'lot's knowledge really ended here and he thought, wisely, that he shouldn't add anything he wasn't sure of, let alone make up a story to add to his importance. "I really don't know where, Ja'eel. If I find out, I'll let you know right away!" A hint of desperation flowed through his words. He desperately wanted to continue this contact with this amazing woman. He needn't have worried.

"That's all right, dear Kal'to-an!" Ja'eel said, her smile broad and warm and she gave his now limp member a quick tweak. "Why don't you come to my village tomorrow evening? We are having a little celebration and I think you might enjoy it all. Eh?"

"Where is that, Ja'eel?" His question was genuine because Ja'eel's people had only moved to their new location a few days before. Their village straddled the Black Boar Track! Like a dysfunctional sphincter on an important passage, this village and its errant population posed a great threat to the Mal'lam way of life on Sht'ah Lee-Set. Ja'eel was more clever than any would have thought. "Just follow the trail up to the Black Boar Track, my dear. And if you come, do bring some food, any kind will do." She rose and slung her muddied wrap about her waist, blew a kiss to Kal'to'lot and turned and strode away, leaving him seated and besotted. Kal'to'lot was immediately converted!

~ ~ * ~ ~

Ja'eel had sent spies to the area of the northern village but all returned pleading ignorance of even a whisper of Sht'ana's whereabouts. Again she sent them out and again they returned, but this time they had news. Sht'ana and the children were nowhere near. They had gone to the villages of the Itin! With a shriek of such brutal rage that her attendants scrambled away from her, Ja'eel picked up and threw any object at hand; her aim was at the universe itself. How dare that she be so frustrated in her just demands? How dare the silly Gods let her down this way! How dare they take my son away from me?' Her tantrum lasted a shocking hour before finally she calmed down.

By that time all her retainers had retreated to well into the background, utterly helpless to know what to do to assuage their dear leader's wrath. And then Ja'eel made the first of several mistakes which would secure the Destiny she inwardly, secretly sought. She went into seclusion for nearly thirty days, allowing only two of her attendants to bring her food and a few special items. Ja'eel was going to metamorphose into something quite *other!* Ja'eel was going to become a Goddess! That thirty days would create a gap in her planning which she would never be able to regain. The curses she had thrown out upon the departing fleet of voyagers were now returning to her. The sea, which she hated, was bringing back those whom she had condemned. Ja'eel Feather-Plait would become the 'Goddess, 'Ja'jan' and so cleverly would she represent herself as that to her devotees that even she would come to believe it.

Chapter Thirty Three - Sht'ah Lee Back at Last

For four days and nights 'Wa'Ran'tar' struggled through a severe storm, ceaseless winds and mountainous seas battering it. On the afternoon of the third day the aft sail panel blew out with a sickening tearing sound. Some unseen weakness in the great woven sheet of pandanus leaf had finally succumbed to the insistent wind. Here was the one reservation Al'malan had about this new sail configuration. With the old system, the seamen would have dropped the damaged sail to the deck and effected repairs even during the storm. But now the whole of the sail assembly, including the heavy outside boom, would have to be laboriously unwound and new panels stitched together and as laboriously raised again. And in these seas and in this wind, that was impossible. 'Wa'Ran'tar' would have to carry on with only its foresail, and thank the Gods, it was the aft sail which had failed! Had the foresail blown out, with only the sail aft pulling, the vessel would have been very difficult to steer. Most likely they would have had to let it blow loose in the wind and lie a-hull in the waves with little steerage possible. This would take some serious thought, once this crisis was over.

Throughout the dark nights it was Al'malan's special hearing which would give the vessel warning of rogue waves, of which there were a number. One, so intense that he detected it fully two minutes before it arrived, caused him to order the canoe to come about to the right to avoid being broadsided. The huge wave bore down on the 'Wa'Ran'tar' with a deafening roar, the breaking crest of the surge visible even in the blackness. "Hold on tight! Hold on tight!" he screamed into the shrieking wind. The canoe had risen on the face of the wave at a frightening angle, been pushed backward for terrifying moments, then it finally broke through the crest of the wave and slipped down its backside, unscathed. That had been Al'malan's most terrifying moment in his short years at sea. Of course, as Sea-Master, he must not let on that he was as frightened as any of his crew and passengers. Those who knew him well, Joha'lan for one, later that night noticed a slight tremble in his voice. Al'malan knew that they all had been within but a few feet of wave-face from dying!

Morning and a belated dawn through heavy cloud saw the storm abating. The wind was shifting to the east and weakening but the swells continued huge. This fifth morning saw all aboard the canoe nearly exhausted. The heavy steering oar had demanded two strong men to attend it constantly, each pair having to be relieved after an hour of straining. Shen'ham, his wounded hand now wrapped in a waterproof mitten of oil-soaked *tapa* cloth, served as dedicatedly as any other seaman. Joha'lan, with his massive strength, was indispensable. Al'malan Sea-Master had slept hardly at all throughout the whole ordeal.

The shards of sail fabric rustled and flapped in the wind as he looked up at the carnage of the aft sail. It would have to wait! "Two hours sleep for all but four men!" he called out to the haggard crew. "And wake me the moment anything looks threatening!" With that the master of the 'Wa'Ran'tar' lay down where he stood on the deck matting and fell to sleep. A crewman ducked into the little hut amidships and returned with a finely woven, soft mat and covered him. Another Sea-Hewn, Shen'ham's compatriot, walked over to his younger mate and insisted, successfully, that the lad go and get some rest. The rain having ceased, Sha'lat now re-kindled the deck fire and began to heat tea for all.

By late morning the sun broke through the thinning cloud cover and a most welcome warmth slowly spread upon the beleaguered canoe and its passengers. Al'malan was allowed to sleep until well into the afternoon. Other seamen too were so exhausted that their comrades let them rest. Nothing was done about that destroyed sail panel except to begin sewing replacement sections for when the whole construction would be brought down and repaired. There was little conversation. All aboard were so grateful for silence after the screaming winds and roaring seas of the past four days that idle chatter seemed an intrusion.

Al'malan awoke greatly refreshed but slightly embarrassed. All day long his crew had stepped over and around him, doing their duty while he rested. It was Joha'lan who eased his conscience in his usual manner. "Good morning, bright eyes! Care to join the day?" attended by a hearty slap on the back. Late afternoon saw that destroyed sail panel replaced and the whole, awkward construction reinstalled. Both Joha'lan and Al'malan discussed better methods as the heavy boom was retied and at last the 'Wa'Ran'tar' was under way with all flags flying again. The two long tell-tales stood out and danced with joy as the speed of the canoe increased and a real momentum was resumed.

Late in the afternoon a large group of dolphins appeared off the Port quarter, moving parallel to the canoe. Suddenly they all disappeared, only to reappear moments later all around 'Wa'Ran'tar', leaping and rolling. These animals were beautifully marked on their sides with grey and cream stripes which wove over and around each other, the top of their bodies a glistening black. Some of them took to running at high speed from off the stern and then between the hulls, exiting with bounding leaps at the bows. They were having a marvelous game with this strange apparition which surely none of these dolphins had ever before encountered.

"'Hoosh'taba', they are!" one of the seamen called out. Found usually only far at sea, these particular dolphin were common on the long route between Sht'ah Lee-Set and the northern islands, when such voyages were still undertaken. Mal'lam canoes no longer made those voyages since no one now survived on those decimated islands. The passengers and crew sat enthralled as they watched these shining acrobats, the only signs of life, fish or animal, which they had seen for many days. The open sea can be a barren and lonely-seeming place. The dolphins remained until dark. They then descended and disappeared as mysteriously as they had arrived.

"Where do you reckon we are?" Joha'lan asked Al'malan, his grin challenging the Sea-Master. "I reckon we're lost!" Al'malan retorted with a grin of his own. There really was no way just yet of knowing their position. Surely the four days of storm had blown them off course but the Sea-Master couldn't even guess in which direction. There had been no stars to guide them of course, and even had they a 'sighted' Sea-Hewn aboard, they were surely too far from land yet for there to be any light-lines beneath the sea. But as darkness fell it revealed a sky utterly devoid of cloud and though moonless, the sky shone with those myriad of stars which can only truly be appreciated far out to sea or in the middle of a wide desert. Al'malan moved to the very bow end of the canoe's platform deck and sat with two other Sea-Hewn and Joha'lan.

When voyaging south those many months ago the Sea-Hewn had naturally studied the sky behind them as well as the new sets of stars before them. Only in this way would they find their way home one day. The Mal'lam Sea-Hewn, as did all Mal'lam, possessed highly developed memories. From early childhood, as soon as they could understand abstract speech, all were given increasingly difficult memory exercises, mostly to do with their genealogies.Crafts such as that practiced by the Herb-Hewn and Plait and most especially by the Sea-Hewn, required a staggering amount of information be recorded. The training of all young Sea-Hewn involved a constant study of the skies and this learning never ceased until a seaman grew too old to sail anymore. Even then, they were invaluable teachers of the young.

The three Sea-Hewn studied the velvety blackness and its pinpricks of light, drawing on those studies engaged in on the earlier trip south. For two hours they discussed, argued and finally came to the unanimous conclusion that they were too far to the west. They were indeed off-course! Headed in the right direction, surely, since the sun told them direction but not their longitude. All the while of their discussion, Joha'lan sat quietly listening. He was also listening within to that special sense, not of direction but of a presence which he could never properly find words to describe. That sense of a presence grew and suddenly manifested itself in the most extraordinary display of *Earth Mother's* magical generosity he and all around him had ever witnessed!

The dolphins had returned! And the waters over which 'Wa'Ran'tar' rode this night were rich in phosphorescent plankton. Too dark to actually see the dolphin themselves, they appeared as elongated tubes of blue-green light, intense around their bodies as their passage through the thin soup of plankton excited that wondrous glow. The splash of the bows through the waves sent out their own bright signature while the thin blade of the steering oar also lent a long, thin trail of phosphorescence behind the vessel. The rapid passage of the dolphin created dozens of long, slowly fading stripes of light. And then they again began their playful frolic of swimming between the hulls from behind, flashing forward and leaping in a great splash of color. Time and time again they performed this maneuver, swimming well ahead of the canoe and then turning right to come around again. They continued to circle to the right, never the left, as they persisted in their delightful ritual.

Then Joha'lan sat up as if startled! Yes! That's it! "Brother!" he said, reaching a demanding hand out to Al'malan's arm. "Look what the dolphins are doing. Do you see it?" The two other Sea-Hewn looked questioningly at the big man, then to Al'malan. What? Joha'lan stood up and urged his dear friends to do likewise; not just stand up but climb the mast! He literally dragged his friend to the base of the foremast and said, "Go up there and see what they're doing. I promise you - this is very important!" Al'malan knew his friend well enough to know that there was no practical joke involved in this instance.

With a boost from Joha'lan he quickly mounted the foot-slings attached to the mast and climbed to about fifteen feet above the deck. Hanging by one arm he swayed outward to be able to see well beyond the bulging face of the sail panel. He looked - watched intently - peered hard again and then looked down at the deck and shouted, "Helmsman! Come right! Sea-Hewn, prepare to adjust sails!" He had seen what Joha'lan had intuited from his seat near the water. The dolphins were not circling around after their show-off dash between the hulls. They were running off at a radical, straight angle to the course of the 'Wa'Ran'tar' and immediately returning on that same course before rounding behind and running forward again. The dolphins were showing the Mal'lam the course they should be following to bring them to Sht'ah Lee-Set!

Al'malan remained hanging from the mast for minutes, unable to keep his eyes from this wondrous exhibition of … what could he call it? And he knew deep within him that what was occurring was a part of his people's Destiny! 'Thank you *Earth Mother'*. What else could he say? With no *sighted* Sea-Hewn aboard, here they were being blessed with the most magnificent appeal to vision! Could the Spirit of that tragic Sea-Master, Ham'sha, be somehow involved in this great blessing? No one can second-guess the *Earth Mother*!

When finally he descended to the deck he went aft to the steersman and spent time showing the man, Sea-Hewn Shen'ham it was, which stars to steer by, which stars to center upon as the field of lights up there moved left as the night deepened. Other seamen gathered around to share the information and finally the sails were set in position to follow the course. The wind this night was most agreeable too. It blew from the southwest, making the northeasterly course easy to maintain. Twelve days later, the winds light and 'Wa'Ran'tar's' speed halved, everyone aboard was getting very hungry. The extra fat which all had endeavored to accumulate was being pared away daily. Even Joha'lan's bulk had diminished until others remarked that they saw ribs showing which they had never seen before. Fish had been few but on this day two *mahi mahi* were caught on the trolling lines.

Periodic heavy showers, assuring adequate water for the vessel, also denied the use of the fire pit on deck for cooking. The two big fish were eaten raw. Near sunset there flew through a nearby squall a flock of seabirds. They were quickly swallowed up by the rain but it was certain that they were flying almost directly in line with 'Wa'Ran'tar's' course. Home! Through that night squalls and scuds accompanied a wind shift to the east. The sails were pulled to their maximum reach against what amounted to a headwind. The canoe slowed even further. That was the longest night of this voyage, longer even than those nights of severe storm. They all knew that they were nearing Sht'ah Lee. Surely dawn would reveal the sacred mountain, Volan Votu! Dawn did not reveal that great mountain but there was no mistaking the land beneath that long, low cloud cover. The land, grey with only a hint of green, was the northern coast of Sht'ah Lee. They had nearly sailed on past their goal in the night!

Al'malan squirmed at the realization as he stood watching the dawn reveal their destination. Finally stirring himself he called for a course change to the east. The wind, capricious this morning, defeated that intent and began to blow from the southeast. He knew this coast well enough to realize that their best option this day was to make for the Itin village of Bant'la'wan. All aboard needed rest and food. A day or two delay in sailing south to the 'Bay of Dolphins' should make no difference. He called for another course change and spread the word of their new destination. Ch'am'lo Sea-Master smiled widely. He was *truly* going home! He turned and climbed the foremast and hung there in anticipation for the two hours it required the canoe to reach the entrance to 'Crab Claw Bay'. When only four hundred yards offshore, that long, flat, rocky island blocking direct access to the harbor, Al'malan called Ch'am'lo down from the mast and said, "Brother. Take the helm please!"

That order, spoken as a softly uttered request, forever endeared Al'malan to his Brother-of-the-Sea. These two seamen now lived with a visceral understanding and affection rare even among true brothers. Ch'am'lo took Al'malan's arm in his hand for a brief moment, smiled and nodded and then turned and began calling out orders. Al'malan went to the foremost position of the foredeck and sat down, his legs dangling over, a smile of complete relaxation on his face.

Ashore that morning, the Itin headman , Jo'lo'tan, had ordered all sailing out upon the sea suspended. The offshore wind was raising choppy swells and besides, the fish weren't running. 'Everyone stay home!' was his message. 'Things might be happening!' He had seated himself on a stony outcrop overlooking the bay, surrounded by five of his seven sons. The sixth was ailing this day from a sprained ankle and had remained at home. Two of his youngest had called out first; "Sail, father! Look!" Jolo'tan's weakening eyes struggled to focus on the point indicated by his son's extended arm. Yes! So it is! And a canoe of that size can only be one of the three great vessels sent southward so long ago. And with no hesitation he called out an order; "Tell Sht'ana Herb-Plait to bring her children to the beach. Quickly!" Jo'lo'tan sat embracing a sensation of fulfillment and anticipation. He knew that his dear eldest son was aboard that canoe. How he knew he couldn't have explained - he just knew!

Ch'am'lo Sea-Master earned his reputation all over again this blustery morning as he guided the big vessel around the intervening rocky islet, took a sudden turn to the left and entered his home harbor with all paddlers straining against the wind. His Voyage-Master-brother, Al'malan, had strained with the rest as the paddlers breached the entrance and drove the 'Wa'Ran'tar' over the waters and onto the beach. Then he laid aside his paddle and climbed onto the bridging deck forward and sat down. Al'malan still sat on 'Wa'Ran'tar's' foredeck, perfectly at ease as the sand appeared beneath him, replacing the sea which had been this vessel's home for nearly two months. Looking over his shoulder at Ch'am'lo who stood close behind him, he smiled up his admiration for the man's seamanship. Ch'am'lo grinned back, then looked toward shore.

His eyes widened in surprise and then with a wide grin said, "Al'malan … look up there." He pointed to the slope above the beach. Al'malan's face was still frozen in that smile of pleasure and admiration. But now his eyes too widened and a whoop of startled joy came from him. With a powerful push of his hands upon the bamboo deck beneath him he leapt off the canoe and landed running on the sand. Coming toward him at a run also was a beautiful young woman tightly clutching an infant. Right behind her came a shorter, look-alike girl carrying a chunky little boy nearly half her size. Tina-an! Sahn'ta! And, 'Oh thank you *Earth Mother*! Sht'ana!'

Joha'lan Canoe-Master leaped the five feet down to the sand, turned and held his arms up. Sha'lat literally leaped into his arms, her eyes never leaving that marvelous vision of her daughters running toward her. Together they ran to where Al'malan now held Sht'ana and the baby in his arms, Tina-an right behind them. All around them there was more such rejoicing as Ch'am'lo's people wrapped him in their joy. His brothers and two sisters nearly forced him to the ground with the weight of their descent.

Behind them their father, Jolo'tan, stood smiling, waiting his turn. He was in no hurry. He knew this day was close at hand. Itin seamen ashore, all grinning broadly and making loud cries of celebration, had the presence of mind to secure the big canoe before wind and tide turned it sideways onto the beach. Grabbing the coiled hawsers from the deck they ran up the beach, eight men on each line and tied them to coconut palm trunks. The whole beach was a scene of controlled chaos; children jumping and running about, dogs yapping and getting underfoot, people laughing and crying at once and the two Sea-Masters both surrounded by a crowd so deep that neither could be seen. Only Joha'lan's bushy head and beard above the crowd denoted the whereabouts of Al'malan and his family. Finally the crowd began to part around Ch'am'lo and he forced his way to an open space, looked toward his father who stood alone and he knelt on one knee. Jo'lo'tan hobbled quickly toward him and as Ch'am'lo rose the two embraced, each burying their faces in the other's neck. Again the Itin surged around their beloved leaders.

One Mal'lam Sea-Hewn stood back from the confusion, waiting for another view of the one person who had been filling his dreams of late on those long, dark nights at sea. Shen'ham, his left hand still wrapped in a bulky bandage and its waterproof covering, hunkered down now and with tears in his eyes, sent prayers of thanks toward the sky, where he understood *Earth Mother* to reside. Wherever She was, She was doing double duty today! Finally, the slim figure of Tina-an Earth-Plait appeared as she managed to separate herself from the loving melee, the little boy Sahn'ta left behind with his parents. She stood for a few moments and looked frantically around the beach, onto the canoe, hoping. Then the object of her hopeful search stood up and smiled at her. She took two steps toward him, halted, then broke into a run which carried her in a leap into his arms. She had not yet noticed his wounded hand. It was only as she finally stood back to look fully at him that her hands slid down his arms to clasp his hands and she felt the bandage and saw a momentary wince.

"Ham-an! What's happened to your hand?" she asked, concern dampening her smile. She took that hand gently in hers, looked at it, then into his face, questioning still. "Oh, not much!" he said. He didn't want anything, including his wound, to come between the joy and love they now were sharing. It was as if a very long, silver cord had been connected to these two youngsters on the day of his leaving; it had stretched those thousands of miles of his voyaging and was now being reeled in on the spindles of their love, bringing them finally together again. Again they hugged and his grasp of her held the meaning … "I will never leave you again!"

AL'MALAN and Ch'om'lo

At last the smothering circle of greeters loosened around the returning voyagers. Joha'lan, his big head peering over the crowd, called out to a group of Itin women standing on the edge of the crowd. "Ladies! We are starving! Any food around?" With giggles and mutual urging they all ran uphill toward the village. Feast time!

~ ~ * ~ ~

The quarter moon was dipping into the sea when silence began to replace the revelry of this night's celebrations. The huge bonfire was reduced to a wide, shimmering platform of glowing coals, a few Itin villagers still sitting around it, talking quietly. A dozen mutts snoozed among them, bellies full of leftovers. Most of the voyagers were asleep, many with stomachs grumbling in protest at the sudden incursion of rich food.

Al'malan, Sht'ana and the children and Joha'lan and Sha'lat sat together in the neat little hut the Itin had provided for the refugees some weeks before. Al'malan spoke little. Mostly he grinned, gazing at his wife, then one child, then the other. The baby, unsettled by all the intense emotion and noise, had become fussy but now she nursed at her mother's breast and was near to sleep. Sht'ana sat as close to her husband as was possible. Sahn'ta lay asleep on his now-remembered father's lap. It was Sha'lat who was telling her daughter of the voyage and the adventures along the way but soon it became evident that they all needed to rest.

There was a rap on the door post and then Ch'am'lo stuck his head through the opening and said, "Joha'lan. I have a comfortable little hut for you and Sha'lat, if you like. Do you want to come now?" They did, and gratefully so, for both were more exhausted than they had realized. Kisses for Sht'ana and the children, hugs for Al'malan and then the elders of this family were away into the night, following their Itin friend's lead. No one had seen Tina-an or Shen'ham since earlier in the evening. No one worried about them. They could all remember the intensity of new love.

A large storm front had moved in during the early morning. The wind was from the west and soon became a howling gale. Rain sheeted down, blowing almost horizontally, confining most in the village to their huts. Al'malan was up early as usual, seeing to the safety of his vessel. His Sea-Hewn shipmates arrived too, most still groggy and not feeling too well. "A good day for resting, eh?" Al'malan laughed. Together the men checked the lashings and covers aboard "Wa'Rantar', double-checked the hawsers and then scuttled back to whatever dry haven they had come from. Shen'ham and Tina-an had somehow discovered where her mother and Joha'lan were sheltering and joined them there. Sha'lat insisted on changing the dressing on Shen'ham's hand.

Tina covered her face with her hands, peering only through her fingers as she saw the extent of the damage to the young Sea-Hewn's hand. Her heart further melted for her lover. How brave he must have been! She now recalled a moment some weeks ago, the time corresponding to his wounding, when sitting in meditation she had seen on the screen of her mind Shen'ham's face and an expression of severe pain. Somehow she had repressed that memory until now. Tears came in spite of her attempt at stifling them. "Look, Tina-an." her mother said, holding that wounded hand up for her to examine. "You should now learn how to dress the wound. I'll show you. Alright?"

Tina-an swallowed, looked at Shen'ham's face, managed a smile and nodded assent. She had never dressed a serious wound before, only nicks and scratches, and mostly on herself. It went well, however, and Shen'ham's gaze never left her face as she followed her mother's instructions. When she was finished her mother hugged her, saying, "That was very well done, daughter. You have a healer's fingers! I mean it." Tina-an wiped away a tear from her jaw. She hadn't been aware that they had been flowing since she began the task. "Thank you, dear Tina-an." Shen'ham said. "Now, do you know where we can find some food?" They all three giggled. Still the big guts; always hungry!

The heavy storm lasted the most part of two days. So strong were the winds that the Sea-Hewn, Mal'lam and Itin, frequently went to the beach to check on their canoes. Once, 'Wa'Ran'tar' slipped a hawser; the connection aboard had come apart through no seaman's fault. The aging, plaited line had simply seen better days. But the canoe had drifted broadside to the beach and the heavy swells, instead of running smoothly up the beach between the hulls were pushing with great force against one hull, threatening the integrity of the cross-hull connecting beams. It took more than three hours in the drenching downpour to get the big canoe back in its proper position. Then, a similar thing occurred with one of the Itin canoes and all the Sea-Hewn were again desperately involved in saving that craft from damage. Joha'lan, bored and relieved to escape the intense emotions still swelling among the women of his growing family, joined his Sea-Hewn friends in their struggles.

When all was assured as safe, most of the seamen took shelter beneath the largest of the canoe sheds. "These Itin are excellent builders!" Joha'lan whispered to Al'malan, both men grateful for the sturdy shelter of this structure. Soon some one of the Itin seamen unveiled a bamboo container of palm toddy. Another made a dash to a hut nearly hidden by the sheets of rain and returned minutes later with a large basket of bananas and some fried taro. The Sea-Hewn did indeed know how to enjoy themselves, given the opportunity! Shen'ham and his somewhat older compatriot joined their elders and the topic of conversation inevitably centered on the developing drama with Ja'eel and her growing movement. As Shen'ham sat listening to the conversation, he idly fingered his sling-weapon with his right hand. Ch'am'lo noticed this and catalogued the young warrior's subliminal urge, adding this thought to his own warrior's reckoning. "That time may yet come!" he thought.

~ ~ * ~ ~

"Voyage-Master," Ch'am'lo said, "with your permission, I would like to remain here with my people a while longer. My father is ailing, I'm sure you've noticed." Al'malan remained silent but put his arm around this dear friend's shoulder and guided him away from the gathered Sea-Hewn preparing 'Wa'Ran'tar' for sailing. They came to a halt some yards away from the busyness on the beach this morning and Al'malan looked him full in the eye, his sincerity obvious to the Itin Sea-Master. "Yes, Ch'am-an. I understand. Your people need you now, very much so. If Ja'eel and her tribe of fools should know of your people's hospitality to my family … who knows what might happen? I think it best that you do stay. And the Earth Mother will protect you, I do so believe." Few words, fewer as the two men came to know each other better, were needed for their mutual understanding.

"Done, then?" Ch'am'lo asked. A simple nod of Al'malan's head settled it. Had Al'malan ever had a brother, he knew that he could never have been closer than to this man. He watched as Ch'am'lo went up the sloping beach to where his father stood, wrapped now against the still-cold wind which blew after the storm had passed. They spoke briefly, then Jo'lo'tan waved a quick gesture, filled with the meanings which friends can impart so simply. Al'malan now turned to his vessel and the final preparations for the voyage down the coast to the Bay of Dolphins. He and his crew and passengers had been well fed by their Itin friends over the past three days. The journey home might take less than twenty-four hours, depending on the wind. And right now the wind was picking up as it shifted from west to north. Perfect. Let's go!

Chapter Thirty Four - *Ja'jan*

Jana'la Feather-Plait, Ja'eel's second cousin and one of her first devotees, carried her mistress's evening meal through the heavy drape at the door to the little village's largest building. As usual over this past month, Ja'eel's meals were small. Never once had she left this building, which actually was but a two-roomed hut. Not even to relieve herself! In an extraordinary decision the woman had decided that, since she had not left her habitation for nearly a month and her excrement had been taken away each day by her 'servant', Jana'la, she would continue the practice. It only befitted a Goddess! And Ja'eel Feather-Plait now considered herself just that! She had decided that an ancient, almost forgotten deity of her distant ancestor's, the 'Goddess of the Skies', '*Ja'jan*', had entered her soul and was now manifested through the soul and body of this woman, '*Ja'jan of the Skies*'! And her followers would now be known as '*Ja'jan'an-lo*, 'Followers of Ja'jan'! The servile woman, Jana'la, as usual left the covered bowl of food, made a shallow bow and turned and left, closing the drape as she left.

"Leave it open, Jana'la!" the order came. "I need some fresh air!" Quickly the middle-aged women complied and wound a cord about the fine mat and tied it to the doorpost. Waiting for another order, but none coming, she turned and went to continue her work. She was fashioning a beautiful feather cape for her mistress to wear on some upcoming, very special occasion. And it was of a most unusual design, dictated by her mistress.

Jana'la was small in stature and walked with a stoop which had no physical cause. Some trauma to her psyche, unrecalled by anyone else, had left her not only permanently bent at the waist, almost in a cringe as if expecting a blow, but she could not speak! She could hear, but no one had heard her utter a word since she was a little girl. And yet she was one of the most accomplished Mal'lam Feather-Plait, her works unique and much in demand. Her subservient character, well known to her cousin, Ja'eel, made her the perfect handmaiden for a budding goddess.

Unknown to Ja'eel, or anyone else, Jana'la also had a special relationship with another woman; someone who had once prevented her from taking her own life in a terrible fit of depression. She felt a deep and abiding loyalty to that other woman, Shen'ha Herb-Mistress! That good woman she loved. Her relationship with Ja'eel, now to be *Ja'jan*, was of another and very complicated nature. As

Ja'eel's servant, she had a role in life which she had never before experienced. And because of her dumbness, her inability to carry tales of her mistress's behavior or her words, she was *safe* in Ja'eel's reckoning. Those demons in Jana'la's mind still assailed the poor woman and now things were becoming even more complicated. Shen'ha Herb-Mistress had approached her clandestinely one day in the forest as Jana'la was hunting for birds. She had asked Jana'la to be her eyes and ears in Ja'eel's camp! She had agreed to it, even been excited by the prospect since in fact she did not really like Ja'eel one bit. Oh, how complex life was becoming for this simple, lonely woman.

The following day *Ja'jan,* as she was now to be known, called for her father to come to her quarters. Sho'sha'lo Sea-Hewn had left his wife of nearly thirty years to follow his daughter's path. Certainly not as an equal. Sho'sha'lo had been inordinately dedicated to his daughter since she was quite young, incurring the displeasure of his wife because he would not apply the usual, gentle and reasonable discipline a Mal'lam father was obliged to enforce. He indulged her every whim and seemed blind to the fact that she was early developing a willfulness and waywardness.

As she matured, her beauty and sensuality further seduced him. When she had married the attractive, talented young Sea-Hewn, Al'malan, he had been secretly jealous to the point of anger, but kept that jealousy from everyone. Only, his son-in-law's special hearing had detected some animosity there. But he could never quite reconcile it. In the moments it took for Sho'sha'lo's eyes to adjust to the dark interior of the hut, he stood in the doorway trembling with anxiety. It had been weeks since he had even spoken to her through walls of the hut, let alone seen his daughter.

"Come in father. Sit down. It's good to see you again!" This was spoken without the warmth one would expect of a daughter. This new woman, Ja'jan, spoke no warmth to anyone any longer.

"How are you Ja'eel?" he asked with true concern. The voice which answered him was harsh and demanding. "Do not ever again call me Ja'eel! My name is *Ja'jan, Ja'jan of the Skies*! The ancient 'Goddess of the Sky'! And the Goddess has entered my heart and my body! I am no longer a mortal like you, father, but the earthly manifestation of the greatest of powers! Do you understand me?" She didn't wait for an answer. She assumed his understanding, for it was all so clear wasn't it? Sho'sha'lo's eyes had adjusted to the dim light now, the bright midday sun outside sending enough glow inside to illuminate this stranger sitting before him. She was thin, very thin. Her hair had been cropped close to her head, her beautiful long tresses were no more. Her face was gaunt and sharp as a hawk's and she wore a flowing wrap of *tapa* cloth, dyed all black. He hardly recognized her. And yet, something of her previous aura remained; something of that sensuality, perhaps the way she sat so strongly upright, her still-youthful breasts pushing against that black fabric. Yes, she was still the daughter he had always loved so unquestioningly, so perversely.

"And no longer shall you be called simply Sho'sha'lo Sea-Hewn." Her voice softened somewhat now, almost intimately. "You are no longer Sea-Hewn. None of my people will be Hewn-of-the-Sea, ever again. '*Ja'jan of the Skies*' is above both the sea and the land and rules over both. My people shall be of the sky also. We must all live on the earth, of course, but no longer will the '*Ja'jan 'an-lo'*, my people, ride Mal'lam canoes upon the sea. Do you understand me?" Again she did not wait for and answer. Sho'sha'lo, never clever or swift of mind, struggled to absorb all he was being told. Although he knew that this strange woman before him was indeed his daughter, he felt as if he was in the presence of someone new, someone even more unique and powerful than she had been before. She continued to reveal to him the 'truths' of her new manifestation, the rules by which he and all the '*Ja'jan' an-lo'* ould live by, and some of these 'truths' were startling:

No mention was to be made any longer of that Mal'lam deity, the *Earth Mother*! '*Ja'jan of the Skies'* would, for all time now, be in command of the blessings and curses which this world and its people would enjoy or endure.

 Marriage was now abolished! No man or woman was beholden to another in the manner of a man and wife. Children were to be raised communally, no natural mother being required to raise a child; but a woman could do so if she desired.

The Itin were *other*! Not humans like the Mal'lam and of course, not like the *Ja'jan' an-lo'*. The Itin would have to eventually be expelled from Sht'ah Lee-Set; eliminated, if they did not leave voluntarily.

"Ja'jan of the Skies"

All the lands, the gardens, the forests and foreshores of Sht'ah Lee-Set belonged to the *'Ja'jan' an-lo'* ! It was with the great generosity of the Goddess Herself that the Mal'lam would be allowed to remain as they were until their stupid plan to sail away upon the sea was completed. But they, like the Itin, must leave within the year!. Until then, the Mal'lam would be allowed to farm and fish and harvest as usual, as long as they returned some of what belonged to the Goddess in the form of payment in kind.

The Spirit of the great Goddess, *Ja'jan*, had informed her, *'Ja'jan of the Skies'*, that blood sacrifices must be reinstated, just as the old myths had described. And she, *'Ja'jan of the Skies'*, would determine when and where and how such practices were to take place.

Sho'sha'lo sat spellbound, his lips parted and his eyes were wide in wonderment. He could hardly believe what he was hearing. How brilliant! Who else could have reasoned such things, spoken them so persuasively. Truly, my daughter is a Goddess! And then the thought came to him that he, too, by virtue of being father to this Goddess, must also be among the special - the blessed. Sho'sha'lo's ego began to soar. And then it went into orbit!

"So, Sho'sha'lo, I have a very special task for you." *'Ja'jan of the Skies'* spoke in tones which sounded as if she had left her father-daughter relationship forever. Sho'sha'lo either didn't recognize the tone or perhaps no longer cared if that relationship pertained. Here was something even more majestic coming! He waited anxiously for her to continue.

"I am appointing you my Chief Priest!" she said, her tone now almost conciliatory, as if she was simply recognizing what was already apparent. His expression changed to one of slight puzzlement. "Forgive me, Ja - *Ja'jan*. What is a priest?"

Ja'jan laughed, forgiving of her father's ignorance. Actually, very few Mal'lam were aware of the histories and their arcane information like one old woman whom *Ja'jan* had the good fortune to come across here on Sht'ah'Lee. This old woman had once been a sensualist and seeker of power like the young woman Ja'eel had been, but she possessed neither her greed for that power nor had she lived in the difficult upheaval which pertained now. But that old woman, passed away now, had delighted in recounting to Ja'eel the tales of ancient gods and practices, sumptuously decorated by her own imagination, and

Ja'eel had absorbed these tales as if through her skin, becoming an unwholesome part of her perception of the reality of this world.

Like everyone, Ja'eel had chosen her own fantasy. Hers however, set her far apart from everyone else's. Ja'eel, now '*Ja'jan of the Skies'*, had become a vortex of brutal energy which had begun to suck up into its dark cloud of origin the very souls of dozens of people around her. Her father had been her first victim, very many years ago. Now he was to be an accomplice, a sycophant, a willing sacrifice himself, if only he could have seen the truth of that.

"Dear Sho'sha'lo, I'm not surprised that you don't know the meaning of the term but let me tell you what I want you to do." She was being gently intimate with him now, knowing that she must be very careful to both inflate his ego and fill that inflation with enough information and guidance to fulfill her bidding. He would be of great importance, *if he had the brains! Ja'jan* could trust no one totally, not even her father. She was dressing herself in the robes of an autocrat but didn't yet know how heavy and cumbersome those robes would become.

~ ~ * ~ ~

It was near midday the following day when a man came breathlessly to *Ja'jan's* headquarters. She was sitting inside the gloomy hut, being fitted with the robe of black feathers which Jana'la Feather-Plait had now completed. The man knocked on the door frame and knelt on one knee in deference to his dear Mistress. She had been expecting him. In fact, he was very late and her greeting was a dark scowl and a grunt. She rose and walked to the doorway. Her shoulders were draped in the resplendent, glossy, ebony feathers of dozens of crows, the black background edged with the white feathers of seabirds. With her short-cropped hair, unlike any fashion familiar in Mal'lam society, the black *tapa* cloth garment she wore underneath completed a visual manifestation of utter *otherness*! Here was not a woman, but truly a Goddess! The man knelt now on both knees and bowed his head in reverence, and not a little fear. "What do you have to report, Cho'sho?" she asked, impatience rumbling in her voice.

Cho'sho Wood-Hewn, a devotee from one of the northern islands, bereft of any family here on this welcoming but strange island and a man desperate for some anchor of relationship like many another, sought desperately to please, to be accepted. But his message was fraught with possible trauma for himself. He knew of *Ja'jan's* temper.

"Dear Mistress. What I have discovered, after speaking with many who should know such things, is that Sht'ana and the children have been taken away, in the dead of night, northward to the Itin villages." He cringed in expectation of a shrieking outburst of temper. All that returned to him was a clearing of *Ja'jan's* throat, the slap of a hand on a thigh and then a long, drawn-out sigh. "Alright, good man. Well done." Cho'sho could hardly believe his ears and exhaled a thankful release from his tension. "Now, go and fetch both Sho'sha'lo and Wol'man Stone-Hewn." Then she added, "Quickly!"

Wol'man Stone-Hewn was from that beleaguered island of Sha'lan'la where the madmen, Tor'na and Mal'atan, had taken over the island and for nearly a year had lorded over it, forcing all inhabitants to accede to their demands. When finally Mal'atan had been slain by one of his own minions, Wol'man had been among those leaders of the reaction who had seen to the violent demise of those madmen's followers. He had killed. He had enjoyed killing. He was now *Ja'jan's* choice for her Chief of War! He was also one of her most frequent lovers and even more than her father, he was able to subtly sway the Goddess's opinion. Wol'man was first to respond to *Ja'jan's* order to attend her. Sho'sha'lo was busy elsewhere, fulfilling another request, really more an order as *Ja'jan* seldom said please.

Wol'man was a big fellow, Stone-Hewn and with features as rugged as the stone with which he used to work. After his first seduction by *Ja'jan*, he no longer worked at his trade but acted as bodyguard for her. Even through that month of her seclusion he seldom left a small, open-sided hut near her quarters. He was a man who seldom smiled, was never heard to laugh and spoke in short syllables. He always carried with him a hardwood club; the very same club which had taken lives back on Sha'lan'la-Set. And yet, strangely, he seemed to have formed a friendship with another Stone-Hewn man from Sht'ah Lee. That rather silly man, Kal'to'lot, whom *Ja'jan* had seduced that day while he worked on the stone walls at a far corner of the taro paddies, now was a member of her community. He still daydreamed of repeating that marvelous session of sex. So far, it hadn't happened. Still chagrined at being fooled into passing on the wrong information to his Mistress, she seemed not to have held it against him. But *Ja'jan* never really forgave anything.

"Wol'man, come inside with me. We need to make some plans." Wol'man quietly followed her into the dark interior of her quarters and sat where he was directed, near the doorway. "I have a very important duty for you to perform and I want it done immediately!" Her tone held not a hint of their previous intimacies nor of any special respect she might hold for this man. He listened impassively, only nodding slightly at the end of each sentence she spoke. "You will have heard by now that the woman, Sht'ana, has taken my son, Sanh'ta, away with her to live with those stinking pigs, the Itin?" She spit the word, 'Itin", as if it was a foul taste. "I want you and Sho'sha'lo and our bravest men to go there and bring my son back to me. And I want her child too, an infant girl named La'teel. I want you to kill Sht'ana and as many Itin as you can!" This she ordered with a growing shrillness. Again he simply nodded.

"You will go overland. No more will my people travel by sea. Do you understand?" He did, but felt it necessary to say that he understood from the locals that it would take four days on foot. His mind had already formed this very solution and he had begun to mentally select his henchmen for such an activity.

"I don't care how long it takes! I'm told a big storm is coming. I want you to leave when the storm comes. No one is to suspect what you're doing. The storm will hide your movements until you're well away from any Mal'lam settlement." Just then her father, Sho'sha'lo, knocked at the doorpost. *Ja'jan* simply said, "Come." And he came inside, nodded to Wol'man and took a seat near him. *Ja'jan*, having forgotten that her Feather-Plait servant, Jana'la, was still sitting in the gloom of the rear of the hut, packing up her feathers and threads, said, "You can go now, Jana-la. Come back again tomorrow morning."

Jana'la hurried to finish packing, picked up her woven bags of materials and with a curtsy toward *Ja'jan,* swept past in her stoop, nodded to the two men and disappeared into the growing grayness of the approaching storm. She stopped at her own little hut, carefully covered her precious feather collection beneath matting and waited in the dark interior of her sad little home until near darkness had fallen. Then she too entered the storm unseen, and disappeared in the direction of the main Mal'lam main village.

Research Notes: Impressions and General Observations

Subject: Tina Pua'lani Kaiser, Honolulu, Fall 1974

It's a girl!! Her name is Lea Malia. Poor Jiro was on the Big Island when she came though. He was attending a conference, there was a big storm and he couldn't get a flight out until the day after! But I had good company; Tina was with me through the whole thing. What an angel! Also, Jiro's son Andrew played surrogate daddy; waiting in the Daddy's Room, pacing and going out for smokes. He's an angel too! But he smokes too much.

Little Lea arrived about six days late but I was not worried or too uncomfortable. I managed to get a lot of work done on the last passages of Tina's story. Boy, complicated it was! Now, with our little one here, my time with Tina will most likely be quite compromised but she is going to record on her own. As I've said in the past, she's a real whiz with the recorder. And I trust her implicitly.

Also, our friend Bill Snakenborg has some encouraging news, language-wise. He's sure now that there are definite similarities between some of the words in Mal'lam and the languages his colleague is studying in Taiwan. One would have to wonder how long it might be before 'science' accepts what I, as a scientist, have accepted: some human beings have psychic capabilities! I don't, personally, that's quite certain or if I do then those capabilities are very subliminal. But my experience over the past two years has convinced me of many things which I could not now present as 'science' to any scientific body. Then how can I justify my pursuit of this study and, in good conscience, accept University funding for this program of research? Because my husband says I can; he says I do it well and he's the one who signs the checks! Hah! So there! I believe it's called 'feather-bedding' but I refuse even to blush.

Speaking of bedding, my daughter needs hers changed. Tina, my willing maid - nurse - *seestah* and dear friend, isn't home from school yet so I'll just have to do it myself. I don't know yet what's going to transpire in Tina's story but I hope it's a bit cheerier than some of what's been happening back there among her Spirits.

Chapter Thirty Five - Hard Lessons for Some

Sho'sha'lo had been late to the meeting because he had been following *Ja'jan's* instructions: gather as many people as possible and inform them of her recent directives concerning the way the *'Ja'jan-an-lo'* were to think and conduct themselves. He did so with relish. Never in his life as a rather lowly fisherman had he felt such power and purpose! His fantasies of his relationship with his daughter were being altered but he have the intelligence to make did the adjustment. He was now '*Her* Chief Priest', a role he had not yet fully grasped but he was warming to the task. In that meeting with *Ja'jan* and Wol'man he had struggled to come to grips with the awfulness of their assignment. Kidnapping his own grandson? Killing his former son-in-law's wife? Kidnapping their child? What must the *Earth Mother* think … No! No, sorry! He must never again entertain such thoughts! *Ja'jan* must surely be justified in her demands! Carry on! Carry on, Chief Priest!

Wol'man, Chief of War, chose but eight men to accompany him and Shol'sha'lo overland to the Itin villages and perform their murderous duty. Of this 'war party' of *Ja'jan-an-lo*, only one other than the Chief Priest was of the Clan Sht'ah'ha. He was Wood-Hewn, and a native of Sht'ah Lee who would know the way northward to the Itin. All the other seven were like most of *Ja'jan's* disciples: refugees from the disasters on the northern islands - non-Clan.

From his home island's Clan he had absorbed a much stronger prejudice against the Itin than ever had the Clan Sht'ah'ha. Wol'man found hating them easy. They stank of fish! They spoke differently! They lived on and from the sea almost exclusively and they were just, *different*! Reason enough, his twisted mind decided and he harangued his 'warriors' until they growled and shouted and swung their weapons with a deadly intention. None of them had any idea of martial performance. To their sorrow, they would face men who did.

In the howling wind and deluging rain, the night so dark that the 'warriors' had to walk in single file, hand on the shoulder of the man in front, Wol'man followed that one Clan Wood-Hewn guide into the gloom and cold. Their rain capes hardly helped keep them dry, so densely did the rain fall but they did make them blend into the night's background. Could they be seen, they would have appeared as like some huge caterpillar. Through that same dark storm, Jana'la Feather-Plait wended her way with relative ease. She had walked this trail many times, often in the dark. *Ja'jan's* new settlement was nearly four miles inland from the Mal'lam village at Dolphin Bay, her goal this evening.

Forty minutes later she spied a glimmer of light from someone's candlenut-lit hut. Then another, another, until she knew exactly where she was. She saw movement as someone ran from one hut to another, hunched over against the rain. She halted until all was still again and then moved on. Not even a dog was barking this night. Jana'la came at last to the hut she was looking for. It was larger than most, serving not only as a residence but as a clinic for the ailing. Shen'ha Herb-Mistress's home! Jana'la knocked on the door frame. No answer, the noise of the storm muffling such a hesitant announcement. Again, and more strongly this time and suddenly the woven *pandanus* drape at the door was swept aside and Shen'ha appeared, squinting into the blackness.

"Who? Ah, Jana-la! Come in my dear. You'll freeze out there. Where have you come from?" As soon as Jana'la was inside the warm, well-lit room, Shen'ha reached for a bundle of worn *tapa* cloth for the woman to dry herself on. She then went to the little fire in the middle of the hut and threw on some small twigs to bring it to life again. Reaching for a ceramic bowl with water in it, she began to make a tea for her guest. Shen'ha allowed Jana'la to dry and warm herself. When she was comfortably seated she handed her a bamboo cup of steaming liquid, redolent of herbs and fruit. Patiently, Shen'ha sat quietly across the small fire , her face composed and quite lovely in this light.Jana'la drank the tea with gratitude, blowing and sipping in turn until she had drained the cup.

"More?" Shen'ha asked. The woman shook her head in negation and added a gesture of thanks. What gesture? With the palm of her left hand turned inward, Jana'la rolled that hand over with the fingers pointing outward toward her host. It was a natural gesture which this dumb woman had begun to use many years ago to thank someone for something. Shen'ha had built upon this and similar gestures and some body-language to create a form of communication between the two women. The young boy, Han, the child whom Shen'ha had adopted two years before, coughed, stirred in his sleep and Shen'ha rose to adjust his blanket. Done, she returned to her seat and smiled at Jana'la.

"Dear Jana'la. What brings you here on this terrible night? I'm sure it must be very important. Thank you for coming." Shen'ha made that same gesture of thanks and then waited for the woman to begin her story. A great part of their 'conversation' involved Shen'ha asking questions and Jana'la nodding or shaking her head. This required all of the Herb-Mistress's insightful intelligence for what Jana'la had to relate was complex and almost unbelievable even in plain language. Over the years, since that dreadful day when Shen'ha had intercepted the distraught women who was nearly ready to cast herself off a cliff, these two had slowly built up a dialog of sign and gesture which allowed them a surprising level of meaning to be communicated.

After two hours of difficult and sometimes frustrating attempts for both of them to meet their minds on the same message, Shen'ha sat back and smiled at her guest. Jana'la rose and excused herself to go out into the rain and relieve her bladder. In a downpour like this it didn't matter where you peed. While Jana'la was outside, Shen'ha choked back tears and reheated the tea. When she returned, the Feather-Plait sat back down and reached again for the *tapa* rags. It was still pouring rain outside.

"I can only thank you with all my heart, Jana'la. This very night I will inform the people here who need to know of what you have told me. My dear friend," she said, "you have saved lives, the lives of some of our most beloved. How can the Mal'lam people thank you?" The woman shook her head but Shen'ha wasn't sure if it was in sadness, denial or what. Jana'la rose to leave, the hour growing late and she still had that long trek through the continuing storm.

"Here, Jana-la. Take this rain cape. You'll be frozen by the time you return home." Jana'la waved the tempting offer away. Her signing finally impressed Shen'ha that, of course ... what if someone back there at the village of the *Ja'jan-an-lo* discovered a new rain cape? Smiling ruefully the Herb-Mistress hugged her friend goodnight and saw her on her way into the blackness. Moments later she donned that same rain cape and set off to speak with Orn'ta Sea-Master.

~ ~ * ~ ~

Orn'ta Sea-Master and twenty men boarded Sea-Master Chom'shul's new canoe on the morning the storm broke. They were on a desperate mission. Shen'ha could not tell them how many of *Ja'jan's* people they might encounter when they had completed their overland trek, so best to be ready. Orn'ta knew that Jo'lo'tan's sons remaining with their people there in the Itin village were quite capable of defending themselves. But what if the *Ja'jan-an-lo* were able to attack them without any warning? Oh, if only Ch'am'lo were there to guide them!

Chom'shul Sea-Master himself, like Orn'ta and two other men, had been involved in the battle with Tor'na-the-Mad. Since the voyagers had left, many Mal'lam continued to practice those skills Ch'am'lo had so assiduously trained them in. They felt confident of protecting Sht'ana and the children, if only they could get there in time. The Mal'lam Sea-Hewn and five Wood-Hewn among them sailed against a stiff northerly breeze, having to tack repeatedly. The sky now, after the storm had passed, was an intense blue with only a few puffy, low level clouds.

The crew searched the shoreline for any sign of *Ja'jan's* people marching north toward the Itin villages. Those men of course were far inland, the Sht'ah Lee man among them guiding them, was leading them through the rugged wastelands. This country was now sodden and the usually dry streambeds rushed with brown water. There was no proper trail but only a vague track, now nearly indistinguishable from the surrounding, muddy ground. The swollen streams were a hazard and constantly delayed the group of men on their murderous quest. Instead of four days travel this journey would require six, time which would condemn their purpose to utter failure.

"There's a vessel ahead, Voyage-Master! It's a new Mal'lam canoe, by its sail!" Al'malan stood and rushed forward on the deck to see for himself. Indeed. It could only be a new vessel with that rigging. But whose? Simultaneously the men aboard Chom'shul's canoe spotted the 'Wa'Ran'tar' and even at that distance, nearly two miles, Orn'ta Sea-Master could swear that he recognized his friend's canoe. Still capable of hoisting himself up a mast, the elder Sea-Master climbed up to just below the lookout already there, to see for himself. He clung there for nearly five minutes, others on deck calling up for his opinion. Finally satisfied, he swung hand over hand down to the deck, a smile a foot wide on his face. "It's 'Wa'Ran'tar', no doubt at all. Al'malan Voyage-Master has returned and perhaps he has already visited the Itin." Chom'shul ordered his canoe to be stopped to await 'Wa'Ran'tar's approach. The lines were let go and the tall sail panels allowed to swing like weather vanes, offering least resistance to the wind.

Al'malan, his vessel riding swiftly with the breeze nearly behind him, ordered his crewmen to prepare to come beside this friendly craft on 'Wa'Ran'tar's starboard side. Soon the two vessels were lashed together and joyous Mal'lam leaped from vessel to vessel, greeting old friends. Orn'ta, these past months a terrible burden of anxiety to him, embraced Al'malan with a crushing hug. Never had he been so glad to see another man! It only took moments for the nature of the northbound canoe's voyage to be revealed to the men of Al'malan's canoe. Their relief was beaming from their faces. However, Orn'ta, his confidence on a high now, reminded all that the Itin still needed to be warned and the Mal'lam who had come to protect Sht'ana and the children might well be needed to help fight off *Ja'jan's* henchmen.

"We can waste no time, brothers!" Orn'ta declared. "Celebration must wait." He turned to his old friends whose tales of their journeys he could hardly wait to hear. "I believe that it's best, Al'malan-an, that you continue to the Bay of Dolphins directly. We will continue on and warn the Itin. I wish we had Ch'am'lo with us." When quickly informed that Ch'am'lo was already there, Orn'ta closed his eyes and sent thanks to the *Earth Mother* for another series of blessings. It required another twelve hours for Chom'shul's canoe to reach the Itin village on Crab Claw Bay. The northerly winds had increased and although the skies remained clear, they rode a choppy sea with increasing swells all the way. This, his third trip to this small harbor, still was a challenge for the young Sea-Master to negotiate the strong current through to the narrow harbor mouth. All aboard attended the paddles and strained mightily but finally they were through and safe inside. Ch'am'lo and his brothers were quickly at the beach to greet them, wondering what they were doing here now.

"Hello brothers!" Ch'am'lo called out to his fellow seamen, and leaped lightly aboard. It was quickly explained to him the reason and urgency of their arrival. Ch'am'lo's face darkened. This was the final insult! "Chan'sha!" he called out to his next youngest brother, "We may have unwanted visitors approaching from inland. You and some of the boys go inland a ways, keep your eyes and ears open, set up a relay back here to the village. Understand?" His brother raised a hand in acknowledgement, the few words of the conversations he'd already heard had alerted him to the nature of the situation. He pointed to three of his brothers and four other young men and they all set off at a run toward the village to arm themselves.

These Itin young men had spent their youth scouting around and through the dry scrublands behind the villages and they knew every watercourse, rise, hollow and flatland. They had hunted birds and wild pig as well as helped collect herbs and healing plants for their own Herbalists. They would divine the most likely course for intruders unfamiliar with these lands to approach undetected. Their youthful enthusiasm for adventure was balanced by the knowledge that this was much more than a game. And most importantly, the young people of the Itin possessed a collective discipline unknown to their Mal'lam cousins. Generations of adversity had created a small society within the greater Mal'lam environment which was only recently being recognized and emulated by their cousins. These fellows really did know what they were doing and why, while their potential opponents were striding, stumbling, slowly making their way toward them. But they were still a day away and suffering now from the strenuous pace which their leader, Wol'man, was setting for them.

Orn'ta, as warrior-leader of the Mal'lam here, sat in council with all the Sea-Hewn and Ch'am'lo. They agreed that there should be a picket line of lookouts, those young men already sent ahead, and a secondary defense line comprising Orn'ta's people and other Itin men and boys. Orn'ta and Ch'am'lo would float about among the two sections together, gathering information and planning for the many possible eventualities. Orn'ta had now regained that old sense of confidence which had brought him to this island's position of Chief Sea-Master. His fear had fled. But he knew that he had aged and was not the man he once thought himself to be. What he was now, would have to do!

~ ~ * ~ ~

Wol'man Stone-Hewn cursed under his breath as the rain of this new storm continued to pour down. Twice today he and his co-conspirators had had to cross swollen streams, one man falling and losing his spear. Disdaining sharp pointed weapons, he clung to his heavy club, slung on a cord around his neck, freeing his hands for the difficult task of fighting his way through the undergrowth. Sho'sha'lo, *Ja'jan's* father and now her 'Chief Priest', followed closely behind the big man from Sha'lan'la-Set; he who had killed. The older man struggled determinedly to keep up and was pleased at his ability to do so. Wol'man, growing more disgruntled by the hour now, kept asking the local man guiding them if he truly knew where he was going. His urge to kill again was welling up inside him like a festering sore. 'Would this wretched trek never end?' he asked himself.

Soon the *Ja'jan an-lo* had found a cave-like overhang, large enough to accommodate them all in out of the rain. There was even firewood piled neatly at the rear of the structure of rock. Surely the Itin must have done this; a shelter for their foraging or hunting expeditions. That likely meant that they were now but a day away from the Itin settlements. The men started a welcome fire. All were drenched and chilled and weary. Now was the time when the *Ja'jan* Chief Priest must do his duty! Sho'sha'lo began a low, humming chant, of his own composition, which extolled the virtues of their dear Mistress and the glorious future which this new Clan of people could look forward to. Surprising even himself, Sho'sha'lo began to sing a song of praise of this woman whom he had held at the hour of her birth. His love for his daughter, warped as it might have been, shone through and he continued with greater enthusiasm. Even Wol'man found himself warming to the story of how this ill-treated wife of a Sea-Hewn had been chosen as the vehicle for the will of a long-forgotten Goddess.

Now her sacred duty was to retrieve her only son so that he could be sacrificed to the gods of their ancestors to ensure the growth of the Mistress's power and the well-being of her people. Such great courage did it require of the Mistress, this sacrifice of her only issue for the good of her people, that all should fall on their knees in devotion to her. And they all did! Kneeling around the fire, those nine other *Ja'jan* devotees bowed their heads to the ground, emulating the Chief Priest. Slowly that evening, the tired men chewed their tough, moldy field rations and then curled up under their soggy rain capes to try to sleep. The fire was stoked to fill the shallow cavern with some acceptable warmth. Men were left in rotation to tend the fire. The skies were clearing, the wind abating, hinting a new day of warmth, sunlight and certainly, victory!

The *Ja'jan an-lo* 'warriors' could not know that the fire they had kept burning all night had led their adversaries to them. Less than two miles from the sea, its expanse was unseen by the invaders during the previous day's storm. On this clearing night the glow of the fire, reflected off the back of the overhang, shone like a beacon. The Itin's knowledge of their own backyard was complete. They all knew exactly where that fire was. By midnight Ch'am'lo and Orn'ta had gathered their forces and quietly set off through the scrubby growth to surround the temporary shelter of those men who considered the Itin their despised enemies. Dawn would hold much more than a warm sun to greet the *Ja'jan an-lo.*

Orn'ta, in his enthusiasm for overpowering this sneaking invasion, urged a dawn attack. Ch'am'lo demurred, citing the fact that sunrise would see the sun in their *own* faces. "No! Excuse me brother, but I think we should wait for them to organize themselves and get ready to set out. After all, we don't know yet how many they are. I suggest that we quietly form two wings, one on each side of their position. Then when we know their strength we can either close in on them or fall back and regroup closer to the village." Orn'ta frowned, thought a moment, then nodded in agreement. As soon as they awoke, those men would discover just how close to the sea they were; it was quite visible from their little hideout. "Alright," he said to Ch'am'lo, "I'll move my group around to the left side, you to the right. We'll need some signal from you, I think."

Ch'am'lo replied, "I think you and I should remain close together still, in the center, and make our decision together. That way we can each move sideways to direct each wing. What do think of that?" Orn'ta was greatly encouraged by the man's easy inclusion of him in the final decision making. So great was his respect for this lean, athletic Sea-Master and his martial skills that until this moment he had assumed a secondary role to Ch'am'lo. Another segment of his self confidence, which had begun to unravel over the past year, rejoined him and Orn'ta Sea-Master began to glow inside with a renewed sense of power and purpose.

One of the young Itin, a young brother of Ch'am'lo it was, had crept close to the shallow cave well before dawn. His approach was unheard. He remained there until the *Ja'jan an-lo* began to stir, counting them as they emerged from their hideout, the predawn light revealing the ten of them. He nodded to himself, quietly backed away and down a slight incline and jogged back to his nearest other lookout. That young man turned seaward, cupped his hands near his mouth and whistled a bird-call, ten times. He waited a few moments and repeated his signal back to the body of the warriors.

"Ten of them!" Ch'am'lo said quietly. "I'm surprised there are not more. They must feel quite confident of themselves." The two leaders sat hunkered down together in the rising dawn, making their last minute plans. Each then called a man nearest in the wings of their formation and whispered orders. Those two men in turn moved silently along the lines of their comrades, repeating the order. Too much danger of misinterpretation if the message was passed from man to man.

Wol'man was surprised and dismayed when he saw how close the sea was. So were his henchmen and they were soon all looking about anxiously, expecting to see their enemies appear any second. As the light level quickly rose, Chief Priest Sho'sha'lo came beside Wol'man and said quietly, "I think we should advance *now*! We may still be able to surprise them before their village is up and about." Wol'man, never one for discussion, simply thought - *simply* - then nodded finally and turned and ordered the *Ja'jan an-lo*, in a low voice, to get ready. This was the day! As his followers gathered up their various weapons, mostly heavy-shafted spears such as the ones used against wild boar, the Chief Priest walked among them, speaking words of encouragement, invoking the name of the Mistress and her blessings. He himself carried a heavy club, like Wol'man, used so often in his past life as a Sea-Hewn to club large fish to death once he had pulled them aboard his small canoe. His fingers gripped the club's handle nervously, the movements meant to increase his courage and commitment, even as he urged similar commitment among his daughter's followers.

Below the intruders the Itin and Mal'lam defenders waited, pairs of young eyes watching their every move. Orn'ta and his co-commander waited in the deep shadows and whispered their assessments to each other. The sun, rising in a cloudless sky, could certainly be to their personal detriment in a fight but their warriors on each wing of their formation would be looking side-on to the *Ja'jan an-lo* advance and their vision would be unimpaired. Then Orn'ta nodded with his head to what Ch'am'lo just then noticed. On the right side of the pathway up the slope was a large, broad-leafed fan palm, its fronds spreading over the track and as the sun now rose in its intense brilliance, it threw a broad swath of shade onto the trail. Now was the time and that was the place.

Both men rose together and Ch'am'lo pursed his lips and gave out a soft, chortling bird song. The signal for both wings of their bird-of-prey formation to close on their enemy. It was the *Ja'jan an-lo* Wood-Hewn who said loudly, "That's not a bird! That bird isn't here this time of year!" Looking toward Wol'man he added, "That's the Itin, Warrior Chief!" All the intruder's eyes now focused downhill, the sun-cast shadows deep and dark and the flickering reflections off foliage making it difficult to see detail. Then, there they were! Two men only! All recognized the Sht'ah Lee Sea-Master but not all knew the taller, leaner man beside him. They stood side by side in the middle of the well worn track downhill, their bodies shaded beneath a large palm tree. The Mal'lam carried a spear and a shield, the other man, yes, an Itin, was similarly armed and they stood silent and still.

Wol'man was about to make a derisive noise when, from all around them, there came rustling sounds. The Chief Priest looked left and right, seeing one, two, five … then many more men stepping from the cover of the surrounding scrub. They too were well armed and shielded, their bodies painted with diagonal stripes of black and white paint."We're surrounded!" Sho'sha'lo gasped. He turned and looked to the shallow rise above the shelter they had so gladly sought the night before. Three men swinging slings nonchalantly but issuing a discreet threat, stood looking down at them! Then the voice reached them:

"Sho'sha'lo Sea-Hewn! You know my voice! You know the man I am! I tell you now, lay down your arms and return to your squalid village and your mad 'Mistress'!" Not a bird sang or called, so startling was that commanding voice which rang through the thick scrubland. "We know why you are here, you *Ja'jan followers* ! Let me tell you this, and with great joy; Al'malan Voyage-Master has returned and reclaimed his family! All of them are now safely back at Dolphin Bay. Your journey here is for nothing. You are already defeated!" Letting the silence return and his words sink in, Orn'ta waited before continuing, then resumed as loudly as before."I see you looking around you. Yes, these men are ready to kill you! But I tell you from my heart … I want no bloodshed this, or any other day! How think *you*?"

Sho'sha'lo knew his answer. He started to speak it but Wol'man stepped quickly in front of him and shouted, his voice high with tension but its force covering his own fear. He looked down the trail and saw his shadow, elongated and broad in the brilliant sun, laid out on that downhill track like a guide to destiny. "I, Wol'man, Warrior Chief of the *Ja'jan an-lo*, tell you this. I am a man of war. I have killed and killing is my Destiny! You stupid fools cannot deceive us. We will complete our mission. Now stand aside and let us pass and perhaps we will spare you unnecessary bloodshed. That is all I have to say to you. There will be no more discussion!" With that, the man raised his club and followed his shadow down the track at a dead run. A death run!

Ch'am'lo stepped forward and raised a commanding arm and swung it around for all his men to see. Even Orn'ta deferred to his mate. This man was trusted to be in control just now. Itin and Mal'lam warriors withheld their sling stones and spears. The only sound now was the slap of Wol'man's bare feet upon the track, his grunting breathing rose in pitch as he approached the slimmer, shorter man who seemed willing to meet his charge. Ten feet out from his adversary, Wol'man raised his club and prepared to bring it down on Ch'am'lo's head. Wol'man's heavy, awkward body contained no subtlety of movement. Ch'am'lo judged his arrival to the instant. Two steps away from delivering his killing blow, Wol'man's legs tangled with Ch'am'lo's expertly thrust spear. Driving the spear point solidly into the ground, the shaft formed a solid barrier to his next raging step. Wol'man fell in a heap two paces beyond where Ch'am'lo stood. The Warrior Chief's club flew from his hand to disappear into the scrub. His painful collision with the ground, even softened as it was by the storm's rain, tore the wind from him, leaving him kneeling and gasping for breath. The Itin and Mal'lam men, expecting his compatriots to follow his charge, arched their throwing arms and cocked their slings. No one up on the slope in front of the shallow cave moved. Not even their spiritual leader, Sho'sha'lo.

In three strides, Ch'am'lo stood above the *Ja'jan* devotee. He threw his spear aside, raised his shield in both hands and brought its edge down on the back of Wol'man's neck. The stiff bamboo edging of that defensive shield became a savage weapon. Wol'man's neck broke and his body collapsed in a heap upon itself. The Itin warrior immediately swung around, ready to repel an expected attack from the dead man's followers. Not one of them followed, let alone attacked.

It was Orn'ta's voice which broke the painful silence which followed that man's death. "Fellow Mal'lam … whomever you call yourselves now, let the killing stop here! You are outnumbered five to one, you have no skills as fighters and your only kill-trained leader is now dead! Need I say more of it? It is time for you all to turn around, leave your weapons behind and return to wherever you see fit. But you must leave. Now!"

Only Sho'sha'lo still gripped his weapon, all the others had quickly discarded theirs and stood in a milling circle of aimless, leaderless, hopeless men. Some sobbed with panic and terror although the defenders of the Itin villages had made no further movement toward them. Except Sho'sha'lo! From somewhere deep within him came a fierce renewal of the 'holy' office his daughter had laid upon him. Sho'sha'lo Chief Priest strode forward to the head of the slope down the trail and declared, "We accept the conditions of this day and the victory of your people."

With that he too cast aside his weapon. "But know this, Masters of the Itin and the Mal'lam … our Mistress leads us to glory, to our eventual victory over those who look to the sea for their strength. After years upon the sea, I have only discovered my true strength here upon the land. This island, this Sht'ah Lee, will be our inheritance." His gaze then centered upon the Itin Sea-Master, a look evident even at this distance to all who watched. "You Itin, non-Clan scavengers of the sea, you will have no place on this land when finally the Mal'lam bless us with their departure. If any of you remain behind when finally we see their sails disappear over the horizon, you will all die!"

The Chief Priest could hardly believe his own words. It was as if someone else had borrowed his voice. But the meaning was his own also and he stamped his own signature upon the moment. "Take word to that foolish man who was once my son-in-law, Al'malan, that he must surrender his son, Sahn'ta, to his mother. It is her right! And it must be done before the autumn harvest ends." Sho'sha'lo halted himself before he carried himself beyond his real capacity. He took a deep breath and gambled all on his next demand. "Therefore, either kill us all now or allow us to return to our own homes. We shall both observe a truce, an abeyance of hostilities until after the autumn harvest. Then we shall see what we shall see!" All the Mal'lam and Itin involved looked to each other while Orn'ta and Ch'am'lo spoke quietly and quickly. Enough death!, was their decision. *Earth Mother* would guide the future!

The *Ja'jan an-lo* began their wearying, thirsty journey back to the Mistress's home village. Weaponless, half starved and despondent, they never-the-less made the return journey in but four days. On that journey the Chief Priest, Sho'sha'lo, began to evolve into quite another man. There was more to be heard from him yet and his daughter would be among the listeners.

Chapter Thirty Six - Back Among the Tarbara'ut

The day had been broiling hot. The two young Sea-Hewn, A'lan and Faldo-in were sweaty and grimy and ready for a bath after a day working in the gardens. They sat in the shade of the coconut grove above the canoe sheds and with a hand axe opened two green drinking nuts each. Ahhh! The cool, sweet liquid ran off their chins and down their chests as they emptied the coconut water from the smooth, green nuts.

"Let's go for a swim!" Faldo-in said, wiping his chin. With unspoken understanding they both surged to their feet and ran across the sandy beach, racing each other. Faldo-in was two steps ahead when they splashed into the cooling water and both dove headlong into the shallow waves. Laughing and trying to dunk each other, the lads played and thrashed about in the water for minutes. "Let's go for a walk up the shady side of the island." was A'lan's suggestion.

In this late afternoon the hills which rose abruptly behind the beach cast their long shadows down to the waterline. In this shade the afternoon sea breeze felt wonderfully cool on their sunburned skins and they set out for the southern end of this island of 'Tara'tor'. As the island began to narrow heading southward, so too did the reef narrow and draw closer to the shore. The young Sea-Hewn picked up chunks of coral and skipped them out over the water as they walked. Once they stopped to inspect a dead seabird in the sand, A'lan plucking out the long tail feathers; white with bands of black. As they walked, A'lan ran the feathers over his face, the soft, smooth caress of them stirring that mix of hormones which in young men his age lay so close to ignition.

Reaching the end of the long, sandy beach they began climbing up and over the wave-washed basalt rocks which formed the base of this volcanic island. They paused again and inspected the salt pans which the Tarbara'ut had long ago chipped into those level areas of the hard stone. Filled with seawater, allowed to evaporate, then filled numerous more times, these basins provided all the salt which the native people on this island required. Each of them dipped wetted fingers into the crusty salt a few times, relishing the replacement of all the salt they had sweated out during their scorching day of hard work.

Ahead of them now was a wall-like structure of basalt crystals; black, five or six-sided columns of smooth rock which rose variously from three to eight feet. Short pieces, having broken and fallen off over the ages lay in a jumble at the wall's base.. The upright sections afforded an uneven but easily climbed stairway up and over the barrier. As they neared the top of this barrier they could see waves erupting against rocks further on. Here was the end of the coral reef and the beginning of deep, blue, open sea. Mounting the top of the wall they stood looking out at the beckoning blueness, that place where both longed to be setting out upon in their people's canoes. A squeal, laughter and movement far below them brought their attention down upon a delightful sight.

There on a small black sand beach, liberally speckled with white coral stones were a group of Tarbara'ut women and young girls. Laughing and chasing, splashing and diving into the incoming swells the group was oblivious to the two Mal'lam voyeurs. All of the maidens on the beach were naked, their broad skirts of soft grasses lay high on the sand above the reach of the waves. Faldo-in instinctively knelt down on one knee to make himself less conspicuous but A'lan remained standing, enthralled by the scene below him. He stood with his arms at his side, one hand filled with white feathers, the other clenched into a fist in response to those hormones which had begun to bubble and boil within him.

Unaware that they were standing in a narrow beam of sunlight, the two Sea-Hewn were soon spotted by the girls. The word was passed around and soon all of them stood looking up at the two stalwart apparitions on the black rock. One girl, taller than the rest, indeed taller than most Tarbara'ut women, walked close to the base of the steep wall of rock and motioned upward to the Mal'lam. 'Come on down!' was the implication, the surf drowning out her words but her meaning was immediately responded to. Faldo-in Sea-Hewn, tutored by his uncle, had become quite conversant in the language of these delightful black people.

While the two fellows carefully descended the rocks to the beach below, each feasted their eyes on the scene, casting their glances about among these nubile creatures, all glistening wet and grinning white smiles at them. Faldo-in called out a greeting in their language and giggling voices returned it. But on their descent, A'lan's eyes kept returning to that tallest girl. She was totally demanding of his attention. And it seemed to him that her gaze was centered on him also.

When they had at last jumped down onto the sand the girls immediately surrounded them, giggling and laughing, flirting with their eyes and body language. Mal'lam girls, once they had been Plait and considered women, seldom revealed all their naked bodies in public. Their breasts, yes, but from their waist to their knees they kept themselves covered in their *tapa* cloth wraps. Only lovers and husbands-lovers saw them totally naked. Not so the Tarbara'ut females! And more than one Mal'lam man had already succumbed to this irresistible, but in Tarbara'ut context, innocent and normal display. Faldo-in, able to converse at least roughly with these ladies, soon had them grouped around him, touching him, gazing into his face, giggling and laughing.

A'lan stood apart, unable to proceed, his eyes locked on those of that lovely girl who now walked directly up to him and stood close in front. Her head came up only to his chin. Her hair, kinky and black, held a wilting cluster of yellow flowers and around her slim neck was a perfectly graded chain of cowry shells. Her left cheek displayed a small scar, surely accidental but A'lan found it quite attractive. Her eyes held his with an unavoidable insistence and she stood looking up at him, searching his face, turning her head slightly this way and that, inspecting this stranger's being. There flowed between them an energy which grew moment by moment.

A'lan's tension mounted and he felt he had to do something … say something! He raised his left hand and offered her the feathers. The lovely young girl … no, she was definitely a woman now … took a step backward, looked at the feathers and then held out her right hand. A'lan reached his hand out and laid them into her palm. He noticed the soft pink of her palm and underside of her fingers as her hand cupped upward toward his. A jolt of passion flowed through his whole body and their fingers touched as she gently accepted the white offering. Her fingers closed softly around the gift and withdrew almost reluctantly. For the first time in his young life, A'lan Sea-Hewn was totally smitten!

Faldo-in and A'lan joined the girls and the two older women among them, and plunged into the breaking waves. They had removed their wraps but were both reluctant to discard their breech-cloths in spite of the teasing insistence of their flirtatious friends. A half-hour of playing in the surf saw first one, then another of the girls retreat to the beach and put on their grass skirts and ascend the rocky ladder up to the top of the black wall. Time to go home. But both

Mal'lam Sea-Hewn remained in the surging waters, each having chosen, or having been chosen by, black-skinned, voluptuous girls. As their friends disappeared over the stone wall, the last two waving and calling out teasing comments which none below could hear, Faldo-in and A'lan stood in the surf with an eager girl nestled tightly, wetly, against each of them. A'lan and the native girl held onto each other's arms, bracing themselves against the crash and pull of the waves which rushed repeatedly from the open sea and onto this secluded beach. She loosed his left arm and patted her chest, between those lovely, firm breasts. "Arawee!" she said, repeating the word and gesture until his mind finally encompassed the meaning. He was not actually at his most acutely intelligent at this moment.

A'lan copied her gesture and said, "A'lan. I am named A'lan!" The girl tried to form the words, looking at his mouth as now he tried to assist her by silently mouthing and repeating his name.

"Aran!" she said, the Tarbara'ut not having and 'l' in their vocabulary. "Aran!" That was good enough for him and he repeated the name 'Arawee' with no lack of pronunciation. Nervous giggles and a step closer were suddenly dashed by a large wave which overwhelmed them and took them both off their feet. Spluttering and choking as they surfaced, they clung tightly to each other and A'lan began to pull her toward shore, gently gripping one arm. The hand of that arm still held those white feathers. Once ashore, A'lan looked around for his compatriot, Faldo-in. Nowhere! He looked urgently out into the surf but there was no sign of him or the other Tarbara'ut girl. Then he thought to look up onto the sands above the waterline. Only one grass skirt lay there in the deep shade and it could only be Arawee's.

Holding hands the two youngsters helped each other up through the increasing strength of the surging waves and regained the beach. Once on the dry sand, Arawee looked down at the feathers in her hand, brought them up to caress her wet face with their wet softness and smiled at him. As if only just noticing, she raised her other hand to his face and laid it gently onto the scar which dominated it. She looked questioningly into his eyes, the questions there gentle and meaningful. He shrugged and looked away and did all those things which men do when an imperfection or an old wound drew attention. 'It's nothing!' was the implication. But he felt her intelligence fly through his eyes and into his soul and deposit a healing intent which would bind him to this person for the rest of his life.

It was Arawee who instigated what occurred next. Letting go his hand, she walked quickly to the dry sand and retrieved and put on her skirt. His eyes of course were on her body as she did so and he was quite willing to assist in her directions from then on. Leading the way, Arawee climbed the rock wall, A'lan close behind, trying to keep his eyes on his footing and handholds. Soon they had crossed the sculpted stone barrier and were upon the now white, coral sand beach, the waves there softly lapping the coral and black stones scattered about. Not touching each other now, they walked closely together, she playing with those white feathers and casting him glances which only increased the flame growing within him. A'lan Sea-Hewn, a young man of intense dedication and discipline found himself happily melting into someone quite 'else'. A dark glade of grass appeared beyond a grove of coconut palms and as if following a newly revealed path, the two went there. A half moon would rise to the center of the sky before they walked together, hand in hand, toward the settlement another mile on. Arawee's hair was now set with white feathers.

~ ~ * ~ ~

The Mal'lam had always been an industrious people and now they turned their industry upon two of these beautiful islands: 'Tara'tor', where first they had landed and where their voyaging canoes remained well above the water, sheltered beneath long, thatched, open-sided buildings and 'Tara'Bet', the 'Snake Island' which the native people shunned. It was that island which was the focus of the majority of the voyagers. Of the ninety Mal'lam who had landed here with the fleet, twenty-four had returned toward Sht'ah Lee with Al'malan Voyage-Master. Of the sixty-six remaining here, thirty-eight had moved almost permanently to 'Tara'Bet'. The twenty-nine remaining on 'Tara'tor' were mostly Sea-Hewn, Faldo Sea-Master among them. Their primary duty was the protection and maintenance of the four canoes but this really required little of their time so most had turned the most of their days to fishing and farming. To the great surprise of many of them, they actually were enjoying these roles and took turn about performing them. Enno Stone-Master, preferring to remain close to his brother, centered his tool-making endeavors in a small hut near the canoes.

He now had a Tarbara'ut apprentice, a man in his early thirties who had some experience with stone-knapping but accepted Enno as the true Master he was. The man's name was Bat'rat. A more jolly and agreeable companion Enno could not have hoped for and the smiling man was even keen to learn to converse in Mal'lam. Enno was amazed at how quickly he learned, and a bit embarrassed at his own slow pace in learning Tarbara'ut. Together they traveled over all the islands of this little archipelago searching for the best stone. On one island they discovered obsidian but it was of an inferior quality for larger tools. But for knife blades, awls and drilling bits it was quite adequate and for those larger tools, the best stone he found was on 'Tara'Bet'. Faldo Sea-Master, now that he couldn't make these treks with his brother, became interested in wood carving and would spend hours sitting near Enno, one creating piles of wood chips and sawdust, the other piles of stone chips and dust. As those things often evolve, it was the Tarbara'ut assistant who had the job of cleaning up. He still grinned and giggled as he did so and Enno was becoming very fond of him. Besides, he had a young niece who visited often while they were working and Enno found her most attractive.

On the island of 'Tara'Bet', the 'Snake Island', the Mal'lam were already making great headway in establishing a viable community. The shallow valley between its two mounded hills was already the site of a small hamlet and the fertile land around this settlement was becoming farmland. The memory of those periodic incursions from the sea by the breeding snakes was another motivation for moving inland from the beaches. The Stone-Hewn were hard at work establishing aqueducts and drainage channels as well as weirs and dams.

Rather than building temporary huts as they did on the island of 'Tara'tor' they began building raised building platforms and substantial structures. Some of the Mal'lam definitely planned to stay here permanently. Those intent on settling-in received lots of assistance from the Sea-Hewn who were temporarily land-bound. More small bamboo rafts were being constructed and a lively little traffic was developing between the various islands. A dugout canoe required weeks of labor to construct and when completed, its carrying capacity was limited. Some of the Tarbara'ut had begun to install outriggers on their own little dugouts and, finding them more stable now, began to go beyond the reef more often and further.

The Mal'lam presence was having many effects on the lives of these native peoples. But bamboo rafts are slow, too slow to suit two young men whose girl friends lived on another island. A'lan and Faldo-in Sea-Hewn now took every opportunity to borrow a Tarbara'ut canoe and paddle hard for the small islet of 'Tara'zin', in the opposite direction to 'Tara'Bet'. Finding these little dugouts not swift or commodious enough, they decided to build their own vessel. With the willing assistance of two Sea-Hewn living on Tara'tor, the young seamen felled and hauled to the beach a softwood log nearly twenty feet long. They immediately set about hollowing it, a Wood-Hewn with much canoe-building experience also guiding their efforts. Enno Stone-Master was happy to keep them supplied with sharpened adze blades. Actually, it was his assistant, Bat'rat who did most of the grinding of the adze blades. It was monotonous, hard work. Bat'rat did it mostly with a smile, humming away to himself.

The basic hull of this new canoe was too shallow for using in any kind of rough weather or for carrying much weight. Only one answer for that! Build up the sides with planks. Here the two lads were out of their depth of knowledge and the Wood-Hewn took over. A tree of another species had to be felled and also dragged and rolled down to the beach far on the other side of the island and floated around to the work area near the big canoe sheds. This straight-grained, fragrant timber was split into planks using wedges and shims and soon the two young Sea-Hewn were put to work adzing the planks smooth.

With the discipline most Sea-Hewn were inculcated with as initiates, A'lan and Faldo-in applied themselves diligently, working until the light failed after a day of other duties - like weeding the *taro* paddies and resetting rockwork on the terrace walls. Their youthful energy, their youthful insistence on maintaining contact with their girlfriends and their realization that what they were creating would remain to benefit the future Mal'lam arrivals to these islands, made the work seem well worth it. Their Tarbara'ut friends, the young lads Jun'tee and Ah'tee, sometimes offered assistance but mostly sat looking on in wonder that anyone could work so hard, so long and with such dedication to a really abstract idea. That was one of the basic differences between these two cultures; the Tarbara'ut saw their existence and life-style as their ultimate finality. The Mal'lam society contained within it a nervous itch for something a bit new, a bit, *other*! These two young Sea-Hewn embodied that characteristic; did they ever!

Among the Mal'lam Sea-Masters there was growing another itch. To be upon the blue ocean again! They looked at their powerful canoes, high and dry on land and like fretting steeds, anxious for release. There was no hope yet of supplying enough preserved rations for an extended voyage. But surely, there was reason to keep seamanship at its peak and this could only be maintained by practice. Time to set sail again. Only one vessel at a time, but it was certainly time for these men-of-the-sea to feel the blue water swells beneath them once more. Both A'lan and Faldo-in were chosen by the Master of 'Wa'Olon', Sh'ban'al Sea-Master, to accompany his canoe's sortie out onto the open sea.

The work on their small canoe was progressing nicely but they were more than happy to down tools and climb aboard the big vessel and prepare it for sailing. All else, even girlfriends, took second place to this fulfillment of their desires. When word had circulated among the Sea-Hewn on the two islands that the canoes were to take to sea again, albeit one at a time, great excitement prevailed. It was a renewal of their energies. The Sea-Masters had chosen A'lan especially because all seamen were impressed with his *sea-sight* and knew that that capacity must be reinforced whenever possible. A'lan would accompany each canoe in turn as its crew exercised itself and its vessel.

'Wa'Olon' was pulled down the sloping sands of the beach and into the water with a rejoicing among the seamen which approximated a formal celebration. Bamboo rafts and Tarbara'ut canoes had ferried Sea-Hewn from the island of 'Tara'Bet' in the early morning hours to assist in the launching. The masts had been raised, their newly-reinforced sails attached and as the canoe lay upon the inner waters of the lagoon, a challenging wind grew from the southeast. Right! Paddlers take your stations! Twenty-two Sea-Hewn were aboard this morning, all but three at the paddles. Unaccustomed work on the land had never-the-less maintained their strength and on Sh'ban'al's command the twenty men dug their paddles deeply into the windblown surf.

Slowly the big canoe made way against the wind, its sail panels lying loose, avoiding the wind's insistence. It was A'lan, his muscles strengthened by those days of adzing the hull of the canoe and its planking members whose voice overtook even the senior paddle master's call; 'Pull! Pull! Pull!' he shouted, as if his strength alone might hasten the canoe's passage through the reef's surging waves. The vessel's Master, Sh'ban'al, noted with admiration the young man's exuberance. More than exuberance, there was mastery, command, irresistible leadership. He marked his own leadership in comparison to that same age in himself and surrendered to the fact that this young man was a born leader.

Faldo Sea-Master stood on his one leg and watched the big canoe take to the sea. Regret was always but a thought away, but this man had long ago learned to overlook such thoughts in light of what his life had led him to experience. "Look at them!" he whispered, "Such a beautiful sight! Our people are again trying their wings! So shall we always fly!"

'Wa'Olon' grasped the incoming swells as a challenge and quickly overcame them. The proud vessel swept through the obstructing waves and plunged beyond into the welcoming blueness. The edge of these islands dropped sharply downward and as soon as a vessel escaped the confines of its reefs, it could fly away in whichever direction it chose. Sh'ban'al chose to turn left and take advantage of the wind and set his course on an around-archipelago journey. The sun was nearing full height, the horizon revealed squalls and sudden wind shifts as the Autumn weather followed its inevitable course. "Take us well out to sea!" the Master called to his crew and paddles were secured and the sails set to run the vessel abeam of the wind.

They ran so for most of an hour, the shoreline diminishing and the horizon tugging at the minds of all aboard. 'Not to be!', however, as the Sea-Master stood trying to hide his excitement. 'This is just an exercise!' he kept reminding himself. 'Soon though! Soon!' That short voyage lasted but twenty-four hours; overnight for the navigators and men like A'lan to peer into the depths of the sea and into the deep of space and its myriad of guiding stars. The following afternoon saw the 'Wa'Olon' follow those same trade winds in an almost reckless rush through the opening in the reef and once again into the embrace of the island's sheltering harbor.

Over the next four weeks all four of the canoes had been crewed and sailed on overnight jaunts. By now A'lan had memorized the sub-surface signatures of this archipelago; its flashes of mauve and gold light radiating outward like beacons to be seen and read from many nautical miles away. As well did the skies, currents, wave directions, the color of the waters, the times and flights of the different sea birds which called these islands home, all were recorded in the well exercised memories of the Sea-Hewn.

Revitalized and fully confident again of their initial quest, the seamen of the Mal'lam returned to those more mundane pursuits with renewed vigor. Wood-Hewn specialists from 'Tara'Bet' remained with the canoe makers on 'Tara'tor', aiding the two younger Sea-Hewn to complete their canoe. Within but eight weeks of the felling of the trees the canoe was in the water and undergoing its trial run. Named, 'Wa'iti' or 'Little canoe', the craft with its double outriggers and tall, narrow sail raced across the shallow reef waters with A'lan and Faldo-in as main crew and Faldo Sea-Master as special guest. It handled well but sat lower in the water than some would have liked. "Don't worry." Faldo Sea-Master would explain, "When it has had time to dry out, it will ride much higher and prouder. The wood is still green, don't forget."

It was he who had applied his newly found occupation of woodcarver to the carving of the canoe's paddles. The paddle blades were long and pointed in the manner of the Tarbara'ut but had a crosspiece hand grip like the Mal'lam used. These hybrid tools proved even more satisfactory than either of their two models. Innovation would seem to result from synthesis, as does romance! In the case of the Tarbara'ut and the Mal'lam, not only the imbalance of male/female numbers within the population of the Mal'lam voyagers but an element of fascination with differentness would surely have been applying.

Within the year, mothers would be holding nursing babies to their breasts which were lighter in color or darker in color than was their previous experience. But to these two people, only the infant counted. To the Mal'lam, the *Earth Mother* had simply added a bit of charcoal dust to this baby or sawdust-hued flavor to another. To the Tarbara'ut, with their declining birthrate, every infant was a blessing, no matter the color. And so the germ of another racial offshoot was forming in these southern seas; a blend of genes which would expand and move southward, then eastward, and the islands of this great expanse would welcome a new divergence of mankind.

Chapter Thirty Seven - Changes for *Ja'jan*

Jolo'tan, the esteemed Headman of the Itin, lay dying. But not in some dark hut surrounded by loved ones stifling their sadness. His wizened body was propped up on a pallet on the sandy slope above the shoreline of 'Crab Claw Bay', a rosy sunset and a gentle breeze caressing him with all the comforting memories of his life. His eldest son, Ch'am'lo, sat at his head while around him his wives and children arrayed themselves in a loose circle. Beyond this family closeness sat or stood his neighbors and friends. A fire had been lit and smothered in herbs and the offshore wind carried the sweet smoke out over the surf and dispersed it upon the very sea which had been his lifeblood through a very long and fruitful existence.

"Father," spoke Ch'am'lo, "is there anything you would like? A drink of water perhaps?" His son's voice was calm and even, betraying none of the anguish which lay behind it. Jolo'tan cleared his throat numerous times before answering and then only answered with a gesture. No! With death so near, water could salve nothing. And this man's life required no salvation for he had lived it to its fullest. He raised one weak hand from the elbow and invited his eldest son to embrace it. Ch'am'lo quickly grasped it in both of his and pressed it to his forehead, then sat back, still caressing the dry, leathery hand which had guided him all of his life. He could now only wait for that other life to depart. The end came suddenly, silently, with no warning. That old hand, in its sudden limpness, signaled to his devoted son that all was completed in the life of Jolo'tan. His choked words unleashed a growing wailing and sobbing. "We are now alone upon our own path, brothers and sisters. Let us rejoice in our father!" Ch'am'lo bent forward and kissed the old man's head, let go of his hand and rose and left the assembly to grieve on his own.

Ch'am'lo Sea-Master returned at dawn to the village and officiated at his father's funeral. Unlike the Mal'lam, the Itin buried their dead in deep graves covered with heavy stones. The strongly built house in which he had lived for so many years was dismantled and the man's body wrapped in *tapa* cloth and woven mats and buried deep in the center of the building's platform. The timbers and thatching were made into another bonfire and a gathering of all the Itin stood watching the smoke rise. Within that smoke they believed the valued man's soul rose and wafted out over his beloved ocean while beneath the earth his body slept finally with no more pain or worry or obligation. 'We rejoice in you!'

~ ~ * ~ ~

Three days hence the Itin were on the move. The weather was glorious; the sea was calm and a gentle, steady breeze was blowing from the northeast. These people were going south to join their Mal'lam cousins - permanently! Before Jo'lo'tan's passing it had been decided in the Council of Elders that life here in their secluded northern villages might soon become too dangerous. Besides, the Mal'lam were moving on en masse as soon as they could build enough large canoes. Like the Mal'lam Sea-Hewn, the seamen of the Itin looked with longing at the open ocean and dreamed of what they might find beyond the horizon. Ch'am'lo's tales of his travels further fired their enthusiasm, most especially his younger brothers.

Only eight elderly Itin refused to join the exodus. Frail and unwilling to make even the journey down the coast they determined to remain and end their days where their own ancestors had lived for over three hundred years. Ch'am'lo was now the uncontested leader of his people and he had promised these elderly loved ones that he would return and insure the proper burial of their remains. Like the Mal'lam, the Itin had a tradition of the elderly simply willing themselves to die on a designated day. This was a morning of great sorrow for all. As soon as the sun was midway in the morning sky the little flotilla of outrigger canoes followed the four double-hulled vessels of the Itin Sea-Hewn.

Ch'am'lo's canoe, inherited from his father, was in the lead. Its upright sail panel with that esoteric, black symbol emblazoned on it ran ahead and slowly outdistanced the rest. They were on their way as quickly as possible to inform their Mal'lam cousins of this sudden arrival of nearly one-hundred souls. Orn'ta Sea-Master had taken word of their likely decision back with him after the confrontation with the *Ja'jan an-lo* but the exact day of arrival could not be known except by a few psychic individuals. Already, like when the Clan cousins from Sh'ham Set were forced from their home island, preparations were underway to assist them in settling in.

The little outrigger canoes, each propelled by both sail and paddle, could certainly not keep pace with those larger vessels and as the sun fell low in the west a well-known little harbor drew near. Time for an overnight stay. Still the sea remained tranquil and the wind constant and tired Itin sailors and their many passengers greeted the little harbor with gratitude. Only a morning's sail, weather permitting, would see them safely into the 'Bay of Dolphins'. Most of the Itin had never been this far away from their safe lands in the north of Sht'ah Lee and it provided an interim adjustment; a gentle introduction to a whole new world. Canoes safely secured ashore, the seamen aided their families in setting up campsites. Food was at a minimum but adequate for a small celebration. Children had fussed with fatigue because it had been a long day. Forced to sit relatively still for hours, when they landed on the beach it was in running mode! Many adults too were not good sailors and not a few had suffered from seasickness. But now they could all relax and rest and have a bite to eat. Tomorrow's sailing would come early, weather permitting.

And so the weather did permit. Another bright and beautiful dawn with sky and wind promising a repeat of yesterday's easy run. By now the van of the Itin vessels was safely on the beach at 'Dolphin Bay'. Ch'am'lo was greeted by his Sea-Brother, Al'malan, and they were shortly joined by Orn'ta Sea-Master and Shen'ham Sea-Hewn and numerous other seamen and Elders of the other crafts. Shen'ham's wounded hand was now bare of bandages, still sensitive to the touch but his use of that hand improved day by day. Ch'am'lo embraced the young seaman as he did his own brothers and Shen'ham glowed with pride and pleasure. Never was there a moment's animosity in his mind over the removal of two of his fingers. Much had been saved by that small loss.

Another hour saw the beach filled with Mal'lam families, all preparing to greet their Itin cousins. The refugees from Sh'ham-Set, more than most, appreciated the importance of these new refugee's impending sense of displacement and no little bewilderment. They would greet them with open arms and generous hearts. Earth ovens were blazing; trussed pig carcasses, mounds of *taro*, yams, bananas, breadfruit, cleaned and plucked chickens and large *mahi mahi* fish lay beneath cooling, protective banana leaves, ready for packing into the carefully structured stone liners of the ovens. The beat of drums grew louder and the rhythm more complex as the hours passed. Ordered lines of young dancers swayed and stomped while flutes and stringed instruments kept pace.

And then, the sun not yet at midday, there they came! Sea-Hewn jumped to canoes and bamboo rafts, racing each other to be first to reach the small outrigger dugouts of the Itin voyagers. Al'malan Voyage-Master, Orn'ta and Ch'am'lo paddled strongly out in one fishing canoe, all three garlanded with leis of flowers and shells to toss aboard the approaching craft. This was truly a day of great celebration.

However, to a discerning eye that morning there was one anomaly among the crowd. A young woman and two children, accompanied by her own mother and her mother-in-law and the oldest child's other grandmother, were cupped in a half-circle of young, well-armed warriors. Wherever the women and children moved to, there also followed their guardians. Sht'ana Herb-Plait, Sahn'ta and his little half-sister La'teel and all of the Voyage-Master's family was now guarded day and night. No one took the warnings of that mad creature, *Ja'jan*, lightly. They had but recently experienced the extremes to which such out-of-control egos could go. A siege mentality quivered shallowly beneath this day's joyous celebration.

Very many of the Itin refugees were overwhelmed by the boisterous reception set for them. All their lives they had believed, not always unreasonably, that they were considered separate and therefore a lesser people in the eyes of the Mal'lam. This morning's rousing welcome dissuaded most of those opinions and over the coming months, all but a few hard-shelled Itin greeted a Mal'lam as a true cousin. There was now a true melding of these two peoples. They both spoke a very similar language, ate nearly the same foods and held the *Earth Mother* as their deity. But it was the same, deep blue sea and its enchantment which had accompanied all their ancestors to this now-failing archipelago, and that same enchantment was now calling them both to journey together again and dance to its song.

~ ~ * ~ ~

Four miles inland from the 'Dolphin Bay' settlement there was no rejoicing. Behind the strange construction which could only be called a palisade, there rested within three specially-built structures the inner-circle of the Goddess *Ja'jan's* servants and advisors. Her father and now Chief Priest, Sho'sha'lo, occupied a small room in one hut while the speechless servant, Jana'la Feather-Plait and a younger woman from another Clan occupied the other half of that hut. The younger woman attended to all of the Chief Priest's needs, whatever they might be. The enclosure was a raw and heartless place. No decorative carvings graced the door frames, the ends of the roof thatching were left untrimmed and ragged and no stone paving protected the bare ground from becoming a quagmire when it rained. One old breadfruit tree was left standing just beyond the rough paling walls of the enclosure, offering some shade on a hot afternoon.

On this day of joyful celebration among the Mal'lam and the Itin, only a morose silence prevailed here. *Ja'jan* had been informed of the impending arrival of those people she hated with such intensity, the evening before. That they had been responsible for the death of her chosen Warrior Chief was insupportable. When Sho'sha'la had returned empty handed and carrying that bad news, *Ja'jan* had flown into one of her signature rages which continued unabated for hours until finally she had exhausted herself and fallen into a deep sleep. Her father had sat close beside her all that time, intoning the words of a liturgy of his own devising. The man was inventing a religion which centered on his daughter's belief that she was divine. He also made room for himself in that invention for, after all, she was his seed and surely he too was imbued with some of that divinity. The sins of the daughters seemed capable of visiting upon the fathers!

Ja'jan occupied the largest of the three structures as her own dwelling, meager as it was, while the third little hut was where she retreated to commune with whatever and whomever it was that inspired and guided her. Not even her faithful servant, Jana'la, was allowed to enter there. The day was bright and sunny and a deliciously balmy breeze caressed the whole island. But the village of the *Ja'jan an-lo* sweltered in a deep funk. No noise was allowed; no calling out, no hammering or clattering of the people at their normal craft work, all conversation hushed in respect of the Mistress's own dark mood.

From time to time a sudden, ephemeral shift of the wind carried the sound of drums to this sad place. *Ja'jan* so seldom left her darkened quarters these days that her skin had begun to look sallow and yellowed. Her long fasting those months ago had left her with little appetite and her once voluptuous figure had begun to diminish into scragginess. She took no new lovers. That once powerful sensuality which had drawn so many of her devotees to her was being replaced with a grim, humorless presence, usually clad in black garments decorated now with black feathers. *Ja'jan's* incitement of fear upon others was working the same effect upon herself. She lived more and more in fear for her own sanity.

Late that afternoon *Ja'jan* sent for her father. Lately she had altered her opinion of the man, even though the mission to retrieve her son had failed disastrously. He seemed greatly changed somehow; more focused, less obsequious to her and even willing to contradict her. *Ja'jan* knew that she was loosing touch with her followers. Some were leaving her and returning to the Mal'lam, others growing restless and questioning. She needed to reinforce her position, renew her power. She needed her father's opinion for the first time in her life. It could be said that Sho'sha'lo Chief Priest was finally becoming a responsible father. But was it too late? Sho'sha'lo been away from the compound and had to be sought out . He returned immediately he was told of the Mistress's call for him and was greatly surprised when she greeted him with, "Thank you for coming, father. Please sit down and join me in some tea." Her tone was strange, as if finding it difficult to deign to speak casually even with her father. He knew something very important was occurring here. In the background was the bent, silent figure of the servant/cousin.

Jana'la busied herself making a sweet-smelling herbal and fruit concoction. The smoke from the small fire at the back of the hut seeped slowly up to the roof and found its way out beneath the rafters. And outside now, the normal sounds of a small village resumed. An hour before, *Ja'jan* had lifted the curfew on normal existence. She had even walked outside her compound and, wearing a white wrap now and a smile, informed a small group of her followers that it was time to return to the normal, blessed life of a *Ja'jan an-lo.* And she had winked at a handsome young man who had not yet been blessed with her seduction. Surprising and important changes indeed. And only hours ago doom and gloom had reigned!

"Father, I believe I have made some mistakes. I have not properly understood the messages sent to me by the emissaries of the *Goddess, Ja'jan of the Skies.*" Her demeanor now was somewhat sad, Sho'sha'lo thought, an expression he had seldom seen even in her childhood.

"I thought perhaps you could assist me in …well, understanding what must be done, now that we have suffered some setbacks." *Ja'jan* leaned toward her father and stroked his cheek, a ploy for sympathy which she had invented as a small girl. It still worked. But then Sho'sha'lo caught a movement in the dim light of the hut. Both of them had forgotten the quiet presence of Jana'la, sitting near the fire, waiting for the tea to heat. A glance and nod of his head indicated that *Ja'jan* should look behind her. Without looking she knew his meaning, gave a small shrug and a slight smile and said quietly, "Not to worry father. She is perfectly safe to have around." He was not so sure but accepted her declaration and returned his thought to the important question being considered. 'Where to from here?'

"I do think it's wise of you, Mistress, to think carefully about the near future." Sho'sha'lo ventured. Even he wasn't quite sure what his daughter's 'people' should be focusing upon at this juncture. Before he could continue she interrupted.

"As you well know, father, I'm a person of compulsion." This was certainly no revelation to the father but the fact that the daughter was thinking in those terms of self-examination was quite startling! "You see," she continued, leaning again intimately toward him and speaking softly, "It was the urgings of '*Ja'jan of the Sky*', which I had not yet learned to interpret, which drove me to make some mistakes. Now that I understand so much more, I am able to concentrate on what is most important at this time. We can forget all those mistakes and failings which were so distressing and begin again to make our people aware and confident of the 'Goddess'." Still there remained in her tone the inference that the 'mistakes' and 'failings' were not all hers. Sho'sha'lo too, by inference, shared some responsibility. That he had returned empty handed from the Itin homeland and lost the Warrior Chief besides, was guilt enough for him to bear. She let the implication float onto the gentle breeze which wafted into the hut and disappear with the smoke of the fire.

"Oh yes, Jana'la. Thank you. That will be all now. You may go." *Ja'jan* had accepted the delivery of the tea from her cousin and dismissed her in a manner so gentle that Jana'la did a double take, gave a shallow bow and left the hut quite puzzled. For all these months she had borne the brunt of her Mistress's bad tempers, tantrums and outright cruelties and yet here she was, calling the Chief Priest, 'father', speaking like a wholly reasonable person and showing kindness and consideration. Sho'sha'lo too took hope that *Ja'jan* was entering a new and more amenable manifestation of her 'holiness'. One hour became three and still *Ja'jan* and Sho'sha'lo Chief Priest sat huddled in consultation. The moon was rising now and quiet, every-night sounds rustled about the little village of this strange assortment of people. The wind had shifted and no longer did the distant echo of faraway drums from the Mal'lam village on the bay intrude on the *Ja'jan an-lo's* evening.

Research Notes: Impressions and General Observations

Subject: Tina Pua'lani Kaiser, Hanalei, Kaua'i, Winter 1975

Good, good news! The war in Vietnam is over! My brother David came back from Asia just last week. I hardly recognized him. He's grown up, of course, but something is not quite right. He hardly spent any time with his new niece and was only here for dinner once. We used to be very close but he's gone away somewhere else. Maybe he just needs time.

We are having a good time on Kaua'i, this time staying up on Koke'e with Aunty Bev and Unca' Warren Kapuna. Yesterday, while Tina and Jiro stayed behind with Warren to work in his garden, I put little Lea Malia in her 'papoose' pack, which hangs off my front for urgent feeding situations, and we went with Tutu Kinau and Aunty Bev up to the baths above Kalalau Valley where Tina and I had gone … yikes!... it's over two years now!

When we got there Aunty Bev asked me to strip the baby down and take her to the pool. Bev stripped down too and climbed into the pool first. I mean, it's winter and even though the day was beautiful and sunny, it was very cool. Not to worry! In Bev gets, hunching her shoulders against the chill and puffing a bit but soon she sits down in that cold water and holds her hands out for me to give her my baby. "Go ahead, honey!" Kinau whispers to me, "It'll be alright."

Motherhood makes changes in a woman's psyche I guess. Before Lea Malia was born I would have been game for just about anything. But this? Give my baby to a woman crazy enough to sit in freezing water and then want to put my baby in there too? Oh no! So I gave Lea Malia to Tutu to hold and I got naked too and climbed into the pool beside Bev. She and Tutu burst out laughing, making jokes about 'crazy *haole* ladies'. Lea didn't seem to mind any of this carry-on. She just smiled and cooed and flapped her arms.

I have to confess that I'd been told in advance what all this was about. Both Jiro and I agreed that it was a wonderful idea, really, just a bit unorthodox! This was to be Lea Malia's *baptism*! It was a tradition which both these women's families had practiced for generations. It was a melding of Christian and Old Hawai'ian traditions and only performed by women on girl babies. It was a lovely little, actually very short ceremony during which both ladies sang and chanted in Hawai'ian, all three of us adults sitting waist deep in the stream and passing my baby around between us, cuddling and kissing her while the soft Hawai'ian phrases embraced her. I felt so blessed myself and so happy for my little daughter. But, God! Couldn't they have picked another season for this? Shit, that water was freezing!

"Tina has a boyfriend! Tina has a boyfriend!" I sang this one day when she'd come home from school, all blushing and mumbling because I'd seen her little friend duck down the street after I'd watched them walking, holding hands. Know what she did? She grabbed the garden hose and was going to spray me. I of course, being the adult here and needing to establish respect and discipline, tried to wrestle the hose from her grasp. About the time we were both soaked to the skin and near to collapsing from laughter, guess who arrives home early from work? Professor Yukihara himself. You should have seen the look on his face as he came up the driveway. I waved the hose threateningly at him, still giggling like an idiot, and he stuck his tongue out at me and then it was on!

When this bit of madness was over and Tina came back out of the house with the baby under one arm and three towels under the other, Jiro and I decided that next year we'd have to think seriously about getting a swimming pool installed. Then I could drown him!

Oh yes; here's some information pertaining to things scientific, which is what I'm supposed to be about.

- Last summer I reported that there was considerable work being done with ceramic and other artifacts associated with what is now called the 'Lapita People'. Well, a new archaeological dig has been opened in Fiji and much information is beginning to accrue from that.

- Tutu Kinau Ho'opai Kaiser has informed me that *her spirit voices* assure her that what is now being investigated in Fiji and elsewhere, having to do with the 'Lapita', is indeed the very same people … the Mal'lam! This is all getting quite scary. I love it!

We - Tina and I - agreed to leave our recorders at home on this holiday. Never mind. Here's another few hours of previous transcription.

Chapter Thirty Eight - Truly a Master

When the column of Wood-Hewn, led by the Canoe-Master Joha'lan, passed up the 'Black Boar Track' toward the forest-clad mountains, the *Ja'jan an-lo* kept out of sight. Their village, now called '*Ja'jan-wan*' was but a few hundred feet off the well-used trail. Only weeks ago the fear had been that *Ja'jan's* followers would attempt to impede the progress of the Woodsmen in their movements up and down the mountain track. On this day, the craftsmen traveling upward were accompanied by warriors! Never had this island seen the like of this display of martial intent and considerable capacity. They meant business. Among the column of men, nearly two-hundred of them counting the protection force which was led by the Itin Sea-Master, Ch'am'lo, were many women and older children. The latter group carried moderately heavy bundles of foodstuffs. In fact, this would be but the first of many such supply trips women and youngsters would make up the 'Black Boar Track'.

The cutting and hauling and completion of the canoe hulls was estimated to take over two years. As soon as the first of the great logs was delivered to the canoe sheds above the beach at 'Dolphin Bay', finishing work would begin. Wood-Hewn craftsmen specializing in building the big, sea-going vessels would set-to immediately but this time the nature of the construction would be somewhat different. Long hours, days and weeks at sea with little to occupy his mind had allowed Joha'lan Canoe-Master to devise new methods of constructing his people's canoe fleet for the coming exodus. No longer would the huge logs which comprised those six hulls of his previous designs be sought-out in the forests. This time it was still the Kan'ta'ab timber for the basic hull, but of a smaller diameter. The canoe hulls would be slightly shorter than the exploratory fleet's hulls but they would be deeper. And depth was all important, for these vessels must hold more people, food , animals and other supplies. This voyage was not of discovery but of resettlement.

Whereas with 'Wa'Ran'tar' and the other two large, new vessels, it was the width of the initial log plus but one course of planking which determined the capacity of the hull, these new canoes would be narrower but higher-sided. The huge effort involved in moving those earlier, great baulks of timber would be avoided. More, smaller logs of Kan'ta'ab would be required and many more logs of Kan'wit'to. Kan'wit'to timber is a semi-hardwood, straight-grained and resinous and is relatively easy to split into long, straight planks. And these planks were what would be the great difference in the Mal'lam fleet which would move nearly all the people and their portable possessions that two thousand nautical miles to the south. But the whole project was daunting.

Thirty canoes of large size would be required to transport the approximately one thousand Mal'lam and Itin who were expected to leave Sht'ah Lee-Set within three years. The Mal'lam survivors now resident on this island, of all surviving Clans, possessed between them but twelve seaworthy voyaging canoes. Bamboo rafts were out of the equation; too slow and unwieldy. That left a minimum of eighteen vessels to be constructed. A system of great efficiency must be devised and maintained and again the big, affable Canoe-Master must find the inner strength and discipline to carry on for those short but difficult years.

Within ten days the first logs of Kan'ta'ab were making their way down the mountain. Guarding them were twenty Mal'lam and Itin warriors, again led by Ch'am'lo. And again the *Ja'jan an-lo* kept their heads down and nearly out of sight. In fact, they could be seen working industriously in their gardens and paddies, hardly casting a glance at the procession of men and timber. The inner-circle of Mal'lam Elders were now receiving information of a surprising and most welcome nature regarding *Ja'jan* and her followers. If what was being reported to them was reliable, *Ja'jan* was turning over a new leaf! She had ceased her strident demands for the return of her son, Sahn'ta, and no more was heard of that rumor of sacrifice!

A source very close to the Mistress herself revealed, very quietly, that the woman seemed quite changed since that abortive attempt to kidnap her own son and take the life of Sht'ana Herb-Plait. Her father, too, was exhibiting a hitherto unknown side; confident without arrogance and very much less obsequious to *Ja'jan*; much given to long discourses on the meaning of life according to *Ja'jan* and most importantly, preaching brotherly forbearance! Too good to be true? Probably, most thought, but it did appear that there was a period of peace and stability on offer.

Ch'am'lo Sea-Master took this opportunity to return to his home village and carry out his promise to attend to the proper burial of the aged Itin who had chosen to remain behind. All of his brothers and one sister and three other Itin Elders journeyed back. It was a sad and melancholy affair, attended to with a not unseemly haste. This was to be the final separation, the final visitation to a homeland which had helped shape a unique, small element within the larger Mal'lam whole. Itin children born from now on would know of themselves as Mal'lam first and as of the Clan-Itin second. On the voyage back down the coast to 'Dolphin Bay', Ch'am'lo mused while his younger siblings took over the sailing of his vessel. He climbed high on the mast, wrapped a safety line around his waist and leaned back into it, enjoying the rhythmic swaying of the canoe and the shoreline's changing features as they slowly slipped by. He had come to love those rich, tropical islands in the southern seas and was as anxious as any of those he had sailed with to return there. The dry, sparse land of his youth was now forever fading into the background as his vessel caught a stronger breeze and picked up speed. A brother called up a needless but appreciated warning of a change in the sail's position.

Ch'am'lo was as aware as any seaman of the dangers which could lurk atop a mast. Another awareness worked his mind on this morning. It was well past time that the leader of his Clan should be married! There was no shortage of women, Mal'lam or Itin, who would consider marrying this handsome, impressive man. Of course he did respond quite freely to the advances of many women and enjoyed a robust sex life when he could. But he found that he was most attracted to younger women, girls even, just beginning their sexual activity. And there was one such Mal'lam girl who was lately on his mind. Just seventeen now, he had noticed her grow from a slightly chubby child of fourteen into a blossoming young woman with a delightful personality. She was a natural born raconteur and sweet natured in the bargain and their eyes had made meaningful contact more often of late. 'Yes! She could be the mother of my sons and daughters! I will speak with her as soon as I arrive back 'home' to 'Dolphin Bay". Her name was Shana'lan Herb-Plait, best friend to Tina-an Earth-Plait.

~ ~ * ~ ~

Shen'ha Herb-Mistress, now regarded as the Mal'lam's premier officer in charge of gathering information on the activities and proclivities of the *Ja'jan an-lo,* had just seen one of her intelligence gatherers off on a mission. Her other spy, in the camp of *Ja'jan,* Jana'la Feather-Plait, had not been seen for many days. Shen'ha was baffled by *Ja'jan's* quiescence of late. Her people had not even come to watch the procession of the Woodsmen into the hills. Surely though, they were being watched. The Mal'lam had fully expected the *Ja'jan an-lo* to make some demonstration after those strong reports of their intention to block the canoe-building project. What was that crazy woman up to? Tina-an and her sweetheart, Shen'ham, were walking hand-in-hand over the raised pathways between the upper *taro* paddies. A hot midday sun beat down and many field workers were taking breaks from the heat under the cool awning of a large tree. As the two young people passed they were hailed and spoken to with more than the usual warmth of a Mal'lam greeting.

"Good day, Tina-an! Do you have that young man well under control?" grinned an older woman, wiping perspiration from her face. Tina only grinned back and moved a bit closer to Shen'ham." Well 'Three-finger'", a man called out, "What mischief are you up to?" Shen'ham's nickname had stuck and he wore it quite proudly. Very many saw this Sea-Hewn as marked for greatness and the fact that he was now the lover of another youngster of imposing potential lent more facets to his persona. To see the two of them together, as with most young lovers, sent warmth and gratitude throughout the whole community. The young lovers walked on until the paddies ended and the scrub forest began. To the left lay the declared realm of the *Goddess Ja'jan*.

"I have to leave you here, my love!" Tina-an said, clinging tightly to Shen'ham's arm in a farewell gesture. His face clouded in concern and he held her at arm's length and looked meaningfully into her hazel eyes. "Are you sure I shouldn't come with you?" She smiled widely and thumped him on the chest. "Dear Shen-an. You are a man of the sea. I am a woman of the bush. Leave me to do what I am best at. I have things to do and I am especially trained for it. My beloved 'Vesa'tan' will be my guide." With that she reached up and kissed him and within a few moments she was gone - disappeared - utterly silent and invisible as he gazed in vain to see her retreat. She was on the mission assigned her by his own mother. 'Oh *Earth Mother*! You have trapped me between two of the loves of my life. I surrender!' he thought, as he returned up the track they had come down, passing the *taro* workers with waves and greetings. Shen'ham stooped and picked up a vagrant stone on the track, slipped it quickly into his sling and fired an unerring missile at a tree trunk. With that, Shen'ham temporarily killed the loneliness of separation which among such young lovers was painfully acute. 'She'll be back tomorrow!'

Tina-an had moved with her usual silent swiftness away from the well-used track and set off northwest toward 'Ja'jan-wan' the village of the *Ja'jan an-lo*. Such facility in the bush was the result of those many weeks she had spent in the mountain forests, alone except for the Spiritual presence of her mentor, The Vesa'tan. Naturally slim and light on her feet, Tina took great pleasure in running full speed through heavy brush, ducking and leaping under and over obstacles. She gauged her progress in this skill by the number of scratches and bruises accumulated. Most often now she could perform this feat of agility and speed unscathed. She ran thus for five minutes until she reached the edge of the scrub. Barely breathing hard she knelt behind a large shrub and peered down a slope toward where she knew the village to lay.

There was little movement visible around the huts and drying racks and storehouses. Only a couple of smoldering fires spread their smoke over the scene, the breeze fitful this day. Crouching low and moving quickly from shrub to bush to tree, Tina crept closer to the nearest hut from which the sound of pounding issued. Almost like the rhythmic beat of *tapa* making, this rhythm was faster and a bit heavier. Crawling now, she moved like a lizard through the tall grass which surrounded the whole site until she obtained a ground level view across the whole of the open area in the middle of the roughly circular arrangement of huts. Yes. There, off to her left, a man sat cross-legged hammering what looked like pegs into a log. Another man knelt opposite him, steadying the object of those hard blows. She couldn't even guess what they were working on but she knew at least one of them was a Clan Wood-Hewn. He was from her own island Clan too.

Then two women came into view, each carrying a large gourd to contain water. They both stooped over a small stream of clean water which ran beside the little village, filled their gourds and without pause, backtracked to wherever they had come from. Tina followed them, retreating back further into the scrub so that she could move more easily and swiftly. The scrub land became more rocky and bare. It was an old lava flow which still had not succumbed to the incursion of vegetation; only a few hardy shrubs and groundcovers here and there offered cover or shade.

Tina stopped beneath the scant shade of a small tree and shaded her eyes against the sun's glare, the two women having dropped from view now behind a rocky outcrop. She reached a hand to her throat and grasped the pendant around her neck. Clearing her mind of any thought, she opened herself to that always-reliable sense which resided in that small stone. Moments later she smiled and uttered a thanks to her mentor. A few yards beyond was a small rivulet of water, more smelled than heard or seen, for she was getting thirsty. Dropping down into a shallow streambed, Tina knelt and drank deeply. She then removed her creamy white *tapa* wrap and folded it and hid it beneath some brush. Scraping up handfuls of soil she created a pool of mud which she proceeded to cover herself with. Her hair she left untouched, most often neatly plaited now that she had a boyfriend who appreciated a bit more neatness and style than she usually displayed. She sat for many minutes while the mud she had smeared all over herself dried. Wet mud would glisten and make her more visible. Dried, it would help her blend into the lava rock and low scrub of the area she was headed for. The hot, dry air and the gusty wind of this day quickly evaporated the water in the mud and soon she set off, crouching low among the sparse, coarse shrubbery. Coming to a high outcrop of lava, hot now with the fierce sun beating down, she crawled to the top and cautiously peered over. Something was definitely happening up ahead. Dust was rising from some activity, still obscured by the rough ground.

Moving with athletic grace, Tina crawled crab-like across the ground, keeping her profile totally hidden and her movements steady, avoiding contact with shrubs, the movement of which might give her location away. It took her many minutes to circle around to the east of where that mysterious activity was taking place but now she could hear voices and what sounded like stones being dropped or broken. Carefully scanning her surroundings she crawled to a grouping of boulders surrounded by thick scrub. On her belly now she inched forward until she could peer through the branches. 'Well! So that's what they're doing!' she muttered.

Seventy-five feet away were at least forty men and women formed up in a long queue and passing rocks from one to another. The last person in the queue threw them onto a growing pile of rugged lava. Another group of men where picking from that pile and placing the rock onto the base of a structure which appeared to be nearly fifty feet long by fifteen feet wide. She recognized some of the people, all Mal'lam but mostly people from the refugee Clans. One seemed to be directing the placing of the rock; a Stone-Hewn whom she recognized as Kal'to'lot, the man to whom Shen'ha had given that misleading story about the whereabouts of Sht'ana and the children.

And then - there she was - the Mistress herself! She stood with her father, Chief Priest Sho'sha'lo and two younger men, both carrying spears and standing a few feet behind them. *Ja'jan* was wearing what had now become her signature mode of dress; a *tapa* cloth robe which fell from her shoulders to her ankles. The cloth was dyed black and a fringing of black Frigate Bird feathers decorated the top of the wrap, blowing animatedly around her shoulders in the gusts of hot wind. She presented quite an imposing figure, for her long, dark brown hair was short and without fashion, maybe three inches long. A single cluster of white feathers was tied to the back of her hair and they too swept back and forth in the breeze. A long necklace of large fish scales glistened upon her chest. In her left hand she held a fly whisk of the long wing feathers of a Gannet.

The Chief Priest also wore a unique costume and Tina-an felt a chill of recognition. She had not seen but had heard of the colored wraps which 'Tor'na the Mad' had dressed his henchmen in. Sho'sha'lo was wearing a flowing robe of *tapa* which wrapped over one shoulder, leaving the other shoulder exposed. The bottom third of that cloth was dyed a rusty red. His head was wrapped in a turban of *tapa* cloth, also dyed red, and a long tail of that fabric fell down his back. His right hand held a tall staff from which blew an assortment of multi-colored feathers. Most striking of all was the design of the painting on his face. One side, the left, was totally covered in yellow paint while the right side sported horizontal stripes in black and white.

Tina then noticed that the two young men, guards obviously, also had red-dyed bands on their shorter wraps, narrower than those of the Chief-Priest's, and they also had black and white bands on their faces but no yellow paint. Tina thought they all looked quite gay and delightful, like the clowns who decorated themselves for the Mal'lam festivals at harvest time. But her mind whispered that a more sinister meaning attended this display of splendor. And there too was the hunched figure of *Ja'jan's* handmaid, Jana'la Feather-Plait, crouched down behind them all, a water gourd held in both hands. But she was looking in Tina's direction. Had she seen Tina somehow? A Feather-Plait always had very keen eyes for they were trained to spot the subtle movements of birds.

Tina-an froze her movements and averted her glance away from the woman, observing her out of the corner of her eye. Some people could sense someone staring hard at them. Jana'la made no movement and seemed not to give any sign of having observed someone or something. Shortly she stood up and offered the water gourd to the two guards, one of them taking it and drinking but the other waving it away rather brusquely. Next she timidly circled around *Ja'jan* and Sho'sha'lo and offered the gourd to them. *Ja'jan* took a brief drink and passed it back. She said something to Jana'la who made a shallow bow and walked away. The woman paused and cast a look toward where Tina lay hidden and then turned and continued walking away back toward *Ja'jan's* village, perhaps to refill the gourd. Tina was sure that Jana'la had seen her; how, she couldn't guess.

Tina was very confident of her ability but the feeling became a conviction and she made a sudden decision. Carefully and quietly she worked her way backward on her stomach until she was well out of sight of those people below. Then she quickly rose to a crouch and retreated back to the streambed where she reclaimed her wrap and put it on, not bothering even to brush away any of the camouflaging mud. Keeping to cover, Tina-an ran as quickly as she could on a parallel course to where she felt Jana'la would be walking. Coming again to the high outcrop of rock she crawled to the top of it again and peered over. Yes! She spotted Jana'la who was herself gazing all about her, obviously intent on observing something. Tina paused, clasped her necklace and closed her eyes, nodded to some internal confirmation and stood up in full view of where the Feather-Plait was looking.

The two women's eyes met across the yards separating them. Jana'la stood motionless for three seconds, gave a quick nod of her head and with a glance in both directions on the trail, moved with a grace belying her apparently crippled back and came toward Tina. Tina lost sight of her for a moment as brush intervened but then she was there. She halted but ten feet from Tina, a look of nervous questioning on her face. Tina held out her right hand and stood quietly, smiling. Reassured now, the older woman ducked beneath a branch and came to stand before Tina. Tina looked around, listened, judged that no one else was near and reached her hand out again and took Jana'la's forearm. The silent Feather-Plait managed a smile of her own then gestured that they should move further back off the trail and into the bush. Tina let her lead the way. This woman would surely know these lands intimately. Those who seek out and obtain feathers and eggs range far and wide and record much.

"My name is Tina Earth-Plait. Your name is Jana'la Feather-Plait?" Tina looked hopefully at the woman, nearly sure that she had the right person. When Tina was a child, this woman had lived in another village on her home island and was not known to her until that great cataclysm which had forced them all to move here to Sht'ah Lee-Set.

Jana'la nodded and smiled, then held out the gourd she was carrying, offering Tina a drink. Tina shook her head and smiled, but still cautious she again looked and listened for sight or sound of anyone following. Nothing. "Let's sit down a while, Jana'la. I need to … speak with you." Tina didn't know of another way to express her request. Communicating with people who cannot speak can be an unsettling experience for the uninitiated. When they had seated themselves on the smooth bark of a tree which had been partially blown down, Tina looked at Jana'la and asked, "How did you spot me? I thought that surely I was well hidden." Tina-an was very proud of her ability to move about undetected in the bush and she was quite puzzled.

Jana'la smiled rather shyly and reached up to Tina's head and gently tweaked her hair. Tina-an then reached up to investigate. Oh my! One end of a plait had come loose and Tina could feel it sticking up and fluttering happily in the breeze. Of course. Jana'la's keen eyes would have picked it out among the background of brush and leaves like a flag flying. Silly girl! Tina thought. She would have to tend more carefully to her hair, and the rest of her appearance, she admitted. She looked down at the remnants of her muddy camouflage and giggled at her own expense. But now it was time to get serious and the next forty minutes was taken up with the two trying, with considerable difficulty, to communicate. Tina, being able to speak, could ask and tell, prompt and question but the silent woman's responses were much harder to understand. Jana'la used hand gestures constantly as well as facial grimaces and smiles, nods and shakes of her head but not so much as a grunt did she sound. Finally Tina-an had to admit defeat. Patting Jana'la on the arm and apologizing to her for her failure to understand, she said, "I really think you must speak with Shen'ha Herb-Mistress, Jana'la. Where and when would you like to meet her?"

Of course, Tina was right back where she had started. All she could do was grin helplessly and roll her eyes. Jana'la grinned widely, gestured with both hands that it was alright, not to worry! Then very carefully she began signing in a manner which Tina-an was beginning to understand. Jana'la made waving, undulating movements which Tina thought she understood."Waves? The beach?" she asked. Jana'la nodded enthusiastically and then made a circle of her thumb and forefinger, hid it behind her other hand then slowly raised the circle to view. "Sunrise?" Tina ventured. Jana'la nodded and reached out and patted Tina's leg. "Tomorrow morning - at the beach - at sunrise?" Jana'la's grin widened and she leaned forward and put her arms around Tina-an's neck and gave her a quick squeeze. Then the silent women rose quickly, tilted her head as if listening to something, frowned and pausing to again give Tina a hug, she hurried off through the brush and disappeared.

Tina-an felt exhausted from the effort of trying to understand the poor woman's method of communication. Her estimation of Shen'ha rose another notch. Such patience it must have taken for her to establish that special means of understanding with Jana'la. Well, she had better be off quickly to tell Shen'ha. If she could find her quickly. Dear Shen'ham's mother was a very busy person and often away in the bush herself, gathering plants. Tina sat quietly and listened for sounds of human movement. Nothing, only birds and crickets and the breeze in the trees. Moments later she was on her way back to the Mal'lam main settlement, running at full speed through the undergrowth, reveling in the sheer joy of it.

~ ~ * ~ ~

While skullduggery and conspiracy flourished on the lowland flats, on the rugged mountain slopes beneath that great, dormant volcano, all was intense planning, preparation and implementation. Joha'lan Canoe-Master was back in his element! With the additional manpower available with the recent arrival of the Itin, and a number of experienced Wood-Hewn drawn from the refugee Clans whose individuals shunned *Ja'jan's* movement, the Canoe-Master had at his disposal more than three hundred workers to employ on this, his people's greatest venture yet. Joha'lan stood with the Sea-Masters Al'malan and Orn'ta as they watched the Woodsmen and their volunteer workers clear the brush from around a sizeable Kan'ta'ab tree. Further on into the dim forest another crew could be heard wielding axes and adzes to clear around another potential canoe hull. It was mid-summer now and even here in the heights the air was heavy with moisture and the sun made any open clearing a hot-box. But it must be done! The workmen chanted and sang as they labored, the sense of teamwork and brotherhood lightened what was indeed very hard work.

"So, Joha'lan, I see that you've bypassed some really huge Kanta'ab trees and are taking smaller ones now." Orn'ta had turned to the Canoe-Master with a question in his voice, not yet understanding the program which Joha'lan had devised those many weeks ago on that long voyage back to this home island.

"Yes, brother. The new hulls will have even more carrying capacity than our other, larger canoes. But we'll be starting with smaller, narrower hulls and building them up on the sides with expanded planking. With the manpower we have now, and applying as many men as we can to getting each log down the mountain, things should go faster." There was a momentary interruption as a Woodsman called to the Canoe-Master for direction, then Joha'lan continued to explain to Orn'ta the reasoning behind this new and unorthodox program. He ushered his compatriots into a cooler, shaded grove further uphill where they could see even more of the working area. "We have decided to use two types of straight grained trees which we have often before used to make planking. But this time we'll use larger trees to make wider planks. There are two crews working far downhill now, cutting and preparing some of those trees for transport. They only grow in the more open forested areas. It's handy too because the terrain is easier and we can move them out more quickly."

Joha'lan carried on explaining the new process to Orn'ta, Al'malan listening just as intently. He continued to be impressed by the big man's, not only passionate dedication, but also his innovativeness. But soon Al'malan's thoughts drifted to another important problem needing solving; how to re-rig those big sail panels so that they could be more quickly and safely removed from the masts when gale force winds threatened to destroy them. It was time he returned to the seashore and attended to the solution. An hour later he bade his compatriots farewell and joined a column of Woodsmen returning downhill for a couple of days rest. Ch'am'lo and five of his warriors joined the procession in spite of Al'malan's protestation that he didn't need guarding. The Voyage-Master found it irksome to have to submit to constant protection by armed men, just as his wife and children were now constantly guarded. But he tried to smile indulgently when his good friend walked beside him, a spear and shield slung over his shoulder.

Ch'am'lo was well aware of Al'malan's impatience with this intrusion on his freedom of movement and helped make light of it by engaging him in conversation whenever it seemed politic to do so. This day they began discussing the sail panel problem and were soon both immersed in the possibilities. They were strolling well behind the rest of the column, the lead being taken by three young, armed Itin, Ch'am'lo's brothers, when a warning shout rang out from one of them. Ch'am'lo immediately un-slung his shield and weapon and took a defensive stance, gesturing with one hand for Al'malam to stand still. Al'malam instinctively put his right hand on the sheathed seaman's knife at his hip.

The Woodsmen all stood stock still on the trail, looking downhill to where the leading guards were focusing their gaze on a point around a sharp corner. Ch'am'lo said quickly, "Please stay back, brother, I'll see what this is about." and he ran downhill to join his siblings. There, around that sharp bend stood a group of men, perhaps twelve, apparently unarmed but obviously *Ja'jan an-lo*. Their newly designed and manufactured *tapa* wraps, shorter than the standard Mal'lam men's wrap and painted a rusty red in a band a hand-width's wide around the hem identified them from quite a distance. In the center of the group stood a stocky man with an all-white wrap and a red *tapa* cloth turban. He was leaning with both hands on a tall staff. He emanated strength and control and as Ch'am'lo strode past his brothers toward the group, his spear at the ready, he noticed the painted stripes on the man's face. Al'malan could not remain behind and soon followed his Itin friend downhill and around the corner. The Woodsmen meanwhile had moved to each side of the track and stood waiting to see what transpired.

As soon as Al'malan turned the corner he recognized the central, commanding figure as that of his ex-father-in-law, Sho'sha'lo Sea-Hewn. He quickly walked up beside Ch'am'lo and stood near. "Good day, Sea-Hewn. What brings you up here to the mountains?" Al'malan's voice held a stern edge. He no longer had any respect for the man who once was his family. And now he understood Sho'sha'lo to be acting in some role of authority in his ex-wife's weird religion.

"Do not address me as, 'Sea-Hewn', Al'malan. You should know by now that I have disowned the sea. All of my people have." Al'malan smiled a bit bitterly. Disowning the sea, to his mind, was like disowning breathing: stupid and ultimately fatal. "And by what name do we now greet you, Sho'sha'lo?" Al'malan's stance carried its own authority and his powerful presence, in contrast to the rather clown-like figure below him on the trail, made the scene almost comical. Sho'sha'lo tried to straighten his frame even more and project his self confidence up the hill. "I am 'Chief Priest' to the Mistress, *Ja'jan of the Skies*! I have come here to give you a message on her behalf. You must now listen closely!"

Al'malan fought to control the struggle within him; he tried to neither laugh nor growl. He had never been impressed by this man's maturity, wisdom or intelligence and now, here he was playing the role of an advisor and esteemed representative to a band of crazy people! He listened as the man who had been his father-in-law, the grandfather of his son, delivered his message.

"I would first ask that that murderer, that Itin, move away." Sho'sha'lo certainly would have recognized Ch'am'lo, war-paint or not. Sho'sha'lo would never forget the swift, brutal efficiency with which he had dispatched the 'War Chief' of the *Ja'jan an-lo*. Ch'am'lo didn't move a muscle except to smile tolerantly at the foolish man there on the trail below him.

"You might as well proceed with what you have to say, Sho'sha'lo." Al'malan replied. "This man is my brother and now a leader among the Mal'lam. Carry on." His words were spoken in a flat, demanding tone, the power of which was not lost on the 'Chief Priest'. Sho'sha'lo's accompanying contingent of devotees shuffled their feet in nervous recognition that a confrontation was about to occur. Glancing at those young Itin men with their weapons held lightly at the ready made them all quite eager to be away from this place. Gathering his flagging courage with a shuffle of his own feet, Sho'sha'lo crossed his arms and puffed out his chest and glared with all the contempt he could muster. He must perform this task which *Ja'jan* had assigned him. This might well be the turning point in his perceived career as the second-most powerful individual to occupy this island when finally these nuisance Mal'lam vacate it.

"Al'malan Sea-Master! My Mistress, *Ja'jan of the Skies*, has directed me to inform you and the Mal'lam people of her demands." Sho'sha'lo heard the echo of his words and an infestation of doubt immediately invaded his perception of the situation. The words sounded ridiculous and what else he was about to say might well sound even more ridiculous. But! He must indeed carry on. The other option was to turn tail and run back down the mountainside.

"My Mistress has directed me to inform you that Sh'tah Lee-Set is now the home of the *Ja'jan an-lo*. Future generations will see the blossoming of our culture here on this island and there will be no place for the likes of the Mal'lam!" Sho'sha'lo avoided eye contact with the recipient of his address. Instead, his eyes swept around the surrounding forest as if already its growth and majesty belonged to him.

Confrontation......

"Further, the 'Mistress' demands that the Mal'lam 'sea people' vacate this island within one year. After the autumn harvest you will fill your doomed canoes with the goods of our land and set sail into your own demise." Sho'sha'lo was nearing nervous collapse; his hands shook and his eyes could not meet Al'malan's. Al'malan's own inner-hearing read the man's fear and for a moment his heart went out in a surge of pity. But only for a moment. This man, his son's grandfather, was participant in a dark plot to remove his son from him, possibly even fatally sacrifice him to Ja'eel's warped construction of her new world. It would not happen! Al'malan cut short the 'Chief Priest's' diatribe.

"I have heard enough of your blather, Sho'sha'lo! No more!" Sho'sha'lo gave a loud sigh of such violence that it left spittle on his lips. He knew he had failed and although he maintained his stance, out of the corner of his eye he saw his company of supporters fade back behind him, leaving him to stand alone in the face of what all around could see coming. Al'amalan strode quickly down the intervening few feet between them and stood with hands on hips as he looked slightly down to the shorter man. Ch'am'lo had signaled to his brothers to remain where they were. He knew Al'malan's force of character was his best defense.

"Sho'sha'lo! You are as silly a man as I always thought you were. I am sorry to have to be so blunt with you, but what you, and my ex-wife are proposing will not happen. The Mal'lam will leave this island when the time is right for that exodus ... not before. You will be welcome to inherit this beautiful land, and what befalls it in the future, but only on our terms. We have much to do to prepare for our departure. If you and your people should attempt to interfere in our work, the result will be dire for all of you. Do you understand me?" That last question was spoken so loudly that Sho'sha'la closed his eyes in a quick blink to avoid the force of it.

"Furthermore, you, as grandfather to my son, should hang your head in shame for your complicity in Ja'eel's mad threats against me, my son, my wife and our child. Tell your *Ja'jan, Mistress of the Skies*, that she, you and all your silly adherents to her madness, must stay completely out of our way. Not for one year but for the three years we believe will be required to complete our work!"

Al'malan was definitely on a role! Never in his life had he let his emotions and his certainties flow from him with such force. Even his dear friend, Ch'am'lo, looked wide-eyed at the back of Al'malan's head as he listened, wondering if he was really hearing correctly.

Ch'am'lo could no longer restrain himself. He strode quickly to his friend's side and laid his hand upon Al'malan's shoulder, a silent request to interrupt and add his own import. Al'malan glanced over to Ch'am'lo, relishing this intrusion, because he had nearly lost control. There were few more words left available to him. A blow would have been his next offering. Sho'sha'lo stood nearly alone in the middle of the trail, only two of his compatriots remaining fearfully but steadfastly a few steps behind him. The others had retreated ten feet back, ready to flee.

"You will well remember our last meeting, Sho'sha'lo!" Ch'am'lo began, standing nearly toe-to-toe with the 'Chief Priest'. "Your life and those of your followers were spared that day because you were rendered impotent by your fear. Oh yes. You had words to throw at us, just like today. Threats and warnings, projections of the fear which was eating your insides, just like today." Ch'am'lo paused and took a calming breath, his own emotions threatening his best judgment. "But today you must carry back to that foolish daughter of yours some truths which even she cannot avoid. The Mal'lam and we Itin, who are now fully a part of the Mal'lam society, rule this island of Sht'ah Lee. You and your people we could crush under our feet in a day. You know that." Again Ch'am'lo took a breath, less to control his rampant emotions than to compose his final sally of sense at this man whose basic intelligence he had to rely upon. In a quieter voice he finished his speech.

"Hear me truly, Sho'sha'lo! Should any harm befall our people, we Mal'lam, due to your connivance, my face will be the last face you will ever see. I will personally kill you!" With that the Itin Headman spat on the ground before Sho'sha'lo's feet and pushed past him, signaling with a wave of his arm for his younger brothers, Al'malam and the astounded Woodsmen, to follow him on downhill. The *Ja'jan an-lo* scrambled to the edge of the track and watched the Mal'lam pass by them. Sho'sha'lo remained standing in the middle of the path, unable to move, tears of shame and terror blighting the stripes of paint on his face. As Al'malan followed, he laid his hand on Sho'sha'lo's shoulder in an instant's gesture of his sorrow at what had come to pass. The 'Chief Priest' misinterpreted that gesture and secreted it away in his smoldering folio of hatreds. He would have his revenge, he swore.

Research Notes: Impressions and General Observations:

Subject: Tina Pualani Kaiser and other events, Honolulu, Spring 1975

Hoo boy! Things are getting curiouser and curiouser! Jiro is over on Kaua'i now, assisting in the excavation of what may be a very old grave site. He thinks it may be Mal'lam (<u>Pre-Hawaiian</u>, is the term he still uses, officially)

John Kou'anani, who owns the property next to Tutu Kinau's at Hanalei, recently had a bulldozer working on site and it uncovered what appeared to be an old Hawaiian house platform. John is an old friend of Jiro's and kind of an amateur archeologist himself so he rang Jiro to ask him what he thought of it. Jiro was on the next available flight over to Kaua'i. I spoke to him last night, after he'd been at the site for two days with a couple of people from the University. He says the stonework is definitely not early Hawai'ian. He says it more resembles the shaped and fitted stones still existing at The Menehune Ditch. As usual, Jiro has sworn everyone involved to secrecy, similar to the situation with the old *heiau* on the hill above Hanalei Valley. He can be quite persuasive, believe me.

Tina is near to completing her second year of high school here in Honolulu. Her grades have slipped a little but I don't think it's anything to worry about. We are all looking forward to our summer holiday at Hanalei and now there's something really exciting to get involved in.

Our baby girl is beautiful and growing like a weed. We are all so very happy!

Update:

Tutu Kinau rang us last night to tell us that her Mal'lam Spirits have told her that indeed the ruin that Jiro is working on is a grave site and yes, it is Mal'lam! If Jiro and the other archaeologists agree that it is pre-Hawai'ian, we may have something very important. She has told Jiro too but he says he doesn't want to hear it - it may interfere with the objectivity of the investigation. Such a good scientist; such a hard-head.

Chapter Thirty Nine - The New Canoes

The confrontation between the *Ja'jan an-lo* 'Chief Priest' and the Voyage-Master, along with Ch'am'lo, produced no immediate response from the 'Mistress' herself nor any other of her devotees. Tina-an continued her surveillance of the *Ja'jan* territory and what seemed to be occurring there. What she discovered was that the *Ja'jan an-lo* were all hard at work building that mysterious stone structure, planting more crops, clearing land for more gardens and improving their living conditions in their village. Tina-an reported that her impression was that they were quite like the Mal'lam in how they carried out their days. There did seem to be a definite hierarchy developing though, and she had seen some corporal punishments carried out. This had really shocked her.

There is a Mal'lam saying: "Should two people trying to find the sense of a dispute, fail, then at least one of them has no sense!" Not even obstreperous children in Mal'lam society were beaten. There were better ways. But even Shen'ha's careful interrogation of her spy within *Ja'jan's* camp could not really explain what the stone structure was all about. The inference which Jana'la hinted at was; a platform for worship of *Ja'jan's* Gods ... maybe even sacrifice? Too soon to know. At least peace of a sort reigned on the island and the Canoe-Master drove the great project ever forward.

Subtle hints from his wife's mother, Sha'lat Herb-Mistress, plus his own concerns for the man's health and well-being, led Al'malan to persuade his dear friend Joha'lan to take a few days off from the intensity of the harvesting of the big trees; come down to the seashore and just hang about and relax. Mention of his wife's concern decided the question. As the two men walked down the 'Black Boar Track' together for the umpteenth time in the past months, Joha'lan began chuckling."I've never told anyone this before, brother, not even Sha'lat. All my adult life, whenever I've come to a crisis or at least a difficult period, it's always the last minute influence of women which decides my course of action. I appreciate your own, genuine friendship, of course!" With this he stepped close and gave his friend a quick hug even as they continued walking.

"But you know . . . The Vesa'tan still communicates with me. Yes! Crazy as it might sound, that mad, wonderful old woman still helps guide my path!" Al'malan noticed the gleam of insipient tears in Joha'lan's eyes as he quickly glanced over at him. "Yes. I know I need a rest. I know that Sha'lat needs me too. Oh, my poor wife has had to endure so much! She is one of the *Earth Mother's* blessed ones!" Al'malan strode strongly, trying to match his friend's long steps as finally they separated from the dark, tall forests of the great trees and entered the lowlands. A family of wild pigs darted across and off the trail before them, Al'malan stooping to pick up a handful of stones should the need arise. They walked on in silence for many minutes, each man comfortable with the subliminal emanations of the other. Unquestioning friendship.

The Itin Sea-Master, Ch'am'lo, had just recently announced his betrothal to the young Mal'lam girl, Shana'la Herb-Plait. Jokes abounded, but no one took the inference as anything but humor. This vigorous man in his thirties was taking for wife a Mal'lam girl of but eighteen. That she was Joha'lan's step-daughter's best female friend was another spur to the Canoe-Master to attend the social happenings of his village. The recent lessening of tensions between the *Ja'jan an-lo* and the Mal'lam opened the opportunity for more celebrations and marriages. Life, for the present at least, was returning to the normal, old days. Still, the guards accompanied Sht'ana Herb-Plait and her children daily.

Al'malan was still struggling with the problem of the sails on the newly-configured canoes. How to reduce sail, even drop sail if the wind became too strong. The near disaster of that last storm which had caused him such fright must never be repeated again. And if a solution was not decided upon, it surely would occur again. He and Ch'am'lo and all the other Sea-Masters had endlessly discussed the problem. Surely there was an answer! Above the three stone quarries on the island rose a thin cloud of rock dust nearly every day. Adze heads, axe heads and stone gouges were being turned out by the dozens every week.

Apprentice Wood-Hewn were creating piles of wood chips and shavings, keeping pace with requirements for tool handles. The sound of the *tapa* hammers resounded constantly, a background sound as natural as the wind in the coconut palms. Elderly Mal'lam men sat in gossiping groups by the hour, rolling lengths of coir string into twine, the twine being spun into rope. Always busy by inclination, there was now an accelerated intensity to the people's endeavors as they began producing and storing all those items which the upcoming voyage would require.

The farmers of the Mal'lam were blessed again with ideal weather for their crops. Bananas and breadfruit, *taro* and yams - the community's staples flourished. The Paper Mulberry trees stretched skyward, creating new branches of a width which offered yet more lengths of *tapa* bark. Every four or five days a new log of 'Wa'pa'la' timber was brought down to the canoe sheds. This rough-barked, straight-grained timber could be successfully split with wedges into long lengths of easily worked planking. Woodsmen immediately set to the task as each log arrived; splitting and adzing to a fine thickness and then soaking the planks in seawater for many days until they were pulled from the sea and stacked to dry. The larger, older canoes of the Mal'lam were converted to that new sail type and crews were trained in its operation. When this training program began, Al'malan knew that the solution to that problem with stifling the sails in a storm must find solution immediately. It would be foolish to train crews and then finally introduce a new regime. What was the answer?!

The answer came one morning as Al'malan sat in the shallow surf, playing with his tiny daughter, La'teel, with his son Sahn'ta swimming just beyond them. To their left was a group of little boys playing with sailing canoes which they had cleverly fabricated themselves. Their rough little models were mounted with approximations of the latest Mal'lam voyaging rig. Soon another, slightly older boy arrived with his model and set it upon the low swell attending the beach this morning.

With mild interest Al'malan watched the boys playing with their toys when he noticed something rather odd about the way the older boy had rigged his sails. He called out to the lad, waving him to come. The young fellow splashed over to the Voyage-Master, beaming with delight that this esteemed man should call him. Arriving with his well made model, he stood speechless, looking down to where Al'malan sat with La'teel on his lap."May I see your canoe, boy?" he smiled, "And what is your name?"

"At'mal un-hewn, Voyage-Master." He looked a bit embarrassed and nervous now but Al'malan's easy smile and friendly manner soon had him sitting near Al'malan and earnestly showing him his pride and joy; his first toy canoe built solely by himself. "And why have you tied the sail boom to the mast this way, At'mal? Is that just for carrying it about?"

"No, Voyage-Master. I tied it up that way ... well, let me show you." and the lad proceeded to point to the clever way in which he had lashed the outer boom to the mast and then pulled the sail and boom close to the mast and lashed all together, making quite a tidy bundle which would greatly reduce the windage of the sail while keeping it bound securely. In effect, reefing a sail which previously could not be reefed. Al'malan slapped his forehead with his free hand, rolled his eyes and began laughing loudly. Young At'mal didn't know whether to be insulted or what, but he soon joined in Al'malan's irresistible mirth. The baby girl joined in the jollity, tiny new teeth gleaming whitely. Finally Al'malan managed to control his burst of ironic laughter, stood with his child under one arm and called out to his son to stay with the other youngsters, enjoying their rowdy swim.

A young Itin Sea-Hewn, armed with a spear, moved closer to the water to keep watch over Sahn'ta now. Al'malan asked At'mal un-hewn to bring his canoe and follow. The boy, still unsure what this was all about, did ashe was asked and followed the Voyage-Master up to the village. Al'malan stopped to leave their daughter with Sht'ana , the two young men guarding them moving closer to the shelter beneath which she sat talking with another woman. Al'malan put a hand on the boy's shoulder and led him to where the Itin Sea-Master, Ch'am'lo, was resting beside his own hut.

"Are you ready for a revelation, my friend?" Al'malan called out, a big grin leading the way. Ch'am'lo grinned in return and stood up to greet Al'malan and the youngster. "What have we here?" Ch'am'lo asked, hunkering down now to scrutinize what the boy was carrying. He reached out, asked permission with raised eyebrows and then took the well-crafted toy from At'mal. Within seconds the Itin Sea-Master had divined the element which had so surprised Al'malan.

"Who would have thought?" he said , looking up at the Voyage-Master's grin. Shaking his head he reached up and placed a hand on the boy's arm and gave him a wide smile. "My boy, I think you should come with us to see the Canoe-Master. What do you say?" At'mal un-hewn was so flustered with the praise that he couldn't reply, but only nod his head in the affirmative. Ch'am'lo handed the boy's brilliantly designed toy back to him and the two Sea-Hewn walked him up the sandy slope to a shady area beneath the big, spreading trees where Joha'lan and two canoe workers were discussing the works in progress. "Here comes trouble, if ever I've seen it!" Joha'lan called out, wondering what mischief his friends were up to. The two Woodsmen with him rose to leave the Masters to their meeting but Al'malan waved a hand urging them to remain seated.

"Stay brothers. We have something of importance to show you too." Al'malan urged the young lad to let Joha'lan inspect the little vessel. The two Woodsmen leaned over to observe what Joha'lan was inspecting, unaware that this nicely crafted little canoe held the answer to a question which had been dogging the experts for weeks. "Do you see it?" Al'malan asked, impatient for Joha'lan to discover this surprise innovation. "Aha! Of course!" With a short gaze at the face of the still embarrassed boy, then glances at the faces of his friends he said, "Three of our people's most experienced canoe men couldn't work it out But this young lad, building his toy, has answered the problem and very cleverly too. What is your name, un-hewn?"

Al'malan and Ch'am'lo sat down now, Joha'lan asking the boy to sit also right next to him. Joha'lan genuinely congratulated the lad on his workmanship in crafting the elements of the vessel, suggesting that surely he aspired to be a wood-worker.

"No, Canoe-Master, not really. I want to be Sea-Hewn!" Joha'lan nodded and added, "Well, before you are *hewn*, don't stop making things with your hands. You have a natural talent. Ah! Wait a moment." and Joha'lan turned as he sat and reached under a mat where many of his finest tools lay. He had been doing fine woodcarving these past days; a form of relaxation he had not allowed himself since the harvesting of the trees had begun. "At'mal un-hewn," Joha'lan said quite formally and with sincerity in his face, "would you consider a trade?" The Canoe-Master drew a beautifully crafted, narrow bladed adze with an obsidian head from the group of equally fine tools and held it out to the boy. "I would trade you this adze ... it's about right for your hands ... for your wonderfully made canoe. What say you?"

The men sitting nearby all smiled and Al'malan nodded encouragingly to At'mal. At'mal looked longingly at the beautiful tool in Joha'lan's hand, his face registering concentration - intelligent consideration. Then the boy looked Joha'lan straight in the eye and made his counter offer; "If you will show me how best to use a real adze, Canoe-Master."Joha'lan looked blank for a moment, then his eyes crinkled with humor and he laughed loudly, the other men joining in. The boy tried to keep a straight face but a grin tickled the corners of his mouth. When he had reduced his laughter to intermittent chuckles, Joha'lan reached forward and laid his big hand on At'mal's shoulder. "You have a deal, young trader! If you will leave your canoe with me now and take this adze with you, come back here tomorrow morning and we'll see what you can do with it."

At'mal, now all grins and giggles, took the adze from Joha'lan's hand and turned and ran away up the beach toward his home. His father, a renowned Wood-Hewn himself, would be delighted.

Ch'am'lo, Al'malan and Joha'lan immediately began focusing on the boy's model canoe which the Canoe-Master still held up before him, their conversation so intense that the two Woodsmen were able to take their leave without being noticed. After an hour's conversation the three got up and strode quickly down to where one of the older canoes was being renovated. This vessel's mast was about to be reseated and now was the perfect opportunity to trial the new design for attaching the sail boom to the mast. It was nearly dark before the base of the long, curved boom and heavy, woven *pandanus* sail were lashed securely to the mast using the newly devised system. Tomorrow the canoe would be sea-borne and the system tried under real conditions. The weather promised change to windy and stormy. Perfect!

~ ~ * ~ ~

In the Canoe-Master's absence from the scene of the tree felling, his second in command, a Master Wood-Hewn named Tan'atal called a halt to further cutting for the time being. Storms were brewing up on the slopes of Volan Votu and at this time of year they could be dangerously severe. Gale force winds over the forests could tear great limbs from big trees and send them hurtling down. Men working below could be at great risk. With one large log already awaiting transport to the building yards, Tan'atal Wood-Hewn ordered the one-hundred-eighty men under his command to pack tools and other equipment. Fifteen men would be required to carry the load of axes, adzes and replacement blades back down the mountain. It was a sign of the times that such was necessary. In the days before the present animosities and growing mistrust between the minions of *Ja'jan* and the Mal'lam, all those tools could simply have been covered and left until the workers returned to the task. Now it was thought best to take the valuable cache of equipment with them.

The younger and more nimble Wood-Hewn and other volunteer workers now took up the task of laying the small, roller logs on the ground for the big timber to be pushed or pulled across. This task required some quick movement back and forth as the log progressed. The small rollers left behind as the big log moved forward had to be picked up and quickly moved ahead and placed again at the front of the line. On a downhill stretch of the long trail, when the dozens of men on the heavy ropes controlling the log were actually in braking mode, these scurrying workmen were soon gasping with exertion. When the trail again turned uphill, it was the men on the ropes who strained and grunted.

Unlike those years before when the huge baulks of timber for those three great canoes were cut and moved to the sea, these logs were but half as heavy. With the increased manpower now available, the future canoe hulls were collecting in encouraging numbers on the beach near the canoe sheds. Since many of those logs would lie out in the weather for up to a year before work began on them, the thick bark was left on, protection against the elements and allowing a controlled seasoning of the wood. These logs were further protected by layers of palm fronds.

A few miles downhill among the many old cinder cones grew the tall, straight trees called, 'Wa'pa'la', meaning 'canoe plank timber'. Here the slopes were long and gentle, the underbrush scant and the task of cutting and hauling much easier. The wood of the 'Wa'pa'la' was much softer than the 'Kan'ta'ab'; straight grained , resinous and easy to work. The workmen had established an efficient routine now which saw a new log of 'Wa'pa'la' debarked, and long planks split off and hauled to the beach for a seawater soak before the final adzing began. Twenty men could reduce a log to planks in one day now.

Joha'lan Canoe-Master's job was much broader also but the consummate skill of so many of the Mal'lam woodworkers was such that he could confidently relegate most of the work of felling and transporting. Still, it was he who selected each tree, calling upon his Spirit mentor, The Vesa'tan, to guide him in his selections. Al'malan Voyage-Master seldom ventured inland anymore, his duties at the canoe sheds and with the training crews keeping him very busy. Also, as a recognized Elder now, although only thirty-three years old, he was constantly on-call to consult with other Elders.

Every traditional ritual and celebration was retained by the Mal'lam; the days, and sometimes a week involved in the preparation and performance, a source of respite from the hard labor of the men and women involved in the ongoing, indeed, seemingly endless task all were involved in. The '*hewing*' required the Master craftsmen's involvement just as it always had and this year saw a bumper-crop of initiates. Not surprisingly, most were for the seaman's craft for in nearly every young boy's vision was the upcoming adventure upon the 'great unknown'!

Harvest time came and went; stocks of timber, coir twine and rope, finished tools ready for application, all the necessary items which their exodus would require gradually increased. By the beginning of the rainy season when Woodsmen would leave the forests and attend to the actual construction of the canoes, Al'malan was satisfied with the progress. He was satisfied also that the re-rigging of the sails and booms was complete. It worked! That young boy's innovation must surely have been a special blessing of the *Earth Mother*! The Voyage-Master vowed that, should he be blessed with another son, he would name him At'mal in honor of that boy's miraculous invention.

But so far, Sht'ana had not been able to conceive again. "More practice!" was his friend Ch'am'lo's advice. Ch'am'lo had obviously been practicing himself because his new, young wife, Shana'la Herb-Plait, was heavily pregnant. Tina- an Earth-Plait insisted that she be an 'aunty' to the new baby and her best friend agreed wholeheartedly. Things were progressing well for the Mal'lam on Sht'ah Lee-Set. The *Ja'jan an-lo* seemed quiescent, the harvest had been good and the people were healthy and well. Still, all minds found a concentration on the southern horizon but a thought away.

Chapter Forty - The Southern Seas

On that newly discovered island more than five hundred miles to the southeast of Sht'ah Lee-Set, the eleven Mal'lam who had remained behind ... twelve now, as a baby girl had arrived, were thriving. 'Win'no'hi' was indeed an hospitable island. The little community's Elder, Ven'ana Herb-Plait, was pleased and enthusiastic, especially now that there was a child among them. Her partner-not-yet-husband, Al'wala Herb-Hewn too reveled in the rich environment they had inherited. Of course, all would have preferred the presence of more of their familiar foods from the earth; *Taro*, bananas, breadfruit, ginger root and especially coconut, but they were all keeping quite healthy with the foods this lovely island already had to offer. The sea around them abounded in fish, shellfish and turtles and also on land the seabird's eggs. Those delicious flightless birds were becoming fewer however and attempts to domesticate them seemed doomed to failure. Primarily insectivorous, when penned-up it was impossible to find enough food for them. All those captives slowly wasted away and died. Chicken would be nice!

In the eleven months they had been separated from their Mal'lam brothers and sisters, most days held thoughts of when, even *if* they would be reunited with their people. But their busy lives left little time for brooding over this. Ven'ana's '*sight*' enabled her to sense what was occurring on their homeland and she was fully aware too that blessings emanating from far to the north assured them that they were certainly not forgotten.

"Ven'ana! Come see what we've caught today!" It was the young Sea-Hewn, Jo'shan, calling up the hill from the beach. Ven'ana had been sorting plants for drying, Ska'sat Herb-Plait assisting her and in the background sat the young mother, Shena'sha, nursing her baby. Nearby, constructing a larger and more substantial hut than most now lived in were four of the men. These Mal'lam were truly settling in for the long haul. The two Clay-Plait were busy further inland at their pottery. Standing and looking down onto the beach, Ven'ana saw the three Sea-Hewn there unloading the canoe after many hours of fishing quite far out to sea. Soon the others began descending the shallow slope to see what the fishermen had landed this day. One of the men was stooped over the canoe's hull about to pull something heavy up from the bottom. He said something to his mate and then the two of them together hoisted one of the largest mahi mahi anyone there had ever seen. It was at least four feet long. Four feet of feast, was the general consensus. And then another, somewhat smaller one appeared and soon everyone was chattering and laughing together.

"Someone prepare the oven!" Ven'ana called out. It was the young Sea-Hewn, Jo'shan who first responded, jogging off to the earth-oven site nearby and beginning to clear the area of palm fronds and debris. He was soon joined by Fal'fan Wood-Hewn and between them they started digging sand away to form the fire-pit.

"Where are the potters?" Mool'lem Sea-Hewn asked. He was quickly informed that ... where else? Up the hill at their worksite. "I'll go get them," he replied, "I need some exercise after being cramped up in the canoe all day with those two boring Sea-Hewn!" Laughter and answering jibes followed his quickening jog up through the thickets and soon he was out of sight. Ven'ana suspected that there was more to this triumphant return than that which had already been revealed. She walked down to the wet sand and peered over the edge of the canoe. Right! She turned and looked reprovingly at the seaman who was now beginning to clean the two magnificent *mahi mahi*.

"Did you forget something, Sho'ja?" Sho'ja Sea-Hewn broke into a huge grin and stood up, fish blood bathing both hands."Oh yes. Sorry, we almost forgot." and now the remaining fisherman started guffawing, the trade in word and meaning tweaking the curiosity of all the others there. Gathered around the canoe now the curious Mal'lam bent over the hull as Ven'ana had done and oooh's and ahhh's followed. A large sea turtle, still alive, lay flapping its flippers against the inside of the hull, struggling hopelessly to return to its home.

"Isn't it a beauty, Ven'ana?" the young Sea-Hewn asked, confident that he and his shipmates had won a great victory. Ven'ana bent again over the edge of the canoe and investigated the carapace of the turtle. There was no sign of a harpoon wound. "How did you catch it?" she asked, her tone a bit inquisitorial and the young seaman stepped back and looked at the older woman, not understanding her lack of enthusiasm for this exceptional largess of food.

"Well, I jumped into the water and grabbed it by its back flippers and was able to turn it over onto its back. That was a hard job!" Jo'shan tried to look proud of his accomplishment but something was not replying to his pride of accomplishment. Ven'ana was looking rather severely at him."Did you catch him before or after you caught the fish?" She was now in one of her moods, the youngster thought, and I'd better be careful. When in doubt, tell all the truth. "Uh, well ... yes, it was on our way back after we'd caught both *mahi mahi*. We caught the turtle just outside the reef before we sailed back in." His eyebrows raised hopefully, waiting for at least slight praise.

Ven'ana shook her head, crossed her arms across her breasts and glared, first at the young man and then at the older Sea-Hewn. Her expression softened somewhat as her glance encompassed all her brothers and sisters who surrounded her; most were puzzled, some just waiting for her decision upon a situation which she alone had apparently laid some significance. The faces of the Sea-Hewn displayed puzzlement too.

"I surely admire your abilities as fishermen." Ven'ana said more softly, "But the two big *mahi mahi* will more than feed all eleven of us for two days. The turtle, if you keep it, would have to lie on land and suffer until it was butchered. I will not countenance such suffering when our need is not great." Ven'ana looked into the faces of all those assembled on the beach, her voice still softly demanding. "Come now," she said, a note of finality there, "let's put this poor animal back into the sea." And now she looked at the crestfallen young Sea-Hewn who had been so proud of his catch. "Don't look so discouraged, Jo'shan. The time will come again when we will all rejoice in your skill as a turtle catcher. But keep this in mind; *Earth Mother* abhors greed and waste, and especially cruelty. *She* has blessed us all with the riches of the sea and the land. But if we forget to be mindful that all these things are blessings, we lessen ourselves."

As Headwoman of this little enclave of Mal'lam, it was her duty to sometimes remind the people of those values which pertained within the larger community. Had this event occurred back on Sht'ah Lee-Set, the result would have been the same. There it would have been a senior Sea-Hewn who would have decided that more than enough was too much. The little drama ended with Ven'ana helping the seamen lift the struggling reptile from the bottom of the canoe and releasing it back into the surf.

"Now!" the Headwoman said, "Who's going to start the fire? I can almost taste that fish." Striding past the youngest seaman, who stood with a faint pout of disappointment on his face, Ven'ana suddenly took a step toward him and locked her left arm around his head and with her right hand, began tweaking his nose. Muffled protestations soon became giggles as, bent over, he had no choice but to follow the woman's lead up the beach toward the fire-pit. She was, after all, his oldest aunty and such playful intimacy was allowed. All those around joined in the humor - that humor shared within a family, which this little community surely was.

Mool'lem Sea-Hewn had reached the site of the two potters little hut and pottery works. Calling out joyfully, announcing the good news of a feast, he received the welcoming waves and greetings of these rather reclusive women. Coming to the large awning attached to their living quarters he was immediately taken with the display of pots and bowls which lay neatly arranged there, drying in the shade before being fired. Squatting down just within the shade he looked intently at these women's latest offerings. Beautiful, he thought! "Sho'at-an," he addressed the youngest of them, "these pots and bowls are really wonderful! So much fine detail on them. May I pick one up?"A generous smile invited him and he gently picked out one of the larger bowls to examine.

The whole of its outer surface was invested with tiny, repetitive details, obviously impressed with different tools into the damp clay. The design ran all around the body of the vessel, the pattern changing every few lines; some were star shapes, some triangles, some more abstract and larger impressions. The whole presented a richness of texture and pattern which far transcended the merely decorative. Here was some esoteric meaning, some intention to portray much more than pleasing decoration. Mool'lem replaced, very gently, the bowl he had first scrutinized and then picked up a smaller vessel. Around its periphery were three bands of diamond shapes near the lip of the bowl. Below were three more lines of another repeated pattern but interrupted by four, no, five figures which looked like human faces. That row was succeeded by three more lines of diagonal slashes. The whole surface of the still-damp pottery glowed with this richness of decoration. He turned the pot this way and that, delighting in the rich flow of shadow and light upon the incised surface.

"I have never seen such pottery, Sho'at-an. These are all so beautiful!" The Sea-Hewn looked over at the older woman, Ba'lee'an, who seemed to be studiously ignoring his perusal of the women's exceptional work. He knew her well enough to no longer be intimidated by her apparent gruffness and short temper."Sister!" he said with loud enthusiasm, "You ladies have thrilled my eyes and warmed my heart with your work of these past months. Surely the *Earth Mother* sits beside you in your work. Now!" he said with what he hoped was a man's strength of demand, "It's time for us all to attend a feast. Will you come?" His tone was not questioning but subtly demanding, attended by a broad smile of heartfelt warmth. The more masculine of the two women finally looked up at the Sea-Hewn and offered an answering smile, but tempered with a sigh which might imply resignation.

"Yes, Mool'lem. We will be with you all, shortly." The older woman rose rather stiffly from a posture long-held in her concentration on working her pottery. "What can we bring to the celebration, Sea-Hewn? Perhaps a few of our latest, fired pots?" This woman could be quite generous when the mood struck. Mool'lem quickly accepted the offer for he knew that the whole community would be enthralled with the wonderful creativity which now flowed from this workshop. "Surely, sister!" he retorted with enthusiasm, "Can I carry them down to the beach for you?" A few minutes later the seaman struggled under the weight of the basketful of pottery, grinning back at the potters, unaware that he was carrying the prototypes of a tradition of pottery making which would be the signature product of a people whom one branch of the Mal'lam were to become.

~ ~ * ~ ~

Further south still, another one-thousand plus miles, lay the islands of the Tarbara'ut. On a secluded, sun-bright patch of water, well beyond any other islet or island or curious eye, that small dugout canoe of Mal'lam construction lay rocking and swaying to an inner convulsion of energy. Two young people lay on the bottom of the canoe, making love. A'lan Sea-Hewn had thrown lots with his good friend Faldo-in, and won. Both lads had girlfriends on two different outer islands of this small archipelago, each an hour's sail, weather being kind. Their work on the gardens and on the readying of the two canoes for a sail southward to unknown lands allowing only sparse time for either to see their loved ones.

A'lan had reached Ara'wee's island in less time than usual, a kind and boisterous wind behind him. She had been waiting, unbidden except by that powerful coupling of minds which young lovers can manifest. Quickly she had run to the sandy beach as he landed and leapt into the little dugout, her wide grin urging him to again launch free of the land. Behind her came running a group of young children and women, all shouting and singing and whistling, and as the canoe fled the sands they showered it with small, inoffensive pebbles of coral. This was the ritual, played out by generations of Tarbara'ut whenever a young man came to claim a lover and carry her away, albeit for just a day or a night.

When their sweating bodies finally parted and A'lan sat up onto one of the canoe's seats, gazing adoringly down upon his still supine lover, he was nearly overwhelmed with the underlying tension which this day's union implied. A'lan Sea-Hewn would soon be leaving these lovely islands. Also he'd be leaving this young woman who now so contended with his earlier, implacable dedication to the sea and voyaging. Within days, two fully manned and equipped Mal'lam canoes would leave these islands and head south for lands unknown, for a time unknown - perhaps forever.

It had been Faldo-in Sea-Hewn who, with his greater gift with language, had been able to explain to Arawee that her beloved A'lan must leave her for a time. She had wept softly and accepted that he and Faldo-in had duties to perform, even though such a journey was quite incomprehensible to her people. But Arawee's comprehension of the world was very unlike that of most Tarbara'ut. Like her lover, she too was drawn by something indescribable which whispered to her soul. And that silent voice also came from the sea.

Recovered from the intensity of their lovemaking, Arawee rose and sat opposite A'lan on another cross member of the canoe. They reached their hands out to each other, clinging tightly, their eyes doing the speaking and their eyes both soon clouded with tears. Then with both of her hands she took A'lan's right hand and pulled it toward her and placed it on her stomach. Never leaving his gaze she uttered a Mal'lam word which she had sought and learned from Faldo-in; "Baby." "Baby!" she repeated and the realization struck A'lan like lightning. His eyes widened, his lips parted but no words came. He just looked stunned and ready to cry. Arawee pressed his hand more strongly against her stomach and again said "Baby!" Her eyes betrayed a sudden fear; fear that he would not understand - fear that he would not want her to have his baby - fear that his going away would mean the end of their love.

A'lan saw this fear and quickly took his hand from her stomach and with a gentle grasp, held her face in both his hands. He bent forward and kissed her long and forcefully, insistent that her fear should be driven away. When he opened his eyes, his special vision returned with a splash of light; Arawee's form was suffused with a rosy glow which the midday sun could not hide. He blinked once, twice, but still it was there. Never before had he seen light like that hover around a human form. It was as definite and demanding as any of those lights beneath the sea. At that moment A'lan Sea-Hewn knew that he had a beacon which would guide him home again safely; home again to this beautiful young woman and now, to their child! Although she was in but her sixteenth year and he in his eighteenth, these two were no longer children.

A'lan and Arawee paddled the canoe back to the beach from which he had gathered her early that morning, the sky now bright with stars and the sliver of a new moon. They then stood upon the sand holding each other with that desperation of parting which was almost a physical pain. Suddenly, from near them came the sound of someone politely clearing their throat, begging to interrupt. It was Arawee's mother, her tiny body nearly invisible in the dim light. She came forward to the couple who still clung to each other and wrapped both her arms around them. Together the three stood, the night's warm breeze caressing them. Slowly the older woman released A'lan and took her daughter by the hand and without looking back, led the girl away. Arawee kept turning and looking back, her white teeth shining a long smile at A'lan. Then they were gone and only the sound of the gently lapping waves remained. The paddle home was only a vague recollection for A'lan. But what he did remember was that it was a soft rosy light which guided him back to the beach near those big double canoes and the adventure which lay ahead.

~ ~ * ~ ~

As when the canoes and crews were exercised one at a time, only three months before, on this day all the Mal'lam and most Tarbara'ut gathered on the beach to witness this most important launching.

The big, newer canoe, 'Wa'Boton', and one of the older, smaller vessels, 'Wa'Salat', lay with their bows pointed out to sea, their sterns lying upon the sandy beach. The former was captained by the non-Clan Sea-Master, Sh'ban'al, a man with the *sea sight*. He had been master of his Clan's vessel, 'Wa'Olon', on the voyage to these islands. 'Wa'Olon' still needed some repairs to one of its hulls so would not be ready to voyage for some months yet. It was agreed by the

Council of Sea-Masters that a 'sighted' master must be aboard at least one of the canoes. Due to his already pronounced gift of '*sea sight*', A'lan Sea-Hewn would crew on the other, smaller canoe, 'Wa'Salat'. Both vessels would have sighted seamen aboard - an indispensable inclusion considering the nature of this voyage into unknown seas.

The master of 'Wa'Salat', A'lan's vessel, was the big, jovial man of the same Clan, from Sh'ham-Set, Fan'al Sea-Master. Although not one with the 'sea sight', he was a man of wide experience, respected and admired by all for his level-headedness and foresight. Also aboard with A'lan was his close friend, Faldo-in. A'lan had campaigned for his presence on the voyage because of his apparent facility with languages. He could now speak Tarbara'ut as well as could his uncle, Faldo Sea-Master. With his own keen foresight, A'lan reckoned that his friend's skills as a seaman might be matched by the need to communicate with other strange peoples they could meet on their way. Besides, the two young men were quite inseparable, except by their girlfriends.

Both vessels had been loaded with enough foodstuffs to last their crews for two months. As well, each canoe hull held dozens of ripe coconuts, bundled tightly together fore and aft. This was a twofold consideration: should a hull be swamped by a wave it would have added flotation at both ends, perhaps critical until bailing could lighten the hull. Also there was the intent to plant coconuts wherever they might find lands without this valuable plant. The larger vessel held a compliment of sixteen men: fourteen Sea-Hewn and two Herb-Hewn with wide medical as well as plant knowledge. 'Wa'Salat' was crewed by twelve seamen, one Herbalist and one Wood-Hewn. Being a voyage of exploration rather than settlement, only the coconuts were taken as seed stock.

Boyish excitement certainly filled the hearts of the younger men like A'lan and Faldo-in but by now they had learned to focus their energies totally on the task at hand. A'lan's service aboard the canoes on those trial runs and his undoubted capacity as a '*seer*' of those all-important 'sea-lights' had led to his being considered quite special by the Sea-Masters. Some thought him a bit presumptuous at times but he was actually without self-promotion or excess ego. He simply knew a great deal and could anticipate needs before they became apparent to most men with much more time at sea. In short, he was indeed a gifted seaman and already exhibiting strong leadership potential.

This morning as he busied himself with the last minute loading of rope and spare lengths of timber and bamboo, he kept snatching glances toward the beach. Where was she? Arawee said she would come to see him off but already most of the small Tarbara'ut canoes were pulled up on the beach. The people from the other little islands should all be here by now! And then, as he turned to gather another bundle of rope from a seaman on the ground, he saw her. She stood alone on the beach as the bustle and rush swept around her. In her hair were those seabird feathers which first he had given her as their souls began to join. Her hands were clasped behind her, her head held high as their eyes met. That wonderful, white, wide smile flashed across the sand to him. He felt torn. Torn between his yearning for the comfort of her presence and the draw of the sea and what lay beyond. Such was his world to become and something in him told him to stop agonizing and simply accept it. He would serve both worlds. Somehow!

A calloused hand gripped his shoulder and he turned to see his Sea-Master, Fan'al, smiling at him. "You have only a few minutes, Sea-Hewn. Go to your woman." Three steps and a leap saw A'lan on the sand and running to where

Arawee stood, her arms now stretched out to meet him. They embraced, they kissed and embraced again and then A'lan slid his right hand from her back and caressed her stomach, yet flat and firm before its swelling began. Baby!" he said softly. "Our baby!" She stepped back now, loosed his hands and placing both of hers on her stomach she smiled with such sweetness that his heart nearly burst. She continued to back away up the beach. He started to follow but she waved him away, still smiling. Just then Faldo-in came by near her, heading for the canoe, as she uttered the words in Tarbara'ut which A'lan could not yet understand. She repeated them loudly and Faldo-in stopped and looked back at her, then to A'lan. "What did she say?" A'lan asked his friend. Faldo-in looked back at Arawee one last time and waved to her, then turned to A'lan and replied, "She called you Sea-Master. Take note, my friend. She is a *seer*!" Then Faldo-in leapt aboard the canoe and called out to A'lan to follow. The vessel was ready to launch.

A'lan paused, sent a last passionate glance toward the retreating form of his beloved and turned and followed his mate aboard. He surrendered this moment to the future when the situation would be reversed. He would return - that he knew! And she would be here to greet him!

Chapter Forty One - A Change in the Plan

Winter had come to Sht'ah Lee and the rain was relentless. The Convocation of Elders this day would be held beneath the cover of a newly constructed but as yet empty canoe shed. Some of the most elderly Mal'lam sat wrapped in blankets of layered and quilted *tapa* cloth while even some of the younger people gathered wraps about their shoulders against the damp chill. Al'malan Voyage-Master, wearing his formal regalia, minus his headdress, stood with the Speakers Staff before him. All around him in the relatively narrow confines of the workshop sat the leaders of the various crafts. Non-Clan and Itin too were in attendance.

In a long arc around the black sand beach of 'Dolphin Bay' these rectangular, thatched structures sheltered twenty canoe hulls in all; ten vessels in various stages of completion. The Canoe-Master and the Sea-Masters had already spent hours over the previous weeks discussing the logistics and scheduling of the upcoming 'Great Voyage'. Now was the day when they would formally present their plan to the combined gathering of the community's decision-makers. Orn'ta Sea-Master was first to ask for permission to address the Convocation. Al'malan handed him the Speakers Staff with a formal gesture and sat down.

"My brothers and sisters of the Mal'lam and the Itin. After much consultation with my Sea-Hewn brothers, our Canoe-Master and other Wood-Hewn involved directly in the construction of our fleet of canoes, we have arrived at a decision which we now wish to put before this assembly for consideration." Orn'ta was never one who enjoyed these formal discussions, either as a participant speaker or as an interested bystander. Too much talk when a few words would suffice! But he wasn't doing too badly in that regard himself today. He was convinced of the wisdom of the proposal which had been given him to present.

"It is the considered opinion of the men for whom I speak today that our plan for the "Great Voyage' must be altered." He paused while the anticipated muttering among the crowd subsided and then he began again. "We believe that the time for a few of our vessels to take to the southern sea is very near. Instead of waiting for another two whole years, that time when it is believed that all the canoes will be completed, when all the fleet would depart together, we should send three canoes south in the spring. Nearly all our present Sea-Hewn have received extensive training. We now have twenty young initiates, new Sea-

Hewn whose training has really just begun. These youngsters will need a year, in home waters, to gain the experience required to crew on the 'Voyage' vessels. Only half of our present, experienced Sea-Hewn are required to provide this training. We have among our Sea-Masters twelve men with the '*sea-sight*'. Two of our recent initiates show some promise in this regard also. We propose that these two lads, and a couple of others of exceptional aptitude, should accompany a voyage of three canoes south to that island which Al'malan Sea-Master discovered and where eleven of our kinsmen and women now wait for us to return to them. Such a voyage will provide navigational experience for the *sighted* Sea-masters as well as all other Sea-Hewn involved, to reach this island and return to Sht'ah Lee. As well, our people on that island of 'New Beginnings' are in need of food plants, chickens and pigs and dogs and many other things to make that island truly livable for our Mal'lam way of life."

Orn'ta had to pause here to take a drink of water. Never had he expended so many words at one go!

"The Voyage-Master assures us that this little island in the middle of the sea is worthy of our effort. He believes it may become of great importance to our future expansion southward. What is proposed is to load three canoes with all those things which will make of that island a valuable stop-over, in time, and then to return here. They would be leaving behind a number of men and women to further the population of our people already there. Spring is the optimum time for such an expedition. New bamboo shoots will be ready for propagation. That island has no bamboo. Yams and banana plants and sugar cane and so many more plant materials will be needed. Pigs will be littering, as will dogs, and chickens will all be laying. Also, the wind and the weather offers a safe opportunity for such a voyage." Another pause to take a breath; many in attendance now enthralled!

"Therefore, we propose that some of our well-trained Sea-Hewn crews and at least twenty people of other crafts - men, women and older children - be chosen during these winter months and prepared for a voyage to be launched in late spring." Now Orn'ta offered his final persuasion.

"For all we Mal'lam and Itin to leave at one time would not only strain our capacity to provide enough food for a long journey - we will not have enough experienced seamen to crew enough vessels to carry us all away at one time.

Our 'Great Voyage' must actually become a back and forth shuttle, taking place over a number of years!"

There was silence for many moments, long enough for Orn'ta to hand the Speakers Staff' back to the Voyage-Master and retreat to the back row of seamen. He desperately hoped that never again would he be called upon to deliver such an address. In spite of the chill air, he wiped beads of sweat from his forehead. The debate continued not for hours but for days. There was considerable consternation. So many Mal'lam had formed a hopeful picture of one grand fleet carrying all together, sailing away from Sh'tah Lee-Set into a great adventure. Well, a great adventure it would be but it would evolve in an orderly and timely, altogether sensible fashion. The Sea-Hewn, and especially the Sea-masters, absorbed the jibes and complaints of their neighbors with as good humor as they could muster. They too were disappointed. But they too knew that the decision was correct. Joha'lan Canoe-Master had declared that the 'Great Voyage' fleet would consist of no more than twenty-two vessels.

Some of the older canoes, originally intended to be part of the 'Voyage', were showing signs of aging which no amount of repair and refurbishment could guarantee as 'voyage-worthy'. The rush was on now to prepare three canoes, one new, two older, for the spring sailing. Already people of all crafts and their families were volunteering to be part of the re-supply journey to 'Win'no'hi-Set'. Sea-Hewn also were volunteering in numbers which would require ten vessels. Al'malan rubbed his chin in frustration, knowing that the final decisions regarding - who and when? - would evolve onto his head.

He and his great friend, Canoe-Master Joha'lan, had already declared that they and their families would be the last to depart, their obligations to their people's safe departure ahead of them paramount. That left Sea-Master Ch'om'lo with an equally insistent obligation to remain and protect these last remnants. He was, after all, the premier warrior of these combined Clans. Surely, as the Mal'lam population disappeared into the horizon, *Ja'jan* and her people would be emboldened to press their claim on the island. That would leave a small group of Mal'lam/Itin people, perhaps less in number than the *Ja'jan an-lo*, to defend themselves against *Ja'jan's* spurious claim upon her son, Sahn'ta. Ch'om'lo's mind was already working on this problem and so far his solutions were colored with blood. There had to be another way, was his insistent thought, but it was slow in developing even in his ever-active mind.

Shen'ha and Sha'lat, the supreme Herb-Mistresses of the combined Clans, were now together involved in a demanding project; organizing the planting, propagation and care and processing of all those plant materials which must be ready for the spring voyage of re-supply and settlement on 'Win'no'hi'. There was great pressure upon Shen'ha to include herself in this voyage and also to remain there on that island and see to the planting and general advancement of horticulture. She resisted, adamantly, knowing that her son, Shen'ham, would surely remain here on Sht'ah Lee until his soul-mate and lover, Tina Earth-Plait, left with her family.

Recently the young boy whom she had adopted, Han, had died during an epileptic seizure. The thought of being separated from her other son was too much to endure. No! She too would remain until the last day. There were many other Herbalists, men and women, capable of fulfilling the role demanded there on that far-away land. So there was again anxiety and uncertainty among the Mal'lam as they continued their preparations for the construction, outfitting and launching of their 'Great Voyage'. Were these considerations not burden enough, still, there in the background, lurked the ominous threat of what that mad woman *Ja'jan* might do.

~ ~ * ~ ~

The woman, Sha'sha, had come to the 'Chief Priest' with the information she had gleaned from her Mal'lam contacts. It was all about the recent developments within the Mal'lam camp; the extension of time for the removal of all Mal'lam from the island and the sequence of events which were being planned. Nervously she imparted to Sho'sha'lo all that she had heard and seemed very anxious to be away. Not so fast!

"Wonderful, Sha'sha!" he said, the smile on his face not really one of admiration. "Now, since you have, through your own clever means, learned what our neighbors are about, I think you deserve to be the one to so inform our 'Mistress'."

The woman looked horrified! "No! Please, 'Chief Priest'! Really, you can tell our 'Mistress' much better than I."

Sho'sha'lo rose from his seat beneath the shady tree and took the young woman by the arm and led her toward the enclosure of *Ja'jan's* inner-sanctum. "It will be alright!" he lied and Sha'sha knew that there was no escape. Sho'sha'lo guided the reluctant woman through the open gates of the enclosure, still gripping her arm, and led her to the door to *Ja'jan's* quarters. He reached out and knocked on the door frame once, followed by a series of prescribed knocks, informing the woman within that something important was approaching. Sha'sha looked up into Sho'sha'lo's face with a last pleading grimace. No hope!

"Yes? Come in now, if you must!" came *Ja'jan's* testy reply. Sho'sha'lo sat himself down on a seat which he had instructed be installed for his convenience and waited, a bitter smile tweaking the corners of his mouth. Sha'sha bent and pushed aside the entry's thick drape and entered. Within two minutes there was an unearthly shriek from inside the 'Mistress's' hut and the poor *Ja'jan'an-lo* woman exited with pieces of pottery flying after her. The woman caste a glance filled with loathing at the 'Chief Priest' as she ran past him, knowing full well that she had been set up to take the "Mistress's' wrath. Sho'sha'lo only grinned in triumph and rose slowly and deliberately and headed toward his daughter's abode. Screams of rage still issued from within, the drape at the door still suffering the odd impact from a thrown object.

"What? More bad news?" *Ja'jan* asked, as her father pushed aside the drape and hung it on its hook at the door frame. He had come to abhor the darkness which his daughter seemed to insist upon when in her lodgings. He needed some light with which to observe her features and expressions. He had known her from her birth but still her utterances held lies and distractions which he had yet to decipher. But her eyes and face always told him the truth of her state of mind now.

"Well, it would seem that our enemies have changed course somewhat." Sho'sha'lo immediately regretted that nautical inference but *Ja'jan* seemed not to notice. She simply glowered!

"So, we have to wait for years yet before those stupid Mal'lam decide to leave us in peace?" *Jajan* sat pouting, her short-cropped hair unable to sustain the light feathers attached, making her look somewhat ridiculous as one by one they fell onto her shoulders.

"It would seem that that is their plan, my dear." Sho'sha'lo's previous obsequiousness had recently become a more familiar form of address, not unnoticed by the "Mistress', but tolerated. She reluctantly recognized that she needed her father's guidance. More so of late.

"It will be alright though," he continued, "Your sacrificial platform is complete now and ready for your direction in its use. Also, we have twenty new converts to our movement and six children have been born to the *Ja'jan an-lo*, another three women pregnant. We are growing in strength and numbers. We must wait a while longer than we had hoped, but what of that?" He waited for her reply. *Ja'jan* was silent for nearly five minutes, her father patiently waiting, familiar with the sometimes retarded reasoning and reply which was her fashion. He also knew that these long pauses sometimes resulted in a sudden flare of brilliance and purpose.

Finally *Ja'jan* spoke again, this time with more questions of her trusted 'Chief Priest'."Al'malan intends staying until the last vessels sail, is that right?" He responded in the affirmative, about to say more but she interrupted. "So when he and his woman and child - and my son- prepare to depart, they will be at their weakest?" Again he answered but with just a nod. "How long would it take us to form a group of warriors sufficient to overwhelm them?" This question took Sho'sha'lo by surprise. Since the death of her 'Chief Warrior' in that abortive quest to capture her son from the Itin, *Ja'jan* had never mentioned the raising of an armed force as such. Her 'Chief Priest' though, could see the reasoning behind her question. It was perhaps possible. But he held no great hope for such a possibility. He knew himself unqualified to train such a group and he knew of no one in the *Ja'jan an-lo* who could fill such a role.

"Well?" she asked, impatience once again in her tone. Sho'sha'lo thought quickly for the right response. Stalling tactics were needed here. "I believe we need more … how can I say it … inspiration, for our younger men?"

"What do you mean?" and she bent forward toward him, demanding clarification. In the past few months the intensity of *Ja'jan's* involvement, day to day, had waned. She was seen less often among her people. The frequency of her famous orgies had declined and so too had the attendance at those mad functions. Women with children were spending more time with their offspring and men too were more often seen acting as fathers to the youngsters, even though they might have no idea of whose sperm sired the infant. Sho'sha'lo knew that his daughter's control was lessening and that she must wait no longer to reestablish *her* power over *her* people!

"You must bring passion and ardor once more to your people, Mistress! You must remind the younger men of your love for them. Only when they think fondly, passionately of their relationship with you will they be able to respond with the fire inside them needed to become warriors!" Sho'sha'lo was once again stirred by his own words and enthusiasm, reaching out to his daughter's consciousness with that old passion of his own toward her. She pondered again for many moments, glancing frequently in his direction, listening to the echo of his words and grasping at their full meaning. Finally she made a decision.

"Yes. I see what you mean. I understand." Her voice was quite flat and emotionless. She was still thinking, weighing the possibilities. Suddenly she brightened and even chuckled mischievously.

"Alright . . . we will have an orgy! Actually, the Gods have been telling me much the same thing." She lied, but her father didn't care. He had her moving again."Tomorrow is the half-moon night. I declare it auspicious! There you are! Solved!" Ja'jan stood up quickly and called through the open doorway for her handmaiden, her cousin Jana'la. While she waited for the woman to come from her small hut in the compound, *Ja'jan* turned to her father and in a voice which had regained its old power of command, commanded him: "'Chief Priest', I want you to organize a feast for tomorrow. I will kill a pig with my own hand and offer it to the Gods and to my people. We shall have a celebration which this village has not seen before! And I shall lie with every young man in turn. Let them all remember again the passion the '*Goddess of the Skies*' will bring to their lives." Sitting again, she looked up at her father. Her expression was one of surprise and impatience. "Well?" she said, both a question and an order. The 'Chief Priest' took his cue and got up quickly and hastened out the doorway. He had much to do. He chuckled to himself in self-congratulation as he set out to organize a long-delayed orgy.

~ ~ * ~ ~

Whack! Quickly again . . . whack! The sling stones struck the target of tightly bundled fiber with deadly force and precision. The young man placed another stone into the coir sling and prepared to let fly once more. Whack!

"Well done, Shal'tet! Now try it from one-hundred paces." 'Three Finger' was instructing a class of newly-initiated Sea-Hewn in the art of the sling. He had a keen and efficient class to work with too. Never before had such training been included in the curriculum of the newly initiated Sea-Hewn. When all of the trainees in Shen'ham's group this day had shown not only improvement but impressive accomplishment, he signaled an end to the session and called the boys to come around him.

"You fellows have done really well!" His manner was always open and friendly and he took much time to assist someone finding hitting the target difficult. In fact, his manner was that of only a senior initiate rather than a battle-hardened veteran and experienced seaman. Shen'ham Sea-Hewn was the idol of many of these young recruits to the sea. He was also the idol of a pretty, slim young woman who sat uphill of the practice ground, hidden among the foliage.

Tina-an Earth-Plait never tired of watching her man in whatever he was involved in. Their love and dedication to each other had grown to become an inseparable melding of their souls. Yet each was so different from the other; often separated for days by her proclivities as a wanderer of the mountains and he with his obligations as a Sea-Hewn trainer and seaman. But their coming together again was always as that first time when he had returned to Sht'ah Lee. It was Tina who still resisted the option of marriage and Shen'ham didn't press the subject. He knew that her reluctance had all to do with her deep devotion to this island; this land upon which her Spiritual journey had begun and which still sustained and encouraged her. She still resisted the call to commit to joining in the 'Great Voyage', the leaving of her now-beloved Sht'ah Lee.

But in her recent meditations her mentor, The Vesa'tan, seemed to be hinting at a need for her to reevaluate her whole situation. Thus was she involved in an internal struggle which not even Shen'ham would understand. But he would simply smile and say, 'Whatever is best for you, my darling." whenever the subject came up. OOOOOH! Sometimes she could hit him! Why was he so understanding, when he didn't understand? Why didn't he just lay down the law and command me to do what he wants? It would maybe be so much easier! But there was no law to lay down! The only law lay in their love for each other. Both knew that. So, my dear Tina, it's still and always, up to you! OOOOOH!!!

She stood up and sauntered down from the cool shade of the trees as the boys were departing. Shen'ham was gathering the pack full of sling stones and preparing to depart himself when he suddenly turned in her direction and stood upright. He could always feel her presence. "Have you been spying on our young warriors?" he called out, looking away to attend to his task.

"There's only one warrior I'm interested in, 'Three Finger'", she replied and began a run toward him. He timed her arrival to the split second, turned and caught her leaping form in both arms. He wrestled her to the ground quickly and fell lightly on top of her, his weight and strength overwhelming, welcome."Not here!" she protested, not caring. They didn't though. From the edge of the open ground where the practice had taken place a hail from a familiar voice arrived. It was Ch'om'lo Sea-Master, come to find out how the practice session had gone. He approached them with a mischievous grin a yard wide.

"I'm sorry if I interrupted a family fight … excuse me!" Tina-an stood up but didn't dust herself off. She seldom dusted herself off, still not quite in tune with the requirements of feminine appearance. Shen'ham just sat chuckling, resting on his hands and grinning up at his own mentor.

"They all did well, Sea-Master. Very well, actually. I think it's time they began working with you now." Tina-an sat down again and looked up at the Itin Sea-Master with genuine affection. "How is my darling friend, Shana'la, today?" Ch'om'lo smiled, bent down and kissed his wife's closest friend on her forehead and replied, "She's just fine, Tina! Actually, she said she'd like to see you. Whenever you're free, that is."

Tina reckoned that this repartee' had gone on long enough. With an extravagant groan and phony struggle to rise from the ground, which caused Ch'om'lo to laugh, she turned to Shen'ham with a quick movement, kissed him on the cheek and ran past Ch'om'lo, laying a stinging slap to his arm. Strangers had become friends; friends become family; brothers and sisters. The two Sea-Hewn sauntered casually downhill toward the village, Shen'ham with the heavy pack of stones carried lightly on his broad shoulder. "Have you considered making the round-trip to 'Win'no'hi, Sea-Master?" Shen'ham asked.

"Yes, of course. We are two of the seamen who know the route there and back. I say that because even though you were still suffering considerable pain from your wound, I was aware that you attended the tutoring sessions studiously. I've always admired you for that." Shen'ham glanced quickly at Ch'om'lo, wondering if there was a joke involved here. He had memories of dragging himself to those evening lessons on the star route they were then following, barely able to concentrate, and often failing to do so.

"My recollection is much less than you might think, Sea-Master." he said. "I surely don't feel I'm qualified to contribute much to the navigation." Then, hoping to lighten what he was afraid might become a tense separation of opinion with his mentor, he said, "Of course, that's all your fault … having cut my fingers off and all!" He risked a grin at Ch'om'lo. Ch'om'lo stopped and looked with intensity at the younger man who nearly stumbled, coming to a stop with his heavy load trying to carry him on down the now steep section of track.

"Shen'ham! You and I have endured much together. We have sailed together, fought together and shared more than most of our people can understand. I believe that I know you as well as anyone, even Tina-an. You will one day be a Sea-Master yourself, of that I have no doubt. Don't you doubt yourself, even for an instant. I am recommending to the Council of Sea-Masters that you be included in the voyage to 'Win'no'hi' as a senior member. I expect you to accept that position because you are more than qualified. I will not be going. I have responsibilities here which require my presence."

Ch'om'lo studied his young friend's face for a moment, saw what he expected and continued, "One more thing, Sea-Hewn. When you and I are together, alone, don't address me as 'Sea-Master'. We are brothers as much as my father's other sons are my brothers. Formalities have value when conducting those things which require discipline, like while under sail. But at a time such as this, I am your brother, Ch'om'lo - nothing more or less." And with a mischievous grin he added, "And don't forget that … or you may be called 'Two Finger'!" With that he carried his grin on down the hill, Shen'ham quickly following, the weight of those stones on his shoulder forgotten, as was any whisper of self-doubt.

Research Notes: Impressions and General Observations

Subject: Tina Pualani Kaiser and other events, Kaua'i, late Spring, 1975

Tina has begun her Summer vacation now, joining us here on Kaua'i. She has brought 5 tapes with her which she has annotated herself. Good girl! I think she's in love with one of the characters in her Spirit's tale; A'lan Sea-Hewn. He does sound pretty groovy! 'He's cool!' she says.

Jiro and his team are nearly finished work on the burial site on the property next to Kinau's. He's adamant that the stonework is pre-Hawai'ian, but do you think I can trick him into saying it's Mal'lam? Not likely!

We've had a long and very interesting letter from one of Jiro's contacts in New Zealand. She (I won't use her name yet because there seems to be a lot of professional bitchiness happening concerning this whole subject of the Lapita People) has been on a 'dig' in New Caledonia for the past year and she and her French colleagues there have found something *very* interesting! An artifact of copper, found in a deposit of much broken Lapita pottery around the bones of a single individual, which they're pretty sure is male.

She has enclosed a sketch of the artifact: it is approximately three inches wide, quite likely a pendant, and in the form of a spiral. No other copper artifacts from a prehistoric Oceanic period have yet been found. Jiro immediately faxed the drawing to another friend at Stanford University for his opinion. His reply: "I'm pretty sure it's Mochica, from southern Ecuador. These spiral symbols are common among coastal cultures, as well as elsewhere around the world among so-called primitive peoples. Where was it found?" Well, Jiro is now having to play some games himself, holding off telling his friend the whole truth while not hurting his feelings. Politics!

Little Lea Malia is wonderful. Jiro says she's the 'banana of his eye'. Sometimes I worry about him!

Tutu is throwing another big *luau* soon. This one's for Jiro. It's his sixtieth birthday and shortly it will be Kinau's sixty-fifth. Look out! It's gonna be a Biiig bash!

Update:

Latest news from the New Zealand archaeologist is that the copper artifact has been sent to France! Supposedly a university there, and she doesn't know which one, is going to run tests on it and try to determine its origin. Jiro says it's quite possible to accurately pinpoint the area where the ore came from. He also thinks that's the last we are going to hear of it. "Don't be so cynical!" I told him. "Experienced, my dear!" he replied, and went on to explain that the whole question of the origin of the Polynesians was becoming so heated and contentious that underhanded tricks were not rare, as people tried to prove their own theories or quash someone else's. He has reinforced in me the need for great discretion. Me? Discreet?

Chapter Forty Two - The Explorers Sail South

The new, larger canoe, 'Wa'Boton', was first out of the opening in the reef. 'Wa'Salat' was three minutes behind, A'lan Sea-hewn standing in his preferred spot when underway - at the very front of one hull or the other. He gazed down into the water, watching the color of the sea change rapidly as depth increased. It seemed many years since the voyagers had landed here on the islands of the Tarbara'ut. It was but two years and four months, time in which much had changed in this young seaman's life. A'lan was going on nineteen years old now. As tall as most men, he was still with the lithe figure of his age but very well muscled. Those months of working in the gardens, laying stone, adzing timber for the canoe, all had shaped his body into a powerful engine of activity. And he was even beginning to grow a reasonable beard. But the beard was not going to obscure that scar. Only a few rampant hairs managed to find their way through the tough, pink scar tissue which ran from the left corner of his mouth to his ear. In fact, the beard was going to accent this singular feature of his otherwise handsome face.

A'lan had quenched the tears of parting as soon as he had grasped a rope to set the sail. Seamanship filled the painful void and the smooth rise and fall of the vessel upon the waves surging through the reef's opening began to sing its song of the adventure ahead. By sunset, the pink and blue curtain of the western sky eclipsed the last view of the tops of the tallest Tarbara'ut islands. The two big canoes were two-hundred feet apart, 'Wa'Salat' slightly behind its larger companion. Ahead to the south lay a bank of towering cumulus cloud - potential storm! Sea-Master Sh'ban'ol signaled from his lead vessel to widen the distance between the canoes. There would be no moon tonight and if that cloud moved in, little visibility. Torches were prepared for lighting when full dark descended, one to be burning on each vessel as long as weather permitted; this a wise precept established by the Voyage-Master, Al'malan.

The Tarbara'ut had seemed to have abandoned their memory of these southern seas. When questioned at length by the Mal'lam Sea-Master, Faldo, prior to these two vessel's discovery voyage, not one gleam of information about these people's distant past seemed to survive. Faldo was confident that, given his years among these gentle people, he would know if obfuscation attended their replies to his questions. The Tarbara'ut had chosen to forget their distant past;

not even myths survived. The Mal'lam Sea-Hewn were truly sailing blind into unknown waters and only their seamanship and, perhaps, blind luck, would attend their wanderings. Did some mysterious predisposition, even genetic in nature, attend these gentle, happy little black people? Their children were few in spite of a wholesale acceptance of sexual activity as a natural function of being who they were. It was as if some strange finality had descended upon them, generations ago, and the Tarbara'ut were simply waiting for it to play itself out. It was all beyond the ken of the Mal'lam and yet Mal'lam seed was producing pregnancies among the lovers they had chosen. Not even the Tarbara'ut men were greatly confronted by this fact. Very strange!

As night settled over the ocean those distant cloud banks retreated, leaving a southern sky clear and inviting of investigation. A'lan Sea-Hewn took the first night watch as senior officer, the first time such a responsibility had been thrust upon him. He accepted that responsibility without hesitation. Night at sea was his favorite time. First he positioned himself astern on the bridging deck, scanning the water for the signature of the islands they had just sailed from. There they were; long, lazy emanations in pinks and greens, flowing steadily from that source which held safely his lover and their child. He believed he could even discern the separate issue of lights from those smaller islands which flanked 'Tara'tor'.

When satisfied that he had memorized the signature of these islands which had now become 'home', he moved forward and rested himself in the bow of the starboard hull. No lights flowed from forward, the dark depths devoid of any such information there. So it was the stars which his keen eyes concentrated on now. Turning alternately to view the sky ahead, above and behind, he registered the vessel's position. He called behind him for another seaman to throw out the line holding a ripe coconut. The nut was thrown forward and outward to a line even with the plunging bows. Seconds were counted until the coconut had come even with the canoe's stern. From this was gauged their speed. A'lan called for an adjustment of the sails' angle's to bring the tall panels more acutely into the southeasterly breeze off their port quarter. He could feel the slight increase in forward motion and the decrease in the pitching of the vessel. Perfect!

The two vessels came into an area of sea full of phosphorescence. The steady starlight from above shimmered upon a sea which signaled back its own visual richness, applauding the smooth passage of the canoes through this dark field which opened tracks of blue-green light to mark the progress of the hulls. Looking down into the black depths, A'lan could see deeper swathes of light as great swarms of tiny animals responded to some unseen stimulation. They were like undersea clouds and over that mass of dim illumination flowed larger sea creatures; hunters of the night, pursuing smaller prey who themselves pursued the descending ranks of the food chain. A'lan Sea-Hewn allowed this enchantment to absorb him, inform him, and enrich his knowledge and speculation by the minute, the hour. Every day and night overflowed with increasing richness for this young man whose life was so intimately tied to the watery realm upon which he rode.

For five days the weather continued to draw the two canoes to the south, the wind direction barely shifting from its insistent southeasterly direction. On the evening of the fifth day seabirds were sighted heading to the east, across their path. 'Wa'Boton' signaled back to its trailing partner to change course to the east, that new course speeding their passage in the more acute angle to the wind. Throughout the night a double watch was kept and the two 'sighted' seamen, A'lan aboard the 'Wa' Shalat', searched the depths for sign of land. There it was! Blue streaks with attendant signals of violet flashing out from the east with increasing intensity as the night wore on. Lookouts were sent aloft, starlight the only illumination. The sliver of new moon had sunk below the western horizon hours ago.

Dawn rose behind a curious accumulation of clouds. An island must surely lay below! The dawn also brought a shift in the wind and again the sail panels were adjusted to accept a more northerly blow. More speed now and those towering clouds were approached with great expectation. Faldo-in Sea-Hewn called down from the mast-top that he could see a dark line beneath the cloud, which could only be land. Land! And as the canoes coursed ahead toward that land, the flights of birds, heading seaward for their day's fishing, flew overhead in increasing numbers until they disappeared to the west.

"Land! Land ahead!" The call echoed from vessel to vessel, every seaman now wide awake and crowding the foredecks in their anticipation. The fatigue of a sleepless night was wiped away by the excitement as A'lan climbed upward on the foremast to join his friend in viewing this hoped-for discovery. The land they were approaching was long and low, only a few rocky peaks reaching up to grasp the clouds above and even those peaks were narrow and abrupt. There appeared to be no chain of mountains, no vast highlands such as Sht'ah Lee had possessed. And as the canoes wore ever closer the seamen could observe the difference in color also. This island was a dull grey-green, with only swathes of darker green along its shores and on the narrow pinnacles and the slopes around them. It hinted at dryness. Another hour's sail revealed the white girdle of surf which surrounded this side of the island, indicating reef, shoals and danger!

Sh'ban'ol Sea-Master signaled from his leading canoe that they both should sail around the island. 'Wa'Salat' was to fall in astern of the larger vessel and follow well behind. The early evening aided the navigators in establishing their course by the stars. The breaking surf along the shoreline remained visible long enough for the Sea-Masters to estimate the direction to follow and the safe distance from shore. Still, the crews must remain alert and the watches were increased. As always when scouting a new and unknown shoreline, the greatest caution must be exercised.

The sets of waves descending upon the island from the open sea were countered by the rebounding waves created by their predecessors which had earlier crashed ashore, creating a lumpy, disturbed surface; a rough sea with sudden currents which had to be carefully considered and anticipated. In the dark of night this was a considerable challenge to even the most experienced seaman. It seemed almost inevitable that new arrivals must endure such a night of anxiety before finding a safe landing. It was here that A'lan Sea-Hewn's extraordinary capacities as a 'sighted' seaman where of such value. Not only could he read the undersea signature of islands but when drawing close to land he could also determine what might be a gap in the fringing reef, allowing entry to a vessel.

He recalled the equally strange capacity of the Voyage-Master, Al'malan, whose hearing could likewise find gaps in the sound of crashing waves. Ah, but wouldn't these two be an awesome combination! A'lan kept that thought in his list of possibilities. This young Sea-Hewn no longer thought like a young apprentice. He was beginning to develop a confidence in his abilities which, once recognized by him, he strove to perfect and apply - insistently and sometimes to the consternation of his superior Sea-Hewn. But on this night he was willing to bide his time and await the decisions of the Sea-Masters under whom he served.

His watch ended, A'lan stayed on deck, sleep the last inclination in his mind. Sea-Master Fan'al was back on duty and stood on the foredeck with A'lan, discussing the dim sight to their left as they slowly passed the length of this intriguing new land. No new light signals or vocal hails had come from the lead canoe. The glow from the torches aboard each was steady. That vessel's commander too was surely awake and attending to his duties on this exciting night. Slowly the sky's expanse of starlight became constricted as clouds drifted insistently over from the southeast. Fan'al turned to A'lan and said, "Those are storm clouds, Sea-Hewn. I reckon that by dawn we'll have increasing winds and rain. If we are to make a landing today, it will have to be on the other side of the island, against the wind. Frankly, I'd prefer to turn about and go further out to sea and wait this out. What think you?"

A'lan was momentarily taken aback. But only momentarily. "No, Fan'al! I would make for land now ... here on this side of the island!"

"What?" the Master Seaman retorted, "How would we know where to land? Sea-Hewn, I think you must be dreaming!" The Master of this canoe was surely upset by what he felt was a stupid, immature response to the situation. A'lan reached out and took hold of his captain's arm, a minor infraction of the established system of rank. He pointed to the area to their left where the continuous splashing of the surf upon reef-rocks captured and echoed the dim starlight.

"We are on the lee-side of whatever weather is approaching. Now is the time to get ashore and out of the worst of the storm. I agree, Fan'al, we are in for stiff weather. But let us do it while we have time to secure our vessels upon the sands of that nearest coast." The young Sea-Hewn stood before his doubting captain with an intensity of purpose which shone through the darkness. Had that Sea-Master himself the 'vision' he might well have seen an insistent glow surrounding A'lan. "Now, Sea-Master!" A'lan roared, "We must turn into the land now!"

Faced with a dilemma totally new to his years upon the sea, Fan'al could only hesitate and try to seek the truth of the moment. For what seemed an eternity to A'lan, his master considered. Then with a mighty roar of his own, Fan'al turned toward 'Wa'Boton' and shouted into the rising sound of strengthening wind and crashing waves and called to the Voyage-Master's vessel, ahead but fifty feet off his bows.

"Sh'ban'al Sea-Master! Do you hear me?" There was no immediate response from ahead, probably the sounds of wind and surf were too loud. Then one of the big canoe's steersmen cupped an ear in their direction and waved. Turning to face forward he could be heard to call out to the master of that vessel. Quickly Sh'ban'ol came aft and gave an order to his steersmen. The men immediately pushed hard right on their long oar and 'Wa'Boton' swung to port, losing speed, allowing 'Wa'salat' to pull closer abeam. 'Wa'Boton' swung back parallel to shore now and the two vessels were side by side.

"You have words for me, brother?" the tall, heavily bearded Sea-Master called out. The distance between the two canoes was no more than thirty feet now and both sets of steersmen had to be very careful.

"In consultation with my 'sighted' Sea-Hewn, A'lan, it is my opinion that we should make for shore, here on this side of the island." He looked over at A'lan who was standing close enough for expressions to be read. "What do you think lad? Can you see an opening for us before dawn?"

Instead of an answer A'lan gave a nod to Fan'al and then walked to the edge of the bridging deck and spoke in a loud voice filled with confidence and insistence. "Voyage-Master, there is a large opening in the reef, well behind us now. My sight has revealed it to me and I know that we can safely negotiate it. However I will lose my ability to see clearly once the sky lightens. If we turn about right now, I will lead us to the gap in the reef and we can be ashore before dawn." With hardly a pause to allow the commander of this voyage to fully consider, A'lan continued. "As we know, the wind is increasing and the storm clouds are covering the stars as we speak. Soon our only option will be to run out to sea and ride with the storm. Sea-Master Fan'al is willing to cross the reef first, Voyage-Master. We must decide very soon!" Fan'al stood behind this assertive young man with some reservations about being volunteered for a dangerous, possibly fatal mission. But something about A'lan's voice finally persuaded him. He stepped close beside A'lan and shouted across to his Sea-Hewn brother.

"Yes, Sh'ban'ol! I agree with the lad. Let me turn about now and lead you to the opening in the reef. We haven't much time!" Though some might find insubordination evident here, such was the manner of decision-making among the Mal'lam Sea-Hewn that the Voyage-Master took no umbrage. But he did wait - what seemed a very long time - and then called out a confirmation. A'lan had anticipated this answer and already was preparing the orders to the crew to come about. Fan'al turned to address A'lan but the young man was already across the deck, giving those orders to the crew. Fan'al shook his head and smiled ruefully. "I might not see out this voyage as Master of this canoe, if this keeps up." He then strode to the stern of the bridging deck and stood by to assist the steersmen in the turning maneuver.

A'lan too, as senior officers usually did, came aft to help. The two seamen on the oars were already pushing hard to bring the vessel around to the right, away from 'Wa'Boton' and onto a reverse course. The new sail plan of these vessels made this maneuver a much easier and faster process than would have been possible with those older, larger sails. Fan'al Sea-Master commented on this as he and A'lan lent their weight to the oars. A'lan appreciated the easy manner in which his superior spoke with him. There had been moments when he thought he might be, quite rightly, admonished for his presumptuousness. But he had been listened to thoughtfully, his ideas carefully considered and now his own judgment enacted. A'lan's mind was filled now with only one question: 'Where is that opening?'

As soon as 'Wa'Salat' had reversed course, A'lan was leaning out over the front edge of the bridging deck, his brow creased in concentration, his eyes focused not on but 'into' the water. Within that maze of radiations from this island's rocky mass there existed specific signatures, so subtle that not every 'sighted' Sea-Hewn could register them. These took the form of slight changes in hue in the colors and a difference in the intensity of the major radiations. There was one! No! Too slight a variation. Five minutes went by. Then ten minutes and A'lan was becoming more than a little anxious. He rubbed his eyes free of the seawater which a large wave had rinsed his face with. Blinking his vision clear again - there it was, for sure! It was a long section of that main radiation which was lighter in hue. It ran forward and out of sight. This was the opening! Leaping to his feet he called out, "Hard to starboard! Hard to starboard! Now! Now!"

The vessel's Master, Fan'al, stood near to A'lan, his one hand gripping a forestay with desperate force. His other hand wiped sweat from his forehead. As his vessel turned to the right and toward that line of surf which the dimming light portrayed as continuous and impenetrable, he braced himself, his teeth tightly clenched. "You'd better be right, lad!' he muttered. The canoe facing into the wind now, A'lan called out to have the sail panels fly loose and for every available hand to take to the paddles. It was beginning to rain and the wind was becoming stronger. The motion of the vessel changed markedly - the stern rising steeply as a large swell lifted 'Wa'Salat' and bore it forward toward the surf ahead. Settling into the slack trough as the wave swept past, the bow rising less sharply, the canoe and its occupants braced for another following surge from the open sea. Unable to handle the tension while standing and watching, Fan'al went to a vacant seat in the port hull and began adding his strength to the paddler's efforts to keep some speed up. The two men on the steering oars were hard-pressed also, but able to keep the bows pointed at - what? To the left were great waves breaking on coral reef! So too on the right! And ahead? Ahead, in the dim light, made dimmer by the falling rain, was only the smooth backs of rollers, breaking cleanly of their own momentum. There was no reef ahead!

"Drive your paddles deep, Sea-Hewn!" came the cry from Sea-Master Fan'al. The vessel was slowing as it was carried over the collapsing waves. They must maintain speed in order to control the motion of the canoe. Now every man aboard except the steersmen dug deep into the roiled water. A'lan, remembering the proper signal to the following vessel, leapt from his seat, discarding his paddle onto the bridging deck. 'Two white flags in the day, two torches at night', signaled a successful entry to a safe harbor. The rain had nearly extinguished the one sputtering torch which each vessel now carried at night. He pulled it's long staff from its mounting and ran beneath the covered cabin amidships. Quickly he picked up two fresh torches and applied the reviving original light to them both until they began blazing. When both were burning he threw the original out onto the sea and went onto the bridging deck behind the aft sail and held a torch in each hand, as far apart as his arms would reach. Raindrops assaulted the torches but their fish-oil-soaked baste resisted and the torches blazed brightly.

"There, Voyage-Master!" a seaman shouted into the wind and rain. "There! Do you see? 'Wa'Salat' is through the reef!" The master of the large canoe stood looking almost incredulous for long moments, temporarily immobilized by the wisdom of his decision. 'How did I know to listen to that young Sea-Hewn?' But then he began a series of loud orders which had every man aboard hurrying in desperation; they had only a few minutes to complete a series of complex sailing maneuvers or they would miss their opportunity to cross through that safe passage. The storm was now upon them. "We need every bit of speed we can muster!" shouted the vessel's Master. "Bring the sails around into the wind. Steersmen! Steer for those two lights!" Sh'ban'ol ran forward to the front of the deck, knowing that the sails themselves would obstruct the steersmen's vision and called back orders. "More right! More! Yes, hold it there" And now they were into the heavy swells which mounted higher and higher and 'Wa'Boton' began its rapid ride toward the opening. Common sense told everyone aboard that they were about to run onto a deadly reef.

"Everyone to your paddles! Let go the sails now - let them swing free!" Quickly the lines were let go and the increasing wind pushed the unrestrained sail panels straight back, no longer resisting the wind's pressure. As with the smaller vessel which had preceded them, this canoe rose and fell to the wave action, first surging forward, then into a trough, then again raised high and pushed forward yet again. The Voyage-Master too sat down and thrust his paddle deeply into the surge, calling out a rhythm for his crew to follow.

For what seemed like an eternity of fear and desperate activity, the great canoe rode through the gap in the reef which darkness and pouring rain totally obscured. Still the Master's cadence rang out and the seamen dug deep with their paddles, most looking up forward to that pair of lights which were now growing brighter, closer. And then 'Wa'Boton' too was safely through the passage, still surging forward, paddle-power assisting the impetus provided by the following swells. Shouts could be heard issuing from 'Wa'Salat' which soon became cheers of greeting. Flashes of lightning began to illuminate the scene and the sight of their sister vessel, now safely ashore, brought cheers from 'Wa'Boton's' men also.

"Light two torches!" Sh'ban'ol Sea-Master called out. "Secure the sails in a downwind position. Get the covers on the hulls before we fill up with rainwater" More orders boomed out from this mightily relieved Master, the power of his voice a release of the tensions which had become nearly unbearable over the past half hour. Crewmen from 'Wa'Salat' ran to catch the hawsers thrown ashore to them and they immediately ran inland to the nearest trees, only small they were and a number of them were employed as anchors. 'Wa'Salat' was already securely tied to the shore and the crew of that vessel also busy securing their vessel against pouring rain.

The storm proved short-lived. An hour after the canoes had been battened down the clouds carried the rain away and like a ripped and tattered cloth, the remnants of the storm began to again reveal a sky bright with stars. Soon fires were blazing on the beach, the light from them a welcome addition to the small torches. But it was too soon for exploring. All the men were very tired and needed sleep. Some crawled back into their accustomed sleeping platforms in the hulls of their vessels while a few others made a bed on the beach, near the warming bonfires.

A'lan Sea-Hewn sat with the Sea-Masters and two other senior seamen, the firelight revealing faces still lined with fatigue, worry, even some fear which still ran through their veins. But A'lan's face was composed, one might even call it serene. His judgment had been vindicated. Firelight shimmered on that long facial scar which his incipient beard could not disguise. Sea-Master Sh'ban'ol gazed tiredly at the young man opposite him. 'This youngster is destined for great things.' He carried that thought with him as he excused himself and returned to his vessel and the comfort of his berth in the port hull.

A'lan and his vessel's Master remained chatting quietly for a time, the other two seamen having also excused themselves. "My boy," the elder seaman said, "what has occurred tonight I would never have believed, had someone told it to me! Even though Sh'ban'ol is one of the 'sighted' ones, he apparently has no sensitivity to the subtleties of the sea-lights which you have displayed. You will appreciate of course, that some other element was also at work here tonight?" Fan'al was referring to the fact that he and Sh'ban'ol, two of the most experienced senior Sea-Masters among the Mal'lam, had relegated the safety of their vessels and crews to what might have seemed the inexperienced whim of a novice Sea-Hewn. Had another young seaman, Faldo-in perhaps, come to his Master with A'lan's proposal, most likely he would have been reprimanded for arrogance, if not insubordination. But Fan'al was right. Both he and Sh'ban'ol had been affected by some strange, outside influence which opened their minds to A'lan's insistence and judged it reasonable. The Sea Gods? The *Earth Mother*? Suddenly Fan'al was too tired to try to understand this strange phenomena.

"Come lad. Let us get some rest. Tomorrow will be a very full day." He rose with a groan, rubbing the small of his back and walked slowly toward his tethered vessel, its glossy hulls shining and casting reflections on the waves that ran in and around them. "I'll sleep here by the fire, if you don't mind Master." Fan'al turned part way around while still walking and waved a tired consent. The tone of respect and affection in A'lan's voice pleased him. 'He's a good lad.' was the thought that saw him to sleep.

A'lan, weariness finally overcoming him, lay down on the still-damp sand some feet upwind of the dying bonfire. As he pulled his warm rain-cape over himself, he again brought that vision to his mind. There had indeed been some strange element at work this night, stranger than anyone would ever know.

It had been just as A'lan was about to order the canoe to make its fateful turn that it had occurred. "It' was a vision of two old men, standing side by side … and standing in mid-air ... there to the right of the plunging vessel. They were fifty feet away, both figures glowing with a shimmering blueness. Then at once both began motioning to A'lan - he knew it was himself they were signaling to for now he recognized them. On the left was his Great Uncle Tal'ma and beside him the old Sea-Master Telan! It was only after seconds of wonder, and a hint of fear, that he called out for the vessel to make its turn. That vision remained at the same distance away all through 'Wa'Salat's' maneuvers; into the plunging swells before the reef, through the opening and forward onto the distant beach.

A'lan seldom took his eyes from the apparition before him. When finally the twin bows of the canoe hushed onto the sandy beach and A'lan had to glance quickly about to orient himself, he looked up again expectantly. They were gone. Flashes of lightning revealed no human forms standing on the sand nor up among the small trees and brush above the beach. He shook himself, disbelief trying to conquer his mind. But no! They had been there, as surely as he was kneeling on the coarse mat of the deck. A'lan fell to sleep. But immediately a dream overcame him:

"Are you all right?" It was Faldo-in, his friend, kneeling beside him, trying to peer into his face in the darkness. A'lan stirred himself and rose and slapped his friend on the shoulder and said loudly, "We made it! Brother, we made it!" By this time more torches were brought out into the open from the hut and A'lan could see the puzzlement, mixed with joy and relief, on Faldo-in's face. All over the canoe, men were shouting and pummeling each other and Sea-Master Fan'al came to A'lan and wrapped him in a big, wet hug.

A'lan awoke for a few minutes, his mind overflowing. Slowly he managed to quiet the raging, disparate thoughts and centered on his personal mantra of calmness. As sleep again took him from this strenuous, challenging, magical day, he thought he could hear two old men's chuckles.

~ ~ * ~ ~

It was late morning before the two vessels were carefully assessed for damage, loose lashings tightened or replaced and the hulls bailed of their mix of rainwater and seawater. The food stores were inspected for water damage … none found. A conference with the two Sea-Masters and A'lan and two other senior seamen brought the decision that the canoes should be hauled higher up on the gritty sand of this island and some days devoted to exploration. It required all thirty of this voyage's seamen to haul first one, then the other vessel up and nearly out of the water. The stern of 'Wa'Olon's longer hulls were but eight feet into water, "Wa'Salat' nearly up and dry.

"I propose that we send two groups in separate directions. I'm eager to see what this island has to offer." Sea-Master Sh'ban'ol was in good humor and high spirits this day. Reconciled to the strange happenings of the previous day, he was ready for more excitement.

"Yes. I agree." said Sea-Master Fan'al, and then added, "I also think we should go armed. And we should leave ten men behind with the canoes. They too should have arms ready." A'lan said, "I am happy to remain here for the day. We need to search a little way inland to see if we can find some water close by." Settled!

Sea-Master Sh'ban'ol took his group of nine seamen to the right, eastward along the reach of the apparently long beach and foreshore which curved very gradually inward and out of sight. Fan'al took his group along a rockier left shore. Had the canoes come to shore in that direction there might have been some serious mishap as fingers of rock extended out into the shallow lagoon. Coral heads too could be seen just below the surface in that direction. All began to marvel at how accurate the young Sea-Hewn's course into this safe-harbor had been. It was as if they had been guided by some unseen hand!

Carrying spears, slings and edged clubs, A'lan's group, five others still at the landing site, walked close together into the sparse, dry scrub above the beach. A'lan had noticed that there was a freshwater outflow on the beach, running gently but consistently into the surf. Surely there must be a stream close inland. There was and quite full too, more than adequate to refill their water supply. There was one Herbalist among A'lan's contingent and he was forever busy investigating every plant which caught his eye.

There was very much to investigate because this island held so many plants of which he had no prior knowledge. No coconut palms were sighted though, nor any familiar food plants. There were many birds but of a relatively limited selection; mostly small, colorful creatures of varied and delightful song. Around the shoreline there flew Gannets and other familiar seabirds. Here too, like on the islands of the Tarbara'ut, there were small, apparently flightless birds which were as tame as domestic chickens and as easily caught. Tonight would see a fowl feast.

Meanwhile, to the east, that group of seamen and two Herbalists found easy going on the long, flat beach, interrupted only here and there by a low outcrop of a rather strange stone. It was of a grayish-yellow hue, hard but malleable and behind the beach were low cliffs of the same stone. As they progressed they came upon a number of freshwater streams flowing onto sand, just as A'lan had noticed. There certainly was ample water here. Most of the trees so far seen were quite low and spreading, a few species familiar, common on the Tarbara'ut islands. There were small lizards of a number of species, one of which gave a sharp clicking sound. That sound would become widespread at night.

Just past midday Sh'ban'ol's group stopped beneath the deep shade offered by a low, spreading tree, much branched and with yellow blossoms throughout the foliage. One Herbalist called it by its Tarbara'ut name, stating that it was a valuable source of bark for rope and that the timber was soft and light, ideal for outriggers for small canoes. All along this shoreline the sound of the surf booming and crashing on the distant reef was a constant accompaniment. The intervening shallow lagoon was a sparkling blue-green which shimmered, stinging the eyes, so bright was the reflection of the broiling sunlight. After a half-hour rest, Sh'ban'ol's enthusiasm urged the men up and onward. The Sea-Master was keeping a sharp eye out for any signs of human activity. So far, none. The land was beginning to curve to the left now, another corner to turn, another level to the adventure. These hardened seamen were all really like young boys today; laughing, marveling, pointing to something else new and wondrous.

The Herbalists were truly in their element. One said that he wouldn't mind a whole year to explore this strange and wonderful island. Another retorted that a year here without women would not be very wonderful. And so the day wore on for the explorers until Sh'ban'ol called a halt and decided it was time to trek back to the canoes. Knowing that the way was easy traveling all the way back, he insisted on a jog pace. No one grumbled because on the way back they stopped to pick up the three fowl they had killed and buried under the sand beneath a shady bush. Everyone was very hungry by now and hoping that their compatriots who had gone the other direction would also have taken some of these easily captured birds.

Around the bonfire that evening, the sun just setting over the island behind them, Fan'al's crew exchanged stories of their own adventures. They too had brought back flightless prey and were waiting for them to cook in the earth oven. They had also brought a few dozen bird's eggs gathered from a large rookery on a rugged headland. With plentiful food and fresh water, the two vessel's crews settled into a calm and happy evening. The senior Sea-Hewn grouped together to plan tomorrow's exploration.

"Until we've seen all the island," A'lan offered, "I think we should still maintain a small crew here with the canoes. When we know for sure that we're alone on this island, then we can explore it more thoroughly." Nods of assent answered him and then another seaman added, "And I'd like to climb that high pinnacle we came close to today. It should give us a good view of most of this island. We could certainly spot any smoke from fires or other sign of people here." So the evening evolved, and the fowl tasted very like the chickens so beloved of the Mal'lam and the slightly fishy flavor of the seabird's eggs went down well too. Laughter, yawns and belches soon saw most of the men seek their sleeping positions either on the canoes or on the sandy beach. A new moon's sliver of silver bade them a good night.

Rain greeted the rising of the Mal'lam voyagers. It fell from a leaden sky which had crept in during the early hours before dawn and now lay like a sodden blanket over the island and all the sea around. Undeterred, the two crews set out as they had the day before, jogging to the place where they had stopped and turned around and then resuming an exploratory ramble. The end of the island which Fan'al Sea-Master and his group were exploring was quite different from that which Sh'ban'ol's people where encountering.

There were small outcrops of that strange, light colored stone but more commonly volcanic basalt prevailed. The soil was heavier too, deposits of clay being found in depressions which were most often boggy, sometimes flooded into small ponds. Much of the land here was covered in small to medium sized shrubbery with few trees. Late in the morning the sky began to clear and allow sunlight to lay down shafts of brilliance, spotlighting large patches of grey-green foliage and sometimes those strange, narrow pinnacles which rose further inland. With the sun came an immediate rise in the humidity and a sticky heat descended on the trekkers.

With no breeze penetrating the scrubland across which they were traveling, Fan'al decided to return to the shoreline, hoping for an onshore wind to cool their progress. They passed the bird rookery, which the day before had been their furthest reconnaissance of the coastline and found themselves looking down on another long stretch of beach. Here the wind did pick up and blew a coolness which was most welcome. This western shore held many differences, both visually and physically.

By now it was evident that the island was long and narrow, the prevailing southeast to northwest trade wind leaving its mark. The relative flatness of the land allowed the winds to proceed with little obstruction across the island and back out to sea. All the taller trees they had so far observed were somewhat warped and one-sided, their branches pointing mostly to the west. On this day there was that cool breeze from the southwest and for most of the Mal'lam voyager's stay here, there was a consistent low moan of wind across the island.

Offshore there lay dotted a system of small islets, most barren rock upon which hundreds of seabirds roosted. The coral reef as on the eastern side appeared not to have taken hold here. Rather even from a distance the swirling eddies and choppy waters betrayed nasty currents. Thank the Sea Gods that they had not attempted to land on this western shore! The decision had been made for these two groups to continue their marches around the island and eventually meet somewhere about halfway. They took enough food and water with them to allow an overnight stay if necessary. And so it proved because by the time the two groups of tired seamen and Herbalists came together near the northern end of this island, dusk was upon them. "Well, Sea-Master!" Fan'al called to his counterpart as the groups approached each other, "did you find anyone or anything interesting?"

"Only scrub chickens, scrub and more scrub!" Sh'ban'ol replied, grinning widely. "Not one coconut palm did we find, but we did find two kinds of smaller palms. Thorny, tough-looking plants they are too." The two Sea-Masters sat down together and shared a drink of water while the rest of the men set about making camp for the night. Sh'ban'ol said, "I don't find this island too promising, to tell the truth. The soil looks hard and poor. We found a number of stagnant ponds but no fish bigger than a little finger. How about you?"

Fan'al leaned back on one elbow and sighed. "I too believe this island doesn't hold much promise for us. I wouldn't want to be stranded here for long. There is no coral reef on the west side. A number of little, rocky islands lie not far offshore but the sea around them looks nasty. Even small dugouts with outriggers would have a hard time maneuvering out there. No, I really think we should move on soon. We can't live on scrub chickens forever." There had been the plan to return inland, through the center of the island, but a short venture in that direction the next morning persuaded them all, except for the inquisitive Herbalists, to return around the easier eastern side.

Although the island had numerous springs with good water, still the overall impression was one of harsh, dry foliage in the main and a general poverty of plant species. A'lan, on that previous day, had himself done some exploring directly inland from the beached canoes. Taking Faldo-in and the Herbalist/Healer, Pash'wo with him, they struggled through thick scrub and thorny bushes. With Pash'wo's encouragement they continued for three hours until A'lan finally called a halt. "Enough of this, Pash'wo! We'll go back now. Let's wait until the Sea-Masters return and hear what they've found." Pash'wo, rather to A'lan's surprise, readily agreed.

The following evening saw a general Convocation of all seamen and the Herbalists. Not one voice dissented of the decision to set sail in two days, time enough to stock up on water, smoke-dry some scrub chickens and gather some shellfish from the rocks. The canoes had already been carefully inspected and any needed repairs carried out. The Sea-Masters were satisfied that the two vessels were quite ready to return to duty. The sea called once again.

Chapter Forty Three - A'lan Sea-Master

A'lan had informed Fan'al and Sh'ban'ol that on the night of their landing he had seen underwater emanations indicating other islands not too distant. He felt that the voyage should resume near sunset. After night fell he could scan the sea and determine a proper course for the hours of darkness. They must avoid coming too close to another island in the dark, even though a half moon now lit the early night sky. Sh'ban'ol, himself with *'the sight'*, was so impressed with this young Sea-Hewn's abilities that he quickly saw the sense of his proposal and agreed, as did Fan'al. On the day, the crew all waited impatiently for evening to come.

The Herbalists planted some already shooting coconuts in damp soil while A'lan and the Sea-Masters napped off and on, storing up sleep for a long night ahead. There was to be a major change in staffing on this leg of the voyage. A'lan Sea-Hewn would now sail with Sh'ban'ol aboard 'Wa'Boton'. Faldo-in also would change vessels and these two would be replaced aboard Fan'al's canoe by two other seamen. Everyone seemed happy with the arrangement except Pash'wo, the Herbalist/Healer. He asked that he too move aboard 'Wa'Boton' for reason of some prescience which he never fully described. After some discussion with one of the other Herb-Hewn, all was settled amicably.

The day dragged seemingly endlessly, so anxious were these keen seamen to regain their natural environment. The days of sitting with part of the hulls resting on the beach had seen sand build up around the canoes, requiring some energetic shoveling, pushing and straining but by midday both vessels lay floating, only short sections of their bows still touching shore. Finally the shadows fell long upon the beach, covering the canoes, cooling the sticky, hot air of the day. Last minute loading took only a few minutes. The canoes had been loaded, loads shifted and repacked numerous times already. The launching was going to coincide with mid-tide when there was still good depth of water over the opening in the reef. The trade wind was gusty but steady in direction, the sky clear of any storm cloud and the surge of waves through the reef were small. Everything was ready for departure.

Long bamboo poles were wielded in order to maneuver 'Wa'Boton' bow-first toward the reef and open sea. A loud order rang out and every man save the steersmen jumped to their paddling positions. Moments later the big canoe was gaining speed and moving offshore. When that vessel was well away and nearly at the entrance to this little harbor, 'Wa'Salat' followed suit. Being smaller and lighter it made the turn more quickly. Both vessels' sails' lay loose before the headwind which continued its steady blow. When safely beyond the line of breakers, the paddlers straining to carry their canoes out to deeper water, the order was given to the steersmen to turn their vessels sharply to starboard. The sails were then set and secured for a long tack away from the island, 'Wa'Salat' trailing its larger leader by some three-hundred feet.

The two vessels followed their lengthening shadows into the mounting gloom of dusk until all was shadow upon the sea. Sh'ban'ol' Voyage-Master changed course to a more southerly direction and ordered the torch to be lit and placed aft. 'Wa'Salat' soon answered with a light forward. After a leisurely meal of left-over scrub chicken, A'lan and Sh'ban'ol went to the forward edge of the bridging deck and sat down near each other. Faldo-in Sea-Hewn sat close behind them, this evening an opportunity for him to learn more of how these sighted seamen worked in tandem.

Sh'ban'ol asked that the torch be moved as far aft as possible now. The *'sighted'* seamen required total darkness around them in order to see properly into the depths and read the sea's mysterious messages. The sky this night was nearly empty of cloud and starlight danced its points of illumination over the surface. A 'light-reader' must accustom his eyes to this interference; look beyond and beneath it in order to focus deeper into the sea. Simultaneously the two gifted navigators pointed to what Faldo-in, leaning over their shoulders, could not see. But, keen to improve his navigational skills, Faldo-in swept his eyes upward to study the positions of the stars. He mentally aligned the direction which the two 'sighted' men indicated as the source of light signals from what must surely be an island.

After an hour of this observation, A'lan and the Voyage-Master stood up and stretched themselves and rubbed their eyes, both asking for a drink of water. Theirs was strenuous work, requiring sitting or lying still for long periods of total concentration. Suddenly there was a small commotion among the deck crew aft of them. A school of flying fish had taken wing, soaring over the waves, fleeing some predator. A number had landed on the deck and seamen were darting about the deck, gathering them up before they could escape overboard again. Fresh fish for breakfast!

A'lan's youth, and the intensity of his dedication, allowed him to remain at this demanding occupation for longer than Sh'ban'ol cared to. The older man retired for a short nap inside the sheltering hut amidships. The sea-dew was heavy tonight and the air held a chill one would not expect in these tropical latitudes. Unbidden, Faldo-in brought warm capes for A'lan and himself and sat on the edge of the bridging deck next to his friend, his legs dangling down toward the water. The two chatted about things navigational for a long while, Faldo-in frequently gazing upward at the stars, A'lan down into the depths of the black sea and its esoteric messages. It was Faldo-in who said, "A'lan-an. Do you notice the motion of the canoe? We seem to be encountering some wave action that wasn't there a while ago."

A'lan broke off his gazing and looked up. Slipping into another mode of observation took him a moment or three, like coming out of a daze. "Uh … oh yes! Yes, I feel it now. It's coming from slightly off to our right." A'lan gave Faldo-in a quick pat on the leg and said, "Thank you brother. I was far away. Too far," he added, "I should have noticed that too." A'lan was admonishing himself when, in the light of a new torch being carried aft by another seaman, a shadow fell over the two young Sea-Hewn.

"Well," said Sh'ban'ol, awake now and standing behind the two, "the change in the waves woke me up. From the southwest I think." The big man came and sat down next to Faldo-in, clapping a big hand on the lad's shoulder, asking, "What have you learned tonight, Sea-Hewn?" A'lan was about to offer that Faldo-in had learned not to presume too much about A'lan's discipline but Faldo-in quickly replied, "I've learned that both the 'sea sight' and a knowing of the surface of the sea are equally important, Voyage-Master." There was a momentary silence as Sh'ban'ol looked at both his young canoe-mates in the dim light. "And is the light signal constant from the southwest, A'lan?" The Master bent forward and peered into the depths as if seeking his own answer. There was much there tonight for one of his skill to see.

"Yes, Voyage-Master, and many other signals too. But I think they are quite distant … far behind the strongest, nearest signal. Southwest of us lies at least one island, if not more. I wouldn't be surprised if we can see it, or them, at dawn." There was weariness in A'lan Sea-Hewn's voice and it was noted by the Master. "Right! We shall see. Now, you two seamen go and have some rest. I'll take the balance of this watch. Of course," he said , anticipating their requests,

"I'll call for you immediately anything happens. Go on now. You both will need your strength tomorrow." That was in the tone of an order and A'lan and Faldo-in responded quickly, both rising and going to their respective bunks, one in each hull. Indeed; they would need all their strength!

~ ~ * ~ ~

Dawn brought a shock to the Mal'lam seamen on both vessels. Directly ahead of them lay a line of surf! Shouted commands brought every seaman awake and on deck and scrambling to follow orders to wear the vessels to port. A'lan Sea-Hewn leaped onto the bridging deck from his warm, cozy sleeping platform and gasped in amazement! No! The island couldn't be this close! But it was, and actually, it was not an island. They were headed for the remnants of what had once, thousands of years before, been a series of atolls.

These atolls of coral and residual basalt had of course once been high, volcanic islands but the many millennia of sea-action and settling had left only this awesome barrier to anything which floated. The two canoe's sails filled with the trade wind at an angle which greatly increased their speed and all aboard them began to relax a bit. For three hours they went due north until at last they saw an end to the barrier before them. "We will keep going on this course for a time yet!" shouted Voyage-Master Sh'ban'ol, cupping his hands as he called back to the 'Wa'Salat'. "Keep well astern, brothers. There are dangerous currents here!"

What both 'sighted' Sea-Hewn had never experienced was an atoll! The mass of an island, rising many hundreds of feet above the sea, sent a strong and easily recognizable signal through dark waters to those who could see them. But a random collection of fractured coral reefs with varying depths of seawater immediately around and behind them would send a completely different emanation of energy. Had there been but another hour of darkness before the fortunate dawn of this day, all would have been lost! Both vessels could have run aground … fatally!

A'lan and his Voyage-Master sat in rapt consultation as 'Wa'Boton' ran swiftly with the wind abeam, safely out of harm's way. Both gifted seamen blamed themselves for an oversight which neither were really guilty of. This was, after all, a voyage of exploration and true exploration always reveals many unknowns. It was the wisdom of the Voyage-Master which managed to settle A'lan's self-flagellation into quiet acceptance. "Forget your anger and disappointment, my boy! That's an order! A'lan Sea-Hewn, sometimes you take yourself too seriously. Did you know that?" A'lan took deep breaths before replying, knowing that his mentor was right. Raising his head from its position of submission to a painful truth, he succeeded in giving Sh'ban'ol a hesitant smile "Yes, Voyage-Master. I do understand. Please have patience with me on this. I very nearly brought us all to disaster!"

"No, no more than I did, young A'lan! Have either of us seen such a thing - a reef with no island to attach to? A sudden rising of coral from nowhere - in the middle of the sea? No, we both have much to learn. I thank the Sea Gods and the *Earth Mother* that the decision was made for both of us to be aboard this same vessel. I may be many years older, A'lan, but you are blessed with knowledge which seems to extend from your birth. Let us continue to sail together, learn together, and hopefully, survive together." The two men gripped hands and bowed to each other in mutual respect.

The two canoes continued on their course away to the north of their frightening encounter until no sign of those perilous reefs remained. A meal was served, the wind dropping to a breeze, allowing the cooking fires of the canoes to be fully utilized. Again A'lan and Sh'ban'ol sat together in the shade of a sail in the late afternoon sun and discussed their plans. In a momentary gap in their conversation Sh'ban'ol turned and looked to the eastern sky. "We have company." the Voyage-Master said quietly, nodding toward the source of one of sailing's awesome moments. There in the east rose the early signs of a very large storm. Thin, low clouds were spreading over the sea, moving with noticeable speed. Behind them was a series of high cloud masses with flat tops. As minutes passed, this phenomenon spread across the eastern horizon and rose higher and higher.

"I think it's time we started preparing for a blow, lads!" Sh'ban'ol said loudly, gaining the immediate attention of every seaman aboard. "Let's maintain our present course. We need to be well away from those reefs when the storm gets to us." Sh'ban'ol continued moving about the vessel, calling out orders, checking on lashings, looking into the hull spaces and generally making sure his vessel was in good order. Glancing behind to where the sister canoe followed, he could see that vessel's crew equally busy. One Sea-Hewn whose duty this watch was on a steering oar mentioned to the Master that he had only just noticed that the approaching cloud mass seemed to be moving around itself from right to left. "Strange, Sh'ban'ol. Back in our home waters a big storm like this one coming moves from left to right, if I'm not mistaken." "Yes," replied the Master, "I was noticing that too. But I suspect this one is going to be a big one, no matter which direction it's winding itself in."

An hour passed, then two and the sea took on a grayish hue, reflection of those frightening clouds which were still far away but overwhelming the sky with their approach. The wind began to shift erratically and grow steadily in velocity. Sh'ban'ol Voyage-Master signaled to the smaller vessel to move further away and behind. It was soon going to be 'each vessel for itself' situation! Extra coverings were wrapped around the food supplies and other materials which might suffer damage from inundation with seawater. Every piece of loose equipment was securely lashed down; coils of rope were cleverly lashed in various sites for quick retrieval in case of need and extra guy ropes were attached to the booms supporting the sail panels. A last minute check-over and all had been done that could be done to prepare for the worst. Sh'ban'ol had a queasy feeling of certainty that this storm was going to be horrendous.

All the Mal'lam voyagers could do now was wait; sit and wait! The low clouds fringing the approaching storm were now blocking the sun and a strange color was invading the whole environment; greenish-grey and almost luminous, every seaman growing more nervous in anticipation of what all knew to be a very dangerous situation. Night had fallen very early, the storm clouds so thick that the light above was shut out completely. The wind was ferocious now, spray ripped from wave tops and rain flying horizontally rather than falling. The wave heights grew and grew and there was more randomness than regularity to their flow.

Two men to each steering oar was the order and four men to each sail. These four men, like the oarsmen, had safety lines wrapped around their waists. Their job was to keep the big sail panels parallel to the wind, offering least resistance but also aiding in keeping the big double-hulls facing into the wind and waves. Theirs was the most difficult task on this day and Sh'ban'ol replaced them with four others in rotation every twenty minutes. The Master himself was not guyed to any safety line but roamed the bridging deck, grasping at ropes and whatever solid object was at hand to steady himself. The motion of the vessel was so random, so violent that every seaman had difficulty in keeping his feet.

No torch could survive in this wind so both vessels had lost sight of each other. The noise was like a physical beating, hammering at the men's bodies, creating even greater tension and fear. Then over this noise grew a louder tone; a fearsome screaming was approaching, a sound no one here had ever encountered. It was a waterspout; a sea-Tor'nado born of the tumult in the clouds high above.

Accompanying its approach were bolts of lightning which illuminated this immense apparition from hell! It was headed straight for 'Wa'Boton! A'lan Sea-Hewn stood between the two masts, both hands gripping a stay as he looked up and watched with horror as this wide, screaming wall of water plunged toward him. About him his mates too stood frozen, immanent death staring back at them. But when the wall of the huge column of water was no more than one hundred feet away, it suddenly lifted and broke its contact with the raging sea below. Lightning bolts seared into the sea, marking its leaving and one of these struck the port side of 'Wa'Boton'. The flash of fire and sparks temporarily blinded any man facing that quarter. Voyage-Master Sh'ban'ol had been standing on the port edge of the deck, helping his crewmen control the foremast. Two men had stood beside him, all heaving mightily on a line. Now they were no longer there!

A'lan Sea-Hewn was one whose glance had been in the opposite direction when the bolt of fire had struck and he quickly turned to his left to see what had happened. Shards of fire still ran across the deck on the port side and along the gunnels of the hull. The flaming ends of two stays whipped through the air, blasted and burned away from their lashing posts in an instant. Another series of lightning flashes allowed A'lan to crawl across to where a man was lying still on the deck and peer into his face. The man, his name was Tan'el Sea-Hewn, stared blindly into the sky, his mouth open wide as if expelling a silent scream. A'lan shouted his name and shook the man's shoulders. There was no response. He was dead.

A'lan swept his gaze wildly around the deck, fore and aft. He could not see his Voyage-Master anywhere. Only two men still stood at their post at the stern, on the big oar, desperately clinging to the long shaft which threatened to throw them overboard. All A'lan could think to do at this moment was to go to the men's aid. Then there was someone beside him as he crawled aft. It was Faldo-in, on the same painful journey on hands and knees. "Faldo-in!" A'lan screamed, "Go help the steersmen. I'll get two more men to help. And tie a safety line to yourself!" Another lightning flash revealed the form of two men struggling to regain the stern of the port hull, wave motion lifting them nearly there but then pulling them back again. A'lan stood up now and ran aft. He paused to grab a loose length of rope, tied one end to a deck spar and one end around his own waist. The deck suddenly lifted on a massive wave and A'lan fell backward heavily. Momentarily stunned, he struggled to reorient himself and get moving again. More lightning, almost continuous now and creating illumination which would allow the surviving crewmen to slowly regain themselves and their vessel.

To A'lan everything seemed to be in slow-motion; his own movements and those of the others about him appeared controlled and sensible - but so slow! 'Get men onto the oar!' was his main thought in this long moment. He grabbed the arm of one of the Herbalists, shouted into his ear and released him. The man made his way aft to assist those steersman struggling to re-board the vessel. Then another seaman joined him and together they hauled the half-drowned men onto the bridging deck. Faldo-in was now standing with the steersman, both heaving on the oar, fighting to redirect the canoe which was threatened with broaching.

Another sweep of the deck by A'lan's watering eyes revealed only six more men standing. All six were hanging onto the sail guy ropes but being whipped back and forth by the force of the wildly swinging sail panels. Looking up at the sails now, A'lan could see a large tear in the foresail and two panels blown away from the aft sail. His response was instantaneous. Staggering over the pitching deck he lunged for one of the guy ropes and held on tightly, shouting at the other two men holding it. "Secure this line to a deck spar. There's no use in trying to control the sail now. Tie it down and help the others do the same. Hurry!"

Another lurch of the deck sent him to his knees but he controlled his fall this time. All the while his anxious eyes sought the form of Sh'ban'ol. A loud ripping sound, its source directly above him, brought his attention to the aft sail panel. There it went! Blown overboard and far away somewhere into the surging nightmare which was his beloved sea. A'lan had to pause, catch his breath, sort out what was occurring. He looked out into the lightning splashed darkness and for a moment thought - yes! - was sure that he saw a dim glow of blue surrounding two human figures! No time! No time now for visions. Too much to do. And what was this?! A sudden realization struck him and he shouted a wordless cry of amazement. His face! His face wasn't aching!

In all his time at sea that old scar had plagued him with neuralgia whenever cold had invaded it. But this night, with the stinging seawater blown constantly into his face and the screaming wind like ice, there was no pain there! A surge of lightness flowed upward from his heart and radiated out to all his body. 'Move!' it told him. 'Get moving! Your vessel and your mates need you!'

A'lan was quickly back on his feet and struggling against the movement of the deck to reach those crewmen attempting to tie the sail booms securely to the deck beams. Shouting as loud as he could he assisted them to strain the ropes tightly and quickly tie them down. Then another two men he assisted until the tall, curved booms, the space between mast and boom now vacant of all but remnants of sail panel, were tightly secured. This would have to do. He was not going to go up a mast to add more ropes nor would he order another man to. Order? Who was he to order anyone? Another sweep of his eyes around the deck told him. Sh'ban'ol Sea-Master was gone. The eager willingness of those other seamen to follow his orders in these last few, frantic minutes assured him. He, A'lan Sea-Hewn, was in charge of this vessel now.

Groping his way around the deck again he made a head-count. Twelve men he counted and that one dead man still lying where someone had lashed his body to the bamboo decking. There had been seventeen aboard before the storm hit. Three are missing! A quick look inside the shattered hut revealed no one. Even the non-seamen Herbalists were on deck and joining in the struggle to stay alive. Faldo-in handed over his place on one side of the steering oar and staggered over to A'lan. "A'lan-an! Shouldn't we have some of the men begin bailing?" It was a reasonable question but A'lan hesitated only a moment before shouting back to him, "No, brother. Let the hulls fill up. They won't sink. But filled with water they'll keep us low and prevent us from being overturned. Do you understand what I'm saying?"

The young Sea-Hewn looked at his friend, not comprehending the wisdom of A'lan's words for a moment. A seaman's most important duty was to keep his vessel afloat, surely! Then he remembered the hundreds of coconuts stored inside netting at each end of the deep hulls. They would certainly help.

A'lan waited no longer for a reply but ordered, "Faldo-in. See that everyone has a safety line attached, yourself too. I'm going to secure the steering oar and then I want everyone into the hulls, six men on each side." It was only at this moment that Faldo-in realized that some of the crew were missing. He hesitated a moment, then nodded to A'lan and turned to attend to his tasks. A'lan made his way back to the steersmen's location and assisted in pulling the oar up onto the deck and tying it down. The wind and the sea were now in charge of the motion and direction of this proud craft. All the Mal'lam could do now was to go hull-down and try to stay alive until this terrible storm passed. It already seemed endless.

A series of huge waves had turned 'Wa'Boton' beam-on to the seas. Each wave arrived with a hissing roar, short warning and even shorter intervals between their arrivals. A'lan had tied a heavy section of rope from one hull across to the other, just ahead of the foremast, and he clung to this rope with grim desperation each time a flood of water swept over the deck. His arms ached with the effort of resisting those walls of water which attempted to sweep him off the deck. He wrapped both arms at the elbow onto the rough safety line and pressed his head firmly to the bamboo deck as each wave engulfed him.

A lull in the arrival of those monstrous waves prompted him to pull himself sideways across the deck to check on the other crewmen. In such a wind, words were torn from one's mouth and cast away unheard into the storm. Gripping another safety line laid lengthwise along the edge of the deck he leaned over and shouted at the man sitting aft;

"Are you alright, brother?" He waited until a series of lightning flashes revealed his crew-mate's strained face, that face usually registering a nod or unheard mouthing. He worked his way along the line of cowering seamen, each clinging desperately to the gunnels of the hull. Abeam of the sea. these men were being repeatedly inundated, having to hold their breaths for many seconds until the water subsided. Satisfied that the men in the port hull were surviving

… for now … he painfully pulled himself across the deck and repeated the procedure with the starboard survivors.

Faldo-in was in the front of the starboard hull and when A'lan reached him, his friend grasped his arm and shouted, "Tie yourself down, A'lan-an. Tie yourself down!" A'lan signaled to his good mate to lean forward toward him.

"No!" A'lan shouted into his friend's ear, "If we capsize I might get pinned underneath. Make sure your safety line is long enough to let you surface if we do go over!"

With that A'lan gave Faldo-in's shoulder a punch and crawled back around to repeat his survey of his crewmen. Halfway back across the flooded deck he tucked his arms under the safety rope across the deck and lay his head down for a few seconds of rest, gasping for breath. Then he quickly raised his head and looked forward. Oh no! This one was gigantic! A'lan threw one leg over the restraint line and tucked it under, his two arms clinging as tightly as possible. With a roar the big wave hit them from slightly to port and rushed across the deck four feet deep. 'Those poor brothers in the hulls!' he thought as he pictured them sitting even more deeply in the sea, desperately holding their breaths.

So great was the noise of this huge wall of water that A'lan could not hear the devastation taking place behind him. The wave tore the shattered hut amidships from its moorings and carried it with terrible force against the aft mast. The big baulk of timber on which the foot of the mast sat split and broke apart, allowing the wave to topple the mast backward, three restraining lines parting. With but three other mast stays remaining attached, the heavy, hardwood member fell off the stern and followed the passing remnants of the surge. The thick, strong coir ropes brought the mast's retreat to a halt ten yards aft of the canoe.

What now occurred was the establishment of a very efficient drogue or sea-anchor which effectively kept 'Wa'Olon's' bows pointed into the waves. Regaining himself, A'lan saw that the vessel had again turned bow-on to the waves and strangely, those big breakers were not rushing aboard as they had been. Rather, 'Wa'Boton' was rising up and over the great swells. The drop down the back of those swells was awesome, terrifying! A'lan was cognizant of being steeply pitched downward, his body slipping forward onto his restraining rope. As suddenly, the 'Wa'Boton' bottomed out on the valley of the wave and began to rise again.

This time as he looked forward, searching for the next wave: there they were again! In a sphere of bluish light stood those same two old men who had guided him ashore those days ago on that last island. Great uncle Tal'ma and the Sea-Master Telan! A'lan shook his head and blinked, looked again … Yes! … still there, about fifty yards ahead of the "Wa'Boton' and standing placidly some feet above the raging sea. To each side of the stricken canoe could be seen the whitewater of the crashing waves as they rushed past with watery growls, but now those waves did not crash onto the canoe's bows but ran beneath, lifting but not battering the vessel. A'lan's head slumped down onto the deck again, weariness such as he had never known beckoning sleep. 'No! his mind shouted! No! Get up and check on the men again.' After that last huge inundation he was afraid of what he might find. Hulls empty of seamen? Bodies sinking beneath the tumultuous sea? A'lan the only survivor?

Again the young Sea-Hewn, now Master by default, hauled his bruised body to the port side, his hands still gripping the safety line. Oh, thank the Sea Gods! A blast of lightning revealed six figures still on their paddling seats, all but one with their heads bowed and shoulders hunched against the continuing spray and driving rain. One was looking around and seeing A'lan's form crawling toward him, reached out an arm to him. A'lan grabbed that cold, slippery hand with gratitude, unspeakable relief bringing tears to his eyes which the stinging spray quickly diluted. A'lan grabbed the fore-and-aft safety line and dragged himself along to each man in turn. Some men he had to pound on a shoulder to attract their attention, a simple tap on the arm would not suffice to bring some from the hunched cocoon position they had assumed. Two men even managed a lightning-splashed grin.

Another painful drag across the deck and the starboard hull was seen to, dear Faldo-in the first of the men he reached. Faldo-in's posture was more upright and alert than some of the others and when A'lan reached him his friend threw him a broad grin and pointed forward toward where that mysterious, benign wave action was occurring. The waves still refused to assault 'Wa'Boton's' bows but insisted on running up and under, lifting the canoe but not crashing upon it.

With a handclasp the two parted and A'lan continued on to the other five, one of them, the Herbalist Pash'wo, was also alert and met A'lan's arrival with a two-handed clasp. What a seaman was this landsman! A'lan registered this man's courage and competency with admiration. Then he moved back to the foremast.

With one arm around the hard, wet timber and its rope lashings, he turned to look aft and at the devastation which the now less- frequent flashes of light allowed. A'lan could sense a lessening in the storm's power and ferocity. Straining against cold, resisting muscles, he pulled himself around the mast and looked over the bows. The two old men were gone. He blinked spray out of his vision and looked again. Gone! 'They've done their job.' ran through his mind but his mind was growing fuzzy and concentration difficult. A'lan Sea-Hewn was approaching utter exhaustion.

Dawn's light began weak and watery, no warmth ensuing, but as the battered seamen's eyes responded to its welcome promise, slowly the exhausted survivors pulled themselves, and each other, from the shallow enclosures in which they had been submerged to waist-level for many hours. The vessel still rose and fell on huge waves but that horrendous wind had fled, following its creator into the distance. Only a light sprinkle of rain remained, as if in gentle apology for its forebears' ferocity.

One by one, a man helping a mate up onto the deck and out of the chill water, the other twelve surviving members of this vessel's contingent pulled themselves onto the bamboo bridging-deck. One, Faldo-in Sea-Hewn, gained his feet and stumbled to where his close friend lay amidships, both arms over and under that safety line across the deck. His body lay so slackly that Faldo-in approached him with trepidation. 'No … it can't be!' he thought, kneeling beside his friend's supine form. A gentle prod brought no response. Another push to the man's shoulder … nothing! He then reached out and put both hands to A'lan's shoulder and shook him insistently. A moan and movement answered. Still alive!

The crewmen were beginning to move around the deck now, most searching for fresh water. Those hours of inundation with seawater had left all of them desperate for a good drink. Cupped hands in the deluge from the skies always resulted in salt-infested water to drink. Two, then a third and fourth long bamboo tube of drinking water was hauled from their strongly lashed positions and shared around among the men. Some drank deeply and almost immediately vomited, purging their stomach of all that inadvertently swallowed saltwater. More was offered them and slowly their stomachs filled with sweet, fresh sustenance.

The swells now emanated from behind the vessel, a change in direction so gentle that few of the shattered men aboard 'Wa'Boton' even noticed. The wispy cloud that had presaged that storm now hurried away aft to follow what was left of the cataclysm's ferocity. Soon there was the tropical sun's warmth to replace them and the ocean sighed in relief. Thirst satisfied, the men began to lie down wherever they could and fell into sleeps as deep and healing as was their Master's, he who lay still wrapped in the strong cords of coir which had saved his life many times.

A flock of seabirds, evidence of land, flew near the wreckage of the big canoe and continued beyond, seeking whatever leftovers that storm may have provided. Two huge whales surfaced only sixty feet from the floating mass of timber and fiber, themselves enjoying the relief of calm seas and bright light. One raised its massive head above the water, its own special vision acknowledging that sphere of blue light and those two still figures within it which floated above and near the canoe. A last inhalation and the two behemoths dove and swam away on their journey to the north.

~ ~ * ~ ~

A'lan Sea-Hewn awoke after midday, hot sun causing his body to be bathed in sweat. For many moments he was disoriented; 'where, when and what' questions mumbled through his mind and he had to wipe his eyes to open them properly. His mouth was dry and sticky and he had a raging thirst. But he continued to lay still for a minute or more before committing himself to movement. When finally he raised himself on one elbow his whole body shouted aches of protest. Grimacing, he sat up and looked around him. All over the bridging deck lay the rest of the crew in various postures of exhausted sleep. The only sign of life was their gently moving rib cages as they breathed sleep's quiet dance.

Pushing himself up on his hands, A'lan groaned as he brought his legs beneath him and stood. Very unsteadily! He ached from his feet to the top of his head. Water! He needed water! Looking around he finally saw a hollow bamboo water container lying nearly at his feet, thoughtful act of one of his brothers. A'lan picked up the half full length and raised it to his mouth. Sweet water, quite cool yet in spite of having lain in the sun all morning, poured from the tube into and around his mouth. He choked, coughed, drank again and then stood struggling to hold the water down in his stomach. He succeeded and after waiting a few more moments he again drank deeply. The world slowly began to make sense again.

After one more deep swallow he corked the bamboo tube and bent and laid it down. That movement's attendant pain brought memory flooding back. "By the *Earth Mother's Grace*!" he said out loud. "We have survived!" A man sleeping near him stirred at the sound of the voice. For at least six hours the only sound heard on this vessel had been the gentle splash of the sea and the odd snore. That man nearby was his friend Faldo-in who had lain down near A'lan to seek his own rest.

Gazing about him he straightened a stiff back and began to take stock. 'Wa'Boton' lay so deep in the water that the gentle swell splashed up through the bridging deck's bamboo floor. Every sleeping body was receiving regular rinses of cooling seawater on one side. Ropes lay tangled everywhere and pieces of timber and bamboo were spread about in disorder. Astern the aft mast lay gently undulating in seas which were themselves resting after that terrible recruitment to the storm's fury. Turning forward A'lan looked up at the sad remains of the foremast and its long, curved boom. Not even a shred of sail panel remained there, only torn lengths of the ropes which had held the proud sail in place. This vessel lay deep but level, he thought, and that's a very good sign.

A'lan staggered aft on stiff legs and relieved himself into the deep blue water below. Then he bent onto one knee and splashed water over his head and arms and body, wincing as his hand brushed his right thigh. He looked down and discovered a long gash on that leg, not deep but stinging at a touch. Ah well, cuts and bruises are part of a seaman's day. He had no recollection of what caused it. Shortly his movements about the deck roused other seamen, although that was not his intent. One man rose on one elbow and looked dazedly about. A'lan noticed that his left wrist was splinted and bandaged. Then he saw another man with a bandage around his head. The Herbalist/Healer, Pash'wo, had been busy those many hours ago at first light, attending to the injured before he also succumbed to his exhaustion. Who could know the many acts of bravery and courage which had taken place through those awful hours?

A'lan had recovered substantially by now and was becoming anxious that things must begin to be done. He picked up the water tube he had earlier discarded and went in turn to those men still sleeping and gently roused them, offering them a drink and assisting them to their feet. There was very much to do now to ensure their continued survival and he had to get the men moving again.

First the hulls must be emptied of the stored goods and equipment. Whatever food stores had survived, if indeed any had, must be dried out and some kind of sustenance given the crew. When the hulls were free of encumbrance they must be bailed dry. And that would take hours because in surveying the number of baling scoops, he discovered that more than half of them had been washed away. The spare sail panels, rope and other repair materials must be dried and prepared for use.

Faldo-in Sea-Hewn was first among many seamen who came to him and asked what they should do next. He was given the task of finding the replacement sail panels and spreading them out to dry, forward of the mast. Faldo-in quickly recruited two men, one the Herbalist, to help him. It took over an hour for the crew to recover adequately to organize a proper response to the need. A'lan began each task - emptying the hulls, sorting the contents, etc. - as a pacesetter, never demanding too much of his men, confident that they would soon all find their natural energy level. Then he would move to the next exercise, all the while carefully observing and planning. It didn't look too promising!

Nearly all the foodstuffs were soaked in seawater! 'We'll get heartily sick of coconuts, I think!' he chuckled to himself as he inspected the still-intact bundles of ripe coconuts at each end of each hull. He personally sought out the fishing gear; the tightly plaited human-hair lines, the seashell hooks with their intricate in-curves, the wooden gaff hooks, stone sinkers. All there! There were still water gourds, both full and empty and waiting to be refilled. Twelve eight-foot lengths of hollowed out bamboo still with fresh water and another twelve to be refilled. So, thirst would not be an enemy for a few days yet if the water was used judiciously. Food was the problem! Even the cleverest, most careful packaging of breadfruit paste, *taro* and *pandanus* could not survive total immersion for nearly twenty-four hours. What little food that had been stored for immediate consumption, in the little hut on deck, disappeared with the hut. Fish would have to suffice for the time being.

Soon after A'lan had fallen into a sound sleep on the deck, seabirds had been noticed flying overhead. That meant land was not too far away. When told of this A'lan asked which direction the birds had come from. Not one of the weary seamen had registered that observation. A'lan simply nodded, understanding, sure that he too might have been too exhausted to notice. Two hours later, all the men aboard having combined to complete those various chores, A'lan gave the order they had all been dreading: 'Bail the hulls, brothers!' Familiarity with this tedious task reminded everyone to pace themselves from the beginning. Wide sections of bamboo were cut and shaped to serve as replacement bailers and soon six men in each hull were dipping into the deep water and throwing it overboard.

The weather in this late afternoon was still calm and the horizon continued to plead innocent of any more storms. A'lan took this opportunity to mount the mast for a good look around. He carefully tested each bamboo rung as he climbed, finding two whose rope wrappings were abraded and possibly dangerous. These he cut away and tossed down to the deck and continued cautiously to the top lookout station. There the rungs and the restraining ropes were sound and safe. First he scanned the sky to the west before the sun set too low for clear viewing. The smooth surface continued all around, no wind gusts ruffling the waters anywhere within sight.

On the northern horizon lay a line of cloud but it was of benign formation. Eastward, not a wisp of white showed anywhere, the same to the south. But something was there to the north, indistinct yet but definitely different than anything else in view. Then a call from the deck brought his eyes toward the north again. Birds! Flocks of Gannets were flying low over the sea from the west and heading north. There is land there, he thought, but there is no land-cloud over it. Perhaps it's a very low island. Atolls, most likely but with no cloud above to reflect an atoll's peculiar color signature. He was only guessing. The sea held so little movement that 'Wa'Boton', while surely being carried on some current, was not swinging about at all.

A'lan mentally aligned that hazy apparition there to the north with the position of the starboard bow. He would double-check that again in a few minutes. More flocks of seabirds winged their way home, one flock flying directly above the canoe, a few even peeling off to investigate this strange thing lying placidly on the surface. A'lan found it comforting watching the sleek hunters in their flight back to whatever piece of land lay out there. Satisfied that he knew that island's direction and confident that this coming night's sea conditions would remain calm, he took a last careful look out across the sea and then climbed down to the deck and went to share in that tiresome task of bailing.

The thirteen tired survivors finished their task only after the stars had risen and a half moon was settling toward the western horizon. A last drink of water was passed around along with some scraps of breadfruit paste, only lightly salted and very welcome. The lightened vessel now took on some motion, reflecting the very gentle swaying of the sea's surface. Tomorrow would see the aft mast brought back aboard and work begun on mounting a new sail panel on the forward mast. A'lan took the first watch with Faldo-in. The watches this night would be but two hours long.

A'lan went to the starboard side of the deck and sat down, looking over the hull and into the blackness below. Indeed there was a signature emanating from that island or islands out there to the north. Faldo-in established the star track to that position A'lan was indicating with his arm and then the two close friends sat quietly chatting, watching the stars and absently counting the flashes of meteors which crisscrossed the black velvet roof above.

"Tomorrow we must properly farewell our brothers who have died." A'lan said somberly, Faldo-in nodding silently in reply. "One man, Tan'el Sea-Hewn, was dead when I found him. I'm sure he was killed by the lightning strike which carried Sh'ban'ol, Fon'lo and Stan'la overboard. One of those huge waves which washed over us carried his body away later." Both young men sat in thoughtful silence until suddenly the surface of the sea out from the port side erupted with splashing and flashes of silver. They jumped up together and ran across the deck in anticipation. Flying fish! But not tonight. Those tasty morsels were being chased parallel to the vessel and too far out to stray onto the canoe's deck. Well, anyway, tomorrow they would try some fishing. It was known that in the open sea after a severe storm, most of the natural clumps of flotsam, usually shoreline plant materials washed into the sea from floods ashore, were destroyed or dissipated by wave action. Around these floating islands of material took refuge many species of fish and mollusks. Abandoned by their shelters, these fish must seek another such home in the open ocean and the presently inert canoe might be just such an option for them. Of course, where there are little fish, big fish arrive to feed on them and these were what the Mal'lam seamen hoped to catch. A'lan decided that tonight was as good a time as any to start fishing, since there was little else to do but watch the stars sink into the horizon on one side and rise on the other.

When the first watch gladly relinquished the deck to the next two seamen, A'lan and Faldo-in gratefully sank onto their sleeping platforms. Through that long night men did fish but with little result. One small tuna sacrificed itself and in the morning the crew shared what was but a tiny, raw morsel.

A rising breeze attended sunrise but still the sky remained nearly empty of cloud. A'lan was first up the mast at daybreak, searching eagerly to the north for sign of that island. Again birds flew past them from that direction. Overnight the vessel had swung somewhat and now the bows were pointed hopefully northward. But now was the time for the requiem for the lost, loved brothers whom the sea had claimed. As the sun rose, bringing welcome warmth after a chilly night, A'lan gathered everyone on the rear of the deck. As de-facto Sea-Master now, it was his role to lead the ceremony of remembrance. He naturally possessed no insignia or raiment of that office and stood as did everyone else, wearing a stained and torn *tapa* cloth wrap, the patterns and designs painted on them nearly worn away. Two seamen had located their personal flutes, an instrument many Sea-Hewn owned and played. They began a quiet and soulful tune, not sad or a lament but one with great gentleness and beauty. A ripe coconut had been husked and cleaned of its fibrous covering and along with an adze, was handed to A'lan. The young Sea-Master took the nut and the adze with great solemnity and walked to the very edge of the deck where the steersman usually stood. He began to intone a solemn chant of remembrance, a ceremony which he had learned during his initiation.

"Brothers of the Sea, those who have been called back home by the *Earth Mother*, you know your names but we shall sing them now in our remembrance of you. We are sorry to have lost you from our campfires, our canoes, our celebrations and our voyages. On returning to our earthly homes we will sing your names to your loved ones. Hear us as we send our love and respect to you.

"Sh'ban'al Voyage-Master!

We rejoice in you!

Tan'el Sea-Hewn!

We rejoice in you!

Fon'lo Sea-Hewn!

We rejoice in you!

Stan'la Sea-Hewn!

We rejoice in you!"

"We rejoice in you!" was repeated in unison by all assembled, including the Herb-Hewn, Pash'wo. When this chant was completed, A'lan held the coconut out over the water in his left hand and with the adze he cracked it with one blow, releasing the clear fluid into the sea. Passing the adze behind him to a crewman he tore the nut in half with a practiced twist of both hands and tossed each separately into the water.

> *"Take this offering of one of the Earth Mother's greatest blessings to our people!*
>
> *We will remember you in our hearts for all our lives.*
>
> *Thank you for being who you were."*

With this simple offering the devotional service ended. A'lan was about to turn away and begin the tasks he had outlined for this day's work. Faldo-in Sea-Hewn spoke and halted him.

"A'lan Sea-Hewn, Brother of the Sea, dear friend to us all! We seamen would ask your attention to our intention." Faldo-in stepped back and an older seaman, his name was Po'wan'win, stepped forward to stand immediately in front of the younger man. Po'wan'win reached out and placed a hand on each of A'lan's shoulders. Looking him straight in the eyes, the older seaman said, "Al'an Sea-Hewn. Our seaman brothers have all discussed this subject. We are unanimous in our request that you formally accept the role and station of Sea-Master! As well, given the unique circumstances of this voyage we are all engaged in, we also ask that you accept the role and station of Voyage-Master!" It was then that every man stepped forward and one by one, slapped a hand onto A'lan's left shoulder in a formal recognition of this young Sea-Hewn's advancement. No man there, let alone A'lan, had any notion of refusal. A'lan Sea-Hewn knew himself to be worthy of his brothers' faith in him but had not expected this to happen in this manner, at this time. Tears teased his eyes and his voice momentarily failed him. All he could do for a few seconds was nod his head and try to look serious and 'Masterly'. He failed of course, especially when Faldo-in mischievously looked cross-eyed at him.

"Brothers of the Sea," he was finally able to reply, "I accept your faith in me with great love and respect. With the assistance of *Earth Mother*, all of you and the Sea Gods, whoever they might be, we shall regain not only land but that land where many of our loved ones reside. Thank you for your remembrance too, of those men who have left us. Keep them in your minds always." He paused for a few moments to sweep his glance around to every face and establish a contact there. He finished this rather awkward moment with a broad grin. "Now, you lazy lot! Get back to work!"

As the gathering broke up with a mixture of tears for the departed and laughter at their now-Sea-Master's opportune sense of humor, Faldo-in stood looking from the sidelines, sure of this dear friend's uniqueness. He would sail with no other man in the future, unless this man ordered it. A'lan was now Faldo-in's chosen leader. Many more would follow this decision as time wore on. A'lan Sea-Master's mind was centered on prayers to the *Earth Mother*: "How am I going to do this?"

~ ~ * ~ ~

The whole of that day was taken up with, first, the retrieval and securing of the aft mast and its attendant lines; secondly, the drying, woven panels of the foremast sail were reunited with that glaring emptiness between mast and boom. Initially, the boom had to be lowered and the outside lashings established, then the heavy assemblage was raised up the mast and secured. Additional stays were attached to the mast and the boom. The memory of that storm's violence was not to be forgotten. A'lan Sea-Master stood looking at the completed construction and thought, ' There must be a better way of attaching these wonderful sail panels so that they don't blow away so readily!"

When finally 'Wa'Boton' again had propulsive potential, and the sail stood out proudly waiting for a wind to drive it, no wind yet arrived! The sea was still resting and so, it seemed, was the sky above. But an insistent current was ever carrying the vessel toward its primary goal: that, or those, islands off somewhere to the north. Another day ended with sea birds scooting homeward, Mal'lam bellies grumbling with hunger and the water supply dwindling. Two hour watches were again instituted, A'lan and Faldo-in repeating their first-watch role. The subsequent watches spent much of their time fishing, to no avail. A'lan had seen more indications of land; land near and maybe even larger than that which had revealed itself the night before. But morning saw the wind return, gently at first, almost teasingly, then by mid-morning it was blowing steadily from the southeast, small whitecaps covering the surface and 'Wa'Boton' was again underway.

In the early afternoon A'lan sat talking to a number of off-duty seamen when Pash'wo Herb-Hewn asked to speak with him alone. This was rather unusual, certainly not Sea-Hewn etiquette but A'lan excused himself from his seamen and followed the Herbalist far forward on the deck. Pash'wo turned to A'lan with a grave, somewhat embarrassed expression.

"Voyage-Master A'lan. Forgive my impertinence in interrupting you, but what I have to say is very important." The man cleared his throat nervously, looking down at his feet momentarily. A'lan was baffled. "You are only the third person I have revealed this to, A'lan-an, but you see, I have over the years developed a special sensitivity. The '*sight*', you might say. I don't see visions, rather I am sometimes overwhelmed with certainty about coming events. All too often this certainty is quite disturbing. I am disturbed now. I must tell you that the course on which we are headed is going to bring an occasion of great sadness for us all. I don't know if what is to occur will be on the island we are seeking or sometime before. I'm sorry I can't be more specific." Pash'wo's face held sad regret and he reached out one hand to touch A'lan's arm. "This feeling has grown stronger over the past hours. Please, be wary and very careful. At this very moment I feel chills of foreboding." He then held an arm up for A'lan to see. The hairs on that arm stuck up on goose-bump skin.

A'lan knew the man well enough to take him very seriously. Even without knowledge of his '*sight*', the man's behavior and commitment had been exemplary and had assured A'lan months ago of his reliability. A'lan could only nod his head in recognition of the man's message. "I will keep well in mind what you say, Pash-an. Is there anything else?

"No, Voyage-Master. That is all. But I hope that for once I am wrong." The Herbalist looked away out to sea, toward some certainty which only he knew of.

"Alright, my friend. Thank you." He turned to go back to the seamen but stopped and turned again to Pash'wo. "Does this '*sight*' of yours have anything to do with your abilities as a healer?"

"A great deal - yes." Pash'wo answered. A'lan thought a moment, looked up and out to the north, nodded again and turned away. As he strode back to the seated seamen he called up to the seaman on watch atop the mast. "Faldo-in! Anything to report?" His friend thought this question rather strange. Surely A'lan knew that had he anything to report he would already have said so. But before he could reply, out of the corner of his eye he thought he saw something strange out there to the north. He looked again, squinting against the sun's glare. Yes. But what can that be? It's not a Hoosh, but as big! "Yes A'lan-an, I do see something … just now in fact. To the north, not quite abeam of us. It's large and lying low in the water. As big as a large Hoosh, but it's not one. I really think we should have a look, uh ... Master." Faldo-in wasn't yet accustomed to calling his old friend by his formal rank but A'lan appeared not to notice.

"Well, call out the heading to the steersmen as we go." A'lan then called four men to prepare to adjust sail to head in a northwesterly direction. With this he returned to the forward end of the deck and joined the lookout for whatever they were approaching. Pash'wo was still there, himself gazing intently out over the whitecaps.

Pash'wo looked over to A'lan and said quietly, "This is what I have been sensitive to, Voyage-Master. I can feel its closeness now! Yes. It's out there and not on that island."

"Can you make it out yet, brother?" A'lan called up loudly to Faldo-in. There was a pause before the young lookout answered and then he quickly bent down and shouted, "It's wreckage, A'lan-an! It's 'Wa'Salat'! I'm sure it is!" Faldo-in was gesturing with one arm, waving it up and down excitedly. "Can you see it yet?"

"Not yet." was the reply and now a second seaman climbed up the mast to add his eyes to the search. Soon that man called down his confirmation. Indeed it was 'Wa'Salat' - rather, what was left of it. "Waaaahooooh!" shouted Faldo-in. "'Wa'Salat'! Can you hear us?" No reply and the men above saw no movement. Now the wreckage was becoming visible from deck level. A'lan ordered a course change. He wanted to come to the canoe from downwind, slow and easy. The maneuver took a painfully long time to execute, every man aboard 'Wa'Boton' calling out hopeful greetings. When the lookouts called down that there was no sign of movement, the shouting faded away. For five tense minutes 'Wa'Boton' ran past the stricken vessel for a hundred yards before turning and coming back against the wind.

"Paddlers, take your positions!" A'lan cried, and himself sat down with paddle in hand. They would approach 'Wa'Salat' on the windward side and allow the wind pressure to push them against the hull of the wreckage. When only fifty yards away the order to the paddlers was given and the sail was let go to swing free with no resistance to the wind. Eight men paddled powerfully while the two steersmen remained at their posts to guide the vessel. Three others remained standing on the starboard side, ready to leap aboard with ropes to secure the stricken canoe to their own hull. Closer, closer, the choppy sea making things a bit difficult. And then they were there!

The decking aboard 'Wa'Salat' was a shambles; bamboo deck pieces were torn loose and lay bunched among a tangle of ropes, large gaps making leaping aboard dangerous. There was no sign of the masts. Both hulls were filled with water nearly to the top of the gunnels. A'lan put down his paddle and joined the three men standing as they carefully made their way from one hull, theirs, to that of the wreck. On 'Wa'Boton's' starboard side the four paddlers there remained on duty, struggling to keep their vessel snugged against the side of 'Wa'Salat'. "Be careful, men! That deck is dangerous. Get a good handhold as you go." A'lan Voyage-Master was as anxious as anyone to get aboard but he could see that the connection between the two hulls was extremely precarious.

Finally 'Wa'Boton' was securely lashed to its sister vessel and more men began making their way across. "Voyage-Master!" Faldo-in said, standing looking down into the canoe's far hull. He looked to see that A'lan was coming, then knelt and climbed down into the flooded hull. A'lan followed closely, stopped and gazed for a moment at something down there and then followed his friend into the hull. Moments later they had pulled the upper body of a man up onto the gunnel. Other hands arrived to assist and soon they had the drowned body of a seaman whom all recognized as Sea-Master Fan'al, laid out on the remnant of bamboo deck. Moans and choked sobs rose in a sad unison among 'Wa'Boton's' crew.

Now another cry for help came from what had been the proud bow of one hull. Another seaman had found something. Scrambling carefully, the would-be rescuers moved to that spot. Again there was the sound of sorrow. Three men took hold of a rope which was lashed to the deck beam nearest the bow and lifted. It was the Herbalist, Selta'lan, who had agreed to swap places with Pash'wo those days ago. But lifting his body aboard was less strain. Sharks had taken both legs and part of his torso. Still aboard 'Wa'Boton' but watching carefully, Pash'wo Herb-Master turned away and vomited. That man had been Pash'wo's closest friend since childhood. The Herb-Master fell to his knees and wept bitterly. His were not the only tears on this awful afternoon for many among the surviving seamen acknowledged the wrenching loss of so many of their compatriots. Of the thirty Sea-Hewn and Herb-Hewn members of this expedition, now only thirteen survived. Sorrow urged return to land, to safety and many more familiar faces. A'lan Sea-Master stood looking at his grieving brothers and the wreckage of half of this voyage's strength. Turn back? To where? The living needed water and food. The dead needed proper burial. Was there any other option? No!

"Brothers!" A'lans voice was loud and demanding. "We must not linger here, sorry as this experience is. Bring our seamen-brother's bodies aboard 'Wa'Boton'. We will give them proper burial later. What must be done now is to salvage what is of value to us, the living. Gather all materials which we may require in the future from the sad remains of our beloved 'Wa'Salat'. All ropes and lines which are useable, bring them aboard. Any water containers, empty or full, bring them too. You all know what we may need on our return journey. Do what is needed, and know that our fellows' spirits sail with us.

A'lan stepped back aboard 'Wa'Boton' and went to the bow of one of the hulls and sat alone for many minutes while his crew went about their unquestioned duties. Minutes later a gentle hand was laid on his shoulder and he turned to face Herb-Master Pash'wo.

"A'lan-an? Excuse my intrusion again, brother. I have something more of importance to tell you." A'lan turned and smiled weakly at the Herbalist, sure that what the man had to say was indeed of importance. "Unfortunately, my previous prediction was gruesomely correct. However, my friend, what I have to tell you now is very much different. My impressions are that tomorrow will see you leading us to a safe haven where water and food will abound. I promise you that! Also, there will be other events which will make this seemingly disastrous voyage full of promise and fulfillment. I share your grief and your sorrow, believe me. I would be the last man aboard to advise you on seamanship, Voyage-Master. You know that. But what I can tell you, with the certainty of my very life, is that the course you have already chosen for this and the many days forward will be the salvation of us all." Pash'wo gave A'lan a warm smile and laid his hand on A'lan's shoulder briefly. Then he rose quickly and went to assist in the tasks which the rest of the crew were engaged in. A'lan too rose and followed this strange man. How could he ignore good news?

Research Notes: Impressions and General Observations

Subject: External Developments of Importance, Honolulu, Fall 1975

Whew! I can see why Tina thinks the man was special. We spent six weeks going over her transcript and doing a lot of editing. Tina's Spirits were very verbose throughout and I have to admit that we did a lot of cutting … but no pasting!

Two months ago I asked Jiro's secretary, Nina, to send a letter I had written to the Norwegian archaeologist, Thor Heyerdahl. Jiro intercepted it and added an introduction of his own, bless his cotton socks! She sent it on his letterhead. A week ago I received a reply. The controversy over his theories is well documented but I won't go into the intricacies of all that business. Suffice it to say that I was staggered by his reply: 'Dear lady,' he said, 'While some of your sources must unfortunately remain suspect, in scientific terms, nevertheless your thesis deserves careful study.' He carried on for a number of sentences and ended with, 'I hope that you will not be dissuaded from your continuing research. I know of Professor Yukihara's reputation and I am sure that, with his continued support, you may well discover another avenue through which we may yet grow closer to the truth of what actually occurred in those shadowy centuries. With kind regards and best wishes . . . And he actually signed it freehand!

Well, when I'd finally come down off the ceiling after Jiro had read the letter to me in his office, he grinned that devil grin of his and said, 'So, what do you say to that?'

For possibly the second time in my life I was speechless - the first time was when Jiro asked me to marry him. I stuttered and stammered and finally he said . . . 'Wassa matta? You got stuck mouf, lady?'

Our baby girl is growing weed-like and her teeth have developed to the point where she now gets her milk from a bottle. I am conducting two more classes this Fall and Tina is growing into a little Hawai'ian beauty and Jiro swears he's going to start setting bear traps around the place, the suitors are so numerous. Tutu Kinau has asked us over to Hanalei for Thanksgiving, saying she has some special messages for us all. Another great year? You can bet your bippy!

Chapter Forty Four - The Relief Fleet

Ven'ana Herb-Plait, the Headwoman of 'Win'no'hi-Set', had been coming here to this high headland for the past three days. Her psychic contacts had been signaling her for days that a number of canoes would be arriving soon. Not how many or exactly when but the messages were clear and repetitive. The Mal'lam were returning here to bring food plants, pigs and chickens and dogs, bamboo plants and many of the items which made life good for the Mal'lam. More people too, Ven'ana hoped, people who would remain and swell this beautiful island's population. A second child had been born and another young Herb-Mistress was pregnant. But with only eleven adults and only two of those of child-bearing age, the population here could only diminish without more immigrants.

It was cloudless but very hazy over the sea today. The haze welded the sea and sky together in a bright grey oneness, the horizon totally obscured. The middle-aged 'seer' and Herb-Mistress sat with her dear friend-not-yet-husband, Al'walla. He was whittling a tool handle while passing time and she was sorting and tying bundles of herbs. From time to time one or the other would squint against the glare and peer out onto the ocean. Al'walla, possessing no 'sight' of his own, nevertheless held complete faith in Ven'ana's capabilities in that regard. He knew the canoes would come. He daydreamed of bananas, chicken baked in an earth oven, young pig similarly baked and stuffed with yams; on and on his wish list grew until he could no longer stand it. Rummaging in a woven basket near him he found the rather stringy, overcooked drumstick of one of the native flightless birds which were becoming ever harder to find on this side of the island. It would suffice, he reckoned.

"There!" Ven'ana shouted. Al'walla nearly choked on his drumstick. "Where?" he responded, still swallowing around the question. "Can't you see? Out there!" He followed the point of her finger, leaning closer to her to do so. Then Ven'ana was on her feet and jumping up and down. Al'walla finished gnawing on the bone, threw it aside and stood beside her. She threw him a glower, as if to say, 'Aren't you excited?'

"It'll take them a while to get here you know. No hurry." but he bent and picked up the basket and other items which were spread out around them and slowly followed her charge downhill to alert the little community. Halfway down she stopped and sent back another glower. He picked up the pace a bit. She shook her head and broke into a run downhill to inform the others.

The view which slowly emerged from the haze brought shouts of joy from the people aboard the three voyaging canoes. The Voyage-Master, Ska'el aboard 'Wa'Cho'sho', accepted congratulations from his crewmembers with a grateful smile. 'How much closer could one get?" he thought. The young seaman, 'Three Finger', was up the forward mast and called down that the opening in the girdle of rock around the island was in view but the vessel would have to approach from further to the left. Ska'el so ordered and crewmen moved quickly to adjust the sails while the steersmen pushed to the right on their oar.

Aboard the three canoes, 'Wa'Cho'sho', Wa' Ter'ora' and Wa'Mal'lan', rode seventy-three Mal'lam. The storage holds in the canoes' hulls held a total of three tons of plants, stone tools and sundry materials needed for the eleven voluntary castaways as well as for the twenty-five other Mal'lam who intended to remain here. Cages on each vessel held chickens and pigs; the small, curl-tailed, 'barkless' dogs were allowed free reign to roam the decks. Quarters were tight on the canoes and all looked forward to some greater freedom of movement. Sea-Hewn were used to the limiting space aboard their vessels but for many of the non-sailors, this relatively short voyage of twelve days had seemed endless. There had been a steady beam wind for the whole of the voyage and only squalls and some large swell action had brought any real discomfort to the landlubbers. The seamen thought it unusually smooth sailing.

Except for 'Three Finger', Shen'ham Sea-Hewn, and three others of the crew of 'Wa'Rantar' on its voyage from this island, all the seamen including the Sea-Masters were experiencing their longest voyage into unfamiliar seas. Shen'ham had reluctantly agreed to Ch'om'lo's vigorous suggestion that he attend this passage and return. Tina-an Earth-Plait had been upset for a time, reluctant for her lover to sail away. He had suggested that she too come along but Tina-an was still hesitant about leaving her beloved island of Sht'ah Lee. She still was of the belief that her Spirit mentor, The Vesa'tan, would be beyond her reach. Talented and independent as she was, Tina still had much to learn.

Once he had made up his mind, Shen'ham could hardly wait to be back upon the sea. He knew that his presence aboard the canoes was vital for only he and one other of his crew-mates from that previous voyage were truly confident of their navigational ability. Each was certain that he could find the way back. Both were right. Youth was definitely in the forefront of Mal'lam sailing at this juncture of their people's progress. It took the wisdom of the Elders to make the right decisions and the energy and talent of youth to carry them out. Perhaps an added strength which aided the Mal'lam was that respect and admiration ran both ways between the Elders and the young. The Elders seldom forgot what it was to be young. The young loved and respected their Elders because of that. This dynamism which now ran throughout Mal'lam society was aided by Spirit; the spirit of those who had passed from this world but always remained to assist. Those Mal'lam with special sensitivity to the Spirit, 'seers', were more than ever imbued with helpful intercession; so much so that some of the most elderly of the gifted complained of not enjoying a good night's sleep without having to reply to a helpful, well-meaning spirit who always seemed to carry some message which must be addressed immediately. 'May we live in peaceful times!' might have been their lament. 'Oh, *Earth Mother*, where are you leading us?"

This group of Mal'lam, with a sprinkling of Itin among them, were about to enjoy the rich destination to which they had been led. 'Win'no'hi-Set', as they neared land, appeared green and inviting. The day's hazy envelopment was thinning and blue sky allowed a bright sun to illuminate the run into the little harbor. It was a wind shift which carried away the haze and suddenly made the approach to land problematic. The three vessels were now confronted with a headwind which blew across the island, the mass of the island creating tricky swirls of breeze. This was when the innovation of furling the sail panels proved most advantageous. "Take in the sails!" was Voyage-Master Ska'el's order. "Paddlers, take your places!" Shen'ham came quickly down from his perch atop the mast and joined his Sea-Hewn mates in preparation to drive the canoe through the gap with arm-power alone. Behind 'Wa'cho'sho' the other two canoes were maneuvering to come into land with a wide space between them, waiting to see the progress of the Voyage-Master's entrance.

Ashore, the waiting Mal'lam could not restrain their excitement. Two men lit a large bonfire. It was no longer needed as an aid to navigation. It was a celebratory signal of welcome and relief. The eleven adult occupants of this island whooped and danced with joy on the sandy beach as they watched the vessels maneuver toward them, the two tiny children being held up to see what they surely could not understand. Nevertheless, their bright smiles responded to the joy around them.

'Wa'cho'sho' breached the opening to the little lagoon with ease, the paddlers driving hard, the swell ever behind and assisting. Five minute later the second vessel, 'Wa'Ter'ora' likewise slipped easily into the calm waters, following its leader toward the beach. "Wa'Malan' was even closer behind, having kept its sails aloft and catching a sideways breeze until the last moment. Its Master, the young Sea-Master, Chom'shul, had become a true expert at sail handling and he didn't give the order to his paddlers until wind alone had driven his canoe onto the first great wave which poured through the entrance. Before the first vessel had landed, all three were within the confines of this little harbor and shouts, chants and cries of greeting rang across the curving, sandy foreshore. The first of the Mal'lam intentional settlement voyages was drawing to a close!

~ ~ * ~ ~

The beach on Win'no'hi rang with shouts and greetings and to the eleven castaways, this was a more wonderful moment than even their fondest dreams over the past two years had conjured. Old friends, some family and loved ones and a few Itin strangers climbed hurriedly from the decks of the three canoes and were immediately smothered in hugs and kisses. Sea-Masters called to their crews to secure their vessels high on the sand and soon every available seaman was hauling on ropes or pushing the hulls. Women too joined in the effort, especially those who were intent that this visitation would not end until those vessels were emptied of all the food and materials which they contained. Never had three large voyaging canoes been unloaded in so short a time.

In response to Ven'ana's declarations that this little fleet was soon to arrive, pens for the chickens and pigs had been constructed along with temporary shelters for the arriving humans. The little dogs ran about excitedly and were picked up and claimed by the 'locals'; not as food but as pets, for such were sorely missed here on this island bereft of furry animals. The young banana, taro, sugar cane and all the other plants and cuttings were carefully carried into the shade and given fresh water. *Taro* paddies and garden beds had been in preparation for months and would soon be full of green shoots and tubers. In fact, so advanced in growth were many of the new imports that they would require immediate attention. But that would wait until tomorrow. Today was party day!

Two of the pigs were slaughtered immediately as well as a dozen roosters and they went into an earth oven along with bunches of green bananas, taro, breadfruit and fish and local mussels and oysters. Drums and flutes and stringed instruments signaled the beginning of dancing and singing and chanting such as this island had never heard. Bamboo tubes of palm toddy were brought out and some of the 'local' men were soon tipsy and leading the dancing and singing, all lost in an inebriation which created endless smiles of joy.

All the newcomers commented on one surprising, unfamiliar visual aspect of this wonderful beach scene; there were no coconut palms! Those few nuts which had been left here and planted on the discovery voyage were but five feet high now and years away from fruiting. But the 'locals' soon availed themselves of the green drinking nuts which had also arrived, savoring the soft, sweet 'spoon-meat' inside. One thousand coconuts, mostly the ripe ones, had been brought. They were first aboard at loading and filled the bottoms of the hulls to a depth of two feet. Five hundred of these were destined for planting only.

The celebrations wore on until first light, a few hardy souls sitting about still chatting.The beach was littered with sleeping forms on this warm pre-dawn and for the first time the sound of the rooster's crow was heard on 'Win'no'hi-Set'. A number of the castaways woke to this welcome sound for they had pined for the morning herald's song. Snorts and snuffles issued from the pig pens along with a distinctive odor. Soon there would be manure to add to the banana crop. The round, stone-lined beds for the plants had already been deeply covered in leaf mould and seaweed in preparation. Great ceremony would attend these joyous plantings, the Herbalists chanting special invocations to the *Earth Mother* while the first watering took place. This was the time for 'new beginnings' indeed, Voyage-Master Al'malan's naming of this island being most apt.

As always, 'Three Finger' was concerned with the condition of the canoes, more so than he was curious about what the few inhabitants had achieved in two years here. There was time for that. After all, he had been here before, although not in very good condition, recovering as he was from losing those two fingers. This was to be a quick turnaround voyage only. He worked steadily with the older Sea-Hewn on the inspection and repair of the three canoes. As with any voyage, short or long, there was always wear and tear; lashings needed tightening or replacing, timber or bamboo members might have split or broken - on the list went. The big sail panels were removed and inspected for weaknesses and this was always a difficult task, even with the newly installed lashing system. All the interior framing and platforms were removed and the interior of the hulls allowed to dry out. Those hundreds of pounds of coconuts, evenly distributed fore and aft in each hull were all removed and distributed; some for the immediate use by the oil-starved 'locals' but most consigned to a number of plantation sites. Many of these nuts were already sprouting, the dousing in seawater during the voyage of no consequence to them because the coconut actually thrives adjacent to the sea.

The newcomers, seamen and landsmen and women alike, spent eager, enthralled days exploring 'Win'no'hi-Set'. The major source of the islander's protein had been, and would remain for a while yet, the millions of shellfish which lined the rocky shorelines. Mussels and oysters abounded everywhere, a delight to the newcomers. The flightless birds were harder to find now but both fascinating and delicious to the newly arrived Mal'lam and Itin. On a large, treeless rock off the southern shore was a seabird rookery, its inhabitant's squawking and shrieking audible from the main island when the wind was right. Up closer, from the small canoe which was so valuable to the eleven inhabitants, the smell was quite overwhelming. But the eggs were delicious. The newly-arrived Sea-Hewn, some of whom had already decided to remain here, declared the intention to immediately begin the construction of new canoes for fishing.

Herein lay a problem for the Sea-Masters, especially for Voyage-Master Ska'el. If too many seamen decided to remain here, and it was their right to chose to do so, then there might not be enough crew to return the three canoes to Sht'ah Lee. Also there was the consideration of the potential disparity in male-to-female ratio. Among the twenty-five new settlers there were only eight unattached women. Already three of the 'local' men were anxious for some female companionship. In consultation with the island's Headmistress, Ven'ana, it was agreed that a closer ratio must be established until the next voyage brought more settlers. Therefore only six men of the crews would be allowed to remain.

Still, that number could short-hand one of the vessels because the canoes had been assigned a bare minimum of crew on the way here. It had been felt that many of the landsmen and women would be able to assist in the sailing in case of emergency. But going back short-handed when the season of sudden storms was approaching could pose a danger to one or all of the returning canoes. There was, of course, a simple option; one canoe would have to remain here! And the more the Sea-Masters debated the prospect the more sense it made. The ten seamen remaining on 'Win'no'hi' could man the canoe, 'Wa'Ter'ora' in local waters, exploring for other islands nearby which '*seers*' had divined. The proper maintenance of the canoe would be assured and future voyages would bring extra seamen to fill its compliment for the ongoing voyages to the islands of the Tarbara'ut. Another asset for the Mal'lam was that the Master of 'Wa'Ter'ora' could take over another vessel back 'home', one of the new canoes now nearing completion. Still the Masters continued their debate for another week before deciding.

But Shen'ham 'Three Finger' took no part in the discussion. He was going back, no matter what. Tina-an's absence was a gnawing ache in his heart. He did take time to paddle and sail around this lovely island in its one double-outrigger dugout. The young Sea-Hewn who had remained here, Jo'shan, with whom he had apprenticed, was a good friend and Shen'ham rejoiced in his company in this lonely time.

"When do you think the Sea-Masters will make their final decision, Shen'ham?" his friend asked, knowing that this seaman had risen in the unofficial ranks of the Sea-Hewn and must surely be privy to more information.

"I'm not really certain, Shan-an, but I think we should know at the general Convocation tomorrow night." Shen'ham spoke candidly for he too wished the Masters would speed up their long debate. The Mal'lam tradition of rather tedious, long-winded debate on almost any subject tended to annoy the young and impatient. "Have you thought about returning with us to Sht'ah Lee, Shan-an?"

"I have. I would like to see my family again soon rather than waiting for the main voyage to get here. "It was then that Shen'ham told him of the decision of the Sea-Masters to send the voyagers in smaller groups rather than in one mighty fleet. "Should I speak with the Voyage-Master soon then, if I want to return?"

"I would, certainly. I suspect that only two canoes will return and that they might already be assigning crew to two vessels." Shen'ham smiled at his friend and said, "I'd be really happy if you did come back with me." Then 'Three Finger' frowned and said almost absently, "I wonder what A'lan and Faldo-in are up to now?" The two young seamen turned the little dugout back toward the beach, seven large fish in the bottom of the canoe testament to their skills.

~ ~ * ~ ~

One month and four days after their arrival the two vessels of the relief fleet turned toward the northeast, biding farewell for now to the crowd on the beach. The crew could just make out the canoe, 'Wa'Ter'ora' in its shed high on the sand beneath the big, spreading trees. Dismantled now, its two hulls separated and braced, it would wait out the approaching rainy season.

This day's sailing was accompanied by strong winds from the west, perfect conditions for the start of their run back to Sht'ah Lee. There were twelve crewmen aboard each canoe. Shen'ham and Jo'shan rode aboard 'Wa' Mal'lan' with Ch'om'shul in command. Kal'lat'on Sea-Master rode as guest Master aboard 'Wa'Cho'sho', quite happy to take his turn at watches so that he could exercise his *sea sight*. Storms there were but none severe and the winds continued to shift from west to south, both advantageous to the little flotilla's progress toward home.

In only eight days the great dome of Volan Votu raised its snowy head to greet them, its lower slopes covered in thick rain clouds. But not before time for all those aboard the canoes; only a skimpy ration of food had been consigned aboard each vessel, nearly all the sea rations having been left behind for the new settlers. Twenty-four seamen looked forward to a celebratory feast upon arrival. Two hours before arrival off Dolphin Bay they sighted another canoe, large and apparently new, out for a training run and now heading home. That canoe, well ahead of the two voyagers, raised a long white pennant in recognition and greeting and continued on its own course for home. Yes! It's good to be home.

But there was not to be a celebration that night. Sht'ah Lee was in turmoil! For the first time in Mal'lam memory, Sht'ah Lee-Set had been shaken by a series of powerful earthquakes. They had begun a little past midday and now as the sun was heading for the horizon, the last and weakest had just ceased its rumblings. The canoe ahead of them had been at sea all day and it too was ignorant of the dramas ashore.

Because Mal'lam dwellings were lightly constructed and relatively small, the collapse of some buildings did little or no harm to individuals in and about them. Huge landslides occurred in the upper forests but fortunately no people were up in the mountains this day. Many days of rain had seen the cutters and haulers of timber retreat back down to the villages and some dry shelter. Very strangely, no *seer* predicted this event. Only vague intimations of some possible calamity occurred. Such was the tenor of these times that most assumed that the warnings had to do with some activity of the *Ja'jan an-lo.* No one was known to have ventured a guess at such a happening. No one that is, except Tina-an Earth-Plait.

Tina-an had sat with a rain cape around her shoulders, trying to decide if she should go home. This rain didn't seem to want to quit. Two days already it had poured down and she was convinced it was never going to stop. Tina was capable of feeling sorry for herself on occasion. She had come here this time especially to try to establish contact with her loved one, Shen'ham. Although she strove continually to develop this kind of sensitivity, it just wasn't working. It wasn't just the rain or the frustration though which was causing a deep feeling of foreboding in her. It was time to try to contact her mentor, her beloved, The Vesa'tan. Her amulet, that small blue stone which she wore around her neck suspended on the woven, shed skins of the 'Bota' snake, she believed was her only passport to contacting this powerful Spirit. As she began packing her damp carry-all with even damper spare wraps and a blanket, the stone began to glow and she could feel its growing warmth at her throat. The Vesa'tan was calling!

Tina-an retreated to beneath a large-leafed tree, partial protection against this nuisance rain. She sat and held the stone in her palm, feeling its smoothness grow ever warmer. Then came that familiar sensation of hearing a voice when no voice should be there.

"Tina-an, my dear. Are you cranky today?" The impression received was one of gentle mockery - an admonition. She didn't reply but sat quietly, nodding in spite of herself, listening. "I have important things to tell you today, my sweet. Therefore, clear your mind of petty annoyances and listen carefully to me."

Tina did as she was ordered, by the only entity on the planet who's orders she attended without argument. She took a number of deep breathes and did succeed in forgetting everything but the fact that now was the time to listen very closely.

"My dear child, and you will always be a dear child to me … our beloved mountain, Volan Votu, is in agony .Within its belly is growing a savage fire which will soon become evident to every living thing upon this land. Just as I had hoped, when still I lived among you, that this island would avoid the terrors our sister islands suffered, so I now hope that my message comes to the Mal'lam people in time. You must all prepare for great changes. Sht'ah Lee too will one day sink beneath the waves. That day is within your own lifetime, Tina-an! I am so sorry to tell you this because I know how much you love this island." The Vesa'tan's voice held a hint of tears and that sound brought a flood of tears to Tina's eyes and they mixed with the continuing rain.

Tina knew from long experience that to ask questions, let alone directly query The Vesa'tan's messages, was stupid. She was here to listen, remember and think and then act if action was needed. The rest of the message was offered to her with great love and concern - from somewhere beyond?

"I have little time now, my dear one, so listen carefully. The *Earth Mother* has surely planned much ahead - again! And She continues to guide those who will listen to her. Just so did your Sea-Hewn plan their voyaging - with guidance! And now you must take to the Sea-Masters and all the Elders this message of urgency: the Mal'lam must leave Sht'ah Lee within a year - no longer! Voyages must proceed as the opportunity arises. And one other thing, my dear child. There must be peace between the Mal'lam and the person who calls herself, *Ja'jan*. In her heart this poor, unfortunate woman is still but Ja'eel Feather-Plait, a child who has lost her way. It is you, Tina-an Earth-Plait, who will help her to find a way to peace!" That statement deserved a hundred questions. Tina asked none. And then that beloved presence was gone, the warmth was receding from the blue stone at her neck and the moment was over.

"Me? Talk to *Ja'jan*?" Tina now gathered all her possessions and began the long descent down to the main village of her people. The rain began to let up but the trail was slippery and dangerous, even for one with Tina's competence. Slipping and sliding, she finally stopped and broke off a sapling to use as a trail stick. That helped. All the while Tina struggled with her mind. "How can I possibly have any influence over *Ja'jan*? She hates me because I'm Sh'tana's sister!" This internal dialog continued until the village came into sight. The early afternoon sky was clear now and the air was warming up. Instead of heading directly for her mother's hut, Tina made for the hut of the Herb-Mistress, Shen'ha. There she found both Shen'ha and her mother engaged in some serious discussion. They greeted Tina with their usual warmth but Tina sensed that they wished to continue their conversation alone. Whatever the subject was, it would have to wait. Tina-an sat down between the two women and cleared her throat twice, still undecided how to proceed with her message.

"Forgive me for intruding, mother and Shen'ha, but I have brought a message from The Vesa'tan. You really must hear this now!" Shen'ha sighed tolerantly and nodded for Tina to continue.
 "We are informed by The Vesa'tan that our island, this Sht'ah Lee which we love, is going to be destroyed!" Tina paused to watch their reaction. Her mother's jaw dropped and she inclined her head toward her daughter as if unbelieving what she had heard. Tina was surprised to see Shen'ha nod her head slightly and look intently into Tina's face. "Go ahead Tina, we're listening."

"I am told that I must bring this message to all the Elders. The Vesa'tan says we have only a year, no more, to leave Sht'ah Lee" Tina then asked for a drink of water for her mouth was dry with the tension and the implied disastrous situation. Shen'ha reached behind her and produced a small gourd of water. Tina-an drank deeply, wiped her mouth and began again.

"And that's not all. I don't know what to do with this part of the message. I need both of you to help me with this." Tina shifted nervously and looked up to the ceiling of the hut, stalling for a few moments before revealing what to her was even more disturbing than the destruction of her beloved island. Her mother and her lover's mother both leaned forward toward her, offering their silent support. And then the first of the powerful tremors struck!

Shouts and screams issued from outside the little hut where the three women gripped the ground with outstretched hands, fighting to maintain even the balance of a sitting position. The three sat with wide eyes, their mouths open. Dry bits of thatching showered down upon them and the hut groaned frighteningly. It was Tina who first tried to stand, failed that and had to crawl out through the open door of the swaying hut. Shen'ha and Sha'lat followed in like manner. Outside was a chaos of violently swinging palm trees, swaying huts and people running, falling, crawling and many screaming in fear. Those who had experienced the demise of the island of Sh'ham were among the most frightened, unbelieving that this island of refuge would itself betray them.

Adding to the cacophony was a shrill squealing from the pig pens and from those pigs allowed to roam free within the village compound. The air was filled with birds flying frantically in every direction and across the open spaces chickens fled in a flurry of feathers. Dogs were howling, even the normally silent short-legged species. In the canoe sheds Wood-Hewn braced themselves against hulls, and then found themselves pushing against them to keep them from falling off their mountings. Some did and one man sustained a broken leg. In the fields and paddies workers fell about in the mud, stunned with disbelief. Then stone irrigation channels and weirs ruptured and those field workers found themselves struggling against sometimes dangerously deep rushes of water.

In the territory of the *Ja'jan an-lo*, less well-constructed shelters collapsed causing cuts and bruises. *Ja'jan's* own hut caved in on the back side and she struggled desperately on hands and knees to exit her private lodgings, a silent handmaiden, Jana'la, right behind her. What would not be known until the following day was that the stone platform constructed for her ceremonies of sacrifice on the full moon had broken right through the center. The platform, four feet high and ten by thirty feet wide and long, had been sited on an ancient fissure in the earth which time had nearly hidden. The workmen who constructed it had only scoffed when the Stone-Master in charge of the project had pointed it out. Nothing could harm the Mistress's special construction, surely! After all, the Goddess had chosen the very site. Don't worry! Well, now one half lay elevated a foot above the other half. The quake had brought that ancient fissure to life again.

The *Ja'jan an-lo* were as frightened as anyone on this stricken island. *Ja'jan* herself was terrified! *Ja'jan,* for all her theatrics, monstrous ego and blustering certainties, knew that what was occurring was beyond even her capacity to comprehend, let alone to prevent. Her own shuddering continued until after the earth fell silent and still beneath her feet. This earthquake and what it foreboded shook her to her core. Those to follow would crush her confidence utterly.

"Do not fear, loved ones!" she finally brought herself to cry out, her voice high with panic. "'The Goddess of the Skies' has come to punish our enemies. See? Everyone here is unharmed." she lied. "Now, return to your tasks. Help with repairing what has been damaged. All will be well." This was said with a hint of certainty with no basis. With this she gathered her closest associates … her father and Jana'la Feather-Plait … and hurried away to a secluded hideaway far from her village, which no one else used. No sooner had she settled into discussion with Sho'sha'lo Chief Priest than the most powerful shock rolled through the earth beneath them. *Ja'jan*, Mistress of her people, self-proclaimed incarnation of a non-existent God, screamed and fell into her father's arms.

Seething with anger he nevertheless tried to comfort her. 'But what kind of a Goddess is this?' he thought. In his mind rose the picture of all that he and she had created, crumbling, undermined by her weakness. 'Stupid girl!'

Among the Mal'lam Elders there was confusion, and no little panic. One Master however, kept his head. He remembered well that as a child he had seen the mighty waves wash over the village below him, carrying many to their deaths and sweeping bamboo rafts and big canoes far inland, crushing them, or dragging them back out to sea.

"Sea-Hewn! Hear me!" Al'malan fairly screamed to be heard above the noise around him. "We must launch every seaworthy canoe and take to sea. Go straight out, at least three miles! Go, seamen, go!" Not only the Sea-Hewn responded but many others ran to the beach, thinking to ride the canoes to safety beyond the reach of a great wave which might yet come. When one-by-one the big canoes were launched, it was all the Sea-Masters could do to persuade the landsmen that they were safer going far inland and away from the beaches. Still some panicked souls managed to clamber aboard. They were allowed to stay and told to shelter inside the small hut on deck, well out of the way.

What the returning voyagers thought at first to be an extraordinary welcoming of their arrival, soon became apparent as something quite different. The canoes coming out through the opening to Dolphin Bay were not flying white pennants of greeting. Their hulls were lined with men paddling desperately, the sails barely pulling in the on-shore wind. The canoe which had been preceding the two returning vessels came close to one of those rushing out and hailed them. Without stopping, the fleeing vessel called back the news. Then that canoe turned about and followed, coming within hailing distance of the voyagers who themselves joined the anxious flight away from land. Some homecoming! Within two hours there were fourteen big canoes lying well out to sea and out of harm's way … they hoped.

What Al'malan could not know was that his considered caution was unnecessary. The mighty shock waves generated by the rupturing within Volan Votu radiated quite evenly outward from the island and away, causing only minor disturbances in local seas. Some of the islands to the north would suffer inundation but this island would experience but small, inconsequential wavelets which no one would notice. The fact that no great wave had eventuated bothered the logic of no one, least of all the seamen. Almost unanimously they hailed their leader for his fast action. After all, what if he had been right in his judgment but done nothing? The answer was obvious and too awesome to consider. But by now all those Sea-Hewn on the canoes were exhausted by their mighty effort. They remained at sea for the night, torches burning to signal their presence to those waiting anxiously ashore. The two great jolts and the two aftershocks had created such fear that it took until nearly dawn, with the aid of exhausted sleep, for calm to return to the villages of the Mal'lam. The Elders too could finally find a place to lie down and sleep.

By mid-morning the canoes had returned to Dolphin Bay and run up onto the black sands where they were all secured by hawsers but kept ready to sail again on a moment's notice. Slowly the villagers gathered themselves and began putting things back in order. Pigs had to be corralled, corrals repaired where panicked animals had broken through. Likewise did escaped chickens need penning again. This task was given to fleet-footed children.

When satisfied that their people were now in control of what immediately needed doing, the Elders gathered in Council. It was raining again and again the Council ensconced themselves in an empty canoe shed. It was the Voyage-Master, Al'malan, who held the speakers staff and the first Elder he recognized was Herb-Mistress Shen'ha. Shen'ha had taken the trouble to wash and braid her long hair and decorate it with feathers and seashells. She looked not only imposing but quite beautiful. Her son sat outside the hut with two of his young mates, watching her proudly.

"My brothers and sisters. Our careful considerations and planning must now be revised. Among our gifted 'seers' there is now a consensus that this recent calamity is but the beginning of the destruction of our beautiful Sht'ah Lee!" Pausing, this highly regarded Herbalist cast a meaningful glance around the assembly, catching every eye. "How this has suddenly come upon us, with little fore-knowledge or intuition is a great mystery. *Earth Mother* has Her own reasons, we can be sure of that. But warning has come from a Spirit we will all remember and whose continuing blessings have been imparted to us by her special student of the Earth Craft, Tina-an Earth-Plait. Tina-an has asked me to relay to you all the words of The Vesa'tan. Shen'ha then related to the Council these warnings and impressed upon everyone those troubling words, 'Within a year and no longer!'"

This day's session of the Council ran on into darkness, people going to attend to other matters and then returning. No debate of greater importance had any man or woman been involved in. It would be days before the Elders completed their discussions and a final plan developed. All precious time taken but that was the Mal'lam way. Meanwhile the work on the new canoes accelerated. Canoe-Master Joha'lan fell exhausted into his bed each night, sleep but moments away. So too did his workers, some doing double shifts. Most seamen became wood workers, spending their days with axe or adze or bow-drill as slowly the remaining six planned voyaging canoes took shape. A number of those hard-won logs which had been destined for use as hulls now lay discarded near the canoe sheds. There was no time left for them. Twenty voyaging canoes would be the maximum of the total fleet and this included ten older, still seaworthy vessels.

The Sea-Masters were finalizing schedules of another two voyages to the island of 'Win'no'hi'. These were to take place soon, carrying as many people aboard as possible. A shuttle to and from that island must take place in all seasons and weathers now. There would be no waiting.

The recent heavy rains and the flooding of the paddies and gardens after the earthquakes also presented a serious problem. Would the voyagers have enough food? Children who would normally be out and about playing all day were now seconded as little Herbalists, working at weeding and carrying, harvesting and sorting. And then was the question of *Ja'jan* and her followers! Even with the animosity, hatred even, which had grown between the two communities, few Mal'lam could countenance leaving these people behind to the frightening inevitability of the death of Sht'ah Lee. What was to be done?

Chapter Forty Five - The Rebirth of Ja'eel

Tina-an Earth-Plait and her lover, Shen'ham, had been able to steal but a few precious hours together alone since his return. This cool morning they walked together down from where they had spent the night in a small, cozy cave a couple of miles from the village. The roosters were crowing now and the mist was rising from the taro paddies and fields of herbs and vegetables. The sun was not yet up but already cooking fires were raising a thin shield of smoke over the village huts. Harvesters could be seen approaching, their figures but shadowy shapes through the mist.

"Why must you do this alone Tina?" Shen'ham was still very uneasy in spite of Tina's assurances that all would be well. She had an appointment with *Ja'jan* to organize a meeting with the Herb-Mistress Shen'ha and her mother, Sha'lat. Shen'ham had been asking her this question since they had awakened at first light. When first she had told him of this meeting, approved by both their mothers, he had been incredulous, then angry, insisting that he should accompany her for protection. But when Tina-an made up her mind, not even her lover and future husband could dissuade her. The only soul who could change Tina's mind no longer lived on this plane of existence and it was her idea in the first place. So there it was! She was going and she was going alone ; this very morning!

Ja'jan had sent word to Shen'ha Herb-Mistress that she wanted to speak with her. She had sent the one speaking person she still had complete faith in. Her name was Shay'la, an older woman and one of *Ja'jan's* first converts. Shay'la still had regular contact with a daughter within the Mal'lam camp. *Ja'jan* still was totally ignorant of her cousin Jana'la's role as a spy within her own camp. And with the level of distrust and jealousy which had over the past months developed within *Ja'jan's* circle, this was quite extraordinary. That silent woman had caused not even a moment's suspicion, even with the Chief Priest. And since the earthquakes, a cool distance had developed between father and daughter. *Ja'jan* had changed. All about her said so and all were growing nervous and unsettled. They were unsure of what their future would hold.

Sho'sha'lo had scoffed at the rumors of the island's destruction, calling them the wild imaginings of a few frightened people or worse, a plot by the Mal'lam to sow fear and dissention among the *Ja'jan an-lo.* Chief Priest Sho'sha'lo, himself, had much to worry about. If his daughter should abandon her role as Goddess what would become of him? He had made enemies among the Mal'lam and he assigned to them the same animosity he held himself. He must protect himself, his role as a leader and, should worse come to worse, assume the title of leader himself. Already his mind had been spinning with scenarios and half-formed plans. But to find some relief from these problems, this morning he was spending in bed with two of the younger, prettier *Ja'jan an-lo*, all three quite drunk on palm toddy.

Herb-Mistress Shen'ha had sent word back to *Ja'jan*, through Shay'la, that in order to assure secrecy she should bring only one person with her. That person would be her handmaiden, the woman who could not speak. *Ja'jan* made the choice herself, still not suspecting any subterfuge. The meeting was to be held at the warm water baths to the east of the *Ja'jan an-lo* village, just inside Mal'lam territory. Tina-an Earth-Plait would meet with her there and together they could arrange for the meeting with the Herb-Mistresses.

Ja'jan had to act, now! Time was fleeing and so was the life she had constructed for herself about to disappear. Her father was very suspicious and becoming aggressive, even toward her. But beyond all that, *Ja'jan* had one overriding desire. And for this she was ready to abandon all her other appetites and ambitions. She wanted to see her son, Sahn'ta, at least one more time. *Ja'jan* believed the predictions concerning Sht'ah Lee's future. She knew the island was going to die and believed that she had so alienated herself from the Mal'lam that they would surely leave her and the *Ja'jan an-lo* to perish. Just one more time! That's all she would ask.

As the sky had begun to lighten, *Ja'jan* had awakened her handmaiden and asked her to help her dress. To be asked rather than ordered was a new experience for the speechless woman and she reacted not with obsequiousness but with even more loving care than was her usual method. Ja'jan had let her cropped hair grow longer over the past few months. It was another indicator that she was undergoing changes in her self-perception. Jana'la combed *Ja'jan's* hair back into a shallow bun and decorated it with cowry shell *leis* and small yellow flowers. Then she dressed her Mistress in a new, bright and unadorned *tapa* cloth wrap, tied up over her breasts and under her arms. Finished, Jana'la stood back and looked at Ja'jan's face and figure. She smiled and nodded. *Ja'jan's* returning smile was thin but hopeful. She knew that today was a new beginning.

Jana'la went to the doorway of the hut and looked around as she often did at this time of morning. No one was stirring. She gestured to *Ja'jan* to come. The two women walked quickly around the corner of the compound and strode for the cover of the nearby brushy surrounds, Jana'la leading the way. It felt good to again be alone - well, almost alone - out into the forests where the breeze blew cool and fresh and the birds flitted about with busy purpose. It was here where she had often come alone on her search for conquests and converts. Now she could hardly recall the path to the warm water baths. They were in Mal'lam territory and she had sworn never to step foot on enemy land again. 'Stupid woman!" she thought to herself.

The trail was dry and easy to walk now that the rains had stopped and within fifteen minutes they were at the pools of warm, misting water. Jana'la signaled for *Ja'jan* to stand behind some bushes until she scouted around. They were alone. Feeling strangely free and unafraid, *Ja'jan* went to the baths, took off her wrap and climbed into one. The natural stone formation which resulted in a dozen small basins was fed by an unceasing spring of heated water which flowed from the slope behind. Then Jana'la clapped her hands once. Someone was coming.

Immersed in the warm waters for long enough for her body to relax, so too did her mind brush aside the fears which had grown to insupportable size; fears which were only of her own making. *Ja'jan* felt the false persona she had constructed melting away as the water flowed around her body. Almost negligently she turned toward the approach of the stranger. It was the slight, quite pretty young figure of the Earth-Plait woman, Tina-an.

"Good morning, Tina-an Earth-Plait!" *Ja'jan* said by way of a warm greeting. "Thank you for coming. I hope that you are alone." There was a strange, distant tone in her voice as if she, at this very moment, cared not at all if a great crowd should accompany Tina-an. "Please come and join me here. This water is just marvelous!"

Tina-an stood still and tense, she too thinking this might be a trap but soon she relaxed, the silent attendant's smile reassuring her. Yes. They were truly alone. Tina's forest-sense detected no human presence other than their own. Tina-an walked to the edge of the pool which Ja'jan occupied and saw that there was plenty of room for two in the water. She undid her wrap and stepped carefully into the slippery stone basin and sat herself down into the water. It *was* marvelous! 'Vesa'tan, don't leave me now!' was her thought.

"We find ourselves in a situation which neither of us has ever considered. Am I right?" *Ja'jan* said, her hands casually swishing the water around her body. Tina tried to read her emanations: falsity? conspiracy? stupidity? No! None of those rose to confront her sensitivity. She glanced at Jana'la who sat quietly nearby, her hands relaxed in her lap. Jana'la smiled warmly, returning the glance.

Not one for small talk or diplomacy, Tina-an immediately went to the point of this meeting. "I am told that you want to see Sahn'ta. How long since you last saw him, *Ja'jan?*" Tina started when from that apparently relaxed and composed figure near her in the warm water came a sudden sob and cry of such intensity that Tina's heart leaped!

Ja'jan had moments before lain back against the stone wall of the pool but now she sat upright with her hands over her face, her shoulders shaking with sobs. Tina knew that this was not more dramatics. *Ja'jan's* pain and sorrow nearly overwhelmed her and she instinctively reached out both arms to comfort this woman who only minutes before was her avowed enemy. Jana'la too came to the edge of the pool and extended an arm in support of her Mistress.

Tina could think of no words to offer. Instead she slipped her body close to *Ja'jan's* and wrapped one arm across her shoulders and hugged her tightly. Ja'jan's sobs continued and her body bent so far over that Tina feared she might submerge her face in the water. "Shoosh! Shoosh, *Ja'jan*. It will be alright. We can talk about it."

Then as if another earth tremor approached, there came a growling curse, a man's voice growing in shrillness and approaching rapidly. Tina turned quickly to see *Ja'jan's* father, Sho'sha'lo, wearing only a breech cloth and a face full of aggression, striding on unsteady feet from out of the surrounding brush, an obsidian knife in his right hand.

"You faithless slut!" he screamed, stopping and waving the weapon in front of him, his drunken body swaying from side to side. "You pig of a woman! You are no longer my daughter. You have destroyed my life!" His voice was towering with rage, growing shriller with each utterance, spittle riming his lips.

"You have used me as you have used so many, you stupid whore! Did you think I didn't know? Did you?!" Sho'sha'lo was nearly out of control and with steadier steps, his madness negating the effect of the toddy, he moved closer to the pool with that knife now held out before him. The gesture was unmistakable.

"I saw you leave this morning, you and your dumb maid. And here you are sitting in the baths with a Mal'lam witch!" Sho'sha'lo's eyes bulged suddenly, he lifted his right arm above his head and lunged toward the pool with the two terrified women still in the water, but standing now.

"NOOOO!" came the scream, "Ja'eel, look out!" It was the voice which had not uttered a word in more than twenty-five years. Jana'la, to this moment frozen with fear beside the baths, leaped to her feet and threw herself between Sho'sha'lo and his intended victims. She had come to hold Tina-an in great regard also but it was the thought of harm coming to her dear cousin which drove her to abandon all thought of her own safety. Love had replaced any sense of iniquity which her years of near servitude might have installed.

Sho'sha'lo pushed her aside with one arm but Jana'la grasped that arm and attempted to pull him away from his intention. The knife was suddenly swung around and thrust with murderous force into Jana'la's chest. Without another sound Jana'la's hands released their grip and she fell backward onto the ground. Sho'sha'lo deigned to stop his forward movement long enough for a look down to see if the poor woman was dead. Then he turned his burning gaze again upon *Ja'jan* and Tina-an. It was those saved moments which allowed the salvation!

The sound of a sling stone in flight is very subtle. Given the utter silence which dominated the senses, that subtle WHIZZZZ!, conquered the moment. The egg-sized, smooth river stone struck Sho'sha'lo just above his right eye. The impact threw his head back violently, carrying his body backward with it. Sho'sha'lo, late the Chief Priest of a mad regime, lay on his back now, his body sprawled awkwardly, blood trickling from his ears and nose. His body twitched its last movements as his shattered brain gave a burst of terminal signals. Then he lay still.

Shen'ham Sea-Hewn ran forward from the place where he had crouched for many minutes, the sling dangling from his right hand, the three fingers of his left clutching another stone in readiness. He stood over the man's body only long enough to be certain Sho'sha'lo was dead. He was.

Shen'ham slipped the ready stone back into its pouch and gave a loud sigh. "*Earth Mother*, forgive me!" he muttered quietly. After a quick glance at the body of Jana'la he turned to where Tina-an and *Ja'jan* still stood in the pool, both dripping and trembling.

Ja'jan's eyes were wide with terror, madness reaching up from within her to clutch her mind. Tina, herself trying to grasp this moment's meanings, stood beside the older woman and led her to the pool's edge and with Shen'ham's assistance, guided her out and onto the smooth stone surrounds. Then *Ja'jan* let out a sharp cry and collapsed onto the stone and curled upon her side. She was wailing and sobbing, tears and mucus wetting her face anew. Tina knelt beside her to try to comfort her. At that moment the sound of running feet was heard and suddenly four men burst from the brush beside the trail, spears and clubs held at the ready. It was Ch'om'lo and three of his brothers.

"Are you alright, 'Three Finger?" the Itin Sea-Master gasped, obviously winded from a long, hard run. He quickly strode to where Sho'sha'lo's body lay, looked without bothering to investigate it and stepped to Jana'la's body. He knelt beside her and laid the back of a hand to her neck. He shook his head and surveyed the surreal scene around him. Tina-an was now in Shen'ham's arms, her face buried against his chest, sobbing. Shen'ham looked over her head at his friend. The pain and helplessness in his face tugged at Ch'om'lo's own heart. "I had to do it, Sea-Master." Shen'ham pressed his face to Tina's hair, momentarily hiding his own face."The woman too?" Ch'om'lo asked, still trying to make sense of this whole scene of carnage.

"No! No, Sho'sha'lo killed her. I was too slow. I couldn't stop him." Ch'om'lo began to piece it together then and his heart went out to his two friends. He went to them and wrapped both arms around them, holding them tightly as their bodies shook with sobs of fear and release from fear. By then Ch'om'lo's brothers had found a wrap beside the pool to cover the trembling body of *Ja'jan.* Gently they lifted her to her feet and steadied her for a few moments. One of the brothers, the strongest and biggest, bent and lifted the small body of Jana'la and slung it over his shoulder, waited until Ch'om'lo nodded a signal and then began slowly returning down the path. Slowly, very slowly, '*Ja'jan of the Skies*' was helped along the same path, once more to her real home, back to where she might one day again be known as, Ja'eel Feather-Plait.

~~*~~

Nothing was known of this event out among the community, until the following day. This was time in which *Ja'jan* was taken to a small hut away from the main settlement, the place where Herb-Mistress Shen'ha concocted many of her herbal and healing remedies. Ch'om'lo had sent one of his brothers to inform the Herb-Mistress and she in turn brought together a small group of other healers, including Tina-an's mother, Sha'lat. The body of the woman who had found her voice at the very moment when her input was needed, Jana'la, was covered in an ornamental length of *tapa* cloth and laid on a raised timber platform beside the hut, one used for drying plants. Shen'ha saw that the shroud was also adorned with fresh flowers. Tomorrow she would be cremated with all due ceremony.

It was Tina-an who took word of the day's events to her sister and Al'malan, Shen'ham accompanying her. "Sht'ana!" she had called out, breathing hard from the run back to the village. Fortunately Al'malan Voyage-Master was at home too, stealing time from his busy schedule to cuddle and play with his children. "*Ja'jan* has relinquished her rule over the *Ja'jan an-lo* and Sho'sha'lo is dead ..." - all this she said in one breath and then collapsed, sitting on the mat next to Sht'ana. Perhaps not the most informative announcement Tina could have organized yet the meaning was quickly gleaned by those two people most involved in that drama which had been, '*Ja'jan'.*

"What has happened to her?" was Al'malan's first question and he reached out and brought his son into his lap. Sht'ana moved closer to her husband as they both waited for clarification of this starling news.

Shen'ham had seated himself behind Tina-an and laid a hand on her shoulder. She turned to him and he said with a gentle smile, "Would you like me to tell them?" Tina shut her eyes momentarily and thanked her mentor, The Vesa'tan, for this intervention upon a story which she hardly knew how to begin. Her mind was still too awhirl with awful events. Shen'ham moved forward now to sit beside Tina and begin his version of the story.

"My mother and Sha'lat and Tina too, have been conducting a secret communication with *Ja'jan's* cousin, Jana'la, for more than two years. You might know that Jana'la doesn't ... sorry ... didn't speak for all her adult life. No one knows why for sure. But, sadly, she is dead now." Al'malan and Sht'ana looked at each other, both puzzled.

"Well, somehow my mother has been able to communicate quite well with Jana'la, even though she couldn't reply except in sign language. In the past few days, according to Jana'la, *Ja'jan* had been experiencing some kind of personal crisis. She actually sent another woman, one of the *Ja'jan an-lo*, to mother to ask for a meeting. That's when Tina got involved again." Shen'ham turned briefly, silently asking if he was doing alright with the story so far. She nodded for him to continue. Little La'teel chose this time to crawl across and into Tin-an's lap and curl up, sucking her thumb.

"Tina agreed to meet with *Ja'jan* and arrange a meeting with my mother. Tina told me about this meeting but absolutely forbade me to accompany her to make sure she would be safe." 'Three Finger' now looked at Tina with a sly grin. "Of course, I always do as she says. I went with her to the forest track which turns off to the Baths. She did her usual trick of distracting me for a moment and then disappearing into the bush. I guess she forgot that last night she had told me where the meeting was going to happen." Tina looked slightly embarrassed and bent to cuddle the child in her lap.

"I was really concerned for her safety. Not so much about what *Ja'jan* herself might do but about her father, Sho'sha'lo. I've never trusted the man. Immediately after she disappeared I ran down the hill for a few hundred yards until I came upon a group of young boys coming back from the paddies. I knew that Ch'om'lo and his brothers would be down at the canoe sheds but it would have taken me too long to run there for help on my own. I told the oldest boy in the group, and he looked like he could run, to take a message to Ch'om'lo for me. He did a good job too, going and alerting Ch'om'lo that I needed his help at the baths, immediately!

"Well, I followed Tina's footprints, like she had taught me to do long ago and when I got to the baths I could hear only women's voices. I crept up as close as I could and hid myself and waited. Just *Ja'jan* and Tina and Jana'la were there but no sign of anyone lurking about." Again he looked at Tina-an, thinking she might want to tell the rest of the story. No.

"Tina and *Ja'jan* were just chatting, both of them sitting in the water. Then *Ja'jan* began to cry - I mean she was just *wailing!*" Al'malan's face betrayed some inner turmoil at this stage but no one seemed to notice, Sht'ana's attention riveted on Shen'ham's story.

"Then Sho'sha'lo came charging out of the bushes, drunk and waving a knife around. I have never seen so ugly a look on a man's face, even when we fought Tor'na and his men. He was cursing Ja'jan, calling her terrible names … his own daughter! When he started to approach the side of the bath, Jana'la screamed out, 'NOOOO! Ja'eel, look out!' Not *Ja'jan* but, *Ja'eel*!" Al'malan wiped a hand across his face to hide the tears forming in his eyes. "Jana'la jumped up and grabbed Sho'sha'lo's arm but he turned and stabbed her!"

Here Shen'ham sobbed and covered his face, but was able to continue. "I was too slow! I didn't see that coming. I was behind the bushes. I had a stone in my sling but I was too slow to save her!" Shen'ham was becoming very emotional now, his voice breaking as he tried to continue. "Sho'sha'lo kept coming toward the bath, toward Tina and *Ja'jan*. That's when I threw my stone and killed him!" Shen'ham couldn't continue. Tina-an laid a hand lovingly on his knee and nodded to him knowingly. She picked up her niece and handed her back to her mother's care and finished the tale.

"Shen'ham's throw was perfect, believe me. Sho'sha'lo died instantly. It was then that Ch'om'lo and his brothers arrived. They had run all the way from the beach to the baths. That frightened me all the more because for a moment I thought it was some *Jajan an-lo* coming. Anyway, we all took *Ja'jan* and Jana'la's body down toward the village. Ch'om'lo sent one of his brothers to talk to my mother and Shen'ha about what we should do next. During that time that we waited, *Ja'jan* never stopped crying. She kept trying to wake Jana'la up by shaking her body. She wouldn't believe that she was dead."

Tina's story was interrupted by Al'malan's own weeping. He sat with both hands over his face, his shoulders jerking with sobs. Sht'ana, like Tina a few moments ago, turned to her man to comfort him in his sorrow. Her own emotions were held in check. There remained a residue of hatred in her heart which kept her own eyes dry. Tina-an turned toward the open doorway of the hut and called out for someone to come and please take the children for a while. Young Sahn'ta, barely six years old now, stood up. He understood this adult drama more than anyone would have credited him for. He picked up the little girl and carried her outside just as someone arrived to answer a neighbor's call.

Tina completed the story, telling how word had come back for them to take *Ja'jan* and Jana'la's body to Shen'ha's workshop, a place away from any other huts or often-used tracks. They had succeeded in avoiding any other people that morning and were met by Shen'ha and her Herbalist/Healer compatriots. Sha'lat's own experience, her temporary breakdown away there on that Tarbara'ut island, brought a special sensitivity to this extraordinary occasion. All she focused on was the fact that someone was in great agony of mind and soul and it was her duty to do her best to save this person's sanity.

The guards who had for so long attended the safety of Sht'ana and her children were now assigned to protect the very person whose mad delusions had threatened them in the first place. It was always possible that some of the *Ja'jan an-lo*, understandably feeling themselves betrayed, might try to exact some revenge on *Ja'jan*. The '*Goddess of the Skies*' had created a mind-set which would now be turned against her by some. But the Mal'lam had regained one of their own and surely many more would return. The *Earth Mother* smiled.

Research Notes: Impressions and General Observations

Subjects: Tina Pua'lani Kaiser and 'Tutu' Kinau Kaiser, Kaua'i, Winter 1975

Christmas this year Jiro and I are going to California to visit my family so we're having an early Christmas in Hanalei with Kinau and the family here. The weather is overcast and cool but so far no rain. Tina, Jiro and I have been out weeding the gardens while 'Tutu' minds the baby.

Kinau, as I've mentioned before, has been compiling her own story, related to her by those Mal'lam 'Spirits' who lived here in Hawai'i long ago. One Mal'lam woman came through to her quite insistently and often, apparently, and she was among those first generations who settled on the islands here. She relates a myth - or is it truly history? - of a Mal'lam Sea-Hewn long before her time who was named A'lan Sea-Master. And then she tells of a great navigator named 'Three Finger', but no proper name went with that. They were contemporaries and how many famous Mal'lam would have been called 'Three Finger'?

I had to check this carefully, suspicious mind that I have, and I'm satisfied that there is something quite compelling in the conjunction of these stories.

Kinau, you see, was aware of the characters A'lan and of his friend Shen'ham. But she has not read or been told of the accident which resulted in the name, 'Three Finger'. However, so far in Kinau's communications with the Hawai'ian Mal'lam Spirits, those names and much of the memories of those long ago times of pre-settlement by the Mal'lam faded away. It will be interesting to see where Kinau's part of this story leads. It's getting decidedly complicateder!

Ah yes! I nearly forgot ... I've been fired! Jiro, still my project supervisor at the University, says it's time I stay home and practice just being a wife and mother. We didn't even argue about it, honestly! But really, just because I'm pregnant again is no reason to make me stay housebound. He'll be sorry! I may take up drinking and get fat and lazy. That'll show him! How do I say 'male chauvinist pig' in Mal'lam?

Chapter Forty Six - A'lan Sea-Master Returns

The wind had failed again. Off into the eastern horizon lay a low mass of cloud and beneath it surely lay an island. A'lan Sea-Master had determined in the dark of last night's easy run, with a gentle breeze attending, that there was indeed an island out there. But now, the sun rising to mid morning, 'Wa'Boton' lay becalmed. A'lan stood on the foredeck, stroking his growing beard, fighting frustration and impatience, emotions a Sea-Master must learn to control.

'Wa'Boton' was now in good order; sails repaired and numerous other maintenance items attended to and ready to allow them to sail onward. The formal burial at sea of the two bodies found aboard 'Wa'Salat' had drawn tears from all the crew. The foundering remains of that vessel had to be left to the whim of the sea after everything of possible value was brought aboard 'Wa'Boton'. There was little to eat aboard the voyaging canoe and in this becalmed state, eight seamen were attending fishing lines from all around the perimeter. Water they had, enough to last for another week and A'lan was sure that squalls would reach them soon or they might reach that island sooner. There must be water there because an island large enough to capture a bank of cloud above it would certainly have groundwater.

Tired from his long night watch, A'lan asked a senior Sea-Hewn to take over while he got some sleep. He lay down beneath the scrap of roof they had been able to raise amidships, a barely satisfactory shelter from the hot sun. Nudging another resting seaman gently, the man moaned and rolled over, affording A'lan just enough space to stretch himself out. As he often did of late, he brought to mind the face of Arawee and tried to send his life-force out to her in a message of love and support. It helped to salve the loneliness which this dramatic change in circumstances had created in him. Friends he had. Faldo-in, his old mate from his younger years and still like a brother and his other crew were all supportive; true brothers-of-the-sea who had unanimously elected him Sea-master. But for the first time in his seaman's life he yearned to be ashore again; ashore with the lovely young, dark-skinned woman who carried his child. Carried?! By now he must be a father! It had been six months since this voyage of discovery had begun and surely she had been two or three months pregnant before he left. 'I'm a father!' he whispered to himself, the thought having just arrived. 'Are you perhaps too self-centered, A'lan Sea-Master? Why hasn't this obvious realization occurred to you before?' A'lan shrugged off the implication of blind self-absorption and quickly fell to sleep. Perhaps best to avoid questions which you are not quite ready to answer.

A'lan was well into an erotic dream when someone began shaking his shoulder, calling his name. "A'lan-an! Wake up. The wind is back with us." It was Faldo-in and he was kneeling beside A'lan, his body casting a cooling shadow on A'lan's sweaty form. The sun had moved around to where it shone through the insubstantial thatching of the hut, overheating but not awakening the tired Sea-Master. A'lan raised himself on one elbow and squinted out onto the sea. Sure enough, there were the riffles of a rising breeze. Struggling up to his feet he cast a grateful smile at Faldo-in and then went to the rear of the starboard hull to relieve himself. Hanging onto a stay, one which needed a bit of tightening he noted, he looked all about him as he slowly gathered this new reality into his consciousness. Wind again! Striding fully awake now he went forward to the center of the bridging deck and looked out to where the pillow of cloud still covered that elusive island. A quick check around the deck and at all the men there and then he called out the orders to adjust sail, catch this southeasterly breeze and let's get going!

"Why is it that landfall is so often reached so late in the day?" mused the Herbalist, Pash'wo. A seaman answered that it was because very often the wind failed around midday here in these waters of the tropics. And then they often died away again in the middle of the night. Quite different from the usual conditions far to the north in the waters of their home islands. Men who an hour before had been groggy and half-asleep in the hot sun were now energetically hauling on lines and adjusting the sails. The steering oars were now manned and beginning to leave long, thin wakes behind. How good to be underway again.

With the setting sun behind them the Mal'lam could now see clearly the dark outline of the island beneath that never-moving cloud. The wind was shifting more southerly, demanding another adjustment to the tall sail panels and the darkening eastern sky was gathering the low, scudding clouds into a solid layer. "Perhaps some squalls tonight." the young Sea-Master said, turning his head all around to scout the evening sky. A large moon, just past full, would rise in another two hours and the night should be bright and affording a clear view of their destination.

Almost simultaneously two sailors hooked into *mahi mahi*, those beautiful, blunt-headed raptors whose flesh was prized by all Sea-Hewn. "We eat tonight!" someone cried and laughter and enthusiasm ran over the decks. Enough stone and sand had survived that fatal storm to provide a small fireplace on the deck between the masts. Soon the fillets of white flesh were searing and the smell brought smiles to everyone. In the gathering darkness the firelight threw shadows about the deck as men moved to and fro. That same light lit the face of A'lan Sea-Master as he stood watching the activity around him, his own belly grumbling impatiently for some of that good food.

That night passed uneventfully; the wind kept blowing from the southeast, a low swell ran diagonally across the 'Wa'Boton's' course and the vessel rode easily to its regular rhythm. A smaller swell, which was the result of waves rebounding off that island, added another regular note to the tuneful slap and hush of seawater against the hulls. The movement of the big canoe, the feel of the swells, the counter swells, all were recorded in the keen minds of the navigators, Faldo-in one of the most sensitive men aboard in this regard. Then, around midnight when the mid-watch was changing, Faldo-in gently shook A'lan awake. This time he was instantly awake and asked Faldo-in if all was right.

"Yes, Sea-Master. It's just that I have noticed another subtle system of waves coming from the southeast. I think there is another piece of land off to the right of the island we're headed for." The implication was that A'lan's *'sea sight'* was called for to confirm this phenomenon. A'lan searched the blackness below them. Yes! Another body of land *was* announcing itself but it was some way off, over the horizon. He complimented his friend on his perception and remained sitting with him on the leading edge of the deck. They sat chatting quietly until the eastern sky began to betray the sun's approach. They both rose and went in search of some leftovers of last night's little feast of fish. Too late! Other hungry hands had scraped up every last morsel. A'lan and Faldo-in chuckled and shared an old joke about Sea-Masters always being hungry and lean.

An atmospheric change was occurring in the pre-dawn and the cloud cap was disintegrating. The island now stood out in bold relief with the bright hues of sunrise silhouetting a long, quite low island with some higher, rounded hills inland. A'lan woke the crew and began preparing the vessel for a close approach within the hour, if the wind was kind. Smaller islands, some far off to the right, and two to the left, now began to reflect the rising sun. The high cloud of the night before which had reflected the bright moonlight were also dissipating, leaving the morning sky wide and clear. Seabirds were off on their day's journeys and dozens flew close by the canoe, curious perhaps about this strange piece of flotsam. A school of dolphin had found 'Wa'Boton'. These were 'common dolphin', with broad swatches of curving white and grey lines on glossy black bodies. They blew and rolled all around the canoe, some leaping high as if to get a good look at this intruder on their private domain. It was only minutes after the sun had risen above the sea that the mast-top lookout called out excitedly. "Sea-Master! I see smoke on the island! Dead ahead, in the center of the island, just a little way inland."

A'lan was quickly up the foremast himself, Faldo-in scrambling up the aft sail structure. Yes, by the Sea Gods! There, and to the left of that, more smoke rising. Morning fires, someone cooking. This island was surely inhabited! With the sun rising higher the color of the waters around the island became visible and the blue-green of shallows over coral reefs became evident. It was a wide reef, much wider than those which enclosed the islands of the Tarbara'ut and now the sound of surf greeted waiting ears. They were all half-expecting to see small canoes leave the shore, as had occurred when the Mal'lam came close to 'Tara'tor', now nearly four years ago. A'lan remained aloft for an hour, squinting hard against the glare, searching for a passage through this broad barrier reef. Inside that reef was deeper water, indicated by the darker color, meaning sheltered water in which the big canoe could probably maneuver safely. This was a time for great caution and alertness. He knew this well from his experiences on previous landings and the general knowledge of those whose experience was much greater than his own. Bringing to the forefront of his sensitivity his special talent, he sought other clues which probably only his eyes, aboard this vessel, could discern.

An hour of sustained breeze from the southeast had 'Wa'Boton' within two hundred yards of the white fringe of surf. A'lan came down from the mast and called for another man whose eyesight he had great trust in. "Stan'la. Take the masthead now, will you? Keep a sharp lookout for big coral boulders out from the main body of the reef. And if you see any movement ashore, give a shout." Stan'la Sea-Hewn was quickly up the line of foot treads and to the highest vantage point, his keen eyes sweeping back and forth.

A'lan had already chosen what he was certain was a break in the reef's structure, wide enough to safely take his canoe through. Stan'la too would spot it soon. He gave the order to clear the covers from the hulls and prepare to break out the paddles. To one seaman he gave the order to bring weapons up on deck, just in case! In the past few minutes two more columns of smoke had become visible, these from just behind what was now appearing as a long and bright sand beach. Whoever these people were, they either had not yet seen a strange vessel approaching or were simply lying low, waiting to see what happened. Surely they knew their cooking fires had been spotted! On that long beach lay what appeared to be three or four small canoes, from this distance looking like fragile little platters made of bark. And such they were.

Ashore, the inhabitants were indeed lying low. Of course, any island dweller living close to the sea looks out upon that sea, whether or not they are expecting to see anything special there. That great, all-encompassing expanse of blue draws the eye as surely as does the blue above. One simply cannot ignore the world in which one lives, most especially when that observation might spell the difference between life and death. The people who on this ordinary morning had risen with the sun's first rays and lit their cooking fires did look outward. What they saw was a vessel unlike any seen before. It was nearly as large as the great rafts made of huge logs which their people had been using to explore the almost endless seas to the west of their homeland for a century. Yet so swift!

And its sails! Two upright, narrow plates of some unknown fabric, held rigid by what appeared to be a curved piece of timber. How many sailors rode with the craft the island's observers couldn't tell at this distance. And an anxious scan of the sea behind them revealed no other vessels. Who could they be?

Alone on this island for eight years, the twenty-seven colonizers did not expect a return of their own people for another two years. It was over five-thousand miles to their homeland, across an expanse of ocean which only the greatest of faith could have inspired the exploration of. Yes, between here and the homeland there were outposts of settlement; stopping-off islands which were part of a purposeful attempt to expand their civilization westward. But their means of transport were woefully slow, cumbersome and ultimately inadequate for the purpose. Every settlement established faced the understood potential for total isolation and eventual decline. Still, how much fortitude and what kind of faith was involved in prompting this kind of courageous commitment? These were truly a people of a uniqueness matching that of those Mal'lam voyagers who were about to meet them. This was a momentous day!

Aboard 'Wa'Boton', Sea-master A'lan had a sudden inspiration. "Everyone! Listen to me. Go by twos and put on your best *tapa* cloth wraps and any decorations which you have with you. Re-tie your hair and pretend you are about to meet some beautiful ladies!" A few unbelieving guffaws and snorts followed but he insisted. "I am serious, brothers! We must present ourselves as self-respecting Sea-Hewn, not bedraggled wanderers. My eyes tell me that this land is home to people who wish to greet us in friendship. Now, do as I say, and quickly!"

A'lan himself went to the salvaged chest, covered in layers of watertight wrapping which had been his own Master's formal dress. Fan'al Sea-Master had been a man who enjoyed wearing the finery of his office and A'lan drew each piece out from the chest with great respect but with urgency. Half an hour passed and 'Wa'Boton' was approaching that opening in the reef which the topmast lookout had confirmed. A'lan stood looking about him at his crew, now all as beautified as the circumstances allowed. With no mirrored bowl of water with which to judge his own appearance, he had to rely on his friend, Faldo-in, to assess his own appearance. "Don't you joke with me, Faldo-in! I'll kick your ass if you laugh!" Faldo-in didn't laugh. He looked slightly awe-struck as he considered the appearance of this newly adorned symbol of Mal'lam Sea-Mastery.

"Brother!" he said, "I can hardly wait to see you in a formal Council wearing that. You look rather awesome. Oh - well, you should comb your beard a bit. Let your scar show." A'lan struggled momentarily with a fine-toothed comb, the teeth catching painfully in tangled beard hairs but soon he raised his head again for his friend's assessment.

"Yes! You've got it now!" Faldo-in turned to go, then swung around and asked, "How do I look?" The grins and laughter they shared then answered any and all questions. But now it was time to enter the opening in the reef. It was as if the Gods of the Sea had spread their hands and opened the way for 'Wa'Boton' to enter into the wide lagoon. With as little effort as any aboard this Mal'lam vessel would ever encounter, the proud canoe surged forward under sail power alone, adequate to carry it over the intervening wave-break. The paddlers waiting for the order to begin stroking, began only as the big canoe was carried beyond the surge of the swells entering the little harbor. They were soon ashore, the two hulls gliding softly onto sands composed of crushed shell and coral - fine and powdery.

A'lan stood now on the foremost edge of the deck, his inner-vision searching the land before him. His vision revealed a glow of pink, almost purple, the colors lending a sense of moderation - complete peace! It was his life which would be forfeit first should he be badly mistaken. But he shrugged off all such thoughts. As 'Wa'Boton' grounded securely onto the sand, the first of the island's inhabitants issued forth from the undergrowth behind the beach. Wearing their daily garb of breechcloth and headband, all the men appeared carrying slings with sling-stones ready. A'lan's mind immediately flew back to his best friend Shen'ham and his expertise with this weapon. A'lan would be totally defenseless should these islanders decide to attack. Well, here we go! *Earth Mother* be with me!

His feet landed in a foot of water and he strode purposefully up and out of the lapping waves and stood still and erect just above the tide line. There were twelve of them, shorter and stockier than the Mal'lam but with similar hair color. So too did their eyes contain a pronounced caste upward from the outside corners, the islander's eyes more slanted. Their faces bore no sign of painting or scarring but were smooth and nearly hairless, only wispy mustaches being visible. These were surely not the 'Itoi' of Mal'lam legend!

A'lan turned quickly to the canoe and said loudly but without expressed command, "Everyone sit down now. Relax and show no weapons!" All the Mal'lam Sea-Hewn responded accordingly. A'lan Sea-Master began slowly walking forward, raising both hands, palms outward toward the encircling group of strangers. He stopped and bowed shallowly toward them, then straightened, his hands now loose at his sides.

The islanders too relaxed their stances of defense and one man among them took a few steps forward. He was if anything slightly shorter than the rest but his movements exuded confidence and authority. His face displayed a sumptuous mustache but only a few insistent hairs invaded his rounded jaw. He too stood erect and faced A'lan straight-on while tucking his sling into the belt of his breechcloth. 'Here was no confrontation!', A'lan's sensitivity registered, and he took a few more steps forward up the sands.

A'lan's eyes immediately fell upon the neckpiece the man was wearing. It was of some kind of shell, pure in color, no striations of texture or ornamentation evident. Very strange and beautiful it was. He diverted that gaze to the man's face. As the two men approached, both scrutinizing each other with intense interest, A'lan was cognizant of the change in the stance of that man's compatriots behind him. They were all looking on with intense attention, not knowing what to expect but following their leader's guidance. It was then that A'lan made a gesture indicating thirst; his hands formed a cupping motion and one of drinking from his hands. The apparent leader of these islanders called a quick order over his shoulder. Movement behind and a few moments later a man returned with a gourd and handed it to the leader A'lan was facing. The man held it forward to A'lan who took it and drank as if greatly relieved. He drank again to reinforce the scenario, then handed it back to the islander, gesturing for the man to join him in assuaging a thirst which both must share; a thirst for knowing and understanding and surviving together in this moment. The island leader's drink in return sealed the opening for these two unique and very different people to begin a dialog which would eventually enrich both their cultures.

With the breeze ruffling the white feathers of his borrowed headdress, A'lan Sea-Master took four more steps toward the man he could only assume was this island's premier leader. He again opened both palms, then sat down in a graceful movement with legs crossed, arms at rest in his lap. It was all up to that man now! Death or deliverance!

Aboard 'Wa'Boton' the crew held their breaths. They could never have imagined such reckless bravery in the face of the unknown! Then again, hadn't this young man steered them through the worst storm any had ever seen and still they survived? A mantra formed among the Mal'lam Sea-Hewn, the Herbalist Pash'wo's voice the loudest as the men aboard the canoe prayed for the presence of the *Earth Mother* in this encounter. Again the *Earth Mother* smiled.

~ ~ * ~ ~

There were no familiar words to share among these strangers, but sign language and shared humanity prevailed to bridge the gaps. 'Wa'Boton' was secured by its hawsers to strong trees just behind the beach. Here again there were no coconut palms but the foreshore abounded in the familiar pandanus trees; their stiff, spiny leaves similar to those which provided the Mal'lam with their canoe sails. The lands behind the beaches were rich in foliage, some of it familiar to the Herbalist, Pash'wo. Sea-Master A'lan dispatched his friend, Faldo-in, to begin an understanding of these people's language. Faldo-in did not disappoint for he quickly engaged the somewhat incredulous islanders in an exploratory sequence of gesture and point, grin and grimace, smile and pat on the arm. His was a very special talent and he applied it with great aptitude, but results were slow to develop.

Water there was, all over this island, and nearly all of it quite potable. There were great, deep swathes of mangrove swamps, salt-water enclaves which harbored shellfish, fish and very hard timbers for construction. Exploring with their hosts the deeper areas of this long, narrow island, the Mal'lam found only medium-sized timber, none large enough to supply hulls for the Mal'lam style of vessel. On the beach they discovered the rotting remains of a large raft, the very one which had carried these brave people to this land. The logs were diminished by time but still over four feet in width, the connecting lengths of rope entirely decayed. One could push a finger into the punk-like timber up to the third knuckle. 'How could one depend upon such ephemeral construction?' was the question repeated among the Mal'lam sailors. Yet, here they were!

The local people themselves were equally astounded by the big canoe and the system of sailing. Slowly, very slowly, a language began to develop between the two groups. One of the great spurs to communication was hunger! The Mal'lam were all past lean and heading for skinny! That was when they discovered the staple food of these intriguing islanders. A tuber it was, growing vigorously in large gardens assiduously attended by the locals. They proudly tried to explain that it was their basic source of food. Much like *taro*, thought the Mal'lam, but these people had none of that food. But wasn't it delicious! The Mal'lam could hardly get their fill and yet the local people seemed to have a never-ending abundance of this food.

Their other staple foods included herbs and green vegetables which it appeared they had brought with them from the eastern seas. Like the Mal'lam, these people were consummate fishermen, their fragile little bark canoes quite adequate to carry them on fishing expeditions within the inner lagoon and its calm waters. But these people had no dogs or pigs or chickens. Perhaps they had been forced to eat them all after they first arrived here. The Mal'lam could only guess. The islanders were delighted with coconuts! There were no more green drinking nuts left aboard 'Wa'Boton' but the flesh of the ripe nuts these people found quite wonderful. A'lan was taking a tour one day with the islander's headman, whose name the Mal'lam could only approximate as Shin-shet-olo. Both the Mal'lam and these people from far to the east had sounds in their respective languages which were difficult for the other to replicate. So after much trying, and even more laughter, some approximation would be settled upon.

Coming to where the Herbalist Pash'wo had planted a hundred coconuts, A'lan knelt and with a small stick tried to illustrate the shape and size of a coconut palm with figures scratched in the damp sand. He drew a rather good approximation of a man standing beneath a tree and indicated the clusters of nuts above him. Then, with a real coconut he pantomimed a nut falling from the tree and landing on one's head. Shin-shet-olo collapsed laughing and rolled about on the sand, hugging his ribs in mirth. A'lan joined him and the two men, uncomprehending strangers but a few days ago, were now like fond cousins. Holding the nut above his head, A'lan again let it drop and mouthed a 'BONK' sound and again the two fell into hysterical laughter - like little boys.

Among the island's twenty-seven colonists were twelve women. Six young children, all born here on this island, brought the total to thirty-three. All seemed exceptionally healthy and robust. The men all wore their straight, somewhat coarse hair loose to their shoulders, a wide band of some wonderfully soft fabric wrapped around and across their foreheads. The women wore their lustrous hair long and braided down the back in one pigtail. They often decorated their hair with flowers and shell *leis* and the Mal'lam found them quite attractive. For clothing they wore only a skirt of that same soft material, tied around their waists with a thick cord of a local fiber. And much like the men of the Tarbara'ut, these men were not at all bothered by the fact that some of their women were having sex with the newcomers. A'lan however, was not tempted. Well, at least he didn't give in to the temptation! Marked differences between races is often a source of strong physical attraction and it was certainly applying here. The Mal'lam mostly stood a head taller than these islander men and taller yet than their women. Stockily built, wide shouldered and very muscular, these colonists were the perfect physical specimens for their role as resilient and vigorous adventurers.

Faldo-in was making slow headway with the language difficulty. There seemed no word or phrase in this new language similar enough to act as a starting point for translation. So it was a matter of memorizing personal names, and that was difficult enough for both sides. Then there was the difficulty of learning the words relating to familiar objects. Faldo-in told A'lan that given two or three years, he was sure he could carry on a sensible conversation.

"Unfortunately, Faldo-in, we don't have that much time. I believe that it's time we began preparing to return to our people. What say you?" Faldo-in too felt that the time had come. In fact all of the crew was missing their families and friends. Also there was the possibility that the rest of the Mal'lam had already left Sht'ah Lee and had arrived at the Tarbara'ut islands. Yes, it was time for the voyagers to sail back to the northwest. Only Pash'wo seemed entirely happy to remain here longer. There was so much more that he wished to learn of the plant materials on this island and these people's knowledge and use of those plants and herbs they had apparently brought with them. And then there was that wonderful food plant which the colonists called, 'kumaru'. Surely they would allow the Mal'lam to trade coconuts for these tubers and some other plants unique in his experience. And so it was agreed. Pash'wo Herb-Master would remain, continuing his explorations and studies, hoping with the little colony of people here that their own would return for them. 'Wa'Boton' would carry but one hundred coconuts on the return voyage, leaving over four hundred for these hospitable people to eat or plant or whatever they wished.

A rousing party was held on the eve of the Mal'lam departure. The colonists were obviously sad to see their guests leave but dancing and feasting brought them close together one last time. Even more than the affable Tarbara'ut, the Mal'lam found these people to be quite similar in their outlook and work ethic. Barring the language difficulty, the Sea-Hewn felt very much at home here. But 'home' was calling. Shin-shet-olo and A'lan sat somewhat apart from the festivities, the night relaxing itself to accept the dawn. Shin-shet-olo had a small child cradled in his lap, sound asleep. The two men with similar characters, the islander probably ten years older, were quite comfortable, sitting and watching the firelight from the big bonfire flickering through the moving crowd beyond. Words to share would have been good but in their absence there was the understanding which had developed between the two men over the past two weeks.

Then Shin-shet-olo reached up and took from around his neck that wondrous shell pendant which had caught A'lan's eye on that first morning on the beach. He handed it to A'lan, nodding his intention that his new friend should have it. A'lan took it, looked up questioningly at the Headman, was reassured, and then began to examine it. It was not shell, at least no shell he had ever seen. It was very hard and glossy, shaped in a spiral. One hole had been made and through it was strung a braided cord of some kind of leather. And it was heavier than shell. Smiling his thanks, A'lan placed the cord around his neck and then let the pendant fall onto his upper chest where it rested at the apex of his collar bones as if satisfied with its new home.

A'lan knew he must offer another gift of equal value in return. But what did he have? Ah, yes. His hands went to his belly and untied the plaited fiber cord which held his seaman's knife in its pigskin sheath. He remembered Shin-shet-olo having eyed it many times. This knife had been made especially for Al'an by the Mal'lam Stone-Master, Enno, shortly before their departure on this voyage. It was his prized possession. He held it out with both hands in offering to his new-found friend. Shin-shet-olo took it and he too looked with questions at the giver. A'lan smiled and nodded. The islander drew the knife from the sheath and held it up to catch the firelight, turning it this way and that, one finger cautiously testing the sharp edge. The obsidian from which it was made, part of the last of Enno's cache of the stone brought from Sht'ah Lee, was hafted with a hardwood from the islands of the Tarbara'ut. The strong glue and pig leather binding were also from Enno's diminishing reserve of materials from the islands of the Mal'lam.

While his new friend sat admiring his new knife, A'lan again examined his pendant. He tested it with his teeth. No, this was not any shell he had ever seen. What was it? The lack of a mutual language prevented any understanding except that it was a precious item. This was the first, but perhaps not the last artifact of copper which a Mal'lam Sea-Hewn might ever hold.

The child in Shin-shet-olo's lap squirmed and dug an elbow into a painful place, bringing a sudden intake of breath and a grunt from his father. He picked the still-sleeping child up and rose to his feet. It was time for some rest. The coming day was the day for preparation for departure. A'lan hated to see the night end for he knew that the likelihood of his ever meeting this man again was small indeed. They shared a great ocean and only happy chance had brought them together here on this small dot within that huge expanse.

The Mal'lam seamen rose late in the morning, some with but few hours sleep behind them. Still they were soon into the heavy work of loading supplies aboard and doing those last-minute jobs which always attended a launch. All the available bamboo and gourd water vessels were filled and stowed away along with a generous supply of that delicious '*kumaru*'. Much of that supply was placed in a specially built holding bay in one hull, up out of seawater which naturally accumulated in the bottom of the canoe. It was covered in dry grasses and wrapped around with layers of finely woven *pandanus*, protection from all but total submersion. There lay a gift from a chance encounter which would forever alter the lifestyle of these people who called themselves, the Mal'lam. And the possession of this food plant would extend out into seas and lands which the Mal'lam themselves would never see. The islanders who had so generously offered this gift would keep for themselves a plant of equal importance; the coconut. Should their brothers from that mysterious continent far to the east manage to return to them and carry this gift from the Mal'lam, so too would it affect the livelihood of another people. The opening of eastern Oceania had begun with blessings aplenty. And it was a product of peaceful brotherhood in the face of complete strangeness. *Earth Mother* smiled again upon *Her* sea.

Enough daylight remained for the vessel, 'Wa'Olon', to launch itself safely through the reef's opening and head out to the safe, open sea beyond. The whole of the islander community plus that one Mal'lam Herbalist, Pash'wo, stood on the beach and continued to shout and wave to the departing canoe until all were certain that those seamen would hear only the wind and the waves around them. Pash'wo stood alone for another hour until the fading light had stolen the view of his brothers' canoe and its tall sails. The tears he shed were not just loneliness or regret. Pash'wo knew that he was dying and would not have survived the journey back. Each tear was a prayer of blessing for his people.

When A'lan had come to say farewell to Pash'wo Herb-Master, his own eyes had held the glitter of tears. A'lan Sea-Master held this man in great esteem and told him so. "Pash'wo, dear friend, we will all miss you. Are you sure you will not change your mind?" A'lan's special vision searched for a reason other than that this dedicated herbalist simply wanted to remain to explore and learn more of the flora and fauna of this island. It was there. Yes, around the strong figure of Pash'wo hovered a faint, grayish fluorescence. A'lan had seen it before. When his great uncle Tal'ma had been near death, there too was that strange blur. "I understand now, Pash-an. Forgive me for not knowing before. We shall not meet again!" Pash'wo only nodded but then he brightened and smiled.

"A'lan Sea-Master, it has been a privilege to sail with you. You are truly an exceptional young man. My senses tell me that your life will be long and filled with adventure." He reached out and tapped the copper spiral which hung from A'lan's neck. "This pendant has great meaning to the man who gave it to you, meaning which our lack of mutual words cannot convey. Keep it always with you. And keep the awareness of the *Earth Mother* always in your mind. Farewell, A'lan-an!" With that he turned and walked to join the islanders who would care for him until his passing, many months later.

Chapter Forty Seven ~ The Great Exodus from Sht'ah Lee

That great mountain, Volan Votu, whose towering pinnacle had greeted generations of Mal'lam sailors with its welcoming presence was now glowering down upon these same people with immanent threat. Daily the mountain's rumbles and growling sent chills of foreboding over its slopes and onto the flatlands near the sea. There the Mal'lam were in the final stages of preparing to flee this last outpost of what had once been a kind and gentle archipelago. Just as she had screamed her childish fears on that day on Sh'ham-Set before that island's disastrous eruption and destruction, Tina-an Earth-Plait, more mature and circumspect now, struggled with the insistent messages her special sensitivity conveyed to her. More often now did her mentor, the Spirit woman, The Vesa'tan, come to her with warnings. "Within a year!" had been the forecast and Tina-an doubted it not.

The third shuttle voyage to the small enclave on the island of 'Win'no'hi' had only just returned, its crews exhausted by a bad-weather passage. 'Win'no'hi-Set' now accommodated over one-hundred Mal'lam and Itin refugees, that small island's young infrastructure stretched to the limit to provide enough food for the new settlers. The Council of Elders had just completed another convocation, perhaps the shortest in Mal'lam history. There was no longer time for the old, traditional method of casual consideration and debate. Voyage-Master Al'malan had assumed almost dictatorial powers, so contrary to his own nature let alone to Mal'lam tradition. But very few voices were raised in objection. Everyone knew that this island of Sht'ah Lee would soon be destroyed as had its northern neighbors and the final, great fleet of voyaging canoes were being prepared for the journey away to a new life for these people.

It would be a long journey. This fleet would not stop at 'Win'no'hi-Set' but would continue on directly for the islands of the Tarbara'ut, perhaps as much as two and a half months away. These twelve voyaging canoes - all but the recently returned four - were in good repair and ready to go. Dozens of Wood-Hewn craftsmen descended upon these four weather-beaten vessels and while their crews rested and regained their strength, completed the necessary refits. Canoe-Master Joha'lan now had a staff of very competent supervisors who lightened his workload. Still, he was a man near to collapse. His wife, Sha'lat, worried constantly about his weight-loss and fatigue and applied all her herbal knowledge to assist him. Everywhere the Mal'lam were working in extremity!

When this last fleet out of Sht'ah Lee sailed it would carry over nine hundred souls, men women and children. Some children had already been carried to 'Win'no'hi' and only one child and one elderly man had been lost overboard. Falling overboard was always a risk for even the most veteran seaman. Special care had to be taken with the little ones, toddlers who might wander away from safety. It would be the added task of each Sea-Master to properly inform and train his passengers as to the dangers when underway. With nearly sixty people aboard these big, double-hulled canoes, each one at least fifty feet long, space and amenity was going to be at a minimum. So too was food and water going to be at a premium. Some seamen joked that while underway there would be so many fishhooks trailing behind the vessels that any fish within reach would be in danger, hungry for bait or not. Already Mal'lam landsmen and women were familiarizing themselves with the vessels, seaman conducting tours and educating them as to the routine of life aboard. As the voyages to 'Win'no'hi' had proven, the Mal'lam and the few Itin remaining already possessed the social cohesion and personal discipline to assure that each vessel's compliment of voyagers would soon adjust.

The woman known as *'Ja'jan'*, now reclaiming her identity as Ja'eel-Feather-Plait, had unfortunately so inculcated some of her previous devotees with the nonsense of her ideology that they refused to relinquish it. Some forty of those people, men and women, refused the obvious signs of this island's demise and clung to the area of their settlement with dogged insistence that all would be right. 'Sht'ah Lee would save them!', was their desperate hope. No one in that group of hold-outs possessed the *'sight'*, although two claimed that capacity. These two vied for control of the surviving *'Ja'jan an-lo'* and contention and fear prevailed there. Their orgies were now held more often and many pigs and chickens were sacrificed to the blind and deaf Gods which they now espoused. No amount of entreaty on the part of the Mal'lam Elders could sway them. They were doomed and preferred destruction to the easier admission that they had been mistaken. Some among them were still voicing threats toward Ja'eel Feather-Plait. That she had betrayed them was not in question. She herself agonized over this truth.

Some ten to twelve days before the voyaging fleet's planned departure, weather being the deciding factor, Ja'eel eluded her guard of armed Mal'lam and slipped into the bush and made her way to what had been her 'sacred village'. Wearing only a standard Mal'lam day-to-day wrap of undecorated *tapa* cloth, her hair even was unadorned, she was setting out on a mission which she hoped would finally reconcile her previous foolishness and allow her full renewal of membership in her Mal'lam people's community. Ja'eel had been given her opportunity to see her son, Sahn'ta but it had been at a distance, at her request. The now-six year old, sturdy and resembling his father, Al'malan, was brought by his father to near where Ja'eel was sitting among a group of Herbalist women. The reluctant mother sat with silent tears streaming down her face but uttered not one word. Al'malan and their son sat beneath a shade tree, the father teaching the lad some rope ties. Occasionally he would glance up at Ja'eel but made no attempt to contact her. Sahn'ta remained unaware that anything was of particular importance and was totally absorbed in what his father was teaching him. He tied and retied knots and chatted amiably with Al'malan until it was clear that he was becoming bored. It was time to leave. Taking Sahn'ta by the hand he began strolling back toward the village, looking back only once to where the women were sitting. Ja'eel raised one hand briefly, a gesture of thanks. Then they were gone. It had been enough. Now she had things to do.

Reaching the now run-down little village she stopped while still hidden in the undergrowth and surveyed the scene. Something was going on there. A noisy debate seemed in progress and the little square of open ground in front of what had been *Her* compound was crowded with those remaining devotees. She listened intently but could not make sense of the loud contention being voiced. Now was the time! Standing up straight, she brushed back her hair and straightened her wrap, took some deep breaths and then committed herself. Striding with an approximation of her old style of strut she came to the back of the crowd without at first being recognized, the emotions of those involved this day so intense. She pushed her way to the center of the crowd. In a small open space two women stood facing each other - she knew them well - and they appeared about to assault each other physically, their faces flushed with anger and aggression. With a courage which only this morning's sudden determination had aroused, Ja'eel stepped between the two.

"Brothers and sisters!" her voice was loud and contained some of that dominance of old. "I have come to you in peace and I wish to have you hear me!" Silence fell like a prelude to an explosion. Then gasps of disbelief, rumbles of outrage and squeals of hope mingled as voices regained themselves. The two contending women stood back a few paces, more surprised perhaps than any there. They had been engaged in the building argument about who was going to succeed '*Ja'jan*' as leader of this diminished, pathetic remnant of a movement which was intended to succeed the Mal'lam.

"I am told that those of you still here intend to remain on Sht'ah Lee-Set. You must not! This island is going to die just as all the others to our north have. You know that!" Ja'eel paused for a moment only, time in which to sense the mood more fully. It didn't feel good. "I know what many of you feel toward me. You think I have betrayed you by my leaving." There were threats being murmured now and she rushed to cut them off. Turning slowly to face everyone in the hostile circle around her she let her tears of sorrow flow. "My leaving you was not my only betrayal. My convincing you that you should follow me in the first place was my real betrayal!"

Those words took some in the crowd many moments to digest. One man in the crowd now moved closer to her, a movement which she saw out of the corner of her eye. It was the Stone-Hewn, Kal'to'lot, one of those men who had been seduced by Ja'eel near the beginning of her 'reign' and the man she had appointed to construct her now-destroyed sacrificial altar. Here is where death will issue from, of this Ja'eel was sure. He, like all the others present, had reason to hate her. "Whatever you wish to do to me - kill me if you must - but you must rejoin *your* people! Remaining here will mean senseless tragedy and a death which none of you deserve. I remember the horror of the death of Sh'ham-Set. It is not a good way to die."

The sturdy figure of the stonemason moved closer now, standing just behind a women to Ja'eel's left. Ja'eel tensed, closed her eyes and sighed, resigned to the inevitable. But she must make one more attempt to persuade them to save their own lives. "I beg you, all of you. Burn this sad little village and let all that took place within it be carried away in smoke. Return to the memories of your childhood happiness among your people, the Mal'lam. You are all Mal'lam and your families and friends there will welcome you. I assure you of this because *I*, the greatest threat to the happiness and stability of *my* people, have been forgiven by them and brought back into their loving embrace. Do what you will with me. I am at peace now with my son and my mother and all who once loved me. I love you too - all of you! May the *Earth Mother* forgive me for misleading you!"

"You filthy bitch!" screamed a woman on Ja'eel's right and rushed toward the focus of her own fear and distractions. Her rush was met by the powerful arm of the Stone-Hewn, Kal'to'lot, his other arm was raised and its hand held one of those murderous, cdgcd clubs.

"Stay back!" and he shoved the woman with a mighty heave, making her nearly fall. She took ten steps back into the crowd and hid. "The rest of you - all of you - listen to me! This woman, Ja'jan or Ja'eel, however she is to be called, is not to be harmed. We all here, made our own minds up one day to follow this woman's teachings. It was good for a while, wasn't it?" Kal'to'lot swept his gaze back and forth among the crowd, his arm with its terrible weapon still held high. The circle of would-be devotees moved back and any sense of unity began to dissolve. "But Ja'eel has had the courage to return to us and say again that which our Mal'lam family has been saying all along ... that we too must flee this island." A man stepped forward from the widening ring of people and made to challenge the Stone-Hewn protector.

"Don't make me laugh, Fol'sho Wood-Hewn. Step back, now!" The determination in the voice of a man for whom life had been nearly wasted on self-doubt, struck the would-be challenger with its deadly truth and he retreated, all aggression dissipated. Kal'to'lot Stone-Hewn then slowly lowered his club and the sigh of relief swept quietly among the gathered ex-devotees.

"Please, my brothers and sisters ... let us begin again. Begin a new life together with all of our true family, our Mal'lam family." Ja'eel's softly spoken words were without tremor or the slightest hint of dramatics. She turned to Kal'to'lot and almost whispering said, "Thank you brother. I will speak to you soon. Please follow me this one last time." With that utterance the former 'Goddess of the Skies' turned and with a wave and a smile, beckoned these people to follow her down the shallow slopes toward the Mal'lam village. Most did on this day and behind them grey smoke began to rise from burning thatch. The rest would come in time.

~ ~ * ~ ~

The return of the *Ja'jan an-lo* to their families and friends was met with rejoicing by most Mal'lam but consternation by the Sea-Masters. Another forty souls to be crammed aboard the twelve canoes! The disposition of the voyagers upon the vessels had been meticulously planned and now the addition of these forty more people was going to throw all that careful planning out of kilter. Al'malan Voyage-Master formally addressed all those forty people and reiterated what everyone else had already been informed of; the proper conduct and the shared responsibilities necessary for the successful journey which may take up to two months. He impressed upon them that there would be hardships and danger. Hunger and thirst were quite possible and those who suffered seasickness would simply have to endure the malady as best they could. It was while he was speaking that Volan Votu sent a heavy impact through the ground and moments later came the sound of an eruption of steam from the great mountain's slopes. It was the beginning of the formation of a vent in the side of the mountain, an opening through which lava would eventually begin to pour. All heads had turned to look into the distance to the source of that sound. Anyone still considering remaining on Sht'ah Lee, young or old, reconsidered very seriously.

To Tina-an Earth-Plait, this latest testament to the correctness of The Vesa'tan's prediction brought added sadness. She had but that afternoon returned from the last of those journeys up the slopes of her beloved mountain. She had hoped for one last meeting with The Vesa'tan. Her Spirit mentor had once more spoken to her, this time in no uncertain terms. "Get down off this mountain, you silly girl! Now, this very minute! Turn around and run! You have no time ... not even an hour. Go!" Tina-an had turned and run, crying like a child who has been loudly scolded. Her eyes filled with tears, half blinding her. She had stumbled and fallen twice, her pack of food and blanket and clothing being emptied in the last collision with the hard soil of the trail. She struggled up limping, dropped the pack's straps off her shoulders and abandoned it and hobbled as quickly as she could until the pains faded and she could run again. Still she cried. Once she ran headlong into a large shrub which she surely should have known protruded into the trail. It wasn't until miles later that she noticed that her talisman, that blessed stone given her by her mentor, was missing. She started to turn around and run back to retrieve it but into her mind came the words, "Run, Tina-an, run!"

When finally she reached the main village, some hours later, she threw herself into Shen'ham's arms, totally exhausted and bereft. Shen'ham picked her up and carried her to his mother's lodgings where the gash on her knee could be cleansed and dressed. He sat beside her through that procedure and remained hovering near until finally she had fallen into a deep sleep. All the while strange new noises were issuing from the mountaintop and tremors occurred every few minutes. Late that afternoon, as rain clouds blanked out the view to the ominous peak away to the northeast, Al'malan and Canoe-Master Joha'lan made a final inspection of the twelve canoes. They walked slowly, chatting in tired voices, consulting with those crewmen and woodworkers still on duty among the big hulls.

"Brother." said Joha'lan, "We can't be any more ready than we are now. It's time!" "I agree, Joha'lan. I will order the loading of supplies to begin at first light tomorrow. The final harvest and preparation of the foodstuffs will require another six to seven days." Then Al'malan turned to face his friend and placed both hands on the big man's shoulders. "And *this* is an order! You are to rest during that time. You have done all you can do and then some. There are plenty of men who can see to the final readiness. You know I mean this well. We have all been concerned for your health of late. You must rest, even if I have to sit on your chest to keep you down." He smiled as he removed his hands and Joha'lan relinquished his frown to the grateful smile which his friend's words finally drew from him.

"Alright, brother. You're about as bossy as my wife sometimes, but yes, I am tired. Come with me. We'll have a drink of toddy and a bite to eat. Then I'm going to sleep until you have to wake me up to sail away with you." The next day no one sighted Joha'lan. With the connivance of his wife, Sha'lat, Al'malan saw that the man's food was lightly spiked with a soporific which would make him sleep for hours. "I think this banana paste is a bit off." he had muttered sleepily, finishing the whole bowl anyway.

The next day saw another glorious sight! Out of the early morning gloom over the sea to the west appeared the double sails of a canoe. It was 'Wa'Ter'ora', the canoe which had been left on 'Win'no'hi-Set' after the first voyage back there, nearly a year before. Shouts of welcome rang across the 'Bay of Dolphins' as Mal'lam seamen and villagers ran down to the shore to greet this most welcome addition to the voyaging fleet. Now those forty last-minute additions to the passenger list could be accommodated without straining the capacities of any of the existing twelve canoes. Not all of them would sail on this vessel, however. Al'malan, in consultation with many other Elders, decided that they must be parceled out among the various canoes and some people shifted from them to this new arrival. There still remained some distrust of these former dissidents. Ja'eel herself would sail on a vessel with only one of her former devotees aboard. It would be the Stone-hewn man, Kal'to'lot, he who still insisted on acting as a bodyguard for her. And their association was developing a deeper quality too.

"Shen'lat-an." Al'malan called out to the Sea-Master of the 'Wa'Ter'ora', "You are a most welcome sight! What prompted you to return just now? Surely the *Earth Mother* must have whispered in your ear." The heavily-bearded Sea-Master let out a loud guffaw and others of his crew added their laughter. "No, no, Voyage-Master. No one whispered ... someone shouted! That mad woman, Ven'ana, gave me no rest. For weeks she pestered me. Then she began shouting every morning, just outside my little hut. 'Get your canoe ready and go back to Sht'ah Lee!' she shouted. Every morning, day after day and often through the day. Such a woman! We came back mainly to get away from her. Why? Is something serious happening?"

It was partially the smell that informed the crew of this new arrival that something serious was indeed happening. It was the smell of rotten eggs. Another vent had opened, this time very near the upper *taro* paddies. The smell of sulfur came in sporadic drifts down onto the populated zones of the island. Not injurious in its concentration but an awful smell nonetheless and another spur to the Mal'lam to be away from here. The weather was not kind. Some thought it in league with the growing ferociousness of the mountain. Not only rain but a sustained wind with gusts of up to forty knots swept across the island from the northeast. At least this kept away the rotten egg smell.

Ripe coconuts were constantly bombarding the land beneath and increasing the odds that someone was actually going to be hit by one. The earth beneath the Mal'lam shuddered and jolted, coconuts flew at innocent pedestrians and the skies kept up a damp assault on the harvesters and made drying and packing especially difficult. Every Mal'lam had a chore to fulfill, most often many different ones within a day. Those seamen, and land dwellers that had occasion to sail and enjoyed it, could hardly wait to be at sea. Anything would be better than this endless struggle just to be free of a land which obviously didn't want them here.

"We can do no more, my dear!" This was the sentiment of the island's Herb-Mistress Shen'ha as she spoke with her compatriot, Sha'lat Herb-Mistress. Both women were now in the same family; one's son and the other's daughter soon to be wed. And they were, in fact, as close in spirit as any sisters could be. "All the plants and herbs, everything we can possibly gather and pack is now aboard the canoes. I don't know about you but, I'm truly exhausted. Oh, by the way. How is Joha'lan doing today? Poor man. All of our men are really such heroes!" Sha'lat offered a little giggle in response. "My hero has slept three days out of the past four. I stopped giving him any sleeping concoctions two days ago. This morning he woke up beside me and wanted to make love. I think I'll give him some more sleeping potion."

~ ~ * ~ ~

The morning of departure arrived bright and nearly clear, the sky tossed with rapidly sailing small clouds with no capacity for rain. Even the great mountain was quiescent. The tide had peaked and on its lowering the fleet sent its vessels, one by one, through the opening at 'Dolphin Bay'. The last two canoes to leave were 'Wa'Mal'lan', under the command of Al'malan's cousin, Chom'shul. Aboard were the Itin Sea-Master Ch'om'lo as second in command and his young family. Also were Shen'ha, Tina-an and Shen'ham 'Three Finger', acting as third in command. Aboard this vessel was Ja'eel and her guardian and forty-eight other Mal'lam and Itin.

'Wa'Rantar' was last off the beach, nearly every adult aboard being required to shove the great canoe free of the black sands and out into the waiting waves. Sht'ana and the children, Al'malan's mother, Sht'ah'et, Joha'lan, fully awake now, and his wife Sha'lat and various cousins, non-Clan refugees and a few Itin made up a compliment of forty-five. Fear and anxiety began to drop away almost immediately the vessels rode through those wonderful, majestic headlands, only to be replaced with great sorrow. Weeping men and women turned to look aft at what was still a most beautiful sight - their beloved Sht'ah Lee-Set!

Of all those aboard 'Wa'Rantar', no one could have sent more intense prayers to the *Earth Mother* than the Voyage-Master. Al'malan had withheld the intense emotions which had been choking his throat for these past few weeks. Upon his shoulders had fallen the most of this, his people's struggle, for the past five years. Still so young at only thirty five, already grey hairs were beginning to dominate his forked beard. He sat on the aft deck dressed as an ordinary seaman; breechcloth and belt with his seaman's knife. Nothing of a signature of office or authority except his hair style. Only with reluctance did he finally turn to gaze upon the retreating scene behind him. As most of the others aboard now turned to look upon a midday sea of unknown promise, Voyage-Master Al'malan looked behind and onto that last view of a world which had consumed his youth. He felt suddenly old; not in body but in spirit. How had he lost that vigor, that sense of the ever-beyond? He felt like weeping but knew he must not. He saw his young son, Sahn'ta, cavorting with three other children, totally oblivious to the depth of his father's suffering. And so it should be, Al'malan thought, "*Earth Mother*, be kind to me now. I am so tired. Bring strength to me again."

As if in answer to his call, two warm, soft hands descended onto his shoulders. Sh'tana! He half turned to greet her but she quickly took his head in both her hands and held his head toward land. "Look long and lovingly, my dearest!" she said, "Most of us are looking away and trying to forget our fear. You alone have looked fear in the face as the rest of us do a morning's breakfast. You are the most courageous of our people, my husband. Come now ... your crew has everything under control ...come and spend time with us." She let go her hold on his head and smiled down at him as he turned his eyes up toward her.

"You are truly the *Earth Mother's* handmaiden, Sh'tana!" he replied, took her hands and kissed them both and then rose and followed her to where his mother and their daughter sat sheltering beneath the shade of the hut amidships. This was his true source of strength. It was the blessing of the *Earth* Mother, channeled through those whom he loved and those who loved him unquestioningly. Al'malan turned his back on the dying island behind and picked up his daughter and kissed her, grinning widely as she giggled and squirmed in his arms.

Chapter Forty Eight - To the South and Another Future

As on that long-ago voyage to the south which A'lmalan Voyage-Master had first led, again he imposed a strict discipline among his fleet of canoes. The vessels sailed in a series of three 'V' formations, five in the first two and followed by the last three. Night would see torches borne by all, weather permitting. For three days the sailing was gentle on the landsmen, even on those who tended to motion sickness. Of the children aboard there were seventy ranging in age from infants to twelve years old. To all of them this was a most delightful adventure. Always, of course, there were a few timid ones who clung to their mothers or aunties but eventually they too began to adjust to this strange environment.

On the fourth day squalls and gusty winds assailed the fleet and the sea became choppy and the motion of the canoes more pronounced. As each squall of rain approached, the tightly woven rain-catcher mats were rigged and water vessels were refilled throughout the damp day. The huts amidships of each canoe were jammed with sheltering Mal'lam. Songs and chants and games helped to pass the time. On the decks the Sea-Hewn stood or hunkered down, their thick rain capes making them look like bushy stumps. Each man also wore a wide girdle of soft matting, wrapped from upper stomach to below the hips, designed to keep the torso warm. When it was raining like this, no fire could be lit on the small sand fire-pit on deck. Cold, damp food was all that was on offer. Neither was palm toddy available, a libation which landsmen might indulge in on a rainy day. Sex and alcohol were proscribed for all on this voyage!

The following week was again a period of fine weather. High but regular and sometimes exciting swells rolled toward the voyagers from the northeast. Some great storm had blown itself out, leaving this legacy of waves to radiate outward in testimony to its strength. The wind remained consistently from the west, the sail panels hardly having to be adjusted. As well, the navigators had determined that the fleet was caught in an eastward flowing current, highly unusual for this latitude.

"What do you think, Voyage-Master? Are we well on course?" The Elder Sea-Hewn, a Grey-Head from Sht'ah Lee and almost toothless, lisped his question to Al'malan.

"Yes, Fo'so-an. In fact we have made progress over the past three days greater than could be hoped for. If the wind and this extraordinary current continue as they have, we may be into the zone of calm within a day. Hopefully we can escape that. I don't look forward to having to endure that again with all these people aboard the canoes. It does seem to be an area which fluctuates. Coming back north from the islands of the Tarbara'ut we met light breezes but still enough wind to sail through the area. "And how is your back handling being at sea again, my dear friend?" Al'malan's question was genuine for this old gentleman was among the most highly regarded of those '*sighted*' Sea-Hewn. Al'malan had, some years before, learned much about navigation from him in one of those long teaching sessions which took place on land, under the cover of a disused canoe shed, during the storm season.

"Well enough." he replied, "But I'm afraid my sight, my '*sea sight*', has failed me!"Al'malan's aural sensitivity heard the echo of a sob of sadness there. He reached a hand over and patted the old man's knee. "Well, I suppose one day I'll not hear so well either. *Earth Mother* does seem to extract strange payments from us as we get older. I can't get it up as often as I used to either!" The two men shared a hearty laugh, Fo'so coughing after a few moments, Al'malan slapping his back helpfully. Recovered but still chuckling, Fo'so made to rise but Al'malan heard his intake of breath. There was pain in that sound. He quickly rose and assisted the old Sea-Hewn to his feet and holding one elbow, walked with him to the crowded hut where snores and heavy breathing could be heard above the rush of the sea on the hulls. Before turning back to the deck, Al'malan peered into the dark interior to where he knew his wife and children lay. Sh'tana, still awake but not wanting to rise and disturb the two children cuddled next to her, recognized her husband's figure silhouetted against the moonlit sky. She raised one arm and waved to him. He waved back, his smile unseen in the dark hut but felt by her. She took her own smile contentedly off to sleep.

Too good to last!? Yes, the doldrums fell upon the Mal'lam fleet after seventeen days of sailing. But the voyagers had managed to penetrate to the lower edge of the band of quiescent airs below the equator and had only to endure two days of windless, hot and sticky weather. It was 'Three Finger', aloft on the foremast of 'Wa'Malan' who first spotted the patterns of wind action on the water, a mile away to the south. Calling down to Chom'shul Sea-Master he pointed and said, "Away about a mile, Sea-Master. And there are clouds appearing well off to the south." Shouts reached across the water to the Voyage-Master's vessel and he in turn looked up to his mast-lookout. "What do you see to the south, Sht'oh'so?" The seaman had been looking eastward for a few minutes, his concentration on a strange apparition growing there. Quickly turning his scan to the south he called down that, yes, there was sign of wind to the south. But what might that be that was rippling the surface off there to the east? He had never seen its like before.

Al'malan thought he knew what it was. Still with the strength and agility of a younger man, he was up the ladder and to the top of the aft mast in seconds. He shielded his eyes against the oceans reflecting glare and peered intently. Of course - the 'Hoosh d'wan'! Again, his Destiny and that of his people had brought this valiant little fleet of vessels into conjunction with one of the sea's great dramatic events. The indicators of a reviving wind were reduced to a lesser consideration by the approach of this marvelous phenomenon. Since the fleet's thirteen vessels had been paddled close to each other and tethered, creating a little island of timber and sweating humanity, the message quickly spread. 'The 'Hoosh'dwan' are coming!"

Those few who had sailed back to Sht'ah Lee with Al'malan excitedly explained to their neighbors aboard the various canoes what a marvelous spectacle they were about to watch. "I hope the wind holds off!" This was a silent wish from the Master of this voyage. Like a small boy's was his enthusiasm, for no one who had ever witnessed this migration of those whales with their big, bulbous heads would ever cease relating the story; perhaps boringly after too many tellings. But now any unbelievers were about to be converted!

But the wind did come, fitfully, slowly increasing, demanding attention. While the passengers watched the approach of this disturbance on the surface with growing excitement, the Sea-Hewn had to return to their tasks. "Be careful aloft, you men!" was a common call from the vessels' commanders as young seamen again carried water aloft to wet down sails and lines, showering those below with a welcome coolness. The Masters knew that their young apprentice's eyes would keep returning to the approaching multitude of 'Hoosh' and might forget their safety lessons. Every Mal'lam old enough to comprehend the drama turned their eyes to the eastern sea. Parents lifted youngsters up and pointed and older eyes too strained to focus on this promised miracle.

It required nearly thirty minutes of extreme effort to uncouple the vessels and paddle them safely away from each other so that sails could be set, lines tightened and oars put in place for steering in response to the renewed breeze. All the while the passengers stood enthralled, getting in the way of the seamen as the men rushed about their tasks on the decks. But soon the thirteen canoes were under way by sail, cutting through the shallow swell, the black cetaceans diving under and around their surging hulls.

Three generations of Mal'lam were introduced to one of the most beautiful manifestations of *Earth Mother's* rich world of experience, reinforcing these people's infatuation with the majesty of the sea. Some Mal'lam aboard, enthralled as they were, dreamt of land and its solidity and safety but most would recount to their children and grandchildren the marvelous day when the 'Hoosh'dwan' blessed them with their presence. Children, boys and girls still too young to determine their course in life as adults, were infused with the desire to spend most of their existence upon this great, watery world. Indeed, the Mal'lam voyagers of the future would include young women whose dedication to exploration of the unknown would match that of any of their brothers. Aboard the canoe, 'Wa'Malan', Tina-an Earth-Plait, she of a childhood commitment to the land and its mysteries, sat and applauded the glorious parade of these thousands of sea-creatures as they swam and dove and sometimes leapt about her. Within her womb grew a child who's future would be dedicated also to the sea, as was its father, 'Three Finger' Sea-Hewn.

But before reaching their destination, these voyagers must endure some less kindly aspects of life upon the waves. The gentle, fitful breezes which had released the fleet from the temporary grip of the doldrums now grew into a sustained storm. The canoes widened their distances from each other, giving sea-room to maneuver in the increasing swell and turbulence. If constant rain were not enough for discomfort, stinging sea-spray, flying almost horizontally across the decks, drove the passengers into the huts again. The usual toilet platforms aft were now too dangerous to use. Special openings had been allowed for in the deck beneath the huts, safe toilets for the crowded, cowering inhabitants. Seasickness was rife and other special openings in the decking had been prepared for just this eventuality. Not even all the seamen were inured against this malady and even seasoned Sea-Hewn sometimes found themselves fighting the enervating effects of nausea. These seas they were now encountering, although not enormous, were rough and random in their flow, a constant challenge for Sea-Master and crew, the steersmen especially challenged and needing rest every hour. There were accidents and injuries among the seamen but the presence of so many Herbalists and Healers among the vessels prevented any severe results of the onslaught of this prolonged storm.

But twenty-eight days from departure, so many of the voyagers nearing collapse from fatigue and fear, the storm receded and a blue sky and gentle seas returned. And seabirds! All the Sea-Masters and navigators watched with thankful wonder as the evening sky revealed the flocks of terns and gannets winging steadily toward home - toward the south. The first clear night skies for nearly a week revealed that the fleet, miraculously still intact and again sailing in formation, was still on course. Not only on course but nearing their destination! But rather than raise the hopes of their passengers unduly, lest there be some mistake in their position, the Sea-Masters ordered their crewmen to hold their enthusiasms and not promote hopes among the landsmen which might not be fulfilled. A wise caution but unnecessary in the event.

Early morning of the day following the bird sightings saw those telltale clouds stationary over an hospitable group of islands, signaling their arrival at the home of the Tarbara'ut! Al'malan Voyage-Master stood alone in the very front of the port hull of his canoe. With all the power of his special perceptions he focused forward toward those green mounds of earth which were growing to view. Yes! We are there! He had been awake all night, in conference with the one 'sighted' Sea-Hewn aboard who was still fully capable and acutely tuned to the 'sea-lights'. Aboard the 'Wa'Malan', Ch'om'lo Sea-Master was making the same assessment and arriving at the same conclusion. The shapes of the hills, the color of the sea, the emerging scene of the whole expanse of the archipelago visible from this perspective ... it was all as it should be, all as he remembered. Yes, we are there.

Psychic signals had poured across the great distance for weeks and now with the proximity of the fleet itself, the 'seers' on shore were awakened with insistent messages;

"Get up and see for yourself! They are here!" And so one, then another of the Mal'lam on the islands of the Tarbara'ut spread the word. On the island once known as 'Snake Island', now renamed 'Sh'ham-ra-Set' or, 'New Sh'ham', the many newly-made canoes and bamboo rafts filled with paddlers and passengers all headed for the beach at 'Tara'tor', where they knew the fleet would land. The excitement among the Mal'lam on 'Tara'tor' stirred a renewed anxiety among the indigenous population. These three years had seen the newcomers, agreeable and conciliatory as they were, come to dominate the lifestyle of the local people. The energetic and mind-boggling activity of the Mal'lam in comparison to these little people's traditional way of life was changing not only the landscape but the future of the Tarbara'ut. Tarbara'ut women were now giving birth with wonderful regularity. But most of the babies were half Mal'lam. The eclipse of a people, begun by some unfathomable local circumstance long before the arrival of the Mal'lam, was now accelerating. And the Mal'lam were absorbing a new genetic component.

~ ~ * ~ ~

The battered and worn vessel, 'Wa'Boton', carried its tired crewmen doggedly onward toward the islands of the Tarbara'ut. This day was windy but the sky was a bright and clear dome of blue. Sea-Master A'lan was sleeping in the little hut amidships, two other men of the night crew were also resting nearby.

The moonless night before had revealed the familiar, sub-surface streaks of light which signaled the close proximity of their goal. The southeast trade winds were fair behind them now and 'Wa'Boton' surged forward over the moderate swell, the sail panels winged out left and right to catch the maximum airs. "We're flying now, eh?" Faldo-in Sea-Hewn commented to the other seaman manning the steering oar. "Yes. The best sailing we've struck so far in all these months." replied his mate, "'Wa'Boton' wants to go home as badly as we do, I think." Just then Faldo-in glanced behind him and nearly lost his grip on the oar. What is that?! "Look behind us!" he gasped, steadying himself with feet wide apart, half expecting a collision.

The other oarsman made no sound but the look on his face displayed his own alarm. There on the surface, just a few feet behind the tips of the oar blade, was the great grey back of a huge whale.

"Hoosh! Hoosh right behind us!" Faldo-in finally managed to call out to his shipmates. The lookout up the forward mast had eyes only for the horizon ahead and had not seen the approach of the monstrous cetacean from behind. Everyone on deck ran aft to see for themselves. Most stopped short of the edge of the deck and peered over cautiously as if afraid whatever it was might suddenly reach aboard and swallow them. It was huge! And then another, somewhat smaller whale surfaced beside the first one and blew a great spray of mist into the air, immediately followed by a loud sucking sound as it inhaled. Here were two of the earth's largest creatures come for a visit. Someone rushed to awaken the sleeping crewmen but Faldo-in's cry had already done that. A'lan had awakened immediately and was on his feet before he was fully awake. Soon the whole of 'Wa'Boton's crew was staring in wonder at this marvelous apparition. All had seen many whales in their days upon the open sea but none had ever been so close to these majestic creatures.

For more than twenty minutes this huge mother, for that's what she was, and her half-grown calf attended the 'Wa'Boton'. Neither whale submerged during that time, both of them simply cruising side by side effortlessly, the action of their huge flukes hidden beneath the surface behind them, keeping pace with the canoe as it ran at nearly maximum speed. And then abruptly both made that great intake of air and dived beneath the vessel. Their massive tails rose high into the air and slowly, gracefully, sank below the surface with hardly a splash. The Mal'lam seamen ran to the sides of the hulls and peered down into the clear blue water. The great shapes could be seen to extend beyond the length of their canoe, dwarfing it in comparison to the mother whale's ninety foot length and massive bulk. Slowly they drifted down into the blue gloom and finally disappeared. The Sea-Hewn could only stand gaping in awe. The man on watch up the mast had the most wonderful view of all. When finally he returned his attention back to the northwest his eyes widened with another wonder. Land!

Dead ahead, in an otherwise featureless horizon lay a bank of small, fluffy clouds trying to coagulate into an island chain's usual tell-tale accompaniment. "Land!" the excited seaman fairly screamed. "Land ahead! It's the Tarbara'ut for sure!"

Three seamen rushed for the aft mast but Sea-Master A'lan was there first and up the ladder rungs to the top as quickly as ever he had done. He hung by one arm from the mast, leaning far out, but the foremast sail panel obscured his view. "Come to starboard a bit, Faldo-an!" he called down to the steersmen. Moments later the big canoe was steered to the right and the view opened for A'lan's anxious eyes. "Yes! We're there!" he muttered, grinning widely, his heart racing with a boyish excitement. He cast his visual acuity forward and was rewarded with the vision of a faint pinkish mist hovering around the little archipelago off there on the horizon. "Arawee!" he muttered again, "Oh Arawee!" and tears welled in his eyes and washed away the vision. But he knew! He knew what that glow was.

The wind remained with the joyous crew of 'Wa'Boton', driving their worn vessel and its patched sails in a steady rush for the islands. Ashore on 'Tara'tor', forewarned by the psychics, lookouts scanned the sea to the south and east. "There they are!" came the shouts from a number of seamen with sharp and experienced vision. But it soon became apparent that there was only one set of sails out there. Surely the two canoes would be sailing together - wouldn't they?

The main fleet of Al'malan's thirteen vessels had reached 'Tara'tor' only five days before but all had been hauled ashore and were being dismantled and prepared for refit. Two of those canoes which had remained here for three years were fit for sea however, and Al'malan ordered them both to be launched and sailed out to greet the returning explorers. He was aboard the first vessel through the opening in the reef and among the twenty-seven crew and eager passengers was one seaman insistent on being first among the greeters.

Shen'ham Sea-Hewn was as anxiously uncertain as anyone but determined to be among the first to know the answer to the universal question: why was there only one vessel approaching? It took two hours for the three canoes to make contact; the canoes heading outward had to tack constantly in the face of that fortunate wind which was driving 'Wa'Boton' so directly. The Voyage-Master Al'malan had given the order for the two vessels from 'Tara'tor' to swing wide to each side of the homecoming-canoe and then circle around to come up abreast of it.

Al'malan recognized 'Wa'Boton' by its beautifully upward-curved and carved bows. "Hello Sh'ban'ol Sea-Master!" he called out across the narrowing distance, hanging out beyond the edge of the canoe by one strong grip on a mast stay. But instead of the familiar figure of the big, bearded seaman whom he had known for so many years, waving back and returning his call, another, slimmer and younger man wearing a Sea-Master's headdress replied. "By the Sea Gods!" he said loudly. "That's young A'lan Sea-Hewn" Others about him mentioned how few crew were apparent aboard the sorry-looking vessel with its patched and faded sails.

"Where is 'Wa'Salat'?" Al'malan could not wait longer to know what had occurred. Quickly the reply came. A voice no longer that of the lad he had last seen here on the Tarbara'ut islands shouted across, "Wa'Salat' is no more! Nor are the Sea-Masters Fan'al and Sh'ban'al. Both they and many crewmen died in a terrible storm which only we few survived. 'Wa'Salat' was found but we had to abandon our brother vessel to the sea." Sea-Master A'lan was loath to slow his vessel's rush toward land. Sharing the news could wait.

Then A'lan recognized the familiar figure of his old and best friend, Shen'ham, waving from Al'malan's canoe. Something was strange about the hand that waved. Maybe he was holding something. A'lan waved back with heartfelt enthusiasm, hardly able to wait to be again with his oldest friend. And now Faldo-in was beside him, calling Shen'ham's name out loudly. The shouts and cries flew across the light chop on the water all the way back to the opening in the reef. Then came the serious business of seamanship and one by one the three canoes entered the wide lagoon and the paddlers drove the vessels the last hundred yards to the welcome awaiting them on the beach.

What a welcome it was, however tempered by the tragic news of the losses. A'lan Sea-Master had shed his Master's regalia before landing, feeling somehow embarrassed. His eyes swept the beach as 'Wa'Boton' grounded. His heart leapt with joy as he spied his mother, Lana'ma Herb-Plait. Beside her was Tina-an whose face was lit with a wide grin. So many others too did he recognize, too many to focus on all at once. The usual disorienting factor immediately took hold, not only of A'lan but Faldo-in and all the rest of the crew. Every long voyage brought this strange sense of disjointed familiarity yet it was tinged with strangeness. Remembering his duty as Master, A'lan saw to the security of his vessel first, the waiting crowd cooperating in this traditional necessity by waiting for the canoe to be secured to land before descending on their loved ones. All the while, pulling his eyes away from those members of his family and his old friends, A'lan cast his view about for that signature of specialness which he so sought. There it was, faintly glowing there at the back of the crowd. That pink glow surrounding the form of a small, black-skinned woman - and she was holding an infant in her arms!

"All secure, Sea-Master!" one of A'lan's crew called to him.

"Then don't wait any longer, brothers!" their Master shouted. Within seconds A'lan was left alone on the front of the canoe's bridging deck, every other man now on the beach and running to greet friends and family. Nor did he wait long before jumping down too. Tradition held that the Sea-Master must be last to leave his vessel, but how long he must wait was not prescribed. His mother was first to embrace him and he thought she might crush his ribs with the power of her greeting. Tina-an joined in the huge hug, then Canoe-Master Joha'lan and Sha'lat and A'lan's body disappeared in a mass of weeping, grinning Mal'lam. Finally his mother was able to free him enough to stand back and hold his face in her hands. She inspected that long scar, admired the now full beard which gave his face a new gravity, touched the plaits on each side of his head, signature of a Sea-Master. She gave him a puzzled look, hardly believing what she saw. From time to time he was able to look over and around his welcoming committee and again search for a view of Arawee. Again the pink glow guided his glance.

Taking his mother by the hand, A'lan led her through the crowd, his friends following. Arawee, her heart nearly shattering with the terror that A'lan might ignore her, even reject her, stood weeping as she held the beautiful baby boy tightly. Then he was coming toward her, his eyes on hers, gripping her with their meaning. He began running, careless of bumping into others of the jostling crowd, Lana'ma struggling to keep up, her grip on his hand tenacious. Then he was there, right before Arawee. He pulled his hand from his mother's grasp and wrapped his arms around both Arawee and the child. Their kiss was long and desperate and the baby began to whimper. The immensity of the emotions which swirled about him was naturally frightening. His was not the only child's whimpers on this beach this day. Finally A'lan turned to his mother, one hand still clutching Arawee as if afraid she might run away.

"Mother. This is Arawee - my woman! Soon she will be my wife!" As if to remind him of something he was overlooking, Arawee poked his shoulder with her free hand, jiggling the baby all the while, trying to appease the little fellow. A'lan's eyes now flooded with tears and with a sob he held out both hands to take his son. Lana'ma had come close beside the couple by now, smiling her joy as tears streamed down her cheeks. Touching her chest she said to the small woman, "I Lana'ma'. I A'lan's mother. Do you understand?"

"Of course, Lana'ma. I do understand." Arawee had learned much Mal'lam language in A'lan's absence. Unabashed, Lana'ma stepped forward and embraced Arawee with great tenderness, chuckles of happiness welling up from her throat. The two women turned to watch A'lan as he held his son for the first time. His mother had never seen that expression on her only son's face before. It was like a child might look holding a little puppy ... full of surprise, curiosity, adoration and unconditional love.

The Tarbara'ut people looked on in increasing wonder. Here were hundreds of these strangers, these high energy people who grew strange things, cooked most of their food, even fish, yet remained gentle and respectful of the local people's needs and possessions. And hadn't they changed the land which the Tarbara'ut had allowed them to settle on!

Shen'ham and Tina-an, their mothers and Sht'ana and Al'malan and their children and other friends found A'lan and his family among the crowd at about the time that Joha'lan and Sha'lat rejoined them. All along the beach, as afternoon melted into soft, tropical evening, the sounds of celebration only grew. Drums and flutes and those small stringed instruments started up. Chants and songs rang from various places along the long shoreline. With the exception of those nearly three-hundred Mal'lam and Itin on Win'no'hi-Set, far to the north, the Mal'lam were together again!

"'Three Finger', eh?" said A'lan, now holding his second cup of palm toddy, the first having gotten him a bit tiddly already. Yes!" Shen'ham retorted loudly, "and it's all his fault!" as he nudged Ch'om'lo who sat beside him. Ch'om'lo was holding his infant son as was A'lan, the night's merriment now totally ignored by the sleeping babies. The women, including Arawee, were sitting together a few feet away, confident that the fathers were in good control of their awesome little charges. Arawee's and A'lan's eyes kept signaling to each other. This would be a long night; and when would all these people go to bed and leave us alone? When finally the revelry subsided, an hour before dawn, A'lan and Arawee left the beach together, the as-yet unnamed child in its father's arms. He had seldom relinquished its warm little body all night, surrendering it only to its mother's breasts when it insisted on nourishment.

Laying the sleeping child down on a soft bed of coconut fiber beneath a copse of young coconut trees, the young lovers embraced tightly. Suddenly A'lan moved back a step, still holding Arawee at arms length. He looked down in the darkness and tried to see what was that wetness covering his chest. Arawee began giggling and snorting. A'lan had never experienced mother's milk on his chest before. The two dissolved in laughter and holding each other tightly, fell to their knees onto the softly woven mat of pandanus leaves which someone had providently left at this spot. The slowly brightening dawn saw the three sleeping soundly together, the morning's soft breeze sighing through the ironwood trees around and above them. A'lan Sea-Master finally knew the meaning of being 'home'.

~ ~ * ~ ~

Six months later, to the day, Tina-an Earth-Plait gave birth to a healthy daughter. On her forehead, to the left and just below her hairline, were three small, purplish-brown birthmarks. "As if her father had touched her while still in the womb!" one Elder Herbalist announced, excited and yet baffled by this surprising manifestation.

Birthmarks were rare and those whose study of the esoteric signs of *Earth Mother's* direct dealings with humanity pondered long on its meaning. Tina-an, after her athletic body had assisted her daughter's entry into the Mal'lam world for but five hours, felt that she knew the meaning of those marks. "The Vesa'tan' sat with my husband and I as we conceived our child. I never told Shen'ham that I saw her there with us. Men can be put off by such things, you know." What Tina-an disclosed to no one, ever, was the certain knowledge which came to her many days later; that one day her husband and their daughter would embark upon a voyage together. He would be a renowned Sea-Master by that time, and she would never see them again. Tina's experiences with 'The Vesa'tan' through these many years had convinced her that wishes and hopes were solely a human involvement; the 'truth' lay somewhere within a mystery which was beyond either hope or wish. Tina-an called it simply, faith.

It was when Tina-an Earth-Plait traveled to the small island of 'Sh'ham-ra' that she discovered a world which she could relate to just as she had to Sht'ah Lee. For here she rediscovered her mentor, 'The Vesa'tan'. That old woman's Spirit had come to her on her first day there. Walking with her baby in a sling suspended from her shoulders, the little one resting against Tina's belly, she climbed at a slow pace up to the hills above the now rapidly evolving lowland gardens and paddies. New gardens were being built for the propagation of those delicious new tubers which A'lan called *kumeru,* a food source which was exciting many far-thinking Mal'lam. And what of that marvelous pendant he now wore constantly? Had anyone ever seen such a rich material? Oh yes, she still loved A'lan as she had as a child. But now it was the love of a brother. How he had changed; just so had her husband, Shen'ham, become quite another person from that chubby boy she had first known. Her musings were interrupted by that familiar voice now heard here in these unfamiliar places.

"Tina-an, my child! Come sit and talk with me." Tina instinctively reached toward her throat as she always had when hearing that beloved voice. But the talisman was no longer there. Less and less did she think of it anymore. The little bundle of warmth lying against her stomach seemed quite a wonderful enough talisman. Tina patted her daughter, now named Vesa-an, the child half asleep and curled up comfortably. Tina found a large stone with a natural seat-shape eroded into it and sat down, her view now out over the island and onto the smaller islands within this archipelago's huge, surrounding lagoon. She felt so at peace. She felt the very real presence too, of The Vesa'tan but after all these years, knew not to bother to look for her physical form.

"Thank you for naming your daughter after me, dear child." The voice was very close and it spoke softly. Tina was covered in chills and goose bumps. This often happened when The Vesa'tan was near but now she was *very* near - Tina could feel a physical presence but a quick look around revealed no one. Then Tina noticed a strange shimmering in the air in front of her, some phenomenon which was distorting the view behind it. Slowly that shimmering took on the rough outline of a woman. Then it disappeared.

"Phew! Well, that's the best I could do my dear." Tina-an began to chuckle at the tone in The Vesa'tan's voice. "That was pretty impressive, just the same. But I'm so glad that you are here." Tina then reached into the baby's sling and gently lifted Vesa-an out and sat her on her knee.

"Can you see your auntie Vesa'tan, Vesa-an?" The infant, her head wobbling back and forth, too young yet to keep her head upright, made a cooing sound, dribbled a long string of saliva and waved her little arms. "That means, yes, she can see me." The Vesa'tan answered. "She is a blessed child, like her mother. All children can see Spirits because they have just come from that world themselves. Now, there was something which you wanted to discuss with me?"

Tina-an had no recollection of making a request to speak about anything specific. She frowned a moment, thinking hard, then smiled. "Oh yes. Yes, Vesa'tan, I do have something which is bothering me somewhat. It's ... well ... it's about a dream, or maybe a message in a dream." Tina-an took a deep breath and fought off the sadness which rekindling that message brought with it. "I know that Vesa-an will be Plait of the Sea. Many Mal'lam females will be. And Dear Shen'ham will become a famous man and one day they will sail away together on a voyage and I will never see them again." Tina's voice broke but she resisted the sob which lay behind it.

"Well my dear, one day indeed you will be parted from your loved ones in this world. But did you not consider that the parting you fear will not be because of any event which would remove them from your world? Did you not consider that it might be *you* who departs this world and it will be their sorrow when they return and you are not there?"

Tina-an shook her head and broke into a grateful smile. "How simple, Vesa'tan. How simple of me not to have seen that. Oh, you are so dear to me! Thank you." Little Vesa-an was cooing and dribbling again and again waving her arms. And something wet was running over Tina's knees. "Oh my!" she said. "Such timing little babies have."

"That's all right, dear child. It is time I was leaving. Do give my love to your wonderful husband. Oh yes, and assure him that those marks on his daughter's forehead are indeed a result of his love for her, while she was still in your womb. Goodbye for now, Tina-an. Goodbye baby." And then she was gone. Tina-an sat quietly in meditation for a moment as she always did at times like this but the rivulets of baby pee down her legs urged her to get up and take the baby to a nearby stream and wash and change the *tapa* cloth diaper. Not looking at the baby but watching her footing on the slippery stones of the stream, she knelt and first washed the urine from her own legs and then lifted the baby with both hands to ease it into the cool water.

"Oh, dear *Earth Mother*! What is this?" Tina's voice was choked with tears and this time she could not withhold them. Through her tears she washed the child and then took her back out of the stream and onto a grassy patch and laid the little girl down on the soft greenness. Around the child's little neck hung a plaited, translucent cord and from it dangled *that stone*! Wiping her eyes she gazed at the face of this tiny blessing of a child. Vesa-an was smiling up at her mother. Her first ever smile!

~ ~ * ~ ~

Four days short of his twentieth birthday, A'lan Sea-Hewn was confirmed as Sea-Master. Only one other man in Mal'lam history had risen to this rank at such a young age. That man had been 'Tor'na the Mad'. His face beaming with pride in this young man whom he had trained so assiduously, and who he already counted as a close friend, Al'malan Voyage-Master placed the newly-made headdress of woven coir fiber and white feathers and seashells on A'lan's head. The young Master already wore a yoke of seashells and Mother of Pearl. Resting on his throat on a shortened cord was that mysterious pendant of that strange material, the spirals of its design glinting in the bright sunlight. The Convocation of Sea-Hewn had taken two days to discuss and debate the merits of this exceptional seaman but everyone knew what the outcome would be. Mal'lam custom and ceremony could drag on!

A newly appointed Sea-Master was given his first formal command on this day and also given the option of renaming his vessel. The whole of the assembled Sea-Hewn, led by the young master, strode to the beach on Tora'tor and up the sandy way to where 'Wa'Boton' sat on logs, undergoing refit in preparation for more voyaging. No one yet knew what A'lan's intention in this regard was but many had guessed rightly. 'Three Finger' Sea-Hewn went to the warm water lapping up onto the beach and filled a small gourd with it and brought it back to his longtime friend. A'lan took it and with his face solemn, his eyes bright with insipient tears, said loudly for all to hear; "I, A'lan Sea-Master, with the authority given me by my Sea-Hewn brethren and with the blessings of my people, name this canoe to honor one of the greatest Mal'lam seamen with whom I have had the honor to sail."

With that short announcement he stepped up to the bare hulls and splashed the seawater over them both. Then A'lan Sea-Master did something no one here had ever seen done. He handed the gourd back to Shen'ham, drew his newly made seaman's knife from its sheath and made a shallow slice across his stomach, below his heart. Beads of blood welled up and began to trickle down his stomach. With a quick movement he wiped both hands over the small flow of blood and placed his hands first on one hull and then the next. "With my life's blood I will commit myself to the success and safety of this vessel, now to be called, 'Wa'Fan'al'!" A'lan then turned to 'Three Finger' and held out his hands. Shen'ham poured the rest of the gourd's contents over those hands, rinsing away the blood and that other close friend, Faldo-in, handed him a piece of coarse cloth on which to dry them.

This unique ceremony was not unprecedented in Mal'lam history but had simply fallen into disuse over the generations. These three young seamen had discussed reviving it at great length over the past few days. Now a new precedent had arisen and it would but add to the mystique which would grow around this young Sea-Master.

A'lan then turned to the crowd around him. That long scar on his bearded face, the tall headdress of white feathers which quivered in the breeze, the shell yoke, that strange pendant and now the trickle of blood on his stomach created an unforgettable impression.

"Thank you brother seamen!" he said loudly, so that some of the most elderly were sure to hear, "Please know that my love and respect for you all will never fail. As surely as *Earth Mother* has guided us thus far in our journeys, *She* will continue to bless us with love and miracles. Now, with your blessings, I propose that we all go and join the feasting which awaits us. I'm starving!" Polite applause from the Grey Heads was drown out by hoots and cheers from the younger seamen. It was time to party! The gathering dissolved into small groups as the seamen turned and headed back to the settlement. Voyage-Master Al'malan, Sea-Master Ch'om'lo, Canoe-Master Joha'lan and A'lan's two closest friends walked slowly together, the older men uttering their personal congratulations and blessings to A'lan in quiet voices.

"A'lan!" The woman's voice was from behind the men and demanding of attention. They all turned to face the figure of Lana'ma Herb Mistress, A'lan Sea-Master's mother. She was striding quickly toward them, something in her hands. Coming directly to A'lan without a glance at the other men around she began unraveling a wrapping of *tapa* cloth and leaves, quite strong smelling it was too. "Raise your arms up, please." It was an order, not a request, so A'lan raised his arms up. Lana'ma looked carefully at the shallow wound across his abdomen, grimaced and shook her head. She laid the bandage of healing plants and *tapa* cloth against the wound. Then holding it carefully, she moved around behind him to tie it in place. As she did so she looked meaningfully at each male face, muttering, "You men can do some stupid things sometimes. What would you think of me if I cut myself across the stomach, eh?"

Finished with her bandaging she stood back with her hands on her hips and extended another meaningful look at her son. The grin that was forming gave her away though. Suddenly she jumped forward and wrapped her arms around the newly dedicated Sea-Master and kissed him on both cheeks, whispering a private message of love into his ear. Then with a slap on his arm she turned and walked away without a backward glance. This small group of major, male players in the Destiny of the Mal'lam people all stood looking a bit perplexed, if not dumbfounded. Then Joha'lan's belly began to jiggle with silent laughter and soon they were all cackling and snorting. "Where would we be without women like that?" Al'malan asked, between gusts of laughter. A'lan tried to look offended but failed and was soon laughing as hard as anyone. They resumed their walk up the beach toward where the fires were being lit for the feast, all semblance of reserve, authority and majesty evaporated, arms over each others' shoulders. Boys again.

~ ~ * ~ ~

Like all Mal'lam weddings, this one was low-keyed. The mother of the bride, Ma'tea Feather-Plait, stood behind her daughter, gladness and relief all over her face. She had come through a terrible time but now life was blooming again. She was going to be a grandmother once more. An elderly Herb-Hewn by the name of Tol'sho'lot officiated but his task was simple. Facing about at the small gathering he looked at each as he spoke. "The *Earth Mother* has called us together to acknowledge the intent of these two people to join their lives together. It is the custom of our people, we Mal'lam, to witness every such joining and add our blessings to those of the *Earth Mother*.

"We understand that you, Ja'eel Feather-Plait and you, Kal'to'lot Stone-Hewn, intend to make a marriage together," He nodded to them both in turn and received a nod and a smile from both. "Then no one of us can deny you this intention. Will you now take these cups of coconut juice and drink to your own futures together?" It was the Herb-Mistress Shen'ha who stepped forward with the two ceramic cups filled to the brim with the sweet liquid. She held them out at arms length, her own wrists wrapped with chains of white blossoms. Ja'eel took her cup with both hands, a shy smile of gratitude softening what had for so long been a visage of haughty arrogance. The muscular Stone-Hewn took his cup and nodded to Shen'ha with his own smile. Then, facing each other and looking into each others eyes, they tipped their cups up shallowly and drank, never breaking that eye contact.

"Now we welcome you both to our community, as married people. Do either of you wish to speak on your own behalf?" Ja'eel looked expectantly at her husband. He swallowed hard, embarrassed to speak at even such a small gathering. Speaking slowly and quietly he began his short address. "Thank you, Tol'sho'lot, for your kind words." He looked directly at the Herb-Mistress now and tears glistened in his eyes. "And to you, dear lady, my wife and I wish to thank you for your very special blessings of courage, dedication and kindness. Without your loving intervention and determined patience over these past years, Ja'eel and I would not be together here this day. We would both be dead." This was said with the man's usual blunt ineptitude but it was a message from his heart. He turned then to his bride's mother, who by now was weeping softly, her fingers wiping tears from her face.

"For you, dear lady, I have the greatest respect also. You have accepted the woman I love back into your heart and into your life. We both promise you that we will be your dearest friends for all your life." Kal'to'lot had finally run out of words and stood looking a bit sheepish and awkward. She of the oratorical skills and commanding presence, Ja'eel, now spoke for herself as well as her new husband.

"Thank you Tol'sho'lot, for your kindness today." Everyone there knew that Tol'sho'lot's youngest daughter had become a devotee of the woman, *Ja'jan*, and at one time he had led the chorus of her condemnation. "I know of no way to properly thank this special woman, Shen'ha, nor my mother - my own mother who suffered such pain because of me. Yet here within this community of Mal'lam, I have been given rebirth. The child I now carry in my womb, both my husband and I have dedicated to the pleasure of *Earth Mother*, to direct to *Her* own needs." Ja'eel suddenly dissolved into tears and both Kal'to'lot and her mother moved to her to comfort her. Shen'ha looked skyward, not in frustration but in supplication.

As if to answer a prayer, the skies opened and a downpour began. Rain at a wedding was considered by the Mal'lam as a good omen of a long and fruitful marriage. A number of visitors to this simple ceremony had stood well to the background all throughout. With the plunging rain came a shout of rejoicing and celebration and a dozen people surged forward to congratulate the newly married couple. Among them was Voyage-Master Al'malan. He held the hand of his son, Sahn'ta, and in Sahn'ta's other small hand was held a large cluster of blossoms and scented herbs.

Behind these two stood Sht'ana Herb-Plait. Al'malan turned and looked at her with an encouraging smile and a twist of his head indicating that she should come forward now. She did. All her fear and resentment had been evaporated by both time and her people's innate forgiveness. In her hands were more flowers and fragrant herbs. It was when Ja'eel, laden now with floral offerings, her tears flowing over a widening smile, that the little boy stepped forward and held up his bunch of flowers. She knelt in front of him and took them from him, tucking them into an armful already overloaded. Sahn'ta turned and looked up at his father who stood close behind him. Al'malan grinned his irresistible grin and nodded. Sahn'ta reached up quickly and wrapped his arms around his mother's neck. That final, encumbering connection with guilt and sorrow broke under the weight of the child's hug. Ja'eel was truly reborn on the day she wed. The rain continued, but no one cared.

~ ~ * ~ ~

Al'malan, Joha'lan and Ch'om'lo sat comfortably on the slope above the beach. The early morning sun was hot already and sweat formed on their skins.

Ch'om'lo passed the water gourd to Al'malan who took a long drink. Joha'lan wasn't thirsty yet. His mind was on canoe-matters.

"These canoes aren't going to last forever, you know." his brow was furrowed with concentration on a thought. "There are good timbers here but none large enough to form the basic hulls." These three men had formed an association of personal and professional depth which allowed them to almost read each other's minds. Al'malan responded with the obvious."Then I reckon we'll have to find some more islands that do have big trees." He shifted his buttocks and reached beneath himself and withdrew an offending rock, then threw it casually away. "A'lan Sea-Master has discovered some fascinating islands, but still none with great forests which would provide us with canoe material. I think that it's time our illustrious Voyage-Master went to sea again!" Ch'om'lo's comment received looks of mixed humor and seriousness.

"Alright. Who's going with me?" Al'malan returned the jibe with a smile. This was not a frivolous chat session. These men, upon whom fell such great responsibility, must soon make some serious decisions. "We'll all have to go!" was Joha'lan's reply and Ch'om'lo nodded his agreement. There was a minute or two of silent thought among them until Joha'lan continued. "Some of the timber panels set onto the solid bases of the hulls are showing great wear. It's difficult to keep them repaired. We can't reduce the depth of the hulls because we need that depth to hold the supplies we need for voyaging. We can't extend the length of our vessels because of the lack of big timber for the bases of the hulls. Even if we could, it would seem that the lengths we're working with now are near to optimum for the sea conditions we encounter. In other words, we've already gotten as long in hull length as we can go and still maintain safety when encountering storm swells. What's the recourse? I'll tell you. Fifty to sixty foot hulls and six foot height. No more and no less."

Al'malan and Ch'om'lo both knew where this discussion was headed. As comfortable as these past weeks had been ashore, very soon the Sea-Hewn must once again hew to the sea. "How many canoes do you think we can safely commit to another voyage at this time, Joha'lan?" Al'malan asked. Joha'lan was slow to reply, his face registering the workings of his mind. Finally he replied. "Six!" he said with definiteness. "And two to sail back north to 'Win'no'hi-Set'. We must maintain contact there. These new, delicious tubers should be taken back to them too."

Ch'om'lo added, "I agree. A'lan Sea-Master's find of those *kumeru*, as he calls them, could well be a very important element in supplying our people's expansion southward. What do you think, Al'malan?"

Al'malan didn't answer immediately but with a wave of his hand asked for a few moments to consider. He was listening closely to the voices and the words within those voices of his friends. He heard some remaining hesitation to commit to voyaging again so soon after the fleet's combined arrival. Of course, there was the consideration of families: new babies, babies on the way, new friendships and lovers, parents and elders growing more elderly. Always this was at the back of any Sea-Hewn's mind. But a Voyage-Master had somewhat different considerations to occupy him. His vision was focused upon a reality somewhere one or two generations beyond his own life. It was a vision the fulfillment or failure of which he would never personally know. Flying blind, another might have named it. Depending on the *Earth Mother* was his recourse to the unknown.

"Right! Joha'lan, I would like you to prepare a voyage of two canoes to go north again to 'Win'no'hi-Set'. Soon. Ch'om-an, I'd like you to lead that voyage but return as soon as possible. Take with you some of our best navigators and make sure that we always have men who can sail back and forth to there. It's nearing time for the '*hewing*'. We can be sure that the number of youngsters applying for inclusion in the Sea-Hewn classes will be large. Plan to take the very best from this group of initiates with you. School them intensively in navigation."

Al'malan's words tumbled from him now and his friends had to pay very close attention. He wanted his own younger cousin, Chom'shul Sea-Master to accompany A'lan Sea-Master in another two-vessel excursion. This time more to the southwest. They should plan for a four month voyage, turning back after a two month exploration of whatever land they might find. This was a time of collecting information which would lay the groundwork, sea-work more exactly, for the Mal'lam to head outward in numbers again.

"We will probably all be Grey-Heads by that time though!" Al'malan joked, but all knew it was not really a joke. It was a probability. And so the policy was determined by these three men. It would have to be ratified by a Council of the Elders, of course, but such was the standing and respect in which they were perceived by their community that it was a given. The Mal'lam would not stop here, as welcoming as this archipelago was. Their future lay upon the rich possibilities which the horizon offered. A Voyage-Master with immense insight, a Sea-Master-Warrior with indomitable energy and wisdom and a Master of canoe design were the very elements which would see the Mal'lam on their way to southern seas. *Earth Mother* still smiled.

Chapter Forty Nine - New Beginnings

"What do you think, Enno-an?" Faldo Sea-Master rested a hand on the base of the hull's stern post, taking a bit of weight off his one leg while showing his brother his latest wood carving.

"It's beautifully done, brother. What do you suppose the spiral means? I mean, what do you think those people who A'lan met considered it to mean? We know it as a symbol for time, for eternity, but they may have another meaning".

These two brothers now worked together almost daily; Enno Stone-Master with his stone tool-making and Faldo Sea-Master with his newly discovered talent as a wood carver. A'lan Sea-Master had asked Faldo to carve some symbols on the sternposts of his vessel in preparation for the upcoming voyage of discovery. They occupied an expanded and sturdily-built workshop, wood chips coating the ground at one end, stone chips the other. Enno Stone-Master now had a group of men working with him including still, the Tarbara'ut apprentice, Bat'rat. The small, black man was by now a specialist in making knife blades and there was no end to work available for him. Enno moved to the other hull and inspected the completed carvings there. He grinned at his one-legged brother and complimented him profusely. "If you had started carving instead of sailing off into the sunset, brother, you might still have both legs!"

"Yes, but I might have fewer fingers. Look at all these cuts and scars! My hands are beginning to look like yours." They carried on with silly chatter all day long, teasing and chiding each other constantly, just as they had done as boys together. But this particular day was one for serious subjects. "Faldo-an, I understand that there is some unhappiness among the Tarbara'ut now that we Mal'lam have descended like a flock of migratory birds. What are they telling you?"

Faldo sat down on the sand in the shade cast by the big canoe hull, Enno joining him."Many of the Tarbara'ut Elders are very sad. They know exactly what we know - that we will eventually inhabit all these islands and that they, as a people, are dying out. I know how I would feel if things were the other way around. It's sad. But even if all we Mal'lam disappeared, still their fate seems sealed."

Enno looked grieved for a moment but then brightened. "At least there are babies being born to the Tarbara'ut women." He looked hopefully at his brother but that bit of information didn't seem to impress him. Enno himself was father to a little girl, her mother a Tarbara'ut.

"Yes, I know. And all children are a blessing. But only one child of wholly Tarbara'ut blood has been born since you arrived and that's been five years now." Faldo shook his head sadly. "Well, anyway, these mixed babies are beautiful and strong. I guess that makes it alright. Help me up will you? I need to pee and my back hurts." Enno reached down and pulled his brother to his foot and handed him his crutch. "Admit it. You're just getting old." The two moved away toward the village again, renewing their usual repartee.

Two other brothers, twin sons of Orn'ta Sea-Master and at only seven years old, both daredevil water-men already, played nearby. Their father sat with a friend in the shade of young coconut palms, watching the boys as they pushed a small, boy-sized dugout into the small surf running inside the lagoon this morning. "You've got a couple of little rascal there, Sea-Master." his friend said, chuckling."By the time they're of *hewing* age they'll already be competent seamen.

"If they don't kill themselves first!" Orn'ta replied. "They are surely a handful. Their mother almost despairs of them. They are good boys though, really. We were a bit of a nuisance ourselves at that age - you may recall." His friend laughed at the memory, remembering the mischief they both had gotten into together.

"Ah, here they come now." Orn'ta said, leaning over his crossed knees to look up the beach. He had appointed to meet here with Ch'om'lo and 'Three Finger'. "Good morning, Sea-Hewn!" he called out when they were still a dozen yards away. Ch'om'lo waved and the two turned and walked uphill toward Orn'ta and his friend. His friend then rose and made to leave the three to discuss whatever their business was. "No, no, An'lat-an. Please stay. This will involve you too, if you wish." Ch'om'lo and Shen'ham reached the shade of the palm fronds and sat down with sighs of relief.

"Whew! It's hot today, eh?" 'Three Finger'said. He was carrying a large water gourd in his three-fingered left hand and held it out to Orn'ta and An'lat Sea-Hewn. As always, the young Sea-Hewn carried his sling tucked into his waist band, a pouch of sling stones swinging from his other hip. And this was the signature of what was to be discussed between warriors this morning. These four men had been involved in the battle in which 'Tor'na the Mad' had been defeated. The past year, what with the withdrawal of the *Ja'jan* threat and the desperate preparations to leave Sht'ah Lee-Set, coupled with the voyage here to these peaceful islands, had seen martial training go by the wayside. Ch'om'lo, as the recognized leader of things martial, was insistent that training must be resumed.

The fact that Sea-Master A'lan and his crew had come across strange but peaceful and friendly people didn't mean that future contacts, which were bound to occur, would not incur danger. Sea-Master Ch'om'lo would soon be sailing for 'Win'no'hi-Set' and would not be able to direct a resumed training program himself. His recommendation was that 'Three Finger' be the one. Orn'ta concurred with no persuasion needed. He had always thought so highly of this young Sea-Hewn, even before he had seen him in deadly combat while still but a boy. An'lat Sea-Hewn actually owed his life to Shen'ham's timely interception of a spear thrust aboard Tor'na's vessel. Yes, indeed An'lat wanted to be involved and his continued, but sporadic, practice with a club and shield he felt qualified him to take a tutoring role. By the time the scheduling and planning was complete, the sun was in mid afternoon and all four men were hungry. Orn'ta's boys had just returned to the beach in their little canoe. All the men laughed as the two lifted a small shark from the hull, its weight requiring both their strengths. Orn'ta shook his head. "If they don't kill themselves first."

~ ~ * ~ ~

Two of the Mal'lam community's leading women, neither quite of an age to be considered matriarchs, sat with grandchildren on their laps in the cooling waters of a stream on the island of 'Sh'ham-ra'. Shen'ha and Sha'lat Herb-Mistresses were like soul-sisters. They could sometimes even finish each other's sentences, which always sent them into a fit of giggles.

"Isn't your granddaughter growing quickly?" Shen'ha exclaimed. "In spite of having little tits, Tina-an must have plenty of milk." "Yes. Just like I did. I was small too, believe it or not." They shared a good laugh as they sat and compared their breasts which were now quite matronly.

A noisy, colorful bird landed nearby. The daughter of Al'malan and Sht'ana squealed and pointed, kicking her legs excitedly while the younger baby tried to giggle but only drooled happily. The two women spent another hour bathing and tending the children until their mothers came to relieve them, Tina-an's breasts needing relieving too. With a bit of reluctance the grandmothers relinquished their charges, the oldest fussing mildly in protest. With the shadows growing longer now the water seemed too cool for more bathing so the women left the stream and dried themselves. They then went to have a snack of bananas out in the filtered sunlight beneath a palm tree.

"I'm glad your son isn't sailing away so soon as some Sea-Hewn." Sha'lat said. "Tina really doesn't want him to go at all. I suppose he will though, in time."

"Yes, I'm happy for him to stay longer. But, you know, his Destiny does appear to be on the sea. And he has become a very good navigator, from what I hear." The women were quiet for a time, each drifting with their own thoughts, each thankful for the existence of such a close friendship. Finally Sha'lat said, "Joha'lan will be voyaging south with Al'malan, maybe in the next year. It will be the first time we will have been apart. I'm so happy that I have a grandchild or two to keep me company." Then she brightened again. "Maybe there will be more before long, eh?"

Shen'ha frowned but quickly wiped the frown away with a smile. "Well, you know that Sht'ana will have no more children. Remember when The Vesa'tan predicted that?" Sha'lat remembered that night on the mountain ... how could she forget? "Other *seers* have confirmed that." Shen'ha continued, "And I think she has accepted that now. Surely she's spoken to you about it recently?" Sha'lat only nodded, remembering her oldest daughter's sadness when they had discussed it. But, then, it's all in the hands of *Earth Mother*. Just then the little, noisy bird returned and lighted on the grass near them. Both women had the same, sudden sense of certainty. The bird was a messenger! They both sat very still and quiet, expecting - something!

The colorful little finch hopped about through the short, dry grass, not as if searching for food but distinctly as if it was performing a dance. Hopping first one way then the other, flying for a few feet into the air and then landing again just where it had taken off from ... surely there was some message here! To compound their fascination, a low whistle from down hill. Head bobbing into view came Tina-an again but this time without her child. She was smiling widely and as she neared, the women could see that mischievous gleam in her eyes. The little bird maintained its dance, if that's what it was, and allowed Tina to come between the two grandmothers and sit down. "Thank you, little bird!" Tina said as she sat. "Thank you very much. You may go now." And it did, flying quickly away into the brushy forest behind them.

"Do you notice anything special?" Tina-an asked, that delightful smile of childish glee on her face. Her mother and mother-in-law looked at each other, then all over Tina's form, then ... wait! "Your talisman!" Sha'lat shrieked, placing both hands to her face. Shen'ha saw it now. How could she not have seen it? It had been lost months ago on Sht'ah Lee and yet here it was, glistening on her daughter-in-law's throat as it had from that day when The Vesa'tan had given it to her. Both older women knew this young woman well enough to know that there was no trickery or childishness at play. "Tell us!" her mother cried.

Tina-an took but few minutes to convince them that The Vesa'tan was actually here in spirit, on this very island. She had not revealed the reappearance of the talisman until this day, not even to her husband. But a little bird had come to where Sht'ana and she were resting after feeding their children. The bird had done a complex dance of hopping and short flights into the air above her. Tina had known what it meant. How she had known she could not explain. No words existed to describe such awareness. It just was.

The magical connection which Shen'ha, Sha'lat and Tina-an had shared since that time on the slopes of Volan Votu continued uninterrupted, and so it would always be. So much had intervened since then that lesser souls might have abandoned the life within that memory. But not these three. On this glorious afternoon there occurred a melding of powers - that of three exceptional women whose own Destiny's would be interwoven with those of their men. And through their men would come a new and dynamic era which would see humans flow over the vast expanses of the Pacific Ocean and the myriad, tiny resting places afforded there. Though forgotten now, the mantra-like sound of their people's name can still be heard in quiet places - **Mal'lam ...**

Final Report: Katherine Feldman-BlakeWinter, Hawai'i, 1975-76

Subject: The Mal'lam people as described by those following

Tina Pua'lani Kaiser

'Tutu' Kinau Ho'opai Kaiser

That's all for now folks! Actually it won't be. Both Tina and Kinau are compiling their own recorded versions of their communications and we will get together again within a year to organize things for a continuation of the dialog.

Jiro's and my second baby is due in two months. However, we won't be here in Hawai'i and that's a bit sad. Jiro has taken the post of Interim Head of Anthropology at Stanford University, a two year job. Of course, he's not excited. Nooooo! *Old Inscrutable* won't let on that he's as pleased as punch. But I know my old rascal and he's dancing in his boots.

As I've mentioned before, I'm now relegated to housewife and mother roles. Wanna bet?! There's too much yet to collect and compile on the story of the Mal'lam as well as studying a lot of data that's accumulating in the field of archaeology to let this go by.

Thanks to all those who helped with this project, even those who still think I'm off my rocker.

Aloha and much love to all - - - - Katherine F-B Yukihara

The End of Book One

ABOUT THE AUTHOR

Jim Leslie was born in 1939 in the American Northwest. Raised and educated on the Oregon coast, his attention was very early drawn to the lure of the unknown beyond that great horizon. Many of his childhood dreams were cast out upon the cold waters of the North Pacific, later to be reclaimed from the warm tropical waters of Hawai'i. Part-time employment in the nursery and landscape industry while attending university led to a full-time career in that field.

A natural artistic bent allowed him to include cartooning, painting and sculpture in his repertoire of skills. Jim was also mightily afflicted with the 'travel bug'! He lived and worked in Oregon, California, Massachusetts and then Hawai'i. It was in Hawai'i that he developed his abiding interest in the sea and most especially Oceanic voyaging.

He carried that interest to his new and present home in Australia where exposure to Indigenous and Islander cultures further expanded his fascination with ancient societies. A daughter's suggestion then led to some experiments in writing, which steadily became a serious focus of his energies. Years of leading and training workers in large-scale landscape construction led to some work as a training facilitator on Government sponsored work programs.

Located now on the Sunshine Coast in the State of Queensland, Jim works as a live-in Caretaker at a Red Cross accommodation facility. With his wife's patient encouragement, he is engaged in work on the sequel to his novel, 'The Mal'lam Voyagers' and a book of short stories.

www.ingramcontent.com/pod-product-compliance
Lightning Source LLC
Chambersburg PA
CBHW080942020726
47505CB00009B/2111